M000191513

The Suffolk Trilogy

KNIGHT'S ACRE
THE HOMECOMING
THE LONELY FURROW

Norah Lofts

CORONET BOOKS
Hodder and Stoughton

First published as three separate volumes:

KNIGHT'S ACRE copyright © 1975 by Norah Lofts
First published in Great Britain in 1975 by Hodder and
Stoughton Limited
Coronet edition 1976

THE HOMECOMING © 1975 by Norah Lofts
First published in Great Britain in 1975 by Hodder and
Stoughton Limited
Coronet edition 1977

THE LONELY FURROW © 1976 by Norah Lofts
First published in Great Britain in 1976 by Hodder and
Stoughton Limited
Coronet edition 1978

This edition 1986

British Library C.I.P.

Lofts, Norah
    The Suffolk trilogy.
    I. Title   II. Lofts, Norah. Knight's Acre
    III. Lofts, Norah. The Homecoming   IV. Lofts,
    Norah. The Lonely Furrow
    823'.912[F]   PR6023.035

    ISBN 0–340–38935–4

*The characters and situations in this book are
entirely imaginary and bear no real relation to any real
person or actual happening*

This book is sold subject to the condition that
it shall not, by way of trade or otherwise, be
lent, re-sold, hired out or otherwise circulated
without the publisher's prior consent in any
form of binding or cover other than that in
which this is published and without a similar
condition including this condition being
imposed on the subsequent purchaser.

Printed and bound in Great Britain for
Hodder and Stoughton Paperbacks, a
division of Hodder and Stoughton Ltd.,
Mill Road, Dunton Green, Sevenoaks,
Kent (Editorial Office: 47 Bedford
Square, London, WC1 3DP) by
Cox & Wyman Ltd., Reading

Book One

KNIGHT'S ACRE

1

WHEN Sir Godfrey Tallboys decided to build his house he was thirty-five years old and at the very peak of his career as knight errant. 1451, still only eight months old, had been a wonderful year for him. He was not only acknowledged as the premier knight in England, he was once clear of debt and had a hundred pounds in hand. The Michaelmas and Christmas tournaments were still to come. Now, if ever, he could give his sweet Sybilla the thing she had long craved for—a house of her own.

He was a man of action, not of thought. He lived for the moment, seldom looking backward—and then only to pleasant things, and even less seldom taking thought for tomorrow. But he accepted, as he accepted everything else associated with his way of life, that the day would come when his eyes would lose keenness, his arms their strength and then he would need a place to which to retire, a wall upon which to hang his armour, and some pasture for Arcol, his great horse. However, when he thought of that day, it always seemed far distant; eight, ten years. He would not have considered building when he did, had it not been for Sybilla and the children.

Not that she nagged. A sweeter more amenable woman never lived, but ever since the birth of Henry, who was now six years old, she had been saying that it would be pleasant to have a home of her own. And in the past eighteen months or so she had drawn his attention to a fact which he—unobservant outside his trade—would not have noticed; the Tallboys family was increasingly unwelcome.

She said, cool and tolerant, as was her way, 'It is understandable ...' She listed the places where she and the children stayed while he rode in tournaments or went to take part in one of the recurrent wars between rival nobles, or against the Scots or the Welsh.

At Moyidan in Suffolk which Sir Godfrey's brother James had inherited, being the first-born, there were two children; a girl, sturdy but remarkably lacking in beauty and grace; and a boy weakly of body and dull of mind. No fond father and mother could help contrasting their offspring with Henry, big and handsome and precocious and Richard, a bare year younger and so forward that he might almost have been Henry's twin. And look at Margaret, an angel child, so very pretty, three years old; and John, now a year old, again big, handsome and forward.

Sybilla well understood why they were no longer warmly welcomed at Moyidan.

At Beauclaire, where Godfrey's pretty sister, Alys ruled as Lady Astallon, there was less cause for that kind of envy. Lady Astallon had produced a son, handsome and lively, and a daughter, very pretty. But Beauclaire was a huge and complicated place and Lady Astallon had waiting ladies who took sides when Henry and Richard squabbled, as they did interminably.

The third family house—that of Godfrey's second brother, who like many second sons had gone into the Church, was at Bywater, where William Tallboys was Bishop, a most estimable man, given to good works. But he kept such a bad table, and children, growing and active, needed food. In her cool, reasonable way Sybilla had said, 'We cannot stay with William again. The boys were hungry all the time, and when I went into the kitchen that sloven who calls herself housekeeper, ordered me away, most rudely.'

It was plain, even to Sir Godfrey that a house of her own was Sybilla's necessity as well as her right.

'I will ride to Intake tomorrow and put the building in hand,' he said.

The choice of place was obvious. Sir Godfrey was not, like many younger sons a landless knight. In this as in so many other ways, he had been singularly fortunate.

'It need not be a large house. Or grand,' Sybilla said. She knew that when he had money he was inclined to be free with it. 'We shall not be able to afford a large household. A hall to live in, a kitchen and four bedchambers will be enough.'

He knew many women who would have wished to choose their own site, give their own orders to the builder, but that was not her way.

In the morning she rose early to see him off, as she always did, even when his errand was peaceful and his absence to be brief. As his horse's feet rang hollow on the drawbridge—they were spending the summer at Beauclaire—she called after him. 'My love, let it not be damp.'

Intake was rather less than five miles from the family manor at Moyidan, and when on the second day Sir Godfrey arrived just as dinner was being served, his brother, Sir James and his wife Emma groaned inwardly, thinking that he had ridden ahead and that somewhere behind him on the road was a wagon bringing Sybilla and her brood and behind them his squire, Eustace and that great horse Arcol who must have corn every day.

Their obvious relief when he said that he was alone, showed even Sir Godfrey that Sybilla had not been imagining the lack of warmth in recent welcomes; and when they heard that his purpose was to choose a site and build a house they became positively joyful. What a wise decision! Children needed a settled home. Sybilla would relish a place of her own.

'The harvest will be in by the week's end if the weather holds,' Sir James said. 'I will lend you six or seven of my fellows to help with the building.'

The institution of serfdom was dying out, but the lord of the manor of Moyidan still had some tenants who paid for their strips of land in the great open fields by tending his as well and by doing at all times anything they were told to.

'That would be kind. And what builder would you commend?'

'Hobson of Baildon,' James said without hesitation. 'He made an excellent job of our new barn. I'll send a boy in to tell him to meet you there, first thing tomorrow morning.'

Anything to speed on the work. Let the house be finished by Christmas!

Intake lay, shaped like a dish, embraced on one side by the

river Wren and on three by Layer Wood. It was not a manor—it never had been; it was, as its name implied, intake land, snatched from the forest. Sir Godfrey's great grandfather had had a surplus of serfs at Moyidan, some of them a bit discontented and one day he had told them that any man who liked to go and hew himself a field, build himself a hovel, was free to go and do so. They could live rent free for five years; after that they would pay ten shillings a year.

A number of men had taken advantage of this offer. The strongest and most determined had survived. Intake now consisted of eight small enclosed farms, each tenant still paying ten shillings a year. Much less in purchasing power than it had been in the old man's time, but fixed in some obscure legal way. And in any case, four pounds a year was spending money for a family who ate at other people's tables and slept in other people's beds. And though Sir Godfrey was careless, inclined to lend and to spend, Sybilla was thrifty and very clever at refurbishing old gowns and headdresses, so that she was always abreast of the latest fashion at small cost.

On this hot August morning—the weather was holding—Master Hobson was waiting; his rather sorry-looking horse tied to a tree. He was a prosperous man and could well have afforded a better mount, but he was cautious; if you *looked* prosperous people thought they had been over-charged. He kept a good table, had money saved, and his wife had the silk gown of every respectable woman's ambition, but it was never worn outside her own house.

He greeted Sir Godfrey with happy servility. This would be a good job, and the money was certain. Before he dismounted Sir Godfrey looked out over his village, seeing, in his single-minded way, nothing but potential sites. There seemed to be unoccupied land near the river, but he remembered Sybilla's last words and turned his attention to a space that lay between the edge of the village common and the fringe of the wood. It had been a farm once and was now covered with light, secondary growth, self-sown saplings, brambles, bracken and gay wild-flowers. The ruins of the original clod-built farmhouse could still be seen. A good spot, he thought, well away from the river. The oak-tree would be a bit of a drawback.

It stood almost in the centre of the site, Layer Wood's last outpost. It had been a well-grown tree when the Normans landed at Hastings, and by the time the first settlers came to Intake it offered more of an obstacle than they could tackle.

Master Hobson looked about with an experienced, calculating eye. The ruined farmhouse would make a shelter for his workmen and save the building of the lodge which was the rule when they were employed beyond walking distance of their homes. He could also see a use for the huge tree.

He gave no sign of satisfaction. It was a sound rule to make any job sound as difficult as possible.

'Take a bit of clearing, sir.' He sounded gloomy.

Sir Godfrey looked rather helpless. He was out of his depths. If the wood had been full of Welsh archers, or the undergrowth crawling with Scottish reivers he would have known what to do; but the decision of whether to build to the left or to the right of the great tree was a difficult one. The site seemed to demand that the house should be in the centre, and this was impossible because of the tree. Not that it mattered; there was plenty of room on either side.

The builder, now applying another sound rule, became helpful.

'We could use that tree, sir. Centre the house round it, like. Spare planting a king post. Good branches, too. Left and right. Beams.'

'You couldn't have a tree growing in the middle of a house.'

'It wouldn't be *growing*. Not with its top lopped and all the bark off, and its roots under the floor.'

Sir Godfrey tried, and failed, to visualise this, and said, dubiously, 'I suppose you know best. But . . .' There was a word he wanted, it eluded him for a second or two as words so often did; a word used of men as well as of wood. 'Seasoned! I thought timber had to be seasoned.'

'Thass right, sir. For planking, panelling and such, anything likely to *warp*. Not a thing this size.' Hobson regarded the tree with covert approval; the time it would save; not only as a king pin, but with the staircase, if Sir Godfrey wanted—as so many people did these days, to have his house on two floors. The inner side of the staircase could be fixed into the great

9

trunk for at least half the way.

Aloud he said, 'It'd take a bit of contriving. But it could be done. Now, what size of place was you thinking of, sir?'

'Not large. A hall, a kitchen and four sleeping chambers.' That was what Sybilla had told him. But he had been thinking. Sybilla had been so patient, had waited so long, the place should be worthy of her. He said recklessly, 'And a solar, and a still-room. And a stool-room.'

Sybilla deserved a solar, a place to which a lady could withdraw from the hurly-burly of life in the hall; she deserved a still-room too, for often enough he had embraced her and said, 'You smell very sweet,' and she had said, 'I have been helping in the still-room.' The stool-room was definitely an extravagance.

In most castles human needs were catered for by places called garderobes, so called because the smell of them was supposed to deter moths, so that furs and woollen clothes hung in them were protected. There was a stone seat—very cold in winter—and a hole; the excreta made a dark, slimy track down the outside wall to end in the moat. In summer not too unsightly, for ferns and other plants took shallow root and flourished.

However, at Beauclaire more civilised custom had taken over; copper pots set in velvet-covered stools.

Why should Sybilla be less comfortable in her own house than she had been in Beauclaire?

Master Hobson approved the order which meant building an extra room; the principle he deplored. Outside the house was the place for *that*; at some distance from the house, screened by a few bushes and emptied not less than once a month. Still, grand gentlemen had their own ways.

'Now, as to the outside. In what style?'

'I had thought . . . something like the new part of Moyidan.'

It was new in that it had been added, by his enterprising great-grandfather, to the haunch of the cold, draughty castle. But it had already been old when Sir Godfrey knew it, his home, from which at nine years old he had been torn away and sent to join the pages at Beauclaire. He would now have denied, and believed himself, that he had ever been homesick,

10

or felt ill-done-by. Those first wretched weeks had been the beginning of his very successful career; page, squire, knight. But something in him remembered, not the bad, because he had a happy nature, the good; and amongst the good was the face of his birthplace.

'Half-timbered,' Master Hobson said. 'With pargeting?'

An unfamiliar word.

'What is that?'

'A way of working plaster, sir. Very pretty.'

It was an art and Master Hobson's son-in-law was an expert at it. Pargeting had become the fashion as timber became harder and harder to obtain, and the width of plaster between the outer beams, widened. Master Hobson did not much like his son-in-law, a sour, scornful young man. A rebel, too. But he was a good plasterer, where plain work was concerned and his other fancy stuff, the pargeting, was much admired.

For Sybilla the best! Sir Godfrey agreed to the pargeting. Then, most crucial of all there was the question of time.

'When can it be ready?'

Master Hobson had another rule; faced with a downright question, say 'Ah.' Long drawn out, giving you time to think.

'Ah. A bit hard to say, sir. Dependent on the weather. You can't plaster in a frost. Better leave that. But we'll waste no time. Of that you may be sure, sir.'

Never give a positive date. If you did, and exceeded it by so little as a day, all you had was complaints; and if luck and weather and all else favoured you and the job was done before the given time, customers expected a bit off the price.

'I'll get along now, sir and draw up a bit of a plan. And let you have it—at Moyidan, sir?'

'No need,' Sir Godfrey said. He was back on his own ground. He had laid out camps in his time. 'We can settle it now.'

He took up a twig and with a sure, steady hand drew in the dust under the old oak. Hall and solar at the front. Kitchen just behind the hall—he and Sybilla had spent such a long time in places where food grew cold between cooking place and table. Behind the solar the still-room. Neat and four-square. Upstairs the same.

11

Then he drew an oblong which completed but did not enclose the shape made by the house with its two back-jutting wings. Stables tended to attract flies.

'And the stables here,' he said.

'Very clear, sir,' Master Hobson said.

The most vital thing—the price—had not yet been mentioned.

'And what would be the cost?' Sir Godfrey asked.

'Ah.' The hesitation was perfunctory, for there again Master Hobson knew the rules. Where a price was concerned it was simple—extract the last possible penny.

'Solar, still-room, stool-room *and* stables,' he said thoughtfully, carefully naming the extras. 'A bit hard to say, sir, and a bit dependent on the weather. I'd say—a bit of a guess, sir, and I could be wronging myself—a hundred and ten. Pounds.'

He waited for the expostulations. They did not come. Sir Godfrey said, 'Yes. I could manage that.' He would have won ten pounds in prize money, or their worth in prizes, by the time the building was completed.

'Oh, one thing I forgot to mention. My brother of Moyidan has promised to lend six or seven men to speed the work.'

A curious expression came into Master Hobson's shrewd little eyes.

'Ah. I'm taking it they'd be craftsmen, sir.'

Sir Godfrey looked puzzled.

Hobson went on, 'Guild members? Carpenters? Masons?' He knew the answer to that!

'Why no. Just ordinary men. As soon as the harvest is in.'

'They might be useful, clearing the gound and so forth. Fetching and carrying. But they couldn't build, sir, not less they'd done their prentice time and joined the Guild. None of my men'd work along unskilled chaps.'

And why indeed should they? Craftsmen spent from eight to twelve years as apprentices, unpaid and often overworked; then they qualified as journeymen, paid by the day; finally, if they were good enough they were taken into the Guild of their particular trade and sworn to observe its standards and its rules and regulations. And how would *you* like it, Hobson

12

thought, if you was called on to play about in a tournament with a lot of chaps straight from the plough-tail?

'I see. I didn't realise,' Sir Godfrey said. There were millions of things in the world about him that he did not realise. He was single-minded, unobservant, illiterate and all his life had been part of a system designed to make him exactly what he was—a first-class fighting machine.

'Thass how it is, sir,' the builder said, and waited politely for the word of dismissal.

'That'll be all, then. And try to have it done by Christmas . . .'

Making no promises, Master Hobson mounted his old nag and plodded away.

Sir Godfrey stood for a moment and looked out over the little village, this time with a more seeing eye. Smoke rose from the smoke-holes of the little low houses, and the fields were lively, men, women and children scything, stocking, gleaning. On this bright day the river looked like half a silver necklace. In the woods behind him doves called softly.

He indulged in a rare, far-forward-looking thought. Quiet old age in his own solid house. He thought—I could be happy here . . .

'The man is a rogue! One hundred and ten pounds! And you agreed! Didn't you realise that he meant ninety and expected you to beat him down?' Exasperation rendered Sir James almost incoherent. He cursed his gout which had prevented him riding to Intake and putting some sense into Hobson. He blamed himself for not asking the builder to come here, in the first place.

The fact was that in all concerned with ordinary living, Godfrey was a witless fool. Charming of course, everybody liked him, but he had no sense. Like a child in a world of men, and like a child, headstrong and stubborn. Look at his marriage!

Look at his marriage, indeed.

For a poor knight—but famous, handsome, popular and well-connected, a good marriage had seemed to be a matter of

13

course. There were hundreds of heiresses in England; so many families seemed to have lost the trick of breeding boys, the great Earl of Warwick had only two daughters. And Godfrey moved in the right circles. For years all the family, except unworldly William, had been finding and displaying likely young women. He'd remained single until he was twenty-eight and then gone and fallen in love with a sixteen-year-old orphan without a penny. The family grieved over such reckless improvidence, and one member of it never forgave him. That was his sister Mary, the clever, dominating Abbess of Lamarsh who had had charge of Sybilla Fitzherbert, since she was orphaned at the age of two. The Abbess had seen in the girl some quality, seldom apparent to others, and had convinced herself that if only the girl could be persuaded, or forced into the right mould, she would make a splendid successor to herself. Sybilla Fitzherbert was very clever; she could learn anything—reading, writing, needlework, domestic skills, work in the infirmary. She would, when the time came, be fit to govern. All she lacked was a sense of vocation; and the very frankness with which she denied having any simply added to the Abbess's certainty that here was a young woman of unusual promise. God would recognise it . . .

All ruined! A whole edifice of hope and endeavour brought crashing down because that stupid Godfrey looked in to pay his respects to his sister and saw Sybilla. It was enough to make angels weep.

Apart from the Abbess, and a few disappointed ladies everybody soon accepted this most unfortunate marriage, and most people liked Sybilla, modest, tactful, helpful, so devoted to her husband that she constituted no threat where other men were concerned.

Sybilla's attitude towards Sir Godfrey was tinged with a kind of adoration. He had come to her rescue; he was her saviour and if she lived to be sixty she knew that she could not possibly express her gratitude to him. When she thought of the cold cloister, of the essentially lonely life that every nun lived while seeming to be part of a community, she was so grateful

14

that the idea of criticising anything he said or did, any arrangement he made, or failed to make, was utterly unthinkable. She was no fool and the Abbess's training had already shaped her judgment; there were times when she saw Godfrey Tallboys as feckless, extravagant, easily imposed upon, unobservant and insensitive, but such clear-sighted moments made no difference; she loved even his faults. And one of the reasons why she ruled her two naughty boys so badly, was that they were his, and so like him as he must have been before the discipline of life tamed him to some extent. To Henry, to Richard would come all too soon the cuffs and the beatings, the rules and the rebukes; but they would come from other hands and from other voices.

At Moyidan Sir James said, trying to make the best of a bad job: 'Well, my summer gout ends next month.' He suffered two kinds; one in hot weather—June to September, one in cold, November to March. 'And I will ride over to Intake and see what Hobson is about. Builders have a bad habit nowadays of getting one job under way and then taking on another, playing put and take. But I assure you, Godfrey, if I find any slackness, I'll light a fire under Master Hobson. A hundred and ten pounds! Have you got it?' The question was an afterthought.

'A hundred. I thought that might be enough. I've never built a house before,' Godfrey said. That was the kind of thing that was so endearing about him, a kind of downright simplicity.

'But I'll get some more. There is talk of a war on the Welsh border. It might pay better than tourneys. Would you be so kind, James, as to take charge of this?' He tumbled his money out. He had had a vague idea that a hundred pounds would build a house and partly furnish it. Apparently he had been wrong.

Sir James said that he would gladly take charge of the money and pay Hobson in stages. And he would see that the house was ready by Christmas. It would be, if he had anything to do with it.

And Emma, no less eager to see Sybilla in her own house for Christmas, said, 'I am sure, Godfrey, that I can help with the furnishing. I will look to it.'

'That is extremely kind,' Sir Godfrey said. He rode happily back to Beauclaire to report the success of his mission.

2

[September–December 1451]

IN no time at all, it seemed, she was seeing him off again, this time to war. Such partings were always heart-wrenching, but she had learned self-control in the convent and from experience the need for keeping a cheerful face and manner. Once, soon after their marriage he had gone to fight on the Scottish border and she had cried and cried. He had been greatly distressed and said, 'Sweetheart, you knew when you married me that I was not a shoemaker plying his trade at home.' He had also explained to her that for a knight who knew his business, who was well-armoured and well mounted the risk of death in battle was small. 'Plainly, a knight is worth more alive than dead. Think of the ransom!'

So now as he was about to leave—this time for Wales—she reminded herself that his armour was good, Arcol, his war-horse an exceptional animal, so especially well-trained that his price had kept them poor for two years. He was also lucky in his squire, a distant Tallboys cousin and completely devoted. Any hardships of the campaign would be mitigated for Godfrey by Eustace who would shove and kick with the best, and was not above a little cheating at times.

Godfrey himself was in high spirits, certain of returning much enriched. There would be loot and ransom money. 'All these Welsh chieftains call themselves princes; and any I take will pay a prince's ransom,' he said. 'Then we can furnish our house fittingly.'

One thing worried him; the house might be completed while he was still away. 'In which case you would be advised to remain here until my return. Or, if you wish to move—with borrowed furnishings, you will have Walter.'

'Oh yes,' she said, 'I have Walter.'

Walter was God's gift to an impoverished young couple. Five years earlier when they were in Dover, about to move on to Richborough, he had approached Godfrey and said that he wished to be their serving man. Godfrey had explained that useful as such a man might be, they were in no position to afford one. Walter said:

'I'm not looking for a wage. I have a pension of fourpence a week. If needs be I can provide my own provender.'

To such an unlikely tale the natural, sadly human reaction was suspicion. The man could be a serf running away from his manor, or a criminal; and a peripatetic, yet respectable family like that of the Tallboys would provide perfect cover. And neither Walter's appearance nor his manner offered much assurance. His clothes were noticeably neat and of good quality, but his face was scarred in such a way that it wore a perpetual sneer, and his manner was off-hand, almost arrogant.

Yet everything he said about himself proved, on enquiry, to be true. He was a freeman born—his name was Freeman. A younger son with no hope of inheritance, he had gone, as an archer, to the French wars with Lord Bowdegrave of Abhurst; and when Lord Bowdegrave was unhorsed stood over him; hence the scar, hence the pension.

Why such a man, of independent means and markedly unservile nature should wish to serve them remained a mystery. Sybilla had a rather romantic explanation; Godfrey had done so well in the Dover Tournament, any old soldier, looking for a new master, and with pay no object, might well have fastened upon him. Godfrey, very modest over most things, said that old soldiers liked to be on the move. Most of those now tramping, hobbling, limping about the roads of England would have fared better, he said, had they stayed in one place where they had relatives or friends. But the habit of movement was so ingrained . . .

So Walter joined them and not only served them well but saw that others did. In the vast, ill-organised households of the time, there was a system of 'vails', presents given to servants.

17

Those unable or unwilling to give substantial vails were remembered and when they came again, ill-served. Servants, from high to low, were in connivance and a bad vail meant, next time, inferior accommodation and neglectful service at table. Walter would not accept what Sybilla had taken for granted and Godfrey never noticed. 'This will not do for my lady.' And there was something about him, his size, his assurance, his sneer that made other servants give way. Nor was he an easy target for retaliation; more often than not, with his family installed and everybody properly intimidated, he would take himself off to eat, drink, sleep at the most convenient inn.

In other ways he served Sybilla and Godfrey well. He had the sharpest eye for a bargain ever known. His expression was, 'I happened on it.' His happenings were always timely and ranged from a roll of blue-green silk, slightly scorched by a fire which had put a mercer out of business, to a four-year-old riding horse in tip-top condition which he had happened on in Winchester. And paid, he said, knacker's price for.

That bargain could hardly be accepted without question, horse stealing being a capital offence.

'Like I say,' Walter said. 'There's this man, leading a horse and howling like a baby. I asked what ailed him and he said his master was just dead and had left orders for the horse to be destroyed. And he'd looked after it since it was foaled and couldn't bear to take it in to the knacker's yard, but must, dead man's wishes being law. So then . . .' Walter hesitated a second. 'Well, I said I was the knacker—at least his nephew, come to help him. I reckoned the real one might be known by sight. The fellow was only too glad to take the hoof-and-hide money and spare himself a nasty job. So I took the halter. You can tell a knacker's by the smell. We went in, waited a bit, and came out.'

Enquiries corroborated this fantastic tale. A rich old woolmerchant had just died, leaving all his money to the Church and ordering his horse to be destroyed.

With his usual courtesy Sir Godfrey apologised to Walter for seeming, even for a moment, to doubt his word.

Walter said, 'I've been thinking. It'd be worth while for

somebody to nip along and ask about the harness. There might be a bargain there. It'd likely be better than yours.'

After that Walter's bargains were accepted unquestioningly. So were his loyalty, devotion and ability. Sir Godfrey, riding off to join Lord Malvern's punitive expedition, knew that he was leaving Sybilla in safe hands.

Sir James kept his word. In his gout-free autumn, September and October, he rode to Intake almost every other day, acting and sounding like a dog dealing with a flock of laggard sheep. He started the campaign with the most acrimonious reproaches about over-charging and did not withdraw them when he realised that the price included solar, still-room and stool-room, though he and Emma exchanged some sharp comments upon this latest proof of Godfrey's stupidity and extravagance. Master Hobson accepted the rebukes in the proper respectful manner, but took leave to point out that things had altered a bit since he last did a job for Sir James. Apprentices now demanded meat three times a week and day workers' wages had risen by a ha'penny a week; in fact, if bad weather set in and this job wasn't completed by Christmas, he'd be out of pocket.

Sir James went on nagging; why this, why that, why the other thing? If on any visit he did not see Master Hobson's ancient grey mare tethered in her usual place, he would bark, 'Where's your master?' and proceed to track the rascal down. On one memorable occasion he found the builder measuring up and preparing to give an estimate for another job. His rage so frightened the would-be client that he withdrew his order.

Sir James did not accept as easily as Sir Godfrey had done, the explanation for the comparative uselessness of the men he had lent. They had cleared the ground, done a lot of work on the digging of foundations, they carried stuff, but they were not, in their master's opinion fully occupied.

'God's blood!' he exploded, one day early in October, 'they could do the stables and outbuildings. No skill needed there. Set them to work, man! Make use of them!' In another, craftier, calmer mood he asked, 'Is there a guild of well-diggers, Hobson?' Master Hobson was obliged to confess that if such a thing existed he had never heard of it. 'Then set my fellows to work on a well.'

The harassing tactics were effective; the house grew apace. It acquired its name. All those early settlers, suddenly emancipated, frenziedly trying to clear land and make a living on a subsistence level had been very conscious of the word *acre*. Most of the little farms, though now wider than an acre, were known by the names of their makers. Robin's Acre, Martin's Acre, Will's Acre. It was inevitable that Sir Godfrey's growing house should be called Knight's Acre.

Coming up, echoing from an even further past was something which nobody now, in the middle of the fifteenth century, was fully prepared to admit to, a superstition, older than memory. Nothing to do with the cheerful custom of putting a green bough on the highest point of a new building, with a bit of ribbon maybe, and somebody saying, 'God Bless This House.' Nothing to do with the equally cheerful custom of spilling a little wine or ale on the newly set doorstep in order to make sure that plenty would be the rule here. Old customs died hard and they died patchily. Master Hobson, a bit of a sceptic, was fully prepared to fix a bough, spill a drop of ale, because, like almost everyone else who had come in close contact with him, he had liked Sir Godfrey.

About the other ritual Master Hobson was not so sure. And when he was not sure he said to himself, 'Ah . . .' and waited. Wait; see how things went, see how the men felt.

Early in November Sir James's winter gout set in, exacerbating his temper but not preventing him from doing his duty though he reduced his visits to two in a week. On a day when early mist gave way to a curious and beautiful luminosity, he arrived at Intake. The grey mare was not there, and to his critical eye the thatching seemed to have made little progress since his last visit. At the front of the house there was a young man on a ladder, doing something very peculiar. The space between the upright beams had been plastered for at least a fortnight, well ahead of the onset of frost; yet this young man had a bucket of plaster slung from the rung of the ladder. He dipped into it, spread it on the space between two of the upper windows, smoothed and pressed it with his hands and then applied to it what looked like a thick wooden dish. He wiped around the dish very carefully, flicking bits of exuding plaster away, and waited, and then withdrew the dish, surveying what was revealed with smug satisfaction.

Sir James shouted, 'Hi, there! You fellow! What do you think you're doing?'

The young man looked down and said mildly, 'Pargeting, sir.' Despite the mildness there was something cocksure about his manner, about that brief downward glance and then back to his work that was infuriating.

'Come down off that ladder.'

The young man obeyed, not with alacrity but with a kind of weary patience—what now? As soon as he was on the ground he studied the inside of the dish-like thing, took an oily rag from his apron pocket and began to rub. Altogether too much!

'Stand up when you speak to me. Take your cap off! Where's your master?'

'Dead, sir.'

For a moment rage gave way to another emotion. Younger than me, and in good health!

'Hobson. Dead? How? He was here on Monday.'

'Master Hobson is not my master. I served my time with Master Turner. Then I set up on my own.'

'Where's Hobson?'

'Gone to Marshmere to complain. The thatchers found straw mixed with the reeds.'

Reasonable; indeed praiseworthy. But anger must be vented.

'Now, what's this pargeting?'

'As you see, sir.' He looked up, drawing Sir James's gaze to the three completed panels.

The design was based on the family badge. A hare, up on its hind legs, defying some invisible enemy, in defence of a little leveret, crouched low behind her.

The badge fitted exactly the family motto—'I defend my own'—for the hare, though usually a timid animal had been known to fly at the nose of a bullock in defence of its young.

The silver gilt light of the morning brought out the shape and contours of this white-on-white decoration, revealing a beauty which Sir James was not in a mood to appreciate.

21

'A lot of nonsense,' he said. 'You can stop it at once and find a job of work.'

Something sparked in the young man's eyes, but he remained civil.

'Pargeting *is* work, sir.'

The mould, cut into solid beechwood, had taken five days to complete. Allowed more time he would have carved the motto, too, and the date. But Hobson, pressed by Sir James, in turn pressed his son-in-law, and apart from the hare and the leveret, both most lifelike in their postures of defiance and terror, all he had added was what looked like some blades of grass, just in front of the hare's hind feet. The intertwined grass blades were in fact his signature—his name was Walter Weaver.

'Sir Godfrey ordered pargeting,' the young man said, seeing that no word of appreciation was forthcoming.

Sir James thought—He would! The young fool!

'You tell Hobson I cancelled that order. Find yourself something useful to do.'

The pressure of the stirrup increased the pain in his gout-swollen foot; the delay in the thatching increased the risk that Sybilla and her horrible children would be at Moyidan for Christmas—they'd been at Beauclaire for a full six months—and he simply could not wait to tell Emma about this latest proof of Godfrey's wicked extravagance: so, contrary to custom, he did not ride round to the back of the house to see how the stables were going up or the well going down. He turned his horse and rode home.

He was no sooner out of sight around the little flint church which his great grandmother had built and endowed; a pious woman and fearful that a five-mile walk from Intake to Moyidan was too much for the young, the old, or men who had laboured for six days, than William Weaver, more often known as William Pargeter, resumed work.

He was, as his father-in-law knew, a sour-tempered, scornful young rebel, far less appreciative than he should have been of his profound good fortune in marrying Barbara Hobson, with her generous dowry which had enabled him to go into business on his own, and her chestful of household linen which

22

many a lady might envy. All he cared for was his work—good work. Even his grudging father-in-law admitted that and found him a job whenever he could. He was not really the right husband for Barbara, too much engrossed in his work— 'Chippings all over the place,' too little grateful for good meals—'He does not care whether his supper is hot or cold.'

In Sir James's presence he controlled himself having no wish to offend, or to do or say anything which would be detrimental to his father-in-law—the only outlet so far, for his beautiful work.

So he had restrained himself, spoken civilly, but at some cost. Find yourself something useful to do. I cancelled that order. Tremulous, despising himself for allowing somebody so wooden-headed as Sir James to upset him so, William Weaver, the pargeter, set about moving his ladder into the next space between the windows. But, upset by anger and the need to control it, he forgot that before the ladder was shifted the bucket of plaster should be removed.

The ladder moved, lurched, and the bucket of plaster tilted.

Master Hobson, coming back from Marshmere where he had dealt with the cheating reed supplier more harshly than anybody had ever dealt with him, was sorry, but not altogether sorry . . . He had never much liked his son-in-law, while admitting his skill.

And William Weaver's death, though not in the old ritual way a sacrifice to ensure luck on the house, was opportune. Master Hobson had been planning to bring a stray cat or dog and damn what his son-in-law might have to say about superstition. The house had been given its sacrifice. It would stand firm and prosper.

THE Lady Emma, though she had not had a convent up-bringing, had mastered the arts of reading and writing and had twice written to Sybilla reporting upon the progress of the building. 'It will be done by Christmas.' Neither letter contained an invitation for the family to spend the festive season at Moyidan and Sybilla could read, between what was said and what was left unsaid, that she and the children were expected to remain at Beauclaire for Christmas and then move.

Emma's third letter arrived on the 20th of December; the house was ready and furnished with most essentials. Emma also had kept her word and listed the articles which Sybilla did not need to bring or buy.

Sybilla had no intention of moving before Christmas. The festival was always observed in great style at Beauclaire, and this year Henry, almost seven and Richard, hard on six, would be able to participate—something to remember—and in the roisterings, with the Lord of Misrule in charge, their rowdy behaviour would give no offence.

It was with a certain innocent pride that she imparted to her sister-in-law the news that the house was ready. Lady Astallon's reaction was astounding, the more so because she was a woman who never seemed to be aware of anything. She seemed to go through life like a beautiful somnambulist. She had been the beauty of the family, had made a grand marriage, was adored by her husband—and by a number of other men who seemed to be content to worship at the shrine of her icy loveliness with no more reward than an inattentive attention, and a remote smile now and again. Sybilla had expected her to say, 'Indeed. I am happy for you, my dear.'

Lady Astallon, suddenly sharp and practical, said, 'My dear, I think you should go at once. Snow always falls immediately after Christmas. I will see that a wagon is ordered for you. And tell Dame Margery to give you anything in the way of stores that you may require. What about beds?'

The Abbess herself could not have spoken more briskly or sensibly. It was the first time that the slightest resemblance between the two sisters had evidenced itself.

Dame Margery, who from the still-room actually ruled much of Beauclaire, had a soft spot for Sybilla who, before the children came—and later, when the boys were small and manageable, had often lent a hand with the making of potpourri and such delicate work as candying violets and rose petals.

'You see to the packing of your own gear, my lady,' she said. 'I'll see to it that you have stores for a month. I'll make sure you have a good horse and wagon, too.'

Fond as she was of Lady Tallboys, Dame Margery would be glad to see the back of those two terrible little boys who had once stolen into the still-room and drunk an incredible amount of raspberry cordial in the making. They had been first drunk and then sick; in the first state they had been destructive and in the second disgusting.

The wagon and the horse selected by Dame Margery's distant but powerful finger, were both good and the wagon was loaded before sunset that day. Lady Astallon, without stirring had been active, too. Emma at Moyidan had provided *two* beds; she added another and some good blankets.

The hitch came over the question of who was to drive the wagon to Suffolk and bring it back.

Nobody actually *said* he would not go, setting out on a journey that would take at least three days—and three back, which would mean missing all the merry preliminaries, the bringing in of the Yule Log, the cutting of holly, ivy and mistletoe, the election of some humble person, servant or clown, to be Lord of Misrule whose most fantastic orders must be obeyed. Nobody refused to go to Suffolk, but everybody was ready with a reason why he should not be the one. Beauclaire like all overgrown establishments was riddled with favouritism, with corruption. In the end Lady Tallboys was to be driven to her new home by a boy, a near idiot who owed his place in the household to the fact that he was related to one of the under-cooks, and could pluck a fowl.

He also could be trusted to return without the horse and wagon. All the servants at Beauclaire wished to protect their master from any depredation but their own, so from some hidden place a rickety wagon was pulled and the load transferred. When, at first light Sybilla emerged into the courtyard, the half-wit was hitching the wagon to a decrepit old horse. Walter who had preceded her by a few minutes, carrying down her clothes chest and her lute, was raging. The boy was an idiot, there was some mistake; if the lady would just go back inside for a minute he'd see it set right.

'There was no mistake, Walter. If it takes us a mile I shall be content.'

A glance at her face enlightened him. He placed the chest and the lute in the wagon and helped Sybilla in. The well-stuffed feather mattress made a comfortable seat, and the framework of the bed—one of the low, truckle kind—covered with a blanket made something to lean against. Walter tucked the other blankets around Sybilla, the baby and the little girl who, strictly speaking was no longer a baby, but who acted like one.

'Up you get, Master Richard. I'll just get my own box . . .' He had it somewhere handy, for he was back in a minute with the old arrow box which contained all he owned. 'And we're not taking that numbskull. So much dead weight. If they want this contraption back they can send for it. Now Master Henry, you can sit alongside me. To start with,' he added, knowing the boys well. 'You'll take turns.'

He looked at the horse and thought—Hit it and it'd fall over! So he clucked to it, it leaned against the collar, the wheels creaked and they were off.

It was still very early in the morning, the sky in the east rose-flushed.

The insult of this shameful equipage stung for a little in Sybilla's heart but was soon assuaged. Perhaps not deliberate, simply a matter of muddle and servants' cunning. The Abbess has taught her that in certain situations a dignified acceptance was preferable to futile protest. Besides she was going home. To the first place which after more than twenty-three years of living, and almost eight of married life, she would be able to

26

call her own, her very own.

Presently Henry said, 'I want to drive.'

'Then want'll be your master.'

Henry grabbed the reins and Walter said, 'Do that again and you'll go in the back.'

'I'm not going to ride with children!'

Richard wriggled forward and from behind took his brother's arm in a known, painful grip. 'Don't you call me *children*.' Henry twisted round and retaliated with another hold, a bending down of the fourth finger.

Walter said, 'Whoa,' and glad of a respite, the old horse stopped. 'You want to fight, get down and do it in the road.' They tumbled out willingly enough. Walter clucked to the horse and said, 'A bit of a run'll do them no harm, my lady. I'll keep them in sight.'

He had more to think about than two naughty, squabbling boys. The horse must be guided, for the mud in the road had frozen into high sharp ridges, and there were water-filled pot-holes, crusted with ice. He was also on the look-out for some place where the horse, perhaps the wagon, too, might be exchanged.

He had travelled this road before on his way to Moyidan or Bywater, but he had not realised how lonely this stretch of it was; only one inn, so far, at a crossroads, near a gibbet, and that as miserable a place as any peasant's hovel. It had some tumbledown stables, but no horses.

Behind the wagon, their breath like smoke on the frosty air the boys would stop to pummel each other, or roll each other over; then they would run to overtake the slow creaking wagon. Their faces were like poppies, Sybilla thought. She had no anxiety about them; they never inflicted real damage on each other. Just a fight could break out for the flimsiest reason—or no reason at all—so it always seemed to stop short of actual malice. And here there was nobody to exclaim, or feign alarm, to say, 'Those boys are at it again,' or urge her to rule them more strictly.

At last Walter found what he thought to be a suitable halting place. There was water in a little stream by the road, a clump of beechtrees.

27

'I'd reckon it's nearly dinner time, my lady. Do us all good to stretch our legs a bit.' Walter had an inborn tact and courtesy. When she came back from among the beechtrees he had covered the sweating, steaming horse with a rug, and was offering it water from his hat—an archer's hat made of stiff felt and leather-lined.

The boys came charging up, a truce declared, for exercise had worked off their surplus energy and they were hungry.

Dame Margery—God bless her—had thought of everything. At the top of one hamper was a bowl of delicious brawn, pork pieces in firm jelly, a long loaf of bread; a stoppered jug of mild ale and two horn cups. As Sybilla prepared to cut the brawn, to the top of which white fat had risen, Walter said, 'I could do with some of that grease. For the wheels.' With his own knife he scooped up a handful, and went around, pushing the grease, half melted from the heat of his hand, into the dry axles.

Nobody had ever talked to Walter in abstract terms about resignation to unalterable circumstances, but life had taught him that in order to survive a man must make do with what he had. And he had been thinking about the horse.

Why at Beauclaire where everything was in abundance and waste the rule, should there have been in the stables such a thing of hide and bones available at just the right moment? Just as somebody had provided for human needs, so somebody else had provided for the horse; a bag of oats. Holding his slab of bread and brawn in one hand, offering the horse oats from his hat with the other—December days were short and there was no time to waste—Walter hit on the truth. This horse was so old that its teeth were worn down; it could not munch. In the midst of plenty, with nobody noticing, it had been slowly starving.

He went round to the back of the wagon where the mood engendered by freedom, by eating in the open air had taken over.

'Can I have the rest of that loaf, my lady?'

Crumbled and soaked, it was the nearest thing to the bran-mash which kept ailing, or over-exhausted horses on their feet.

By sun-down they reached a village and an inn which

28

Walter remembered as a stopping place for dinner on former, swifter journeys. He threw himself into the business of compensating for the shabby wagon by being as demanding as he could. Lady Tallboys must have a fire in her chamber and a roast fowl for her supper; did The Three Pigeons stock no wine? then Lady Tallboys's supper ale must be mulled; the shoes of the young masters must be dried and cleaned. Henry and Richard had amused themselves by jumping on ice-covered puddles.

In the morning he looked anxiously at the sky, less clear than on the previous day. Snow was his dread. He imagined that two thirds of a loaf of bread and two bran mashes had done something for the horse, but not to the extent of rendering it capable of contending with snow clogged roads. In fact snow, though threatening for the next three days, did not begin to fall until midday of Christmas Eve when they were within a mile of their destination.

It was through a veil of snow that Sybilla first saw Knight's Acre.

She knew its position for once or twice in the early days of her marriage she had ridden with Godfrey to look at what he called his little estate, but she had had no clear mental picture of what the house would look like. He had no talent for describing things and having said that it would be rather like the new part of Moyidan, though smaller of course, he had exhausted his powers; he had not mentioned the solar, the still-room or the stool-room because he wished them to come as a surprise to her; and he had not mentioned the pargeting because he was still uncertain what it meant.

It was rather bigger than she had imagined and had more windows; two to one side of the door, one on the other, and five above. It looked solid and strong against its background of leafless trees. It also looked entirely unwelcoming. This, she quickly realised was because nobody was in it, and just as this was the first time she had ever looked on a building and been able to think—Mine! so it was the first time that she had ever approached a place, at this time of afternoon, in such weather, without seeing a glow of light from fire, or candle.

She was aware suddenly of a decline in spirit. It went further and deeper than the mere lack of welcome which the blank-eyed house presented; she thought—If Dame Margery did not think to put in candles, we shall have no light; and abruptly that was typical of the light-hearted, unprepared way in which this whole thing had been undertaken. Insufficient forethought. She had said that it would be pleasant to have a house of their own, Godfrey had ordered it; and here it was.

She had been too much surprised by Alys's behaviour, too busy concealing her surprise and in making ready to go that she had not thought about candles.

Nor had she thought about what owning a house involved—with the only *certain* income, four pounds a year. Taxes!

It would all have been different if there had been a glow from those windows. But Sir James and his lady had discussed the question of providing servants and decided against it. They did not expect Sybilla to travel before Twelfth Night; servants chosen by other people were never satisfactory; Intake, though not a manor, must have a certain feeling of obligation—and young people to spare; and Sybilla had Walter.

'Here we are, my lady, and just in time. It's thickening,' Walter said. He helped her down, John sound asleep in her arms, and Margaret clutching at her skirt. The boys ran about painstakingly scooping up enough snow to make snowballs with which to pelt each other.

Master Hobson might be a rogue, but he was an honest rogue, what he built he built and the new house had a good solid door; oak, two inches thick and on the outside an iron ring which lifted the latch within and could also serve as knocker.

The door had no lock, though it could be bolted from within. Walter threw open the door and stood aside. Sybilla stepped in.

Darker than out of doors, and almost as cold. The smell of fresh plaster, the smell of lack of use sharply called to mind the convent parlour.

Outside Walter shouted to the boys, 'Gather wood and take

30

it in.' He edged himself through the doorway, her chest under one arm, the lute and the blankets clasped in the other.

'Get a fire going it'll be all different, my lady,' he said and hurried out again. Next time he came in he was carrying the hampers that Dame Margery had provided. The baby was awake now and Sybilla put him down on the floor where he began to crawl about vigorously.

Dame Margery had visualised a new house lacking Christmas provender; she had visualised some makeshift dinners on the road, but she had not foreseen an unlighted house. There were no candles.

The boys ran in and out bringing wood of all kinds, the débris of building. The competition between them had now focussed upon who could find and carry most. Sybilla heard the snow-muffled clop of the old horse's hoofs as Walter led it around the house. Next time he entered he came in from the kitchen, his hands full of straw and thin wood shavings. He knelt on the hearth, worked flint and tinder vigorously and abruptly the room sprang to life.

My first fire on my own hearth, Sybilla thought, but joy refused to come at call. Walter chose the driest and slimmest pieces of wood and placed them, tent-like over the first flames.

'We have no candles, Walter.'

'I'll get my box. I've got one and a half. And a lantern.'

He went out to the front where he had left the wagon and returned with the old arrow box.

Thrift rather than generosity had governed Emma's giving. There was a table, old and battered and unsteady because it had one leg badly worm-eaten; there was a backless bench, capable of holding four people, and a three-legged milking stool. Nothing more and the lack of furniture made the place seem larger than it was; voices and footsteps sounded hollow.

Instead of the interest and curiosity which would have been natural in the circumstances, Sybilla felt a disinclination to move about, a temptation to remain near the bright-burning fire. Such weakness must not be pandered to.

'I'll take the foodstuff into the kitchen,' Walter said.

31

'I'll bring a light. Boys, see that John and Margaret do not get too near to the fire.'

Walter was bi-lingual, his two brands of English, Foul and Decent, being as far apart as any of Babel's tongues. He never confused them. In Foul he had been communicating with himself ever since he saw how the lady had been fobbed off at Beauclaire; to see how she had been treated here—and not by servants, by her own kin, rendered even Foul inadequate.

In the Decent, from which he never varied in her presence, he said, 'It's a good kitchen, my lady.' It was a good kitchen, with a wide hearth, and a bread-oven in the wall. It contained a table, bigger and more solid than the one in the hall; it looked as though at some time it had been used as a carpenter's bench. Laid out on it were such items as Emma had thought essential and which could be easily spared. It was the kind of collection which anyone, living poorly, and suddenly inheriting a fully furnished house, might be expected to throw out from his own humble abode.

'We'll get this straightened out in the morning,' Walter said, eyeing the rusty spit; the pewter candlestick, so bent that no candle could live in it for long, the pile of platters, wooden, potsherd, battered pewter.

Alongside this the contents of the hampers looked munificent. There was even a game pie with what was called a raised crust, patterned and highly glazed.

'We'll eat this for supper,' Sybilla said, 'and then the children must go to bed. All else can wait until morning.'

Upstairs there were two beds, akin to the one brought from Beauclaire, a frame and a mattress, no more. Bleak. But adequate. And what right had she to expect anything to gladden the eye and say, 'Welcome'?

Walter carried up the clothes chest and placed it in the room which contained the larger of the two beds; and then, for the first time in all the years he had travelled with them, she gave a thought to his sleeping arrangements.

'The children will share this bed with me,' she said, 'and the boys will sleep next door. That leaves two empty rooms, and

32

the bed we brought with us. Make yourself comfortable, Walter.'

'I've found myself a place, my lady.'

His old-soldier's eye had spotted it as he led the horse to the stable. Slightly to one side, the remains of the original farmhouse, used, and patchily repaired by the carpenters, masons and casual labourers who had worked here. Watertight, windproof; what more could a man ask? There was even a bed of bracken upon which Walter Freeman, who had standards of his own, did not hesitate to lie. Bracken did not harbour lice as hay and straw and flock and feather did.

When Walter had gone to his own place—wherever that might be—Sybilla experienced something new; loneliness. She had spent years at Lamarsh, where if voices were muted and footfalls soft, they were there. Then Godfrey had whisked her into places where voices were louder and gayer, and footsteps rang. Here with the boys, rolled together like puppies in one room and the two babies fitted like spoons together in the bed she was about to share, there was a ringing silence, an emptiness, a feeling of isolation.

I should have bargained for this when I said I should like a house of my own. I am under my own roof, my children are sleeping peacefully. I should be thankful. God, I do thank you ... She managed two Our Fathers and two Hail Marys before she slept.

4

[*Spring 1452*]

FATHER Ambrose was the first person in Intake to be aware of the arrival. The snow had ceased during the night and looking out into a glittering white world he spied the hump of the snow-covered wagon which obscured his usual view of Knight's Acre's front door. He called briskly for his heavy boots—so well-greased as to be waterproof—and wrapped himself in the shawl which was his winter wear.

'And not even a fire to welcome you, my lady. Had I but known . . .'

His kind heart was genuinely grieved to think of anyone arriving at an unlit, unheated house in the middle of a snow-storm—and on Christmas Day, too; but he was also concerned for a missed opportunity for ingratiating himself with the lady who was to be his most important parishioner. He had been very much excited about the building of the house. Ladies were usually pious and charitable; they did embroidery, altar clothes and copes; they could usually be relied upon to set a good example which God knew Intake could do with. Had he been warned he would have seen to it that the fire was lighted, have been there himself to offer words of welcome. He hast-ened to repair the situation.

'You will need servants, my lady. I think I can put my hand on the very couple. Both named Wade, a woman and her nephew. They have both known service in great houses, but are temporarily out of employment.'

God had called him to what at first sight seemed a sinecure but which had turned out to be hard labour in a very stony field. In the period before Sir Godfrey's great grandmother built and endowed the little church the people of Intake seemed to have lost the habit, and in some cases, even the outward forms of piety. The founders of the village had, after all, been an unruly lot, men whose master at Moyidan had been glad to be rid of. And while Intake had no priest, and during the en-cumbency of Father Ambrose's immediate predecessor who was lax in such matters, there had been a good deal of in-breeding which had hardened the mould. Father Ambrose had never succeeded in breaking it, though he never relaxed his efforts. Just before Christmas he had made a round of the farms, reminding everybody of the seasonal obligations. They knew it was Christmas; they were boiling bag puddings and chopping mincemeat; the young children had dragged in the festive greenery—ivy, holly, mistletoe, and they seemed to resent the reminder.

In the house at Wade's Acre—once a single room of clods, and now a substantial place with six rooms, he noticed that

34

Bessie and Jacky were back. He had said, 'Home for Christmas?' and the unacknowledged head of the family, an old woman of incredible age, had muttered sourly, 'Back for good, by the look of it.'

The two were misfits. The in-breeding against which Father Ambrose had set his face, twenty-five years ago; yes, a quarter century; how time sped! had curious results. Most of the Wades were strong and sensible and very hard workers, far from witless; but the woman, Bessie, nearing forty and very fat, the boy Jacky, fifteen and thin as a rail, were, to put it at its kindliest, simple. The woman was said to be a good cook, but undependable, the boy willing enough but forgetful.

Father Ambrose felt it unnecessary to mention this, or the catalogue of jobs found and quickly lost, to Sybilla. Neither of the pair had ever been employed in Intake—for who was there to employ them? And perhaps in far places, Basildon, Clevely, Muchanger, they had suffered from that debilitating ailment, homesickness, and had lost jobs because they wanted to lose them. Here, within easy reach of their relatives, and under his own eye, they might well do better. Without hesitation he recommended them to Sybilla.

She felt better this morning; everything seemed better. She was faintly ashamed of her overnight feelings of which nothing remained except a kind of caution, the feeling that this was rather a big house to be sustained on such slender resources.

She was not without money. The Intake tenants paid their rent twice a year, at Michaelmas and on Lady Day; two pounds. And at a Michaelmas tourney, Godfrey had won a silver-gilt cup which Walter had sold, happening upon a buyer who wanted a cup as a christening present and had not quibbled at paying ten shillings for a thing which on an open market would have brought no more than eight.

Godfrey had left it all with her; he was taking service under Lord Malvern's standard; he was well provided for, and hoped to come home rich. But something about that looming bulk, the reach of the roof, the widths of the hearths, and the extra rooms which had indeed surprised her, had made an impression that remained, even in this blue and white morning and

35

she said cautiously that she could not afford *expensive* servants. Like everybody else who knew the family Father Ambrose had assumed that Sir Godfrey was well-to-do and Sybilla's remark roused surprise and disappointment; however, he assured her that Bessie Wade would probably be content with three shillings a year, Jacky with eighteen pence, 'And their keep, of course,' he added. 'I will walk across to Wade's Acre and arrange it at once.'

In the doorway he looked about at the waste of hard trodden, wood-littered ground on which the new house stood, and another dream revived. 'I expect your ladyship will be making a garden.' Ladies cared about such things, farm wives did not; he visualised the altar decked with roses and lilies. The only flowers it now knew were occasional offerings from young children, primroses, oxslips, wild daffodils and bluebells, all gathered much too short and damaged by hot little hands.

'I shall hope to—in time,' Sybilla said. She also looked at the unpromising ground and once again felt the weight of the task she had undertaken. As she had slept in other people's beds and eaten at their tables, so she had enjoyed their gardens, their roses and lilies and gilly flowers, their lavender and rosemary. Would this waste ever flower?

Self-pity was not an actual *sin*, but it showed weakness of character. She braced herself. Here is the house I wanted and asked for and here in due time will my garden be . . .

Walter looked at the cleared land before and around the house with a different eye. Fourth son of a yeoman farmer and as much the victim as Sir Godfrey of the Norman institution of primogeniture, he had always been land hungry. Now here it was, enough even for a land-hungry man; acres of it. Sir James's men, fearful of seeming idle, had cleared the ground well. Walter could see that, even under the covering of snow.

This year it would be hit or miss; no autumn sown seed, lying there waiting. It would mean spring ploughing and spring sowing; but he'd manage.

Because he must.

He knew far more about Sir Godfrey's finances than either Sir Godfrey or the lady knew about *his*. Four pounds a year and some prize money soon earned, soon spent, did not, in Walter's view represent security. A place of this size should, must, be self-supporting. And would be, if he had anything to do with it.

Walter bitterly resented the twelve wasted days of Christmas; all very well for the rich, playing the fool and guzzling. And the poor, blind, stupid, copied their betters. Everything stopped for Christmas and it was twelve days before Walter could really get to work. What could be done in the interval he did. He coddled the old horse which responded gallantly, he bullied the Wades, who, if they had as the lady said, ever been in service before, showed no signs of any training. A great fat slob of a woman, a flibberty-gibbert boy. The lady, as always, had listened to soft talk—this time from the priest and Walter distrusted priests, and monks, and friars; even the one Bishop he had encountered, William of Bywater who literally starved himself, and his guests, in order to support a Lying-in Hospital for fallen women and a Foundlings' Home for the children who were the product of the falls.

In Walter's opinion, William, Bishop of Bywater should have fed his guests better, and as soon as he heard that the lady, his brother's wife, was about to move in, should have sent wall hangings, some chairs, a settle with cushions.

The lady would have such things in time, because Walter would obtain them for her, in the meantime, first things first . . .

The men of Intake no more liked Walter than the servants in great houses had done. He had an unpleasant manner and they could not as they said, 'place' him. He was only a serving man, but his manner was brusque and lordly and they thought his speech affected. It was not Suffolk. Bessie and Jacky Wade reported unfavourably on him, too. He'd threatened Bessie with the sack unless her cooking improved, he'd given Jacky a clip on the ear. Such behaviour from a master would not have been worth remarking, coming from a fellow servant it bred resentment.

Dislike of him took the form of refusing any of the mutual aid usual in a small, isolated community. Nobody was prepared to *lend* him a plough; he could *hire* one and it'd be a farthing a day.

From afar they watched his first ploughing with malicious curiosity. Ploughing with a horse; what ignorance! Some of them were interested enough to inspect his furrows, certain of finding many crooked ones, dog's legs. Ploughing was an art and straightness of ridges was closely related to evenness of planting and ease in reaping. There were no dog's legs in Walter's field; in the last of the daylight the furrows lay straight and sure, washed with a faint mauvish light on one side, deep brown on the other. Such a skilled performance—and comparatively quickly done, since a horse moved faster than an ox—was not endearing, and when Walter went the round again, this time offering to buy seed corn, nobody had any to sell.

Walter made the first of his raids upon Baildon.

What sort of fist would he make of the sowing? Disappointingly good. He had the rhythm of it; striding along and matching the throws to his paces. Walter, with a stern father and even sterner elder brothers had been well-trained. As he sowed the boys followed, dragging branches like rakes, to cover the seeds.

With two fields ploughed and sown, he turned his attention to making a garden; the house would need peas and beans, carrots, onions, cabbages. He made small spades for Henry and Richard, so that they could help with the digging. 'And he's nigh as strict with them as he is with us,' Bessie said.

A household also needed livestock of its own. Sharp-eyed in the market, Walter found a bargain, a cow with two defective teats. It took longer to find a sow going cheap, but his luck served him again; an elderly sow, in pig; she was a known good breeder, but savage tempered. Her owner had recently died, his widow was afraid of the beast, and in fact the sow was offered for sale, immobilised in a fishing net. Everybody knew what that meant!

'And the net thrown in,' Walter said gleefully. 'Handy for catching pigeons.'

Pigeons mattered.

Dame Margery had not envisaged a household with no re-

38

sources, no pork or beef salted down in casks, no sides of bacon in the smokehole. She had merely seen that, leaving so suddenly, on the brink of Christmas, Lady Tallboys needed the festive season's trimmings. She had packed the game pie, and that delicacy, a sugar-cured ham, cooked and garnished. Once they were consumed, the household had been dependent upon what could be bought from the grasping villagers, snared, trapped or shot in Layer Wood.

Walter had not even been able to indulge in ritual swapping. When you kill your pig, let me have a half, or a quarter and when I kill mine, you shall have the same. Presently he would be able to do so.

Once he had shot a deer and Sybilla, glad enough of the meat, had been rather dubious about the law.

'There are so many rules about venery, Walter. We may have no rights in Layer Wood.'

'It was on our field, my lady.'

'I am not sure that that justifies . . . I seem to remember . . .' The convent at Lamarsh had included amongst its properties a belt of forest and the Abbess had been very meticulous about her rights.

'Never mind, Walter. Just this once. I will ask Sir James when I see him. He will know. Meanwhile, roast venison! Can you fletch it, Walter?'

'I should hope so, my lady.'

When I see him, Walter thought, dealing expertly with the deer's carcass—once, in a forgotten siege in a forgotten place, he had flayed what remained of a dead horse. To himself, in Foul language of an extreme sort, Walter denounced Sir James of Moyidan. Not a . . . visit, yet! . . . his gout, could the . . . not have come in a . . . wagon? . . . well ashamed to show his . . . face, to look at the . . . stuff he had allowed his . . . wife to send! . . . her and him and all connected with them.

It was over the deer's carcass that Walter found a fault in the house. It had no smokehole, that wide chimney in which meat could be hung, with a slow burning fire of turf or sawdust burning below. But he improvised. The hearth cold he set a stool amongst the ashes and reached up as far as he could and drove in a nail. Anything hung on it would be beyond the scorch of a flame. The whole process might take longer than usual. In his home, with a proper smokehole, a ham and a side of bacon took about a month to be cured; here with the smoke anything but steady, reckon six weeks.

'Walter,' Henry said, 'why don't you *shoot* pigeons?'

'Because there'd be nothing left. Just a smear. I've sent an arrow through a four inch door. Ask yourself what a pigeon'd look like.'

To Walter, as to everyone else the boys had been almost indistinguishable, handsome, noisy, badly behaved. But since the move had been made Walter, somewhat surprising himself, had taken a fancy to Henry because, given a job, Henry would stick at it till he dropped. Henry was the stuff out of which men were made. About Richard, Walter was not so sure. Always wanting to be treated as an equal, but not prepared to measure up. Henry, Walter had concluded, was teachable in a way that Richard was not.

Now that the boys spent so long doing things with Walter the house was reasonably peaceful for long hours at a time. Sybilla tended the two young children, John just beginning to totter about and Margaret, soon to be four, still very childish. Reaching back to her time in the kitchen at Lamarsh, Sybilla resurrected her domestic knowledge and tried to teach Bessie who was incapable of remembering anything from one day to another, and seemed not to care. Really, Sybilla sometimes thought impatiently, it would be quicker and cheaper to do things myself!

Whatever she was about, so long as daylight lasted, she was listening. For a hoof beat; a knock on the door.

Godfrey could not write, but he knew that Sybilla could read, and over the years she had received brief, stilted letters from him, written by another. More usual was the verbal message. The invisible lines of communication covered the country, a web woven by knights on the move, foot soldiers, pedlars, cattle-dealers, wool-buyers. Anybody would carry a letter or a message because it was the rule that in the main payment was made by the recipient.

Nobody came to Intake except an old woman hawking fish; and presently, as soon as his winter gout receded, James of

40

Moyidan. He was still a little lame and hobbled in and sank down thankfully on the comfortable high-backed, cushioned settle and said that he was glad to see, and he was sure Emma would be glad to hear, that Sybilla was so well installed. As he looked around it struck him that nothing he saw was familiar, but Moyidan was a big place. He had left the furnishing of Knight's Acre to Emma, and as usual, Emma had done well.

It was Walter who had furnished the hall and made it fit to live in.

From the first Walter had been forming his scheme, letting it wait until more essential things were done; but when she said that she was not certain about her rights to the deer in Layer Wood, he thought—Oh! And what about those two young oaks? He had adjusted his programme. Slightly sooner than he would have done had he not felt the pressure of time, Walter sought out a man who made furniture to order and proposed a reasonable deal. Two standing oaks in exchange for a table, cushioned settle, a cupboard, four bedposts.

Oak was becoming scarce, especially in a neighbourhood within easy distance of the sea. Ship builders grabbed all the oak.

'What girth?'

'One I can just put my arms round. The other a bit larger.'

A trick somewhere. The old man who made beautiful things but who shuffled and mumbled and blinked and left all dealings to his son, said, 'Very well, I will send my son out to look at the standing timber, tomorrow.'

Walter assumed his most disagreeable expression. He said, 'Take it or leave it. I want the things *now*!'

'For Lady Tallboys?'

'I told you, didn't I. Lady Tallboys.'

'Moyidan?'

'Knight's Acre.'

A reliable name.

'Very well. The difficulty is, I have no cupboard.'

God forgive him the lie! Pushed into a corner, shrouded in sailcloth was the most beautiful thing he had ever made. Years ago, a thing made for the joy of making, without any thought of selling. A thing of his own. Long ago, when he was an

41

outdoor working carpenter, mending broken floor boards at Muchanger, he had seen what was called a court-cupboard, or livery cupboard. A beautiful thing. For the sheer joy of making, in snatched minutes from ordinary day-by-day work, the carpenter had made such a cupboard. The doors that enclosed its lower compartment were carved in the linenfold pattern; its two upper, open shelves were carved with oak leaves and acorns. And into the arch, above the upper shelf, he had set his sign. 'J Woodey maid me 1440'.

He had intended the cupboard to be a gift for his wife and she had rejected it. 'Take all day to dust,' she said; not meaning to be cruel, simply sensible.

'So what would you call this,' the scarred man said, twitching at the canvas that had so long covered the masterpiece and the dream.

'Well . . . Yes, it is a cupboard. But not for sale.'

'Belong to somebody?'

'Well, yes in a manner of speaking.'

'Who?' Walter was relentless. It was a beautiful thing, the kind of thing the lady should possess, and there was something shifty about the man's manner. People in illegal possession of things for sale sometimes wore that look, and they were easy prey.

'Well . . . me.' The admission was made with reluctance.

'Then you can sell it.' A course of action frequently urged on the old artist, by his wife, by his son; and doggedly resisted.

'I don't want to. I didn't make it for sale.'

'Then the deal's off. I'll offer the oak to somebody willing to do business.'

Sweating the old man thought of how his son would scold. He'd hear somebody boasting about *his* bargain; two standing oaks!

'I never thought of selling it. I got fond of it. I spent a lot of time on it . . .'

Walter knew the signs of submission.

'It'll have a good home with Lady Tallboys,' he said, speaking as though of a pet animal.

And that is more than it would here, when he was gone; his

42

son would sell to the first bidder.

'Well ...'

'Right then. Now for a table and a settle.'

Sybilla was delighted, but dismayed at the thought of the price such good things must have cost.

'Not a penny, my lady. A straight swap for a couple of trees.'

Whose trees?

So now, when James had finished admiring the things which Emma had not provided, Sybilla, without mentioning either the shot deer or the swapped trees, asked an artless question about Godfrey's rights in Layer Wood.

'Difficult to say. For one thing there were never any fixed boundaries. All the manors, Clevely, Muchanger, Nettleton and half a dozen more meet somewhere in the wood. I'll get Emma to look it up. There's a document somewhere, granting the Intake people a right to take pigs in at acorn time and to gather dead wood for fuel. Not to cut trees—once their houses were built; or to take game.'

'Strictly speaking, then the wood around here is still yours —part of Moyidan.' How unfair that one man should have inherited so much, his brother so little.

'Strictly speaking yes. But between brothers ... When Godfrey comes home if he and friends want to hunt, or you need a tree for any purpose, I shouldn't go to law about it.' He gave her one of his infrequent smiles. He was making a concession, with—he thought—good grace, but it was a concession nonetheless, and he hoped she was aware of it.

She was. She said, 'Thank you James. That is very generous of you.' She gave him not a smile exactly, but a look which reminded him that in the past, once the monetary disappointment of Godfrey, so poor, marrying a girl equally poor had been accepted, he had been inclined to think, from time to time, that in fact Godfrey hadn't done so badly for himself. Sybilla had always been welcome at Moyidan until she came with those two great healthy boys, a girl who bade fair to be pretty, and then a third son.

What a court-cupboard should have, and this one lacked,

was a display of silver. Drinking cups, bowls for salt.

No man of his generation had won more silver cups than Sir Godfrey had—a drinking cup, either with or without some coins inside—was the universally acknowledged prize. The Tallboys family had never kept one for much longer than a fortnight though Sybilla had expressed a wish that each child should have one, a thing for every day use and also a memento of his father's prowess. Something had always cropped up to render sale imperative and Godfrey had always said, in his light-hearted way, 'Time enough'.

Tournament prizes were in fact growing less valuable. In this, as in everything else, fashion worked downward and King Henry VI was not a good patron for tourneys. He was scholarly—even monkish, far more interested in founding a school at Eton, a College at Cambridge ... Some people said he was slightly mad.

And Godfrey Tallboys was almost equally unworldly. Some contests in the lists were run under the rule that any knight unhorsed forfeited his horse—in some cases even his armour, to the one who had struck him down. Of this rule Godfrey had never taken advantage; 'Bad enough to be so shamed, without being stripped.'

Once she had made a mild protest, saying had things been reversed, *he* would have been stripped and he had laughed and said, 'Time enough to think about that when it happens. And God pity anybody who takes Arcol. He'd soon learn that he'd got the wrong cat by the tail.'

She did not argue; there was something about his eyes, very blue—not that the colour was worthy of notice because blue eyes of varying shades were commonplace—but his had the candour of a child's. Transparent, concealing nothing. It was sometimes a little difficult to associate that mild, candid look with the precise ferocity with which he fought, or with the innocent pleasure with which he received adulations—the shouts and cheers, the flung flowers ... and ribbon bows and bits of lace from headdresses. Sybilla had sat in the space reserved for ladies at more tourneys than she could count, knowing that she was envied.

Walter owned a silver cup, won in an archery competition.

44

A silly prize, he'd thought at the time, to offer to men who would far rather have had its worth in money; but over the years he had grown attached to it, often used it for drinking and kept it well-polished with fine woodash and spit.

He thought it would look well upon the cupboard and smuggled it into the hall at a time when Sybilla was not there. Another surprise for her! But ... It was worse than nothing. He'd always known it was a little cup, but not *so* little. On the beautiful, massive cupboard it looked trumpery and silly. He put it back in his pocket.

It was just possible, he reflected, that this time Sir Godfrey would come home with a sackful of loot; possible, but not likely; he wasn't very good at acquiring things, and even worse at keeping them. Wales was a long way from Knight's Acre and somewhere along the road the silly —— (foul word) would be accosted by starving widows with multitudes of children, by old broken-down knights gone wrong in the head; and he'd get into a card game, or a dice game with some —— (foul word) swindling rogues. Walter liked Sir Godfrey and at times admired him, but he had no respect for his acumen, or even his good sense.

Sybilla's next visitor was William, Bishop of Bywater. Once again at the sound of hoofs, the momentary halt of the heart, the running to the window.

William had remembered the amiable custom of bringing a gift to a new house and fortunately had the very thing to hand so that the poor Magdalens and the foundlings need not be deprived. It was a wall hanging which some well-meaning parishioner had bequeathed him—possibly because she had heard that on taking up his appointment he had sold all those that his predecessor had acquired. A well-meant gesture, but the tapestry was far too secular to be hung on his walls. It depicted some very lightly clad women, one indeed so lightly clad as to be wearing almost nothing, bowed over a casket from which some strange thing was emerging, a kind of winged serpent.

As he had guessed, Sybilla was delighted with it—he had always thought her, with her pretty headdresses and fashion-

45

able clothes, curiously worldly for a convent-bred girl—still mourned by Mary, over at Lamarsh. ('What you do not realise,' Mary had once said to him, 'is that Sybilla had an almost infinite capacity for adjustment. Soft as dough on the outside, iron at heart. I shall never now find such another.')

He asked about Godfrey; agreed that no news was good news; explained why he had not come before. His was, except for those in the extreme north perhaps, the widest diocese in England and he was conscientious about the visitations which he must regularly make to all the Abbeys, Priories, Convents within this wide area. He loathed these visitations. One day he dined in princely splendour with the Abbot of Baildon—and no fault to be found there; next day he was at Clevely where a few old women, good women, lived in extreme poverty, in a decaying house—nobody's fault. And even at Lamarsh which was typical of many, nothing much to put a finger on; the women, not nuns, who walked about with little dogs in their sleeves were merely being temporarily accommodated; this one a widow, his sister Mary explained, quite broken-hearted, the little sleeve-dog her only solace; and this one ... an orphan, an heiress who had taken a dislike to the man whom her guardian wished her to marry.

In a way William, Bishop of Bywater was as singleminded and superficial as his brother Godfrey or his brother James. He was happy to see Sybilla comfortably established and well served.

(Out in the kitchen Walter had said to Jacky, 'This is the first guest my lady has ever had at her table. You make a mess of serving and I'll —— (foul word) break your —— (foul word) neck.' It was a remarkable fact, one which Walter had long ago observed; Decent could be misunderstood, Foul was universal.)

On his good horse—the one luxury he allowed himself, because time mattered, William Tallboys trotted away content that he had no cause to worry about Sybilla, well housed, well served.

5

HORSE hoofs again. And a very splendid young man, quite dazzling in the March sunshine. News at last!

'Lady Tallboys?' And well might he ask for she had come straight from the kitchen, from the latest, hopeless attempt to instruct Bessie in the making and baking of bread.

Hastily she pulled down her sleeves, rolled up above the elbows; and was glad that—great as the temptation was to discard such an inconvenient thing, she was wearing her head-dress, six months ago the latest fashion. Godfrey, when he came, must not find her like a farmwife.

'At your service, my lady. I bring a message from Sir Godfrey.'

'God bless you . . .'

'Sir Simon. Simon Randall. I am on my way home to Cressacre and it was only a short detour.'

'Is he well?'

'In most excellent health, I assure you. Disappointed about the war—as indeed we all were.'

Not that it mattered to him, with all Cressacre behind him. He had only gone to the war for the sake of excitement and to please Lord Malvern who was both his uncle and his godfather—and, a knight should be truthful, if to nobody else, at least to himself, to escape for a season his masterful mother's matrimonial schemes.

Gently, but firmly, Sybilla broke Margaret's clutch on her skirt. 'Darling, go and play with John . . . Yes, Sir Simon?' She knew that this was an occasion that called for wine, and she had none.

'Sir Godfrey asked me to tell you that he is bound for Winchester—the Easter tourney there; the war being so unprofitable.'

Unprofitable indeed! The Welsh fought like devils and any place, hard-taken, offered just about as much loot as this place would, and men who called themselves princes could only offer for ransom some lean-barrelled, long-legged sheep, wild in the hills. Covertly he looked around. What a poor place! Not at all the background he had imagined for Sir Godfrey Tallboys. The lady was a surprise to him too; so very young to be the mother of four.

She apologised for having no wine, no saffron cake to offer. 'We have but recently moved in.' She managed to imply that as soon as the move was really complete wine and cake would be plentiful, silver would shine on the cupboard shelves and the one, rather narrow wall-hanging be joined by a multitude of others. She had pride and dignity as well as a kind of look which he found attractive, something tranquil and delicate. He found himself wondering how Sir Godfrey could bring himself to absent himself for so long. Easily answered; money. He repeated in his mind the wish he had expressed upon parting with Sir Godfrey—that he would be victor ludorum in the Winchester lists.

He set himself to entertain her, picking out the lighter episodes of the campaign against the Welsh and not mentioning the hardships or the dangers. They laughed together over the difficulties of telling one Welsh name from another. Time went quickly. Once she excused herself and rose, 'I must see to the bread. My kitchen wench is not to be relied upon, yet,' She went out, leaving the door ajar and presently the sweet, appetising scent of fresh baked bread came through.

Outside Walter looked at the sun and said, 'Dinner time.' He and the boys had been planting peas and beans in what would one day be the kitchen garden. 'There may be company. I heard a horse. Wash your hands before you go in. And mind you behave yourselves.' He had given them the same instructions before they went to greet their uncle James, their uncle William; boring times. Both men, meaning well, had commented upon how they had grown. 'It'd be funny if we hadn't,' Henry said afterwards to Walter.

Now he said, 'Oh, Walter, must we? Couldn't we fetch our dinner and come and eat it with you?'

'You know the answer to that! When I want you in my place, I'll ask you.'

He didn't want them or anybody else in the place he had

48

made his own. He was having a little trouble with Bessie whose attitude towards him had recently undergone a most unwelcome change, from sullen resentment to fawning devotion. It was not the first time this had happened and he judged himself capable of deterring unwanted attentions, such as offers to mend or wash his hose; but the more stupid people were the more thick-skinned they were. Even a snub like, 'You want to wash anything, wash yourself!' bounced off Bessie's dull mind just as Sybilla's culinary instructions did.

'Boys, this is Sir Simon Randall who has kindly brought us news of your father. Sir Simon, this is Henry. And Richard.'

She had managed to instil some rudiments of manners and both boys bowed. After that they stared. Sir Simon was indeed something to look at, for after the filth and mud sweat of a campaign, however brief, finery was imperative. He wore on this day the latest in men's fashions, the parti-coloured outfit. One half of his tunic was the colour of turquoise, the other cherry-red; hose the same, the turquoise leg under the cherry of the turquoise; even his shoes were half and half, the cap which lay beside him on the settle was turquoise, with a cherry coloured feather and an ornament of ruby stones. On one finger he wore another, single, large ruby.

To this very elegant young person Sybilla could offer only a very humble meal, some cold boiled belly pork which Walter had happened upon; but he ate with apparent enjoyment and—judging that she had had a hand in it, praising the bread.

The two boys, he thought, were handsome little fellows—as was to be expected, considering their parentage; and he was disposed to like them, for the same consideration. He did not mind their staring, any new fashion was designed to attract attention; nor did he resent their ill-concealed amusement. Rustics—and some not so rustic; reacted in a similar way. It was when, the sharpest edge taken from their hunger, they began to quarrel for some obscure reason, and checked by their mother, reverted to kicking one another under the table, that he felt that they were out of hand. He was pleased to hear that Henry was presently bound for Beauclaire. He had himself been a page in his uncle's household, and if Beauclaire was

49

anything like that, Henry Tallboys would soon be brought to heel.

For the rest he only noticed that the baby of the family, his chin almost level with the table, fed himself with energy and neatness, once his meat had been chopped, whereas the little girl, some bit older and larger, had to be fed, coaxed and persuaded to eat.

The time came to leave.

At the end he hit upon something he could do for her.

'You will be making a garden, Lady Tallboys?'

'I hope so—in time.'

'My mother *grows* roses—I mean, not that roses grow for her, she propagates them. She has found a way of grafting a real rose on to a good wild briar. I am sure that it would give her great pleasure to send you a few of her trees.'

And so it would. If only it could be concealed from his mother that at last, at last, he had seen a woman whom he would willingly marry, and could not.

Up to a point, in falling in love with Sybilla, Sir Simon was conforming to pattern. Every young man was supposed to cherish a hopeless passion for the unattainable one; active to do her any small service, to beg a favour to wear in the lists and if he had any talent make verses, make tunes in her honour. And then from the impossible he turned to the possible and married, as advantageously as he could.

Not for me, Sir Simon thought.

The Easter Tournament at Winchester, Sybilla knew, began on Easter Monday and lasted three days. Any minute now she thought. But he did not come and there was no message.

She told herself that perhaps Winchester had proved unprofitable, too, and that Godfrey had accepted another invitation, another challenge.

And then, on a beautiful early May morning, with Layer Wood full of bluebells and cuckoos, he came home.

As always, at the slightest unusual sound she ran to the window and saw, nearing the house, a flat cart, drawn by the horse that Walter had saved, and driven by an only-just-recognisable Eustace. Arcol, wearing only a halter was attached to the back of the cart.

Godfrey was dead! Brought home for burial.

There was a second or two of blackness. Then dizzy, sick, supporting herself by clutching at the wall, she made her way to the door, which stood open.

'It is all right,' Eustace called. 'Only an accident . . .'

Unaware that she was crying, she ran to the cart.

What kind of accident could reduce a man in the prime of life to skeleton, all skin and bones, with sunken, senseless eyes? And the boy looked little better—except that he was in his right mind. Godfrey seemed not to know her. She said, 'My dear! My darling!' and he seemed not to hear.

Stiffly, moving like an old man, Eustace climbed down.

'He took a fall, my lady. He made light of it and we set out for home . . . Then the fever set in. People thought we carried the plague . . .' As he said that, he attempted to laugh and produced a woeful, hooting noise. He was near breaking point, but sensible enough, when she had shouted for Walter and Walter had come, to say, 'It is his knee. Mind his knee. That is where it started.'

Walter took charge.

One thing about mean, truckle beds they were light and easily moved. On the one brought from Beauclaire and never yet used here, Sir Godfrey was placed, and carried into his home.

She knew a dozen febrifuges, but she had nothing to hand; not even sage or mint or lime from which to make an infusion. Walter said all that was needed was cold water, inside, outside, and he would deal with it.

Father Ambrose, seeing the cart, had come along, and asked what was afoot and told, plodded down to the village to Watson's wife, a woman about whom he had, in his deepest heart, both a dislike and suspicion; but she made good brews.

Eustace made his last effort. 'I must see to Arcol; nobody else . . .' And that was true, Arcol, besides being an exceptionally valuable horse was an exceptionally difficult one. Then, Arcol stabled and Sir Godfrey in good hands, the boy who had not had a sound night's rest for a fortnight, lay down on the settle and slept for two nights and a day.

By that time Sir Godfrey was himself—or almost himself again; allowing for the accident and the fever. Either Walter's cold-water cure or the rather sinister black brew which Father Ambrose had brought from the village had been effective. Behind those frightening, fever blanked eyes, there was Godfrey.

But not as he had been.

Almost the first thing he said to her was, 'I was unhorsed; by a beardless boy!'

Eustace, waking from a long, restorative sleep, explained and elaborated. It was true. For the first time in his whole career, Sir Godfrey had been unhorsed and had hurt his knee—his right knee. A mere bruise, he said: and, since they were now almost without funds, they had set out for home. By evening the knee was discoloured and swollen and very stiff and in the morning he had had the utmost difficulty in mounting. Next day the fever struck.

With any kind of open wound, or after loss of blood, fever was expected, but for a bruise . . .?

'I found a doctor, my lady, and he said dark swellings and fever were signs of plague. He held a pomander to his nose and did not even wait for payment. Sir Godfrey was in his right mind then, and said it was not plague. And he said he wanted, above all things, to get home. So I bought the cart . . .'

So Eustace had bought the cart. He did not dwell much upon the nightmare days and nights that had followed, with Sir Godfrey out of his mind; hurting his injured knee by tossing about, and whimpering like a child; attempting to stand up and hurting himself more, screaming like a trapped hare; mistaking Eustace for an enemy and trying to grapple with him. People at inns and at private houses, people who passed or met them in the road all shared the doctor's opinion, summer being the time for plague. Luckily the weather was warm and camping out no hardship.

'At the worst, my lady, I was obliged to tie him down to save him from injuring himself more. And then some people thought I was taking a lunatic to Bedlam!' This time the boy managed a proper laugh; for he had done what he had set out to do—and his beloved master was home, and back in his senses.

'You have been wonderful, Eustace. I shall pray God to reward you.' She turned upon him that look of gratitude which seldom failed to reach the mark. 'I have always felt that whatever happened, Godfrey was safe with you.'

Embarrassed, the boy muttered, 'It was nothing . . . It was the least . . .' But privately he thought he had done rather well. A few acts of larceny which he had been forced to commit did not trouble his conscience.

Walter examined the knee. His hands were enormous, but they had a delicate touch. He listened as his fingers probed around the swelling and the fading bruise. 'Nothing much, Sir Godfrey,' he said hearteningly.

'Only enough to lame me for life.' An invalid could be excused his peevishness.

Privately Walter said to Sybilla, 'Something's splintered there. I could hear it grate.'

'Oh dear! Ought we,' she faltered over the dreaded word, 'a surgeon?' An operation performed by a barber-surgeon was the last resort of the desperate.

She was relieved when Walter said, 'Best leave it alone. It might work out. If not, I'll see to it.'

Day by day, almost hour by hour, she became more aware that Godfrey ailed more than an injured knee. He was silent for long stretches and when he did speak it was always to say something either petulant or melancholy.

He needed nourishment, so Walter killed one of the six recently acquired fowls, and she made chicken broth in the way she had learned at Lamarsh.

'We can't afford fowl now,' Godfrey said. 'I suppose you realise that we are ruined.'

'Not quite. The rents were paid on Lady Day, and I have spent very little. You mustn't worry about such things. You must just think about getting better.'

'I shall never be better. In any case, I was unhorsed. By a beardless boy! Who'd want me now?'

He always came back to that. One day she said, with

feigned lightness, 'Beardless boys have to start on somebody. You did yourself.'

He gave her a glance of something that looked dangerously near hatred.

He took no joy in the children—of whom he had always been so proud and fond. He didn't want them near his bed—they might jar him—though in fact even the boys were awed at first and simply stood and stared. He couldn't bear their noise, and when one of their fights broke out in his presence, he shouted at them in a frightening way. Formerly their antics had amused him and he had called them his two young fighting cocks. Once he said a very cruel thing about his angelically pretty daughter—'There's something about her that reminds me of James's Richard.' The remark had just enough of truth in it to be shocking.

But worst of all were the moments when, alone with her, he broke down and wept, using the old endearments, but in the wrong fashion, 'Sweeting, you got a bad bargain when you married me. Darling, I wish I'd been killed. You'd be better off without me.'

Fever, she told herself, often left an aftermath of melancholy. Perhaps company would cheer him. She suggested that Eustace should ride to Moyidan, and to Bywater and tell his brothers that he was home.

'They'd gloat. I used to poke fun at James and his gout ... And William would talk about the will of God ...'

He'd always had a sweet, sunny nature. But then he had always been healthy, happy and successful ... And that is no way to think of the man you love! No! Think rather that he always gave his whole mind, his whole self, to the thing of the moment, and now for him, poor darling, the moment had narrowed down to pain and a sense of failure. And to that he was devoting all his singlemindedness.

Walter was right. One morning through the now naturally coloured skin of the knee, a tiny protrusion showed itself, white and sharp. It had made its way so gradually that no blood had come with it. Walter greeted the needle-like thing

54

with enthusiasm; it proved what he knew, left alone and not messed about with, the body had a way of healing itself.

'You'll be up and about in no time.'

'And lame for life.'

'But, sir, that does not follow. I once knew a man . . .'

'Spare me your memories, Walter. I have my own. And bitter they are. Unhorsed by a beardless boy.'

The bit of bone, pointed like a needle, and no thicker than a bodkin, did work its way out, leaving, Sir Godfrey said, his knee weakened.

The melancholy did not recede.

He who had never looked far ahead, now made plans for a desolate future.

'We must let Eustace go. I had the best horse, the best squire; but Eustace must go and take service with some able man, and get his knighthood.'

That was just and sensible; but when Godfrey suggested giving Eustace Arcol and his armour as a parting present, she was bound to protest.

'Arcol would be an embarrassment and an expense to a mere squire, dearest. And your armour would never fit him. Give him the other horse and I will write, recommending him, in the warmest terms.'

It was perhaps too early to say that one day he would need his horse and his mail again; but one day she must.

So Walter drove nails into the wall and hung up the armour, and Arcol went out to pasture on the village common, tethered beside a donkey to whom he took an inordinate fancy.

Godfrey remained sunk in gloom, a gloom which deepened at the sound of a would-be cheering word.

James and William eventually heard of his homecoming and paid brotherly visits.

James said, 'You have my true sympathy. I know what it is like to be lame.'

'But not ruined and done for. Old and finished at thirty-six!'

'You'll be better. Able to ride again.'

'With dotards and beardless boys!'

55

William did, inevitably, mention resignation to God's will, and suggested that Godfrey should be thankful that he had not sustained worse injury. 'After all,' he said mildly, 'you might have broken your neck.'

'I wish I had! I wish to God I had. Then your infinite charity could extend to my widow and orphans.'

Both brothers missed the real nub of his misery—a career ended without dignity, almost in ridicule. As for the circumstances, both for various reasons, ignored them. James did not wish to feel responsible, and William saw nothing much wrong. Godfrey had a house, two fields under cultivation and a third waiting; hens clucked and pecked about in his yard; there was a stye full of pigs, a cow soon to drop a calf . . .

Only Sybilla who had loved the man he had been, and still loved what he had become, saw the truth. Her mental similes were homely—let a garment go unmended and the hole would widen; let a crumb of mould stay on a cheese or a loaf and it would grow and take over; the same with rust; one speck, a patch, a collapse.

He still limped, the injured knee weak and from disuse, stiff; health restored, temper still uncertain. The worst things —the moods of weeping and self-reproaches became fewer; the gloomy silences had prolonged themselves. And the situation threatened to harden. By mid-August, he could climb the stairs and share her bed. To no purpose.

She had had no training in the arts of seduction and was not in truth, a hot-blooded, passionate woman. Fourteen years in a convent had tempered her. Always, from the first moment of real marriage, she had sought rather to please than to be pleased, and during his absences she had missed his cheerful talk, his smile, his laughter rather than . . . Well, what? Like Walter, she knew another language. And for its most used word . . . that she could do without, except that the lack of it indicated something badly wrong.

The old Abbess had said of apparently unassailable situations, 'We must work around. Nobody is completely invulnerable.' She had been speaking of some complicated rights about a mill and Sybilla had forgotten all but the general principle. 'Work around.'

So, how could one work around a man who had a weak, somewhat stiff knee and a broken spirit?

Work around.

6

[Autumn 1452]

SYBILLA said, 'We must make some decision about Arcol. He is growing fat on grass and becoming extremely unruly.'

'And what is there to decide about that?' This was the kind of thing he was more and more inclined to these days, and had she been a crying woman she would often have hurried away to shed a few tears when he sounded so sour and so hostile. 'I would have given him to Eustace, but I have no intention of selling him.'

Eustace, with many expressions of regret, had gone off to Lord Bowdegrave at Abhurst. His regret was genuine enough, he admired Sir Godfrey and in the fashionable way imagined himself to be in love with Sybilla, but his over-riding emotion was excitement and the anticipation of a bright future natural to his youth. Arcol did not like Walter and always behaved awkwardly when being tethered out in the morning and brought in at night. Walter said, 'Let Jacky try! Arcol's very fond of one donkey!' Really it had come to something when, with Godfrey in the house, she could be pleased with and smile at such a simple joke.

The suggestion was to Jacky's simple mind the last straw. He had always been scared of Walter, he was terrified of the master who had even less patience with clumsiness or forget-fulness, and now the idea that he should go near that great rearing, iron-shod, tooth-flashing beast filled him with panic, and he fled.

'Good riddance to bad rubbish,' Walter said: and Sybilla thought—He wasn't much good, and his going has saved me eighteenpence a year.

She had known that Godfrey would not wish to sell Arcol.

She was working round.

'He is in need of exercise—and grooming.'

'I daresay I could groom him. I shall never ride him again.'

'Why not?'

'I could never mount him.'

'Then I must.' That, at least penetrated the surly gloom.

'You! My dear, don't talk nonsense. A woman on a war-horse.'

'It has been done. That French girl, Joan of Arc rode a warhorse.'

'Yes. And wore hose like a man, and was burned for a witch.'

'I shall borrow Henry's hose and ride Arcol round and round the fallow field. And if that makes me a witch, then a witch I must be.'

Sir Godfrey knew his wife. The iron core was seldom much in evidence, but it was there. That afternoon he brought Arcol in from the Common himself, and, reverting to the days when he had been a squire, spent two hours grooming him until the amber-coloured hide shone like satin, mane and tail, a shade darker, like spun silk.

Next day he said he would harness Arcol and try to mount; if he succeeded he would ride to Moyidan.

'That would be wonderful,' Sybilla said. 'Those dark red apples will be ripe. Ask Emma for a bagful. And ask her, too, if her Richard has outgrown any clothes. Henry grows so fast.'

Arcol was, as Sybilla had said, growing fat and flabby on his grass diet; even when Sir Godfrey had given him the ritual punch to make him breathe out while the girth was buckled, it had to fasten three holes farther along.

Then came the mounting. Clumsy and slow, a climbing into the saddle rather than springing—an old man's performance. But it was accomplished.

It was a morning in late August, sunny and warm, but just touched with a hint of a change of season to come. Going out to see him off Sybilla saw for the first time that there was a touch of silver in Godfrey's bright fawn-coloured hair. Four months of pain and misery had aged him by five years. But at

58

least, she thought modestly, I have got him into the saddle again and from that who knows what may result. At Baildon and at Bury St Edmund's and Thetford there were tournaments, not of the very first class, but not to be entirely despised. She turned back into the empty house. Harvest was in full swing; Walter was scything; the two boys were gathering the severed stalks and binding them into sheaves, as Walter had shown them, the competitiveness between them put to useful purpose. And behind the boys Bessie was stooking, five sheaves to a stook. She had volunteered for the job and it was obvious that she was more useful in the field than in the kitchen.

Outside the kitchen door Margaret and John were playing.

Resolutely Sybilla ignored the truth that now it was less a matter of Margaret looking after John, than of John looking after Margaret. Almost as soon as he could stand steadily on his feet, the little boy, as precocious as his brothers, had taken charge.

There was bread to make, and a rabbit pie. Rabbits were at their best when the corn was being cut.

Thump thump on the front door. Father Ambrose! He called almost every day. The only road out of Intake ran past his church and his house, he had indubitably seen Godfrey ride past and had come to say how glad he was to see such an improvement.

It took a certain amount of resolution in order not to regard Father Ambrose as a rather silly old man. One must remember that he had brought the black brew. But he had, since then, shown a lack of tact, telling Godfrey that he should come to church as soon as he could walk, even with support, saying what a pity it was that he did not read, a book could offer so much consolation.

Once Godfrey, the new Godfrey had said, 'Keep him away from me. Tell him I'm dead!'

However, when she opened the door it was not Father Ambrose who stood there. It was a Dominican friar. A black friar.

Lamarsh had been a Franciscan house, and all Sybilla's

59

training there had been, despite an underlying, personal strictness, liberal. After all, St Francis had preached to the birds and called his Donkey 'Brother'.

The Dominicans were different, more concerned with organisation, with politics; and the very word 'black' when applied to them had significance, for their garb was in fact not wholly black; it was black over white; the blackness referred more to their general temper, their strictness, the assiduity in sniffing out and hounding down heretics.

In fact when Sybilla first saw the Dominican her heart gave a little jolt and she thought—Walter! Not that Walter had ever been known express any heretical sentiments, but he had resolutely refused to go to church, even at Easter. Father Ambrose had tried persuasion, Sybilla had added her word. Walter had remained obdurate. It occurred to Sybilla that the priest might have sought some support from the Order known to be stern in principle and in argument unbeatable.

She made her curtsey and said, 'Good morning.'

'Good morning. I am Father Andreas. I wish to speak with Sir Godfrey Tallboys.'

'He is away from home at the moment. He will not be back until evening.'

She was aware of his giving her that remote, slightly disparaging look which most celibates turned upon women. In fact he was wondering about her status. Sir Godfrey had been reported to him as being hard on forty. Daughter? Young sister?

Behind him in the space where the garden was yet to be, stood a mouse-coloured mule, very sleek and lively looking.

'If you would care to wait,' she said, and gritted her teeth a little. With Godfrey out for the day and everybody in the field she had planned to carry out a makeshift meal of bread and cheese. 'I am Lady Tallboys,' she added as though to confirm her right to invite him in.

If possible his scrutiny became even more impersonal and at the same time more intense. Men were uxorious. Would a man married to this very young, very comely little creature . . .?

He said, 'I thank you, no. I have another errand. I will come back. At Vespers.'

He mounted the mule and rode away. She stood for a moment in the doorway, staring after him and then turned back to busy herself with the bread and the rabbit pie.

In the field, handing Walter his portion and a cup of water, cold from the well, she said, 'Walter, a Dominican, Father Andreas, came this morning and is coming back later. To see Sir Godfrey. It could be about your refusal to go to Mass.'

'Could be,' Walter agreed.

'It worries me a little, Walter.'

'It shouldn't,' he said. 'I know what you're thinking, my lady. About the church-going. So far as I know there's no law about it. I'm no Lollard. I never said anything *against* the Church. I simply stay away.'

'I know. But *why*, Walter? I never understood why.'

'Too much of it when I was young.' For the first time he lifted the curtain and gave her a brief glimpse into the past. 'My old granny,' he said; 'very religious. Church every day; she was past being useful and I was too young to be. So she'd haul me along ... Once—it was a dry year—she prayed for rain. So did I; little boy doing what I was told. *Not a drop fell.*'

Sybilla knew all the arguments about unanswered prayers; but this was not the time or place for them. She knew about Lollardry, too, a movement fully as much political as religious. Lollards had been persecuted years ago, less because they had protested against certain Church practices—such as selling beforehand a pardon for an offence one intended to commit – than because they had advocated freedom to all serfs.

Sir Godfrey had had what should have been a happy day. James and Emma welcomed him warmly and James, in the middle of his summer gout which this year had encroached into his eyelids, was pitiable, even by the standards of a knight with a weak knee. Emma had most graciously taken Sybilla's request for a few of Richard's outgrown clothes, for Moyidan's Richard had grown, too; upwards, not outwards. Weedy. And why did one use that word, weeds being the toughest things on earth?

He rode back through the rather hazy sunlight of a late

August afternoon. He rode slowly, for a heavy warhorse like Arcol, was not bred for speed. Arcol and all like him were made for short charges—the length of a tourney ground, the length of the distance between two opposing forces. Arcol had two speeds, full charge and idle along.

On one side of Sir Godfrey's saddle as he rode home through the lingering sunset, was a bag of the dark red apples which Sybilla had asked for, and on the other a bag of Richard's outgrown clothes. A successful errand. I have mounted again, I have ridden, I am healed. Not enough; the inner wound still bled, quietly leaching away, day by day, all confidence and joy.

In the stable at Knight's Acre, with everything done that a good squire would do, Sir Godfrey leaned for a moment against the great amber-gleaming shoulder. 'Arcol, old boy, we're done for, you and I.'

Carrying the bags he limped in, by the kitchen door and Sybilla, nodding towards the hall said, 'There is a Dominican, Father Andreas, waiting to see you.'

No Christian denied the possibility of miracles; the blind man healed, the dead man restored to life; but unlike Walter's old granny few reasonable people expected to see a miracle performed, under their very eyes, except perhaps at shrines, like Walsingham and such places. Yet one seemed to have happened here.

When Godfrey entered the kitchen he was limping badly and his shoulders sagged in the new way they had, his face was gloomy and his voice flat. 'Emma sent what you wanted,' he said, putting the two bags on the table, and Sybilla thought— Alas, the outing has done him no good! When she told him about the caller waiting within he had shown no interest, simply limped on wearily towards the door of the hall.

She waited. She could hear the voices but not the words. It was supper time, the children, Bessie and Walter came in, waiting to be fed.

She cut the pie, sparingly, aware of the obligations of hospitality towards a stranger under her roof at meal-time. Soon she must go in and extend the invitation to supper. She chose the three less battered of the ill-matched platters, three of the least shabby of the horn cups and then, as an afterthought, went into the larder and drew a jug of wine from the small cask which she had asked Walter to buy in Baildon so that she could offer sops-in-wine to an invalid with no appetite.

That done she straightened her headdress and went towards the door into the hall.

'I shall be there!' Godfrey's ordinary voice, strong and ringing.

The outer door thudded as she opened the inner one. Godfrey turned from it and came the length of the hall to meet her. He hardly limped at all. He greeted her as he was accustomed to, after any absence, lifting her from her feet. 'Darling, I have such news!'

And in fact it was as though he had been away for three months and had now returned. Over her shoulder he saw the cups and the jug ready and said, in his own voice, 'How did you know?'

'Know what?'

'That we had cause for celebration.'

'Tell me.'

He told her. One must not question or carp at a thing which had in an hour restored him. And Dominicans, whatever else they were, were no liars, in fact they dealt with the truth, even when it was unpalatable. Yet it was a fantastic story.

As usual he told it badly and had to be helped out with questions, but soon she had a gist of it.

In the south of Spain, a part known as Andalucia, there was a nobleman, the Count of Escalona, vastly, vastly rich, who wished to give a tournament of the utmost magnificence with such prizes as had never been heard of; the first the equivalent of a thousand English pounds. (Disloyal to think—But you were unhorsed at Winchester!) And not prizes only; pay of a kind, five hundred pounds to every man who presented himself; and all expenses paid.

Surely too good to be true. Was that why, secretly, her heart doubted and her mind resisted, and aloud her tongue questioned? Why English knights; had he none of his own, so great and rich a lord? A simple answer; English knights were known to be the best in the world.

Why a Dominican as his errand boy? Another simple answer; the Count of Escalona was a patron; the Order owed him much and wished to make some return; besides he needed somebody who knew England and spoke English.

And that emphasised the foreignness of the whole affair. It entailed a voyage on the sea! Is that what I fear?

William's abode at Bywater, called a palace because a Bishop lived there, though it was far from palatial, stood a little above the port of Bywater, and Sybilla remembered the sea—her first glimpse of it—so huge, and the ships so tiny. Yes, that might lie at the back of her resistance to this thing.

She asked, 'When?'

'We sail on St Michael's Day. An omen for good.'

'It leaves only a short time to prepare.'

'If I exercise Arcol every day . . .' He looked at the armour on the wall. 'That needs a good going over, too . . .'

As from a distance she observed that he was no more really aware of this change than he had been of the other. He would not deliberately have become surly, melancholy, bad-tempered and despairing, unloving. In the same way he seemed to be unaware of this change for the better, lameness ignored, appetite restored, cheerfulness in the ascendant.

A weathercock nature? No! No! Simply a man as trained and conditioned as Arcol—And for that I should be thankful; a less single-minded man would never have married *me*! He'd have listened, been dissuaded—and I should now be at Lamarsh! Now—and here was the irony—she had regained him, only to lose him again.

It was being *wanted* that had worked the cure. If he told her once he told her a dozen times about the little book which Father Andreas carried, a book in which were written the names of those worthy of invitation. Again and again he said, 'And I thought I was done for. Arcol, too.'

He was confident—as he always had been—of coming home safe and sound; and this time with certain money. Knight's Acre would be transformed; there would be proper servants, proper beds; there would be new gowns for Sybilla, a dowry for Margaret, now his 'pretty little dear'. And when Henry went off to Beauclaire he would go not as a poor relation. Richard, too, in time. And John. He no longer minded their noise, thought their quarrels amusing.

Sybilla kept her head. Could they, she asked, hope to get Eustace back?

No, he said gaily, it would be unfair to the boy. A knighthood bestowed by a Spanish Count, however rich and grand, might not be valid in England.

'And I need no squire. I have not forgotten the tricks.'

Happily, happily, he hauled down his armour, and polished it, whistling as he worked. And she stitched away, repairing the faded or frayed work on the emblem, the hare at bay, on his blue mantle.

There were so few days, and each one shorter than the one before. But they were happy days, followed by happy nights, for, remanned, he was again her lover.

Exercising Arcol he rode to Moyidan and she had the slight hope that James might call this a wild-goose chase and suggest life at home with little affrays at Baildon, Bury St Edmund's, Thetford and such places. And James, very level-headed and clear-sighted, might even spot the flaw—she was sure it existed, though she could not put her finger on it. But James regarded the whole thing as wonderful; five hundred pounds, win or lose, with the possibility of double that amount.

And what about William, so unworldly. Would he not speak out about being too much involved with money, of a man's first duty being to his wife and children, and how dangerous the sea was; William, of all people, knew how dangerous . . .

But William failed her too. He had—as she had—seen a man soured and prepared to sit down and rot, and now restored, eager and happy. Godfrey, not far from the brink of despair, that ultimate sin, had been snatched back, just in time; and although the sea did claim some victims, roughly four out of five ships that put out from Bywater did come back.

No support anywhere.

The old Abbess had said, 'In the end you must be prepared to be alone with God.'

She prayed often—not for some direct intervention, but for the courage, the strength, the cunning that would enable her to deter him from this venture without casting him back into gloom. When he spoke of what he would do with his money she said that they had all they *needed*. That people could be happy without curtained beds and silver drinking cups. 'After all, darling, we have always been poor and we have always been happy.'

'Not always. Not lately. Not until Father Andreas came. I used to sit and think ... Thinking was something I'd never had time for.' He gave her his old, sweet smile, but then added with sudden violence, 'You cannot know how I *hated* being poor and useless.'

Although the physical signs of age had disappeared, he was older in himself, his prolonged boyhood outgrown at last.

She fell back on feminine wiles, how lonely she would be, how helpless she sometimes felt when the boys were unmanageable. His reception of such remarks was sensible, but all wrong; how about asking one of Eustace's sisters to come and live with her; how about buying a palfry and riding over to visit Emma sometimes? As for the boys, he would speak to Walter and give him leave to chastise them when necessary. In any case Henry would be going to Beauclaire ...

On the verge of tears she said sharply, 'I don't mean that kind of loneliness! I mean being without you.'

'But sweetheart, you have been without me often. This is unlike you. Why are you *against* this?'

'I don't know. I only know that I am.' Now the time had come to speak frankly, 'I know that you are happy about it, but I am not. I never have been, from the start ... From the very start, when I opened the door to that black friar. There must be a trick. No man could be so rich and so crazy ... Godfrey don't go. I beg and beseech you, *don't* go.'

He ended all that with a simple statement. 'I gave my word.'

'There's one thing, my lady,' said Walter—the only one who seemed to understand, 'Sir Godfrey won't drown.'

'How *can* you be so sure?'

'I got him a caul. That Bessie knew where to lay her hands on one.'

It was an old, and prevalent superstition. A baby born with a caul—a bit of membrane over its head, would never drown; what was more the caul in itself could convey its protective powers to anyone who possessed it.

Bessie, so anxious to please Walter, had dragged up this tale and offered to procure this emblem of magic and Walter, insufficiently impressed had said that he supposed it could do no harm. In a place like Bywater there was a ready sale for such things, and even in Baildon a caul was easily disposed of. This one had been; but Granny Wade was equal to the occasion: a pig's bladder, shrivelled and darkened by exposure to smoke, and torn about a bit would deceive anybody.

'That was kind of you, Walter. But—there are other dangers.'

Like Sir Godfrey, Walter thought that this was unlike the lady; in all the time he had known her she had been as brave, in her own way, as Sir Godfrey in his, never fretting, never crying.

'Is it foreigners you're thinking about? Can't speak of Spain, never having been there, but the French. Well, this'd surprise you, but they're just people. We were led to believe they had tails, and they thought the same thing about us ... First prisoner we ever took, we stripped him, just to make sure ...'

Maybe that wasn't quite the thing to say. He fell back on safer ground. 'As for danger, my lady; after all you could stay at home and choke to death on a fishbone.'

So the last, precious days ran away. The last Mass together; the last meal; the last night. Early morning of St Michael's Eve. Misty, everything swimming in a blue haze. He had to make an early start because Arcol, with brief charges and longer amblings would take almost all day to cover the twenty miles to Bywater; and everything, men, horses and gear were supposed to be on the quayside at Bywater by late afternoon, so that the ship could sail on the morning's outgoing tide.

He had no send-off from the village which was not a manor.

From all that he represented, Intake had long ago broken away; the old feudal sense of belonging severed when Sir Godfrey's great-grandfather had said to their great-grandfathers, 'Go make what you can of it,' and trees had been felled, the first acres turned by the plough. Not one of them had ever seen a tournament—which was a practice for war; they had never been threatened by any enemy worse than those that threatened any rural community, a bad harvest, animals sickening, drought when rain was needed and rain when dry weather was essential. Sir Godfrey meant nothing to them; a landlord who could not even—and God be thanked—even raise their rents.

Sybilla did not shed a tear at parting. They embraced; she said, 'God keep you. You take my heart with you.'

'And I leave mine with you.'

Rounding the corner of the little church, he turned in the saddle and raised his hand in a final salute. He had not realised how small she was, or how small she seemed standing there between those two great boys.

7

[September 1452–January 1453]

LATE for the trysting place. And Arcol to blame. Arcol had tolerated a bag of apples, a bag of outgrown clothes; but the leather bag of armour was heavier and noisier; every time he obeyed the word 'Charge', the thing, whatever it was, clanked and bumped, so in the end he refused to charge at all and simply went forward at his other, plodding pace. So, despite his early start, Sir Godfrey was late.

But he was there. Fifty, Father Andreas thought. Not easy to gather, the English were very insular and in the main curiously content with what they had, unseduceable. The company he had gathered divided itself rather sharply into young men, attracted as much by the adventure as the money and men a little older than he would have chosen had choice been free.

Sir Godfrey did not know it but he had been low on the list of desirability.

Riding in he saw several familiar faces—an old friend and rival, Sir Stephen Flowerdew, Sir Ralph Overton, Sir Thomas Drury. Greeting and being greeted by them gave him a sense of homecoming, and of excitement, and also the comforting assurance that this was not quite such a fantastic adventure as Sybilla had made it seem. Ralph Overton was a much travelled man and shrewd as a lawyer, not one to undertake anything with a possibility of trickery in it.

Now, an unfamiliar face. A very young man, so brilliantly clad as to dazzle the eye. He bared his head and bowed in most respectful manner and when Godfrey had returned his greeting, wondering who? wondering where? said in the rather affected way fashionable nowadays amongst the young, 'Now my happiness is complete. No squire, Sir Godfrey? Here! Gilbert, take Sir Godfrey's gear and stow it with mine.'

Raised, in that masterful, authoritative way the voice at least was remembered. The voice that had said at Winchester, 'Take him up gently. No, of course I shall not take his horse!'

Lord Robert Barbury. The beardless boy!

Bywater was a busy port, but almost entirely devoted to commerce; fifty knights, with their horses and other belongings was a sight to see. Embarkations and disembarkations during the French wars had been at the Cinque Ports, Romney, Hythe, Sandwich, Hastings and Dover. Everyone who could spare time now stood about to watch the colourful show which included the biggest hound anyone had ever seen. As big as a donkey. But the most entertaining performance was given by Arcol. Word went round quickly—There's a mad horse!

Arcol's nerves had already been strained by the clatter of the armour bag; he did not like the smooth, slippery stones of Bywater's jetty; he refused absolutely to be coaxed or compelled to step on to the little gangway which connected *The Four Fleeces* with the jetty. The whole thing frightened him and he knew just what to do when he was frightened. Even blindfolded he was resistant and dangerous.

Sweating and breathless, Sir Godfrey said, 'I'll try him again in the morning,' and led the horse, now meek as a lamb, to the stables at the rear of the inn, *Welcome To Mariners*.

'If he continues to be awkward,' Father Andreas said, meaning well, 'I am sure that the Count of Escalona can provide you with a mount.'

But the relationship between a knight and his horse—or in the case of a rich man, his horses—was a thing not easily assessed. They were one. The Count of Escalona had been aware of that when he made an order for fifty knights, their mail and their horses. It had taken Sir Godfrey long hours to become one with Arcol when his first destrier had failed.

He said, 'Without Arcol I cannot go.' His happy mood, so many old friends, such cordial greetings, had clouded when he recognised Lord Robert. Weeks and weeks in the company of one who courteous and civil as he was, would always be a reminder ... There were two ships, but the order, 'Stow his gear by mine,' meant close contact.

Once a bad mood began, it grew and darkened. A year ago, without a thought, except that he had a noble in his pouch, he would have gone gaily to join the crowd who were merry-making in the inn. He'd joined such gatherings hundreds of times, often when he had nothing to pay with, but confident that when somebody said, 'Toss for the reckoning,' the dice, or the coin would favour him. In the unlikely event of its not doing so, well, one could always borrow ...

But broken confidence was less easily healed than a broken knee. He had a good gold piece—Sybilla had insisted upon his taking it: 'Darling, you never know what might happen.' But he was not going to risk it in frivolity. And he had a perfect excuse; he must go and take leave of his brother.

As he toiled up the incline to William's so-called palace, melancholy deepened.

He thought he had done with it, done with it on the night when Father Andreas had talked to him—but here it was again, as persistent as an unwanted dog, or the three-day fever which haunted the marshes. And a meal of William's unidentifiable meat did nothing to cheer him.

'William, if anything should happen to me, have a care to

70

Sybilla and the children . . .' Never in his whole carefree life had he said such a thing, never before had he looked ahead to an untoward happening.

'But naturally,' William said. He had noted the difference in mood. None of the elation Godfrey had shown on the visit when he announced that he was off to Spain. It was the parting, he assumed. Godfrey never looked all round a subject; he probably had not realised until yesterday that what he had called a golden opportunity, such a chance as came to few, would involve parting from his family for a long period. William set himself to be cheerful—there was the voyage, of course, but on the sea, if anywhere, a man was in God's hands. He knew *The Four Fleeces*, she was a sound ship, and Captain Briggs a skilled, experienced seaman. And once ashore—well, going to a tournament was not like going to war.

Godfrey kept saying, 'I know, I know.' But without looking much happier. 'The terms were, five hundred pounds to any man who presented himself . . . I've been thinking, if I get there and become entitled . . . And then should anything happen to me. Somebody would see that Sybilla got the money, no doubt. But it is a large sum—and she has never had much.' Completely unlike himself.

'James and I between us would see that it was well handled . . . And now, I think, your last evening, a glass of wine.'

William's wine was as bad as his meat and did little to lift a heavy mood.

Arcol was no more amenable in the morning; a near ton of frenzied, fighting horse. The companion ship, *Mary Clare* loosed her ropes; clear water showed between her hull and the jetty, and still Arcol would not go aboard. Captain Briggs was dancing with impatience and cursing, Father Andreas, more controlled but equally concerned about the tide, said, 'Sir Godfrey, you must leave him.' Amongst the spectators was the old fishwife, loading her donkey's panniers. Inspiration visited Sir Godfrey; he called, 'Good mother, may I borrow your donkey for a moment?'

The little donkey, well schooled in obedience, trotted along the jetty and on to the gangway, down into the hold. And

Arcol followed the familiar, the loved donkey shape and smell.

'Cast off!' Captain Briggs yelled.

The old woman, lifted her skirts, showing skinny shanks and large flat feet, and ran along the jetty. 'My donkey! My donkey!' The watchers laughed and shouted.

Feeling something almost like physical pain, Sir Godfrey put his hand to his pouch. A whole noble, six shillings and eightpence for an old donkey worth a shilling at most.

Then coins rattled on the stones. Screams and imprecations changed to blessings, 'God bless you, gentlemen all. God bless you.'

Turning to see who had forestalled him, Sir Godfrey found himself face to face with Lord Robert.

He said with no marked gratitude, 'Thank you, my lord. I must reimburse you.' He held out his coin. No great perception was needed to see that it was his only one; full pouches clink when handled.

'I was afraid she would have a fit—or curse the whole outfit. Could we defer the repayment. I flung her all my small change.'

'I shall remember that I am in your debt, my lord. And for the second time. You could have claimed my horse that day.'

The boy laughed. 'And who would want Arcol?'

It was meant tactfully, a joke to explain a gesture, but Sir Godfrey seemed to take it amiss and did not smile.

Lord Robert said, 'I wonder how many men you have unhorsed, Sir Godfrey, fighting under similar rules.'

'One. But the fellow was a bad knight and a bad opponent. I reckoned it would be to everybody's advantage to have him on foot for a bit.'

'In any case, my unhorsing you was pure accident. I know and you know that we could meet again, a thousand times and you would win.'

'That may be put to the proof in Escalona, my lord.'

Stiff, unfriendly, denying absolutely his reputation as not only the best knight, but the most courteous, the most merry. Until the Easter Tournament at Winchester Lord Robert had never seen Sir Godfrey Tallboys, but he had heard of him, even in his native Yorkshire which though part of England was so far away as to be almost a different country. For a man who had an almost legendary quality the boy had developed a kind of hero worship. How sad, he now thought, that that purely accidental happening should have had this effect.

A sailor coiling rope said, 'So now we have a donkey aboard as well as a priest! Sure bad luck.'

Even more than most men in a superstitious age, seamen were superstitious. Bishop William had said that on the sea if anywhere, men were in God's hands; it cut both ways; on the sea, if anywhere men were in the hands of blind chance, or the Devil. Priests were bad cargo; so were donkeys, and corpses—the last worst of all. In fact dead men, soldiers killed abroad who had relatives rich and important enough to want them brought home to be buried with their fathers, were often shipped in the most ignominious fashion, crammed into barrels, rolled up in tapestries. Captain Briggs himself, an enlightened man in his way, had been a bit sorry when Father Andreas chose to travel on his ship and not on *Mary Clare*. And he had suffered a moment's indecision about the donkey, sail with it or wait while it was taken off. The sailor's remark, chiming with his own unacknowledged feelings, provoked him. He administered a clout on the ear. 'Lay off that. Talk of bad luck invites it.' Privately he determined to get rid of the donkey. That proved to be impossible; the little animal shared Arcol's narrow space between the bulkhead and the buffering wall of straw bales and the only person allowed near was Sir Godfrey himself. And he, tactfully approached—'Your horse would have more room and be more comfortable, sir,' said that the donkey might well be needed again.

No bad luck was immediately apparent; a brisk following wind sent *The Four Fleeces* skimming down the channel. The way the ship handled though was a constant reminder to her master that her cargo was lighter than usual; knights and horses were great consumers of space in proportion to their weight. In the Bay *The Four Fleeces* would bounce about like a walnut shell. Knights and horses were also extremely demanding; but Captain Briggs had struck such a bargain with

73

the Dominican who seemed to have unlimited money, that it made the whole thing worth while. Half the charter money was already paid and safe with the captain's wife in Bywater, the other half was to be paid in Seville. Not only that, Father Andreas had guaranteed a return cargo, a full cargo of real sherry wine, a thing practically unheard of.

The price agreed included food for men and horses; and there again some profit might be made, with management and cunning, meticulous though Father Andreas had been about details; fresh bread every other day, fresh meat twice a week. Captain Briggs had carried a few passengers before but they had either provided for themselves or eaten whatever was available; now he carried sheep, pigs, calves, fowls; all closely penned and all—by the sound of them—ill-contented. But the Bay, even at its best was a great curber of appetites. He derived a sour amusement from the thought of a pig killing and a pig roasting with *The Four Fleeces* attempting somersaults.

But at the end of it all with God's blessing and a modicum of luck—peace. Just this one immensely profitable voyage—a chance that came to few men—and he'd sell out and retire. Not as many old sailors did to a place within sight and sound of the sea; he wanted no more of it. A little house in that part of Baildon called Saltgate; on winter nights the shutters closed—he did not aspire to the luxury of glazed windows, a blazing hearth and let the wind blow where it liked. His son should be apprenticed to an easier and safer trade . . .

'It occurs to me,' Sir Ralph Overton said, 'that God, if He is up there, must often have a good laugh.'

The older knights had naturally gravitated to one another, finding out and becoming tolerant of, the little physical habits, mental quirks which had not been noticeable in larger, looser gatherings, but on shipboard did obtrude.

Sir Ralph was terribly, boringly, given to extraordinary statements, near blasphemous; or, as an alternative, sentences beginning, 'When I was in Calais . . . Rome . . . Pamplona . . .'

On this, the last peaceful evening they were to know for a while, Sir Stephen Flowerdew, orthodox to the core said, with

74

some irritation, 'What do you mean. If He is up there. We know He is. And why should He laugh?'

'At us, my dear man. All rushing about and busying ourselves. And all playing Blindman's Buff. Whereas He knows. Why we are here, for example.'

'I know why I am here. I have four daughters; the eldest needs some dower now, the others, presently.'

'Oh, that,' Sir Ralph said, dismissing an excellent reason with a shrug. 'By the same token, I am here because my sister, rich as she is, refused to allow me a penny, or pay another debt. She called me a wastrel.'

Sir Godfrey made his contribution. 'I have a wife and four children, and but a small estate.'

'And you could ask every man and get a reason. But not the one God knows. I sometimes myself hazard a guess.' He said the last words in his irritating, half mysterious manner. Neither of his hearers encouraged him by a question. 'You see, when I was in Pamplona—my first visit, as a very young man, Escalona was there.' That at least was new and interesting, and he had their attention. Indeed Sir Thomas Drury, conscientiously exercising his wolfhound, halted and said, 'What's that? Did you so. What's he like?'

'A very strange fellow. Not mad, but given to fits of madness. He fell in love with Princess Blanche of Pamplona, a mere child. Asked for her hand, in fact and took the refusal so badly, her father asked him to withdraw and never set foot in Navarre again. She's Crown Princess of Castile now.'

'Interesting,' Sir Stephen said. 'But no concern of ours.'

'That is what you think. I ask myself whether we may not find ourselves engaged, not in a tourney—in a rebellion. All this,' he waved a hand in comprehensive gesture which included *Mary Clare* somewhere out of sight, left behind on the first day, 'seems to me rather a high price to pay for a tournament, even for so rich a man.'

Sybilla had said almost the same thing. And now Sir Thomas, fondling the wolfhound's head asked a question that she had asked.

'Then why the Dominican?'

'John of Castile is unpopular with them—indeed with all

75

the Church. He is an open blasphemer; and dabbles in alchemy.'

'If you are right it would put us in a very grievous position.' Sir Stephen said; orthodoxy told him that Kings were Kings, God's anointed. On the other hand—those four sweet girls! 'Not that we owe any allegiance to the King of Castile.'

'Why should you think such things?' Sir Godfrey remembered feeling relief at seeing Sir Ralph on Bywater quay, so knowledgeable, so shrewd.

'I only said that I asked myself. Well, we shall see when we get there.'

Then came the time when it seemed likely that they might not get there. The Bay of Biscay, dangerous at any time, was a giant cauldron, stirred by the autumn westerlies. All but the most hardened seamen were prostrate, and even they went about, green-faced and reeling; even Captain Briggs abandoned his idea of a mocking pig-killing.

Above deck it was like being in a plague-stricken camp under constant rain; below it was an Inferno.

('You will need three men accustomed to stable work,' Father Andreas had said. 'All knights will not have squires— and in fact I have discouraged them.')

The hold had been most thoughtfully prepared for a cargo of horses; bags of chaff and bales of straw, held by nets and steadied by ropes, separated the horses from one another, and in ordinary conditions prevented too much lurching about. The place had been kept much cleaner than any stable because odours tend to rise and nobody wanted to live, to eat and sleep in the odour of horse dung and urine; droppings were removed almost as soon as they fell, and complete swilling down twice a day was the rule.

Lord Robert had again offered Gilbert's services to Sir Godfrey but Arcol would not tolerate him, so Sir Godfrey did his own feeding, grooming and cleaning. He did the feeding, doggedly, even at the worst, feeding and watering other horses, too. Cleaning was impossible, and though horses were physically unable to be sick, when frightened they staled frequently. The few hardy men still active, joked about the smell—it was that which kept them on their feet, they said. But the evening

76

came when Sir Godfrey found himself singlehanded, wading over ankle-deep in filth which swilled about from side to side and from end to end as the ship rolled and pitched.

He had succeeded in watering six horses when he was aware of the sound of vomiting. He turned and there, at the foot of the ladder, was Lord Robert. When he straightened up his pallor was almost phosphorescent in the gloom. 'Better now,' he said, wiping his mouth on his velvet sleeve. 'Able to ... lend a hand.'

During the earlier, pleasanter part of the voyage Lord Robert had been one of the younger men who did not observe, more or less, the gap between the young and the older. Second son of the extremely wealthy Earl of Thorsdale, he had come aboard well-provided with his own wine and every kind of delicacy in the way of food; and often enough he would break away from the rather sycophantic group by which he was always surrounded and invite Sir Godfrey and his cronies— 'Do us the favour of joining us.' Or he would join them. 'May I sit with you? I find Sir Ralph's tales so entrancing.' Entrancing, but now and again somewhat questionable and the boy did not listen with the apathy or full acceptance of the others. Immensely courteous, always, he would sometimes say, 'But Sir Ralph, I always understood ...' He was, what? between eighteen and nineteen, with a girlish complexion, extremely long eyelashes and the fashionable long hair, chestnut coloured and curly; he appeared to have brought a lot of clothes—all most unsuitable; he was, in fact a type which older, harder men tended to despise. But he was extremely well-informed, and once Sir Ralph, corrected twice in an hour—and with wine in him—showed irritation. 'My lord, you are so well-informed. Were you intended for the Church?'

'No. What I know I owe entirely to my grandmother. A most remarkable woman. German by birth and a woman of the people.'

What an admission to make!

'Her father made stained glass and she travelled with him acting as assistant—so many processes being secret. She spoke four languages and was fluent in all. Her father died, somewhat suddenly and she was stranded. Rescued by my grand-

77

father. In return she made his fortune. She knew coal when she saw it and recognised its possibilities.'

That was strictly true and no more than her due. Coal was a fuel that gave, weight for weight, bulk for bulk, more heat than any other, logs or turf. And under the thin skin of sheep-nibbled, rabbit-gnawed surface of Lord Thorsdale's many acres, it lay there, just waiting to be scooped out. People were slow to change, but coal was making its way; smiths and armourers and bakers had begun to use it because it gave a more equable heat; and there were cities, London, Norwich, Lynn where year by year the distance between the hearths where wood burned and the trees from which the wood was brought, increased, every mile adding to the cost of every log. The coal, just under the surface, easily hacked out, easily transportable, by sea—it was known as sea-coal—was becoming increasingly popular.

As a rule Sir Godfrey, whenever possible avoided Lord Robert, the living reminder of something he preferred to forget, but on this terrible evening, in this hideous place, he felt differently, glad of that helping hand, and after a while respectful of the resolute temper the boy displayed. He was sick three or four times before every horse was watered and fed, but he kept on, tottering and slopping about and from time to time essaying a mild joke.

They worked alone for the next two days, and by then the term 'beardless boy' had completely lost its sting; for this was no ordinary boy. Sir Godfrey developed for him a feeling which he thought was paternal.

The Four Fleeces, battered, filthy and stinking, staggered in to Mondeneno, a small, sheltered place on Spain's north coast. It was comparatively sophisticated for a place of its size; sea-borne pilgrims to the shrine of St James of Compostella used it—chiefly in summer—and it was accustomed to and equipped for the reception of ships which the Bay had battered; many of them in far worse case than *The Four Fleeces*. It boasted three taverns, two acknowledged brothels, a Dominican house, several men skilled in ship repairs and even more men skilled in the making of fake relics.

The ship was to be cleared. Arcol, last in was first out, led by the donkey and giving no trouble at all. In this sheltered corner pasture was available even at this late time of the year. Men and horses, cleansed and freed were disposed to enjoy this respite for the four days which Captain Briggs deemed necessary.

Lord Robert, now on such terms with Sir Godfrey as he had despaired of, settling a sky-blue tunic, tricked with silver over hose the colour of ripe mulberries, said, 'Sir Godfrey, you intend to sample the wares?'

'No.' In the past, a time infinitely remote, when he was this boy's age he had taken a sample or two and found them ... well, disappointing to say the least. Nothing to it in fact until he met Sybilla.

The boy said, blushing his ready blush, 'If it is a question of cost ... I could accommodate you, Sir Godfrey, without the slightest inconvenience to myself.'

'I could buy myself a harlot for half an hour, if I wanted one,' Sir Godfrey said harshly. 'I am a married man.'

'But ... but so are many others ...'

'And I have something to do. Run along, enjoy yourself. And keep an eye on your purse.'

A whore in Westminster had made away with his once when he was about this boy's age.

'My wife,' Sir Godfrey said to Father Andreas, having finally tracked him down, 'can read. I cannot write. But I would like to send her a letter.'

'I will write it for you, Sir Godfrey. With great pleasure.'

Father Andreas was capable of changing his mind. This man, not amongst the most eligible, nearing forty and lame, had seemed at the end of a long and disappointing recruiting campaign, rather like the scrapings of the barrel. But, much less lame, much less old, he had kept his word, shown sound good sense about the donkey; never missed Mass and recently when almost everybody else lay prone, wishing to die, had kept about. And now, when all the others had gone off to eat and drink and fornicate—let's not mince words—he was here wanting a letter to be written for his wife. A man in a thousand, ten thousand.

'Yes,' Father Andreas said, dipping the quill's point.

'Tell her, please, that I am safe and well and that the worst is over now.' He changed his rather tentative dictating voice to ordinary speech. 'Captain Briggs said so—fairly plain sailing from here.'

'That is the general experience. Yes? . . .' Pen poised, the single word asking the question; what next?

'Tell her I am well—no, I said that before . . . Say that I hope she is well. And all the children. And Walter.' He paused and the quill squeaked.

'And that is all, Sir Godfrey?'

It was not; but he realised that the man wielding the pen was a man vowed to celibacy. How to put it?

'Would you write that I regret the waste of time . . . in the summer . . . when we were together. She will understand.'

Father Andreas thought that he understood, too.

'Sir Godfrey, can you sign it?'

'Oh yes, I can write my name.'

He wrote it, bearing down so hard, as people unaccustomed to writing did, that the nib of the quill splayed out and the ink sprayed.

'Could you so arrange it that the next ship to put in here, bound for England, could take it. I was told that there was traffic . . .'

'There is. Even in winter. Rest assured. One of my Order will be watchful. No, no, Sir Godfrey, there will be no charge.'

Soft-footed and saying little Father Andreas had been observant. Sir Godfrey never gambled, had brought no extra provisions of his own, and when asked to share others' either excused himself or partook most abstemiously. Plainly a poor man. A man who had behaved most admirably during the difficult days. And now, when all the rest had gone hurrying off to satisfy this appetite or the other, he had come to dictate a letter to his wife.

Father Andreas took out the little black book in which every knight's name was listed and against Sir Godfrey's he made a cryptic little mark. Then he looked at the letter and thought about how far it must travel, of the many hands needed to get it to its destination. It should be made worthwhile. He took up his pen again and above the signature wrote—Your loving husband and faithful knight.

They spent the five days while the ship was repaired and cleansed in exercising the horses and practising their skills against one another. To the boy whom he now looked upon as a son, Sir Godfrey said, 'Your eye is clean out, Lord Robert. And will be if you go a-whoring.'

It was a generally accepted belief that sexual exercise detracted from performance; and certainly some of the most redoubtable knights in the world were vowed to celibacy.

'I shall have time to recover before we reach Escalona,' Lord Robert said.

Also generally accepted was the convention that whereas women of one's own kind must never be discussed, prostitutes could be talked about freely. Sir Thomas Drury could remark that the girl who had fallen to his lot was very young, very small, very dark and very expert.

'In all probability a Moor,' Sir Ralph said, always ready to air his knowledge. He informed his somewhat indifferent audience of all he knew about the Moors; how they had over-run and held the whole of Spain until the re-Conquest, when the Castilians had won it back, city by city, province by province, until only the south-eastern corner remained in their hands. 'Escalona,' he said, 'was the last area to be retaken. The present Count's grandfather took it and thus gained his title—and his wealth. Escalona said that his grandfather would have gone further, but for the mountains. As it is, when we reach Escalona we shall be on the very edge of Christendom.'

'And the Moors are kin to the Turks,' said Lord Robert who had unobtrusively joined the group.

Nobody much relished the mention of the Turks who had over-run much of western Asia and were now threatening Constantinople, the centre of the Byzantine Empire. And Sir Ralph, when he was talking did not welcome interjections. 'You could, I suppose, say kin to. Much as all Infidels would call English, Scots and Irish akin. They look on Christendom as one, and we look on Islam as one . . .'

So with water casks filled, with fresh onions, some very bad wine and some very good dried grapes, with every man and every horse in good health—no mean achievement, *The Four Fleeces* made her way, out of the sea, into the mouth of the Great River, the Guadalquivir, where there was nothing to fight but the current. Easy now.

Father Andreas said, 'To the right—you call it to starboard, there is a landing stage and a tower. Put in there. Then go on to Seville.'

8

ONE bright October morning a gaily painted cart arrived, bearing the gifts which Sir Simon Randall had promised; six well-grown rose trees, young bushes of lavender, rosemary and southernwood, many other plants in baskets and bundles, all labelled, 'Here be lily bulbs', 'Roots of Columbine'. Lady Randall loved her plants and was anxious that they should be treated properly in their new home, so she had sent the cart in charge of an experienced gardener who proceeded to instruct Walter. Walter hated being told what to do and the Cressacre man resented the lack of hospitality in this place—no cakes or ale. They managed to quarrel in the time it took to unload and for Sybilla to write an appreciative letter. She also wished to be civil and send some small gift in return, and she had it handy, for amongst the things which Dame Margery had packed was a sizeable bag of pot-pourri. It should have been opened and its contents stood about in wide-mouthed bowls, but at Knight's Acre every bowl was needed for a more utilitarian purpose; so all the sweetness was still sealed within the waxed cloth bag. Sybilla wrote that she had helped to make this pot-pourri from flowers and shrubs grown at Beauclaire, and that next year, thanks to her Ladyship's great kindness, she hoped to make her own from her own garden. (That was another thing the Abbess had taught her—the turning of a pretty phrase.)

One thing the Cressacre man had said was that the roses should be planted at once and that they liked muck. Walter was slightly torn between his farmer's commonsense—there was more to do in October than plant roses; and other things than roses liked muck—and his wish that the lady should have everything suitable. Sentiment won and, having ascertained where Sybilla wished her roses to be, he fetched manure in pails—when he had time he must make a barrow—took his spade and told Henry and Richard to bring the miniature ones which he had made for them.

They all set to work in the mellow autumn afternoon. Walter did the real work, breaking the soil and leaving the boys to widen and deepen the hole. John stamped about, fell into a hole, fell over something, picked himself up with invincible good humour, and Margaret kept, as always within reach of Sybilla.

Sybilla was holding the fourth rose tree straight while Walter stamped its carefully spread roots down to the muck it would thrive upon, when the quarrel between Henry and Richard broke out, unexpectedly because it was usually allowed to lapse when they were fully employed, and more violent than ever before. Ordinarily they punched and kicked, this afternoon they were armed, hacking away at one another with their small spades, using them like battle axes. Sybilla cried, 'Boys! Stop it!' Walter took action. He strode over, seized each by the scruff of the neck and pulled them apart, holding them at arm's length, kicking and struggling and then threw Henry to the left, Richard to the right and said, 'That's enough of that!' Sybilla was finishing the stamping in from which Walter had been disturbed and he said, 'Leave it, my lady; you'll foul your shoes,' when the incredible happened. Both boys, yelling, and still armed with their spades, closed in on Walter.

Sybilla said, 'Let go, Margaret,' and shook off the clutching hand. She took Henry, nearest to her, about the waist and when he struck out at her wrested the spade from him. Walter with only Richard to deal with did much the same. It was all over in a few seconds. She said, 'You are very naughty, naughty boys. You will go to bed at once and have no supper.'

83

Nor comfort for the wounds they had inflicted on one another.

They slouched off, defeated, but just at the doorway before which next year roses should bloom, they put their arms around one another; comrades in distress. Margaret stood rigid with fright and needed to be reassured and John to be pulled out from the muck-filled hole over which his brothers had quarrelled. And Walter was bleeding.

'It's nothing, my lady,' he said, dabbing at the gashes. 'These should be got in. There'll be frost tonight.'

'I do apologise,' Sybilla said. 'And so shall they, or go without breakfast. Also—I don't know, Walter, whether Sir Godfrey told you—he did tell me. You have leave to chastise them.'

Walter had his own ideas about that. Boys should be hammered. But a clout on the ear, a kick on the backside, three or four cuts with a stick or a strap, administered at the time of the offence, or because somebody was in a bad temper differed somehow from a formal flogging performed at a later date. That savoured too much of the army, or of the law.

'I've been thinking about this, my lady. They get worse, not better. Apart they're all right, but together they're more than anybody can handle.'

'It will not be for much longer. Henry goes to Beauclaire at Easter.'

That meant five months to get through. And for Walter it was in the wrong order. Of the two boys he preferred Henry, nicer natured than Richard who was sly, and inclined to be cheeky.

In the evening Walter gave his mind to finding some method of driving a wedge between the two, something that would give him a hold over Henry and put Richard down a peg or two. How about making Henry a bow of the right size, and teaching him to use it?

Sybilla was also thinking, and the result of her thought was a letter to Alys at Astallon, asking could Henry possibly go to Beauclaire at Christmas instead of Easter. She wrote it unwillingly for, though she always acted with impartiality and loved both boys, Henry was her favourite too. He more closely resembled his father, both in looks and in nature; he had the same extremely candid blue eyes, the same lack of guile.

Lady Astallon seemed to share Walter's opinion, one of the boys would be tolerable while together they were unbearable. And of course poor Sybilla, left alone for so long was finding them difficult to manage. One of the Beauclaire ladies wrote a cordial letter; Henry would be welcome for Christmas; and if he could be got to Chelmsford by December 12th, he would be met there.

'But, Mother, I don't want to go. I want to stay here, with you—and Walter.'

Hundreds of boys in the same situation had doubtless said the same thing. She set out to coax and persuade, using the Christmas festivities as a lure.

'You have no idea of the merrymaking, darling. Last year we missed it altogether and the year before you were too young. This time . . .'

'*Why* do I have to go?'

Sybilla explained the custom which she and everybody else accepted as they accepted night following day. Boys of good family left home, joined other households, became pages, squires and knights.

'But I don't want to be a knight. I want to be a bowman, like Walter.'

She realised that he had no conception of what knighthood meant.

Because I must have a house of my own! Had I stayed at Beauclaire, Henry would by now have been admitted to one end of the Ladies' Gallery; seen knights in full panoply going into action. As it was the only knight he knew was an irritable lame man, then a man preoccupied with preparations, and then riding off in plain, serviceable clothes.

In fact Henry knew more about knights than his mother guessed. Wittingly or unwittingly, during the archery lessons and the talk about archers, Walter had imparted his own opinion of knights, which was not high. They wore armour which was not as impervious to an iron-tipped, six-foot shaft, as they liked to think; and once they were unhorsed was a positive disadvantage. 'Once they're down they're as helpless as beetles on their backs. Can't even *run*,' Walter said. The long-bow had proved its superiority again and again. It was the weapon of the future. Archers were capable of swift, secret movements, they could operate anywhere where there was a foothold and a bit of elbow room. And they were cheap: look at what a horse needed in the way of food to keep it going and the time needed for the feeding and the watering. Bowmen could eat as they moved, sleep in their clothes, get up and be ready at a moment's notice whereas it took the handiest squire at least ten minutes to get a knight into armour.

Bit by bit, mainly in the way of stories, all this information had seeped into the boy's impressionable mind.

Sybilla said, 'You will think differently, Henry, when you know more.' She was tempted to make a class-conscious statement about the low status of archers, but refrained out of loyalty to Walter. The best thing to do, she decided, was to go quietly ahead with her preparations, ignore Henry's protests and his glum looks and assume that all would be well.

Then one cold, snow-threatening evening, Henry's place at the supper table was empty.

'Where is Henry, Richard?'

Richard hunched his shoulders in a sophisticated, unchild-like shrug.

'With Walter, I should say. Playing with bows and arrows.'

The scorn was cover for envy. Walter's scheme had worked well. Henry was secretly pleased to have his eleven months' seniority established in a way which Richard could not possibly challenge. Richard was mortified and humiliated by being excluded. The exclusion was total; 'No, master Richard, you're too young,' or, 'Maybe this time next year, if you behave yourself.' And for the first time Henry was unwilling to share either the tricks or the tools of the trade. 'It's a kind of secret, Richard.'

'Run across and fetch him,' Sybilla said. She had noticed Henry's increased attachment to Walter during the last few weeks and was secretly, perhaps unworthily, glad that it would soon end. Walter was wonderful, clever, faithful, loyal; and she had never heard him use a bad word, or even a coarse expression. But, after all, Henry was Godfrey's son, not his . . .

John could now feed himself, competently if not neatly;

Margaret still needed urging and helping, her attitude towards food as remote as her attitude towards most things. Sybilla served, chopped and spooned the children's portions, while her own and Richard's and Henry's kept warm on the hearth.

Richard rushed in, panting, fresh-faced, bright-eyed from the cold.

'He isn't there and Walter says he hasn't seen him since milking time.'

That meant dusk which came early in the first week of December.

A kind of panic seized her. She remembered Henry saying, 'I will not go to Beauclaire.' She remembered that Godfrey was stubborn, that she was stubborn.

'Help Margaret to finish; keep John away from the fire. Your supper is there,' she said and ran out. The wind was bitter.

Walter said, 'If he's where I reckon, he's all right.'

'Where? Where?'

'Where he'll take no harm, my lady. He'll come back home when he's hungry.'

That was the voice of experience. Walter had made two ineffectual attempts to escape when he was young and being hammered. And fond of Henry as he was, he was not worried about him. Whatever the outcome of this escapade, whether her ladyship won, or the boy did, a night's sleeping rough and a meal or two missed would do no harm.

'*Do* you know where he is?'

'I could make a good guess. But he won't come out for the asking. You know what sent him into hiding?'

'Beauclaire? Then please, Walter, find him and fetch him at once. It is so cold ... Tell him he needn't go.'

'Better think for a minute, my lady. It's giving him his head.'

It was only fair to warn her, even though the turn of events pleased him.

'Never mind that, Walter. This is no time to argue about such things.' That from Lady Tallboys was curt speaking.

87

The place of which Walter had instantly thought was in the wood, under a half-uprooted beech tree, almost a cave in which a vixen had had her lair. Henry had remarked upon it, saying in the soldier-to-soldier fashion that now existed between them that it would make a good hiding place.

'That'd depend what you were hiding *from*. Anybody with a lance or a dog'd have you nailed. Give me the open every time.'

Now, striding along the path he knew so well that he hardly needed the dim light of the lantern, Walter thought in Foul language what a fool he'd look if the boy wasn't there. He began to shout 'Harry' while he was still some way away. No answer, but then anybody hiding would be a fool to give his whereabouts away. And the boy was no fool.

He stopped at the mouth of the cave and saw the faint light reflected from Harry's eyes. With the roughness of relief he said, 'Come on, out of there.'

Henry said in the bitter voice of one betrayed by a friend, 'I might have known. Well, you can stand and shout till you're black in the face. I've got my arrows and I'll use one like you used yours at Vernay. So don't reach in.'

'I don't need to. I've got a message from the lady, your mother. She's changed her mind.'

'About sending me away? Oh, Walter ...' His voice shook with relief. Then suspicion came. 'Or is it a trick to get me out? Will you swear on your word of honour?'

It was strange, Walter reflected how the terms of chivalry came so easily. He said, gruffly, 'Did I ever tell you a lie? Honest men give their word and I give you mine. Now then, out of there.'

The boy had bested his mother. Somebody must now take over control.

Smelling very strongly of foxes, Henry crawled out. Walter had a small quiver of the heart at the sight of the bow. But he acted coldly, giving such short answers that finally Henry said, 'Are you very angry with me, Walter?'

'You expect me to be pleased? Dragged out from my fire and my supper. And your mother half worried to death.'

'I'm very sorry, Walter. But it was the only way.'

88

'Left to me,' Walter said, thumping the lesson home, 'you could have stayed there till hunger brought you out.'

'I'd sooner starve than go to Beauclaire.'

'Don't talk silly rot. You don't know what hunger is, leave alone starvation. You've never missed a meal in your life.'

'Supper I have.'

'And made up for it next day. Now, listen to me. You go in and tell the lady, your mother, that you're truly sorry. *And mean it.* Moreover you don't go telling Richard where you've been, or why. You know how he copies everything you do.'

'What can I tell him, Walter?' Very meek now.

'You just say, "I can't tell you", or "mind your own business!" See? This is between us, the lady, your mother, you and me.'

Already, rather cloudily, Walter saw the next step.

A few days later, when Sybilla said, 'Richard, Henry does not wish to go to Beauclaire, silly boy that he is; would you like to go instead? Richard was not merely willing but eager. The wedge between the brothers which Walter had inserted had been driven home by Henry's behaviour. There was some mystery, some secret about which Henry would not talk, even when they were in bed together, the time when, in the past, all differences had been made up. Richard whose knowledge of the world was small, visualised Beauclaire as a palace where he would not be Henry's young brother and kept out of things. He had also overheard some of Sybilla's coaxings.

So Walter had his way. He had not deliberately manoeuvred Henry's escapade, though he had prepared the way for it by his stories—Henry had heard how bowmen could live off the land, and given two bits of dry wood to rub together make a fire. Sending Richard to Beauclaire in Henry's place, had been Walter's idea entirely. After all, he asked, what was the difference between them? Eleven months and less than two inches in height; Henry was slightly broader, but did that matter in a page? And look, he admonished Sybilla, how their intermittent quarrels had hardened down to permanent hostility. So sensible and logical.

By accident, Lady Astallon, chanced to notice Richard and said, 'Welcome back to Beauclaire, Henry.'

Richard straightened up from his bow—both boys could be mannerly when they cared to be—and said clearly, 'My name is *Richard* Tallboys.'

The correction conveyed nothing to her, but the need to make it sparked off something in the mind of the boy who had already discovered that Beauclaire was not exactly as it had been pictured. Here even more than at home, was the need to assert and prove himself. His name was Richard Tallboys and one day it would be a name to be reckoned with.

Nothing so crudely undignified as a tug-of-war for Henry went on in the now peaceful home; but Sybilla made conscious efforts to prevent Henry becoming a mere farm boy. The present state of affairs was only temporary; Godfrey would come home with money and Henry would take his proper place in the world. So her insistence upon a certain standard of manners became more stringent, and to Henry, tedious. Once she rebuked him for coming to table without washing his hands and he said, 'Mother, I did. This is *ingrained* dirt.' He sounded proud of it.

Perhaps, she thought, a little learning ... But Henry, like his father, was content when he could write his name. She tried to entertain him with stories, myths, legends, tales from the Bible, but to him they seemed poor, remote stuff compared with Walter's stories, which always began in the same thrilling way, 'I remember one time ...' Walter had been *there*, seen with his own eyes, played his part.

The words, 'Walter says,' cropped up continuously.

'Walter says he's going to try his hand at brewing. He says his old mother made the best ale in Kent. Did you know that you start off with a dead rat in the mash?'

'How horrible!'

'But it is strained before it goes into the cask,' Henry explained with something, a kindly condescension in his voice which made Sybilla say, 'I hope, Henry, that you do not copy Walter and speak of me as your old mother.'

He gave her Godfrey's candid blue look and said, 'Of course not. Walter always says "the lady, your mother" and I say, "the lady, my mother". Once I said, "she" and Walter said, "who's she? The cat's aunt?" '

Walter, indeed could not be faulted, except over his steadfast refusal to go to Mass, which made Henry demur occasionally.

Upon this one point Sybilla intended to have her way; Henry must be seen, properly scrubbed and scoured, properly dressed, every Sunday morning. So she spoke. 'Walter, I should be much obliged if you would not speak of your Sunday morning plans to Henry—they almost always concern something he would like to do too.'

Walter understood immediately, he gave her his rare, lopsided smile.

'My lady, this coming Sunday I'll clean out the pigsty.'

Father Ambrose, welcomed in few houses, struggling against apathy and indifference had made a habit of having a word with as many members of his congregation as possible. Those who could dodge past unaccosted, did so, for the kindly words often savoured of reproach. 'I hope your mother's rheumatism is not worse.' 'Is Robin ailing?' Sometimes, as the weeks went by Sybilla wished that she could sidle past and avoid the inevitable question. 'Any news of Sir Godfrey, my lady?' And always the same answer. 'Not yet, Father.' Question and answer marked the passage of time, emphasised the distance, the immensity of the sea . . .

9

THE tower had been built as a fortress but it had not been used for years. The Count of Escalona had two powerful neighbours who were almost perpetually at war with one another, and, wanting no part in their quarrel, he had made a three-cornered treaty, promising to help neither in return for a promise from each of them to respect the neutrality of that part of his province adjoining the river.

Father Andreas did not wait to see knights and horses disembark; he went ashore himself, climbed the slight slope and eagerly examined the door of the fortress. The mark he hoped to find there, a newly scratched Cross was not there. So the *Mary Clare* had not, as he had hoped, arrived first, and her contingent of knights would not be waiting at the little mountain town, Santa Ana del Monte, which was regarded as Escalona's real frontier.

With his own knife he made the agreed sign, raw-looking amongst the graffiti of sentries long-since dead and breathed a prayer that the *Mary Clare* might be safe and not too far behind. And he added a prayer of thankfulness that *The Four Fleeces* had made the voyage without loss. Shambling about, finding their land-legs, men and horses came ashore, the animals led by the donkey, who preceded Arcol. Alone of the four-footed voyagers, the donkey had improved in condition, and now, fleshed up and lively, was, Sir Godfrey considered, capable of bearing his armour sack. Presently Father Andreas mounted his mule and led the way.

To everyone—except of course, Sir Ralph—this was a strange kind of country, rugged but not grey with, in sheltered places, the green of trees, in January. In the north only grass was really green at this time of the year; or garden plants like laurels. The warmth of the sun on their backs after midday, was strange too. Sir Ralph enjoyed pointing out orange trees and lemons, and the grey-green olives and Sir Godfrey who knew the borders of Scotland and of Wales wondered where were the people who tended the trees, gathered the crops. The borders he knew were scantily populated, more sheep than men, but they were not deserted, as this country seemed to be.

Santa Ana del Monte, when they reached it, was strange too—a small town, completely walled and still contained within its ancient boundaries. The knights from the north knew that all towns had once been walled but four centuries of freedom from invasion had resulted in walls allowed to crumble, the gateways which led out of them only remembered by the names of streets which now ran into sprawling suburbs. Santa

Ana del Monte was still as tight as a drum; red walls in good repair, a guarded gateway. Strange houses; in fact a street seemed to be one long wall, with no windows on the ground floor, a heavily grilled gateway or two giving entrance to several houses; upper windows protected by out-curving bars.

The curious street along which they clattered, their shadows now streaking long before them, debouched into a wide square with a fountain spilling over into a kind of horsetrough. A few women were washing clothes in the trough, beating the stuff against the stone verge. They were there, and then they had vanished. In such debatable land anything strange was suspect; go inside, close the gate, that was the custom, the inherited wisdom. So, out by another gate, and there were the silk pavilions.

'Now,' Father Andreas said, 'I can offer you welcome to Escalona.'

Nobody, not even Sir Ralph at Navarre, had seen such a camp. Heated water, braziers lighted as soon as the evening chilled, as it did, rapidly, once the sun went down. Such food, much of it familiar, but all delicious, and such wine.

They lingered, lounging about except while exercising their horses, for four days. Father Andreas was waiting, hoping, praying for some sign of the *Mary Clare*. None came, and with the resources of the temporary camp exhausted they must move on; and it seemed that Father Andreas must face his patron with this handful of knights—all good; but so few!

The next day's journey was easier, the narrow trail sloping gradually downhill. There was another camp, again wonderfully well provided, and then, towards sunset of the second day they came to the ferry. The water across which it plied was dark and still, not a river, a moat, but such a moat as none of them had ever seen, so wide, stretching so far to left and to right. It was in fact part of the vast irrigation system installed by the Moors who had occupied Escalona until the present Count's grandfather won it away from them, and drove them over the mountains to the east into Zagelah.

There was only one raft, poled by two men and capable of taking three horses and a few men, a little baggage at each crossing. It was growing dusk before they were all on the far side and Lord Robert said, 'Just as I always imagined the Styx. And old Charon must have his penny.' He gave each of the raft men a coin. Sir Godfrey had no idea of what he meant, but Sir Ralph said, 'I seem to remember there was no return passage across the Styx.' His suspicions about their having been brought more than for a mere tournament had hardened at Santa Ana del Monte. 'Why not hold the tourney here?' he asked, gazing about the wide plateau on which the little town and the spacious camp stood. 'Think of the time and expense it would have saved.'

However, as they approached the city of Escalona itself, even he felt that any man who owned such a beautiful place would naturally wish to show it off. In the last sunset light they saw the rose-and-white city with its domes and towers. One dome struck a note of a different colour, turquoise blue against the evening sky. In its centre stood a great cross of gold. The building under it had once been the main Mosque of the Moslems and was now the Cathedral Church of St James. Seen from a similar distance London was a low huddle of drab-coloured buildings.

They approached the city through gardens and orchards, clattered through streets which, though secretive, were not stamped by the fear that had been plain in Santa Ana del Monte and similar places they had passed through. Here and there the gateways to the houses were open, giving glimpses of courtyards, in which trees grew and fountains played. There were even—and this in January—some flowering shrubs. It was much warmer here, for the heartland of Escalona, of which the city was the centre, was a wide valley, sheltered on north, east and west by mountains or high hills.

Lights began to sprout everywhere. 'Oil lamps,' Sir Ralph explained. 'Oil from the olives. In such places the olive tree is as the pig is to us.'

Their journey ended in a vast, brightly lit courtyard, swarming with servants, who led away the horses, carried away the baggage. Arcol went willingly enough, following the donkey, into a stable of great splendour, but once there refused the attentions of anyone but his own master; so Sir Godfrey was a little late at the bath house. This was a great hall, walled and floored with marble with a sunken pool in its centre. The water was warmed, and perfumed. All the knights had been in the saddle for a long time—after a long time out of it and they were all men who even when lodged in palaces and great abbeys had thought themselves fortunate to have a squire who could obtain a bucket of hot water. They shed their years and splashed and wallowed like schoolboys, calling to one another in voices which in this place had a curiously hollow yet resonant sound.

Servants waited with towels. But what towels, so soft and absorbent, so almost furry.

Sir Ralph said, 'I retract. Plainly the fellow is rich enough to have brought us here, simply for a tourney . . .'

Juan Enrique de Mendez, Count of Escalona was indeed rich. Far, far richer than his own King, or any other European monarch. His grandfather had taken Escalona with all its accumulated wealth, had demanded vast sums in ransom from those who could pay and sold his poorer captives as slaves. He had been a simple soldier, but developed into a shrewd man of business, exploiting every resource of the conquered County, investing his money wisely and luckily.

His son had married an heiress of whom it was said that she could ride from the border of Portugal to the border of Aragon without ever leaving her own land.

While the knights were enjoying their bathing and the expert attention of barbers, Father Andreas was explaining why he had brought so small a contingent.

'. . . and of course, my lord, the other ship may yet arrive.'

'She will not,' the Count said, his voice light, almost merry, his pale eyes glinting with mischief. 'Don Filipe saw her in his glass, wrecked on a desolate shore, all sand and pine trees. No survivors.'

The Dominican felt a small chill at the back of his neck but he answered stoutly,

'My lord, you know what I think of such nonsense. Worse than nonsense . . .'

'That may be. But, he was able to tell me her name. *Mary Clare!*' That slight chill again. 'However, it is of no matter. I have maintained close contact with Hassan ben Hassan. All that is needed is a *show* of force, and that can be provided by twenty-five men. I assume you chose the best.'

Father Andreas brought out his black book, evidence of enormous effort, miles of travel, hours of seductive argument.

'The best available. Even to recruit fifty was no easy task. My lord, something is brewing in England. No open breach as yet, but an atmosphere like that which precedes a thunderstorm. As a consequence any man with something to defend wishes to be there to defend it. Nobody said so: their excuses were most courteous, and, as one would expect of the English, devious. Of those who accepted your invitation about half are young men with their way to make. There is one exception. The rest are considerably older, men of small estate.'

'One very lame.' The Count's eyes sparkled again.

'I brought no lame man.'

'Ah well, I suppose Don Filipe's inner eye is capable, like all eyes, of error. Or perhaps he misled me because I *asked*. He dislikes to be *asked*, he likes to *tell*; but naturally, my dear Father Andreas, I was anxious about you and your welfare, so I asked and he said that he saw you in a barely furnished hall with a knight who was very lame.'

Father Andreas remembered how Sir Godfrey had limped into the hall at Knight's Acre, and later, seeing him to the door, had limped hardly at all. Without realising that what he said was almost an endorsement of the warlock's claim to magical power, he said, 'Sir Godfrey Tallboys is acknowledged the premier knight in England. He had suffered a slight mishap. But he is sound now. And of those here the best *man*. Indeed it is thanks to him and the young man whom I mentioned as an exception, that all the horses survived.'

'They shall have their reward. Land and resounding titles. You also, Father Andreas, anything you wish—except, of course, Don Filipe's head on a charger.'

Father Andreas ignored the jibe. He and the Count were conspirators, their ambitions interlocked.

Serious again, the Count said, 'Soon I must meet them. Tell

me what you know.'

What Father Andreas knew would have amazed—and in cases, annoyed—the men he had so closely observed. He knew which knight drank too much, was a womaniser, a gambler. When he came to Sir Ralph Overton he said, 'A good knight, but spendthrift. And the kind of wine-shop gossip who knows all. He even claims to know you, my lord.'

'How could he? I was never in England.'

'Sir Ralph was in Navarre, in Pamplona.'

Your turn to wince!

But the Count of Escalona bore the hurt of Navarre and Pamplona as calmly, outwardly, as Father Andreas had borne references to Don Filipe's magic.

'Indeed,' he said. 'I find these English names so difficult, so barbarous. I must ask you, Father to point him out to me. Sir Ralph Overton. Then I can pretend to recognise him—that is always flattering. I should also like my attention to be drawn to the man who was lame and now is not; and to the young man who did not come for money. What is his name?'

'He is Lord Robert Barbury. His father is an earl.'

'I must remember that. May I see the book?' The names of those with whom Father Andreas had failed were deleted by a firm black line. 'I will try over the names. My English has not improved during your absence; the young man you left me as substitute tutor was far inferior to yourself.'

Unflattered, Father Andreas listened and corrected the Count as he named his guests, and then practised his little welcoming speech.

The knights were conducted to a great hall which was dazzling by its decoration as well as the plenitude of lamps. There were no wall-hangings, the walls themselves were the ornamentation, all complicated, symmetrical, geometrical patterns inlaid with ivory, various coloured marbles, silver and glass. The ceiling appeared to be all of silver and from it on silver chains, hung clusters of silver lamps which shed their light upon a table, all aglitter with gold. While they stared in awe and admiration their host, accompanied by Father Andreas, made his entrance.

'He has changed very little,' Sir Ralph murmured. Escalona
had been a very handsome young man and was handsome still,
tall, slender, upright, silver hair and pale aquamarine eyes
sharply, yet pleasantly in contrast with smooth, sun-tanned
skin.

He addressed the whole gathering first, in the slow, careful
English he had acquired in the last few years.

'Honoured Sirs, welcome to Escalona. I hope you will have
happy times here. I wish to make your visit to be enjoyed. I
thank you for coming. Please ask for anything lacking.' He
then made his round, prompted by Father Andreas who murmured the name of each man. His memory was retentive; to
Sir Thomas Drury he said, 'You have brought your hound. We
must find sport for him.' He told Sir Godfrey that he was glad
to know that he had recovered from his hurt. Pausing before
Sir Ralph Overton he said, 'We have met before. In Pamplona, was it not?' But whereas he had looked every other
knight straight in the face, with a smile, he avoided Sir
Ralph's eye. When he had passed on, Sir Ralph murmured
again, 'Quite a *royal* progress, is it not?' He was nearer the
truth than he knew.

The Count took his place, midway along one side of the
table in a chair slightly higher and more ornate than the
others, and the supper a veritable feast, began. Dishes of every
kind of meat, cooked with no sparing of spices which in England were costly and used carefully even in rich households. To
most of them rice was a novelty, and the salads much appreciated. Salads were available in England only in summer and
even then in no great plenty unless one had a well-established
garden. There had been Salett gardens on the banks of the
Thames, but the spreading city had encroached upon them.
The meal ended with dishes piled high with what looked like
outsize jewels, fruits candied into semi-transparency by cooking in sugar—another luxury in the north. There was no lack
of it here, for the Moors had brought sugarcane as well as rice
and many other things to Europe. The green figs were emeralds, the apricots topazes, the peaches amber and the mulberries amethysts, the cherries rubies. Spiced or sweetened
the food conduced to thirst, and the gold cups were filled

before they were emptied.

Lord Robert said, laughing, 'A few more meals like this and I shall need new armour.' Sir Stephen Flowerdew, his tongue loosened by wine, said, 'I will now confess that I thought the number and the size of the prizes rather too good to be true; yet I felt bound to take the risk. Now I see. The gold in these cups, platters and dishes would keep the Royal Mint working for ten years.'

After a few days they were mystified. Partly because their host, such a good organiser, seemed to have done nothing about the tournament to which he had invited them. There was ample room for practice and for exercise, but nothing even remotely resembling a tourney ground.

'Is it possible,' Sir Godfrey asked Sir Stephen, 'that he does not know how to lay one out?' After all the Count for all his wealth, his impressive appearance and personality, was a foreigner.

'Of course he knows,' Sir Ralph said brusquely. 'I told you, he was in Navarre.'

'Then I wish he would lay out the ground and begin,' Sir Stephen said. 'With you here, Godfrey, I cannot expect to win any great prize, but the promised sum ... I wish to earn it, quickly and get home. My Elizabeth ... Waiting does not improve a girl's looks, or her temper.'

Sir Thomas Drury fondled his hound and then made his contribution to the conversation. 'What strikes me as extraordinary is that he seems to have no knights of his own. Maybe here in Spain everything is different, but I should have thought that a Count would have some obligation to his King.' It was something that had not struck anyone else, but it was true.

'Even the Abbot of Baildon,' Sir Godfrey said, 'supports twenty knights. I know, because I could have been one of them if I had been content to be hired and sit about kicking my heels.'

In fact the Count of Escalona supported fifty knights, all well-armed and well-mounted, but they were stationed in one of the fortresses, far to the north. He had removed himself from the Court and immured himself in Escalona, dreaming his dreams and making his plans, but he was aware of his legal obligations.

For most of the knights this was an agreeable holiday. The Count organised deer hunts and boar hunts, expeditions to some of his outlying estates, lavish entertainments to enlighten the evenings. The only women in his household were servants, but there were houses in the city, too grand to be dubbed brothels though they served the same purpose.

Even those who most enjoyed his hospitality considered the Count to be eccentric; he seemed to have no neighbours, no friends. It was with surprise that his guests learned that their host had a six-year-old son who lived in a separate part of the palace and had his own household. 'As though he were Prince of Wales,' Sir Stephen remarked, when he, one of a favoured few, had been taken to see the peevish child, a tyrant in the making. It was assumed that the Count was a widower who had lost a wife so dearly loved that he had adopted an almost monastic way of life. The happily married men in the company could sympathise, and in part understand. Sir Godfrey felt that if Sybilla died, he would never want close contact with a woman again; and Sir Stephen agreed with him.

Sir Ralph who liked to know everything, and was a gossip, rapidly adding to the little Spanish he already knew, in order to be able to gossip, never knew Escalona's history. How, baulked of his one love, the pretty, delightful Princess who could only be allowed to marry a *royal* person, the young Count had become slightly mad; married—because a man must have an heir, a woman of low birth, likely to bear sons, being the one girl in a family of seven, used her as a tool, sired two daughters, utterly despised, and then a son. The two little girls had been put into a convent, on the far away northern border of Escalona; and once the boy was born, the Countess joined her daughters there. She had a peasant's down-to-earth sense and knew that as a rich woman, with a title, she would be better off in a worldly convent where such things counted, than in her husband's palace where she had never mattered at all, except as a breeding animal.

None of this was known to those who saw the one result of

the Count's marriage, but some of them thought his attitude towards his son rather peculiar. There was no sign of fondness; and everybody knew that fondness was the basic reason why boys must be sent away from their own homes to be trained. The fond father, the doting mother were unlikely to provide the necessary discipline; nurses and other servants who had known a child from birth were still inclined to regard him as a baby. But until the boy was sent away from home affection showed itself in smiles and casual physical contacts. The Count of Escalona treated his son as though he were fully grown, a very important guest whose every wish must be respected, but with whom no intimacy was possible.

Real intimacy was impossible between the Count and the knights, for Father Andreas seemed to have vanished and the Count's English was unreliable. At the end of ten days Sir Stephen mentioned the tournament and behind the pale, smiling eyes a shutter seemed to come down. 'He looked and acted as though he did not understand,' Sir Stephen said, 'and that *I* do not understand. After all, it is the reason for our being here. Sir Ralph, *you* must ask him, in Spanish.'

Happy to display his knowledge, Sir Ralph did so; and gained no satisfaction. 'He asked were we not happy,' he reported. 'And I said yes, of course we were happy, but that some of us were anxious to get home.'

Neither in Spanish nor in English could the Count explain that he was waiting for two things, willing them to coincide. He must have a final word from Hassan ben Hassan; and a final word from Don Filipe who was busily consulting the stars for a fortunate date.

Faced with Sir Ralph's lack of success, Lord Robert offered his explanation of the delay. 'Of course!' he exclaimed. 'He is still waiting for the *Mary Clare*.' Everybody said how stupid, how remiss of them not to have thought of that.

Then one evening when they assembled in the great hall, there were differences. Father Andreas was present, attended by a young friar who carried a big golden cross. Against the wall, behind the Count's chair a low dais had been placed, and fixed to the wall above was ... what? A picture? A map?

Most of them were familiar with maps of a rudimentary

kind; this was very elaborate, many-coloured, showing buildings, mountains, even trees as they might appear to someone viewing them from an immense height. At the top, in the margin were two symbols, to the left a painted gold cross, to the right painted black, the crescent of the Moslems.

For the first time since their arrival food was served without wine. The golden cups stood on the table, but they remained empty. One or two of the more bibulous knights drew the servers' attention to this fact and were ignored.

At the end of the meal, all servants withdrawn and the doors closed, the Count mounted the dais and took up a long, slender staff. Father Andreas stepped up and stood beside him, and the young friar went to the other side and stood like a statue, holding the cross aloft.

'My friends and honoured guests,' the Count began his well-rehearsed speech; 'no wine has been offered this evening, because I wished you to make sober decisions. I will explain as well as I can. Father Andreas will answer questions.'

He began by explaining the terrain; the point of the staff travelled. Here, buff, was Escalona, and here in the centre of the largest mass of foreshortened buildings was the place where they sat. Here were the mountains, at one point not high, little more than hills; and to the west of them, coloured pale purple, the kingdom of Zagelah, Moorish territory. This blue ripple was the river Loja which had its source in the hills, which ran through the city of Zagelah and then on.

Even the least sensitive of his listeners felt the tension. The Count was plainly labouring under some strong emotion, strongly controlled. The hand that held the staff was not quite steady and having explained the map, the man faltered and turned to Father Andreas who spoke swiftly in Spanish and then prompted him, in English, saying, 'I will not insult you . . .'

'I will not insult you,' Escalona said, 'by asking you to give me your word of honour never to divulge what you are about to hear, but I would ask any man not willing to pledge himself to silence, please to go away.'

Nobody stirred; curiosity alone held them, rigid and attentive. Even when the sheer fantastic, idiocy of his long concocted plan was revealed to them, they sat almost stunned.

He told them that Zagelah was ruled by a young king, Abdullah, at twenty-four a monster of depravity; a pederast who kept a harem of young boys, a cruel, extortionate tyrant; and a bad Moslem. That was the turning point of the argument. All over Zagelah, in the main city, in the smaller towns, in villages, there were good, orthodox Moslems, and their leader was a lawyer, Hassan ben Hassan, a true follower of all the rules laid down by the Prophet. All these good Moslems had formed a sect—the Hassanites, and were willing to do anything, even make an alliance with the Christians, in order to unseat Abdullah. So what he was now asking of them was to take part in a small Crusade.

The word still held a kind of faded magic. Most of them had an ancestor, linked to an earlier Crusade, a stone effigy in some quiet village church, every link in his chain mail faithfully reproduced, and his legs crossed—proof that he had been to the Holy Land, warring against the Infidel. And of all the stories upon which little boys were reared, that of the greatest Crusader of them all, Richard the First of England, Richard Coeur de Lion was the most common and the most potent.

But that was a long time ago. Since Richard's time—he had actually been within sight of Jerusalem when his so-called allies failed him—there had been other so-called Crusades, all brought to nothing.

The knights now looked at one another, dubiously, questions in their eyes. And presently questions on their tongues.

Lord Robert or Sir Godfrey must be spokesman, first as they were by rank or seniority. The young man acceded the right and Sir Godfrey's simple question rang out loud and clear.

'My lord, why us? Why Englishmen.'

'That I can answer myself, I think,' Escalona said. 'They have not lately been fortunate in France, but English knights are still the best in the world. There at least we are in agreement, eh?' There was a little laughter. 'I have also another reason . . .' He signed to Father Andreas to take up the tale in his more ready English.

The Dominican said the Count had always been much impressed by what happened in Portugal in 1147 when Portugal was small, only just recovered from the Moors and having difficulty in holding them at bay. A small contingent of English Crusaders on their way to the Holy Land put in at Lisbon, and the King of Portugal said to them, '*Why go so far to fight the Infidel? Meet him here, on my doorstep.*'. They had done so and Portugal had been Christian ever since.

Giving the one explanation himself, listening to Father Andreas give the other, the Count hugged his third reason. He did not intend to employ, on this venture, anyone likely at the end of it, to remember an allegiance to the King of Castile. The English would fight, take their pay and go home.

Lord Robert asked his question.

'Why should strict Moslems ask aid of Christians? They have Moorish neighbours in Granada. Why not appeal to them?'

'I myself asked that,' the Count said swiftly. 'Abdullah has sisters, all pretty, all clever, and all married to kings. In Granada, in Marcia, even in Aquilleras. They would not allow their husbands to help rebels.'

Sir Stephen put his question in the form of a statement.

'My lord, we are a muster of twenty-five men.'

'It is enough. As you will hear.' He used the staff again, and now it was steady. The Count felt that his ordeal was past. Nobody had said that the thing was impossible, what questions had been asked showed that his proposal had been seriously considered. With easy confidence he revealed the details of the trick that he and Hassan ben Hassan had planned.

It was possible that if Zagelah had been held by Christians, some knights would have demurred, for although things were changing and the sternest ideals of chivalry on the wane, many men still regarded war as a kind of game, to be played according to the rules; but when you were fighting heathen who did not acknowledge Christ or His Virgin Mother, all rules could be ignored. It was also arguable that what the Count planned was a form of ambush, and even Christians ambushed one another.

(Walter had told Henry about ambushes and said how much preferable for such an exercise, archers were to mounted men. 'Horses will snort and snuffle and jingle their harness. And

104

then look at the space. You can hide twenty bowmen in a coppice that wouldn't give cover for four like Arcol. I remember, one time ...')

There were no demurs, but in case anyone had a doubt, Father Andreas proceeded to speak, with all the force of fanatic conviction of the benefits which a Christian victory would confer upon the conquered. They would all be offered a chance of conversion and of baptism. When the knights' work was done, his would begin. He was sincere; he had no doubt of his ability to convert even Hassanites; for there was so much that a strict Moslem had in common with a real Christian; regular hours of prayer, abstemiousness in the matters of food and drink, a disregard of possessions. He knew he would have one very tough problem since Christianity meant monogamy and the Prophet Mahomet allowed a man four wives. But monogamy, Father Andreas knew, would come easily to the next generation, for the simple reason that once Zagelah was taken and very systematically looted, one wife would be all that any man could afford.

The looting was to be controlled. There was to be no robbery, no rape. A fair distribution of confiscated property. And Zagelah, as a whole, the city, the kingdom reaching down to Andara where the river Loja emptied itself into the Mediterranean was for its size very rich indeed. Zagelah specialised in a woven cloth of silk, fine as a cobweb, and of colours nowhere to be matched. There was something about the water of the Loja river which allowed the dyers there to produce very subtle colours.

In the ears of a few of the knights the word now struck an echoing note. Concerned with headdresses; privileged women spoke of 'my Zagelah'. Sybilla had never owned a length of the filmy stuff; but Sir Godfrey, sitting there and listening, thought that he would take her a supply that would last her a lifetime, blue; harebell blue, bluebell blue, Canterbury-bell blue, cornflower blue.

Escalona, with everything explained said, 'I leave it to you to think and talk over.'

There was a great deal of talk, but at the end of it only one

105

dissident—Sir Ralph Overton. As they stood about and muttered, balancing this with that, slightly fired by the word 'Crusade' and the word 'loot', thinking that having come so far ... and not oblivious to the fact that to refuse this extraordinary challenge might smack of cowardice, Sir Ralph spoke.

'I'm having nothing to do with it. He tricked us once, saying *tournament* when he meant *war*. I'm going home. If he gives me the promised five hundred pounds, well and good. If not maybe my sister has relented or my creditors think me dead.'

They all thought—Cynic! and remembered that they had never liked him much. In that muddled moment not one of them gave him his due and realised that it took courage of a sort to stand up, alone and say, 'My lord, I came to Escalona for a tourney. I now propose, with your permission, to go home.'

'Sir Ralph, there is no question of permission. I want no *pressed* men.'

The others were all of one mind, for various reasons and Sir Godfrey, forced to speak for all, said, 'My lord, we ride with you.'

'Then we will drink to our enterprise. Bring in the wine!'

10

'The English as a race are nothing if not practical,' the Count said. 'And twenty-four out of twenty-five regarded it as a practical plan.'

'I confess,' Father Andreas said, 'that when Sir Ralph Overton withdrew, I feared others might follow.'

He looked back on the many acts of faith which had been made necessary; to continue recruiting in the face of such poor response; to embark with only a quarter of the number demanded; to face the Count with a mere handful. It had been a steady winnowing down, similar to that of Gideon, in the Old

Testament story . . .

'Hassan ben Hassan says that he will be ready on the thirteenth. Five days' journey without over-tiring horse or man. I have already set in motion the establishment of camps. Have you chosen your companions?'

'In my mind. I have not yet informed them. I think six—as a beginning. We do not wish to alarm Hassan until we are established.'

During this waiting time, Father Andreas had fasted and prayed, and watched, selected and discarded. The Dominicans who were to form the spearhead of Christendom in Zagelah must be young, malleable, yet strong and forceful—not a common combination. But he had six.

The Count would have enjoyed telling his fellow conspirator that Don Filipe's casting of horoscopes in order to find the most fortunate date had ended with the prediction that February 13th was favourable. But this was no time for teasing; so they parted in amity, yet each concealing something from the other. Father Andreas did not reveal to the Count, that once made Archbishop of Zagelah he was not going to rely upon gentle persuasion to make converts; when persuasion failed, force would be used. And the Count made no mention of the fact that to his original intention of snatching Abdullah's kingdom and title an even more ambitious hope had now attached itself. Rumours reached him even in his self-imposed isolation, and the latest was heady in the extreme. Prince Henry of Castile was seriously intending to divorce Blanche of Navarre, giving as grounds that they were impotent together. The Pope was likely to regard Henry's petition favourably; sterile royal marriages led to squabbles about the succession. And if that happened . . .

In Navarre the immensely wealthy, handsome young man who had never been thwarted in his life, had been curtly told that only royal personages could marry princesses. His scheme to make himself royal—in title at least—had stemmed from a desire to be avenged upon the world, from a determination that his son should never suffer such humiliation. His attitude towards the child, noticed by some of the knights, resulted from his regarding him as an instrument for his ambition, while feeling no affection for the product of a loveless marriage.

If, as now seemed possible, King Enrique I of Zagelah made suit to a Princess who had been discarded, all his dreams might yet come true. And he would breed other sons, happy, healthy, merry, lovable children.

That he had a wife still living was no cause for concern; an unwanted woman was easily disposed of.

Parting from Father Andreas, the Count found himself irresistibly drawn to Don Filipe's apartments at the top of a tower in a remote part of the palace.

The old warlock, well aware of his worth, allowed himself a certain freedom of speech and manner. He gave a sigh of weariness and said,

'My lord, I have nothing more to tell you.'

Unruffled, the Count said, 'I have something to tell *you*, Don Filipe. You said that Zagelah would be taken by twenty-five of us. And you were right. One Englishman chose to go home.'

'That is no news to me.' Don Filipe's voice was peevish. 'He will not get far.'

'No, he will not get far.' There was a short silence and then Escalona said, 'I know you dislike being *asked* to see, but there is something I need to know.'

Don Filipe disliked being asked to use his gift because he had spent so many years answering fatuous questions, eking out an occasional bit of genuine second sight with inventions, lies, evasions. Until he had been taken under the wing of this very superstitious nobleman, he had led a precarious life as an itinerant fortune-teller, caster of horoscopes, finder of lost property, a diagnoser of mysterious ailments. He had never been able to stay long in one place—the Church disapproved of his kind; and he had always been poor because he worked only just enough to keep himself alive. He believed in his gift and knew that every invention, lie, evasion, frayed it slightly; it was like taking a length of Zagelah gauze and using it to mop a rough floor.

'I worked out the date for you my lord; I saw a great city

taken by twenty-five men. What more can you ask of me?'

'What comes after?'

A great lord, a generous patron, but now almost on a level with country girls wanting to know if they would marry, whom they would marry. A man whose amiability was a mere veneer over arrogance, humble for once.

'How long after, my lord?' Useful to have some sort of guide, in case nothing came, though the inner eye had been more reliable since its owner had not been harried, forced to improvise, and often hungry.

'Whatever you see, Don Filipe.'

'Very well, my lord. There may be nothing.' At least to *this* patron it was possible to say such a thing without being called charlatan, wizard, warlock, scoundrel, heretic.

From amongst the clutter on the table, the old man dug out his ball of crystal, faintly clouded, faintly green. He moved his lamp a little, cupped the ball in his hands and stared.

'Nothing new,' he said at last. Then his expression sharpened. 'Yes! Wait. I can see your losses. Four in the open by the river ... two in the gateway. And an eye will be lost. Another death, too, but of no importance ... There, now it is gone. I see nothing.' But he was pleased, in the circumstances, to have seen anything at all, and to have seen it so clearly. He looked to his master for approval.

The Count, who believed in Don Filipe absolutely, said, 'Interesting, only seven dead. You give me assurance. But what I want, Don Filipe is some sight into the further future.'

'It comes as it will, my lord.'

'I know.'

That was a thing that endeared the Count of Escalona to his wizard; he respected the art and understood that a gift was a gift, not to be commanded or harnessed. Because of this, and the way in which he had been housed and fed, given the courtesy title of Don, and protected from persecution, the old warlock, after some thought, said, unwillingly, 'There is another way, my lord. For you, if you wish, I will attempt it.'

'I should be grateful.'

Don Filipe had tried it seldom; only three or four times; it was dangerous. Despite what priests might say there was nothing evil in practising a God given gift; in his crystal Filipino had done little more than to *see*, just as ordinary people saw their reflections in a puddle or a bucket of water; and in casting his horoscopes he was no more guilty of sin than any man studying a map. But this was different, and he knew it.

There was a priest-like ritual about his preparations; he cleared a space on the marble-topped table, lit and fanned a small brazier to a glow, took from the back of a shelf a stoppered flask. Then he said, 'Sit over there, my Lord,' and indicated a bench as far from the table as the size of the room allowed. 'Do not speak. Do not lean forward. And do not be alarmed if I appear to be—overcome.'

From the flask he shook a little greyish-green powder into his palm, hesitated for a second and then spilled it on to the red charcoal. A dense, evil-smelling smoke arose and slowly formed the shape of a large mushroom, its stem rooted in the brazier, its cap level with Don Filipe's eyes. He put his hands to the sides of his head, like the blinkers of a horse, and leaned forward. His whole posture was different from that he adopted when looking into the crystal, taut and wary.

The smoke hung motionless, keeping its shape, but the stench filled the room. The Count wished that he had brought a pomander ball. He wondered how Filipe could remain so close to it, could lean even nearer, staring, staring. He thought—He is doing this for me; he must be rewarded. But how? The only gold the old man cared about was that which he was trying to make from base metals.

Suddenly Don Filipe said, 'No!' using the voice of one faced with something unbelievable, or utterly unacceptable. He moved his right hand and attempted to cross himself, but his head, deprived of half its support fell forward, so that to the stench was added the smell of singeing hair. Escalona moved swiftly, lifted him—how light he was—and carried him to the window. Still holding the old man with his left arm, he threw open the window with his other hand. The night air, cool and fresh, streamed in.

Don Filipe looked dead. He had closed his eyes—against what sight?—and his lips were blue. Escalona thought, selfishly—He died without telling me! But when he fumbled and found the old man's heart it was beating, though feebly, and after a second or two he took a gasping breath, enough to enable him to speak in a weak whisper. He said, 'Such—great—slaughter.' Then he said, 'King . . .' not as an isolated word but as though a name should have followed. It did not. After that word he was silent.

The Count remembered that the warlock had told him not to be alarmed, and, unalarmed, he thought of wine as a restorative. There would be wine here, for Don Filipe was always, by order, well-served. In fact, on a separate small table, supper was laid out and there was wine in a jug, and there was a cup. Escalona who had been holding Don Filipe's head against his knee, reached out for a huge book, pillowed him on that and crossed the room to the supper table.

In the short time that it took to fetch the wine, the old man died. And what he knew went with him. Just for a moment Escalona forgot that and surprised himself by feeling some emotion. Over the hollow old chest he made the sign which had not been completed; then, crossing himself, he said, 'God rest you in peace.'

He thought—He died in an attempt to serve me, and he shall have Christian burial, no matter what Father Andreas and the rest of them may say.

Curiosity revived. Greatly regretting what had not been said, the Count examined the few words that had been spoken.

Such great slaughter. Well, naturally; Abdullah would have those about him who would fight fiercely, if only from self-interest; betrayed from within, they would be mown down. Escalona knew what his own loss would be, seven men. He also knew the Moors' method of fighting. They depended upon speed. Wearing light armour, or none, mounted on swift horses, they swooped to attack, slashing with their curved scimitars and yelling. Repulsed they turned, as if in flight, and then turned again, in their saddles, and used their other weapon, the bow, discharging, over their horses' tails, arrows dipped in deadly poisons. But Hassan ben Hassan had sworn that there would be no poison on any arrow; no man awake in any of the frontier fortresses. If only the Count could arrive on the given day.

King. Spoken like that, inconclusively, it might well be interpreted as the dying man's effort to give his sponsor his new title.

One word left unexplained, that horrified *No*! Perhaps he had seen in the smoke, his own death.

The road along which the knights moved eastwards had been made by the Romans, to whom Hispania had been one province; to the Visigoths who had taken over from the Romans, the country had been one, also; and to the Moors who had driven them out. The splintering up into small provinces and petty kingdoms had begun with the re-Conquest, but as late as the time when Escalona's grandfather had set out to carve a place for himself with his sword, Escalona and Zagelah had been one and the road that linked them had been much used and kept in good repair. It ran for the first day through fertile and well-populated country, scattered with little villages and a few larger places where some mineral deposits had bred industry. By evening, when they halted at their first camp, the range of mountains which the first Count of Escalona had been content to regard as the limit to his conquest, showed, smudgily against the sky.

Next day the road climbed, gently but inexorably; the olive groves, the terraced vineyards, the sheep-loud pastures fell away. They came to almost barren land, dotted with gorse bushes, here and there a stunted pine tree. Then all was rock, weathered red sandstone, the skeleton of the earth laid bare. But still the good road, and another comfortable camp.

After that Sir Godfrey rode, not uneasily, but alertly. The good road went on, but now it was often a narrow defile between two heights, places where half a dozen determined men could hold up an army. Outside his profession his imagination was not lively, but he could see that three or four well aimed arrows or flung lances could throw their cavalcade into lethal confusion in such a place. Equally dangerous, to his mind, were the twists and turns which the road took in order to avoid sharp ascents or descents; how could you know what was just around a bend? And sometimes the road was merely a shelf with a steep wall of rock on the one hand and a drop into an abyss on the other.

But his fears seemed to be unfounded. And surely, if the Count had anticipated trouble here he would not have brought his son who travelled sometimes in an ornate litter, borne by four men, sometimes on a very pretty pony.

'You may have observed,' Lord Robert said, slipping into place beside Sir Godfrey and Sir Stephen, 'that I am in deep disgrace. My turn to eat supper with his lordship, and not invited. Should I weep? Go ashamed and unfed to my bed?' He pulled a miserable face and then laughed. 'Or dare I tell you the *hideous* crime of which I am guilty? Will you, too, avoid my company if I tell you that I *struck* that sacred child?'

They laughed and Sir Stephen said, 'Long overdue.'

'He was riding and kept stealing up behind other horses and giving sharp cuts with his whip. Imagine the confusion! Pluto and I almost fell into a ravine. So I approached the Count and complained and he said something about boyish high spirits. Not even a word of rebuke. I warned him; I said that if Don Juan struck another horse, I should strike him. He did, of course; and I gave him a cuff he will remember—I hope.'

Lord Robert did not know it, but by that one simple action he had lost all chance of a title and an estate when Zagelah was subdued. The Count did not love his son, was indeed prepared, in certain circumstances to waive his rights, or even dispose of him, but at the moment he was heir apparent and to insult him was to insult his father.

The fourth day's march brought them, several times, into situations which Sir Godfrey had visualised, places where the road, running narrowly between two heights, or along a narrow shelf, was overlooked by fortresses which except for their colour, red instead of grey, and the shape of their arrow-slits, their tops horse-shoe shaped instead of pointed, were not unlike the Peel Towers of the Scottish border. They were not derelict, like the one at the landing stage on the river, they were in good repair, but they were deserted. Hassan ben Hassan was a thorough man. The contemptible little company of invaders passed into Zagelah without so much as a challenge.

113

The road, still avoiding steep gradients by curving brought them down to tree level again; the beech buds were swollen, but still unbroken, some of the chestnuts showed flecks of green. 'I never knew until now what trees meant to me,' Lord Robert said. In what Sir Godfrey would once have thought an affected manner, he flung his arms as far as they would go around a grey beechtree and said, 'Dear tree!'

'I like trees, too,' Sir Godfrey said. 'In fact I built my house around one.' That was a statement unusual enough to evoke questions, but as always his inability to describe prevented him from giving his listeners any very clear mental picture. And his own mind wandered off to Sybilla and Knight's Acre. By now she should have received his first letter. And his second was on its way, written by Lord Robert and carried by Sir Ralph who had promised to find a carrier for it the moment he stepped on to English soil. He had written cautiously, not to alarm her, no mention of going to war, simply that one tournament led to another and that he hoped to come home rich; that letter also—because it was not dictated to a celibate friar, was more loving.

The pity of it was that his more loving letter—almost poetical in places, for Lord Robert had a way with words—was never to be read. As Don Filipe had foreseen, and as Escalona had determined, Sir Ralph did not get far . . .

Their final camp was different from the others, secret, behind the last belt of trees before the cultivated land began. No lights, no fires, no pavilions except the small one which sheltered the child and his attendants, the larger one where Father Andreas had set up his altar and the great golden Cross. Every man made his confession and was absolved. Many of them were reminded of the preliminaries of being knighted.

Then early to bed in a way which to most of them seemed more natural than the luxury of former camps. Not far from where they bedded the river Loja made splashing noises as it tumbled over the last of the falls on its way to the lowlands, through the city of Zagelah and then on, past another city, Andara, and so to the sea. From their darkened camp, knights who cared to look, could see faint lights in Zagelah.

They took up their positions in the grey, predawn light. Sir Godfrey and the eleven men who made up his company were concealed in an orange grove slightly to the south of the city's great gateway, with nothing but a few trees and the width of a road between them and the red and white walls. As the light brightened towards sunrise they could see that the gates were of bronze; inset was a smaller opening, wide enough to admit a cart or two riders abreast. The gateway was flanked by outjutting towers, with battlements and openings that commanded views in all directions. Filled with men prepared to shoot arrows tipped in henbane, to lob down heavy stones, pour boiling water, the place would have been as nearly untakable as a place could be. It would have meant a siege. That Zagelah was dependent upon the surrounding countryside for food was proved by the number of laden donkeys and people carrying baskets who were beginning to line up in the road, awaiting the opening of the smaller gate. They were all preoccupied with their own affairs, getting and keeping their place in the line, prodding their donkeys, greeting acquaintances; is the sole of my shoe flapping again? Shall I get home before labour starts?

The rim of the sun appeared on the eastern horizon. From the minarets the muezzins called and all good Moslems turned towards Mecca and prostrated themselves in the first prayers of the day. Then the gate was opened and they shuffled and jostled their way in. Not one of them had looked north-westwards across the valley and seen the unusual activity going on there, in full view. Those whose function it was to keep watch on walls and towers were either members of Hassan's party and deliberately blind or they had been dealt with, would sleep for twelve hours, perhaps never wake again. Hassan ben Hassan, like the Count of Escalona and Father Andreas, knew exactly what he wanted and held that the end justified the means.

Abdullah IV of Zagelah did not respond to the call to prayer, did not even hear it. In the heart of his rose-coloured palace—compared with which that of Escalona was a modest place indeed, in a bed of silver and gold and pearl, pillowed and covered with silk, he lay asleep, exhausted after a night of excess with his latest favourite, very pretty, very young and at the moment very humble. He had actually gone to sleep on the floor at the foot of the bed, like a dog. It would not last, of course; it never did. All favourites, sooner or later demanded favours in return, enormous gifts, remunerative posts; always given because even when the first fervour had expended itself, something remained. And Abdullah delighted in giving. In fact his last thought before he fell asleep was that he would give the boy Sheba's ruby.

That was a drunken thought, for before, during and after their parody of lovemaking, he and the boy had emptied two jugs of wine.

Nobody knew how the ruby, said to be the last present the Queen of Sheba had ever given to Solomon the Great, had come into the possession of the Kings of Zagelah. It was as big as a hen's egg, but more rounded; it was not set, simply pierced and slung on a chain of gold. It had had a curious history, about which nothing was known. A child in a black felt tent in Kurdistan had cut his teeth on it; an ignorant candle-chandler in Damascus had used it as weight on his scales. It had been bought, sold, pawned. Nobody knew that it had been a gift made in anger not in affection or respect and that in the giving the Queen had thought—And may you and all who wear it, suffer ill-fortune. It had been lost sight of, regarded of no value and then, suddenly at least half identified, in a legendary way by the same Arabic scholar who said that the oversized golden lion which now stood just inside the door of Abdullah's treasure house, was one of those which Solomon had ordered for his temple or his palace. This extremely beautiful and lifelike thing had never been displayed in Zagelah—to the orthodox Moslem as to the orthodox Jew representational art was forbidden. But Solomon had ignored such petty rules—and so, given time, would Abdullah. That was his last thought as he drifted into sleep; Solomon's golden lion and its exact replica, on guard beside his throne; and Sheba's enormous ruby dangling from the boy's slender neck.

On the momentous morning the boy, with the resilience of youth, woke and yawned and stretched; waited, became hun-

gry and presently with diffidence—masters being so unpredictable—touched Abdullah on the shoulder.

'My lord, would you wish to wake and drink kaffe? Shall I
fetch it?'

Fetch. In a week's time he would be saying—Shall I order
it?

Abdullah groaned, muttered 'Go away,' and then remembered that today he must entertain his second cousin, Selim, a
man whom he heartily disliked but must make some show of
respect to; his father's cousin, the eldest surviving male of the
family.

'Dear child, yes. You did well to wake me.' He knew what
Selim had come about; marriage. Selim was strictly orthodox,
mindful of his duty towards his kinsman; disapproving of the
wine, the kaffe, fairly tolerant of the boys but urging marriage
as a political necessity; ready to say, 'A boy for pleasure, if
that is your fancy, but a woman for use. The meanest peasant
needs a son to inherit his old donkey.'

Stretching and yawning, fighting off a heaviness in his
head—the kaffe would cure that—Abdullah thought that this
promised to be an interesting day. He would agree to marry
whomever Selim would come to suggest; then he would tease
Selim a little; tell him that he should wear the patched clothes
which fanatics wore; tell him about the plan to have the two
golden lions; parade the new boy with the great ruby bobbing
on his navel.

The waiting seemed interminable. With so much traffic on
the road it seemed safe to talk, in quiet voices. Lord Robert
said, 'It is an old idea, you know. I believe it was Darius the
Great who employed it against Babylon. But with a difference,
of course.' Nobody knew what he was talking about.

The Count had decided to trust half the operation to Sir
Godfrey; telling him to choose his eleven.

He had a slight, nagging doubt. Father Andreas thought
highly of Sir Godfrey and it was obvious that all his comrades
respected him; but was there a certain almost dangerous simplicity, a naïvety about the man? Unquestionably brave;
given an order he would do his best to carry it out; told to hold

117

a position he would probably do so until he died; but had he the flexibility, the quickmindedness, the resourcefulness to deal with an unexpected situation? Asked to choose his company, Sir Godfrey had named Sir Stephen, Sir Thomas—both men of the same stamp, and then Lord Robert, younger, livelier of mind ... Not that the unexpected was to be expected; everything planned and timed.

The river Loja rose in the hills, a waterfall, joined by others, and swelled and tumbled down into the valley; into and through the city, entering by one great archway in the red and white wall, and going out by another, and so down to Andara and to the sea. How soon would somebody notice that just at the point where it tumbled out of its rocky cradle and spread and slowed, it was being dammed? By rocks, loosened beforehand and needing no more than a push; by trusses of straw and the feather beds on which the knights had slept at their last comfortable camp, by folded tents, folded blankets, anything, everything which might for a little time halt the river's flow.

People who lived inside the city but worked outside in the gardens and orchards began to emerge. One of them gave the alarm. A great host, he said. Fifteen fully armoured knights on their great horses, backed by an army of workmen, looked formidable from a distance.

Panic began and spread, with shouting, with horns blowing. In no time at all the palace was loud with preparation.

Abdullah's first and main thought was, 'No siege!' He had never lived through one, but his grandmother had survived one when she was a child and had retained the most vivid memories of its horrors. People had been reduced to eating dogs, those unclean animals, and rats. And the gasped out words—'They are damming the river,' indicated a siege of the worst kind. The Loja was Zagelah's lifeblood; men could live with little food, even no food for several days; a city without water—with the rainy season over for the winter—could hold out no more than two days.

Dissolute as he was Abdullah did not lack courage. He would himself lead the charge. He did not even stop to think of the safety of anonymity but flung on the robes of royal reddish purple which were handiest. As he raced down the stairs and into the courtyard—a scene of orderly confusion—someone with presence of mind flung over him one of the uniform white outer garments.

He had two hundred men here, all picked and proven, and although in his day there had been no real fighting, mimic warfare and constant exercise had kept them fit and ready. There were few among them who could not with a single slash sever a cow's head. This was a routine practice; it was according to the Law which decreed that an animal must bleed to death; and it saved the butchers a job.

He had other forces posted at strategic places throughout his little kingdom; had he had only a day's warning. No matter, no matter; he and his two hundred had an ally in Allah. Allah! He was aware that he had not observed the Law as laid down by the Prophet, but Allah was merciful.

He did not even notice that not all his two hundred had turned out.

The prospect of immediate physical combat did something to men—unless they were born cowards. Hearts beat harder and higher, breath quickened; nobody thought at such a moment of the wounds he might sustain, only of those he would inflict. When the great bronze gates of Zagelah creaked open, the Christian knights in ambush looked at each other and smiled, not one of them aware that his smile was wolfish—the old, age-old grimace of showing the teeth.

In one of his several preparatory talks the Count had said, 'Hassan considers that no more than a hundred, or a hundred and ten ... Sir Godfrey, allow about forty to emerge.'

And who, at such a moment, could be bothered with counting? Four abreast at a time.

'Ready?' Sir Godfrey said. '*Now.*'

Many of the Moors, attacked suddenly and heavily from the side, never saw what had struck them. Some swerved to meet this other enemy, and so lost the momentum upon which their form of charge depended. Others, some bleeding and dying galloped on. Within two minutes, outside the gates there was the great slaughter that the old warlock had foreseen.

Up by the river where the dam was, it was worse. A white

wave of warriors still, after all these years waging war as their desert forefathers had done, repulsed by so few—but each of that few a miniature fortress.

And Escalona had been extremely cunning. He had recruited his workmen from a class of men accustomed to defend themselves or die. Lonely people, shepherds who in winter must fight wolves or lose their gravid ewes; men who hacked from hillsides things like millstones and grindstones and, coming back from markets where such things were saleable must be on guard against robbers who, unwilling to work themselves, were only too ready to grab the money which long labour had earned. They were all well chosen, stupid men, glad of an easy job with good pay and their keep. They had never bothered to ask what was the ultimate end of their activities. But when the Count of Escalona called, 'Defend yourselves. We are attacked!' they knew what to do. Out came the slings. Just here the now dwindling river showed its bed, floored with water—rounded stones—and a rounded stone carried best. A chunk of rock, intended to be part of the dam, powerfully pushed, did damage to the delicate legs of the horses.

The Moors could not on this morning follow their usual procedure when swoop and slash failed; the Christians' rear was guarded by the river. They wheeled, loosed their arrows which should have been lethal and today were not. Something was wrong, terribly wrong. They turned, charged again, and then, with weakening impetus, a third time. Then it was over and the Count had lost exactly four men.

The walls of Zagelah were so incredibly thick that Sir Godfrey's company fought its main battle in a kind of tunnel between the gateway and the open space within. In such a place weight was an advantage and the sword a more effective weapon than a scimitar. Once through the tunnel and into the sunshine of space beyond, they performed a manoeuvre so swift and so nimble as to be unbelievable with such heavy men and heavy horses. They lined up, knee to knee, offering the same solid, fortified opposition as their friends were offering by the river. There was an empty saddle, but the horse who

120

wore it knew his job and lined up with the others.

Hassan ben Hassan had reckoned shrewdly. Of the two hundred only a hundred and ten had responded. Sir Godfrey, slightly impatient and no great counter at any time had let thirty-two emerge before he said, 'Now!' Eight or nine Moors had been killed in that sudden flank attack; more in the dim tunnel; and amongst those now left to throw themselves against the Christians there were many who were aware of something wrong; terribly wrong. Where were those—the rest of the two hundred, who should now be supporting them? Where were the archers who should be manning the towers?

A Moor, practising the skill he had exercised on cows, took off the head of Sir Thomas Drury's horse in one marvellous stroke—destriers' necks being thicker than cows' and partially protected. The headless horse stood there, spouting blood just long enough to enable his master not to come down in the inevitable crash. Sir Thomas scrambled up into the empty saddle of Sir Alan Brokehampton's horse.

But we cannot keep this up for ever. Rock against battering wave; battering wave against rock. Just as the next wave was about to break—had indeed gathered itself together and launched itself somebody yelled and all the beautiful Arab horses rose on their hindlegs and pivoted and galloped away to the far side of the open space out of which three streets opened.

In the dim tunnel behind them, in the open, sunny space before them there were dead men and dying men, dead and dying horses.

The Count had said, 'At all costs keep the gates open.' But who could close them? Wedged open as they were. By corpses.

As they drew breath one arrow flew and hit Sir Stephen Flowerdew in the left eye. The Count had promised, saying that Hassan had promised no poisoned arrows, but this was an arrow, and it might be poisoned. So he plucked it out, bringing his eye with it. Afterwards he said that when the arrow struck he felt pain, but none as the eye came away. 'And my wife will look on me with even less favour,' he said, wryly.

They were waiting again, obedient to orders. No pursuit; hold the gate and await his coming. When he came he brought

121

workmen. One perched behind every saddle. They jumped down and cleared the tunnel and the knights clattered in over the blood-washed stones.

As they did so a fountain in the centre of the square shot silver spray into the sunshine.

'Four,' the Count said. 'And you?'

'Two. Many Moors got away.'

'Not far,' Escalona said in a gloating voice. He moved his hand towards the fountain. 'They were making for the water arch; escape by the river bed. Now ... We make ourselves look as many and as formidable as possible and move to the Palace, where Hassan will meet us.' Three streets led out of the square; six men to each of two streets, seven to the third.

Presumably from behind the lattices and shutters eyes were watching, counting perhaps, but they might have been riding through a city of the dead. It put the final touch of strangeness on the whole fantastic operation. When towns were taken people watched, with sullen hostility, or dull resignation, or simple curiosity. Here nothing stirred except a few slinking, scavenging dogs.

Of the six in this narrow, balconied street, Sir Godfrey and Lord Robert rode side by side, and last. It was a short street, and shadowed; at its farther end lay another square, bright with sunshine.

Suddenly from a balcony some unseen hand tossed something. That was more natural and ordinary; hostile watchers threw stones, people who welcomed invaders threw flowers or favours.

This was nothing that either of them had ever seen before. It landed, quite softly, in the centre of Lord Robert's breastplate, clung there and began to glow. He tried to brush it off and as the unprotected inner part of his hand came in contact with it, said, 'God's blood! Red hot!' He then hit it with the gauntleted back of his hand, a few bits broke off, fell on to his armoured thighs and began to glow there. The original piece stuck fast.

A secret weapon! An invention of the Devil!

Sir Godfrey reached out and struck at it. A fragment fell on to Pluto's mane and there was a stench of burning horsehair;

another fragment clung to Sir Godfrey's gauntlet and glowed and grew hot.

'Get down,' he said. 'I must unharness you.' He dismounted himself and pulled off his gauntlets.

His own armour was rather more than twenty years old and all that which he had worked on when he was a squire had been in the same style. Lord Robert—a rich man's son—had new armour and fashions had changed. All the straps in the wrong places, all the buckles unfamiliar and complicated. Oh God! God! Help me.

Inside his red-hot carapace Lord Robert began to scream. His horse, aware of its smouldering mane, screamed too, and galloped away. Sir Godfrey, his fingers burned to the bone, went on struggling...

No fighting man could afford to be squeamish and in his time Sir Godfrey had looked, unmoved, on many an unpleasant sight, but nothing quite like that disclosed when at last the armour—still aglow, clanked into the gutter. Roasted alive, the boy he had loved like a son.

Overwhelmed by grief, stunned, single-minded as ever, he knelt—but not in prayer—by the charred thing which had lately been a lively, laughing boy.

And so it happened that he was the only prisoner taken that day. By evening, the only Christian alive in the city.

11

THE letter came in April. 'Threepence,' said the old fishwoman who had brought it from Baildon.

It was sealed in three places and marked with dirty fingerprints. With shaking hands Sybilla broke the seals and read the words in a single glance. Then she turned dizzy and had to lean against the lintel of the door. Did people faint from joy? She drew a deep breath, read the letter again, kissed it and gave the old woman sixpence.

Well, no doubt about it, when your luck was in it was in, and when it was out it was out. Her good luck had started with the sale of her old donkey for such an unbelievable sum, had continued with the getting of a firm, regular order to supply fish to the place for bad women and the orphanage; and now, sixpence for delivering a letter. And seemed to be going on; for when she ventured to ask, 'Will you be wanting fish today, my lady?' the lady said without looking up, 'Yes. Yes. Two dozen of each.' You could trudge about for an hour to sell so many.

I am safe and well and the worst is over now. He could be on his way home.

Such wonderful news must be shared—if only to make it seem real.

She ran out to the byre where Walter was milking, watched by Henry.

'Walter, Henry, I have news. A letter. He is safe and well.'

Walter rose from the three-legged stool and said gravely, 'That is good news, my lady.'

Henry slipped on to the stool and said, 'Now may I finish her off, Walter?'

'Yes, if you do it properly ... My lady, is it over? Is he on his way home?'

His servant asked that; his son milked a cow!

Sybilla read the letter again. 'That he does not say. He says he is safe and well and that the worst is over now. Oh Walter, I am so happy!'

To Walter's ear there was something a little strange about the words—the worst is over. A tournament. Would Sir Godfrey, who enjoyed tournaments have written thus—unless he had had bad luck again. And if he had back luck how was he safe and well? To Walter it sounded more as though Sir Godfrey meant the sea voyage was behind him when he wrote. But he would not say a thing to mar her pleasure.

'Does it say where it was written, my lady.'

It did, but she had taken no heed of that, and now, read out, the name meant nothing to either of them.

William, when he came as he did, a few days later, was more knowledgeable and less considerate. He lived in a sea-faring community and had never shirked contact with ordinary people.

'Mondeneno,' he said. 'Yes, I have heard of it. On Spain's northern coast . . . I think, my dear, that this letter indicates that Godfrey had survived the Bay of Biscay.'

'Not . . . not that he is on his way home?'

'That could hardly be. The date—All Souls' day in the Year of Our Lord 1452. I am no traveller, my dear, and my knowledge of geography is small; but I feel bound to say that no man could leave Bywater on St Michael's Day, go to the south of Spain, fight a tourney and be back in Mondeneno by All Souls'.'

Was it possible to faint through disappointment?

'This letter,' William said, 'has been long on the road.'

And that was true. Father Andreas had left the strictest instructions that the letter should be delivered into the hands of the captain of the first English ship that put in to Mondeneno's welcoming harbour; and he had been implicitly obeyed. The fact that the ship to which the letter had been entrusted was bound for the Canaries was merely incidental.

The year went on. Walter's fields grew green and the wind blew over them, a kindly, a rough hand smoothing hair. Lady Randall's vigorous roses put out copper red shoots which changed to green and changed again, a wealth of roses, two trees bearing red flowers, two white, and two mixed in the way called damask; all sweet scented. The lilies grew tall and beautiful and the bees buzzed about them. Sybilla cut an armful and carried them into the church—thus fulfilling one of Father Ambrose's dreams. She knelt on the cold stone, alone, as the Abbess had said all must be, with God. God keep him, protect him, wherever he may be; and in mercy, bring him back to me. There was, she realized with a start of surprise, something about the scent of those lilies. She had never been one for musk, or attar of roses—both extortionately expensive and both used artfully to attract men—but now the lilies smelt of love-making. A fierce longing gripped her.

Late-sown as Walter's wheat and barley had been it had

125

been sown on land that had lain fallow for years and by August he had something to harvest.

'I'll stook it for you, Walter,' Bessie Wade said.

'That's for her ladyship to say.'

Walter was always administering such snubs and Bessie was either too dim-witted or too thick-hided to be deterred by them. She concocted excuses to go across the yard to his little house.

'Walter, you only had half a supper. I brought your piece of pie.'

'I've had enough. Give it to Master Henry, he's always hungry.'

'Ooh, Walter, you have made this place nice. Neat as a pin.'

'More than I can say of your kitchen.'

' 'S'not really mine, is it Walter? Ooh, if I had a little place like this, of my own, I'd keep it neat as a pin.'

The very way she said his name, the frequency with which she used it set his teeth on edge. Her devotion, her persistence insulted him. Just because he had a scarred face . . .

But in the field, anxious to please, she worked well. Sybilla had said that of course Bessie could stook and she would take charge of the kitchen. So Walter scythed, never hurrying and yet covering a great deal of ground in a day; Henry bound the cut ears into sheaves, and Bessie stooked. It was fine sunny weather, perfect for harvesting and she sweated a lot. Not a word of thanks or appreciation.

Yet Walter *could* give praise. He said he had never had such a good rabbit pie as Sybilla had made. And he said, 'I'm sorry you have to work so hard, my lady. Such a hot day, too.' And he said that in the hearing of the woman who on that hot day had plodded up and down, up and down in the field behind him!

People who could afford to do so stacked corn and kept it until, late in autumn, prices rose. Walter, with some reluctance, decided against this, just for the one year. They needed the flour that could be made from the wheat; they needed the money which the sale of the barley would bring. He made a threshing floor and two flails, a large one for himself and a smaller one for Harry, and then ... another large one for Bessie.

'Truly, Walter,' Sybilla said, 'I find it almost as easy to do things myself as to direct her. If she is of help to you...'

All this was makeshift; a holding on, a bearing up until Godfrey came back. The year tipped over and it was September again. On St Michael's Day he would have been gone for a year.

James, between his winter gout and his summer gout had made conscientious visits and said vague, soothing things, about Spain being a long way away, and the necessity of patience; but he was self-absorbed, taking her news about the letter and what William had said about it with, 'Good. Good!' and proceeding to talk about the betrothal of his gawky daughter to a young man of good family, but, alas, small fortune.

On William's next visit Sybilla said, 'William, you hold high rank in the Church and the Dominican Priory is in Bywater. They have Houses in Spain, too. If you asked, do you think they would make a few enquiries? It is such a *long* time. And if he could find someone to write for him in Mondeneno, he would have found someone in Escalona.'

'And may well have done so. Remember how long the other letter took to arrive. But I will certainly ask.'

He had a good memory but was inclined to be absentminded, having so many things to think about; so she made him write a little note to remind himself.

It was now September, with just that hint of coming change in the air which was stimulating to sexual appetite; mornings came with a faint mist, like the bloom on a grape, midday was warm, and at night the harvest moon hung like a great bronze globe in the sky, making night-work possible for people whose reaping was belated. Walter was not one of them; by the middle of the month even the flailing was finished.

In a way winnowing was an unpleasant job; husks worked their way into one's hair and under one's clothes. On a warm late afternoon, scooping up the last grains of barley and tying the neck of the sack firmly, Walter said, 'Well, that's over for the year. I'm going to take a bath. You, too.' He spoke to Henry, not to Bessie. It simply wasn't safe to speak to her except to snap out an order.

Bessie decided to take a bath, too. It was in the course of it that she realised that Walter had never seen her one real beauty, the compensation for being too fat all over—a fine bosom with firm, well-mounded breasts, white-skinned and tipped with rose. She was thirty-two years old, and desperate ... desperate enough to rip, deliberately, one of the two shifts she possessed.

Walter had heated a pot of water and poured it into a shallow bowl. Stripped to the waist he bowed over the bowl, washing his hair, face, torso. Then, discarding his hose, he stepped into the water.

Not a position in which a man would wish to be caught by an unwanted woman.

Enough to anger any man, but what was worse was the sudden, involuntary response of his body to the sight of those white breasts. A revolt against years of discipline and self-imposed celibacy. He snatched up the towel to hide his shame, said, 'Get out,' and broke into the language so foul that much of it was incomprehensible to Bessie who had spent her life in circles where even abuse was limited. But she understood that despite a second or two of promise, she was being rejected again. There could only be one reason, and she spat it out at him.

Holding the towel about him with his left hand, Walter used his right to slap her, forehand, backhand, across the face.

The people of Intake, freed of feudal domination had reverted to an earlier, more truly English institution—the Council of Elders.

Sybilla faced the deputation, four venerable men in their tidy Sunday or market day clothes and said,

'I cannot believe it.'

'But the girl's face is swollen and bruised, my lady. She got a black eye one side, a split lip the other. And what about the torn shift?'

128

'Granfer Wade,'—he had been excluded from the deputation for various reasons, too closely concerned in the matter, liable to get angry, certain to feel shame, 'Granfer Wade said Bessie went to his place, near naked, and bawling like a calf just taken from the cow. And all hurt about the face.'

'I was here,' Sybilla said. 'Should I not have heard? Bessie said she would take a bath—after supper, in the kitchen. Where was this assault supposed to have taken place? And when?'

About that Bessie had not been explicit. But shift implied bed.

'In her bed.'

'But she slept above stairs.' Bessie had indeed been privileged. In many places, even now, and even in magnificent places servants, male and female slept all hugger-mugger in the hall of the kitchen; Bessie had had a room.

'I sat here,' Sybilla said. 'Bessie took her bath. I went up, as I always do, to look in on the children, to see that they were covered. I thought that while I was looking at them, Bessie followed me up and went to her bed. It was not until this morning ... All her outer clothes there in a heap in the kitchen ... I thought ... when she did not appear, that she was taking a rest, well-earned. I can assure you, this alleged attack did not take place in this house. What is more, Walter Freeman has been with me for many years. In places where sonsy girls were on display and fully available. And never in all those years have I heard one word against him—in that respect.'

'He set about Bessie last night, my lady.'

'Not in this house. Her clothes are there in the kitchen where she left them. Her grandfather says she went to his house almost naked. If Walter laid a finger on her last night it must have been in his house; and she went there. *In her shift.*'

They thought it over. Bessie Wade lost some of the aspect of innocent victim.

'If she done that,' old Martin said, 'she were asking for trouble.'

'Did you hit her, Walter?'

'Yes, my lady.'

129

'Why?'

'She broke in on me while I was washing myself. I told her to get out and she just stood there.'

All too often Bessie's response to any order or suggestion was just to stand there. Almost asking to be smacked.

'You seem to have hit her very hard.'

'Not hard enough . . .' Suddenly, under the weathered tan his face crimsoned as he remembered the vile thing Bessie had said. Suppose she went saying it about the village. He thought —I should have *killed* the bitch!

'Those old men seemed to think that she would not work here any more.'

'I'll find you another woman, my lady. A better one.'

'That should not be difficult,' Sybilla said.

Yet it proved to be. Bessie's story might not ring quite so true as it had done at first telling, but it confirmed something that everybody had felt all along—there was something not quite right about Knight's Acre. Big should be big and rich should be rich; Knight's Acre was neither one thing nor the other; a servant who did not behave like a servant ruled there, and her ladyship stuck up for him. Even at the Michaelmas Hiring Fair several likely young women who would willingly have gone to be bullied by Lady Emma at Moyidan, or to be half starved in William's palace at Bywater, shrank away when offered employment at Knight's Acre. The woman Walter finally found was stone deaf as a result of having had measles when fully adult; but she was a good cook and a conscientious cleaner. Anxious to please, too, and gifted with a kind of extra sense as the afflicted often were.

Downhill into winter. In the house one woman who heard nothing, and one whose ears were constantly alert for a footfall or a hoofbeat, for the news that never came. Henry growing every day more and more like his father in appearance— sometimes the likeness smote her to the heart; Margaret grow- ing a little in size, but in no other way, and John as precocious and sturdy as Henry and Richard had been.

From Beauclaire good news of Richard. Hateful to think that two letters from Alys—written by one of her waiting women—had been sad disappointments in a way. Lady Astallon, through her henchwoman wrote that Richard had settled down very well and was well behaved. Richard was in fact not only behaving himself, he was enjoying a back-wash of public opinion; if the young Tallboys didn't kick and bite, then he was a good boy.

Lady Astallon's second letter informed Sybilla that Richard had outgrown his first outfit of the Astallon green velvet and that he had, of his own accord, taken lessons in reading and writing. Proof of that was at the foot of the page. RICHARD TALLBOYS, carefully and plainly written.

I should be glad. I am glad. But this is not what I am waiting and watching for.

12

GRAVELY, for both were men of dignity, Selim the new king of Zagelah and Hassan ben Hassan laughed in their beards and congratulated themselves. They had hatched and put into action the perfect plot. There would be no civil war—as might have resulted from an uprising; no interference from Abdullah's brothers-in-law which would have resulted from an assassination. The Christians had attacked Zagelah, killed Abdullah and most of his loyal adherents—all bad Moslems; Selim of Andara had simply happened to be in the city at the time, and strong enough to rally the faithful and gain a great victory. And Selim's inheritance by conquest was backed by his legitimate claim. He was kin to Abdullah.

And this was only a beginning. A reformed and purified Zagelah would presently move against Escalona and reclaim it.

'And that,' Selim said, 'will bring the Christians against us.'

Against his will he had been impressed by the performance of the Count and his small company. Fools, all of them; but for so few they had done a vast amount of damage. A matter of training and equipment. He had begun, even on that first day to toy with the possibility of forming a squadron of his own, similarly trained and armoured. With this in view he had issued an order to take prisoners when possible, to house them and feed them well. Despite this only one had survived—the man with the burnt hands.

Just upriver from Andara Selim owned a marble quarry, worked by slaves of almost every nationality; most of them were seamen who had been captured by the Barbary pirates and offered for sale in the port's slave market. Selim, as a strict Moslem would not own another as a slave and since despite comparatively good treatment his slaves seldom lived long, he was always in the market for able-bodied men. He now sent a messenger galloping to Andara with instructions to bring back an English slave.

Sir Godfrey's hands were beginning to heal. The Moorish treatment for burns was very peculiar: In England the practice was to smear a burn with some kind of fat and then to exclude the air. Here it was immersion of the burnt part in cool, slightly salted water. At first touch the water stung, then the coldness seemed to numb the pain. The burns were then exposed to the air, immersed again. An endless repetition.

The pain was the least of his woes. He was bereaved, and he was a prisoner in a heathen land. In a Christian country his ransom price would by now have been fixed and James and William and Alys—and maybe a friend or two—would be getting the money together. Here there was no hope. He lived in a state of utter dejection, not even noticing that he was being well-treated. His thoughts went round and round, like an ox treading corn. I shall never see Sybilla or the children again. I shall never go home. Robert is dead. His death was horrible. I shall never see . . .

The English slave—his name was John Barnes and he was one of the few men who worked in the quarry without developing the cough which was a death sentence—wore the quarry uniform, a pair of short drawers, a sleeveless shirt and a pair of rope-soled sandals. His grizzled hair was neatly trimmed, his

132

face freshly shaven. He looked well-fed, but his face had the tallowy pallor of long exclusion from fresh air or sunlight. Sir Godfrey looked to be in worse case. They had taken away his armour and the quilted garment he wore under it and given him a long Arabic-style gown, once white, now soiled. The good treatment that Selim had ordered had meant to his Arab gaolers enough to eat and no active ill-usage, but not the use of a comb or a razor. His hair was rough and clotted and he had just enough beard growth to make him look dirty.

'Th'art English, lad?'

'Yes. I'm English.'

John Barnes said, hastily, furtively, 'Do what th'art towd, lad. No matter what.' Then they both waited. Selim, in Arabic, spoke to John Barnes and he in turn spoke to Sir Godfrey.

'What's thy name, lad?'

'Godfrey Tallboys. Sir Godfrey Tallboys.'

Deep down in the marble quarry near Andara, John Barnes had heard nothing about the doings in the outer world. All he knew was that he had been brought out into the open, had a ride on a horse and several very good meals because his services as a translator were needed. But he knew what it meant when a man prefixed his name with *Sir*; and he did not use the familiar *lad* again until the very end.

He obeyed his master's instructions. Selim was offering Sir Godfrey an honourable post. All he had to do was to train men to fight in the Christian way; overlook the making of armour, copied from that taken from the bodies of dead men; show men how to school horses. Arcol had made his mark. In that narrow, balconied street with Sir Godfrey crouched in the gutter beside Lord Robert's armour—removed too late—and the charred body, Arcol had behaved valiantly as a destrier was trained to do, if for any reason his rider was smitten down; four iron-clad hoofs, strong teeth. It was in fact to Arcol that Sir Godfrey owed his life. His spirited resistance had gained that moment of time for the order from the centre to penetrate—a few prisoners . . .

'No,' Sir Godfrey said, hearing the proposition but not giving it long thought. Connive with these infidels, against his

133

own kind. No!

John Barnes said, 'Best think it over, Sir Godfrey. They have a whip, the khurbash, I've tasted the rope's end, twice. It's nothing compared. Save thysen.'

'Tell them, No.'

'Th'art a fool, Sir Godfrey. They'll beat thee. Me too, they'll say I didn't tell thee proper...' The man's tallowy pallor took on a greyish tinge and out of Sir Godfrey's despair, deep enough to welcome death in whatever form—I shall never see Sybilla and the children again; never go home. Robert is dead—and so many more; all my friends—a tiny bud of something else started.

'If you stand still,' Sir Godfrey said, 'I'll show them otherwise.'

He clenched his fists and the new frail skin on the inner side of his hands crumpled and split. He hit John Barnes twice, light, but telling blows; right fist to the left of the chin, jerking the head back, left just under the right ear.

It was the only indemnity that he could give his fellowcountryman. And as, under the first blow, John Barnes' head jerked, he said, 'Thanks, lad.'

'A spell in the quarry may make him think again,' Selim said.

The quarry just outside Andara was an awesome place. When God made the world out of darkness and chaos He had laid down a streak of pink marble at the base of a limestone ridge. It ran sideways and inwards. The Romans, in their day had tapped its upper outward end, and done well, for this marble was of peculiar beauty, pink, its colour shading from palest rose to deepest, not flecked, or striped. It had been greatly in demand for palaces and temples. Later for churches and ornate mansions. Besides its colour it had another unique feature, it was layered, slab on slab, like the leaves of a book, and the interleaving limestone layers often produced garnets. As the centuries went by the productive working face of the quarry retreated into the hillside and by the time Sir Godfrey went to work there there was, between the ordinary daylight world and the pink marble a series of caverns and tunnels, emptied of their treasure, providing excellent living accommodation and workrooms for slaves. There were air shafts, conduits for water, plentiful lighting by means of lamps that burned olive oil. It even had a climate of its own, equable and unaffected by either winter's snows or summer's baking heat. From a slave-owner's point of view it had yet another advantage; it had only one entry.

Into this subterranean world Sir Godfrey Tallboys was conducted, as hundreds of other men had been, to live and to work and to die. Perhaps, in his case not to die; for an order came with him. Light labour only and no ill-treatment; the King might have another use for him.

He was set to work with some old men, a few survivors of the régime, or weak men, racked by coughs, or men who in more vigorous work had suffered accidents. The 'light work' consisted of polishing small pieces of marble, the débris of the quarry's produce. The marble was brittle; sometimes a slab broke as it was heaved out of its matrix, sometimes one was dropped. Nothing here was wasted. A little jagged piece no bigger than a thumbnail was marketable for use as part of a mosaic floor or patterned wall. The polishing was done with a woollen rag, dipped first into oil and then into a grey abrasive powder.

His arrival aroused no interest—less in fact than a strange cow would arouse in a field of cows. There was here the apathy of hopelessness which he fully shared. Wait for the next meal, wait for bedtime, wait for death.

There were two meals a day, always enough for everybody. In the morning rice with small chunks of meat; in the evening rice with sugar and bits of dried fruit.

There was provision for nature's other need, not unlike the garderobes of castles, except that here the outlets were small.

There were guards or overseers who carried whippy canes and used them freely on anybody who had not turned enough jagged bits into smoothly polished pieces. Each man's finished work lay by his feet at the end of the day and every day Sir Godfrey's pile was smaller than any other, but he was not caned.

There was nobody to whom he could speak. No Englishman

here. The guards shouted or scolded in Arabic which Sir Godfrey did not understand, or intend to learn. He did what the others did.

For a full fortnight.

At the end of the second week, in accord with the deadly, soul-killing routine, he was taken out into the air, blinking and blinded as they all were by the sunshine. But he saw . . .

There, dark and yawning the great arch, entry and exit to the quarry, and immediately before it the hard trodden ground, a space where laden men and laden donkeys delivered what the quarry needed and took away what the quarry produced. Herded by the guards, shouting in Arabic and using their canes freely, Sir Godfrey and those who worked with him turned to the left. And there was half a meadow and beyond a stretch of river. Half a meadow because it had been carved away, made into a pool, curving inwards.

For the first time since he had been taken in that narrow, balconied street, Sir Godfrey's eye for terrain went to work.

The pool was a semicircle carved out of the river bank and separated from the river by an iron grille, slightly wider than the opening of the pool into the river. Upstream, downstream the iron grille, very spiky, reached into the green meadow.

If I could swim!

With that thought he began to live again.

The fortnightly bath was a ritual. Gang by gang, on differing days all the slaves of the Andara quarry were taken out, stripped, made to go into the water, brought back, clad in clean clothes, given into the barber's hands to be shaven and shorn. Not for their comfort, who cared? A guard against lice and all the other things which unwashed bodies produced.

The pool, Sir Godfrey thought in the mind that had begun to work again, is shaped like a C; the grille that separates it from the river extends, ten, twelve feet upstream, downstream. Are those points guarded?

It seemed not. So he worked it out. All that he needed to do was to go into the far edge of the pool, step out on to the bit of grass confined by the iron grille, run across it, plunge into the river and *swim*. Swim down to Andara, find a ship with an

English name. The masts and spars of the ships in the harbour were visible from the pool.

His time in captivity in Zagelah, his fortnight of sedentary work had slackened his muscles. That must be put right. He started his surreptitious exercises; stretching and bending, swinging his arms, flexing his legs, first thing in the morning, last thing at night. Not enough. He took to wolfing his food and thus gaining a few seconds in order to perform his antics which his fellows watched with complete lack of interest and every time he went to the garderobe place he stayed a little longer than was necessary. He observed that every now and then one of the men he worked with was assailed by cramp and with yelps and grimaces of pain would stand up from his working posture and stamp about to relieve it. He had not yet suffered this affliction himself but he now pretended to, as often as four or five times a day. His pile of finished work was still always the smallest, but he was still never caned. In this place as in all others under Selim's control, an order once given remained in force until it was rescinded.

There was a legend in the quarry that once upon a time a slave had attempted to escape on the way to the bathing pool; on the trodden forecourt he had turned right instead of left, thrown himself on a waiting mule and galloped off. It was a long time ago, but the guards were always particularly vigilant at that point. Once the slaves were in the water they relaxed a little, nobody could escape from the pool; all they had to do was to see that the slaves went far enough in and really washed themselves. On his second visit Sir Godfrey investigated the depth of the water. It grew deeper as it neared the grille. He waded out until it was chin high—that was about the centre; another step and he could feel the buoyancy of the water. He had never swum himself but he had seen it done. You kept your nose and mouth above water and made certain movements with arms and legs. He began to practise such movements. It was slow work, it was hit and miss, but his whole heart was in it and he made progress.

He was still dissatisfied with his physical shape; despite all his exertions it seemed to him that day by day his belly which had been flat as a board bulged a little more while his chest

137

shrank. He began to wonder whether the food had anything to do with it. Most slaves in the quarry looked well-fed though two meals a day was not really very much and if you looked closely at the unvarying dishes—as he did—the amount of meat in the morning meal was very small indeed, and the fruit pieces at evening were equally sparse. Was it the rice which made his belly bulge? He didn't know, but he could find out. He began to pick out the meat and the fruit and eat only a spoonful or two of the plentiful rice. For some days he suffered hunger pangs, then they eased; but the bulge was, if anything, even more pronounced.

In this place there was no day and no night; nor any way of telling one day from another; only the fortnightly cleansing marked the passage of time. The guards changed from time to time, but they all looked and sounded alike, and their behaviour varied so little that they might have been one man.

Outside the seasons progressed; the weather became warm, then hot, so that the bathing became a pleasure and there was no need for the guards to shout, 'Farther!' The grass in the meadow became yellow and brittle. July? August?

Sir Godfrey knew that the attack on Zagelah had been made in mid-February. After that he had been too dejected to bother about time. Say he had come to Andara early in March. And say this was July. Five months. He should have been home by now. Sir Ralph had promised to go and see Sybilla and take her a message. He was *not* to say that it was war, not tournament, and for his own premature return he was to use the excuse of ill health. Sybilla knew how long a tourney lasted. She would be worried now.

He must make his attempt as soon as possible, not wait until he swam better. Another consideration was that shipping was more plentiful in summer, and voyages speedier.

The guards, more observant than they appeared to be during the washing time, were now accustomed to the sight of one man venturing into the really deep water and performing antics. They were not worried; he could not escape by the grille which was heavily spiked and at its top turned inwards.

138

It was an afternoon of somnolent heat; not a time for swift movement or swift thinking. He splashed about a little, sure now that it was just possible. He had only to heave himself out of the pool, run like a hare to the end of the grille, throw himself into the river.

Now!

He did it. As the water closed over his head he heard the shouting. He surfaced and clumsily struck out.

What he did not know, and couldn't know, was that some of the pink marble was transported downstream to the port in small boats. Somebody in one of these hit him over the head with an oar and dragged him aboard.

Far less heinous offences than attempted escape were punishable by flogging, but this man could not be flogged without the King's direct permission. And Selim had lost interest in Sir Godfrey. For one thing Hassan ben Hassan, a firm traditionalist had been opposed to the idea of new-fangled methods of fighting and found the thought of aping the unbelievers most repulsive. For another, when, as he planned he moved in on Escalona nobody had made so much as a murmur of protest. The nearest two great Christian lords were busy with their interminable squabble; and the King of Castile had other things than the loss of a small province to think about. Divorce, remarriage ...

In due time the new order came—Treat this man as you would any other.

Sir Godfrey had regained consciousness in a place so dark and so narrow that when he had felt about a bit he had been seized with panic. He had drowned and they'd buried him alive.

It was a rational assumption. During his time in Andara he had seen two men die and seen how casually their corpses had been treated—literally dragged out, feet first with no more ceremony than would have been given a dead dog. His head hurt. He had no memory of the blow that had stunned him and thought that his head had been injured by similar rough handling.

He felt about; stone under him, stone on both sides; then

139

wood. Wood? Yes, wood. The lid of the coffin? The door to the vault? He hammered on it and shouted. There was no answer.

A man not yet dead, but buried alive and soon to die, should make his peace with God.

He had never been a very pious man; he had accepted the teaching of the Church, kept the rules. He had been faithful to his knighthood vows and to his marriage vows, he had never cheated or told an unnecessary lie, but his religion had always been a matter of form rather than of feeling; except when he knelt there in that narrow street and asked, from his heart for help in getting Robert out before he roasted. That help had not been forthcoming ... How then approach God now, except to say, as to some remote, indifferent overlord, 'My God, I am sorry if by word or deed I have given offence. I beg forgiveness.'

A creak, a narrow streak of oil-lit light. Something pushed in and a voice. 'Take this, you swine!'

Without knowing, without wishing, Sir Godfrey had picked up a small knowledge of Arabic. Terms of abuse were always the most easily acquired in any language.

He had not been buried alive; but he was still a prisoner. He had failed in his attempt to escape and was back with his hopelessness. Sometimes in the darkness, he wept.

Floggings were not frequent in the quarry, partly because they disabled a man for work for some time; but it was good for everyone to be aware of the existence of the dreaded whip and to see it in use from time to time. The procedure was therefore made as public as possible, with the offence which had occasioned it chanted. 'Look well and learn. See what befalls one who would run away. See the punishment for defiance.'

Sir Godfrey would have said that he was hardened to pain; to bear it without fuss was part of every boy's training. At the first stroke of the many-thonged, metal weighted whip he bit through his lower lip in order to keep silent. At the second both bowels and bladder failed him and he screamed like a trapped hare. Then he lost consciousness again.

140

He was now, in every sense of the word a marked man. Even an abortive attempt at escape was resented by the guards as a reflection on their vigilance, and this man had for months been immune from even the most desultory punishment. As soon as his back and shoulders and ribs and buttocks were half healed he was moved to heavier work, at the rock face itself.

Had he, in this new misery been capable of finding consolation in anything, he would have found it in the fact that he now worked alongside John Barnes with whom he could at least exchange remarks now and then. Much talking was not allowed. The atmosphere here was also less dour and sullen than in the mosaic chamber where everyone was half dead of age or ill-health; this was the place for the younger and more able-bodied slaves. Their plight was just as hopeless, but they chose not to recognise it quite as fully as the old, sick men had done. They were of many nationalities; Italian, Dutch, French, Norwegian, German, but they had developed a kind of polyglot language with a good deal of Arabic in it.

One day when Sir Godfrey had been at the quarry face for some time there was a new arrival; a Greek who also spoke Latin and quickly made himself understood by the two Italians who managed to impart the news he brought, to the rest of them. The Turks, he told them, and they told the others, had taken Constantinople in May.

'And that should stir up the Pope and the rest of 'em,' John Barnes said. 'There'll be big war now, Christian against Infidel all over t'place. We might yet see t'light of day; if we bear up.'

It was a frail hope, but anything, however small, was better than nothing.

AT the point where the road to Moyidan met the lane to Intake Bishop William halted his horse. James was head of the family, after all. And breaking bad news to a woman was a woman's job. He was tempted. Then he admonished himself for wishing to shirk, and rode on down the lane.

Sybilla, at the sound of his horse ran out, her headdress blowing in the gay April wind. At the sight of his face, she said, 'Bad?'

'I am afraid so.'

'Dead?'

'Nobody knows. It seems likely.'

She did not break into the storm of tears which he had feared. Her face blanched and hardened, that was all.

Inside the hall she said, 'I have felt for a long time . . . from the very first . . . I was against it. What does it mean—nobody knows?'

He took out the letter which the Head of the Dominican House in Seville had written.

The Count of Escalona, the knights who were with him, Father Andreas and six of the Dominicans had simply vanished. They were known to have gone into Moorish territory in February 1453. No word of what had happened to them had ever been received. In March 1453 the Moors had overrun Escalona itself, and so far as could be ascertained there had been no refugees. All hope for the priests had been abandoned and the chance of any man's survival was small; the Moorish custom was to take only women and children as prisoners.

Sybilla sat perfectly still with her hands pressed to a point just below her breast as though easing a pain. Stunned, poor woman. Now he found himself wishing that she would cry.

He noticed for the first time how thin she had grown during these months of anxiety. He remembered, with startling clarity, a dress she had worn on one of her early visits to him. Not a modest dress, he had thought at the time, either in colour or style. It was bright scarlet, cut low and with sleeves that were so wide and loose that every time she lifted her spoon, her right arm had been revealed to the elbow; white and dimpled.

To be honest, in those days he had not either liked or approved of her much; too worldly and given to fashion; and then when the children came she had spoiled them shamelessly and tried to interfere with his household arrangements which suited him perfectly. But now he was genuinely sorry for her, as he was for all the afflicted, and his words of comfort, though well-worn, came from his heart.

Godfrey, he said, was now in God's hands and safe for ever. Dying in a battle against the Infidel—as must be assumed—he had died in a Holy War. And it could be certain that he had died bravely. 'He was a brave knight, and a good man.'

In his experience, praise of the dead, however little deserved provoked more tears in those already shedding them, but applied comfort at the same time.

'He was a brave knight and a good man. *And he died because I must have a house!*'

'He died,' William said, 'because this Count of Escalona, having gathered knights for a tournament, snatched an opportunity to lead a small Crusade. In effect, Godfrey took the cross—an act which even with men of evil life, shortened the pains of purgatory. Godfrey is now in the presence of God.'

He then bethought himself of his last talk with his brother. There would be no money now to be brought home and looked after.

In his own way William Tallboys was brave, too. He had broken the bad news, given what spiritual comfort was available and now took a decision that was likely to cost him dear.

He said, 'My dear, I should be very happy if you would come and make your home with me.'

And if ever a man told a lie, he told one then. For more than the mere disruption of his household was at stake, though that would be bad enough ... Henry was old enough to go to the monks' school, but even so it would leave two and John bade fair to be as noisy and hungry as his brothers. But there was also an undertow; the Lollards had been put down, but some

143

of the things they had said during their attacks on the Church, had echoed . . . the words 'housekeeper' and 'nephew' had been smeared; and something of the smear clung. Conscientious clerics were careful to have only old, ugly women about them; and seemed to have fewer nephews . . . Still, if at his age and with his unblemished reputation he couldn't invite his brother's widow to share his home things had come to a fine pass.

'William, that is very kind. I am grateful. But I must stay here.'

'Alone?'

'Except for those few short months I have always been alone here.'

'But with hope,' he said gently. 'Now you will be . . .' He left that sentence unfinished. 'I am sure we could make some very comfortable arrangement. Those rooms that face the sea. A kitchen of your own.'

'Thank you. That is most kind and generous. But I must stay here; in the house that Godfrey made for me. His last gift.'

'The offer will remain open, my dear.' She was in no state to be pressed. He felt that she was making a wrong decision: and although to make the offer had been an effort he did not like to see it rejected so promptly. Nor did he like the idea of leaving her here alone. Such unnatural control must surely snap. On whose shoulder would she weep?

He offered to stay overnight. Offered to send Emma from Moyidan. Offered to send a well-mounted messenger to fetch one of Eustace's sisters. She said, 'I need nobody, William. I have been prepared for this. For many months now.'

But then, he thought, so were women who had watched through hopeless illnesses—yet they wept. For the first time William understood what his sister Mary had seen in Sybilla.

James came next day and made an offer similar to William's and that had cost him even more of an effort—hours of argument with Emma who did not favour the idea at all. And he had come a cropper. In the course of the argument he had pointed out—meaning no ill—that in June Margery was to be

144

married and that Sybilla could, to an extent take her place. Emma took that much amiss. 'Are you telling me that I am old enough to be Sybilla's mother? I thank you for nothing! She is full twenty-six, maybe more if the truth were known.' He had tried to explain; he only meant that Sybilla would do the errands, the running about, the waiting on. Emma refused to be pacified, refused even to discuss the matter further until by one of those curious twists that a quarrel takes they came back to something she had long wanted and James had been reluctant to give, holding as he did that as he inherited property so he should pass it on. And there was something—unpleasant—in this asssmption that she would surely outlive him, obvious as it must be considering their ages. And she had been well-dowered; but her argument was that values were changing so rapidly. A noble, once worth, in words six shillings and eightpence, was now, in words worth eight shillings and fourpence, but it bought less; and she could not really trust Richard to look after her—good mother as she had been to him. He was so *weak*; even in the midst of this quarrel she could not bring herself to say simple-minded; weak and stubborn. He'd choose his wife—as Godfrey had done—and then live under her thumb and where would Emma be?

By the end of the quarrel, Sir James had pledged his word. Emma should have land and money enough to build a house when she needed one, not as a bequest in his will but now. A bribe for doing what was merely a duty—offering a home to a widow and her children.

Sybilla gave him the same answer as she had given William. Kind. Generous. But she must stay here. And she could manage. Knight's Acre was even now virtually self-supporting, next year it would do even better. She could manage. Sir James was so much impressed by her attitude that he made another effort; he said that if ever she needed money—or advice—she had only to ask ...

Time now seemed to change pace. While she had awaited news, it had been both speedy and slow. A week of waiting an age and yet the Sundays seeming to crowd one another. Different now.

She had broken the news to Henry. 'Henry, I have something sad to tell you; I heard today that your father is dead.' No impact. Henry said, politely, 'I am sorry, Mother.' He would have been more concerned if she had cut her finger.

Walter struck a truer note. 'I am sorry, my lady; but I had begun to think ... And he died as he would have wished. If that's any comfort.'

There was that to think of. She had not wanted him to go; but he had wanted to, and had whistled, merry as a blackbird as he scoured his armour and rubbed neat's-foot oil into its straps. He had gone happily to death. And since death must come to all men ...

Father Ambrose asked, 'Any news of Sir Godfrey, my lady?'

Senile; she had told him in those first bitter moments, and he had said, 'I am very sorry. I will say a mass for his soul.'

But he asked the question every time he saw her; not on Sundays only; as the days lengthened and even the twilights were warm he would come, knock on the door, ask the same question, receive the same answer, make the same promise. She outlived the stage of being exasperated and was able to think—Poor old man!

In that April William of Bywater had had another thought. What of the rest? Who else should be informed? He plodded up the hill to the Dominican Priory, and because Dominicans were scrupulous about records, he was given the names of fifty knights, half embarked on a ship named *Mary Clare* which, after so long a time must be assumed to be lost, and half on *The Four Fleeces* which had been luckier, at first.

He went back and sat at his wide table and cogitated. Urged by Sybilla he had put enquiries afoot; and been answered. Other women, living with anxiety and suspense that ate the flesh from the bones, still knew nothing. It was his duty to write and he did it, until the repetition dulled his mind and the writing cramped his hand. He had a perfectly adequate clerical staff, but he felt that such a letter should be personal.

The mystery surrounding the event kept interest alive and it was still being discussed when Sir Simon Randall went to the

Lammas Tourney at the Abbey of Bury St Edmund's. There he disported himself less well than usual because his mind was distracted; should he or should he not pay a visit of commiseration to Sir Godfrey's widow? It would be a perfectly conventional thing to do; he and Sir Godfrey had been comrades-in-arms during the Welsh war; so why not make up his mind and go? Because, after only five months, bereavement would still be raw and he shrank from seeing her in a lachrymose state. He'd been a child when his father died but he had a vivid recollection of how his mother—a strong-minded woman, too—had behaved for a full year. (He could also remember how his parents had quarrelled; but he had not associated his mother's violent grief with feelings of remorse and guilt.)

In the end he decided to go; sent his squire home with his great horse, and a message to his mother, rode to Baildon and spent the night there and arrived at Knight's Acre at midmorning.

Sybilla was in the kitchen. Madge, the deaf woman, was helping with the harvest: she worked less ostentatiously hard than Bessie had done, being older and not inspired by a wish to impress Walter, but she did well enough. John and Margaret were also helping this year, gleaning stray ears for the hens. Their development had reached the stage where whatever John did Margaret would attempt to copy.

Sybilla no longer listened for horses' hoofs and when the knock sounded on the door, she thought—Father Ambrose again! She stopped only to throw off the coarse apron. She had abandoned headdresses now. Even in those days of declining hope, or near hopelessness, while there had been the slightest chance of Godfrey ever returning, she had been careful of her appearance. Now there was no reason to suffer inconvenience.

The hair thus fully exposed had changed colour; Sir Simon remembered it as being the soft amber of fresh-run honey. Now it was primrose pale. And that look of youth which had made her so surprising a mother to four children, two of them big boys, had vanished. He felt something twist inside him as she greeted him. Poor lady, she has felt her loss keenly.

There was, however, nothing tragic about her manner; she actually smiled as she said, 'Sir Simon, how very kind of you to visit.'

'I was near by,' he said a trifle awkwardly.

'I have for so long been meaning to write to your mother. To thank her. *Everything* she sent me flourished and gave me much pleasure. The roses are over now, but I believe, I really believe that one tree, one of the damasks, is preparing to bloom again.'

'That does happen sometimes—with damasks.'

She still had not wine, no saffron cake for mid-morning hospitality. But she had ale.

'Walter,' she said in a light, sociable manner, 'has taken to brewing—and does it as well as he does all else. And I have learned the art of making harvest buns.'

Harvest buns were meant to be eaten in the field; they contained a little finely chopped suet which prevented them drying out as slices of bread did. They were flavoured, too, a pinch of nutmeg, a pinch of cinnamon and just before harvest started Walter had 'happened upon' another of his extraordinary bargains, a little old battered chest, regarded as rubbish by those who had inherited it and hoped to find gold. The spices in its small compartments which ignorant heirs had opened with hope and shut again in disappointment, had found their way to what Walter called 'the rubbish market' at Baildon.

Sir Simon was at a loss; he had been properly reared and taught what to do in most circumstances; but how could you mention a dead man to his widow who talked about roses, about ale, and harvest buns. It was like seeing a woman, and talking to her, through a window.

Finally he forced himself to say what he *almost* believed he had come to say. 'Lady Tallboys, I was most profoundly sorry to hear...'

The glass between them should have shattered then; but it did not. She said, 'Yes, it was a terrible thing. My only consolation is that he went happily. That is true. He whistled as he made his armour ready, and as he prepared Arcol. To be honest I was never in favour of that enterprise; I sensed something wrong ... from the very beginning. But he went happily ...' There was a sombreness now in her voice, and on her face the look of sorrow which had hollowed the youth away. But almost immediately she was again a hostess entertaining a welcome visitor; asking what he had been doing since they last met.

How astonished she would be, he thought, if I told her the truth—sedulously avoiding my mother's matrimonial lures! He gave her a brief account of his recent activities, one half of his mind intent to be as entertaining as possible; the other deeply concerned for her. Poor and alone. And sad—for all that brave front! Finally, feeling self-conscious about it, he managed to get in his question; did she propose to stay in this house? Oh yes, she said, everybody had been exceedingly kind; she told him about the homes she had been offered. 'But I prefer to stay. I am not lonely. I have three children, and Walter, and Madge. At the moment they are all in the field.' Where shortly, she should join them, carrying ale and harvest buns. The corn was thicker this year and no part of a good working day must be wasted by dallying over dinner. Supper was the main meal at this busy time of the year; she had been in the act of preparing it; a mutton and apple pie ...

When he rode away Sir Simon was deeply, and now legitimately, in love. *Thou shalt not covet thy neighbour's wife*: and Sir Godfrey had been in a way his neighbour in several bloody little affrays. Now he was dead—God rest him in peace and Sybilla was not a wife, she was a widow.

Lady Randall *knew*. For Simon who had always shied away from anything that was not completely pleasant, to go out of his way ... This Lady Tallboys ... typical widow ... she had known several, one man lost; all agog to catch another. Experienced. Wily.

She had an erroneous picture in her mind. After Simon's first—and completely explicable—visit to Knight's Acre he had spoken of Lady Tallboys, mentioning the four children, two big rather naughty boys, mentioning also her youthful look. That implied a liberal use of cosmetics.

Now, after his second visit he sounded concerned about the woman in a way that could only mean one thing—concern for others not being one of his outstanding virtues. Knight's Acre was such a remote place, and although Lady Tallboys denied that she was lonely, she must be, left with only children and servants for company. Had she no relatives? Yes, and both Sir Godfrey's brothers had offered her a home, but she preferred to remain in her own. A woman out to catch another husband, Lady Randall reflected, would enjoy far more freedom of action under her own roof.

Open opposition would be worse than useless, all mothers knew that. Lady Randall could only hope that this infatuation would wear off; that some man nearer at hand would forestall Simon; that if the worst came to the worst, Lady Tallboys was capable of bearing another son. She had a great longing for grandchildren, but was prepared to make do with one, if a boy.

In October the Cressacre orchards yielded their final offering for the year; particularly excellent pears, long-keeping apples, walnuts. 'Lady Tallboys has no such things,' Simon said. So the gaily painted cart was loaded again, and into it went two casks of good wine as well. Sir Simon followed his gift and was prettily thanked and given a good dinner, for Walter had killed a pig that week.

That morning there was a good fire in the hall, but partly because it was so sparsely furnished, it still struck cold. Of course, no rushes on the stone floor. On his way home he turned aside and went to a place called Shimpling where a special kind of reed grew; scented, so that every time a step was taken, a pleasant odour was emitted. He paid for a load to be delivered to Knight's Acre.

It was that gift which wakened a suspicion in Sybilla's mind.

Presents of surplus produce were usual enough, costing the donor nothing; but she knew this particular kind of rush and how much in demand, how extremely costly it was.

Dismiss the suspicion as ridiculous! Take a look in your mirror! A boy, twenty-three at most. And are you so old?

Twenty-seven. But one ages not only by one's birthdays. In all but years' reckoning I am old enough to be his mother!

He is a young man with a kind and generous heart; he had a fondness for Godfrey. I wrong him. I flatter myself.

But he came again, just before Christmas, bringing not only gifts but an invitation which Lady Randall had extended in a spirit of resignation. If Lady Tallboys had no previous engagements, Lady Randall would be most happy if she, and her family would come to Cressacre for the festive season.

'And I thought,' Sir Simon said, 'that if you travelled with the younger children in the wagon, the cloak would keep you warm.'

It was of sable; the costliest fur known, coming as it did, all the way from Muscovy.

The Abbess of Lamarsh training a promising girl had said, 'Of two possibilities, think of the worst first. One can always retract.'

Time to make things clear; but gently. She used his name without its prefix for the first time.

'Simon, such a gift no honest woman could accept—as you must surely know—except from a wealthy kinsman, or a husband.'

Playing straight into his hands. 'And that is what I wish to be to you, Sybilla. I fell in love with you at first sight.'

The very words Godfrey had spoken in the cold convent parlour. And then, all innocence and defiance and with a feeling of being let out of trap she had been able to say with all sincerity, 'And I with you.' That was not possible now.

'You must put all such thoughts from your mind. I shall never marry again.'

'I spoke too soon . . .' He had indeed been precipitate; he had intended to make his declaration at Cressacre.

'No. In ten, twenty years. I shall still be of the same mind. A proposal is always a compliment, and I value yours, Sir Simon. But I cannot accept it.'

'Why? What have you against me?' What indeed? He was young and handsome and rich and had gone out of his way to show fondness; he was prepared to treat the children as his own.

'Against you? Nothing! Nothing. But it would be impossible for me to marry any man.'

They were now talking at cross purposes. He felt that he had blundered—though she had known of her widowhood since April. He attempted to defend himself.

'Sybilla, I should have waited. But, beside my love, there is another reason ... Time may be short ... The threat of civil war hangs over us all. Next year, or the one after at latest. If you do not love me,' as plainly she did not, 'consider your safety and that of your children. Cressacre is well fortified; moated. It could withstand a siege. Also, married to me, you would be on the winning side. York!'

Sybilla had heard talk of civil war as long ago as when she was staying at Beauclaire: her brother-in-law, Lord Astallon, had been sure that it would come and equally sure that a cautious man could remain neutral. He never went to Court—much to the chagrin of his lady; he did not allow political talk in his hearing; he avoided people with strong views.

'I shall be safe here,' she said. 'I take no sides and I have nothing that anyone could covet.'

In any other woman he would have regarded such reasoning as idiocy; in her it indicated a touching innocence.

'I beg you,' he said, 'reconsider. Do not refuse out of hand. I will accept that you do not love me—but you might come to do so. Marriages are made every day with no fondness on either hand—yet love comes. And I love you so much. I could *make* you love me, given half a chance.'

She shook her head. 'I loved Godfrey. I love him still.'

He *had* spoken too soon!

'Think it over,' he said again. 'I will come again, after Christmas.'

'That would be foolish. You must forget all this. There must be so many girls, with love locked in them, waiting to be freed. So it was with me. Find one of them. And I wish you happy.'

Their leave-taking had, on her side at least, an air of finality.

He did not ride home directly. Temporarily defeated, he

152

felt the need of allies—and found them.

James at Moyidan said, 'It would be the most wonderful thing for Sybilla. She has, as you know, so small a substance. Four pounds a year in rent and what the farm—it is only a farm—brings in. We do what we can, of course,' he said deprecatingly, and in fact when their bees swarmed they had sent Sybilla a hive, 'but times are bad and getting worse.'

(You are a fat selfish pig, Sir James Tallboys, and every twinge of your gout is well-deserved, Sir Simon thought.)

But he was an ally, saying yes, and yes, he would make the great effort and some time over the Christmas season go and have a talk with Sybilla.

William at Bywater was equally obliging if less outspoken. In his long and on the whole, sorry, experience, women who had once known the joys of love, as they called it, needed it again. Time after time a woman, betrayed, rescued and placed in a position which promised security, had fallen again. And he knew about widows, too. Only a few, disappointingly few, were content to live on in loneliness and leave their goods to the Church.

'It would be an excellent thing for Sybilla,' William said. 'If you could be patient, Sir Simon. I think she has not yet realised what loneliness—without hope of relief—can mean. And she is a comparatively young woman, still.'

'She has requested me not to visit her again.'

'And that, surely, is discreet. But you may rely upon me— and upon James, I am sure—to advise her for her own good.'

'She refused me,' Sir Simon told his mother. 'And also your invitation.'

To her already unpleasant vision of Lady Tallboys, Lady Randall added another stroke—Coy! She then made a blunder.

'Perhaps, my dear boy, it is as well. A widow, with four children. Not an ideal match.'

'The only woman I ever wanted to marry—or ever shall. I can tell you this. Unless Sybilla changes her mind, I shall never marry.'

'Nonsense,' his mother said briskly, 'if you can stay away

153

from her for six months you will forget all about her.'

Lady Randall was a practical woman and, anticipating that Lady Tallboys, falsely youthful, would be spending Christmas at Cressacre had invited also two very pretty young girls.

'And you cannot *not* marry, Simon. Cressacre needs an heir.'

'My uncle of Malvern remained a bachelor. I have no nephew, but doubtless I shall find a godson.'

Christmas passed; the pretty young girls doing their best and winning from their host nothing more than a host's due civility. In his lordly surroundings Simon Randall awaited the coming of a messenger just as Sybilla had waited. Sybilla could have changed her mind; the persuasions of her relatives could have been effective; but there was no word from Knight's Acre, Moyidan or Bywater. January, by measure of days one of the long months of the year, but of itself the longest, painfully climbing out of the trough of winter, came and went. Early in February a baby born at nearby Bradwald was christened—with Sir Stephen Randall as his godfather; and Lady Randall, looking with unfond eyes at the squawling, red-faced, scrap of humanity, asked herself—Was it for *this* that I managed during Simon's minority?

Oh, better a widow—still of child-bearing age, one hoped.

Bang, bang, bang of the iron ring on the solid door. Father Ambrose again. A form of discipline.

'Any news of Sir Godfrey, my lady?'

'Yes, Father, he died in Spain.'

'I am sorry to hear that. I will say a mass for his soul.' Again and again, impatience become tolerance and tolerance melting into impatience again. This time she would not even remove the apron, then he would see that she was busy and not make some remark about the weather and then repeat the question. Madge, taking advantage of the fine, bright day, was at the washtub, and Sybilla had been dealing with a piece of bacon which Walter had taken from the smokehole in the kitchen chimney before taking a sack of wheat to be ground at the mill.

A poor household indeed, Lady Randall thought, where the

door was opened by a little kitchen slut with black hands and a smut on her face.

'I wish to see Lady Tallboys.'

'I am Lady Tallboys. And you, I think, must be Lady Randall.'

Dumb from astonishment, Lady Randall who had walked straight into the hall, turned and stared at Sybilla who was closing the door. Outside, on the wide path flanked by Lady Randall's roses, Lady Randall's attendant stood holding Lady Randall's two tall horses.

'There is such a strong resemblance,' Sybilla said, and smiled.

Since Simon had always been considered handsome and Lady Randall, even in youth not even pretty, this was a compliment indeed.

'I beg you, excuse my appearance. Had I had warning . . . I was doing a rather dirty job. Pray be seated.' With one soiled hand she indicated the cushioned settle. She then divested herself of the coarse apron. On the cleaner parts of it she rubbed her hands, taking off the worst, but leaving them still far from clean. She rolled the apron and dropped it out of sight behind the settle and then seated herself on the plain wooden bench.

Then, since Lady Randall was still speechless, Sybilla said, 'I am so happy to see you and to be able to thank you, in person. I asked Sir Simon to tell you that everything had flourished most wonderfully—but a message is not quite the same.'

Lady Randall recovered sufficiently to say that it always gave her great pleasure to give a few plants to appreciative people. But as she spoke she was taking stock. What *can* he see in her? Somewhat over thirty; colourless; no figure to speak of. A kind of grace, yes, a pleasant voice, a composed manner, and dignity—despite the smudged face and the rolled up sleeves. Nothing to account for the boy's infatuated behaviour. Nothing that could not be matched a dozen times, with youth and prettiness thrown in.

'I am—thanks entirely to your generosity—able to offer you a cup of wine, Lady Randall. If you will excuse me. My maid-

155

servant is completely deaf.'

While she was alone Lady Randall could study the hall, the bare cupboard, the single wall hanging. Her mystification grew; and curiosity alongside.

When Sybilla returned she was clean. She had dabbed her hands in the washing tub, and Madge, saying 'Excuse me, my lady,' in the harsh toneless voice of one who had been deaf for years, had removed the smudge.

'I came,' Lady Randall said, accepting a cup of wine and a wafer-thin slice of something that was neither bread nor cake, 'to talk to you about my son. I understand that on his last visit he made you an offer of marriage, and that you refused it. And said you did not wish to see him again.'

'I hope—no, I am sure—that I did not speak so harshly. I refused his offer. I advised him to go away and forget me. I advised him to find a young woman who would love him as he deserves to be loved.'

'As you cannot?'

'As I cannot.'

'Why? If you think him worthy of love?'

'Because I loved my husband. It is too long a story to tell ... He loved me and I loved him. What feeling is left in me is for his children, *because* they are his. I have nothing to spare, even for someone so charming, so kind, so handsome, so altogether delightful as Sir Simon.'

Lady Randall who had come in desperation to plead with a coy, flighty widow who might—one never knew, men being so stupid—have another, even more eligible man on a hook. Now, again confounded, she said, 'Perhaps Simon spoke too soon. I know. I have myself been widowed ... I wept every day for a full year. But my dear Lady Tallboys, life must go on.'

'It goes on here. Every day.'

Lady Randall brought her hands together in an ungraceful way, the right fist clenched and banging into the palm of the left.

'Listen. Within a year there will be war. My brother-in-law, Lord Malvern—informed me privately, only the other day. The present situation cannot outlast the summer.'

And God knew that she had meant to mention Lord Malvern in another connotation, bait for the coy, flighty widow. But this was bedrock stuff. If this stubborn, stupid woman persisted in her refusal, and Simon, stubborn and stupid persisted in his determination to marry nobody else, and the war came . . .

'Has a reluctance to give your children a step-father any bearing on your decision, Lady Tallboys? I can assure you that Simon . . .'

'Far from it. I know very well that they would benefit. Indeed, I am not very happy about Henry—that is my eldest. He is eleven and has had no advantages at all. But . . .'

'You must have married very young.' A cunning interruption.

'I was just sixteen and Henry was born within a year.'

Twenty-eight then; and four children living. A good breeder!

'Naturally any son of Simon's own would inherit Cressacre. But—not to put too fine a point upon it—Simon is very well-to-do. My husband was rich; I brought him a good dowry; and in the years before Simon came of age, by thrift and good management I added to the estate. There would be enough for all; even without regard to the fact that Simon will in all probability inherit Lord Malvern's lands—and *title*.' Surely as glittering a bait as was ever dangled before a poor widow with four children.

'There are times,' Sybilla said, 'when one's mind moves quickly. I thought of all the advantages as soon as Simon had spoken. But even as I thought I knew that it would be impossible for me to remarry. I regret the impossibility—but not the decision.'

'I fear that you will, Lady Tallboys. Privations lightly borne in youth become burdensome as one ages.'

'And some ease,' Sybilla said—again that smile. 'A few years ago it would have mortified me to wear such a dress. I should have sat up all night to refurbish it. Now I do not even notice.'

To Lady Randall the most infuriating thing was that she found herself liking the woman, positively *wanting* her as a daughter-in-law—a very different thing from the grudging

157

acceptance, the better-this-than-nothing mood that had brought her here. She was now even prepared to admit that Sybilla had beautiful eyes and an entrancing smile. She tried persuasion; Cressacre with its castle and all the most habitable living accommodation that had been added was big enough for four or five separate households; Sybilla need not fear any interference or overlapping. She made the final, sacrificial offer. Sybilla could have her garden, she would make herself another, begin from the beginning again.

And all Lady Tallboys said was, 'I am sorry. I am very sorry.' Lady Randall, like her son—and like the Abbess of Lamarsh—was accustomed to getting her own way. In the end she was angry and said some very unkind things. But long ago, as a child at Lamarsh, Sybilla had learned not to meet anger with anger. The soft answer was supposed to turn away wrath. The Abbess had said that—a quotation from Holy Writ, early on, before she had need for wrath or Sybilla need for soft answers. Later Sybilla had learned that when the soft answer turned wrath to rage, a harder one served, provided it were politely phrased and towards the end of this extraordinary interview she said, 'Lady Randall, you are wasting your time.'

<h1 style="text-align:center">14</h1>

THE war which Father Andreas had foreseen in 1452 and which in England had been a matter of talk for years, came in 1455, in the beautiful month of May. It affected the part of Suffolk, of which Baildon was the centre, hardly at all, for it was a war between great lords with their own private armies and this was an area of manors, large or small, of fields and sheepruns owned by people who had no political ambitions. At one point of the long see-saw struggle there was a possibility that the French might send aid to the Queen and that French troops might attempt to land at Bywater. Then even the Abbot of Baildon, Lancastrian at heart because King Henry was such a friend to the Church, remembered that he was English and turned Yorkist, temporarily, sharing the general feeling—*We want no French here.*

Apart from this short-lived scare, the war meant mainly a rise in prices, and for people who produced things this cut both ways; if you paid more for what you bought, you gained more for what you sold.

However, as time went on and the see-saw tilted this way and that, and there were truces, followed by fresh battles and other truces, even this peaceful corner was touched by war's aftermath—footloose men, some wounded, some simply dismissed, turned off to make their own way home, if they had homes. Some merely begged, some demanded what they wanted, with menaces. The civil war weakened the structure of law and order and the bands of 'sturdy beggars' as distinguishable from the pitiable were much dreaded.

Intake, for two years escaped even such visitations; it lay at the end of a lane which led nowhere and on the whole the sturdy beggars infested busy roads where travellers and merchants could be robbed. Isolated houses of medium size were also a target; larger establishments with able-bodied men-servants about were avoided.

The six men who came to Intake towards the end of a March day in 1457, did so by accident, misled by one of their number who claimed to have knowledge of the area and said that the narrow lane was a short cut which would bring them out on to the road to Colchester. And was a sheltered road, with thick woods on both sides.

On an ordinary March day, to hardy men, that would not have been much of an attraction. But this was no ordinary March day; a blizzard was blowing, laden with something midway between snow and sleet. Hungry weather. They were all hungry men. Behind them, three bad days. A long tramp up a long drive to a house that looked likely, only to find it a blackened shell. An attack on Baildon market, where almost everything was for sale—or for the taking, even hot pies, kept warm on a charcoal brazier, but as they moved in, preparing to take what they could not pay for, the pie-woman screamed and immediately all the other stall-holders formed a ragged, but effective, amateur defence force. Out from under a stall offering butter and eggs, came the club, from another the long knife, the hammer . . . even a pottery bowl, aimed well, was capable of breaking a nose.

At the miserable end of a miserable day, Intake looked promising; a house, big enough to promise food, not big enough to offer much resistance. Food and shelter for the night.

Civility first.

'Lady, we're hungry. Got a bite to spare for old soldiers.'

Walter had spared her from the harrowing tales he had heard, and he had not been to market that day. Supper at Knight's Acre was over, and had been an eked out, somewhat meagre meal. The farmhouse routine had been adopted here; when work in the fields was possible dinner was makeshift, supper substantial; in winter the business was reversed; dinner was the main meal and supper simply something to stave off hunger until morning.

'You are welcome to what I have—bread and cheese.'

There was no question of asking them in; they were in, looming large in the kitchen. Margaret, as always when faced with any unusual situation went rigid. The deaf woman looked startled, having heard nothing; she stared at the six men as though they had sprung up out of the floor.

Sybilla made the signs which Madge understood, pointing to Margaret and to John and then to the floor above.

Sybilla brought out the bread and the cheese; not much for six hungry men and now she half understood the situation. Hungry beggars stood humbly by the door waiting for whatever was handed out. These men, uninvited, had walked in.

'This all you got?' one of them asked, cramming cheese and bread into his mouth.

Another said, 'We're meat hungry.'

She had the courage, partly inbred and partly acquired, of her class. This was, she now realised, a raid, but the idea that anything untoward might happen to her never once occurred to her. But she might be robbed—was in fact already being robbed insofar as the men were devouring a month's supply of cheese, a week's supply of fresh baked bread. One of them had

160

even followed her into the larder.

'You live poor, lady and no mistake.'

'I am poor,' she said.

Henry stood staring and a thought occurred to her.

'I could offer you ale ... Henry, run across to Walter; tell him we have guests—old soldiers. Ask him to bring a jug of his ale.'

'How many, Harry?'

'A lot. Six or seven.'

'Now listen. Where are they?'

'In the kitchen. Eating.'

'Then you take this ... And these ... Think you can manage? That's my boy. You go in at the front and lodge them all handy, in the hall, near the door to the kitchen. And then go to bed.'

'You going to shoot them, Walter?'

'Not unless I must. I'll try getting them drunk first.'

The bleak, bitter, near-freezing day had ended in a clear, frosty night. Carrying not a jug but a cask of ale across the yard, Walter calmly made his plan. He could not fight six men within the narrow bounds of the kitchen; but with any luck he could get them drunk and incapable. What happened after that somewhat depended upon the men themselves or upon his judgment of them. To a degree he had sympathy with the plight of soldiers, turned loose upon the world, unwanted as soon as their masters had come to terms. He proposed to drink with them and talk to them; those he considered fundamentally honest, driven to villainy by circumstance, he proposed to drag by the heels and deposit in various parts of Layer Wood, and he would leave them their clothes. Real rogues he would strip, and men so exposed, full of ale, on such a night, would die.

He entered the kitchen with an air of conviviality.

'Brought you some ale, mates. I know what soldiers like. Been one myself.'

To Sybilla he said quietly, 'Go to your room, my lady. Bar yourself in.'

He sat, plying them with ale and pretending to drink with

161

them. The first effect, as usual, was to make them garrulous. Even in this stage they all seemed decent fellows enough; boasting a little of brave deeds, desperate engagements, narrow escapes; but not of cold-blooded murder, or rape. They seemed to be united in their hatred of Lord Delamount, whose men they had been; he'd switched sides so often that in the end neither Lancastrians nor Yorkists could trust him and he'd run off to Scotland without paying the money he owed them.

Presently they were all drunk, laughing, singing bawdy, scurrilous ditties. But the next stage, the one for which Walter was waiting, seemed long in arriving. No heads sagged forward on to the table. Nobody fell to the floor. Strange! They had come in from the cold to the warm kitchen, they had eaten—for the first time in three days if they were to be believed, and they had consumed a vast quantity of ale—October ale, always considered the best and most potent.

Walter took a meditative sip of his own cup. Yes, good ale.

Yet they seemed to grow livelier. And hungrier.

They now accepted him as one of their company.

'We're hungry for meat, mate. You got pigs around here.'

Useless to deny the presence of pigs. They had only to go into the yard, take twenty paces and use their noses.

'Old sow. Tough as the devil,' Walter said, thinking of the seven piglets snuggled in the straw beside their mother. Anything to save them! 'Tell you what, though; there's pickled pork in a barrel.'

'Then why dint that bitch bring it out?'

'And why dint you spot it, Joe? You follered her in.'

'We don't want no pickled pork. Lived on it for months.'

'That weren't pork. That were horse. Went into the cask shoes and all.'

'And harness! Believe me, mate what we ate, and fought on. Owd sow'd be a treat.'

They were good humoured enough, but ready Walter knew, to turn otherwise. He made one last effort.

'Take an hour to get ready, she would; and three to cook. I could boil us up a bit of the pickled in no time at all.'

But now their minds were all set on fresh meat, the fat

162

translucent and sizzling.

Somebody said, 'Make up the fire.' He tossed a stool on to the embers. Somebody threw on two of the wooden plates. They were all on the move now. And potentially dangerous. Likely to set the house on fire. They were drunk, but not in the way he wanted them to be.

'Where's this owd sow?'

Walter's aim now was to get them out of the house. And he had one small hope left. Sometimes men not ostensibly drunk in a warm room went into the cold and were suddenly very drunk indeed. It might happen now.

The clouds had blown away; a thin layer of snow lay on the ground; in the sky the stars and a half moon shone frostily bright. It was very cold.

The men, laughing and shouting, keeping together, jostled out into the yard.

'Over there,' Walter said, 'to your right. I'll just make the fire up properly.' He stooped and picked up some wood from the pile just outside the door and stood for a second, watching. The cold did not have the desired effect, but they were drunk in a very peculiar way, they seemed to be dancing, making little leaps into the air.

Very quietly he closed the door and barred it.

His long bow and the six iron tipped shafts stood just where he had directed Henry to put them. Taking that precaution he had not been able to visualise clearly how he could use them, now he knew. Passing the front door he barred that, too; and then climbed the stairs. Outside Sybilla's door he called. 'My lady, it's me. Let me in.' Her big bedroom had two windows, one overlooking the garden at the front, one the yard at the back.

'Have you got rid of them, Walter?'

'Far from it. But I've got them out. It'll cost us one of the sucking pigs; maybe two. Men like that are wasteful.'

'In that case we shall have escaped lightly,' she said. She seemed unperturbed still. She had retired when Walter told her to because ordinary men, with ale in them would use language unfit for female ears. His other instruction, to bar herself in she had ignored—in any case, with what? And when

163

the noise in the kitchen increased, Margaret had waked and screamed, and John, for once copying Margaret had yelled too. Sybilla was so uninformed, so unsuspicious and so confident ... Six men, plainly hungry had come and asked for food and she had given them not all she had, but all she could spare. In the larder she had purposefully placed herself between the rather rude man who had followed her in and the cask of pork.

'I hoped,' Walter said, taking his stand by the window, 'to get them drunk. Then I could have dealt with them. But it didn't work. My lady, there'll be a bit of trouble when they find the door barred. Better stand away.'

Still with that extraordinary dancing, prancing gait they came back from the sty. Joy; joy; joy. Not an old sow, tough as the devil but that rarest of delicacies, a sucking pig. A dish which only the very rich could afford. People who reared sucklings never ate that tender meat, because a young pig must be fed and coddled along until its weight outran its edibility. Sucking pig ... no dressing needed; no bristles to be singed off; no real hide to be scraped. And taking no time to cook. The old sow would have been a different matter but even for her they had been prepared to wait. Within an hour this young, but sizeable body would be edible. They pranced and danced, tossing the little corpse from hand to hand.

And now, between them and the cooking fire a barred door. The seeming old comrade had betrayed them.

They hammered on the door and shouted; unless Walter opened the door at once they'd ram it in.

From overhead Walter's voice, cold and level, said, 'The first man to touch that door, I'll nail him to it.'

From another window a younger but equally confident voice called, 'And so will I.'

They drew off a little. They were used to making shift. There were outbuildings. Easy enough to make a fire any-where.

At that moment a log on Walter's untended fire shifted and blazed up, making the window bright in his little house. A cottage! Leaping and laughing they made towards it.

'They've gone to my place now, my lady,' Walter said. 'But

better there than here.'

They'd ransack the place, of course. They'd find in the second little room, his other cask of ale. His original plan might yet work.

He watched and saw the window glow more brightly as the intruders broke up his bed, his chair, the big stool which served him as a table, the shelves he had made to hold his few belongings. Presently sparks as well as smoke emerged from the clay lined hole which served him as chimney. Distance slightly muted the noise, but there was a lot of it, and increasing.

As though speaking to himself, Walter said at last,

'It must be the rye.'

'What rye, Walter?'

'I used rye for my brewing this year, barley being such a price, my lady. It looked all right and tasted all right. The ale, I mean. But it made them drunk in a funny sort of way.'

'Do you think they will leave tomorrow?'

'I can't say. Probably not. Maybe not till they've eaten all we have—including the horse. The one thing I can say is they won't set foot in this house again. You're safe enough, my lady.'

'I always feel safe with you,' she said simply. 'Of course, I should never have let them in. But they said they were hungry; and I felt sorry for them.'

'So did I—at first. But not now. I took against them as soon as they mentioned the pig.'

Sybilla moved about. She looked in on Margaret and John, both sound asleep again. She took a blanket from her bed and offered it to Henry who scorned it. 'Mother, I must have my arms free.' Walter refused it too, so she wrapped herself in it and sat huddled at the foot of the bed, cold even so. As the night aged the cold grew sharper.

Suddenly Walter exclaimed, 'God's eyeballs!'

She ran to join him at the window.

'Walter, what is it?'

For a second he struggled between his two languages, Foul which came naturally at such a moment, and Decent because she was here. There was a stammer and a choke before he

165

managed to say, 'They've set my place afire.' She pushed beside him in the narrow window opening. It was true; sparks from the recklessly heaped fire had ignited the thatch at a point where the thin covering of snow had already melted from the heat within.

'And I hope they all roast,' Walter said.

For quite a long time those inside Walter's little house were unaware of what was happening overhead. The little pig was not well cooked, but even its slight rawness was pleasurable. They dragged it from the fire and set it on the floor, pulling it apart with their fingers, cramming the charred, crisp outer skin and tender, only just heated flesh into their meat-hungry mouths. They were men of varied experience—the veteran of the party had been able to match almost word for word, Walter's experiences in France, the youngest was only six months away from the plough, but not one of them had ever known such happiness, such elation, such a desire to dance, to sing.

Walter's house, like all the others in Intake—except Knight's Acre, was built of clay clods. It had a beam or two, and its thatch, vulnerable to fire; at shoulder level for a tall man, head level for a shorter one it offered more resistance. When the roof and the beam that upheld it collapsed, four men were engulfed in smoulder and flame. Two, nearer the door, tore it open and escaped. The incoming draught fanned the conflagration and gave the others a mercifully swift end. The two survivors, out in the yard went through some antics. It was as though a puppet master had muddled the strings. And to the stark black and white of the moon and star light reflected from the now frozen, diamond bright sprinkling of snow was added the red glare of the burning house, and in the yard two madmen danced and then disappeared, into the shadow cast by the outbuildings.

'But Walter, should not they all—even the ones who burned —have Christian burial?'

Four charred corpses—even their mothers would not recognise them, and two, frozen stiff—no need to strip them, in

166

their dancing frenzy they had stripped themselves, just by the pigsty.

Walter said, 'There's a bit more to it, my lady. Oh, I know Father Ambrose would get busy. He's lost his memory for near-by things but he holds to the rules. He would very likely say suicide and he wouldn't be far wrong. And then the Coroner's Court . . . and talk . . . A place like this; one man and a boy . . . it could be a temptation to others. Better do it my way. And the first thing to do is to find out if they were seen. That might make all the difference. I'll go down to the village and ask.'

He put his questions craftily, 'My place got set on fire last night. Did anybody see anybody lurking about?' In every case the answer was 'No.' And Walter believed it. Had anyone seen the strangers he would have said so, if only to make plain the exculpation of any mischievous Intake boys. The men had arrived at dusk and in such weather everybody was within-doors and the shutters closed.

Reporting back, Walter said, 'What's left in the house I shan't bother about. I'd bury the other two, but the ground's too hard for digging. I'll get the barrow and dump them in the wood.'

'Will that be safe? Suppose they were found . . .'

'There won't be much left to find, my lady. This is hungry weather for foxes and weasels and such.'

Sybilla gave a little shudder. 'It sounds such a horrible . . . But I suppose you are right, Walter. Try to do it while Henry is asleep.'

Henry had actually fallen asleep at his post and Walter had carried him to his bed.

'If he wakes while I'm gone, tell him the rogues ran off. And not to go near my place in case more roof should fall in.

Walter had made the barrow to his own pattern out of odds and ends and four wheels bought from the wheelwright's; its main purpose, so far, had been the carting of manure from yard to field. He dragged it out and pushed it to the place where the two stiff corpses lay and was about to load it when a flash of colour caught his eye; colour and movement on the edge of the wood, near the blackened ruin of his house. People had

167

come to stare at the scene of catastrophe. They hadn't quite dared come along by the track that led around the house and stable; they'd slunk along the edge of the wood and stood there, staring; they'd stand all day and unchecked might even venture into the yard to get a better view. Sod the buggers! Unhurriedly Walter lifted and threw first one body and then the other into the pigsty. Unhurriedly he strolled across to the ruin and shouted, 'Don't come any nearer. It could blaze up again any minute.' They stood there, hoping that it would.

Sybilla said, 'Walter, in all the excitement and confusion I did not say what I should have said. I am so sorry about your little house. You had made it so snug and neat. I am indeed *very* sorry. But there is room in the house. John can move in with Henry, and Margaret with me.'

She attributed his lack of enthusiasm about this plan to the fear of losing his independence.

'It would be *your* room, absolutely, Walter. I know it would not be quite like the little house, but I would see that nobody disturbed you.'

'Well,' he said, still with some reluctance, 'if what happened last night is likely to happen again, it might be as well. For the time being.'

He did not mind sharing the kitchen fire with old Madge; the bedroom was comfortable enough, and when he started his next brew, Sybilla offered him the still-room. But it was not like his own place, all of a piece.

As soon as spring came as it did very quickly after that bad spell, Walter said, 'With your permission, my lady, I'll sell the old sow and her litter. There's another breed I've heard of, better doers. I could make a good deal.'

He was a hardy man but the idea of being a cannibal at one remove revolted him. At the end of that frost-bitten day there had been as little left in need of burial from the pigsty as from the burnt-out house.

There was a little plant called Periwinkle which, given half a chance would climb and hold its bluish-mauvish open-eyed flowers to the sun; by mid-summer what had been Walter's house was pretty. And time moved on.

ONE of the first things that John Barnes had said was, 'Don't look at the women. Don't even *look*, lad.'

'What women?'

'Whores for the use of the guards. Time they're unserviceable they earn their keep picking over. And time th'art sound enough to carry a slab, thee'll see them, in the far chamber. Don't even look.'

This was indeed a highly organised community and it included a brothel. Years earlier Selim's grandfather, or great-grandfather had decided that unmarried men made better guards and that their needs should be provided for; on the spot. Their naturally hard characters and the inhuman occupation they plied did not detract from their maleness and the alternative to an integral brothel was to have them for ever capering off down to Andara; or forming homosexual relationships very prejudicial to good discipline. The ideal arrangement would have been to employ eunuch guards, but eunuchs were themselves slaves, and their state inclined them to become fat and lazy—suitable guards for women in harems but not for men in quarries. So Selim's agent in Andara was always on the look-out for healthy, youngish female slaves; not necessarily the youngest or prettiest on offer, since their price was high.

On the whole the young women led tolerable lives in a set of cave-like chambers, comfortably furnished, with hangings on the limestone walls and carpets on the limestone floors. One large, communal chamber even had glazed windows, narrow apertures cut into the outer wall of rock. They fed well and were not stinted of perfumes and unguents and pretty clothes, for it was necessary to make them attractive enough to compete with brothels of the port.

The post of Madam in this place was a covetable one, and had for many years been the perquisite of some respectable, impoverished, widowed relative of the owner. The present incumbent was an elephantine old woman named Soraya.

When the women were as John Barnes decently expressed it, 'unserviceable'—that was for roughly one week out of every four, they were employed in the 'picking over', the searching of the limestone incrustations which clung to every marble slab for the nodules in which garnets were encapsulated. Somebody in the past had discovered that female eyes were quicker, female fingers nimbler, at this work.

The women welcomed it, for there was a system of rewards. In a locked chest Soraya kept a mass of trinkets of no great value but all pretty and at the end of a picking over session the woman who had by industry or luck done best in this treasure hunt, was allowed to take her choice of trinkets.

So every morning one of the lamplit passages saw a procession, moving slowly, at Soraya's pace, well-guarded, to the place where the newly-ripped out slabs were sorted over. They carried a supply of delicacies, always more than even Soraya could consume in a session, the surplus of which they would enjoy. And wine also, for Soraya did not share her kinsman's strict observance of the Prophet's rules. She seated herself in a well-cushioned chair, exchanged pleasantries with the guards at the entrance, was pleased when two slaves staggered in with a new slab, pleased when one of the girls—to her they were all girls—found a garnet, or one of the other nodules, which delicately attacked with miniature chisel and hammer, yielded another, less valuable but still saleable stone, colourless, crystal clear—a diamond without a diamond's fire and sparkle.

Don't even look, John Barnes had told Sir Godfrey. An instruction easy to obey—at least so far as looking implied desiring. When he was sound enough to help carry a slab into what was called 'the far chamber', though in fact it advanced just as the quarry face did, he could glance at the women, waiting to ply their small implements and at the fat old woman who supervised them, with no feeling at all.

He was again low-spirited; for what the Greek slave had said about the Pope and all Christendom driving all Moslems out of Europe had either not happened, or had failed to affect Zagelah. The timeless time went out; the seasons' relentless march observed every other week on the day of the bathing which was pleasant in warm weather, and so unpleasant in cold that only the vigorous application of the canes could force shivering bodies into the water. Sir Godfrey lost count of the seasons as well as of the hours and the days.

He worked like an animal, a two-legged pack donkey. Because of the disablement of his hands he was judged to be unfit for the most skilled work of all—the loosening and prying away of the precious slabs, but he could carry them in a kind of wickerwork basket, held to his back by bands of coarse webbing which came over his shoulders, crossed one another on his chest and then buckled behind his waist. He carried the rough, lime crusted slabs to the place where the women worked, and then on to the place where the polishing was done, and from there to the place where they were stored. Beyond that point no slave was allowed to go except on the fortnightly outings.

At first the rough wickerwork, weighted with marble, re-opened the wounds which the flogging had made on his back, but they scabbed over and healed again. The webbing straps chafed his chest raw, but there again the body's defence took over and the skin became calloused and hardened.

When did John Barnes begin to cough and grow thin and spit blood? There was no means of knowing in this timeless place.

John Barnes said, after a bout of coughing, 'Well lad, it seems to have got me. I hoped to see the day of liberation, but now I doubt it; though I've stuck it out longer than most.'

Even in this hopeless, subterranean, lamplit world there was a hierarchy of a kind and those who worked at the rock face regarded themselves, and were regarded by others as superior.

'I pray,' Barnes said, 'for a quick end; not to end where you began lad, with a lot of half dead men.'

He had his wish—or his answered prayer. He died with an abruptness which took even the guards by surprise. One minute—or so seemed, eye as skilled, hand as skilled ... and then his load already fixed, Sir Godfrey found himself on his knees with his best friend in this infernal place saying weakly,

171

words making bubbles in the last haemorrhage, 'God keep thee. Hope on. Trust . . . in . . . God.'

In a way Godfrey Tallboys had been more fortunate than many of his fellows; the lack of religious exercises had not meant much deprivation to him. And his last contact with God had been in that narrow, balconied street . . . But John Barnes had been pious . . .

What did priests say? He should remember. Only a few words could be recalled; but leaning forward, so that the marble slab in his basket slid forward and hit the base of his skull, he said into the ear of the dying man, 'Go forth, Christian soul.' And then a Hail Mary. Past speech now, the dying man thanked him with his eyes.

Sir Godfrey would have doubted whether he could be more wretched, but when John Barnes' body was dragged out he felt the same sense of bereavement as had followed Lord Robert's death, so why a short time afterwards he should bother about another person's plight, he could not, and never would understand.

Stooped under his load and followed by his working companion, similarly loaded, he plodded into the picking-over chamber, where he lifted out the other man's slabs and was then unloaded by him. As usual two guards were on duty here. One of them said, 'You, wait! There's one about ready to turn over.' That was normal custom, and a not unwelcome chance to snatch a moment's rest and get back one's breath.

Ordinarily in this chamber the strictest decorum prevailed. Soraya was feared, even by the guards. The girls were allowed to talk a little as they worked, not too much and not too loudly, and not at all to the guards. This morning she had absented herself for a while and the atmosphere was different. No strict Moslem would touch a woman in an unserviceable condition, but half-joking, salacious talk was permissible at any time, and the opportunity was being snatched. Only one girl stood silent and unsmiling. Sir Godfrey had time to observe her because serious work on the slab that needed to be soon turned over would not be resumed until Soraya returned.

The girl was very young. About fourteen.

And she was new, he thought, judging partly by the way she held the little pick and hammer, and partly by the colour of her hair—dead black. Men liked prostitutes of exotic colouring, and even in this lost place their tastes were catered for and bleached or hennaed hair was the rule.

Sir Godfrey had acquired by this time enough basic Arabic to enable him to obey orders and so avoid trouble. He knew the names of common articles, and a few phrases of rather cringing civility which could on occasions ward off a blow; but he did not know enough of the language to know what one of the guards said to the girl or what she said in return. Whatever it was it seemed to anger him. He snarled out a term of abuse, recognisable and offensive, and she retorted with another—even worse. He lost his head and began to beat her with his cane.

She certainly *was* new. She fought back, trying to snatch the cane, failed and suffered heavier blows.

Sir Godfrey then lost his head. He sprang at the man, seized him by the collar, swung him round and dealt him a fist blow on the chin which sent him reeling back, straight into Soraya as she waddled in. She administered a push which righted him and into the deathly silence asked, 'What happened here.'

Free men speak before slaves. The guard said that this man had attempted to meddle with the girl and he had gone to her aid.

'He was beating the girl,' Sir Godfrey said.

To Soraya neither story had the ring of truth, both sounding so unlikely. Slaves knew that the women were not for them; and a carefully calculated diet, constant hard work, carried to the point of exhaustion, emasculated them within a month or two. Guards knew that the women were not for them to beat; any correction the girls needed was meted out by Soraya herself. Momentarily puzzled, she turned to the five other women, now all ostentatiously busy. Five false witnesses. Four said that what the guard said was true; the fifth, with an air of smug virtue said she had been too busy to notice what was happening.

Another unlikely story!

It would have ended there, with another flogging for the

173

man with the bad record, but for the girl.

'They lie! All are liars. He only is telling the truth.'

She ripped at her clothing, baring her shoulders and the upper part of her arms. The red welts were already rising.

That was evidence.

Soraya said, 'Back to work, all of you.'

In the evening Soraya sent for the new girl and gave her a little of the wine which Selim, in his folly, eschewed. Wine not only gladdened the heart it loosened tongues.

'How old are you?'

'Fourteen.'

'And where were you born?'

'In the Maghreb. In the stronghold of my father.'

'Free born?'

'We were all free, until we lost the battle.'

'How many masters have you had? How many times have you changed hands? When was the battle? What happened after? Tell me. Tell me exactly what has happened to you since the battle.'

'I cannot. I do not know. I fought beside my father on that day. And was wounded. You do not believe me? Look!' She parted her cloud of black hair and showed, on the crown of her head, a puckered scar over which new hair was growing. Then she flung back her head and the wound was hidden.

'I was insensible for many days.'

'And then?'

'Then I was destined to be a present to the Grand Turk. In Constantinople. But the ship was taken; and I am here.' A bitter little story told without tears.

Soraya framed her next question with cunning.

'And who took your maidenhead?'

Imagine finding in a place like this a girl who could blush? A slave who could look so proud and offended.

'It was never taken.'

'Oh, come, come,' Soraya protested. 'You were taken prisoner—presumably by men. On a ship bound for Constantinople you were a slave, amongst sailors. Even in the slave market at Andara . . .'

174

'My father's enemy is a great rogue, but he is not a fool. Nor a stranger; his tribe and mine have been at war for years. He knew my worth. A Nagulla of the purest blood. Do you imagine that he would himself tamper with, or allow any of his men to touch the gift he intended for the Grand Turk? On the ship I was treated like a queen. And when the ship was taken by pirates, all they thought about was to sell us and get away as fast as possible ... If it is customary to rape slaves before selling them in Andara, then I must consider myself fortunate. Or give thanks to haste again. We were sold within minutes of our arrival.'

Soraya thought—Well, virginity is a condition open to proof, and if the girl's story is true, what a present for Selim! Fourteen years old, and beautiful, and with spirit, and with just that touch of something exotic, likely to appeal to a somewhat jaded taste. Soraya had always been extremely grateful to her cousin Selim for appointing her to this sinecure, which was also a place of power. Now she could repay him.

Discipline must be maintained, however. For striking one of Soraya's girls—a prerogative reserved for herself, the guard was demoted; for striking the guard Sir Godfrey was flogged. But either the hand wielding the dreaded khurbash was less powerful, or his back had hardened. Or complete hopelessness brought its compensating insensibility.

The timeless time went on; and then one morning, bowed under his load he was aware of something different. The fat old bawd, never before seen at the quarry face or any other working area, stood there, panting a little, beside a man who bore every mark of a minor official; sober, decent clothes, serious, self-important demeanour.

Soraya raised and pointed a fat finger. 'That is the man.'

So what now? Another flogging? If so, may it kill me! Death and the Judgment of God would be preferable to this death-in-life, with no hope.

In fact that pointing finger had indicated, if not freedom, a more tolerable life in captivity.

Over the years Sir Godfrey had acquired more Arabic than he realised. He had never set himself to learn it, repudiating it in his mind. He knew enough to get along with. But it was to

175

his imperfect grasp of the language that he attributed the slight craziness of the conversation between Soraya, the official and the overseer of the quarry, which, if taken literally, implied that one of the ladies in the King's harem in Zagelah was discontented with that part of the gardens in which Selim's wives and concubines took air and exercise, and somebody had said that the English were very good at gardening, therefore an English slave was required to make improvements.

Sir Godfrey's sense of humour had always been simple and forthright, untinged by the sardonic or cynical—a kind that would have lasted longer in adversity. John Barnes's had been of that variety and very occasionally one of his dry, sour yet comic comments had made Sir Godfrey laugh. He had not laughed since John Barnes had died. Yet inside him now, as he listened, and was eventually convinced that he did understand aright, something very like laughter took him by the throat. The idea that a knowledge of English gardening—even if he had it—could do anything to improve a garden in Zagelah! That was almost comic. And all he knew of gardens was that they looked pretty in spring and summer, and were pleasant places to walk in at the end of the day. He recognised a rose when he saw one ...

However, he was now well trained in the slave apathy, accustomed to standing by like a donkey, and did so now while his future was being arranged. It meant release from the hateful quarry, work in the open, a sight of the sun.

The word 'garden' brought Sybilla sharply to mind. She had so loved other people's gardens, had always wanted one of her own. If she had attained one, it was not of his providing. He had ceased to visualise her at Knight's Acre now. She could not possibly have managed on those meagre rents, fixed for ever by a well-meaning, but short-sighted old man. Sometimes he saw her back in his sister's house at Beauclaire, Henry and Richard old enough for the discipline of the master of pages. Sometimes he imagined that—giving him up for dead —she might have married again. He hoped that wherever she was, she was happy. In his mental pictures of her she was unchanged, untouched by time.

176

His new work was infinitely preferable to the old. The outdoor slaves, those who worked in the gardens and the stables, lived in comparative comfort in a building made for the purpose and they were well fed. Those who tended the ladies' garden were far from over-worked, often no more than two hours' rather hurried labour early in the morning when even at mid-summer the air was pleasantly cool. All their work must be done before the women's quarter was astir. The exposure of his ignorance of gardening, which Sir Godfrey had rather feared—fear being the foremost emotion in a slave world—never came; there was in fact no mention of his Englishness or of anyone's wish to improve the garden. He was simply one of three slaves, admitted, soon after sunrise, to shave and water a piece of grass about the size of a tennis court, take from every rose tree and every flowering shrub any bloom past its perfect best, see that no stray petal or leaf clogged the fountain, renew and tend flowers in the tubs which stood on the steps, and the terrace up to which they led, the garden entrance from the harem itself.

It was a very secret garden, surrounded on three sides by high walls with no windows. One wall was broken by the gateway of iron grille work, opened to admit the workers, locked behind them, opened so that they could leave, and locked again. The fourth side of the garden was the outer wall of the women's quarters; three steps, a terrace, and another grilled doorway, hung on its inner side with Zagelah gauze, so closely gathered as to be opaque. Once, planting the tubs—they were of silver, glazed in some way so that they did not tarnish, with lilies of a kind he had never seen before, huge, pink flecked with purple and almost overpoweringly scented, Sir Godfrey spared a thought for the women who would presently enjoy them. They were slaves, too! He thought of the freedom his own countrywomen enjoyed; at every level, from the independent old women like the fishwife on Bywater quay, to the Queen whose lightest word was law to the King of England. Briefly he pitied these women, more enclosed than nuns of the strictest order. But in the main his thoughts, now that food and work in the open air had restored him, and his back so long

177

bent under the heavy marble slabs straightened again—was escape.

From the quarry it had been impossible; he had tried the only likely way and all that resulted had been a flogging. Here things were different. Slaves seemed to come and go almost as they pleased; they were sent on errands into the streets, into the market; and certainly the comings and goings of those who worked in the secret garden were most loosely overlooked, once the two hours of rather hurried work was complete. Ermin, Sir Godfrey's new overseer, fat and lethargic— eunuch?—opened that gate, sat down, supervised in a way, occasionally said, 'Hurry.' He wielded no cane. Then he ushered them out and disappeared, to sleep, to follow his own pursuits. His underlings were free to do the same unless they were 'borrowed' to work in some other part of the palace grounds, a practice Ermin did nothing to encourage, not because he feared his men would be overworked but because he was immensely proud of his own post of trust and felt that some of his importance reflected on his small staff. His usual answer when asked for the loan of his men was, 'No, they must see to the tanks.'

The roses and other flowers in the ladies' garden liked muck, but it was unthinkable that the eyes and noses of the ladies should be affronted by stable manure in its natural state. So it was placed in tanks filled with water, stirred three or four times a day for several days and then allowed to settle. The water was then drained off and strained, and carried to the garden and applied. A faint odour of stables was perceptible for a few minutes but vanished as soon as the liquid was absorbed.

Sir Godfrey, in his free time, drifted naturally to the stable yard where beautiful horses lived in conditions far preferable to those of the quarry slaves. It took him a little time to break the habit of enforced silence acquired at Andara where talk during working hours was regarded as a waste of breath and time, and where, when the gruelling day's work was over, there was no energy left for chatter. After a day or two in this easier atmosphere he found his tongue and showed himself know-ledgeable about horses, thereby making himself welcome to

178

this community within a community. One day he said to the friendliest of the stable slaves, 'That horse is of different breed.'

'A true word. That is a son of Shaitan. A vicious horse, taken from the Christian invaders. He killed two men and maimed several before he was turned loose. The King set high store by him and forbade the treatment that would have tamed him. And perhaps he was right. He sires good colts.'

The horse they were studying had a brown hide, with a golden glimmer.

Arcol's colt?

I had three sons.

Now again, definite plans. A runaway slave must not immediately draw attention to himself by begging. Food for at least three days must be saved, and that meant bread and cheese. And perhaps by design, the clothes of a palace slave though of finer quality than those of the quarry workers, were less adaptable for hiding things. The outfit which Sir Godfrey had been given on his arrival in Zagelah was a pair of drawers, longer and more dignified, halfway down the shin, and a jacket, short-sleeved, somewhat skimpy. Both garments were of far finer substance than those the quarry-workers wore, and they were not without decoration. Around the edge of the trouser legs, the front and the sleeves of the jacket there was a kind of braid worked in red and white.

In such a uniform with no pockets, no pouches, enough of even humble bread and cheese to keep a man for three days, was difficult to conceal; he got it away from table openly, 'I'll eat this later. I tend to wake, hungry, in the night.' Nobody questioned, nobody suspected. It was high summer, August; he had been released from the quarry in July; under his mattress in the slave dormitory the cheese sweated and the bread dried.

He carried the food—all he owned in the world—openly, in a little linen bag, when he set out to make another bid for freedom. It had seemed to him, so recently released from the quarry, that palace slaves came and went as they liked, but even on this heavy, somnolent afternoon there was a man at

179

the gate used by slaves and other inferior people.

'Where are you going?'

'Ermin, my master, has shoes to be mended.' That explained the parcel.

He made for the market. Morning trade was over, the best of everything had been sold; this was the waiting time. Four hours after midday the muezzins would call again, for the third prayer hour of the day; then business would brisken again, selling off cheaper stuff, wilting, bruised, not worth carting back home. Meanwhile in the narrow shade of buildings or awnings, the market people rested. Sir Godfrey found a patch of shade and chose the family he would accompany. There was concealment in numbers and this was a sizeable family; an old woman, brown and wrinkled as a walnut, two men, a woman and three children, and a donkey. His mind observed, without knowing that it did so, that whereas all the family had sought shade from the afternoon's glare, the donkey had been left tethered in the full sun.

The call to prayer came, and with the rest he obeyed it, bowing towards Mecca and saying, 'God help me.' Then he hung about while the evening market rush went on, and attached himself, unostentatiously, to the family he had chosen as his stalking horse. Out of the still sunlit market square and into the cool tunnel that pierced the wall, the place where Sir Stephen had lost an eye, the place where victory had seemed certain.

Usless to think back; grieve yes, grieve for the dead, all part of a past that in retrospect seemed golden and gay, but the past was gone beyond recall. There was only the present; this moment.

And a bad moment.

There were guards on the gate.

Unchallenged the old woman, the donkey and the children, quarrelling vociferously, had gone through, Sir Godfrey, thinking that anywhere two men could go, three could go, had attached himself to the two men, in the company of men, less noticeable. Out of the cool dusk of the tunnel, into the evening glow; and a harsh voice:

'Here you, where do you think you're going?'

'On an errand, for my master.'

'Then you'll have a pass.'

He had no pass; he carried a bag which was in itself evidence of ill intent. Over and beyond that he must be mad, for every border of every garment he wore announced that he was a palace slave.

The expression on Sir Godfrey's face when he realised that he had failed again, and been so *stupid*—how could he have overlooked so vital a thing?—justified the guard's assumption that his wits were astray. And a certain kindliness towards the mad was traditional among the Moors. Also the guard, though in public employment, did not favour the régime of King Selim and Hassan ben Hassan, it was too strict for a man who had liked his kaffe and his wine. So instead of holding this demented fellow and later taking him to the palace, there to be flogged and possibly branded as a would-be runaway, he gave him a half-rough, half-friendly push and said, 'Be off with you, fool.'

16

WALTER disliked living in the house. It meant that he had no privacy and that the places with which he was concerned—the kitchen where he lived and ate, the still-room in which he made and kept his ale, the bedroom in which he slept, were distant from one another, and since the one staircase, and the still-room both opened out of the hall he must for ever be crossing and recrossing that apartment. He always said, 'Excuse me, my lady,' or 'I'm sorry to disturb you.' Sybilla was usually sewing, occasionally writing, and she invariably looked up and smiled and said a few amiable words, but he always felt like an intruder, and if he had a jug in hand he felt self-conscious about it.

He always liked his ale, but in moderation. Drunkenness he despised; since the burning of his little house he had drunk more and he spent a good deal of time arguing with himself, producing proof after proof that he was not a toss-pot.

Drunkards reeled about and shouted and laughed at nothing. He was never even slightly unsteady on his feet and his behaviour did not vary.

Drunkards slugged abed in the morning, neglected their work or their business; their sight was not true, their hands grew unsteady. He was always brisk and early in the morning, did the work of two, even three men, all day, was as good an archer as he had ever been.

Drunkards craved the stuff, couldn't do without it. He could. On market days when all other men resorted to inns, he came straight home. It was just that lately, if he went to bed sober, he could not sleep. He tossed and turned and groaned inwardly as a sick man might. He had tried to discipline himself by going sober to bed for as many as three nights in succession, thinking that weariness must win and sleep come. It did not except in brief, dream-haunted snatches, just before morning, and after such nights he felt good for nothing.

Now it was October again, one year and seven months since the raid; and apart from his need for the lulling effect of ale, Walter had good cause to feel pleased with himself. Knight's Acre now had three fields under the plough and the crops had been so heavy that hired labour was needed. Walter had chosen carefully and well; one of the young Robinsons, a boy called Tom, hardworking and teachable.

Walter had also 'happened upon' a good young horse to replace the old one from Beauclaire, which, coddled along had done marvellously, but was now failing. The very way in which Walter had set about obtaining a new horse, cheap, was proof that he was not a drunkard; drunkards were incapable of making clever plans and carrying them through.

Walter had begun to haunt the horse-market in Baildon—it was separate from the general market. His attitude was casual, he studied what was on offer, noted the prices, which were iniquitous, what with the lessened value of money, and the brief, but inconclusive war. However he did at last find exactly the animal for which he was searching; a black horse, young, thickset, strong enough to pull a plough or wagon, but not too heavy to trot. Nice-natured, too; it suffered Walter's inspection with calm.

'How much?'

The dealer named his price, iniquitous, of course to anyone old enough to remember the old days, but by current prices fair enough.

'I'll give you half that,' Walter said.

'Don't be daft.'

Walter said, 'You take what I offered, or I'll call the market overseer and the constable and ask if anybody has lately lost a *grey* horse.' Surreptitiously—Walter never believed in calling attention to his undertakings—he held out a bit of damp soapy cloth, black, and at the same time indicated the small pale patch on the horse's neck.

The dealer turned as pale as the patch—horse stealing was a capital offence.

'All right,' he said.

Adding insult to injury, as he took possession of the horse, Walter said, 'Next time try walnut husks, not soot.'

He went home jubilant.

October produced some of its golden days. Tom Robinson could be trusted to thresh out what remained of the corn, and Henry was eager to try out his skill with the bow on some worthy target.

For deer it was known as the 'grease season', full-fed through summer they were at their best.

'We'll take a day off, Harry, and go hunting.'

'May I try, Walter? With my new bow?'

It was the third that Walter had made for him, but it was not full size and Walter doubted whether any shaft launched from it would be lethal. Not that it mattered. Walter would be there, just behind the boy—who was his boy now.

Layer Wood had gained its name long ago, when 'lay' meant 'pool'. The pools, after the fine summer which had brought the good harvest, were depleted; the first two or three were mere puddles, surrounded by dried, cracked clay. But they came on upon one at a lower level, its mud edge marked with hoofmarks. They hid themselves and waited and presently a deer—a lone young male—came down to drink. Henry

183

looked at Walter, a silent question; Walter nodded. Henry loosed his arrow and missed, by that little which had given rise to the saying that a miss was as good as a mile; and as the animal raised its head, alarmed, alerted, Walter shot it dead.

Henry was momentarily depressed and apologetic, but Walter said not to mind, everybody missed a shot sometimes and after all they had the meat, which was what mattered. 'We'll gut him here,' he said. 'Easier to carry.' Bearing the carcass slung on a pole between them, they went home, happy hunters at the end of the day.

Before Walter sat down to his supper he fetched a jug of ale from the still-room and offered Madge a cupful, as he often did, but she refused.

In the hall, with supper over and Henry gone yawning to bed Sybilla sat down to write a very difficult letter, the latest of a number in what was surely a very peculiar correspondence. It had begun with a violently vituperative letter from Lady Randall. Simon, her only son had been killed at St Albans in the first battle of the civil war; and Sybilla was entirely to blame! Had she married him and made him happy, he would have settled down at Cressacre and not gone running off to fight in a war which did not concern him at all. What was more, Sybilla had not only robbed Lady Randall of her son, but of her grandsons, too, for Simon could never bring himself to look at another woman. Lady Randall was left to face lonely old age with a broken heart—and all because of Sybilla.

Sybilla thought—Poor woman, she is distraught with grief. She wrote a brief letter of sympathy, such as one would send to any bereaved mother. That should have been the end, but was not. Gifts began to arrive, accompanied by letters which were not denunciatory, but still not quite in order; 'Simon wishes you to share our plenty . . .' The letters became fond as though the lonely woman at Cressacre had transferred some of her affection from her dead son to the woman of whom he had been fond. Rather as a mother might cherish a dead child's toy.

Every letter had been answered, kindly, civilly, but without undue sentiment. The cool common sense, which the Abbess of

184

Lamarsh had inculcated, still held against all the wear and tear of the world. But Lady Randall's last letter was difficult to answer. She wrote that she was certain that Simon would wish her to adopt John. That extraordinary statement was followed by a lot of facts and figures all meant to show that Cressacre was an independent property. Nobody, no great lord, not the King himself, had any claim upon it. Between her husband's death and Simon's coming of age, she had held it, and improved it ... 'where only rabbits ran, sheep now nibble and dung the land as they nibble. Next year there will be grass, and cattle ...' She listed the acres that comprised the estate, rents that were paid, income derived from the sale of produce; 'in addition to which I have monies of my own'. All this wealth would in due time pass to her adopted son.

To a mother who could just about feed and clothe a growing boy it was a tempting offer indeed and Sybilla gave it serious consideration for several days. She sought no advice from James or William, knowing what form it would take. William was unworldly, up to a point, and lavished his own money on the poor, but he had a sensible man's respect for security, and this was security indeed, a chance in ten thousand. But ...

Sybilla had kept all Lady Randall's letters, and before beginning her own, she read them through again, taking especial heed of the sentences which roused unease. Simon was often mentioned, sometimes as though Lady Randall realised that he was dead, but just as frequently as though he were still alive, and were in close communication with her. Perhaps the strangest letter of all was the one which had arrived together with a blaring heifer calf. In it Lady Randall wrote, 'Simon seems to think that you have lost a calf. Please accept this in its stead.' The fantastic thing was that about a fortnight earlier the Knight's Acre cow had aborted.

The letter proposing the adoption only said 'Simon would wish,' but it ended on a disquieting note. After the facts and figures Lady Randall had written, 'After all, you owe me a son.'

It was just possible that the whole campaign of friendliness had been mounted by a demented woman with one end in view—retaliation. Far-fetched, of course. But John was only

185

seven; handed over completely to a woman who had a grudge against his mother, his life could be made a misery—it might even be short!

And there was another way of looking at it. Sybilla thought —I bore three sons; one I have lost to Walter; one to Beauclaire; must I give away the third?

She wrote, 'Dear Lady Randall,' and then the door to the kitchen opened and there was old Madge, making her bob and saying good night on her way to bed. Sybilla smiled and said, 'Good night, Madge,' and resumed writing, doing it slowly, testing each sentence in her mind before committing it to paper, trying to sound firm, and at the same time kindly. For her suspicion of the poor woman's motive could be unfounded and unworthy. And now and again she paused, wondering what the future held for John. William, when offering the whole family a home had spoken of sending Henry to the monks' school at Baildon perhaps he would do as much for John. Such schooling did not inevitably lead to priesthood and celibacy; it could be the first step towards a secular profession. The law perhaps.

She read Lady Randall's last letter again and had a rebellious thought—The rich think they can buy anything!

In the kitchen Walter emptied the jug, stood up and went out on his last, necessary errand—he did not acknowledge the existence of the stool-room and had told Henry that such places were meant for women and sick people. He breathed deeply of the cool night air and for the hundredth time assured himself that he was not drunk, though he was now using a larger jug.

He was not drunk. Drunken men did not care where they relieved themselves; nor did they bar doors with care and see that fires were left in such a state that no log could flare, no spark fly during the night. He did these things, because he was not drunk. He doused and towelled his face, and rinsed his mouth because, while Sybilla in the hall had been making her decision, he, by the kitchen fire, had made his.

Once and for all, he would put an end to his agony, the thing that kept him awake at night, unless he dulled his senses with ale.

He came into the hall where Sybilla was making a fair copy of her letter, but he did not say either, 'Excuse me, my lady,' or 'Good night, my lady.' Instead he said, 'It is cold in here,' and placed a fresh log on the moribund fire, a dry log which broke instantly into a blaze which eclipsed the candle by whose light she had been working and made Walter, on the hearth look enormous.

'I've got something to say to you.'

'Just a minute Walter and I shall be done.' She wrote her name and laid the quill aside. She was reasonably certain of what Walter was about to say. Nobody could be expected to *make* a farm out of wasteland, work it, bring it to moderate prosperity—and all for nothing. Some time ago she had offered Walter a wage and he had turned surly and said when he needed money he'd ask for it. Now he was about, she thought, to ask, not for money, but for land. She was prepared to yield. Walter could have the third field—and any other land he could clear, in return for overseeing her two remaining fields and her stock. Tom Robinson, with some help from Henry, was capable of doing the actual work. It was the kind of arrangement becoming common in these shifting times.

She straightened herself, folded her hands in her lap, and because Walter for once looked so awkward and unsure of himself—he who had always been so self-confident; and was sweating, though he had remarked upon the coolness in the hall, she spoke most kindly.

'Walter, sit down. And speak freely. What is it?'

He did not accept the invitation to sit—he never had done so in her presence. Over the years—thirteen of them now—though other people's servants had called him arrogant and overbearing, and the people of Intake, she knew from talk with Father Ambrose, detested him because he treated them with contempt, towards her his manners, as his devotion and loyalty, had never once failed.

So when he said in a strange, half strangulated voice, 'I'm asking you to marry me,' she could not have been more astounded had the roof fallen in. She was momentarily dumbstruck and by contrast, Walter, ordinarily so sparing with words, was now articulate and fluent.

187

It all poured out, from the moment at Dover, when she had played the lute and enchanted him, inspired in him the simple wish to serve, on and on. This, he thought, hearing himself, is not ale talking, it is me, the very core and centre of myself.

'Women,' he said, 'I never cared for. But I fell in love that night, and stayed so. I reckoned it'd be enough to serve you, help to take care of you. And time you was married, I managed . . . Time I had my own place, I managed . . . It's the nights I can't do with. Nothing but a wall between us . . .' The words came out jerkily, interspersed by hard breathing as though he had been running.

Sir Simon's declaration of love had not quickened a pulse or made her face colour; unmoved, untouched she had been in complete control of the situation. Now she was not. She attributed her hot-faced confusion, her jumpy heart to shock, to insult. She made a clutch at dignity, but she was short of breath, too.

'Walter, you know that I shall never remarry, I refused Sir . . .'

'A silly boy! And you were right there. You'd had one, hadn't you? Here today, just long enough to get you in pup and off again. Took the very ring off your finger to help buy that great horse. Never thought of putting a roof over your head till everybody was so sick and tired . . .'

The old Abbess had said that it was unwise to show anger; anger merely begat anger; but Sybilla was past heeding such precepts. She stood up and said,

'Stop! I will not listen to such talk. You are drunk, Walter Freeman. Go to your bed.'

He was drunk, more so than she realised, or than he would admit to himself. He did not stir, he stood there, a great hulking shape between her and the fire. He said, 'Try me! You've never had a real, loving *man* yet.'

Abruptly she realised the precariousness of her situation; alone in a lonely house, with children, a deaf old woman and a man, drunk and lecherous. It was as though he sensed her fear—as dogs were said to do. He moved, he took her into his arms. He said, 'Don't be scared, my lovely. I'd not hurt you . . .'

She fought him and she screamed, idiotically since a scream was a call for help and here no help could be forthcoming. She screamed twice, and then Walter's mouth came down on hers and something she had never known and was never to know again, overwhelmed her. Her very bones melted; she was weak, yielding, willing, eager ... it lasted only a moment, but it taught her something not to be learned in convents or in years of placid marriage; it was a moment to be remembered with shame, but it changed her life. It lasted only a moment because Walter, holding and caressing her as though she were a kitten, suddenly collapsed and fell, bearing her down with him to the floor, and something warm and wet, spouted from his neck.

Halfway down the stairs, his face as white as chalk, Henry stood, fitting another arrow ... The one he had already launched stood quivering for a second or two in the great vein of Walter's neck, and then fell away.

Henry said, 'Walter!' in a voice of utter amazement. And she tried to staunch the wound with a wadded handful of her skirt. Useless. Walter died there, on the floor. And Henry cried.

He said, sobbing, 'How could I know? I thought it was another raid; I heard you cry out ... Walter! He made me the bow and the arrows; he taught me ...' It was a cry of desolation.

'Darling, it was an accident. Walter had taken too much ale, and he was angry with me ... about ... about something I was writing ...' Must one thank God that one's son could not read?

All the letters lay there on the table and it was extraordinary how blood, more than any other liquid spread itself about. The papers were all soiled.

'He'd changed his clothes,' Henry said. 'I thought it was another ruffian. And it was Walter ...' In a voice of intense bitterness, he added, 'I missed the deer.'

'It was an accident, Henry, and I am entirely to blame. I was writing a letter, the content of which Walter did not agree. In his sober senses he would never have done such a thing, but he

189

was drunk and tried to take the letter from me. So I screamed . . .'

'And I heard and came and killed my best friend.'

'By accident, Henry, sheer accident.' On one remote fringe of her mind she noted what Henry had said about Walter's change of clothes. Yes, in order to prepare for his audacious, impossible proposal, he had clad himself in his best.

Time enough to think of that afterwards. Henry went on sobbing and accusing himself. 'I didn't even know that he had a blue jerkin . . . And now they'll hang me. And I deserve it.'

'Do I?'

He stopped on a gulping intake of breath and stared with wide, tear-smeared eyes.

'You? They couldn't blame you. You didn't do anything.'

'I meant did I deserve to see my son hanged—because of an accident?'

She already knew what she intended to do; but she needed Henry's help—and his full consent. There must be no chance of his thinking her callous.

He was silent, except for a few more gulps; and she waited.

'I suppose we could . . . Could we? Bury him somewhere and say nothing?'

'I think it is the only thing to do.'

'I know where . . .' The resilience of youth was already coming to his aid. 'We can't dig much, and the place mustn't show . . . I could dig a little by the wall of his house, and then pull the wall and the rest of the thatch down to cover . . .' Now healing self-justification came along. 'I loved Walter, but he shouldn't . . . have laid hands on you, whatever you wrote.'

'He was drunk.'

'I'll fetch a blanket,' Henry said. She noticed that he brought one from his own bed, not Walter's. Not without difficulty, for Henry, though strong and tough, was only fourteen, and she was small, they got the heavy corpse rolled into the blanket, an enormous sausage. Henry lit the lantern—Walter's lantern, and fetched the spade, Walter's spade and placed them both by the fire blackened wall and the now leafless periwinkle. The lantern gave them something to steer by.

190

Then he went back into the hall and said, 'Take his feet, that's the lighter end . . .'

His voice had been in process of changing, alternating between a growl and a squeak, all his lamentations and self-accusations had been made in shrill, childish tone. Now he used the voice that would go with him all his life, and despite all the differences of upbringing and background it was curiously like his father's. But the way in which he handled the spade to dig a shallow grave, and then from the inner side of the wall pushed it, and the remnant of thatch down, was Walter's, purposeful, sparing of effort.

He allowed himself one sentimental thought; he said, 'He will feel at home here.'

It was an unhallowed grave, but Sybilla felt none of the scruples which she had felt about the raiders. Walter had always sedulously avoided the church, and would not, she felt, have desired Christian burial. But as the clod wall, brittled by fire, crumbled down and the last of the thatch rustled into place, she crossed herself and murmured, 'God have mercy and rest you in peace.'

The best, most loyal, most devoted servant any woman ever had. But in a cold, convent room the Abbess had said, *Bear in mind that none but the very devout, and they are few, ever act without some ulterior motive.*

There was still much to do. Everything concerned with the 'accident' must be disposed of; the soiled papers, the bloodied rushes on the floor, her own blood-soaked dress. The mended fire on the wide hearth consumed them all.

Deaf Madge was the first to miss Walter because, rising early, he kindled the kitchen fire and brought in enough water to last her for the rest of the day. But for his absence she gave herself and everybody else, a simple explanation.

'He never was happy or settled since his little house was burnt. I noticed. Always on the fidget, he was. He liked his house and once it was gone one place was the same to him as another. So he took off.'

Outside the house interest in Walter's disappearance was minimal. Nobody in Intake had liked Walter. His fourpenny pension, when given a considerable and generous sum, but now nonsensical, had come to him, by way of a complicated method of exchange tokens, through a wool-chandler in Baildon, an honest man, who for weeks put the now miserable sum away and waited for the claimant who never came.

At Knight's Acre there was the farm, and the work to be done on it.

'Mother, I can manage,' Henry said. 'Everything I was taught, I remember, I swear. With Tom ... But I must be master, though it is for you to tell him so.'

It sounded ludicrous; a boy of fourteen, helped by another, four years older; and about to be helped by a child of seven, for Henry gave John a baleful look and said, 'He can start to help. When I was his age I made myself useful.' She would not commit herself, saying, 'I must see. I must think.' Much of her thinking was done in the dark, in the night when cheerful thoughts were rare and no prospect pleased. She would wake and think—What is to become of us? The only alternative to staying at Knight's Acre and trying to manage was to seek shelter with one of the family, meekly dependent after all, and would Henry fit in anywhere now? Would he even try? And where else but in her own home would poor Margaret be so happy, free from criticism or comment?

Sleepless, in the dark, Sybilla looked back and regarded decisions that had possibly been erroneous; setting up house here; refusing to leave when Godfrey was known to be dead; refusing a perfectly honourable offer of marriage.

There was always the comfort of touching rock bottom with the thought that at least starvation was not imminent; the hens continued to lay, and to produce clutches of fluffy yellow chickens. The sow farrowed. Somehow the makeshift arrangement—I must see; I must think—took on a permanent air.

Presently the lilies bloomed again. Sybilla took an armful to the church. 'How very beautiful,' Father Ambrose said. 'Our Lady's own flower. Any news of Sir Godfrey, my lady?' 'He died in Spain.' 'I am sorry indeed. I will say a mass for his soul.' Going back, past the lily bed, Sybilla snapped off another and dropped it amongst the periwinkles and nettles under which Walter lay. Three men loved me, she thought; and I have outlived them all. And now I must feed the pigs ...

ALTHOUGH his latest attempt at escape had passed unnoticed, the failure—and more particularly the cause of it—threw Sir Godfrey into deep depression. How could he have been so unobservant? So witless? The answer was that slavery unmanned a man.

So he must remain himself and plan better; obtain, by hook or by crook some clothes which would pass unnoticed in that crowded gateway. Not easy, for even cast off clothes cost money and he had none; nor any means of obtaining it. But he must try . . .

Then something strange happened. He, the least fanciful man in the world, began to fancy that he was being watched. Employed in his proper occupation, he would have understood exactly what that slight uneasiness, a crepitation between the shoulders and at the back of the neck implied. An enemy, in hiding. Here he could only relate to it his escapade; somebody knew, though nothing had been said, somebody was watching for him to put a foot wrong again. More than once, at work in the quiet, secret garden he was so conscious of an eye upon him that he had straightened up from what he was doing and wheeled round. And there sat Ermin, half asleep as always, having assigned jobs, knowing they would be done. The other slaves busy. So who was watching? Not only in the garden. It sometimes happened in the stable yard.

That summer the silver tubs on the steps and the terrace had been planted with orange trees of a peculiar kind, they flowered profusely, but did not fruit. They had a strong, heady scent and they needed watering every morning. In early September they were still in a state which elsewhere would have been highly regarded, but Ermin ambled round and said that they were past their best and on the morrow must be replaced by hyacinths, forced into unseasonable flowering by a special method of rearing. 'Water the tubs well,' he said, 'it will loosen the roots for tomorrow. And we shall need a lot of liquid from the tank. Be ready with it when I open the gate tomorrow morning.'

A voice said, 'Do not look round. Come to the tub nearest the doorway, but turn your back. And listen—if the answer is yes, stand still; if not walk away. You wish to be free?' He stood still. 'You will take a risk? Flogging? Branding?' He stood still. The voice was very soft, hardly more than a whisper, but it had an incisive quality. 'Death? Unpleasant death?' He stood still. 'Tomorrow, immediately after the third prayer. The street of the shoemakers. The shop of the blind man. You will ask for red shoes, lined with blue.'

He waited, diligently watering the little orange tree, but no more was said.

He was now in a quandary. It could be a trap. Confirmation of his suspicion of having been watched, that his attempt to get away, though unremarked upon, had not gone unnoticed.

Why should someone within the harem seem to plot with him?

One appalling answer did present itself. He was the man who had refused to train Selim's men in western methods of warfare; he had been sent to the quarry and forgotten; brought out by sheer chance. Had the King identified him, remembered a grudge and planned to destroy him in the most hideous manner? The King's women were sacrosanct—there were shocking stories whispered about concerning the fate of men who, even inadvertently, came into contact with one.

Deeply troubled Sir Godfrey went along to the stable yard where everything was in a bustle. At dawn next day the King was leaving for Escalona where another attack from the Christians was expected. Horses and harness, weapons and gear were being put into a state of perfect readiness and even the garden slaves were pressed into service.

Despite an exceptionally active day, Sir Godfrey slept little. He would take the risk; he would not take the risk. It could be a trap: it could be a chance. In the end he decided to keep the rendezvous, but to go armed, so that if it were a trap, he could kill himself rather than be taken and doomed to slow death by impalement.

As in all slave communities there was here in the palace of Zagelah, a natural caution about allowing slaves to handle, for any length of time, anything that might be used as an offensive weapon. Slaves worked as armourers, as smiths, as builders, but they were always closely supervised and the tools they used carefully checked. Slaves whose work entailed a certain amount of freedom, were not allowed to carry even that ordinary thing—a knife for the cutting of meat at table. Usually their meat and their bread was cut for them, but if they were served with a dish which made a knife essential, some rather blunt, round ended knives were counted out and counted in again. Such precautions were not taken for fear of slave revolts—very rare occurrences—but as a guard against slaves fighting between themselves, or in a moment of madness, turning upon an overseer who was indulging in a little persecution. Not all of them were as easy going as Ermin, who, next morning, when Sir Godfrey said that his pruning knife was blunt, told him to take it along and get it sharpened.

After that came the problem of concealing it. He managed by tying a piece of cord high on his left arm and pushing the knife into it, as though it were a belt. After that all his movements were very careful, for he honed the knife until it had the shape and sharpness of a sword.

He was in the market place again when the call to prayer rang out, and he prostrated himself with the others. Then as the last market activity broke out, he turned into the street of the shoemakers in search of what sounded somewhat unlikely —a blind man following that trade. He was easily found, a man not particularly old, but with eyes as white as pebbles. He sat on a stool near the front of a small booth whose walls were hung with shoes of many colours, and slippers richly embroidered.

'I want a pair of red shoes, lined with blue.'

'Red. With blue? The custom is to match leather and lining as nearly as possible.'

'It is my fancy. Red, lined with blue they must be.'

'Then it will be a special order. And such things take time. Be so good as to tell me—if I give you my attention, shall I keep other customers waiting?'

'There are no other customers.'

'Then follow me.' He walked briskly, and with the confidence of a full-sighted man, to a door at the back of the shop. There was a long dark passage; cooking smells, women's voices. Sir Godfrey slipped his left arm free of his jacket and retrieved his knife.

'Ten steps down,' the blind man said. At the foot of them he pulled aside a curtain and Sir Godfrey saw a little room, with a door and a window looking on to a street, parallel to, but at a lower level than the street of the shoemakers. It contained a divan upon which sat an Arab woman, a veiled, shapeless bundle.

'Is it right?' the blind man asked.

'You have done well.' Her voice was harsh, rather unpleasing, a voice accustomed to making itself heard above the noises of the market. 'Burn the clothes and you will have done,' she said. On the divan beside her lay a pile of clothes, white, reasonably, but not too conspicuously, clean, the clothes of a fairly prosperous peasant, and a hat of woven straw.

'Dress,' she said. 'I will wait by the donkey.'

She moved heavily, a fattish, middle-aged woman, he judged.

Dressed—and now with a girdle into which he could push his knife—he went out to the quiet sunny street. It was very different from the streets adjoining the market, and something about it—Silly to think that it was the street where Robert had died and Arcol had fought and he had been taken, but it was very like it.

'Pull the hat farther down,' the woman said, 'and get on to the donkey.' It was an animal in fair condition, but rather small, and it wore the usual panniers. 'Crouch a bit, you are too tall. Don't talk unless you must, pretend to be half asleep.'

The gateway again. No challenge this time. They turned right—northwards. He sat, uncomfortably hunched, eyes half closed. The woman talked sometimes, always in that grating voice, so exactly like the other women's. They had only one theme; what wickedly low prices produce taken to market fetched, and what wickedly high prices were charged by those

196

who sold things country people must buy. Here and there people turned off from the road, taking trails and paths that led to their various villages or holdings. Every departure thinned the crowd. When only three other groups were left, the woman stopped the donkey, and said in a loud, complaining voice. 'And now this misbegotten son of the one-eyed one, has a stone in his shoe.'

Nobody else stopped; why should they?

There was no trail or path leading off here. Groves of olives on both sides. She pulled the donkey to the left hand side of the road and once in the shelter of the trees said, 'Here we take to the hills. You take this—' she loosened one pannier and handed it to Sir Godfrey who had thankfully dismounted. The other she shouldered herself, and set off, leading the way, and moving with a swiftness surprising in so heavy a woman.

The donkey, relieved of its triple burden, sighed with relief and began to follow. He had not had a happy life, but he had learned that those who used him—however unkindly—provided, at the end of the day, food and water.

They were now at a point slightly north of the pass between Zagelah and Escalona, where the mountains could be called mere hills. The ground rose steeply and the belts of vegetation succeeded one another less gradually. Olives, rough pasture, gorse, pines, bareness. At one patch of pasture, with a little stream—one of the tributaries of the Loja—running through it, the donkey decided to halt. Across this little stream the woman jumped like a mountain goat. Presently their headlong, upland flight brought them to another, wider and deeper. Into this she plunged, not bothering to lift her skirts, and walked upstream for several yards before stepping out on the farther bank. He followed. There, behind an out-jutting rock she halted, put down her pannier and said in a voice only slightly breathless, 'That should defeat the hounds—if they bring them out.'

It was the first time she had spoken since the helter-skelter uphill climb began. She had led the way, seemingly certain of her direction and he had ploughed along behind, far less nimble. Now he was astonished because she spoke in a different, far more pleasant voice than she had used before.

'I am most deeply grateful to you,' he said. 'Who sent you,

197

to guide me?' He was dazed by the speed of it all, by the fact that he stood here in the free air, able to look down upon Zagelah, which from this height and distance looked very much as it had looked on the Count's map.

The woman shrugged off the voluminous, dusty-black peasant-woman's dress, and stood clad in a bulky sheepskin coat. It reached to her knees and accounted for her heavy look. She threw it off. 'It made running hard,' she said, still from behind the ugly veil. She stood, half-revealed in what Sir Godfrey, though he had never been inside a harem, recognised as harem wear because amongst the slaves in the stable yards titillating little pictures had been furtively handed about. Then as he stared, the woman, with a dramatic gesture, removed the tent-like veil with its little eye piece of coarse threadwork.

'Now you know,' she said, and looked at him with a smile which expected, demanded recognition.

To the best of his knowledge he had never seen her before in his life. A mass of silky black hair, drawn back and held in a net of gold, studded with pearls; skin the colour of ivory, thin arched eyebrows over exceptionally steep eyelids and black eyes, a delicate, high bridged nose, a sharply curved mouth, the colour of a dark red rose. And while his eyes observed, his nose breathed in the sweet odour, the product of a body which baths and unguents and perfumes had impregnated so thoroughly that even hard running inside a fleece-lined coat merely emphasised it.

Such observations of eye and nose took only seconds, but for her too long. The expectant smile faded. She said, 'You do not remember me?'

He knew that people often took non-recognition as a kind of insult. Obviously she was from the harem, the owner of the voice which had spoken from behind the grille. Then a terrible thought struck him—somewhere a mistake had been made; he was not the man for whom escape had been planned.

She said, 'I have remembered you. *For two years.*'

And even then he was not enlightened, having lost all sense of time. It was only from stray remarks in the stable yard about the length of Selim's reign—more than six years, that he had realised how long he had been in the quarry. In that lost, timeless time two years was meaningless.

Utterly at a loss he did the best thing he could have done in the circumstances. He offered her the singularly candid, blue-eyed smile which in the past had made so many people like him, even while admitting that he was stupid, or stubborn.

He said, 'Madam, I am at a loss . . . My memory was never good, and six years in a quarry, trying *not* to remember, has not improved it.'

'But it was in the quarry. The man was beating me . . .'

Confusion upon confusion. He remembered the day, the girl, so young, so new, his own impulsive action, the second flogging . . .

The sun sank suddenly, as it did in mountainous places, cut off by the peaks to the west.

'I remember now,' he said. But he could not see the connection.

'It took me so long,' she said. 'It was months before Selim even looked at me. He had another favourite then . . .' Something, not a smile, though it moved her lips, changed her expression as she remembered the cunning, callous mechanisations which had led to the former favourite's downfall. 'It takes time to establish oneself in a position of favour—and power. I had you out of the quarry as soon as I had that power.'

'I never even guessed . . .'

'I think we should eat now,' she said. 'And then sleep, to be ready for the morning.' She pulled the black, tent-like dress over the satin and silk, bent over the pannier she had carried and produced a large, double-handed, silver cup.

'If you will fill this . . .'

When he returned, in the rapidly fading light, she had laid out on a square of linen, what to him seemed a feast; a fresh roasted leg of mutton, a loaf of newly baked bread, some figs, bursting with ripeness.

'I had so little time,' she said, apologetically. 'I was ready . . . but never sure. Even after I had spoken to you still not sure. At the last moment Selim could have demanded that I go with him . . .'

'It amazes me,' he said, 'how you could arrange so much.'

'Money will buy anything—even loyalty, of a kind. We are not yet safe. We shall not be safe until we are in Spain, and that is to the north. I have studied maps. Selim thought I had interest in them because they were *pretty*.' She laughed, sardonically. 'I brought a coat for you, too. In the mounains nights are cold.'

'You know these mountains?'

'No. My mountains are in Africa. But mountains are much the same. In my *mind* I know this country.' She dipped a finger into the water cup and drew on the rock. 'This is roughly the border between Zagelah and Escalona, this the border between Escalona and Spain, and this between Zagelah and Spain.' It was like a letter T with a sharply sloping cross bar. 'We must somehow cross this ridge and go down to the west—when we are far north enough. Just here,' she made a dot, 'is a place called Santisteban. That is in Spain.'

He sat and tried to think what it would be like to be amongst Christians again; of finding some travelled friar like Father Andreas who could understand English, of borrowing money to take him home.

'I have food for a week—with care,' the girl said. 'Dried stuff when the fresh is eaten.' She handed him a sheepskin coat, and put on her own. 'We should sleep now.'

'I can never thank you properly.'

'There is no need. I too am escaping. You could promise me something . . . If we should be taken, kill me. Women from that place who offend are sewn into weighted sacks and flung into the river.' She knew because she had seen it done.

'I promise. But we must not think about being taken.'

She woke him in the first dim light, offered him water from the refilled cup, gave him a piece of bread. 'We can eat as we go.' Again she led the way, upwards and northwards over ground that became rougher and more broken all the time. The sun came up and the red sandstone took on colour, muted pinks and purples. She halted for a second, bowed herself, touched the ground and then her veiled forehead with her right hand—not a Moslem gesture—and hurried on. He looked back and Zagelah was now hidden from view. Ahead, due north, was a peak which reared itself above its neighbours and which had weathered into a rough resemblance of a helmeted head. He took it for a landmark.

It grew hot again as the sun rose higher; they divested themselves of the coats, stuffing them into the panniers. Whenever they reached a waterfall, or a little stream, they drank. At one such halt they heard sheep and the girl said, 'We must avoid people. In a place like this we should be more remarked than in a crowded street.' She led the way up, up again.

A foot soldier reckoned twenty miles an ordinary day's march, though he could do more under pressure. Sir Godfrey calculated that they must have covered more than that distance by the time they halted for the night, but they had ascended, descended, veered to avoid too steep slopes or wide stretches of scree, and the landmark peak seemed as far away as ever. It took them four strenuous days to reach its base. Each of these days was much like another, except that they now ate dried food, slices of bread rebaked until it was too dry to go mouldy, a little smoked meat, flat dry figs.

Over the food they talked, desultorily, learning each other's history; Tana—that was her name—was more voluble and painted for Sir Godfrey a picture of a strange way of life, half nomadic, half pastoral. Aspects of it were sometimes reminiscent of life on the borders which he knew, raids, feuds, banditry, though her clan or tribe appeared to operate either in the mountains or in desert country which he found difficult to imagine. They were not Moslems, she said; they had come from somewhere far away to the east and were settled long before the Arabs arrived. They had once had their own language—'My grandmother still remembered it and spoke it when she was angry, which was often.' Their women were not secluded nor veiled and seemed to enjoy unusual power; girls chose their own husbands and if a man wished to take a second wife, his first had a voice in the choosing. That, he thought, sounded civilised, but when she spoke of fighting alongside her father and brothers, and showed him, as proof, the scar on her head, his sense of chivalry was outraged. Ladies should be protected! Yet there was little about her to appeal to the protective instinct; she out-ran, out-walked, out-climbed him

201

every day and that despite the fact that she, for two years, had led a most cushioned life while he had worked. She was at home in this empty, hostile terrain as he could never be; her instinct for direction was instinctive—he was always searching for landmarks, observing the position of the sun. She never failed to find water, sometimes making a diversion in order to do so. When he offered to carry both panniers she said, 'Why should you? It would make you slower.'

They talked about horses—it had been agony, she said, never to see a horse, except through a window; her father had owned the best horses in the world. Hounds too. She had had two of her own. 'Trained to fight. They were both killed.'

In exchange he told her about Arcol, also trained to fight—but he cut that story short, it evoked painful memories, and told her instead of Arcol's wilfulness and how it took an old donkey to get him aboard. That amused her and she laughed like a boy. It was, on the whole, rather like travelling with a tough, ingenious young squire, incongruously disguised as a Moorish woman.

She told him that Selim, because he had taken the crown of Zagelah by a trick, was deeply suspicious of treachery and had built up not only the best spy system but the most efficient courier service in the world. 'That is why,' she said, 'we must avoid even a shepherd. By now Selim knows that he has lost a concubine and a slave. Everybody in Zagelah and Escalona will know too. When we come down it must be in Spain.'

He asked, idly, stupidly, 'If we manage it, will you go home?'

'Home? I have none. We were wiped out. Do you imagine that if one of my tribe had been alive and could crawl and had strength to cut my throat, I should have been left alive to become a slave? No, in future your home will be mine.'

'Of course,' he said, 'of course.' Honesty compelled him to add, 'I may have no house of my own. But I have family, and friends.'

More and more as day followed day and they made, though slow, steady progress, he had considered what a man might find after an absence so long that death must be presumed.

Tana said, 'We could buy a house; many houses, I think. Do

202

you think I came away empty-handed? From the stronghold of an enemy? Look!'

She loosened the ugly black dress. And the rose-coloured, heavily embroidered satin jacket which she wore under it. Between the base of her long neck and the jut of breasts, small but firm, there were three strings of pearls; around her slim waist was a band from which two pouches were suspended. She pulled them out with an apparently unself-conscious gesture and tipped out their contents. Gold coins, a tangled mass of jewelled ornaments, sapphires, rubies, diamonds which even in this dimming light, glittered. He had never seen, he thought few men had ever seen such a collection of wealth.

Tana said, 'Spoil! I took everything I could lay my hand upon. I thought that if I ended in a sack, in the river, it should be for some act of which my tribe would have approved.'

Innocent then, he was able to contemplate her future in England. Young—he knew her age, sixteen, so two years ago, in the quarry, he had been right in thinking her very young—rich. But in England she would, for a time, be a stranger. He determined that whatever he found—Knight's Acre sold, Sybilla remarried—he would take care of Tana, see that nobody took advantage of her, find her a decent husband; in short behave to her as though she were his sister.

'I must eat less,' she said, on the fifth or sixth evening, snapping her slice of the brittle bread in two. 'I think maps are liars, we should have been out of the mountains by now.' She scowled fiercely.

'I will eat less, too,' he said, and put his whole piece back into the pannier and took the half she had returned.

They were not only not out of the mountains, but trapped in them, with peaks to east as well as west. Even had they been sure that they were far enough north to have Spain, not Escalona to the west of them, they could not have reached it; and never would unless they found a gap.

They had retained both panniers because they were a convenient means of carrying the sheepskin coats during the heat of the day. What food remained, wrapped in the linen cloth, lay at the bottom of one pannier when they settled themselves for the night. The idea of guarding it had not occurred to them; they had climbed into heights where they were the only things living. Yet something came in the night and robbed them. . . .

'We might as well have eaten it all,' Tana said, bitterly, but not without humour. 'I heard something snuffling and gobbling. I *hit* it.'

'What was it?'

'How could I tell in the dark? It was hairy.'

Wolf? Wild goat? Mountain hare? It had left no footprints on the bare rock.

'You should have called me,' he said. Women wakened in the night by a mouse's activity behind the wainscot, or an owl hooting, or a roll of thunder, ordinarily turned to the nearest person.

'You could have done no more than I did. I hit it, and it was hairy and slipped away.' She must have hit it hard whatever it was. The side of her hand and the little finger were swollen and bruised. She had exceptionally narrow, fragile hands.

She said, 'So today or tomorrow we must find food. I once hungered for three days, but my horse carried me.'

'I once hungered for five, but then we were besieged and could not move.'

Inaction lessened hunger.

Their experience of going without food, different as they were, interlinked. Hold on and you survived. So they survived that day. And part of the next. By that time the shape of the country had changed, the corridor between two impenetrable ranges, a path littered with boulders, with scree, always descending. The last thing that Sir Godfrey saw at the end of that hungry day, was a glimpse of green. Pasture? Tree tops? but far away, deep down, and for their purpose, on the wrong side of the brutally rugged range.

Abruptly, on the third day of hunger, although towards the north peaks still towered, shaped as one decided, a castle, a church steeple, a mushroom, a tree, underfoot the land sloped down and neither of them, fully in control of the mind, followed it. Everywhere lay bare rock, gorse and pine, beeches. And from somewhere came the plaintive cry of sheep.

Tana said, 'I think we should still be careful...'

So they were careful, and hiding behind the grey boles of the beeches in a way of which Walter would have approved, they watched. A Moorish shepherd, leading his flock to lower pastures, stalking along as though sheep did not concern him; a woman, clad exactly as Tana was, and two children acted as sheepdogs did in countries where both women and dogs had more worth.

This was still Moorish territory, and they must be glad that the shepherd had a wife, not a dog. They must also be glad that amongst the surplus, or the diseased fruits of their branches, the beeches had shed a few early and edible nuts. Enough perhaps to keep a man alive, not enough to stay hunger or give strength.

Cautiously they crossed the sheep trail, left the trees and grass behind and below, and re-entered the hostile land of rock. And there, after a day in which they had eaten nothing at all, Tana broke down.

He had heard the expressions, beating one's breast, tearing one's hair, but he had never seen anyone actually performing such actions. Now he did, for Tana's self-recrimination was as thorough and wholehearted as everything else about her.

'I have doomed you to death,' she cried. 'I over-estimated myself... In the garden you were not overworked and you always had food... Now you will die, and I shall have killed you!'

She beat her breast, she tore her hair, she banged her head against the rock.

'We are not dead yet,' he said, appalled by the sight of such distress. 'And if we do die... at least we shall die free.' It was all he could think of to say; fasting had not improved his mental processes or made him handy with words. He could, he thought, prevent her from hurting herself, and with this in mind he took her hands and pulled her away from the rock. He said, 'My dear ... You are not to blame. I came of my own free will. I ... I encouraged you ... Perhaps I should curse myself...'

Then the incredible thing happened, and with incredible speed. At the touch of his hands she changed from a woman wild with misery and self-reproach to one wild with desire, something only a dead man could have resisted. He was idiotically surprised by the violence of his own response.

He had always brought to the matter of sex the straight-forward simplicity he had brought to life. As a young, un-married man he had made occasional visits to brothels because not to have done so would have seemed eccentric. But the traffic of flesh without genuine feeling had always repulsed him slightly. Until he met and fell in love with Sybilla, he had never experienced a genuine feeling towards any woman, and once married had been contentedly faithful. Opportunities to be otherwise had not been lacking. There were many ladies, beautiful ladies of very high rank disposed to favour a hand-some young knight who had distinguished himself in the lists. But intrigue had never appealed to him; at its best it involved furtiveness, at its worst, scandal. More than one angry lady had decided that he was too stupid to take a hint.

He loved Sybilla, Sybilla loved him and their love-making had been placid and pleasant, entirely satisfactory to two people not passionate by nature, but loving, considerate and kind. The six years of enforced celibacy had bothered him little—if he couldn't bed with his loved one, he was content to bed with nobody.

As for this girl, the thought had never once occurred to him though they had been alone together, living in close intimacy for so many days. She was sixteen, he was forty-three—and felt far older. Also, absurd, perhaps, but true, he was not merely a one-woman man, he was a one-type-of-woman man. Sybilla was his ideal and Tana was about as different from Sybilla as a female could be . . .

However, there it was, it had happened, and it was a stun-ning experience.

Afterwards, depleted, completely drained, just before he fell into a sleep of exhaustion, he found himself hoping that what she had said—about loving him from that moment in the quarry and similar things—was the result of hunger-light-headedness. But what had *he* said? Light-headed from hunger,

206

taken out of himself by joy he had not even imagined, *he* had said, 'I would die now, content.'

But death, which would have solved everything was not to be theirs. Stumbling along next morning, now taking the easiest way, they heard sheep again; sheep first and then market place voices and rounding a bluff in which a peak was rooted, they found themselves on the verge of what seemed a busy town.

Santisteban?

Hope cleared their eyes and they saw that this was not the place they were seeking; no streets, no houses, no church.

Centuries ago shepherds had realised that sheep from the uplands were hardier, long of leg, and thicker of fleeces. Those from the lowlands were fatter and more docile, less likely to go back to the wild. So they had met and made exchanges, a ram for three ewes. Then people who owned no sheep, realised that men were hungry and thirsty, and came with food and drink; and then other people who owned nothing, had realised that people craved entertainment.

Here, in a most unlikely place a market had established itself, step by step over the years. Boundaries, never very certain in such rugged country, and the rule of kings, of popes and prelates, had affected the gathering place hardly at all. It was an international, multilingual market where one could buy almost anything and the money-changers were busy at their benches. One day to be called banks.

Tana said, 'I think we should not go down together. It is not Santisteban. Selim's rule might even extend ...' She gave him one of the solid gold coins and said, 'Buy what you can, and ask the way. I will do the same.'

'Perhaps,' he said, 'we should not be seen to leave together, either. Whichever of us first learns the way will go in that direction and wait.' It was necessary to ask, for apart from the way by which they had made their entry which was not a real trail at all, better trodden ways led off in all directions.

The place reeked of food cooking. Moorish women were grilling mutton and boiling rice and frying doughcakes and rolling them in powdered sugar. A woman who looked like a

207

Spaniard was stirring a great pot of something he did not recognise; it looked like white worms; as she stirred she talked and he decided that her speech did not sound like Spanish, so he passed on to a table where a man was slicing ham. Ham! Something he had not tasted for six years—the pig being regarded by the Arabs as an inedible beast. He indicated his wish for a slice and stood and devoured it. Nothing had ever tasted so good! He ate three slices while he listened. The man was undoubtedly Spanish. So he ventured to put his question. Santisteban?

He had never seen the word written, had only heard it said, by Tana, in Arabic, and now pronounced it as she had done, but in his English voice. The ham-seller looked blank, shrugged his shoulders, spread his hands, answered in Spanish that he had never heard of such a place. Sir Godfrey pointed towards what seemed to him the westerly of the trails, and the man understood. 'Escalona,' he said.

But this was a friendly place. Wars might be waged on either side of the mountains, but in this old upland market place there were only buyers and sellers, so the man was disposed to be helpful and turning away from his table, enquired of his neighbour who sold knives, saying the word as Sir Godfrey had said it. He also looked puzzled for a moment and then said, 'Ah! *Sant*isteban?' He gave the word the correct stress. Sir Godfrey nodded and then pointed vaguely, regretting very much that he had learned no Spanish at all; he could not even say 'Thank you,' or 'How far?' He simply had not bothered. He had a sharp, self-reproachful memory of Sir Ralph who had practised so assiduously, acquiring as many as ten words or phrases in a day. He had no means of knowing that Sir Ralph, with all that he knew, his taste for gossip, his keen sense of self-preservation, lay at the bottom of a gully, not far from the city of Escalona, a mass of greening bones.

But, the right trail—it seemed to lead to the north-west—indicated to him he smiled and held up his fingers. One, two, up to ten miles. The gesture was not understood. No matter, he thought, we shall find out.

Then he had a bad moment. He had bought three slices of ham, and now bought more; a whole heap of pink and white

208

succulent meat slapped into a fig leaf. He was uncertain about how Tana felt towards ham. In their talks she had always emphasised her tribe's difference from their Arab neighbours. Some pretence at being converted had been necessary, but her tribe still worshipped the sun, giver of all. He thought—Well if she will not eat ham, she can eat what she has chosen; and he placed the big, folded fig leaf in his pannier and proffered the big gold coin. The ham-seller looked at it, not entirely with suspicion, but with curiosity, turning it this way and that. The three slices of ham, eaten too hastily and gulped down into an empty stomach, threatened for a moment to rebound. For a moment he thought he was going to be sick, and in the same moment he contemplated the wisdom of turning away, vanishing into the crowd without waiting for change. Commonsense alone kept him still. Such extravagance would be remarkable—and he had already indicated his destination. So he stood, with the stolidity that had so often been mistaken for stupidity and waited while the ham-seller placed the coin between his teeth and bit it and then dropped it on the table. It was gold! And here gold in any form was acceptable, just as any harmless man was acceptable. Sir Godfrey took his change and sauntering deliberately, bought bread, apples, figs, and then, ignoring the invitations to enter enclosures inside which bears danced and dogs fought, and all the booths that sold trivialities, even amber from the far north, made his way towards the trail, slightly north of west. He looked about as he went, but Tana, covered from the crown of her head to her ankles was not to be distinguished from any of the other Moorish women in the milling market place. So he went along, sat down on a boulder and waited. Now that he had time to think he realised the folly of his behaviour on the previous evening. It had been, in a way, an act of despair, death seeming so likely as to make what one did or did not do of small importance. It had been a failure of self-control, a violation of his marriage vows, a contradiction of his principles. And would colour the whole of his relationship with the girl in future. Armoured in innocence he had been able to visualise himself presenting Tana to Sybilla, to James, to William as his deliverer, expecting nobody to think evil because none had existed. It would be different now; he felt that guilt was written all over him.

It must never happen again.

Having decided that he began to be uneasy because she had not yet joined him. Had she not seen him leave? Had she misunderstood the direction, or been misdirected? Or—his heart gave a lurch—had the worst happened? He remembered the curiosity which his gold coin had evoked, suppose hers ... and suppose Selim's spy system operated even in this distant, Tower-of-Babel place.

The thought brought him to his feet and set him running back towards the noise and the stench when a moment's cool consideration would have sent him galloping towards Santisteban, for if she had been taken there was nothing he could do; he could only doom himself as well. But he ran marketwards, and at a turn in the trail met her, hurrying too, and heavily laden. For a second the breathlessness of haste and agitation prevented speech; they could only lean against each other in a way which any Arab onlooker would have found highly suspicious. Finally he said, 'I was afraid that something had happened ...'

'It almost did ...' Behind the veil she laughed, but shakily. 'I almost died of fright ... The woman selling doughcakes did not like the look of my money ... She took it to the money-changer, and Godfrey, I could not move. I knew I should ... melt into the crowd ... but I was paralysed. I did not know that one could be so frightened...'

However the money-changer had declared the coin good and fear unlocked its hold. She had bought bread, fruit, cheese, smoked mutton and two portions of the fresh meat which he had seen an Arab woman grilling; cubes of mutton not much bigger than a dice, threaded on to a piece of wire, the meat cubes interspersed with onion and some other vegetable, green.

'One for you,' she said, 'and one for me, I am so hungry.'

'Have you not eaten?'

'Oh no! I thought we should break our long fast together.'

His hastily gobbled slices of ham were uneasy again, spurred this time not by fear but by self-reproach. But he took the proffered handy meal and learned, as they walked and

210

munched that Tana had been more successful than he had in extracting information.

Santisteban was four days' easy walking away. 'And that delayed me too,' she said. 'First I said the name wrongly and must be corrected. Then I was warned that it was in Spain and Moors were not welcome there. I said that it was a place I wished to avoid, and that was why I asked. And I took a roundabout way to this path. Just in case . . . but I do not think we are being followed.'

She ate her portion of meat on the skewer, two slices of ham, half a loaf, three of the doughcakes. She seemed to be insatiable—but she had waited, to take the first mouthful with him.

And whoever had told her that only four days of easy walking would lead into Santisteban had never followed this trail which led upwards, to the last summer pasture, and a little hut in which some shepherd had sheltered. After that the land fell away in a series of steep declines, more difficult to descend than to ascend since in climbing upwards handholds offered some momentum. The journey took a full five days, but they knew on the fourth that they were in Spain, because on that day they reached sheep country again, and this time the flock was led by a bell-wether, an experienced old ewe who knew which way to go.

'All Arabs are terrified of bells,' Tana said. 'We are in Spain. Beloved, we are free!' She lifted the ugly veil from her head and threw it down, and then turned and embraced him.

It was the moment for which he had passionately longed and hopelessly hoped for; but it was marred for him by what had taken place immediately before. The thing he had vowed should never happen again, had happened, and the statements which he had hoped were the product of hunger light-headedness had been repeated many times. It still seemed incredible to him that one so brief encounter with a man old enough to be her father should have kindled such intense and lasting devotion, but there it was!

She had hidden nothing from him; the scheming and plotting—a horrifying harem intrigue—by which she had attained the position of favourite and the title—Light of The King's

211

Eyes; her dangerous contacts with Soraya in order to find out his name, his nationality. 'She is a relative of Selim's and could have betrayed me. To think about another man is a crime . . .' He had simply saved her from a few strokes of a cane, and she, in return, had risked her life many times. 'I made up the story that being English you would know about gardens; had you been German or Italian I should have said the same. It was necessary to have you in the garden. Heart of my heart, I used to watch you, wondering when the moment would come when I could act . . .'

He did not love her—he assured himself of that whenever he thought about the situation in which he found himself. He was deeply and everlastingly in her debt, he admired her wholeheartedly, but he did not love her, or at least only with his body, formerly so disciplined and now out of control. Sometimes he wondered whether it were possible for a man to be in love with two women at once, in two very differing ways. It was a question with which his simple, single-minded nature was not equipped to deal. And now as sheep country became cultivated country and their longed-for destination, a huddle of red roofed tiles and white walls became visible, became near, his happiness was diluted with guilt and foreboding.

He said, as they approached the little town, 'Tana, we must now be careful. We need help from the Church, and if they knew the . . . the truth about us, help might not be forthcoming.'

'Why do we need help from the Church or anybody. We are free, we have plenty of money.' She sounded defensive.

He needed to make contact with the one international body that he knew of. After all, William was a Bishop, able to read and write the Latin which was the Church's common tongue. William, he thought, would not have accepted his complete disappearance without some enquiry, and where a question could penetrate, so could information. He was not so stupid as to imagine that anyone, friar or priest, in this little country town on Spain's border, would have information of what had been happening at Knight's Acre in his absence, but it was possible that they could put him into touch with someone who did.

212

His natural delicacy—remembering last night and all the other nights—prevented him from explaining honestly; so he said that what he craved was some news of what had been happening in England during the past six years.

Tana, prey to no such scruples said, 'You mean your wife!'

She had known of Sybilla's existence—and of the four children—from one of the first of their supper-time talks. He had offered the information then with no thought of being defensive. She spoke of her past, he spoke of his. Nor since the flight of innocence, had he in any way deceived her, careful to point out that in England a man could have only one wife. Nor had he been free with endearments; nothing more than 'my dear', never, even in his most abandoned moments, using any of the terms which were Sybilla's, 'Darling', 'Sweeting'.

If Tana sensed any reticence in him, she gave no sign; her own endearments were fervent, picturesque—had he known it, Oriental in flavour.

She now asked, 'What do you mean by being careful?'

'Sleeping apart.'

'It will take the heart out of my breast. But if it is your wish . . .'

And so they entered Santisteban.

18

AT first their welcome was not very warm; their shoes were in tatters, their clothes in rags and much soiled; they looked like beggars, and foreign at that. But they had money, and by chance the first inn they saw was the best in a town that boasted four. Tana proved herself capable of communicating by mime; they needed food, they needed wine, hot water for washing; after that she needed more hot water in order to wash her hair; they both needed clothes, and sleeping places—she folded her hands together and laid her head on them in sleep's posture. She gave Sir Godfrey a look that he could not interpret, and held up two fingers. Two rooms.

Life in Santisteban, except on market days was dull; a small crowd gathered to peep through open doorway or window to view this couple who had come from nowhere, looked so poor, yet acted as though they were rich. Somebody ran for the priest.

He was a fairly young man and intelligent; he had more Latin than many of his kind who knew just enough to stumble through a ritual. Sir Godfrey had never known more Latin than was needed to make the correct responses, and even those phrases, through long disuse were rusty; also his Latin was English-Latin, Father Pedro's was Spanish-Latin and the two things were different; but Sir Godfrey crossed himself and said a Hail Mary, quickly and badly, but just well enough to establish himself as a Christian. Then Tana mimed again; on the white scrubbed table she drew a Crescent, enemy of the Cross; she pointed to the mountain range, and then ripped from Sir Godfrey's shoulders what remained of his Moorish peasant robe and exposed the scars which the scalding khurbash lashes had made.

And the priest, understanding the mime, said, 'Where is Fernando?'

He was easily found. An old man now, crooked and crippled, willing—if he could be caught sober, to undertake any job which a one-armed man could do. But, like Sir Ralph Overton and many another man he had once, until he was disabled, worked his way about the world. He was a professional mercenary.

Partly to compensate himself for his now humble status, and partly to lure an absorbed audience into paying for another cup of wine, Fernando told long, boastful stories about his adventures and the priest sensibly decided that if there was one person in Santisteban capable of understanding these strange tongues, Fernando was the man. He knew less than he claimed to do, but wine emboldened him to bridge any gaps with guesses. He informed his hearers that Sir Godfrey was English and a Christian and a martyr; he had been a prisoner with the Moors and beaten very often for refusing to give up his faith; he confused six with sixteen, thus increasing the captivity by

214

ten years, and failing to understand Tana's role in the story, explained that she was Sir Godfrey's daughter.

To his audience—few of whom had ever been more than twenty miles from Santisteban, Fernando's cleverness was impressive, and Sir Godfrey's story so moving that tears were shed, generous and pious resolves taken on impulse. There must be a feast to welcome back this man from the dead; two feasts, in fact, one given by the civil authorities and one by the members of the Hermandad, that ancient, self-elected body of men who were responsible for the keeping of law and order. Kind ladies ransacked their wardrobes in order to provide Tana with an outfit and the tailor's two most respected customers managed to convince him that it was nothing less than his duty to enlarge the suit of clothes upon which he was currently at work, to make it fit Sir Godfrey, too tall for borrowed clothes, and to do so fast and without charge.

Father Pedro also knew a generous impulse. A prisoner with the Moors this good Christian must certainly have neglected his religious obligations, and probably committed sins as well; but he had suffered for his faith and entitled to leniency, an overall absolution and a mass of thanksgiving. Never an ostentatiously pious man, and for years a stranger to God, Sir Godfrey was greatly touched by this consideration for his soul; and although he knew that the priest would not understand, he confessed that he had committed adultery, many times. He also knew that absolution always included the adjuration to avoid the *occasion* for sin. This, in his mind, he was determined to do; and he asked, as he had not formerly done— God's help in resisting temptation.

Tana, miming sleep had indicated a wish for two rooms, but that was because Godfrey had said they must be careful; she had every intention of waiting until the house was asleep and then creeping along to his bed. In this she was thwarted because the inn-keeper's wife though sharing the charitable impulse and saying that she would not charge for accommodation, was thrifty, too and did not prepare guest rooms. Tana was to share the bed of her own daughter—what more could anyone ask? Sir Godfrey had a bed in a room which held four,

215

one occupied by the son of the house, and one by a permanent guest, a childless widower who found living at the inn more convenient than keeping house on his own.

So they slept apart; and the civic feast and the Hermandad feast were both strictly male gatherings. 'I did not think it would be like this,' Tana said, looking more miserable than she had done during the hungry days. The wives of the leading citizens of Santisteban were kind to her but she was not grateful. 'It is like being back in the harem again. With dumb women! They give me things—which I could buy—and they *pat* me. Like a pet monkey.'

He felt sorry for her, the more so because he was beginning to enjoy himself. He was back in a world which though strange was not completely alien to him; he could talk only to one person, Fernando, and that imperfectly, but then he had never been much of a talker, and when men lifted winecups and smiled in his direction, he understood. And smiled back, growing, minute by minute more into the shape that he had once known, a man among men. There were even moments when he dared to think hopefully of Knight's Acre; James and Emma only five miles away; William at Bywater, Walter close at hand . . . All his family and many of his friends had thought at one time or another that he was feckless, and now that quality in him which had made him buy Arcol and thus run into debt, and build a house a bit bigger than he could really afford, took over. He had a naturally happy nature and all his training had been directed at a certain *insouciance*. A man of forethought— what if my horse stumbles or, riding at the ring I do not withdraw my arm soon enough and break my shoulder—such a man could never have become the knight he had been, reckless, feckless.

As he was restored, Tana dwindled. She had her moment, astride a horse again. Fernando had understood the word horse, the two uplifted fingers and the word 'good'. He was also capable of understanding that though clothes, accommodation and feasts might be free, horses must be paid for and he had provided the best that Santisteban offered.

Tana could not get away from this disappointing place quickly enough, and she rode as Sir Godfrey had never seen a woman ride before, crouched low, her hair—what had happened to the net?—mingling with the horse's back-blown mane. Wicked, absolutely wicked to think that she brought to horse-riding the same violence and skill as she brought to love-making, and to remember, and yearn . . .

They now carried with them what was virtually a passport, written by Father Pedro, warmly commending to anyone who could read Latin, this Englishman who had come back, as from the dead. The letter repeated Fernando's errors about how long the imprisonment had lasted, and about the relationship between the man and the girl. It also mentioned something very near to Father Pedro's heart. He judged it unlikely that a man regularly beaten for adhering to his faith would have been able to have his child baptised; since the baptism of those of mature years demanded some collaboration from the subject, and since he himself could not communicate with the girl, Father Pedro could only hope that should this letter fall into the hands of some English-speaking priest, he would take action.

For the first four days of their journey the letter was very helpful—even in one small village where the priest could not read it completely. He recognised Latin when he saw it, however, and gave the missive due respect. The village inn being so poor and squalid, he invited Sir Godfrey to sleep in his own house and arranged for Tana to be accommodated in the home of a parishioner. Tana said, with some justification, 'You are using the Church as a shield against me.' She hoped very much that soon they would be forced to halt for the night in the open, or in some village with an inn and no priest, both hopes doomed to disappointment for they were riding through a countryside relatively highly populated, and Spain, though its civil life was falling into chaos, was still the most ardently religious country in Christendom; every village had a priest.

On the evening of the fifth day they reached a town which had what Sir Godfrey had been hoping for—a Dominican Priory in which lived a friar who understood English, who had in fact spent some time in London. For Sir Godfrey to be able to communicate was like being freed from another form of captivity. But the interview took an embarrassing turn. He had already handed in his letter and there were discrepancies. Sir Godfrey said six years, the letter said sixteen.

'That was a mistake, Father. I was in captivity for *six* years.' He tried to explain about the man in Santisteban who knew a very little English; he mentioned being in Escalona in early 1453, in the attack upon Zagelah in the February of that year. His congenital inability to narrate and explain did little to allay the ever ready Dominican suspicion. Nor did it account for the young woman, described in the letter as his daughter. Unless English knights had begun to take girls with them when they went into battle. Even that Father Ignatius could almost believe, having lived in England ... At the same time, Zagelah, six years ago had made a mark on the collective Dominican consciousness. Father Ignatius switched his impersonal, celibate gaze from the young woman, admitted to the only room in the Priory in which women were allowed to set foot, said:

'There was a report that the Count of Escalona took certain members of my order with him.'

Sir Godfrey did not regard this as a test of his genuineness, but he gave the right answer.

'Oh yes. There was Father Andreas and six others, younger men.'

'Of their fate nothing was known; death was assumed. Any detail would, of course, be welcome.'

'I cannot say what happened; only what was arranged ...' his clear, candid gaze clouded. 'In a battle one does the part assigned ... There is no time ... The Count of Escalona had his son ... It was arranged that he and the religious should follow when we had made an entry—and cleared the streets ...' Impossible now not to remember Robert, roasting inside his armour. 'It was a disaster. The Moor, Abdullah we betrayed, and so were we in our turn. I never heard of any other prisoner. I think *my* death has been assumed.' That brought him back to his real reason for seeking out an English-speaking member of the loosely-knit but widespread Church. 'My brother is Bishop of Bywater ... I rather hoped, or wondered if enquiries ... or news from England.'

'Enquiries would hardly have reached us, here, Sir Godfrey. In Seville, possibly. Some news seeps through from time to time. Civil war, I understand, brief and ending in a compromise.'

This news did not affect Sir Godfrey much. War was still something that involved only fighting men; his sons were too young, James was too old, and William had never been a militant cleric. He had himself once fought in a battle on a field between two others; in one a peasant was ploughing, and in the other a boy was flying his hawk.

Then Father Ignatius said, 'And the young woman? *Is* she your daughter?'

'Does the letter say that? In Santisteban there was this one man ... an old soldier who knew a few English words. No indeed. This lady was also a prisoner. In Zagelah; and I owe my freedom to her. But for her I should still be there ...' Suddenly the weight of his debt to her settled on his mind as heavily as the marble slabs had pressed on his shoulders. But for her ...

Tana sat there, upright, immobile, scowling, so obviously aloof from it all, and yet disapproving, that only someone with a rightful regard for her immortal soul would have ventured on the next question,

'Is she a Christian?'

'No, Father.'

'A Moor? A Moslem?'

'No. She ... she has a faith of her own. But I do not understand it. The lady speaks only Arabic—and my knowledge of that language is limited.'

'There are Moors in Seville. Converts,' Father Ignatius said, not sorry to defer the matter, but adding that Sir Godfrey must be mindful of his duty and his responsibility. He then changed the subject by enquiring whether they needed financial assistance and seemed relieved to learn that this was not so. He recommended a certain inn.

That night he woke, and in the dark, in the haze of being aroused from a deep sleep, found her in bed beside him. For a moment he thought that he had only dreamed the awakening

219

and was now dreaming this, for like all cautious travellers in unfamiliar places he had bolted his door. But she was real enough—and importunate.

Once, hotly and openly pursued by a lady intent upon dalliance he had felt ridiculous, so much so that he had cancelled his name from the lists of remaining events in the week-long tournament and simply fled, feeling even more ridiculous. But for that lady he had had no feeling at all; with Tana his flesh at least was in love. And although he had vowed to God— What could God do, short of striking one of them dead, or him impotent, which was far, far from being the case . . .

Afterwards she snuggled against him, soft and content as a cat. He asked how she got into his room, and she said, through the window. That should perhaps have sounded ludicrous, too—and would have done with any other woman—but with Tana it was simply further proof of devotion, unintentionally inspired and completely undeserved.

'Now that I belong to you again, I shall enjoy this country,' she said.

With another woman it would have been possible, even easy, to think an uncouth thought—A bitch on heat; but not with this woman who had been willing to die for him, and with him.

And a fall from grace was a fall from grace; depending only upon his own will, he had made a resolution and failed; asking the help of God he had made a vow and broken it; repetition of the offence could hardly worsen it.

So there followed some days and nights over which, in memory, an enchanted air seemed to hang. They were free, and for the first time since they had attained freedom, Tana was happy. It was still fine weather, and away from the hills warm, even at night. They now avoided villages and towns, or paused in them only long enough to buy food. Money knew no language, coins in a palm, a finger pointing obtained them all they wanted.

They made no further contact with the Church. News, if there was any, would be in Seville—where this happy gypsy journey must end.

He had occasional bad moments, realising that when there

220

was no sexual traffic between them—as in their first days in the mountains, and in their first days in Spain, he had been able to see himself taking Tana to England, of somehow fitting her into his life. So long as she was his saviour, the thing was possible, while she was his lover, it was not. That must be thought about—not today, tomorrow. Some obscure instinct told him to make the best of *now*. And now was travel through country where the first-harvested grapes had already been crushed and made into wine, unmatured, something one drank like water and within a short time felt the effects of; where the later-harvested grapes were being gathered and carted, in donkey panniers, on low carts, on the backs of women; where, because the wine harvest was a season of plenty, meat was available. And Tana could cook, in two ways. She could make a tripod of green branches over a fire and from it suspend a joint, much in the manner of somebody using a spit, or she would dig a hole, line it with stones, light a fire in it and then put meat and onions, wrapped in leaves, into the red-hot cavity and close it down with the clods.

Once or twice he had a demented thought—We could live like this for ever. A thought to be dismissed instantly.

Insulated as they were, by language and by their way of life, they had received no warnings of the perils of the road. All roads, everywhere, were infested with robbers, but those of Spain were worse than most because although in some remote, backward places, like Santisteban, the Hermandad might be active and respected still, in more central regions it had become completely ineffectual. In many towns the chief magistrates were either in league with the bandits, or intimidated by them and so reluctant to pass sentence.

Outwardly Sir Godfrey and Tana did not appear to be likely prey for thieves; the clothes they had been given were plain and simple, they wore no jewels, carried no goods. But they had horses, and every evening before settling upon a suitable place to camp, Sir Godfrey made a sharp reconnoitre. He then unsaddled and tethered the horses, and fed them—grass was wilted and yellow at this season—and Tana cooked.

One evening, with a fine leg of lamb suspended, hissing over

221

the flames, they were surprised to find that they had company. They were camped on open heathland and Sir Godfrey had made sure that there were no other nomads in the vicinity, no likely hiding places; but there the two men were, looming up silently, grunting out greeting in Spanish and eyeing the meat hungrily. Both carried bludgeons, both wore knives, far larger than Sir Godfrey's ground-down pruning knife. Tana said, 'Be amiable!' She returned the greeting, in Arabic, and indicated, by gesture that the intruders were welcome to share the meat. As a token of good will she broke the long crusty loaf into four and gave them each a portion, instantly devoured.

Sir Godfrey watched uneasily, cursing himself for not having provided himself with a sword. They might be simply two hungry men, attracted by the scent of cooking meat, they might, having eaten, go away, but there was something about their manner, both furtive and arrogant, which made him suspicious. One of them pointed to the joint and then to his mouth—an order to Tana to serve. She looked very amiable indeed, and acted sensibly. She tested the meat by running a sliver of wood into it, and the blood ran red. She shook her head and held up her ten fingers; wait ten minutes. The men laughed and then spoke together. That in itself was not sinister, not necessarily secretive, Spanish was their tongue, but it made him uneasy. They were both a good deal younger than he was. He was acutely aware not only of the wealth Tana had concealed about her, but of the fact that she was female. Even in England, sturdy beggars were dreaded; men divorced from home, from womenfolk had been known to hunger for other things than food, and to snatch when they could.

Tana appeared as unperturbed as though she were cooking in her own kitchen. Smiling again she held up five fingers and as earnest of this promise, fed the fire more sticks. That done, and the flames leaping wildly, she said, 'Godfree. Leave this to me, *please*. Do not come near.' There would be no trouble, he thought, until after they had eaten ... She served the meat as she always did, pushing over the tripod that composed the makeshift spit so that it fell away from the flames, and then lifting it complete, the meat being too hot to handle. With a gesture that was even pretty in its wholehearted hospitality,

222

she laid the meat before them, and they took out their knives. Their bludgeons lay close to their sides; could he grab one while they concentrated upon the food? A bludgeon in his right hand, his knife in his left, he could hold them, long enough at least for Tana to loose a horse, mount and ride. Then it happened so swiftly that he, as well as they, were taken completely unawares. She turned back to the fire, snatched a blazing brand in either hand ... Straight to the eyes ... Through the howls of pain her voice carried. 'Get the horses! These may have friends ...'

In the course of a lifetime not lacking in action he had never seen a movement so swift, so callous, so effectual.

It was no distance to where the horses were tethered and as he threw over the saddles and tightened the girths he could see the men, blinded, screaming, eyebrows and beards aflame, and Tana backing away towards him, the still blazing brands ready to strike again. At exactly the right moment—horses being terrified of fire—she flung them down and flames began to snake through the dry heather and the gorse. She got herself into the saddle in the way that she had sometimes displayed for amusement, a cat's leap, ignoring the stirrup.

He had been suspicious, on guard, working out a plan of defence; now he suffered a bout of the inborn English disease—sympathy for the defeated enemy. When, easing from a headlong gallop Tana said with unimaginable viciousness, 'I hope they enjoy their meat—if they can find it!' he knew a pang. The men had been potential, but not declared enemies ... and now they were blind.

And this infinitely crafty and resourceful, callous wild girl was somebody whom he must take back to England; introduce to a way of life where ladies played lutes and did embroidery, busied themselves in sweet-scented still-rooms.

But—and it was a fact to be faced—she had again saved him, if not from death, from injury; for had he succeeded in snatching the bludgeon from one man, the other would have been alerted. And the result debatable.

After that they slept in inns, sharing a bed, and so they came to Seville one of the busiest ports and for all but people

223

with parochial prejudices, the most beautiful city in Christendom. And in its harbour the most beautiful sight in the world—an English ship, loading oranges—not yet fully ripe, and hides, and wine. Her name was *The Mermaid*, and Sir Godfrey remembered the ancient story of the Bywater man who had caught a mermaid in his fishing net and taken her home and been unhappy ever after. He could hardly believe that this vessel was out of Bywater, that would be too good to be true, but so it was; here amidst all this foreign shipping, in the meaningless chatter of foreign tongues was a link not only with England, but with Suffolk; and the name Tallboys meant something. The brother of the good old Bishop, given up for dead, years ago!

In Santisteban his welcome had been warm, once Tana had explained, but it had been impersonal, he was a Christian, delivered from Moorish captivity; this was different, a great welcome, but tinged with respect for his rank. And the news, when he could bring himself to ask the most vital question, was overwhelming.

'Lady Tallboys, God love you, Sir Godfrey, alive and well, and at Intake. Or so it was when I last heard.'

All the colour and noise of the harbour, the sunlight flaked and dancing on the river water went into blackness. He, he, Godfrey Tallboys, proven knight, was about to faint like a green girl! From a great distance his voice, but not his voice, said, 'When?'

'Three months since. July. We made landfalls at Amsterdam and Lisbon.' The captain of *The Mermaid*, himself a family man, obliged by his calling to absent himself from home for long periods, but never, naturally, anything like six years, did not wait for the next question but volunteered the answer. 'I know, sir, because my old grandmother sells fish. Intake is on her round. I've heard say more than once that Lady Tallboys was a good customer—and pleasant with it . . . Sir, may I fill your cup?'

A GOOD customer—and pleasant with it—Sybilla went to the door, for Madge could not hear the loudest knock, and said to the old fishwife, 'I am glad to see you.' True enough. Tom Robinson did not sleep in the house because he was expected to go home and do his share in the work of keeping his bed-ridden grandfather comfortable and fairly clean, but he ate his midday meal in the kitchen with Madge. Henry ate in the hall, often impatiently. They were both boys doing the work of full grown men; John had the hearty appetite of a healthy growing boy, even old Madge enjoyed her food, so a visit from the fishwife was welcome.

'I hope I see you in good health,' Sybilla added. The old woman prided herself upon being so active at the age of—she guessed—well over seventy. However on this sultry September morning she did not respond as usual, saying that she was as hale and hearty as ever she was, due to a fish diet and life in the open: instead she said sadly, 'I don't know, my lady. I'm beginning to feel my years.'

'It may be the weather—so hot for the time of year.' She gave her order, and Madge came forward with a dish while Sybilla went upstairs to fetch the money.

All that year the weather had been so unseasonable that pessimistic people had talked about the world coming to an end; in early spring, when rain was needed not a drop had fallen for two months; April and May had been very wet, and in late June the hay had been cut and gathered between thunderstorms of great violence, some accompanied by hail. July and much of August had been cold and sunless, so that corn was still green when harvest should have begun. Then, halfway through August intensely hot weather had set in and continued. Everywhere the harvesting which should have been almost finished, was in full swing.

'If you'll pluck me some rosemary and a bit of thyme, my lady, I'll stuff the fresh fish. And if the plums are ready I could make a bag pudding. That should stick to their ribs,' Madge said.

Sybilla went into the garden, accompanied by Margaret whom Henry, backed by John, refused absolutely to have in the corn-field; 'She's more trouble than help,' he said. In the garden she was equally useless, didn't know rosemary from lavender, a rose from a marigold, went into one of her rigid fits at the sight of a wasp. She did not even, poor child, offer company, to be with her was to be virtually alone.

So many of the things which now flourished had come from Cressacre that it was impossible not to remember Lady Randall who had ceased all friendly overtures when Sybilla refused to allow John to be adopted. Walter haunted the garden, too—he had planted the roses. And Godfrey had died without ever knowing that she had her own garden.

Think quickly of other things! Attend to what you are doing!

She cut the rosemary, gathered the thyme and the plums; assured Margaret for the hundredth time that wasps were not dangerous. Margaret had never been stung so far as Sybilla knew, it was the sight of the insect that upset her. On the way back into the house she tested the lavender, it, like the corn, had ripened during these last sunny days and was ready to be gathered.

In the kitchen Madge had gutted the fresh herrings and begun to get together what she needed for the bag pudding—so-called because it was boiled in a cloth.

She was, she reflected, very fortunate in having Madge, so willing and co-operative. They exchanged smiles as Sybilla laid the herbs and the fruit on the table.

Outside again, cutting the lavender and noting that the roses which in June had never produced a proper flower, the sodden buds rotted before they could open, were now coming into full flower, she thought again about pot-pourri, as she had thought every summer since she wrote to Lady Randall that next year she hoped to make her own. This year? It was a pity she thought that sweet lavender, scented roses, bright, aromatic marigolds should—by way of pot-pourri—lead to sordid thoughts about money. But there it was, in order to make proper, long-lasting pot-pourri one needed not only things one could grow but others which must be bought, and were costly.

Despite the fact that Henry and Tom had managed unbelievably well, Knight's Acre was still, though self-supporting in most respects, very poor. Money, or so it seemed, lost value every day.

Once, realising how her Intake rents had become ludicrous, she had mentioned to James the desirability of raising them a little. He had listened with apparent sympathy and promised to consult again the document to which he had referred when she asked about deer-shooting. The answer was displeasing; the rents had been fixed, 'in perpetuity'. No such clause governed what he had inherited; he had raised the rent of all his free tenants, and inaugurated a vigorous campaign to encourage his serfs to buy themselves free. He said he was sorry, but there it was, 'in perpetuity' meant what it said. He did not offer financial aid to his brother's widow who, had she had a grain of sense would now have been comfortably installed at Cressacre. And the sight of Henry did nothing to endear the Knight's Acre family to the father of a boy whose weakness of mind and body seemed to increase with his age. Irrevocable as the gout. Gout encroached; one day, Sir James knew, it would reach his heart, and he would die, and leave Moyidan in his son's incapable hands.

We all have our own troubles!

On this unusually warm September day, having gathered the lavender, Sybilla went through to the kitchen where nothing had been done. The silvery herring lay there, gutted, but unstuffed; the plums, the suet, the flour, the cloth for the bag pudding, unrelated entities on the table and the fire almost out. Madge sat, her arms on the table, and her head on her arms.

Dead? Everyone must die, and like the woman who sold fish, Madge was old, but unsure of her age. Sybilla approached tentatively and gently touched Madge on the shoulder. Perhaps asleep.

Madge said, 'I feel ill all over.' She raised her head a little and then let it sag again.

The terrible thing was that with a woman so deaf one could

227

not expect an answer to a question—In what way do you feel ill? Nor apply a word of consolation—You will feel better soon. At Lamarsh bed rest was esteemed a palliative for most things, but to get Madge upstairs, without help, without Madge's co-operation, would be impossible. Sybilla touched her again and Madge responded by raising her head, but a gesture towards the upper floor, the offer of a supporting arm brought nothing but a moan and a violent shudder.

Fever? Yes. Oh, pray God, not the sweating sickness, so dangerously contagious, so often fatal.

Margaret stood staring and Sybilla thought—Oh, for a daughter who could help, could be trusted to fetch a blanket and a pillow! Margaret would go willingly enough but she would have forgotten the errand before it was completed. Sybilla herself brought a pillow and a blanket and lowered Madge to the floor.

The midday dinner hour was close at hand and the boys would be coming in hungry. Give them the bread and bacon which they would have had had the fish woman not called? But in this weather the fish, called fresh to distinguish it from the smoked kind, would stink by evening; it was always at least three days old by the time it reached Intake. So mend the fire, stuff and cook the herrings, and at the same time heat two bricks, one for Madge's feet, one for the small of her back.

When she heard them in the yard she called through the open door; 'Stay outside. Madge is ailing ...' She handed the food out to them, as though to beggars. Eating out of doors in such weather was no hardship and not knowing about the bag pudding they did not miss it, they ate the plums raw and hurried back to the field. Now, given time, she could think about febrifuges, marigold buds, lime leaves, marjoram—all steeped in hot water.

Madge, still hot to the touch but shivering still, was a good patient. She drank what she was given and halfway through the hot afternoon, said that she felt better. 'I'll get to my bed,' she said. 'Johnny is waiting for me. He promised to wait.' It was fever talk, Sybilla knew, but even delirium was a step forward from inertia, and Madge, clutching at the stair rail, at the wall on the other side, heaved herself towards her own bed.

228

And lay down, with a sigh almost of contentment. 'It'll all come right in the end,' she said.

Since no word of cheer or comfort could penetrate, Sybilla touched the hot dry hand, which turned under hers and clutched with sudden strength. Apparently the lime infusion was working, for when Madge spoke after a long silence, what she said was sensible. 'I'm being a sore bother to you, my lady.' Sybilla gave the hand some reassuring pats and presently the old woman seemed to fall asleep. Standing back from the bed, Sybilla thought—Not the way sufferers from the sweating sickness behaved; they tossed and raved wildly, sweated profusely and were insatiable in their demands for water. Just a touch of summer fever.

Downstairs, tidying the kitchen and making an onion and bacon dumpling for supper, Sybilla remembered that at Lamarsh the first thing patients were offered after any fever, was chicken broth, the liquid in which a fowl had been boiled so gently that the pot hardly bubbled. She'd get Tom to kill a fowl for her before he went home. But this evening he did not, as he usually did, come into the yard, hopeful for a handful of something to munch as he made his way across the common to the village.

'He went straight home,' Henry said in answer to her question.

'Oh dear, I wanted him to kill a chicken.'

'I can kill a chicken,' Henry said confidently. He then reflected for a moment and said, 'There's a knack to wringing a fowl's neck. I never learned it.... I think I'd better cut its head off. Which one, Mother?'

'It can wait till morning, darling,' she said and went up to administer another dose to Madge, should she be awake.

In such a short time, a change for the worse: Madge was breathing as though through some thick, gluey substance, each breath a battle. 'Please ... the priest. Dying...'

Supper must wait. Sybilla ran down, out by the front door and the long-shadowed evening.

'He ain't here, my lady,' Father Ambrose's housekeeper said, surliness thinly veneered by civility. The lady had been a great disappointment. While the big house was a-building the priest had confided to his housekeeper his hopes about the improvement which the arrival of a better kind of parishioner would bring. And a few flowers was all. Father Ambrose understood Sybilla's position, his housekeeper did not and attributed all the lady's failings to sheer bad management. She couldn't even rule her own household. Look what had happened to Bessie Wade! And that Walter, for whom the lady had stuck up so stoutly, running off like a thief in the night.

'Where is he?'

'He was sent for. Down in the village. Ah, they know where to come when there's trouble. Most times he ain't welcome. And horses' work to get them to church, 'cept Christmuss and Easter. Give they will not!' (And that goes for you, too!) 'And him so pious with the money the good lady left. Better a leak in my roof than in God's, he says. And his very bed swamped every . . .'

'*Where* in the village?'

'Martin's. Leastway it was one of them red-headed lot . . .'

She had lost her audience. Sybilla was running towards the common.

She saw the old priest shuffling towards her, carrying his little lidded basket. When she was near enough, she saw that he was crying, slow gummy tears oozing and dispersing themselves in the many furrows of his face. From the lid of his basket a fold of his stole protruded. He had been to one deathbed and now she must call him to another.

As soon as he saw and recognised her he stopped and held up one hand. 'Do not come close, my lady. I am straight from a death-bed. Plague!'

For all its familiarity a heart-stopping word.

'You are sure?'

With uncharacteristic testiness he said, 'Of course I am sure. I've lived through it twice—both kinds. And this is the worst. I asked you . . .'

'I'm safe enough. I also have lived through it, Father.'

It was so long ago, when she was so young, that she had no real memory of it; only of the nuns saying, jokingly, 'You'll die of old age; even the plague couldn't kill you.' And everyone knew that you couldn't have the plague twice.

Falling into step beside him she said, 'My old Madge is asking for you . . .'

'What ails her?'

'A sudden fever. And her breathing . . .'

'That is the worst.' He wiped his face on his sleeve and quickened his step a little. 'With the other kind . . . carefully nursed . . . once the buboes break, there is hope. But this is deadly.'

Attempting to fend off what she did not wish to believe, Sybilla said, 'But she was quite well this morning.'

'Robin Martin was scything his corn.' Thus reminded of the swiftness of this enemy, he broke into a shambling trot. But Madge was dead before they reached her bedside.

Father Ambrose shed a few more of the difficult tears of old age. Sybilla stood dry-eyed, the knot which tears might have melted, hard and painful in her throat. The dead woman, he said, in an attempt to comfort himself as well as Sybilla, had been a faithful Christian, a regular attendant at mass; only last Sunday . . . But in a way that made it all the greater pity that the last rites, the formal phrase that sped the Christian soul on its journey should have been denied her, while Robin Martin . . .

However such matters were best left to God. Man must deal with what he could deal with.

'In such times,' he said, 'burial is a problem. I know from the past. Anybody can dig a grave, it is the handling. A man needs to be very drunk . . .' That was the terrible thing about plague; only the most devoted family—or the most devout religious—would nurse the stricken, only reeling drunkards carry them to their graves.

'I am sorry,' Sybilla said, 'I have nothing . . .' The last of the Cressacre wine, the last of Walter's ale, had been drunk long ago.

'I can manage that,' Father Ambrose said firmly. 'I shall use the sacramental wine. It is but wine, until the moment of consecration.'

He hurried off to plant the red-painted wands at the village entry, a warning that this was an afflicted place.

Eating heartily of the dumpling, Henry said, 'I thought it was just an expression running about like a hen with its head off. But it did.'

'Halfway round the yard,' John said. 'Very comical.'

Margaret laughed because the boys laughed. The candle-light shone on their faces, young, lustrous-eyed, healthy-looking. The thought of the peril looming over them moved her to an unusual display of emotion; 'My darlings,' she said and embraced them all. Henry shrugged free and went into the yard, disapproving, she thought of being treated like a child.

When he had been gone long enough for any natural purpose she went to the kitchen door, ravaged by fear. Robin Martin was scything his corn! She was about to call when she heard him retching. He knelt, bowed over, supporting himself by the lower rail of the pig-pen. He said, 'Go away!' but she went and knelt beside him, her left hand supporting his forehead— no fever yet!—her right arm steadying his heaving body. Spasm after spasm. Could it start this way?

Finally it was over and he leant against her for a moment, exhausted, grateful for support. Then he braced himself, stood up, essayed a shaky joke. 'I bolted my supper and it wasn't hasty pudding!'

'How do you feel?'

'Empty. I shall be hungry in a minute.'

Inside the lighted kitchen she examined him covertly; slightly pale, slightly watery eyed. Not flushed. Could it be that beheading the fowl had been more of a strain than he would admit? John looked up from the simple game which he was—a concession now—playing with Margaret, boring because he invariably won, and asked, 'What happened to you?'

'I threw up, if you must know. Mother, I am hungry now.'

She made him a bowl of bread and milk, salted, not sweetened, the way he preferred. Immediately John was hungry, too, and Margaret. She made more bread and milk.

'Two suppers,' John said gloatingly. 'I wish you'd throw up every evening, Henry.'

In their extremely dull lives supper in the kitchen, after the excitement of seeing a cockerel, headless, run about the yard, and then an extra meal, made an occasion. They went noisily to bed and Sybilla did not hush them, as she should perhaps have done, with a dead woman in the house.

She kept a candle burning and hardly slept at all, prowling about as though vigilance could protect. She thought about Madge's burial. On his way out Father Ambrose had said that in time of plague there was no time for coffins; the dead must be buried quickly—'And after all, Our Lord had only a shroud.'

She had a blue dress, her best, once carefully kept for occasions, then even more carefully kept against Godfrey's return. Useless now. Madge, who had lived in homespun should go to her last bed wrapped in silk.

In the morning they were all still well and lively, thank God.

Two youngish men whom she did not recognise, not direct tenants, both happily drunk, took Madge away and laid her in the ground not beside Johnny, whoever he was, but by Robin Martin, a real sinner, reclaimed at the last.

With the corpse removed, Sybilla went through the house with the purifying shovel, heads of lavender smouldering on a few hot embers, scooped from the kitchen hearth. It was not a guaranteed guard but it was a ritual.

Father Ambrose said, 'Three days, my lady, and no fresh case. It is early for hope, this thing obeys no rules—except that it is always *carried*. In this case by the herring-seller, God rest her.'

'How do you know?'

'Because when I went out to plant the wands at the village boundary, she lay dead in the lane.'

Sybilla thought: I made them eat in the yard because Madge lay ill in the kitchen, but what they ate was fish the old woman had handled! That was too piercing a thought, so she said, 'She was old; she told me that morning that she was feeling her years. And if she carried it, why only to two households? She visited others.'

'It strikes where it will,' he said. The crisis appeared to have cleared his mind and concentrated it upon the present; now it clouded and slid back again. 'In the confusion, my lady, I have been forgetful. I forgot to ask you. Any news of

233

Sir Godfrey?'

'He died in Spain, Father.'

'I am very sorry. I will say a mass for his soul.'

On the fifth day—dare one hope now?—she was kneading bread dough in the kitchen when she heard sounds from the yard and ran out to see Henry and John awkwardly supporting and moving Tom. Henry had drawn Tom's left arm around his own neck and held it there with his left hand, while his right was as far about the bigger boy's waist as it would go. John had his shoulder under Tom's right elbow.

'He fell down,' Henry gasped. 'Heat stroke, I thought and we dragged him into the shade, but he got worse.'

She had a thought of which she was ashamed—Oh, *why* did he come to work this morning? Then she thought—Where? Not the kitchen in which we cook and eat, nor the hall through which we have to pass. The solar. She took John's place on Tom's right hand and said to the child, 'Take the cushions from the settle and put them in the solar.'

Tom, groaning and moaning, was hardly prone before Henry said, 'Come on, John. There's only us now.'

It was immediately evident that Tom Robinson would be less easily handled than poor Madge had been. He was younger and stronger and put up more fight against both the discomfort he was suffering, and any efforts to relieve it. He seemed lucid. He wanted no brews, he said, repudiating the lime infusion; he'd seen what brews could do.

Sybilla spoke sternly. 'Tom, if I am to nurse you, you *must* do what I tell you. Otherwise I shall send for your family to come and take you away.'

'They wouldn't come.' That might be true. He struggled weakly against the blanket that she snatched from her own bed, and against the hot brick. 'I'm roasted enough. I'm on the rack.'

'Just try to lie still. You will be better soon.'

He threw himself about and moaned. 'I'm in hell. Satan and all his imps. With red hot pitchforks.'

The three cushions from the settle slithered about. He needed a more solid mattress.

In accordance with custom she had hauled down and burned

234

the one on which Madge had died, with the pillows, the covers, and the old woman's scanty clothing. The one on the bed she had once shared with Godfrey and now shared with Margaret, was double size, so was the one in the boys' room. It must be Walter's . . .

Respecting his privacy, she had never entered it during his occupancy and since his death she had avoided it. Probably Madge, industrious and conscientious had gone in from time to time to wipe off the worst of the dust, or to air the room. It was with a definite effort of will that she now opened the door.

And it was not because the room was scattered with his belongings that he seemed still to be in possession. On the night of the fire he had lost everything except his bow, his arrows and the clothes he was wearing. The bow, unstrung, and the arrows stood propped in a corner. The few fresh clothes with which he had provided himself hung limp from a peg. She remembered Henry saying that he did not know that Walter had a *blue* tunic—perhaps he had been wearing it for the first time when . . . This was no time for such a thought . . .

There was nothing else in the room that said—Walter! For he had never tried to make this place his own as he had that other room. Yet he still seemed to be here, a just not visible or palpable presence.

She moved to the bed which Madge must have stripped and made tidy. Madge's mattress—too hastily disposed of, had been easily handled. Walter's, though not much larger, was not; it was a trifle thicker and stuffed with horsehair, resilient, bouncy. But she must get it down because—the thought flashed—if Tom's fever increased and affected his mind, and lent his body a spurious, brief strength, he could be dangerous; firmly tied down to this mattress . . . Where did that thought come from? Or the strength which suddenly enabled her to deal with the recalcitrant thing. Almost as though stronger hands had come to her aid, and, at the stairhead, a more resourceful mind. Let it slide . . . It slid, impelled by its own weight and bounciness to the turn in the stairs which Master Hobson had regretted, but which had been unavoidable, and then a mere push landed it into the hall, a few jerks took it into

235

the solar and Tom was installed.

In the kitchen, Margaret, unsupervised during this commotion, had pummelled the bread dough, dropped it on the floor, recovered it in pieces, slightly soiled. On the whole insensible to admonition or rebuke she seemed on this day to take Sybilla's mild, 'Oh dear!' seriously, and allowed her head to droop sideways. Contrition?

Maternal rebuke. 'Margaret, sit up and eat your dinner.'

'Margaret's neck hurts.'

John said, 'So do my legs . . .'

So the nightmare began.

The one glimmer of hope the old priest's words about good nursing; the one miracle that Henry, dearest of all, was not stricken. 'I think,' he said, 'that maybe being sick saved me.' And who could argue with that, the whole thing so mysterious, taking such varying forms. Tom Robinson in the solar raving about devils and poisonous brews and toads, which he abhorred, crawling over his bed; upstairs, Margaret wailing, tracking every pain, her head, her neck, her arms, legs, teeth all hurt. John did not complain or demand attention, but his torpor was frightening and he was the first to have the difficulty in breathing, once so much so that Sybilla resorted to an action which she had seen performed on a man who had fallen into the moat at Beauclaire and taken out, seemingly dead. She worked John's skinny little rib cage between her hands, press, release, press . . .

Henry said, 'It would be easier for you if they were all up *or* down. I doubt if I could manage Tom. The others I can.' He carried John down, and then the bed, fetched Margaret.

'Now we,' he said, 'can take turns at sleeping on the settle.'

'That I cannot allow, Henry. Not while you work as you do.'

For doggedly, single-handed, he was proceeding with his harvesting. 'I'm sorry, Mother, not to help you more, but somebody must get the corn in.'

He forbade her to cook. 'Bread and cheese will do for me.'

He was there, fortunately, when Tom, having suffered all the torments that the devil could inflict, refused to be strangled by him, and with fever strength threw himself about the

236

solar, howling, trying to dislodge the enemy by dashing him against the wall. Henry hit him, knocked him down and hauled him back on to the mattress. He rejected Sybilla's idea of tying Tom down to the bed. 'It would just make him more difficult to deal with. I'll tie his feet and his hands together.'

The timeless time went on. Father Ambrose called once to tell her that every household in the village was stricken; 'And those who are not are sitting about, waiting . . . Nobody works, my lady. I have often thought that for one the plague kills, fear kills four.' He was justified in this harsh judgment, for unlike Sybilla, he had never suffered the plague, he had merely lived through two outbreaks and now, with less certainty of immunity than she could claim, went fearlessly about, not only administering to the dying, but tending the sick. In a village which barely tolerated him. After that one visit to Knight's Acre he came no more. The sick there were in good hands.

She had, in reserve, a small quantity of a dark, viscid liquid, a specific for toothache. A few drops, slow-dripping as Father Ambrose's tears, ensured, even for a sufferer from toothache, release from pain and sleep.

In the short interval that Henry allowed himself from the field at midday—not to eat, one could eat bread and cheese anywhere, but to see that in the house things had not got beyond his mother's control—he saw her, measuring drops.

'It seems to ease Tom's delusions. It certainly eases Margaret's pains.'

'Couldn't they *all* have a dose? Tonight? So that you and I could sleep?'

There was no real reason why he should not sleep, but despite her determination to be in charge on the ground floor, resting her bones on the settle, Henry always seemed to know, to hear when Tom yelled, or Margaret said, 'Mother', or when she rose to make certain that in the night John was still breathing.

She said, 'I have so little of it. It must be kept for pain, or waking nightmares.'

'I see,' Henry said.

He went out, she thought to the field.

Momentarily relieved from delusions and from pain, Tom and Margaret seemed to sleep. Sybilla worked on John, again in difficulty with breathing; press, release, press again. He gave a cough and ejected some sticky, grey and yellow-streaked, bloody matter.

'I can breathe now,' John said, and turned on his side and slept.

Despite all her care the pest-house stench had crept about. It followed her into the kitchen and mingled unpleasantly with the sweet smell of baking bread.

She went to the kitchen door for a breath of fresh air and felt the unseasonal heat of the afternoon. She was so weary that she felt ill. She realised now the price that must be paid for independence and pride. In bigger households people fared better at such times; there would be someone not yet stricken, someone who shared Father Ambrose's immunity, somebody like herself who had survived. Isolated here she was fighting almost single-handed, against death, and at the same time doing ordinary, essential things like cooking, since Henry must be fed.

Lack of proper sleep, constant anxiety, had reduced her to something near self-pity; though she knew she had only herself to blame for her plight. And she must not stand here wasting time; she must go and hunt for eggs if Henry were to have the supper she planned for him.

Days were drawing in now, and Henry always left the field in order to milk the cow while the light lasted. This evening he was late—then very late. She remembered how Tom had fallen down in the stubble and had to be helped indoors. In panic she ran out, across the yard, through the space between the stable and the burned-out house and across the rough track which served as a side entrance. It was bounded on its further side by a bank, from the top of which she had a view of the field. Nothing moved in the dusky light. The stooks of cut corn, each made of four sheaves stood on end and leaning slightly towards one another, stood in even rows, like small tents. The cut stubble lay in even rows, alternating, like velvet stroked this way and that. The still uncut wheat stood straight

238

and tall, stretching away in this half-light, to an immeasurable distance. Henry could have fallen at its verge, his scythe beside him; or, feeling unwell, sat down against a stook . . .

The final blow! She moved to descend the bank on the field side; she must find Henry, bring him in; but her legs failed her, wilted like candles in an over-heated room and she fell, not into the field, but back, on to the track.

'Christ in Glory!' Henry said, 'I could have killed you . . . Are you hurt?' The grey horse stood puffing and blowing within inches of where she lay.

'No. Not hurt. I stumbled . . . Looking for you . . .' She took his outstretched hands and pulled herself up. 'No, not hurt,' she said, though pain stabbed at her hip. 'Where have you been?'

'Moyidan. For what we needed. It took so long because . . . Let's get in. I'll tell you all about it.' She tried not to hobble, thankful for his proffered arm.

The cow lowed plaintively.

'I'll just milk her,' Henry said. 'Could you take these? There'll be no need to cook for days . . .'

The grey horse was saddled with a sack, wore only a halter, but carried, slung over the sack, two well-stuffed bags.

'They've barricaded themselves in,' Henry said. 'With guards. I had to shout, who I was and what I wanted. And the barrier is at least a mile from the house . . . Two gates, about four yards apart and the space between filled in with brambles and branches. All this'—he indicated what he had brought— 'was handed out to me at the end of a long pole.' He laughed.

Emma had always been a good housekeeper and now for once she had been generous, mindful of the needs of the healthy as well as of the sick. She had sent a huge flask of the brown, poppy medicine, which was all Henry had asked her for, and another flask, labelled 'For cooling fever,' as well as a cheese, a brawn, a joint of spiced beef and a game pie. And a pomander ball, an orange stuck all over with cloves and dried as hard as iron.

239

'Now,' Henry said, eating voraciously, 'they can all have a dose. And we can sleep. I'll tell you another thing, too . . . Maybe at Moyidan they're harvesting, I couldn't get near enough to see. But down there . . .' he jerked his head towards the village, 'and all along the road I didn't see one single man at work.'

It confirmed something that Father Ambrose had said, 'At such times people simply sit about, waiting for death. I have often thought that for one killed by pestilence, four die of fear.'

'It looks to me,' Henry said, 'as though corn will be scarce and dear this winter. And we shall have some to sell.'

Perhaps Emma's medicine for cooling fever contained some powerful ingredient; or perhaps the plague, like other ailments mounted to a crisis and then receded. For whatever reason, gradually but surely all three invalids began to improve.

20

'You wish to be rid of me,' Tana said.

'I want you to be happy.'

'Without you?'

He said, miserably, 'My dear, wherever you are, it must be without me.'

He thought that parting would hurt them both, but his wound would cut deeper and be slower to heal because he was older and bore a burden of guilt, but that was the kind of thought which he could never put into words.

'And all behind my back,' she said. 'You trade me away like an old horse.'

No statement could have been more unjust. He had been most meticulous.

In the house of the Dominicans, to an English-speaking friar who remembered Father Andreas, painstakingly explaining and asking help; in the mansion of the rich merchant, a second generation Converso Moor with two lively daughters, one about Tana's age, one a year younger, and a mother who spoke Arabic. 'Absolutely to be trusted,' the friar had explained; 'he is a good Christian. Too rich to be interested in whatever wealth the young woman may have; and, like all Conversos, much in awe of the Church. If *we* commit her to his care, she will be safe.'

The idea of making some such arrangement had occurred to Sir Godfrey when, elated by news from home, slightly flown with wine, he had left *The Mermaid* and stepped back into the polyglot streets. He heard Arabic being spoken by unveiled women, caught glimpses of inner courtyards of Moorish-style houses, felt the warm sun of the autumn day. *If* Tana could be persuaded, *if* proper safeguards could be found, would she not be happier here than in England where he would be the only person who understood a word she said, and where he would have his family. So he had turned to the Dominicans and found just the aid he sought.

He was aware that he was not being honest, either with himself or anybody else; he had given Tana her due—the girl who had liberated him—but he had not said that she had been his mistress, and before that a member of the royal harem; he had not explained by what savage means she had gained the position of first favourite, or that her wealth was the result of robbery. He had allowed it to be assumed that she was a Moor. He had shied away from the truth which Tana now put into words—'You wish to be rid of me.'

He did so wish. He had in the past months foreseen a difficult situation, but only vaguely; now, with the news that Sybilla was still his legal wife, still at Knight's Acre, his mental sight cleared. If Tana would only understand and consent, his happiness would be unclouded—and yet . . .

Even as he blundered on, and saw on her face the expression of scorn which is so readily assumed, he was bound to admire her anew; for what other woman in the world would not have rounded on him, accused him of ingratitude, said, 'After all I have done for you . . .' She was too proud for that.

He had wanted to be near the shipping area, and on arrival in Seville had sought accommodation there, though inns in that district were not of the best. 'So long as there is a bed to lie upon, and some hot water so that I can wash my hair, I ask no more,' Tana had said. And she had not protested when he had indicated that two sleeping chambers were required. When asked for how long he made a helpless gesture, not understanding; but here foreigners were no rarity and whether they stayed one night or four the charge was the same. He had then gone straight out to look for an English ship and had found *The Mermaid,* conceived his idea and spent the afternoon in putting it into effect. Tana meanwhile had washed her hair, her first act after a gypsyish period; she had washed it in Santisteban after their sojourn in the mountains, she had washed it in Seville, after their long ride. And now, dead straight, black as night, shining and silky, it hung about her, as she listened, rejected, and accused.

The room which she had been assigned faced the river and had a little balcony, no great advantage now with the dockside so near: it was a soiled river which now, at its lowest, just before the winter rains, ran below the out-jutting stone ledge with its crumbling rail. In the time that it took him to explain that far from trading her away, he had made most careful arrangements, refuse from ships and from houses, including a broom and the grossly inflated body of a dead dog, drifted past.

Tana said, 'And this is what you wish?'

'What I think might be best.'

Swift and sudden as her action against the putative robbers, she flung herself over the rail and into the sullied water.

Swift and sudden as anything he had ever done in his life, he followed and the Great River engulfed them both.

In Andara he had taught himself to swim, ineptly, but well enough to keep himself afloat. The body, like the mind, had a memory. He snatched at the nearest thing which said, 'Tana,' a great hank of floating hair; he made some clumsy strokes, only his legs—booted and heavy, and one arm, operative, and by great good luck managed to snatch at a pole, solidly planted at the foot of some steps for the convenience of a boat delivering goods. He clutched at it, heaved himself and his dripping burden out of the sullied water and sprawled for a moment, physically and emotionally exhausted.

Tana said, 'So you do love me . . .'

With that she became content and amenable. Aboard *The Mermaid* she made no demands, no complaints. In fact with that last violent, would-be self-destructive gesture, she seemed to have turned in herself, to have become resigned. Sad, in a way, like a wild creature caged. But she now understood; this bucking rearing ship was part of England, where he belonged; its captain and most of its crew were from Bywater, where his brother was part of the Church which she hated and feared; the most discreet behaviour was called for.

Bywater, its roofs and trees just rimed by a light night frost, loomed up out of the sea. Presently, amidst all the shouting and manoeuvring needed to bring *The Mermaid* alongside the jetty, her captain found time to speak to his distinguished passenger. 'Here we are sir, and I can just imagine how you're feeling.'

Sir Godfrey had no idea of how he felt. People spoke, he thought, too lightly about the movements of their hearts, saying over trivial things that their hearts rose, or sank. His seemed to be doing both in such rapid succession that rise and fall were simultaneous. This was not the homecoming he had envisaged.

It was not the homecoming any of them had envisaged. Captain Fletcher had imagined himself at the *Welcome To Mariners*, the centre of awed attention, the man who had brought Sir Godfrey Tallboys back to England; the crew would also share this glory, see their families, present the gifts expected of returned sailors, make love to, or quarrel with their wives, get married, see a child for the first time.

The harbour master and the customs official—wines being dutiable—came aboard and one of them said, 'Well, you missed the plague!' The word spread as rapidly as the thing it stood for. It shattered all homecoming dreams.

Sir Godfrey had intended to go straight to the inn, hire two horses and ride to Intake. Now he must see William, because

243

William would know . . . Sybilla, alive and well in July. How now? He had one terrible thought—A judgment on me! He could not speak. He could only seize Tana by the wrist and charge up the slight rise which only in flat East Anglia would be called a hill, at the top of which the Bishop's residence stood.

She seemed to go reluctantly, dragging him back, she who had always gone ahead, so lithe and nimble. Suspicious, poor girl, because she did not understand. He forced himself to master his breath, his tongue. 'My brother . . .' he gasped, and pointed. 'Bad news!'

He should have been warned. William had no use for formality, he had always been accessible to anyone. Now the outer door was barred and Sir Godfrey, trembling with impatience had to tug the bell twice, three times before it opened, narrowly, cautiously.

'The Bishop . . . I must see him. I'm his brother.'

'His Grace is not yet in residence.'

But William had always been there. The good shepherd tending his flock. He ignored conferences and convocations . . . And now, through the narrow space of the guarded doorway Sir Godfrey could see William's hall, rich dark hangings on the walls, the glitter of silver on cupboard and table. All new: all prepared for another man.

William was dead! How many others?

'Go and fetch somebody who was here—before. Chaplain, groom, secretary. Move yourself, man.'

It was the recognisable voice of authority though used by a shabby fellow.

William had never maintained an adequate entourage, and dying suddenly, had left his affairs in a muddle, made worse by the fact that there had been other deaths, but one man seemed to have survived both the plague and the new Bishop's ruthless clean sweep; he had been retained because he had a good memory, knew where to find anything which was there to be found, and wrote a good clear hand. He was brought, blinking to the door. He stared, with disbelief and then with recognition.

'Sir Godfrey! Wh ... wh ...'

'Never mind that. Do you know anything—recent—about my wife?'

There had been weeks of complete confusion, of genuine grief for a good old master, of trepidation, wondering about his own job, of being asked to find this, refer to that, of trying to accommodate himself to the new and very different régime; but the good memory served. He produced the required information as a well-trained dog would offer a retrieved thing.

'Lady Tallboys and her children suffered from the plague, Sir Godfrey—but they all survived.'

He said, 'Thank God!' and broke into such a sweat as might have marked the end of a fever, or the onset of the sweating sickness.

'How do you know?'

'Lady Tallboys wrote a letter ... It arrived ... It was too late.'

Sybilla had written; pride, independence, joy in her own house all brought low by the common sense which informed her that to manage was impossible.

Doggedly, growing haggard and old, Henry had proceeded with cutting and carrying the corn. But who would thresh it? Tom Robinson had survived, but as a shaky, feeble wreck of himself. He tried, pathetically grateful for the nursing he had been given, but he fainted the first time he ventured into the field and Henry had shown a disquieting callousness. 'Let him potter about the yard, Mother. I have enough to do without swoons.'

Father Ambrose, so valiant, not only doing his duty by the dying and the dead but caring for the very old and the sick, had undertaken to tell her that nobody, nobody in Intake, could pay rent for at least a year; the village was ruined, most of the breadwinners dead or so weakened as to be useless.

'I have always tried,' he said mournfully, 'to use what the lady willed for God's use, for the purpose she intended. It is no longer possible. Rain may drip on the very altar. The living must be fed; the holdings restocked.'

Restocked? All that was left now of her poultry was a wary

old cock who seemed to have observed the fate that had over-taken his trusting fellows.

What added to her feeling of weak despair was her own lameness. Such a slight fall. She had limped about, tending the sick in the final hopeful stages of their illness, and then, when the voracious hunger of post-fever set in, cooking and cooking, ignoring the pain, thinking always that it must be better tomorrow. But it was not.

So she had capitulated and written to William, sending the letter by the first person who entered the village after Father Ambrose, counting days, had thought it safe to pluck out the wands. A pedlar.

Of the three refuges offered to her she had chosen Bywater because in William's house there was no woman except his bad-tempered, slovenly housekeeper who might by gradual stages be ousted; because William was kind and had power, could get John into the monks' school at Baildon, and poor Margaret, perhaps, into some kind of religious house; the only safe future for a half-wit.

She made her decision and despatched her letter without consulting Henry.

When she told him he was angry in the worst way; not hot and argumentative, as she had feared—and was prepared to deal with, but cold, polite, relentless.

'Yes,' he said. 'For you and the children, that might be best. But I shall stay here. In my own place.'

'Darling, that is impossible . . . One of my reasons . . . I can no longer stand by and watch you work yourself to death.'

He ignored that. 'What would you do with the house? The fields?'

'We might,' she said, careful to include him, 'find a buyer.'

'Now? With land going back to the waste wherever you look? And is it yours to sell?'

A little flurried, she said, 'Why yes. Yes, of course. Your father being dead . . .'

'I am my father's heir, Mother. If he had left an estate of more value, it would have been taken into custody, to be kept for me until I was of age. I should have been somebody's ward.'

Over a few of the words, estate, custody, ward, he hesitated slightly, unfamiliar words, learned by rote.

'If my father had left three hundred fields, that would have been the law.'

Walter! Walter, who knew a great deal about many things and a little about most, had implanted this unlikely piece of information, these strange words into Henry's mind as soon as Godfrey was deemed to be dead.

'Apart from which,' Henry said, 'the land is mine because I have toiled and sweated. I helped to *make* this farm. And nobody is going to take it away from me.'

'Darling, nobody wishes to. Henry, we must be sensible. It will be a year before Tom is useful—if he ever is ... You cannot manage what it once ... once took three of you to do. And when I spoke of selling I had no intention of defrauding you. I thought ... Some kind of business, in Bywater ...' Brooding over the letter, chewing the quill, she had realised that Henry was too old now for schooling, too old to be left idle. 'Timber,' she said diffidently, 'or wine.' Both very respectable trades.

'Or a well-fitted pedlar's pack!'

She was sharply reminded of the Abbess of Lamarsh, so skilled in the dealing of verbal wounds—and Henry's aunt, after all.

'It must be faced,' she said. 'I have tried to do the best for us all. It is not as though I can help much, now. So lame ... And I look at all the corn you have hauled in. Who'll thresh it, winnow it, sack it up?'

'I shall. It will take time, but time is on our side now. The later to market the better, this year. You go to Bywater, Mother, and rest and live like a lady. I stay here.' He gave a little snort of unmirthful laughter. 'Before you go, show Tom how to bake a loaf. It's about all he's good for now. But I can manage.'

She could just imagine how they would live. Who'd wash and mend for them, change bed linen, have a hot nourishing meal ready?

'You haven't really considered it.'

'I could consider till my beard grew down to my knees, and

247

still think the same.'

'Very well, since you are so set. I will write again. Try again.'

The old boyish grin brightened his face.

'That's more like my mother!' He lifted one of her work-roughened hands and kissed it. 'You shan't regret it. I don't intend to be poor all my life.'

'Yes, Lady Tallboys wrote,' the little clerk said. 'His Grace had expired on the previous day. I took it upon myself, since there was no one else to do so, to send her the sad news.'

'I see. Thank you.' Sir Godfrey had been fond of his brother, was sorry that he was dead, but at the moment the good news outweighed the bad and he had a practical thought. Whatever else William had spared upon, he had kept good horses.

The horses, willingly, even eagerly provided once the clerk's recognition had established his identity, were good, but Tana who on an inferior animal had ridden like the wind, now rode like an old market woman carrying eggs. Plainly she was un-willing to arrive.

'There is nothing to fear,' he said, forced for the tenth time to rein in and wait for her to catch up. 'If we hold to our bargain . . .' A bargain made on a rotting balcony overlooking the Guadalquivir, by two people emotionally exhausted, pre-pared to settle on almost any terms. She should stay with him, have his protection, his brotherly love, his companionship in an alien land; she was to forget, make no claim, do, say nothing that would cause Sybilla a moment's unease. The un-usual thing about this bargain was that the terms were on both sides, volunteered, not exacted. Neither of them was, at that moment in a reasonable state of mind. He was shaken by the latest proof of devotion—she would sooner drown than be parted from him; she so elated by the fact that he had not, in fact, wished to be rid of her—as he could so easily have been, simply by doing nothing, that they were both prepared to build, upon an illicit love, some plan for the future. A post that happened to be handy had saved them both from death; they were enjoying what was almost a sense of resurrection.

248

The brief winter day was just ending when they reached Intake. 'That is my house,' Sir Godfrey said. Knight's Acre presented to Tana the same bleak, unlighted face as it had turned to Sybilla. Sybilla had thought it large, Tana found it disappointingly small. She had never lived in an ordinary house; her father's strong mountain fortress, tents, or sometimes, on the extreme borders of his domain, grass-roofed huts; the quarry, and then the palace at Zagelah; after that sometimes no roof but the sky, and then inns.

Passing the turn-off to Moyidan, Sir Godfrey, without slackening pace had turned his head and said, 'That is where my other brother lives. Where I was born.' And the old castle, reared long ago by a man who, if he could have written his name would have spelt it Taillebois, just showed above the trees. Tana also understood, from the behaviour of everyone who understood English, the captain and crew of the ship, the people in the rich-seeming place at the top of the hill, that Godfrey, in his own country, was a kind of chieftain. So the plain stolid house that Master Hobson had built and his son-in-law had plastered and decorated did not strike her as impressive; a house unworthy of him; and too small to contain two women.

Lady Randall's rose trees, now well grown, still held a few frail leaves on their almost stripped branches. He was glad, momentarily that Sybilla had attained some kind of garden. He said, 'This way,' and took the track to the yard. It had changed somewhat during his absence, more outbuildings, Walter's house gone. But the well was there, and a woman was drawing water. She was bareheaded and the wind teased her white hair. With a slow, weary, old-woman's action, she unhooked the bucket and steadied it on the rim of the well with one hand while with the other she pushed back her hair with a gesture of careless impatience. She did not look towards them, the time when the sound of a hoof alerted her was long past. Any movement at the yard's entry meant that Henry and Tom and the grey horse were back from the field.

As she brushed back her hair he recognised her, but with an almost stunning incredibility. Old, bowed over, doing a serving-boy's job! His Sybilla.

249

He spoke her name. Then she looked, stared and gave a cry that could be heard down in the village. The bucket tilted and fell into the well as she ran towards him, arms outstretched. He had slipped from the saddle and run to meet her, lifting her, holding her, as in the old days, as in his dreams . . .

Tana, still mounted, unnoticed, sat and watched. The sun, just before plunging down behind the woods to the south of the river, sent one last gleam, cruelly revealing. The feminine eye, turned in assessment upon another woman, missed nothing, the white hair, the thin, slightly crooked body, the heavy clumped shoes that dangled from the edge of the shabby skirt, even the red coarse hands which clutched and clung.

With cold hostility, with hot jealousy, with hope, with fear, Tana watched that long embrace and listened to the broken, incoherent exchanges of endearment in a language she did not understand.

On the broken balcony in Seville he had said, 'Sybilla must never know.' But Sybilla would presently know, without a word being spoken. The children of love always resembled their fathers.

The embrace ended. Sybilla said, 'Darling, set me down. But hold me, still. I am so weak with joy.'

So with one arm around his wife, Sir Godfrey—the least likely man to be in such a situation and the least competent to deal with it—reached out his hand to his mistress. He said, in Arabic, 'Welcome to our home,' and in English, 'darling, this is Tana who set me free. But for her I should not be here.'

Somewhere along the journey Tana had discarded the rough sheepskin coat and acquired a hooded cloak of mulberry-coloured cloth. She had worn it throughout the voyage, huddling, he thought, against the cold. Now, without assistance from the offered hand she dismounted and at the same time loosed the loop at the neck of the garment, so that the hood fell back and the front gaped.

Another instant feminine assessment. Beautiful in a strange way, shining with youth, black hair as sleek as satin caught back in a pearl-studded net.

Of course! Of course!

Be sensible. No man could be expected to live like a monk for seven years. But more than sense was at work—the memory of the night when she herself had felt the brush of sheer, unthinking, physical passion. Walter, living, had always tried to make life easy for her, and now, rotting in his shallow, unhallowed grave, he made this easy.

She said, 'I thank you from my heart.'

'She knows no English.'

An embrace then.

The face she pressed to Tana's was damp, from the mingled tears of the joy, from the long kisses. Tana turned her face away. The old woman smelt like a peasant, of onions, of woodsmoke, of cooking.

Released, Tana stepped back, bowed, put her hand to the soil of an English farmyard and then to her forehead.

'A gesture of the utmost respect,' Sir Godfrey explained.

Sybilla matched it. She made to Godfrey's deliverer the deep curtsy due to one's social superiors. The injured hip screamed its protest, but she ignored it, and standing again, as straight as she would ever be, she said, 'My love, tell her how grateful I am, how welcome she is.'

The gleam faded; twilight flooded the yard as Sybilla thought—And the child—his child—shall be welcome, too.

Book Two

THE HOMECOMING

CHAPTER ONE

Sir Godfrey Tallboys and Sybilla, his wife, lay together in Knight's Acre's second-best bed. They had been separated for almost eight years.

The first dizzying ecstasy over, she felt, under her fingertips the ridged scars on his back, and said, 'Dearest, what did they do to you?'

He decided not to mention the dreaded *khurbash*, or the two floggings. Why permit the memory of past humiliation and pain to intrude upon this joy?

'For much of the time I carried slabs of marble on my back,' he said. It was true.

'And she — that girl — saved you from that?'

'Yes. She saved me from that.'

'I'm glad that I gave her the best bed,' Sybilla said.

She already knew — it had been said at the moment of meeting — that Godfrey owed his freedom to that girl, so beautiful in a dark, foreign way, but from exactly what conditions she had freed him Sybilla could not imagine in any great detail. There were no slaves in England. A few serfs, rapidly diminishing in number, but no slaves.

Now, with her man miraculously restored to her, the man to whom she had been, except for one incredible moment, strictly faithful, she saw in the eye of her mind, Godfrey being used like a pack-pony. The furrowed back was more eloquent than words.

Sir Godfrey wished that Tana had not been mentioned just then. He had put himself into a position with which his honest, single-minded nature was ill-equipped to deal. All through the years he had thought about Sybilla, loved Sybilla, made doomed, abortive attempts to escape and return to her, his first love. Yet, on a bleak mountainside between Moorish Zagela and Christian Spain, faced by imminent death by starvation, in company with the girl who had saved him, and loved him, he had experienced something new.

He was not innocent or unworldly; in fact until he went to

5

Spain on that ill-fated expedition, he had moved in the most sophisticated society. He knew that adultery was anything but rare; there were men who acknowledged their bastards without shame, but he had never suffered even the temptation to infidelity. This he regarded, not as virtue but as good fortune. He had married the woman he loved and loved the woman to whom he was married. Even at the height of his passion for Tana his singularly uncomplicated mind found it difficult to admit that a man could be in love with two women, and in two very differing ways. Now he was forced to face another contradiction. His homecoming would have been happier, had he come alone; and even to think thus was proof of the blackest ingratitude, since without Tana there would have been no homecoming at all.

In the next room, in the best bed which seemed to her anything but luxurious — she had spent some time in the royal harem of Zagela — Tana lay thinking long thoughts, backwards to the moment when she had fallen in love with Godfree, the scheming and the plotting that had led to their freedom; forwards to the time when she would come into her own. As she must, she must. She knew what was taking place on the other side of the wall and was not actively jealous because she had always lived in a polygamous society. In the tribe into which she had been born, a man had as many wives, or concubines as he could support and divided his favours between them. Certain courtesies were due to the first wife whose position was reinforced if she bore a son. That old woman, now in Godfree's bed, certainly scored there. One tall boy called Henry, the image of his father; another, younger, John, and yet another, Richard about whom Godfree had asked as soon as he had embraced the other boys and the girl, called Margaret whom Tana's keen eye had instantly assessed — very pretty, probably resembling her mother when young and definitely simpleminded.

She is his wife, Tana thought, and I saluted her with respect. She accepted me; and in accepting me, the child I shall bear. I flung open my cloak, and she saw.

I shall accept her, too. But she is old, and lame, and poor. Poor in fact past belief. A servant to servants . . .

It was true, when the miracle happened, and Godfrey came

home, Sybilla had been drawing water at the well in the yard. The last unkindly glimmer of the winter sunset had struck, revealing the three to one another with merciless clarity. Then they had all gone into the kitchen, where the only fire in the house was burning on this cold afternoon. There was a bare scrubbed table, exactly like those in cheap hostelries, plates and drinking vessels that did not match and a meal which though plentiful, was lacking in all refinement — boiled pork with beans, and bread. They drank water. Henry and John and an older youth called Tom came in from work in the fields, and they were all dressed much alike — as ploughmen; only a certain clarity of feature, a likeness to Godfree distinguished the sons of the house from the hireling.

There was a great deal of talk, largely incomprehensible to Tana. Once he had made his decision to bring her to England Sir Godfrey had begun to teach her English and she had learned quickly, anxious to please him, but confronted by six people all speaking English — and to her ear, very rapid English — she was unable to make out more than a few isolated words. Although it was an exciting occasion, a family reunion which animated everyone except the girl Margaret, Tana was not allowed to feel excluded. From time to time Godfree had turned towards her and spoken in Arabic. That pleased her because it excluded everybody else. Right here, in the very heart of his family, he and she had something that nobody else could share. Her shrewd, cunning mind took note of this and she decided that however quickly she learned to understand English, she would speak it as little as possible. While he spoke to her in Arabic she could command his full attention.

CHAPTER TWO

Not, outside his knightly business, the most observant of men, Godfrey Tallboys could not be blind to the circumstances in which he had found Sybilla. It grieved him to think that had things in Spain gone otherwise, he would have come home with money in his hand.

'Sweeting, it seems to be my fate — ever since I had a house to come back to — to come back to it a pauper. I went to that Welsh war to get money; to the Winchester Tournament for the prize; and then to Spain. And again I return penniless and find you in worse case than I ever imagined. What happened to Walter?'

'He died,' Sybilla said shortly, not wishing to say what had happened to Walter in any detail. 'But that was long ago. Until the plague struck I had a good serving maid. Her name was Madge. She died in the plague. And the village was so stricken that women are at plough.'

He had already enquired about his elder brother, Sir James at Moyidan and learned that the plague had not touched that place.

'James could have helped you. William would have . . .' William, the good Bishop of Bywater had succumbed to the plague.

Sybilla said, 'It was my fault. I annoyed them both. When . . . when it was understood that you were dead, my dearest, both William and James offered me and the children a home. I chose to stay here. Later I annoyed them again. Security — as they saw it — was offered from another source — and I refused that also.'

'Marriage?' Deep in the marble quarry, tending the palace garden in which the ladies of the royal harem walked in the cool of the day, scrambling and starving on the mountains, riding helter-skelter across Spain, he had often visualised Sybilla as re-married.

'Yes. But there is no need to consider that — except to remember him as kindly and honest and charming. He is dead now.' She no more wanted to think about Sir Simon than she did about Walter, so she added hastily, 'I think you should let James know that you are home. Darling, at the worst, in the most desperate hour when we here had no medicine and little food, Emma was generous. Very generous.'

'I will go tomorrow.'

'That would be well. But I think . . .' For a moment Sybilla reverted to what she had been before Sir Godfrey had rescued her — the pupil, the novice whom the cunning old Abbess of Lamarsh had been training to succeed her. 'I think some rather ordinary explanation of *her* presence would be desirable.'

'She saved me,' he said simply.

8

'That I know, and am truly grateful — as I have endeavoured to show. But ... Godfrey, so far as I can see she is neither wife nor widow and by summer will be a mother ...'

'God!' he said. 'God!'

So many things now fell into place. Tana's determination to drown herself rather than be left behind in Spain; her scrupulous observation of her promise to behave well — never once on the ship had she attempted to lure him; the buying of the cloak and the refusal to remove it — 'Godfree, it is so cold.' And how slowly she had run, once they were on English soil and he was hurrying towards the place where he expected William to be; how sedately she — such a wild rider — had ridden from Bywater to Intake. It all fitted.

'I hoped you need never know,' he said in a voice of the utmost misery. 'I cannot exonerate myself. I will try to explain...'

She put her hand, once soft and white, now coarsened and hardened, over his mouth. 'Love, there is no need. I understand. She had saved you. You were alone together. You did not know whether I was alive or dead — or remarried. There is no blame. I shall look upon her child as my own, the child of my middle years. My Benjamin.'

This magnanimous, this truly noble statement served only to emphasise his feeling of guilt. How could a man with such a wife ...? And although she had summed up the situation almost exactly so far as external things went, speaking indeed almost the very words he would have used had he attempted to explain, there was much that she did not know. That upsurge of joy, so overwhelming that he had thought — perhaps even said — that after this he was willing to die.

'But we must be practical,' Sybilla said, and he recognised, even in his misery, the manner of his oldest sister, the Abbess of Lamarsh. 'She is young. When — when this is over, she will need a husband. She must have a name, some status. In that language you speak together, that Spanish, what is the equivalent of *lady*?'

'I do not know. We were only a few days in Spain — I mean before the disaster — and we saw no ladies. After the Moors took me I was a slave, consorting with slaves. And it is not Spanish that we speak, it is Arabic.'

'And have *they* no ladies?'

9

Abruptly, disconcertingly, Sir Godfrey thought of Arcol, his wonderful but arbitrary warhorse — now happily siring foals in the pastures beside the Loja River. Of Arcol somebody in the stableyard at Zagela had used the Arabic word for noble — *serriff*.

Humbly he offered the word.

'It will do well,' Sybilla said. 'Not unlike our own word, Sheriff. Lady Serriff. Yes, that comes easily. Can you explain to her?'

CHAPTER THREE

Sybilla knelt in the cold church where years ago she had knelt and prayed for Godfrey's safe return, and then, believing him dead, prayed for his soul. Now, with tears of joy and gratitude pouring down her face she thanked God and the Blessed Virgin for bringing him back to her.

She wished she could have brought something, a thank-offering some white lilies and roses for the altar and the little niche in which Our Lady's image stood, its once bright colours fading and peeling from age and exposure to damp. Sir Godfrey's great-grandmother had built the little church and endowed it with what, in her day, had seemed an adequate income. But the value of money had changed since then, and though old Father Ambrose put the needs of God's house before his own and lived more meagrely than any peasant, he could not keep the church in repair.

He met Sybilla at the door and asked the inevitable question. 'Any news of Sir Godfrey, my lady?' He must have asked it a thousand times since Sir Godfrey, mounted on Arcol, had ridden away on a crisp autumn morning in the year 1452. At first she had replied, 'No, not yet, Father.' The old man had said, 'I will remember him in my prayers.' Then there had been one letter, written by somebody else, but signed by Sir Godfrey, and saying that the worst was now over. Informed of this, Father Ambrose said, 'I am glad, my lady. I will pray for his safe homecoming.' Then the blow fell. She was obliged to say. 'He died in Spain.' Father Ambrose made the right answer. 'I am sorry. I will say a Mass for his soul.' But his mind had never absorbed that piece of information. It could take in nothing new and he went on and on asking the question, making the same reply. Yet when the plague struck, Father Ambrose had understood, had behaved admirably, his mind stepping backwards to former outbreaks and knowing exactly what actions to dictate.

Now the lady said, 'Father, he is home. Home! He came home yesterday. Safe and well. Is it not wonderful? After all these years.'

The rooted, trained mind produced the right response. 'I am happy for you, my lady.' But the ability to grasp anything really new had deserted him. He recognised Sir Godfrey when he saw him, but any chance encounter with Sybilla alone would provoke the same anxious question.

On this winter morning Tana made her ritual obeisance to the brightening East. It was all that remained of the old Sun Worship which her remote ancestors had brought with them from Persia when Alexander's empire collapsed. Settled in North Africa her small tribe had held its own, having the best horses and the best swords, the strongest will to survive. The great wave of Arabic people which swept over the north of Africa and from there into Spain, into France, in the ninth century had affected her tribe in some ways, made them adopt the Arabic language, methods of weighing and measuring, but they had not become followers of Mahomet. They had lived too long without any rules to take kindly to those which Allah, through his Prophet, had laid down. No alcohol; no pig-meat; women relegated to the status of beasts of burden for the poor, segregated toys for the rich. Until the final disaster, the battle in which she had fought alongside her father and her brothers, Tana had lived a life of almost unlimited freedom; untrammelled by religious obligations apart from the ritual bow to the Sun, the begetter and the giver of all things. What moral content had ever been involved had been forgotten, centuries before she was born. There were rules of course, you never forgave an enemy, or betrayed a friend — a friend being one whose salt you had eaten. Tana had most scrupulously avoided Sybilla's salt, offered in the plain wooden bowl.

Sir Godfrey's welcome at his brother's manor of Moyidan was hearty and unfeigned. Sir James and the Lady Emma his wife, had always been fond of him — while thinking him a fool. A fool to have married a penniless orphan; that most of all. And then to allow her to spoil her great quarrelsome boys to such an extent that they were intolerable. Indeed, in their view, the only sensible thing he had ever done was to build a house of his own so that his unruly brood need never again trouble their relatives.

Dead, as they thought, they had mourned him; alive they welcomed him back with joy. A miracle, no less.

Sir James's winter gout, which differed in some ways from his summer gout, was in full spate, but he forgot the pain in his feet as he listened to Sir Godfrey's account of what had happened to him in the past eight years and four months. Not that the story was well told; Godfrey lacked the ability to describe, to tell a coherent story, just as he lacked the ability to manage monetary matters. But bit by bit, prompted by a question here and there, the gist of the story was told. And James and Emma intercepted now and then to show that they had not been completely neglectful of the woman left alone in a remote place. Godfrey must know that when he was deemed dead they had offered Sybilla and the children a home. So had poor William. That established, James and his wife exchanged a look, a marital signal. Better not mention that infatuated young man, Sir Simon Randle who had offered more than a home.

'Yes,' Sir Godfrey said, 'Sybilla said that you had been very kind and very generous.'

'Well,' Lady Emma said, 'due to most careful precautions, we were spared the plague. It was our duty to help the less fortunate.'

In this household money was very highly regarded and mention of it was never long absent from even dinner-table talk. It was painfully plain that Godfrey had returned as poor as he went away. Also it was more than eight years since he went away; his high reputation was forgotten, his skill possibly impaired; he would not be in such demand. Admittedly he carried his forty-four years well, the silver streaks in his fawn coloured hair were not unbecoming; there were new lines in his face; but hard physical labour had kept him slim and lithe and his blue eyes had retained their astonishingly candid look.

Over the meal Sir James pondered for some way in which he could help his impoverished young brother without dipping into his own purse; and presently said, 'After dinner, Godfrey, I will show you what I have done at Moyidan, to make the place more profitable. You could do the same at Intake.'

'And more easily,' Lady Emma said. 'So many of your tenants being dead.'

Gouty as he was, Sir James made shift to climb to the top of the old castle keep. He wrapped his head in a woollen shawl lest the cold wind should bring on another attack of gout in his eyes.

From the castle ramparts the whole of the manor of Moyidan and far more was visible; the road from Bywater, the course of the river. The castle had been built to overlook and to defend this vulnerable, flat hinterland.

'See any difference?' Sir James asked.

Where terrain was concerned Sir Godfrey had the trained soldier's eye.

'Changed completely.'

Changed indeed. Moyidan had once been a typical manor; three great fields divided into strips, of ploughland, divided from one another by unploughed banks called baulks; and one of the three lying fallow in turn. There had been a number of low humble houses, huddled together, and an open common with geese and goats, oxen.

There was still the huddle of houses, and the church, but everything else had changed.

'I enclosed,' James said. 'Turned everything I could into a sheep run. Fellows with inalienable rights I accommodated with the equivalent ...' He pointed with his puffy hand at a patchwork of small fields, hedged or bordered by bits of fencing, even by stones. 'They much prefer it. They say they fare better and certainly there are fewer quarrels about boundaries and about which day ploughing, or seeding or harvesting should start. So they are happy and so am I. With my sheep run. Look a little farther, Godfrey.' Sir Godfrey looked and saw a vast open space, reaching to the horizon, some sheep, a man and a dog.

'Land that it took thirty men to till,' Sir James said, pulling the shawl closer, 'turned over to sheep, needs only one.'

'And what happened to the others. The ones with no inalienable rights?'

'Some are employed here, either by me or by the small farmers. Some sought work elsewhere. A number of likely young men went to sea. Oh, and of course, there is always seasonal work. Shearing, for instance.'

'And the common land?'

'Ah! There again, a few had rights, and were compensated by an extra half acre on their holdings. But most, although they had enjoyed common rights for many years, had no legal claim. The common land became part of my sheep run. With wool rising steadily in price, this is the most profitable move I ever made.'

Sir Godfrey had no quarrel with that; a man had a right to do what he liked with his own.

'I thought I would show you,' Sir James said, turning away towards the worn stone stairs, 'because you could do the same. And far more easily. In a manner of speaking, Intake is already enclosed. It was never a manor.'

That was true. Intake — as its name implied — was land clawed from the forest by twelve men, malcontent serfs, of whom Sir Godfrey's great-grandfather had been happy to be rid. He'd given them permission to take what land they could, the right to call themselves free, five years rent free and after that a rent which yearly became more absurd. This unusual village had been left by Sir Godfrey's father to his youngest son who had thought himself lucky to have anything at all. The rent, fixed, 'in perpetuity', was now all but worthless; but the land had enabled him to build his house on a space once cleared, then deserted as a result of an earlier plague. And Walter, the most wonderful, most faithful servant — and the most resourceful, had got one field under cultivation by the time Sir Godfrey left for Spain. Now there were three, looked after by Henry, Tom Robinson and John.

A natural transference of thought. Following James down the stairs Sir Godfrey said,

'I was sorry to hear about Walter. Often while I was ... away, I sought comfort in the thought that Walter had charge of things.'

Typical, typical, Sir James thought. Never an eye for the real issue. Here am I trying to tell him how to make a little money in this difficult world and he talks about that rogue! This feeling lent a certain sourness to his voice as he said, reaching, thank God, the last stairs,

'It was disgraceful. Mark you, no more than could have been expected. I never liked him. Nor did Emma.'

Deaf?

'I spoke of Walter, James.'

'So did I. Whom else? Running off like that. No notice given. Leaving Sybilla stranded, after the way she had favoured and spoiled him!'

'But he died. Sybilla said so.'

'She may have had information. Since. At the time we were given to understand that he had simply walked away. No matter, come to the fire. It is a bitter wind.' In the warm room, over the mulled wine — Emma was a good provider — Sir James spread out the parchment, the original deed of gift that concerned Intake.

'Twelve men,' he said, 'all named. Hodge, Martin, Robin, Wade, Fisher, Smith, Archer, Alan, Edmund, Egbert, Eldred, Alfred. This grant to them, and to heirs of their body, in perpetuity. How many, Godfrey, do you think can claim to be direct heirs?'

'How could I know, James? It is different for you, you have always lived here, on your manor. I have never lived at Intake, in the real sense. Granted I was there for a while before I went to Spain, but lame as a three-legged donkey. Then I was exercising Arcol, getting my armour into trim. I do not even know their faces; far less their rights.'

'That is what I am advising. How many direct heirs? I take it that the priests have kept a Kin Book, to prevent incest.'

'I suppose so,' Sir Godfrey said vaguely.

'Then it should be easy. And remember, daughters and illegitimate sons have no rights.'

Sybilla, explaining why she had no servants, had mentioned that since the plague women had been at plough. How many of them, Sir Godfrey wondered, working on land to which they had no right?

He made a remark which was characteristically unworldly — and in view of what Sir James had just told him, extremely tactless.

'I should be loth to turn anybody out. They might be homesick. I know I was when I first left Moyidan, and in captivity I was homesick all the time.'

Useless to argue, Sir James knew. Godfrey could be stubborn as rock. He said briskly,

'Time enough to think about *that* when we know where we stand. At least it would be interesting to know how many of these,' he tapped the parchment, 'have direct heirs still alive.'

Godfrey would pursue the enquiry half-heartedly, or make a muddle of it, or be put off with lies.

'I'll lend you my man, Jocelyn. He managed the change here. But the common is unquestionably yours — there is here no mention of common land or rights to it. I'll start you off with a nucleus to your flock. A young ram and six ewes. And a boy who understands sheep.'

'That is most generous, James. And now, I need help in another matter. Could Moyidan provide us with a cook woman and a serving boy? Sybilla is doing it all. And now we have a guest.'

Emma who had entered the room during the conversation, said, 'A guest?' Her tone expressed astonishment and disapproval. How could that poor house possibly entertain anybody? But how like Sybilla and Godfrey to attempt it!

'Yes.' Explaining things never came easily to Sir Godfrey, and now he was aware of trying out Tana's new identity for the first time. 'It is a Spanish lady. She is a widow. I told you I was helped to escape. She is the one. I had to bring her with me, because, in helping me, she put herself at risk.' He hoped that sounded convincing. He need not have bothered. The eyes exchanged another signal.

'Of what age?' Lady Emma asked.

'Oh. Young. Sixteen or so.'

'And a widow?'

'She was married young.'

Into both minds the thought shafted — A possible bride for Richard!

For the last two years they had been searching and without success. Curiously enough, the fathers of marriageable daughters found themselves able to overlook Moyidan Richard's poor physique and mental backwardness. They looked to the wide acres, the wealth to which the boy would be heir. Mothers were the difficulty. One had even gone so far as to say that she did not wish to be grandmother to a pack of idiots!

A Spanish woman, without relatives, and probably herself knowing English imperfectly and unlikely to notice that Richard, when he spoke, sounded simple, and when silent, looked witless, might be the answer to some really heart-felt prayers.

Tentatively they put forward the suggestion and Sir Godfrey found himself unaccountably in violent opposition, although from the moment when he knew that Tana had organised not only his escape, but her own, he had planned a suitable marriage for her — to some man who would not marry her simply for all that wealth that she carried.

In his heart he knew very well that Tana was fully able to look after herself; but he also knew that Emma and James should not be rebuffed too sharply, because they had been kind.

He said, 'At the moment she is pregnant. Better leave it for a while.'

'I can find you servants,' Lady Emma said. There might in some places — where the proper precautions had not been taken — be a shortage of labour. Moyidan, untouched by the plague, but touched very much by the enclosure had labour to spare. Some families, during the upheaval, had split up, others had clung together, the man with the inalienable rights supporting, however unwillingly, dependent relatives . . .

CHAPTER FOUR

Sybilla was glad of the servants. Freed from kitchen duty she could rest the lame leg which had bothered her ever since her fall, during the plague time; she could give Margaret a little more attention; more attention, too, to her own hair and hands. But the fact remained that Knight's Acre was now supporting five more people than it had done in the immediate past; all mouths to be fed; Godfrey, Tana, Jill and Eddy, the servants sent from Moyidan, and Young Shep who had come with the seven sheep.

She was not, by nature, mercenary, but she was practical.

Knight's Acre, thanks to Henry who had shouldered the burden of it, had just survived, just managed to be self-supporting. Now it was over-loaded.

'I must look about,' Sir Godfrey said. 'I may have lost skill. I have no destrier, no armour, but in some minor tourney, if Astallon can fit me out, I might win something. In the old days even the smallest prize he offered was a silver gilt cup.'

It sounded terrible, even to think that a man, so lately home after so long an absence, must be off again. But Sybilla knew that Lord Astallon's tourneys at Beauclaire were relatively mild affairs and that Alyson, Lady Astallon, Godfrey's sister, would give him a hearty welcome.

'There is also,' he said, 'the matter of Tana's jewels.'

'That pearl-studded hair net?'

'Oh, no. She brought away with her a king's ransom, in rubies, emeralds, diamonds and pearls. Nowhere, except in London,' he said, 'would such things find a market. And Alyson would know how to go about it.'

'That is very true.'

CHAPTER FIVE

'I abandoned tournaments,' Lord Astallon said. 'In this quarrel between Lancaster and York, I have tried to remain neutral. But what we live in now is not peace. A truce, frail as egg-shell. Take Bowdegrave, at Abhurst. He held his usual tourney and some silly girl flung a rose — a red rose — to the knight she favoured. He put it in his helm and the civil war broke out again, there, with servants sent to strip the garden of flowers and the tourney ground becoming a battlefield.'

'If many feel as you do, the outlook for me is gloomy,' Sir Godfrey said.

'From what I hear, genuine warfare is likely to break out again at any minute.'

'Of that I have had a bellyful.'

So far, a disappointing visit. He had hoped to see Richard, his second son. Sybilla had told him how Henry and Richard had quarrelled and actually fought so often and so fiercely that it was impossible for one house to contain them; and how Henry had refused so absolutely to be sent to Beauclaire to become a page, squire and eventually a knight, that Richard had gone instead. Sir Godfrey had not spent much time with his children even in the days before he went to Spain, but he was attached to them all, and actually had a sneaking feeling of sympathy for Richard who had never accepted his place as second son.

Lady Astallon, Sir Godfrey's beautiful sister, Alyson, explained in her remote, languid way why Richard was no longer at Beauclaire.

'He was so clever, Godfrey. Within a week he had learned all a page should know. Then he learned to read and write and cypher. He acquired Latin from our chaplain and French from one of my ladies. The Bishop of Winchester came here and was much impressed. He begged to be allowed to take Richard away with him.'

'To become a clerk!' The natural scorn of the man of action for the scribe rang loud and clear.

'It offered the more promising future,' Lord Astallon said.

Well, one son lost to the plough-handle; and one to the pen. And no tournaments. I have come back to a strange world.

There was, however, one area in which his visit to Beauclaire might yet be satisfactory. He produced the jewels with which Tana had entrusted him; only a fraction of her loot from the palace of Zagela; one string of pearls, and a necklace, five sizeable rubies suspended from a golden chain.

'The Spanish lady, Lady Serriff — I told you, she saved me — asked me to dispose of these for her. I thought perhaps you could tell me how to set about it.'

His beautiful sister — in youth all white and gold, and still, growing old, beautiful, white and gold — snatched at the pearls.

'Humphrey, I want them.'

'Then they are yours,' her husband said. He had always been a rich man, well able to indulge his beautiful wife's whims, and the abandonment of the tournaments had saved him considerable sums of money. 'What is the price, Godfrey?'

'That I do not know. I hoped that you . . .'

Typical! A fool, likeable — they were both glad to see him back, safe and sound, but a fool. Offering for sale something that even Lord Astallon could see was practically priceless, and without any idea of its value.

'There is a man I have had dealings with,' Lady Astallon said, and for a moment Sir Godfrey saw the resemblance between his elder, plain sister, Abbess of Lamarsh and his younger, pretty one, mistress of Beauclaire. 'I will send for him. He shall value both,' she glanced from the necklet which she did not covet, to the pearls which she did — and were almost hers already.

The man for whom Lady Astallon sent first thing next morning, was a Jew, and strictly speaking no Jew had set foot on English soil since Edward the First had banished them all, bowing to popular opinion. But a few, here and there, practising Christians so far as anyone could see, and with names subtly changed by the addition, or omission of a letter or two, had come back and established themselves, and flourished.

The Jew came and within minutes understood the situation. Lady Astallon, always a good customer, wanted him to put a low value on the pearls, which she proposed to buy, and to make a good offer for the rubies.

The pearls, one experienced glance told him, were exceptionally fine — dredged up from eastern seas by men who dived and dived until their lungs burst. They were well-matched, and unlike many that came upon the market, not sick from having been locked away in darkness. He could see no actual flaw which would account for a low estimate: his subtle, supple mind could, however, produce a reason.

'My lady, they are superb. But were they offered to me, I should hesitate a little. Few people could afford such a rope, yet to divide them would be a shame, they are so perfectly matched.'

'Too good to be readily marketable,' said the lady who in the ordinary way appeared to drift through life in a dream. 'What of the rubies?'

He cupped the necklet in his hand, estimating the weight; held each stone to the light, revelling in the deep, rich colour.

'Of these the same might be said, but here division is possible, perhaps even desirable. With five, each detracts from the other. Re-set they would be marketable.' Any one of them would make a hat ornament, a pendant, a splendid thumb-ring. He wondered idly how such things had come into the lady's possession; the gold work of the necklet had not been wrought west of Damascus.

Over the price they haggled a little, but amicably. Then Lady Astallon said, with seeming aimlessness.

'These belong to a lady of my acquaintance, recently widowed and suddenly poor. She has others . . .'

The Jew understood that, too. The others, in due time would be offered to him, if he made a good offer now.

Sir Godfrey was astonished and delighted by the sum thus raised, and, ingenuous man that he was, allowed astonishment and delight to be seen.

'You have done well, Alyson! Tana — Lady Serriff — will be pleased.' The name slipped out because part of his mind was recalling that night in the mountains when Tana had tumbled what she called 'loot' out on to a flat-topped rock, and the last rays of light shone on the jewels, while over them she bent with three ropes of pearls falling from her neck into the valley be-tween her firm young breasts. He had felt then, with relief, that she would be well provided for. How well he had no notion.

Lord Astallon was also pleased. He was not — and actually never had been — in love with his wife in the ordinary, earthy way. She had never seemed quite real to him, though she had, amazingly, given him an heir and a daughter. His devotion to her had an almost mystical quality and when he gave her things he was not unlike a peasant making an offering at the foot of Mary's image.

In all other departments of his life he was a hard-headed man and in thinking over his brother-in-law's predicament, had arrived at what he considered a possible solution.

Over the wine-cups Godfrey had spoken, in his unen-lightening way, all halts and diversions and gaps, of what had happened to him during his long absence. And of what had happened to those who had gone with him to Escalona in Spain and then to Zagela in Moorish territory.

One name stood out. Lord Robert Barbury, son of the Earl of Thorsdale, said to be the richest lord in England.

'I think,' Lord Astallon said, 'that you should go to York-shire, and inform Lord Thorsdale.'

'Impossible. The truth was so horrible. It haunts me still. Even to you, who never saw Lord Robert, I could not give the full story. After all, Humphrey, I am seasoned, but I never saw a death like that.'

'I am not proposing that you should carry a harrowing tale. In fact the contrary. You said yourself that once in Spain, supposedly for a tournament, you — and those with you — became involved with what was virtually a *crusade*. Would that not comfort his parents?'

And would not Lord Thorsdale *do* something for the man who brought such news? An obviously poor man who had gone out of his way to bring comfort. Some kind of appointment.

It was well within Lord Astallon's power to have offered a place in *his* household to his brother-in-law, but that would have involved bringing in Sybilla who managed her children so badly. The fact that Sybilla was to blame for their misbehaviour was proved — was it not? — by the way Richard had conducted himself, once removed from her influence.

Blind, as usual, to all material advantage, Sir Godfrey said, 'I suppose it might comfort all the bereaved. It *was* a crusade, in a way. And they took part — except Sir Ralph Overton. He refused. I gave him a letter for Sybilla. She never received it, so I am afraid . . . Strange,' he said, 'some names I do not even remember. Sir Stephen Flowerdew, the best of company; Sir Thomas Drury, with his great dog . . .'

It was all long ago and far away. His great horse, Arcol, had saved him from death, and Tana had, in the end saved him from slavery. The clearest memory that had stayed with him, even through his own afflictions, was the way in which Lord Robert had died. Roasted within his red-hot armour.

With seeming irrelevance he said, 'I did my utmost,' and looked down at his hands. Thanks to the Moorish way of treating burns, they had healed well, were flexible and in no way unsightly; but they lacked the padding on palm and inside the fingers that they had once had; taut skin over hard bone.

'I should not propose,' Lord Astallon said, 'a visit to all. You would ride for a year — even could you recall names and where the men came from. But I do think that Thorsdale should be informed.'

'I will think about it. But first I must go home and take all this money to Lady Serriff.'

CHAPTER SIX

'And now,' Tana said, 'can I have my own pavilion? A place of my own?'

In her father's great mountain fortress each wife had had her own apartments, her own courtyard, her own servants. When her father went out on a peaceable errand, collecting his dues from the oases that studded the Spice Road from the East, the Gold Road from the South, he took women with him; and each had her pavilion. In places where fuel was scarce food might be cooked on a communal fire fed by camel thorn, but always there was privacy.

And here at Knight's Acre there was none.

With the arrival of two servants, the family had moved into the hall. The old, white-haired, lop-sided first wife no longer cooked or served food as she had done at first, but she spent some time in the kitchen overlooking things there; when she sat in the hall she was always busy with some kind of needlework. With smiles and gestures she invited Tana to join in this despicable pastime, slaves' work! Tana refused to learn. The weather was horrible, cold and dull, day after day; the hall was chilly and uncomfortable, only one settle and some backless stools; nothing of colour or brightness anywhere. And with Godfree gone nobody to talk to. The lanky boy called Henry stared and stared; and sometimes addressed the girl whom he had regarded from the first moment as the most beautiful creature he had ever seen. He told her the names of things — some of which she already knew. 'Fog' however was new to her, both in name and actuality; and detestable it was.

All through Sir Godfrey's absence Tana cheered herself with the thought of her own pavilion, silk-lined, carpet spread, furnished with many cushioned divans upon which one could sit or recline, warmed by braziers upon whose glowing charcoal sweet-smelling substances had been scattered.

Answering her question Sir Godfrey said, 'Yes. You can now build or buy yourself a house.'

His mind made a comment — how strange that two women as different as women could be, had used the same phrase. 'A place of my own'. Sybilla had said it in English — and Knight's Acre was the result; Tana said it in Arabic, and he visualised for her the establishment which he had once, in the days of innocence, planned for her; a snug, comfortable house in Baildon; near enough for him to keep a brotherly eye on her, see that she wasn't cheated or seized upon by some mercenary fellow attracted solely by her wealth.

'I want a pavilion, Godfree.'

'It wouldn't do here, Tana.' He knew what he was talking about; in his time he had lived under canvas and more than once plodded through mud to his bed, or wakened to find his bed almost afloat. And he had seen splendid pavilions, erected to accommodate knights at magnificent tourneys, flattened, uprooted, tattered by wind. 'The English climate,' he said, 'is not suitable for temporary structures. You must have a *house*.'

'About that you know best,' she agreed. 'But I want it here. With you, Godfree.'

That had always been her plea — or rather her demand. And it was her right. She had by resolute will and exploitation of her physical charm, reached a position in the royal harem of Zagela from which she could organise his release from the marble quarry at Andara, that nightmare place, and into the relatively mild enslavement of the palace garden at Zagela; and from there, at imminent risk of her life, she had organised his escape and her own. On one shoulder he bore the debt of gratitude, on the other the burden of guilt. Shuffle both off and think in practical terms.

'It could be arranged,' he said. 'There is ample room. I will see to it.'

He explained to Sybilla — to whom no explanation was actually necessary. Tana was here, she was going to bear a child, naturally she desired what every woman desired — her own place. But when Godfrey said that so far as he could see the best place for Tana's house would be the site on which Walter's little place had stood, Sybilla said, 'Oh no!' in a voice so sharp and positive that he was astounded.

'Why not? It was burnt, I know. But not to the ground. I had a look, the foundations are still there, sound and good . . .'

Yes, and go digging under that bit of charred, tumbled wall, and you will — or the builders will, come across Walter's bones! She remembered all too well, that hasty interment, by lantern light. Walter, the best servant anybody ever had, shot dead by Henry with the weapon that Walter had made for him, and taught him to use. By mistake, a very natural mistake. The servant, so good and faithful, had wished to become lover. And she had screamed . . .

No need to mention Walter now, Sybilla thought. Walter had his memorial, because in his moment of madness he had taught her something, something which had enabled her to understand the relationship between Godfrey and Tana. Only a moment, but it sufficed.

'It is not a good place,' she said. 'In fact it is a charnel house. I told you about the raiders . . . They set the place on fire. A few came out and danced in the yard, but most stayed within, roasting a pig, and were themselves roasted, when the roof fell in . . . Darling, let us not disturb the dead. Let us think of the living. That Tana should wish for a place of her own is under-standable, but not *there*. Could we not build out on the other side of the yard? Beyond the still-room? Truth to tell I have never used it, having so little to preserve and so little time.'

Sir Godfrey, in planning his house, drawing lines with a stick in the dust under the old oak, had been ambitious, want-ing the best for Sybilla who had so long waited for a place of her own. He had ordered a solar — a room which a lady could retire from the hurly-burly of the hall, and a still-room where she could deal with stuff too delicate for kitchens. He had, in fact grossly overestimated.

'She could, in fact have the still-room for her kitchen. It has a hearth, and shelves.'

He thought, rather sadly, that Sybilla's willingness to sacrifice her still-room reflected upon their hopeless financial position. Short of a miracle, he would never now be able to afford all the costly things that went into still-rooms. Still, he was determined to go on trying to find some kind of knightly employment, however modest; something that would bring in a little money so that the family was not entirely dependent upon Henry's farm. Surely every great lord in England had not adapted Astallon's and Bowdegrave's attitude towards tour-naments. Perhaps in the North, further from the storm-centre of London, there were still cups to be won, and hastily sold for cash, as every trophy he had ever won had been.

He would set Master Hobson to work on Tana's apartments,

and then ride for Yorkshire, keeping a sharp ear and a sharp eye open as he went.

Nine years earlier, when Master Hobson undertook the building of Knight's Acre, he had ridden a poor looking horse lest any of his clients should suspect him of being unduly prosperous; now he had no choice in the matter for substantial jobs were rare. There had been a time when men whose businesses had prospered were moving out of towns like Baildon and building houses — often more grand than Knight's Acre — in the countryside. Unsettled times had changed all that; in times of danger people tended to huddle together and ever since the first battle in the civil war Master Hobson's work had consisted mainly of patching, or extending old houses within the town walls. And plain work at that, for he had never managed to replace his disagreeable but gifted son-in-law who had done such beautiful pargetting — and at Knight's Acre died in the doing. Young men these days didn't take to a trade that demanded such skill, such long training.

Master Hobson still said 'Ah', as a sign that he understood, and 'Aaah' long-drawn out to give him time to think before answering a question. He understood what was wanted. Two additional rooms, both on the ground floor; one of fair size, one smaller, with a communicating door between them. There were to be no windows looking out on to the yard; only one in each room giving upon the garden. The larder room was to have a door from the garden, too.

The foreign lady for whom these rooms were to be built stood by Sir Godfrey as he explained things, and somehow Master Hobson got the idea that although she never said a word of English, she understood it. When Sir Godfrey explained that the still-room of the main house was to be the kitchen of the extension, Master Hobson said, 'Aaah. Then that'll mean knocking a door in that wall.' He was thinking of serving food.

Instantly the lady broke into her outlandish talk and Sir Godfrey answered her in the same. She did not wish for a communicating door. The still-room already had a door which gave access to the yard.

'Aaah. But Sir Godfrey, sir, that'll mean every bit of food'll have to be carried right round, if you see what I mean; out of

26

what'll be the kitchen, into the yard, round the house and in at the door facing the garden. Inconvenient to say the least.'

But that was what Tana intended. Her privacy was going to be very private indeed. No servants spying and gossiping.

'That is how Lady Serriff wishes it to be,' Sir Godfrey said, when he and the lady had had another consultation.

Now, as to cost?'

'Aaah. Let's say a hundred and fifty pounds, give or take a bit.'

'God's eyeballs,' Sir Godfrey said, shocked. 'You built *my* house for a hundred! Two rooms, no stairs . . .'

'Sir, things have changed. Excuse me — you've been away a long time. You might think that with so many men idle — through no fault of their own — labour'd be plentiful and cheap. Sir, that ain't so. The Guilds closed in. Even apprentices. Meat once a day, and river fish, even salmon, they don't count as meat. Aaah, and there's another thing to remember, if I may remind you, sir. In *your* house there was that oak, the trunk as king-pin, the two main lower branches as beams. I took that into consideration. Here we start from the bare ground.'

'And when could you start?'

'Aaah. Next week, if the weather holds.'

It held, in fact an exceptionally early and clement spring.

CHAPTER SEVEN

Lies had never come easily to him and faced with Lord Robert's parents, both elderly — Robert being their much youngest son, Godfrey, to his own dismay, found himself breaking down and telling the truth, the appalling truth about how Lord Robert had died in that narrow, balconied street.

He did not realise that the mere telling, in all the horrible detail, too horrible to be explained even at Beauclaire, he found relief, the kind of purging that came from confession and absolution. He told the simple truth — linked to the comforting statement about the crusade.

'It was a crusade,' he said. 'We were fighting the Infidel. And

27

of us all there was not a man more gallant, cheerful, noble than Lord Robert. At the first setting out I had ill-feeling — that summer at Winchester he had unhorsed me, the first knight to do so for many years. I did not care to be reminded. But long before we reached Spain. I knew his worth. I loved him as a son ... What was thrown, I shall never know. A terrible weapon, ten times as fierce as the fiercest fire. And his armour was new-fangled. I did my utmost, to no avail ... Afterwards I knelt there and committed his soul, so far as I could, to the mercy of God.'

(Deep in that marble quarry he had also done his best to commit another good Englishman's soul to God. But he did not think of John Hawkes now.)

He said what everyone would wish to hear of the dead.

'He died very bravely, and in a good cause. And his suffering was short.'

Lady Thorsdale said, 'He is an honest man. Can nothing be done for him? When he spoke of Robert he looked at his hands. I looked, too. And they *had* been burnt.'

'I could, of course, give him money. But there is his pride to be considered. When Robert unhorsed him, all those years ago, at Winchester, Sir Godfrey was the premier knight in England.'

They were able to speak of Lord Robert quite calmly because their grief was old; they were now long accustomed to thinking of Robert as dead. And they were both old, too. Lady Thorsdale had borne Robert at the unlikely age of forty-four and had he lived he would now have been nearing thirty. In all but one thing — a firm and dedicated devotion to the Yorkist cause — they had almost finished with this world. Lord Thorsdale, even older than his wife, was indeed becoming forgetful; but always, at his elbow was his chaplain and man-of-affairs.

To that shrewd and lively-minded young man Lord Thorsdale presently said, 'I wish to do something for this good knight. He has a house and some small portion of land in ...' he tapped the side of his head to set his memory to work, 'in Suffolk. Do I own anything there?'

The chaplain and man-of-affairs, a young man who had climbed up the ladder which education offered, and was at heart almost a revolutionary, almost at one with Wat Tyler,

John Ball and Jack Cade — but with this difference; he was a churchman and knew that any attack on entrenched authority meant an attack on the Church, the most entrenched authority of all, thought — How *wrong* that one man should own so much that he cannot even keep count of it!

His answer gave no sound of grievance.

'There is Bywater, my lord. There the river runs, one bank in Suffolk, the other in Essex. And the jetty. Yes,' he shuffled papers. 'That is on the Suffolk side. If I may remind your lordship . . .'

Quite an ordinary story. The coal-carrying ships, called cobs, labouring down from the mouth of the Humber to the mouth of the Thames, sometimes needed a half-way stop, somewhere to shelter, somewhere to take on supplies, somewhere, now that coal was more and more in demand, to unload. The cobs had not been welcomed at Bywater's busy established jetty, so Lord Thorsdale's father had built his own. The coal-cobs had priority at its moorings, but in slack times other ships used it, paying a small fee to Lord Thorsdale's overseer. There had been a succession of men in this post, and not all were honest.

Bit by bit subsidiary interests had added, a small repair dock, some storage sheds, strings of pack-ponies, a few wagons; and naturally houses for all those directly employed upon Thorsdale business. One quite sizeable house had for years been occupied by couples, or widows of good reputation who paid no rent but earned their house room by taking in and caring for men who worked on the cobs and had sustained injuries or fallen sick.

This small, self-contained world was a mere fragment of the Thorsdale estate and its present owner had never set eyes on it. But it offered an opportunity now.

'I wish,' Lord Thorsdale said — and apart from the difficult area of political activity, his wish had been law ever since he could speak — 'to appoint Sir Godfrey my agent there. How much, do you think, I should offer as salary:'

A chance here for a young, able and ambitious man to strike a blow! Keeping accounts, Lord Thorsdale's man of affairs had not failed to see that of late those who worked with their hands were out-racing those who used their heads. Masons, carpenters, smiths all had their Guilds, sitting in solemn conclave and saying what wages should be. Outside the Guilds was a vast reservoir of hand-power, head-power, but it could never be channelled unless the Guild opened the ever-narrowing gate. The men like himself, who could read, write and reckon, had no Guild, except the Church, where, in fact, preferment meant far more than merit. A topsy-turvy world.

'I would suggest, my lord, a hundred and fifty pounds a year. If he is as honest as he seems, he will save you far more.'

And on the horizon, no bigger than the cloud, the size of man's hand which had brought such abundant rain, was the thought — When the time comes, I shall be able to say, in all honesty, If Sir Godfrey Tallboys was worth a hundred and fifty pounds a year, what am I worth?

Astounded by his good fortune, riding home to tell Sybilla, Sir Godfrey nevertheless, turned aside. In that horrible place, the marble quarry at Andara, he and the man called John Hawke — the man who had warned him to beware of the whip — had finally come together and talked as much as possible, in fits and snatches. The Moorish guards had distrusted talk and discouraged it by the free use of the whippy canes, but Sir Godfrey had learned that John Hawke had been born at a place called Tadcaster where his father was a saddler — a man with a heavy hand. A hand so heavy, in fact that it had driven the boy to run away and go to sea — and be captured by the Barbary pirates, sold as a slave, and die, as the result of the prevalent cough, deep, deep inside that quarry.

So Sir Godfrey turned aside, wishful to bring as much comfort to John Hawke's parents, as he had to Lord Robert's.

And that was a wasted errand. John Hawke's parents were hardly remembered and the saddler's business had changed hands three times.

So, home to Knight's Acre; to tell Sybilla the good news that he now had an appointment. To see that Master Hobson was going ahead with the building which Tana insisted upon calling her pavilion and to take up his new duty as Lord Thorsdale's agent.

CHAPTER EIGHT

At the foot of the stairs Sybilla called, 'Margaret! Margaret! Supper.'

Until very lately Margaret's whereabouts had always been easily ascertainable; at twelve years old she was as dependent, as clinging as a child of three. Quite useless; in the worst days of her single-handedness, Sybilla had never been able to rely upon her daughter to set a table, wash a dish, sweep a floor; but not troublesome, except over the matter of eating. Margaret still had to be encouraged to eat, urged to get on, not to keep everybody waiting. She had always been very pretty in an ethereal way, and seemed to grow prettier as she grew older. In fact she closely resembled her beautiful aunt, Lady Astallon, but who would marry her, Sybilla often wondered, as the years brought physical maturity and no flowering of intelligence. A pretty simpleton with a dowry might just be acceptable, a penniless half-wit had no future outside a convent and even in convents some kind of endowment, if only the ability to work, was desirable.

'She was in the yard when we came in,' Henry said. And that was some while ago, for since the order of their lives had been changed, the boys no longer simply washed their hands before coming to table — a rule upon which Sybilla had always insisted — but put on their better clothes. Henry infatuated by Tana, willingly made this small extra effort, wishing to appear well in the eyes of their guest. John saw no purpose in the performance but was now accustomed to doing whatever Henry did. So here they were, clean, neatly clad and hungry.

Tana sat in the place assigned her from the first; the warm place on the bench nearest the fire. Eddy, the serving boy from Moyidan, brought in the pigeon-pie which Jill — also from Moyidan — had cooked.

Sybilla said, 'Henry, you serve. Look after Lady Serriff. I shall not be long.'

At the back of her mind a thought, not yet firm enough to be suspicion, had formed. Margaret, with no capacity for doing anything herself, found entertainment in watching the activities of others, and ever since the foundations of Tana's house were being dug, had spent much time simply staring. She had been known to eat — quite willingly, a portion of one man's noon piece, a very hard piece of bread, some cheese and a raw onion. The man had probably attributed her wistful stare to hunger.

On that occasion Sybilla said, 'You must not allow my daugher to be a nuisance to you.' The man had replied, good-naturedly, 'She don't bother me none, my lady. I got little girls of my own.'

The workmen ate lightly at mid-day — not wasting the precious daylight hours — but well at night, and Margaret must have drifted away with them to the 'lodge' which they had built for themselves, making use of the biggest bit of wall left standing of Walter's little house, some struts and some well-tarred canvas. Margaret would be sharing their supper. They'd feed her, much as they would a stray dog, and then go away and say that up at Knight's Acre Lady Tallboys' little girl didn't get enough to eat — a statement borne out by the child's appearance.

Hurrying towards the makeshift shelter Sybilla reflected that exhortation and explanation were wasted upon Margaret; she could not understand. She recognised a scolding tone of voice, and scolded, would cry, but the tears were as meaningless as all else about her.

The men had made a bright fire, above which salt herrings were suspended.

Margaret was not there. Nor was the man — a carpenter — who had little girls of his own! The gravest suspicion now, and alarm; but both controlled, subject to common-sense and swift thinking. First to explain this visit, an unprecedented thing.

'I had a message for the carpenter — the one with red hair.'

'That'd be Joe, my lady, just stepped outside for a minute.'

'Ask him to have a word with me before he starts work in the morning.'

'I will that, my lady.'

Outside in the moonlit yard again. She had no doubt in her mind now that the idiot — but recently nubile — girl and the man who could occasionally make her laugh, were together somewhere, and up to no good, though Margaret must be held blameless. Where?

Behind the house Layer Wood stretched away. But the night

was cold. The man, at least, would have had sense enough to seek a sheltered place. The stable, with its store of hay on a kind of low platform which Walter had built to keep the hay from the muck of the stable floor.

Sybilla saw and heard simultaneously; moonlight streaming in from the opened door showed her just what she feared; and there was hard-breathing, small whimpers — of pleasure, not fright — the hay rustling.

Now, not at all controlled, impelled by red fury, Sybilla sprang. She had the strength of ten. With her left hand she seized the man by the hair and pulled, with her right, clenched into a fist, small but hard, she struck him again and again, on the nose, the mouth, the eyes. And at the same time she noticed that although his clothes were in disarray Margaret's were not — yet. At least, not below the waist.

Self-possession returned. To the man, caught in the most vulnerable situation, surprised, guilty, afraid, Sybilla said fiercely, 'One word of this and I'll see you hanged!' She then reached down and jerked Margaret to her feet. Abusive terms came to mind, slut, hussy, bitch, but to utter them was a waste of breathe. Think in practical terms. The girl's bodice was open, there was probably hay in her hair.

Go in through the kitchen and there would be Jill, and Eddy and Tom Robinson and Young Shep, all eyes. All country-born too; knowing the word for it — a roll in the hay. God be thanked the front door opened very near the foot of the stairs; Tana and the boys would be intent upon their supper, and the only candles would be on the table, the rest of the hall in gloom. So they went in by that door. Margaret was whimpering in another way now; the pleasure cut short, the hard hand on her arm pulling and jerking.

John did spare a glance, a second's interest. 'So you found her, Mother.'

'She'd lost her way,' Sybilla said, hustling Margaret up the stairs.

No *real* harm done, the brief distasteful examination proved. But what of the future? You couldn't keep a girl locked up, or under constant surveillance. You couldn't make this girl understand. A convent seemed to be the only answer, and there was now some hope of finding the necessary dowry.

Sir James had wasted no time. Jocelyn, his man of affairs had been sent to make strict investigations, comparing the original deed of grant with the Kin Book. A state of affairs very promising for Sir Godfrey had been revealed; of the twelve men who had made Intake, only five had founded families whose descent could be clearly traced. Holdings had been divided, and sub-divided; illegitimate sons had inherited, so had daughters; widows had assumed rights — and sometimes remarried. Out of an intricate maze, Joycelyn emerged triumphant; only five men could claim those inalienable rights; all the rest must pay a reasonable rent or be evicted. And even the five whom the ancient document protected could claim no rights to the common land of which there was no mention on the parchment.

'Oh, yes, my lady, I assure you, it is perfectly legal. It is indeed the letter of the law. The common land is Sir Godfrey's property, absolutely. In fact, had anyone been so rash as to build on it — as fortunately is not the case — any such building could be destroyed.'

'Well done,' Sir James said. 'Now the thing to do is to get it fenced, no matter how roughly, before my brother returns. He is prone to sentiment ... Order Young Shep to begin fencing immediately; he has nothing else to do at the moment.' And out of the increased rents Godfrey could buy more sheep, get a proper flock which under Young Shep's care would flourish.

The villagers watched, impotent and resentful. This was a blow even to those who — with inalienable rights — had felt superior to those without. It was *their* common; their forefathers had made it. They were not grateful to Sybilla who, acting for Godfrey and knowing his mind, ordered that a path should be left on the edge of what was to be the sheep run — a means of access between the village and the church. Why be grateful for what they regarded as something of their own? Why be glad that the young man from Moyidan, sparing of his labour, left rather more than a path, left indeed enough of the common to accommodate a few geese, some goats, a donkey or two? A seething grudge towards Knight's Acre took the place of indifference; a grudge that was nourished, revived, reinforced every time any Intake man looked out and saw what had been the common, and was now known as Grabber's Green.

CHAPTER NINE

Sir Godfrey came home, this time jubilant. He had obtained a post involving responsibility and authority, and he had, for the first time in his life, a settled income of a hundred and fifty pounds a year. Not great wealth by some standards, but riches by his and comfortable by any.

He was so happy that Sybilla forebore to tell him the truth about Margaret, contenting herself by saying that she thought the time had come for the girl's future to be considered and that given the promise of five pounds a year, the convent at Lamarsh would probably take her — not as a novice, since Margaret could never understand what was required of her — but as a permanent guest.

He made one small protest. 'You were not happy there, Sweeting.'

'Only because the Abbess, your sister, was always trying to force the veil upon me. Before she conceived the idea of making me her successor I was very happy. And later I greatly envied the guests, with their pretty clothes and little pet dogs. At Lamarsh she would have company — here she has none. Also to be considered, is the future, Godfrey. Nobody will marry her, and you and I shall not live for ever.'

Sybilla was, in truth, tired of keeping guard over a girl who, once sexually aroused and feeble-minded, was a problem, demanding constant vigilance.

'I will see to it,' Sir Godfrey said. 'I must ride down to Bywater and see that all is in order there. That is my first duty. After that, Lamarsh.'

Something intervened, however. Tana wanted divans, and he was at first a little uncertain as to what they were. He had never been in a well-furnished Eastern household. Escalona, his destination when he left England for the tournament that had turned out to be a crusade, had been Spanish-furnished with ordinary tables and chairs. Of the Moorish customs of Zagela he had seen nothing; cast into slavery, seated on the floor, bedded on straw pallets. But as Tana explained, faint and far away the memory rang. In that vital interview when he, the

35

last surviving knight, the last outpost of Christendom had refused the easy way, Selim, King of Zagela had sat upon a kind
of bed, eight inches from the floor, many-cushioned.

Yes, he knew what a divan was.

'A sort of bed, sir,' the old carpenter-turned-cabinet-maker
said. 'A truckle bed?' He had made many in his time, beds with
no head-pieces, no foot-piece, capable of being pushed under
an ordinary bed and brought out only when guests overflowed
the available accommodation, or a child was ill and needed
attention by night.

'Not exactly,' Sir Godfrey said; he had occupied many a
truckle bed in his time. 'Wider, softer . . .'

Whether the thing, when finished, held a mattress stuffed
with horsehair, with wool or with feathers was no concern of
the man who made the frame, so that could be disregarded.
How long, how wide, how high on its legs? The more Sir Godfrey tried to explain the more the old man thought — but that
is what I said in the first place, a truckle bed!

A vast quantity of silk was needed too. Far more than the
one mercer who also stocked woollen stuff and linen, had in
store. The average woman, lucky enough to have a successful
father or husband, looked to have one silk gown and make it
last a lifetime. What silk was to be had was in modest colouring, black, blue, buff, grey. Scarlet and crimson, purple and
ochre could be ordered, of course, from London where young
popinjays went for their clothes. Sir Godfrey ordered. He happened to mention that the silk was needed to cover walls and
the mercer thought that either his ears were failing him, or Sir
Godfrey had come home, after a long absence, not quite right
in the head. Still it was a good order.

On the whole Sir Godfrey's shopping expeditions went well.
He was able to buy, for Sybilla a length of silk in a soft, pretty
colour, not unlike a dove's neck feathers, and it delighted him
to be able to pay for it.

Bywater was under control; Tana's pavilion well under way;
Intake, little knowing the threat that had hung over it for a
while had settled down to the loss of half its common; and now
he could give his full attention to Margaret, his only daughter.

About her he had observed — unobservant as he was in general — something that Sybilla, thank God, had not observed. At least, it was more a matter of feeling than of sight. Young as the girl was, slight as she was, and stupid as she was, she was ripe, perhaps even over-ripe for marriage. Man-hungry. He knew by the way she flung herself into his arms greeting him, after the briefest absence with kisses and clutchings which eight, nine years ago, he would have welcomed as proofs of affection. Then they had not been forthcoming, in fact Margaret had hardly recognised his existence until lately and now her recognition of him was not as a father, but as a man.

He rode to Lamarsh willingly. And there was rebuffed. The first battle in the Civil War, followed the peace which Lord Astallon had called a truce, frail as egg-shell, had had repercussions on convents — reputable places, like Lamarsh. Widows, young women whose putative husbands were dead, crowded its walls.

'I could,' Sir Godfrey said, desperately, 'manage even twenty pounds a year.'

The calm-faced woman who had succeeded his sister as Abbess here, said, sweetly, 'I am sorry, Sir Godfrey. Money cannot buy space — unless in such quantity as to allow us to build. We are overcrowded now, and a long list of names waiting. I hesitate,' she said, 'to suggest Clevely; it is a decayed house. But five pounds a year might mean much there.'

So he rode on to Clevely. A decayed house indeed. A place so tumbled down, inhabited by a few old nuns, deaf, blind, toothless, that the idea of consigning Margaret to it was unthinkable. In fact as soon as the place was in full view — it stood the width of two fields from the road — he would have turned and ridden away, but one of the nuns came screeching out, gabbling about a pig. She was under the misapprehension that he had come to buy a pig. Times were so hard, she explained, and flour an absolute necessity, so they must sell the pig. It was young, and this was the wrong time of year, but it was a good little pig, and if allowed to live until autumn, would be double its present size. She spoke loudly, being stone deaf, and at the sound of her voice speaking to somebody, other old women came out; visitors were an event in this forgotten place; even the good old Bishop seemed to desert them. Two of the old nuns made a pathetic sight, one very lame supported by

another whose eyes were opaque with the sightlessness of extreme age. In the hope that somebody here had the use of her
ears, Sir Godfrey explained that he had not come to buy the
pig. He was prepared to say that he had lost his way and was
asking direction. However, as soon as he spoke of not buying
the pig, the blind woman said,

'Holy Mother of God! Then we shall starve!' She began to
cry, and seeing her tears the others began to shed theirs.
Fumbling in his pouch, and gratified to be able to do so, Sir
Godfrey brought out three nobles and handed them to the deaf
woman who happened to be nearest.

'Three,' she exclaimed, passing from misery to jubilation. 'I
did not expect . . . It is a lot for one pig.'

The lame woman said, very loudly indeed, 'the gentleman
does not want the pig, Dame Martha.'

Unhearing or unheeding she said, 'When will you send for
it?'

The blind nun said, 'It is a gift from God. An answer to
prayer.'

Addressing those who could hear, Sir Godfrey said, 'Buy
flour; and eat the pig yourselves.' They had, as well as old age
in common, the wan, frail look of long under-feeding.

He bowed for the benefit of those who could see, replaced
his hat and re-mounted. Blessings followed him as he rode
away.

CHAPTER TEN

Sybilla stitched diligently, now on the beautiful silk that was
her own, and now on the crimson velvet which Godfrey had
managed to procure in Bywater for Tana.

The problem of Margaret she had set aside for a while.
Tana's apartments, needing no stairs and granted no pargetting, were almost ready; the workmen would go away, vigilance could be relaxed, presently. As to the far future, a convent
the only answer, it could wait a little. There were other religious houses. One — though a terrible scandal was attached to
it, at Bury St Edmunds. But that could wait; the clothes could

not; and the clothes presented a very delicate problem.

Tana's measurements — until about June — were predictable; the gradual enlargement allowed for by a complicated system of tucks and gussets.

What of my own? Have I come to the second great watershed of a woman's life or am I pregnant? Has that remark, about Tana's child being my Benjamin, rebounded upon me? Shall I in this silk, the colour of a dove's neck, make deep seams and tucks to allow for letting out as the year ages? Shall I ripen with the harvest and bear another child in September? Not so old yet; pushed, in fact into premature age by uncertainty, worry, bereavement by predicaments which few women had faced; Henry's refusal to conform; the raid which Walter had managed so well; Walter's death; the plague, and the long, grinding process of being poor, of having no time ... not to think of the fall, on that terrible day which had inflicted a hurt which had left her lame for ever. A rest *then* could well have been effective, but she had had no time. Alone with three plague victims to be tended, how could I rest a mere lame leg. Give my hair, my hands attention?

Now, stitching away here, I am I; but also she, that lonely woman, bent on survival and little more. Now, blessed as few women could have been, the husband restored to her, a mind sufficiently expanded to accept Tana, and the faint, but day-by-day growing hope that the disturbance of regular cycle might mean not an end but a beginning. Presently she was sure, and hoped for a daughter, one with her wits about her; a girl to whom could be passed on all the things which Sybilla had acquired; the arts of reading and writing, fine needlework and embroidery, still-room work, and even — since nobody knew what life might bring, the down to earth household skills, baking bread, making butter and cheese, preserving meat.

Spring came to this cold northern country. The dark woods became speckled with green, Henry, at the far end of the farthest field saw a bank all starred over with primroses and gathered a few; fair-minded — loyal to his old love though infatuated by his new one — he laid a small posy by Sybilla's plate as well as Tana's. Pale, frail, insipid, Tana thought them; just like the sun which occasionally gleamed from behind the greyness, only to retire again, but which made everybody say,

'Oh, what a wonderful day!' She now understood English very well, but concealed her knowledge because the Arabic which only she and Godfree could understand was the one thing that was their own.

Now and again, on his way to and from Bywater as the days lengthened, Sir Godfrey turned off and went to Moyidan. It was curious — and he recognised the fact — that of the thing he had been trained to, reared for, become expert at, he had never for a moment been proud. The fighting man that was Sir Godfrey Tallboys, Godfrey Tallboys took for granted. Of his suddenly acquired and quite unforeseen ability as agent and administrator, he was proud. He had enjoyed telling James and Emma about his appointment; they were suitably impressed. He enjoyed taking them little presents, things had fallen into his hand by virtue of his new office. Bribes he would not accept, and one or two ship's captains who had thought that a timely gift might gain priority at the coal jetty had suffered crushing rebuffs. On the other hand a man who was *there*, unbribable and incorruptible, but with money in his hand, often hit upon a bargain, and it delighted him to be able to give things to Emma and James who had given him and his family hospitality in the past.

That year Sir James enjoyed no intermission between his two gouty seasons and although he often declared that next week he must surely be better and able to ride to Knight's Acre to meet Lady Serriff, he had not in fact been able to do so. He and Emma had not, however, abandoned their intention to make a match of this — if a match could be made. Emma had never ridden except as a pillion passenger, and she felt that to make the errand alone, either behind Sir Godfrey, or a servant, would show that she was losing hope for James. So they dallied and privately thought Godfrey was unhelpful in not offering to bring the girl to them.

'Many women,' Lady Emma said to her husband, 'take journeys while in her condition and no harm done. I do not wish to sound suspicious of Godfrey, but he said the girl was sixteen, which is just Henry's age.'

'That is true.' Sir James brooded and then gave orders that his lightest wagon should be fitted with a padded seat at the back. 'I will make this last effort, for the boy's sake. Once the girl has shed her load ... And Henry is big and strong ...'

Godfrey proved obstructive again.

'The lady will be in no condition to receive you. Sybilla reckons that she will be having her baby towards the end of June.'

'Midsummer Day is not the end of June,' Emma said firmly. 'And first babies are invariably late. We shall make our visit as arranged. On Midsummer Day.'

He felt sorry for them. Moyidan Richard could only appeal to a poor woman, past her prime. And all other considerations apart had Tana intended to marry would she have built and furnished her pavilion? When he left after that visit Lady Emma came with him, beyond the outer door and said quietly, 'I fear it is the last visit James will ever make. When gout reaches the eyes there is little hope.'

Sir Godfrey repeated this to Sybilla when she exclaimed, 'Of all the ill-chosen times!'

Henry said, 'Must John and I come in that day? *What* a waste of time! Washing and changing clothes in the middle of a hay-making day!'

The arrangement was irksome to him because it was part of a general feeling of having been reduced to second place. Ever since Walter's death Henry had been the man of the house; the prop; the stay; the provider. When the plague struck he had not sickened but stood by his mother's side, staunch tough weary — and had worked the farm, too. Then Father had come back, taken his rightful place as head of the household, and soon, without soiling his hands or shedding a drop of sweat, was bringing home money which made Henry's income, so hard earned, seem pitiable. In addition to this there was jealousy — not consciously sexual because to Henry his father seemed old. What Henry envied was his father's ability to talk to the beautiful lady, and to make her laugh. Once Henry had conceived the idea of learning this strange, clicking language himself, but his father had discouraged that, saying that the best thing Henry could do was to speak in English, very slowly and distinctly, so that Tana might learn. This Henry had conscientiously attempted, to the point of sounding as though he himself were learning English. 'It — is — a — sunny — day.' The beautiful eyes looked at him blankly.

Knight's Acre, in fact no longer revolved about Henry and this asking for guests to dinner on a hay-making day was proof of the change.

On the bright sunny day of the visit it was plain that Sir James was pitiable indeed. His feet were so swollen that he could not wear even slippers, but had his feet tied, like puddings, in velvet bags, and he wore, not only a hat but a black scarf over his eyes to shield them from the sun. The driver of the wagon, helped and admonished by Lady Emma, hauled him out on to the ground.

'Is Richard here? Where is Richard? We will enter together,' Sir James said. Richard had learned to ride, and mounted on a meek horse, looked well. He arrived while his father was asking about him.

'He is here,' Emma said.

'Are we watched from the windows?'

The fond yet shrewd old mind had reckoned on their being looked for. He wished the arrival to make a good impression. Richard, in tawny slashed with yellow, and on horseback, was looking his best.

'Something moved,' Emma said. And then the door was flung open and there was Godfrey extending a hearty welcome. Once out of the sun Emma whisked off the scarf and blinking a little through the slits which his puffy lids had formed, Sir James advanced towards the settle upon which Tana sat, looking pretty and not — in the cunningly fashioned crimson velvet gown — as pregnant as Godfrey had implied.

Introductions were made. Sybilla, in the purple-grey silk rustled in from the kitchen where she had been seeing to a few last things, and instructing Eddy: and really Richard did not look at all bad until Henry, followed by John, came clattering down the stairs. Then the contrast was as sharp as it had been when the boys were young; Henry lean and brown, upright and alert; his cousin wilting, drooping and vague.

It was disconcerting, too, to find that the lady, after six months in England was so completely ignorant of the language as to be impervious to hints. This is my son; my only son; my heir. Richard will inherit Moyidan. Meaningless!

Tana had perfected that blank stare. Lady Emma had never before encountered a person of foreign birth and fell back on insular instinct. Shout loud enough and something would get through. It must! She shouted to Tana about Richard being heir to such a prosperous estate; so many tenants, all paying regular rents, so many sheep.

Finally Tana turned to Godfrey and asked, in Arabic, 'Is this woman angry with me that she speaks so loudly?' Assured, in that same barbaric tongue that this was not so, she said, 'I am glad. I wished to ask everybody to see my pavilion and to drink wine with me.'

The visit had coincided with the completion of the pavilion. It was now ready for occupation. Godfree had found her a waiting woman called Ursula who could cook and clean and look after babies. (Ursula was a middle-aged woman, thrown out of work by the running down of the Foundlings' Home at Bywater) Sir Godfrey translated the invitation which was accepted eagerly. Only Henry was irate. He'd had a glimpse or two of the beautiful place while it was in the making and would have loved to go in now that it was finished and sit on one of the divans — as near Tana as possible. But he had been trained by Walter, to whom work had always come first, and who had used such old country sayings as, 'Make hay while the sun shines'.

Grumpily, Henry said, 'Come on John. Back to work.'

John was by disposition idle, and only ten years old. For his youth Henry made no allowance, having gone to work himself at the age of six.

John said, 'Oh, must I?'

'You'd better!' John took swift stock of the situation; here with the family assembled, he might successfully rebel, but there would be tomorrow, and tomorrow. Better go.

Tana led the way; out at the main door, passing Sybilla's roses and round to the side, to her own door. Sir Godfrey gave his brother a helping arm, Sybilla and Emma came behind.

'I thought a pavilion was a tent,' Emma said. 'This is an ordinary house.'

'Godfrey used the word without thinking,' Sybilla said. 'Inside it is far from ordinary ... I am sorry to see James so much afflicted.'

'Yes. He is failing in other ways, too; and he does so long to see Richard settled . . .' Sybilla made sympathetic noises. What could one *say*?

With malice and amusement Tana had realised the purpose of this visit. The procedure was not so different from that followed by her own tribe, a display of elegibility. She had understood every hint, every shouted word, and had issued her invitation in order that they might see how rich she was, how immensely far from needing to marry a boy, not without a certain girlish prettiness of face, but weakly built, mumbling, senseless. A male version of his cousin Margaret.

The ceiling of the pavilion was lined entirely with sky-blue silk, stretched taut. The walls were draped with pleated silk, crimson, white, yellow, green. The two divans which when bare much resembled truckle beds were covered with silk and piled with cushions of varied colours. In the angle where they met stood a low table upon which Ursula soon placed silver cups and jugs. Under the window another table bore candlesticks and a silver bowl of red roses. In the whole of their lives Sir James and Lady Emma had not seen so much silk and even Moyidan could not show more silver. James, blinking, could hardly believe his eyes; Emma believed hers and understood.

Tana's wine was excellent; sweet and red — the colour of her gown. But the divans made uncomfortable seating for people accustomed to chairs, benches, stools; they were so soft and so low that to sit on them in the ordinary way brought the knees very near the chin. Only Tana was fully at ease.

Due to give birth almost any day now, Sybilla thought, but so young, so taut of figure that she is more graceful and active than I am, with three months more to go . . . And that made her think of children. She realised suddenly that Moyidan Richard and Margaret, bringing up the rear of the procession, had not entered the pavilion. They might, in their aimless way have followed Henry and John into the hayfield; they might have lingered among the roses. Instinct told her otherwise.

'The children,' she said, heaving herself with difficulty, to her feet, gathering up her skirt, making swift if clumsy progress round the out-jutting wing of the house and into the yard. To the hay.

This time, too late. On the new hay, still sweet-smelling, the half-witted boy and the girl with no wits at all were locked in

44

ecstasy; doing the one thing that needed no sense at all.

Emma's son; Sybilla's daughter. Hands which had tended, patted, soothed, now tore the two apart. Interrupted from a boyous mating neither of the semi-idiots showed shame; simply resentment. Margaret clawed Sybilla's face, Richard pushed his mother with such force that she almost fell.

Father's arrived, late because Sir Godfrey had been obliged to heave his brother to his feet, and then in the dazzling afternoon sunshine, guide him.

Sybilla, still holding Margaret by the arm, ashamed before Emma, just as Emma was ashamed before her, barely felt the nails' raking. Another, more familiar pain lanced her, low down in her body. A warning pain. She bent over it and said, 'Emma . . . I think . . .'

Emma took charge, issuing crisp, purposeful orders.

'Godfrey, carry Sybilla to bed.' 'Wat, Wat, where are you? Get the wagon ready. Take Sir James home.'

'James, take Richard home. Richard go home with your father.'

'And what about you, my dear?' Sir James asked. He had not seen anything and was bewildered.

'I am needed here — at least until tomorrow. Send the wagon then and if I can I will come home.'

She seized Margaret's arm in a clasp that left marks visible a fortnight later and hustled her into the house. She thanked God that James seemed not to have seen that shameful sight; she prayed God that Richard would not be able to explain. She did not speak until they were on the stairs and then she said, 'You wicked, wicked girl,' and administered a sound shaking before bundling her into the nearest room, which happened to be the right one and locking her inside. Then she went into the room where Sir Godfrey, having laid Sybilla on the bed, was loosening her clothes.

It could not be even a premature birth; Godfrey had been home less than seven months. A miscarriage so late could be lethal. And all that wicked girl's fault! She did not blame Richard at all; he had never shown before the slightest interest in sex.

She sent Godfrey running to the kitchen for what was needed — none of the items that anticipated the birth of a living child, just provision against the inevitable mess.

'Send your kitchen woman up with them. And then, God-frey, ride after James. I forgot his scarf in the confusion. It is in the hall.'

Racked with pain Sybilla said, 'I am sorry that this should have fallen to you, Emma.'

'Be thankful that I am here. Between Margery and Richard I had two miscarriages myself. I know what to do.'

Presently it was clear that this was no miscarriage. It was a birth. A boy, no bigger than, and much resembling, a skinned rabbit, but alive. Lady Emma applied common-sense. Ejected so abruptly from the womb the little creature would need a makeshift one; must be kept warm, handled as little as possible. If it could be saved Lady Emma was the woman to do it, even though she thought with some bitterness — This is Sybilla's *fourth* boy!

Tana had not joined the rush to the yard. The children — by which she understood the idiot girl and boy — were no concern of hers. She reclined upon her divan and finished her wine, and then Godfrey's; it pleased her to drink from his cup. She was nearing her time, but the thought did not perturb her; she came of a tribe resistant to pain and from living so much among women, she knew what to expect. In both her lives, the one in North Africa, the one in Zagela, women had rallied around a birth. The old wife would see to all the necessary business, just as she had seen to the making of tiny garments.

She heard nothing of the bustle in the yard, for Master Hobson built well and she herself had decreed that her pavilion should not even have a window on that side. Everything was very quiet. When the first pain struck she thought I will wait a little, then call Ursula, who will call Sybilla; a baby takes a long time to be born. Ursula should have been in Tana's kitchen which had once been Sybilla's still-room, and which had a window on the garden side, quite close to the door of the pavilion. When, eventually, Tana did call, the sound should have carried and brought Ursula running by the inconvenient way which Tana herself had insisted upon, through the kitchen door, into the yard, round the out-jutting wing and so to the door. But Ursula had been drawn by the drama going on in the main house. The heating of blankets, the heating of bricks to be wrapped in flannel to be laid alongside the little rabbit-like baby in the plain wooden cradle which Sybilla had ordered for Tana's baby and which had not yet been carried into the pavilion. The second cradle, not expected to be needed for three months was still in the making. Lady Emma was fully occupied with Sybilla who, having suffered something that was not quite a birth or quite a miscarriage, was in a very poor way.

When silence answered her calls, Tana pressing her hands on either side of the yielding mattress of the divan, heaved herself up and staggered to the door of her pavilion. It was late afternoon now and roses and lilies swooned, heavy-scented. In the doorway she realised that some births did not take long. It was happening now, she could no longer walk. Crawl perhaps. She crawled towards the front of the house and then screamed, at a fortunate spot, just under the window of the room where Lady Emma was beginning to be hopeful that Sybilla would not bleed to death, and at the same time being worried because the child having come so untimely, there was no milk for him.

She said, crossly, 'And what is to do now?' And went down to deal, competently, with whatever was to do. The second task was far easier, a full time baby, a girl, and curiously, girls were tougher than boys; and Lady Serriff had, thank God, enough milk for two. And Emma thought — We must not go jogging that poor little thing up and down stairs. So the two babies lay, side by side in the cradle.

Few women, Lady Emma thought had managed two deliveries in so short a time. And that after a shock.

She did not forget Margaret as everybody else had done. She opened the door, took the idiot by the arm to the stoolroom, locked her in again with a hunk of bread and a cup of water. 'That'll cool your blood, you little bitch.'

Next day, as instructed, James sent the wagon which went back empty. It was impossible for Lady Emma to leave Knight's Acre while Sybilla was still so helpless and her baby in need of such diligent care. The foreign woman could, at a pinch, have taken control — peasant women often gave birth and cooked a meal on the same day — but she understood nothing and only Sir Godfrey understood her. And neither of the hired women was fully to be trusted. Men were useless at such times, hanging about and asking, 'How is she?' twenty times a day; so Emma devised an errand for Godfrey.

'Ride over to Moyidan and explain to James why I shall be

here for at least two days more. Take your dinner with him, and for my sake make sure that it is a good one. And see that his shutters are closed.'

'*Two* babies on the same day,' Sir James said. 'Poor Emma! Still they could not be in better hands. One is yours, Godfrey.'

Both are mine, God forgive me.

'Yes, the boy, born untimely is mine.' The girl, twice the size and twice as lusty, he must not claim.

Behind the swollen watering eyes there was an active mind at work. Richard, hustled out of Knight's Acre in summary fashion had said something which had struck home and Sir James feared that shortly he would need his foolish young brother's consent and connivance.

'Then you need two cradles, Godfrey.'

'They are managing. Sybilla had ordered one for Tana's, that is Lady Serriff's baby — and that was delivered in good time. The other is still in the making.'

'No need for that! Somewhere . . . I think in the old castle, near the stairs when I last saw it, under a bit of sailcloth, is the one we were all rocked in. Take it. Make use of it for your son.'

The head-piece of that cradle was carved with the family emblem, the timid hare rampant in defence of its young. It had been painted once, but like all painted things, it had faded and in places flaked. But the lending of it was a gesture, brotherly, imbued with family feeling, and awkwardly as it balanced across the pommel of his saddle, Sir Godfrey carried it home with pride.

CHAPTER ELEVEN

It took Margaret's slow wits two days to realise that the way of escape lay open to her. From her window to the roof of the new building was not much of a drop; from that roof to the garden was a bigger one, but she did not flinch from it. No definite purpose drove her, she was following an animal instinct to escape, to be free of the deadly routine, bedroom, stool-room, bedroom again, to be away from that hostile eye.

She had no sense of direction, but that did not matter; there was only one way out of Intake, and that was the lane. Its verges were white with the big daisies that Mother had said was her name flower — the marguerite — and Henry called bull-daisies. Of the smaller kind of daisy Sybilla had once shown Margaret how to make a daisy chain. The instruction, seemingly not much regarded at the time, had made an impression and as she walked Margaret made herself two. One for her neck, one for her head.

Halfway along its length the lane was crossed by a little stream, a casual, nameless tributary to the river, it was unbridged because even in winter rains it was still shallow, merely a water-splash. Its banks were thick with wild strawberries, so many and so ripe that they scented the air. Margaret did not notice this immediately. What she saw was a man.

He was a carter. Somebody called Wade, of Wade's Acre at Intake had commissioned him to bring — with all his belongings — an extremely old man from Nettleton. The enquiry, earlier in the year, though nothing had come of it, had shaken Wade whose claim to Wade's Acre was shown to be poor. But old Uncle Arthur's claim was good and valid, and Wade of Wade's Acre was not the man to miss an opportunity.

Having delivered the ancient man and his belongings, the carter, offered no hospitality, had turned about and was making for Baildon. He had no settled home there, he was in fact a homeless man, sleeping, eating where he could, but he frequented markets because there were to be found a good number of men with goods to be carried — things that could not be transported on a donkey.

The carter was mindful of his horse; not in a sentimental way, but because it earned him his livelihood. So he halted by the stream to let the horse drink and graze a bit, to drink himself and eat his bread and cheese. As an addition to this fare he had gathered a big dockleaf full of the wild strawberries.

'Margaret likes them,' a sweet voice said.

The carter turned and stared, his eyes bulging and, despite the heat of the day, a shiver between his shoulder blades. Strange tales were told of Layer Wood. The Little People were said to live there. And here was one! Never in his life had the carter seen anything so beautiful. The fall of yellow hair, the blue eyes, fair skin and a mouth the colour of a hedge-rose. She

49

was a child in height, but with a woman's breasts. She wore a crown and a garland of flowers.

If he could have run then, he would have done so, but fear held him captive. Then, gradually fear receded, for the fairy was looking at him kindly. She sat down, close to him, and ate a few of his strawberries. He had never seen anybody eat so delicately before. Sybilla had instilled table manners into all her children, and Margaret had never eaten with heartiness.

'Margaret likes you,' she said, and began to give proof of this liking, kissing him, taking his coarse brown hand and pressing it to her cheek, to her breast. With awe, with astonishment, with delight he discovered that a fairy woman was much like any other — except that she was so different. His traffic with women had been confined to hirelings, bored and indifferent, doing what they did for pay.

It was an experience that he would never forget, never speak of, something out of this world.

At the end of an afternoon of the sweetest dalliance, the real world made sharp impact again. He had thought that she would vanish as suddenly as she had appeared, but she said, 'Take Margaret with you.'

'I wish I could, my pretty, but I ain't got no home. Mostly I sleep in the wagon.'

'Margaret sleep in wagon. With you.'

Abruptly into his mind came the memory of another old story.

Long, long ago, a Bywater man, fishing for herring, had dredged up a mermaid in his net, fallen in love with her and taken her home and lived unhappily ever after.

'No,' he said, 'that wouldn't do. That wouldn't do at all. You must go back where you belong. And I gotta get to Baildon.'

When she saw that he meant it, she began to cry, and that again she did differently. No snuffling or blubbering. Tears filling the eyes and spilling.

Now he was anxious only to get away, for fear he might weaken. Lucky he hadn't unharnessed. He ran to his wagon and jumped to its seat, with shouts and blows rousing the drowsing horse.

For a while she followed, calling piteously, 'Take Margaret with you. Take Margaret . . .' When he reached the end of the lane, the place where it joined the road which led in one direction to Baildon, in the other to Moyidan and eventually to Bywater, he ventured to look back. She had crossed the water-splash and was still in pursuit. He turned the horse into the Baildon road and hurried it along.

When Margaret reached the fork she turned towards Baildon too, and the light wagon from Moyidan missed her only by a minute or two.

Sir James' man of business had written at his dictation.

My dearest Emma, I am sending the wagon for you. You must come home at once. My eyes are much worse and Richard will not eat anything. He has not taken a crumb since that dinner at Knight's Acre, and swears never to break his fast until he can marry that idiot cousin. Please come. Whatever their need it is less than mine . . .

This was heavy news. Whenever Richard's will was crossed, which was not often, his parents being so doting, he had refused to eat. And worry of this sort was the very worst thing for poor James. Lady Emma took a look at the situation here. Sybilla lay upstairs, still very weak, but mending. Lady Serriff, young and strong was feeding both babies, and eating heartily herself. The two babies were with her, the cradles side by side, so that the poor little boy should not suffer the handling, the jolting which being carried up and downstairs would entail. Lady Serriff's new maid, Ursula, had her experience in the Foundlings' Home behind her, and Sybilla's maid, Jill, now understood how to make good chicken broth and how to infuse lovage, that herbal specific for female pains.

Yes, I am free to go. I have done my best. Then she remembered Margaret. Well, presumably she had now learnt her lesson and could be allowed to rejoin the family. Mounting the stairs Lady Emma decided to speak strictly to Godfrey, handing over to him the responsibility of looking after his wicked daughter. Sybilla must not be bothered. Oh, and she intended to tell him another thing, too. It would be most unwise for Sybilla to risk child-birth again. She was so crooked. Emma had not realised how crooked Sybilla was. If that baby had gone full-time Sybilla would have had a very difficult — possibly fatal — delivery.

Godfrey had gone to Bywater that day, but he had said he

51

would be home for supper. Emma proposed to delay her departure until he arrived, say her say and then go about her own business.

Thinking thus she unlocked the door of the empty room. The open window told its own tale.

From experience with her own son — though compared with Margaret he was almost sound — Lady Emma knew that what those defective in sense lacked they often made up for with cunning. That sly little bitch had clambered out and made for Moyidan. Pray God she hadn't reached it. Two stupid creatures, impervious to reason, acknowledging no rules but their own, and James, so afflicted . . . And so worried.

She kept her head. Wat who drove the wagon, had just come from Moyidan.

'No, my lady. Nobody extra was there when I left and I didn't see nobody along the road.' So the idiot girl had not gone in that direction. There remained the woods — the river. If she wandered, lost and starving in the one, drowned dead in the other, what a blessing!

But Sir Godfrey, arriving just then, repudiated either idea.

'Oh no, Emma. Margaret was always frightened of the woods. Sybilla told me — Margaret liked flowers, but she would never venture far in unless Sybilla held her hand. And to get to the river she would have to go through the village, and she was frightened of that, too. Frightened of the boys and the dogs.'

'Then where can she be?'

'I can go and look.'

With a jolt of his heart he remembered that this was the week of the Midsummer Fair in Baildon. Margaret's understanding was limited, but who knew where the limits ran? Somebody might have said something which had attracted her vagrant attention . . . A pretty girl among that riff-raff!

At the lane's end he turned in the direction of Baildon and rather more than a mile along, found her, walking in the middle of the road, looking about from side to side in a frightened way and crying, quietly, but with infinite desolation. Dusk was thickening here because two spurs of Layer Wood almost met, branches linking across the road. It was getting dark, and she was afraid of the dark, when she was alone.

He called her name, and she turned.

She said, 'Da-da,' her name for him when she was very young. He scooped her up and set her across the saddle in front of him. She smelt of wild strawberries and crushed grass and wilting daisies. The garland had been broken but a few flowers still clung to her hair. He felt relief and exasperation in equal measure. And also a slight repulsion. He had not seen her since he had caught one horrified glimpse of her, skirts tossed up, legs asprawl, face set in ecstasy, changing to sullenness. It seemed to him suddenly that some faint odour of that encounter still hung about her . . .

In the shuttered room, Sir James said testily, 'Don't keep saying "Cousins, cousins," Godfrey. We know that as well as you do. It's *our* boy who won't eat! Do you realise that it is almost a week? If it could be arranged, would you consent?'

'Of course. A girl like that would be far happier here — and married, than she would in a nunnery. But the marriage of first cousins needs a dispensation.'

'It needs a little cunning. And a very old priest with poor sight. That you have on your doorstep. Sybilla was telling me that day how almost blind, how astray in his wits your Father Ambrose is. He *still* asks for news of you. Did you know that? I've worked it out. So far as I know Father Ambrose has never set eyes on Richard in his life. That they — my boy and your girl — share a surname means nothing. Richard Tallboys could well be a brother of that Eustace you once had as your squire. Very distant relative.' Sir James wiped his eyes, shifted his painful feet. 'If any,' he said. 'Now what do you say?'

'I am agreeable. Sybilla might have scruples about the deceit.'

'You must talk her out of them. God's teeth, Godfrey, can we see the boy *die*?'

Lady Emma said, succinctly, 'The fact that Sybilla and her baby are alive today, is due to me, Godfrey. I think you owe us a small accommodation.'

This small accommodation Sir Godfrey was willing to make. He had never been very pious and he had spent a long time in a place where the rules of the Church, of Rome, did not apply. Emma and James had sent for him in sheer desperation, and he understood, indeed shared their point of view.

'I will try,' he said.

Ramming her point home, Emma said, 'It is astounding what you can do if you set your mind to it. If anyone had told me that I should deliver two women in one afternoon . . .' For her the most immediate thing was to get some food into Richard. She went away and told him that so soon as arrangements could be made, he should marry Margaret.

As Sir Godfrey had predicted, Sybilla had scruples. Such a marriage, unless by dispensation, was against Church law and it was a shame to take advantage of Father Ambrose. She told Godfrey how heroically the old man had behaved during the time of the plague, how he denied himself in order to keep the church in some kind of repair. 'We should be doubly breaking the law to play such a trick on him,' at the altar he has served so long.'

She was right, of course; and added to that it was difficult to pursue an argument which caused distress to a woman still far from well. He could only say mildly that Richard's health — perhaps even his life was at stake, that the worry was hastening James into the grave and that the investigation of the Kin Book, ill-kept as it had been until Father Ambrose's coming, had revealed marriages between first cousins which seemed to have been attended by no ill results. Sybilla held firm and Sir Godfrey was obliged to ride to Moyidan and report failure.

'Then you must try again, and harder,' Emma said. 'I have already told Richard that he can marry Margaret — and he ate a whole piegeon pie! And it seemed to me that his understanding has improved, too. He asked some quite sensible questions, about how soon, and where. You must assert your authority, Godfrey.'

'Sybilla looks so frail,' he said.

Relentlessly, Emma said, 'But for me she would probably be dead! And you probably exaggerate her ill looks by comparing them with those of Lady Serriff who gave birth as easily as a cow.'

There might be truth in that.

For Sir Godfrey this was a miserable time. And then, with no word of warning, Sybilla capitulated. She gave no reason except that she had given the matter more thought and come to the conclusion that this was, after all, the best way.

What had made her change her mind was the matter of the

monthly cloths, regularly used, soaked, scoured, put out to bleach in air and sun, stored in the clothes chest. Margaret should have needed some a day, or at most two or three after her misbehaviour with her cousin. The need had not arisen, and added to all Godfrey's arguments about Richard's health, Sir James' happiness in his last days, and their unquestionable debt to Emma, was the fact that a pregnant girl needed a husband, and a baby a father.

Once, halfway through the ceremony, it struck Father Ambrose that the young couple he was uniting in holy matrimony looked curiously *alike*. But his eyes were failing, he knew only too well, and perhaps they looked alike because they both looked so happy. God keep them happy always.

After the wedding was to be a double christening, and about the baptism of the foreign lady's baby, Father Ambrose had entertained some qualms. She had lived in his parish for quite some time — he could not remember exactly how long — and had never once set foot in his church. Admittedly, most of the people of Intake were irregular in attendance, but they came at Easter and at Christmas. Still, he had faith in Lady Tallboys who certainly would not have offered to be a god-mother to the child of a heathen, or to have her own baby baptised from the same font, at the same time.

Sybilla had wanted the baby to be named Geoffrey, a name not unlike Godfrey while unlike enough to avoid confusion, but Godfrey had wanted him to be named Robert, in memory of Lord Robert Barbury upon whom he had come to look as a son.

Tana — the daughter a disappointment, for although within her tribe women were allowed an unusual freedom, sons were actually valued more, and the woman who bore them had power — had suggested the name Jamil, meaning in Arabic, beautiful for the little girl's name. But Sir Godfrey had reminded her that she was supposed to be Spanish and the child could have, if not an English name, a Spanish one. In their helter-skelter ride across Spain — neither knowing any Spanish — they had heard several women called Juana. So they settled upon that. However, at the end of a day with so many ceremonies, Juana was more than Father Ambrose could manage so he said, 'I name thee, Joanna.'

CHAPTER TWELVE

Through all this troublous time, Sir Godfrey had been mindful of Lord Thorsdale and of his duties towards the patron. He would perhaps have denied that it was relief for him to get away from Knight's Acre where two women were tending children both sired by him, but that was the truth of it. Get down to Bywater, see that no ordinary ship put in at the coal jetty without paying his dues, that the coal cobs from the North were unloaded, quickly, sheltered, repaired, sent on their way properly provisioned. He was an honest steward and he enjoyed his work. In the communal house, kept by a woman of good reputation, he made himself a little office with a clerk, named Harold, to keep meticulous accounts, a narrow, hard bed upon which, when winter brought short days and bad weather, he could sleep if necessary. He thought he was prepared for everything. What he was not prepared for was a ghost.

But it came, and announced itself. 'Sir Godfrey? I am Sir William Barbury. Lord Thorsdale's nephew. At your service, sir.'

Like Father Ambrose at the altar, Sir Godfrey saw the cousinly resemblance. A spitting image of Lord Robert who had died in that narrow, balconied street, long ago and far away. Even to the way his hair grew, and the certainty, allied with grace, of manner.

Sir Godfrey welcomed the boy, and steadying himself under what had been quite a shock — though ridiculous, waited to hear what his errand was.

It was simple, and yet not simple. War had broken out again and there had been a battle at Northampton, a victory for the Yorkists.

'But my uncle,' the boy said, 'does not think the Queen will be content to leave it there. He is reasonably certain that she will now appeal to the French — her kindred. He wants Bywater held against any French who might come to help the Lancastrian cause. But not so openly as to invite retaliation. I am to be your aid; and cost does not matter. So he said.'

'Not openly. That is wise. People here are not concerned

with the quarrel. Sir William, I doubt whether you could go into the town, the inn or any place within thirty miles and find a man committed to red rose or white.'

'Sir Godfrey, are *you* committed?'

He thought for a bit and then said, 'No. Not in my heart. I was absent from England when this festering boil broke. To be frank I don't understand what it is all about. Two claimants to the throne. And who am I to say? I am not a political man, Sir William.'

'You owe my uncle some allegiance, Sir Godfrey.'

'That I could not deny. In fact I willingly admit it.'

Now that he came to think about it, Sir Godfrey saw that free as he had always seemed to be, he had almost always owed somebody some allegiance — even that mad man in Spain. And a conversation with Henry flashed back into his mind. He had suggested to Henry that now that they were not so poor there was no need for Henry to work so hard; they could hire hands. Henry had retorted that *hands* was an apt word, you could hire hands but not heads and that he had no intention of leaving his harvest to mere hands. Sir Godfrey had then suggested that Henry should come down with him to Bywater and learn, pre-pare himself to take over the stewardship, and that also Henry had despised, his voice polite, his eyes scornful, 'Sir, I prefer to tend my own fields.'

Exasperated, Sir Godfrey had said, 'Oh, get back to your hay!' and Henry, with an unusually merry look, had said, 'Sir, the hay is safely in. Today we start on the oats.'

Now, not on his own field, not truly his own man, Sir Godfrey said, 'What does Lord Thorsdale wish of me?'

'That Bywater should be prepared — secretly — to repel any French forces who might come to the aid of the Lancastrian cause.'

The trained mind sprang into action. Even the need to make preparations in secret was in attune with experience.

'We need a look-out tower, for early warning,' Sir Godfrey said. 'And that need cause no stir. This is my Lord Thorsdale's jetty, and on it he might wish to have a tower to keep watch for the cobs from the North. There is also a device of which I have heard though I never saw it put to use — the fire ship. We could place one on either side of the harbour. What about men?'

'They are on their way; twenty archers and twenty pikemen, all trained, hired men, and loyal to the white rose and to their lord. My uncle judged that to be sufficient force because the townspeople themselves will rise against the French. Even uncommitted men, like yourself, Sir Godfrey. Four knights are also coming — the greatest number that can be spared. With you and myself that makes six.' He smiled with his dead cousin's charming, confident smile.

'The presence of so many men can hardly be concealed,' Sir Godfrey said.

'We hope so, with Master Johnson's aid.'

Christopher Johnson was the most prosperous wool merchant in Suffolk, possibly in all East Anglia. He bought wool from as far away as Yorkshire and a good deal of that wool was Lord Thorsdale's. Johnson was a shrewd enough man to take advantage of Bywater's exemption from the Staple — a favour granted it long ago in return for some singular favour the town had rendered the king of the day.

'Master Johnson,' Sir William said, smiling again, 'is about to employ some singularly ablebodied pack-drivers, woolpickers, general handy-men. Sir Wilfred, Sir Giles and Sir Martin, my brother Philip and myself propose to buy or hire a house and set up a disreputable, merry knights' lodgings of our own.'

'It would have given me great pleasure to offer hospitality,' Sir Godfrey said, truthfully. 'But my house is twenty miles inland.' And small, and bare — and ruled by a lady not yet fully recovered in health.

However, the word hospitality, reminded him of what he could offer, wine and food at the Welcome to Mariners.

Over the wine Sir William explained a little more about the political situation, and Lord Thorsdale's attitude. Lord Thorsdale was a Yorkist, everybody knew that. The Battle of Northampton had been a Yorkist victory — but not decisive enough to end the war and put Richard of York on the throne. So there was certain to be another battle which the Lancastrians would lose, unless help came from the French; and there were still enough Lancastrians alert and alive to take note of any sudden defence measures taken in such a place as Bywater.

'Frankly, I think that if they come, they will make for the

Cinque ports, nearer to France, nearer to London. And indeed, they may not come at all. The King of France has other things to think about, and would stand to gain nothing. Nonetheless, my uncle said, "Prepare" and prepare we will. Enjoying ourselves along the way.'

It could have been Lord Robert speaking.

Through all that fine summer Sir Godfrey did enjoy himself in a way he had not known since his old tournament days. Of the five knights three were young, boisterously merry; two older and completely responsible, but never dull. The young were respectful, too, and when Sir Godfrey, Sir Martin or Sir Wilfred reminisced they were all attention. And of course nobody had such a tale as Sir Godfrey had to tell. Nobody else had been to Spain, taken part in an assault seemingly insane, won and lost a city, been a slave, escaped by the most romantic means. He was a bad story-teller and perhaps for that very reason, never boring. He had to be prompted, asked, 'What then, sir?' There were things that he still could not bring himself to speak of, and perhaps they sensed that, prey, as all men were to curiosity.

He had found for them an old spacious house, empty since the plague, and tradesmen in Bywater, butchers, bakers, dairy-women, fishmongers, revelled in an increase of custom and never questioned the origin of it. Carpenters did not question the purpose of their work, which was to erect a tall tower of no great substance, really no more than a skeleton. Trusted men from the contingent ostensibly lodged and employed with Johnson, took turns to man the watchtower. Out in the harbour two old ships crammed with straw and tallow and dry wood, rocked. They were also manned, turn and turn about — and for a perfectly good reason which everybody in Bywater understood, left unguarded they would have been stripped down to the water-line.

Sir Godfrey went home as often as he could. The two elder knights — Sir Martin and Sir Wilfred — were able and experienced men, and it had been proved by experiment that should the man at the top of the tower sight a conglomeration of vessels which might hint at invasion, and set fire to the combustible materials always ready in an iron pan, the blaze and the smoke could be seen at Knight's Acre. Lord Thorsdale had said that cost did not matter, so Sir Godfrey always had one fresh, swift horse in reserve, so that should the beacon flare just as he had arrived home he had only to remount on a horse ready to run twenty miles at top speed.

The French did not come in July, in August or September; it began to look as though the Queen's appeal to her country-men had been in vain. Tension relaxed. October was the month of westerly gales. November brought fog. As for December, singularly few wars broke out, or were renewed in that month.

When he went home Sir Godfrey passed abruptly from the carefree masculine society which was his true element — one he would never have deserted had he not met Sybilla — into one heavily charged with femininity. By October Sybilla was strong again and Tana's supply of milk had ceased; and where simply looking after babies was concerned, Sybilla had come into her own. After all, she had reared four with little help, never having been able to afford what she considered a proper nursemaid. Tana completely lacked the maternal instinct and was happy to leave the care of the babies to Sybilla.

Joanna gave little trouble, anything she could swallow she could digest; Robert was more frail and prone to coughs and colds and stomach troubles. Presently Joanna cut her teeth almost unnoticed while Robert was miserable, flushed, feverish and peevish. When in good health however, he was lively and merry and Sybilla's great fear — that one of these children could turn out like Margaret or Moyidan Richard — soon re-ceded. Robert and Joanna greatly resembled one another, both being blue-eyed and fair-haired, when they were asleep, with only their faces exposed they might well have been twins. Now and again, when Sir Godfrey saw them thus he felt a pang. His daughter had no real name; was in fact a bastard.

Sybilla's behaviour over the whole affair, the equality with which she treated the two, evoked his sincerest admiration; she was a woman in a million and although the ultimate intimacy between them was now forbidden, he loved her, if anything, more dearly than ever. That thought always brought him back to the problem of Tana.

So far she had kept her promise to be good, but now his animal instinct informed him that he was being hunted.

Dozens of times Ursula would come and say, 'Sir, please will you come? My mistress cannot make me understand.'

It was always some trivial thing, often something that could have been demonstrated if not explained in words. One could not expect a middle-aged serving woman from Bywater to acquire a working knowledge of Arabic, but Tana could have, should have, by now picked up enough English to enable her to give simple orders. She had once been eager to learn, had learned. All this nonsense was simply an excuse. Yet how could he express even the mildest irritation when, but for her he would still have been labouring away in the marble quarry at Andara — or dead of the cough that had claimed so many?

The nonsense disposed of, Tana always said, 'Now that you *are* here, take a glass of wine with me.' Everything in her pavilion had been planned to be seductive, and Tana herself, her figure restored, was seduction personified. He had never before seen her against the background that suited her so well; the silken scented background; he had trudged with her over the mountains, ridden across Spain with her, seen her in mean inns, on shipboard, and then in his own hall, with its one half-comfortable settle.

Sometimes she said, 'When will you be home again? Good. Ursula by then should have mastered the kebab. Come and take supper with me.'

Then he would mention that one of the knights had been invited to Knight's Acre for that evening, and she would say, with a most recognisable air of one retreating only to remuster and fight another day, 'He, too, will be welcome.'

One by one he brought them, and one by one they all — even the older men — succumbed to the charm of which he was so well aware, but to which he must not, must not succumb. She resolutely refused to speak any English, outside a few formal phrases, but the grace with which she served them, her smiles, her poses, the seemingly innocent way in which, seeing them laugh, she would join in, were all designed for a single purpose.

Sybilla never once evinced a sign of jealousy. The old Abbess had trained her to logical thought; it worked now, informing her that if Godfrey had been completely enamoured with this girl, so pretty, and as it had transpired, so rich, he would have gone off with her somewhere, not brought her back here, to his home. At the same time she was not blind; she saw through all the tricks and sometimes felt a faintly complacent pity for the girl who had almost everything except the one thing she wanted. Such an *empty* life. She did not even care for her own child.

October came, at first with gales from the west which would deter any fleet setting out from France, and then passing on to sunny days, invigoratingly chill at dawn and dusk, summer-warm at mid-day. Layer Wood was a riot of colour.

This year they could afford to eat fresh beef from the steer they had raised, and when, in the second week of the month Tana issued one of her invitations — having seen Sir Godfrey come home alone — he was able to say that this was one occasion when she must take supper with them, since they had a fine joint on the spit.

Towards the end of the meal, Tana turned to Sir Godfrey and asked when he would go back to Bywater. He told her, next morning. Although he came home whenever he could he was scrupulous about taking his turn of duty. She said, 'I wish to go with you. There are things I need to buy.' Hitherto he had made her purchases and offered to do so tomorrow but she smiled and said that there were things that only she could buy. He then made another objection; it would mean upsetting his careful shuttle service of mounts with one horse always fresh, crammed with corn, at Knight's Acre. But she was insistent; just this once. And he, like Sybilla, had thought what a dull life she led; no friends, nothing to do all day. He said, rather grudgingly, 'Very well.'

'It is like old times,' Tana said, as they rode through the coloured woods. She had never seen an English autumn before; she had not been on a horse for nine months; nor, so cunningly he had managed it, had she been alone with him, for more than a little while, for, failing other support, on a few rare occasions, he had brought Henry, the staring, infatuated boy with him. Now, so stubborn he was, he refused to admit that this was merely a continuation of their ride through Spain; he said, 'This is England, Tana.' England, a place where a man had one wife and no concubines. A state of things which Tana intended to change before this day died. And Sir Godfrey, exhilarated by the morning air, the colour, the leaves, lemon yellow, scarlet, crimson, bronze, dropping gently down, making a path for them, thought — but for her I should never have looked on this again . . .

With an eye as keen as his for terrain, Tana marked the spot. An ancient tree with low branches, suitable for the tethering of horses.

They clattered into Bywater and stabled at the inn. They arranged their meeting time.

When she failed to appear, he was not immediately anxious. She could hardly be lost. All the main streets in Bywater led down to the quay, and the side lanes from which the sea was not visible did not contain the kind of shop that Tana would be likely to patronise. He went into the inn and ordered wine. The delay was probably because at the mercer's she could not decide between two colours; or perhaps she was being measured for new shoes. There was also a possibility that being a stranger she had mistaken the bells which marked the day's divisions.

Presently, however, he began to worry. He remembered her method of shopping when they were in Spain, point to what she wanted and display money. Had she been a little careless in her display of money, been noticed, followed, dragged into one of those squalid narrow lanes and robbed? Had her beauty attracted some undesirable attention? There were always disreputable characters hanging about a port.

People came and went. The landlady who knew and liked him, hovered and then approached to tell him that the fresh pork was almost gone; unless he ordered now there would be nothing but salt beef. 'No matter,' he said, 'I will wait.' The landlady turned the hour glass and by that simple action reminded him that he had been waiting for more than an hour. Something must have happened to her, he must take action, alert the knights and ask them to help him to comb the town. He must also take precautions against Tana arriving here and finding him gone.

'If a lady comes, tell her to wait. I shall not be long.'

'What lady, sir?'

'You will know her. Young, very pretty. She is wearing tawny velvet. With fur, and a little cap of the same colour. And she has . . .' He was about to mention the black hair, most unusual in this district, when there was a clatter of hoofs outside and the landlady who was facing the window said, 'That looks like her now.'

He ran to the door, and there was Tana mounted — could a man believe his eyes? — on one of Tom Thoroughgood's horses — a stallion!

She must have stolen it. There was no other explanation. No Thoroughgood stallion was ever sold; only mares and geldings. England was riddled with monopolies but none was more strict than that exercised by successive Tom Thoroughgoods over this particular breed. Even their stallions' services were restricted either to Thoroughgood mares in the Nettleton pastures or to strange mares with no strain of the original blood. Because of their rarity, and their beauty — they were all pale cream with manes and tails a shade darker — they were in great demand and very costly. Queens and other ladies of high rank were proud to own a Thoroughgood.

'I am late,' Tana said. 'I am sorry. But that is a stubborn man. And the other horse delayed us.' The horse which she had ridden in the morning was on a long leading rein. Sir Godfrey had considered it an excellent horse, but comparison diminished it.

He had not missed the remark about the stubborn man. He could just imagine Tana pointing to the horse she wanted and Tom Thoroughgood refusing to sell. Then she'd hung about and stolen it — saddle and bridle, too! Terrible! There was nothing for it but to ride to Nettleton at once and explain that she was a foreigner and did not understand. He glanced at the sky; the West was already brightening and he'd told Sybilla they would be home early.

'We must take it back at once,' he said.

'But why? He is mine.'

'No Thoroughgood ever sells an entire.'

She laughed.

'So the stubborn man said. And he did not *sell*. I won him in a wager. I will tell you as you go.' She had lost or discarded the little cap and her hair flowed free. 'He does not like to wait.'

Sir Godfrey called for his horse and when it was brought round Tana said, 'You lead the other. It makes Jamil restive. Now I will tell you ... Last night you said, Godfree, that to lend me a horse would upset your arrangements; so I thought to myself — I will have a horse of my own! And I asked, where are good horses? The boy in the yard said at Nettleton and told me a short way to reach this place. And it was true, many,

many beautiful horses, but this the most beautiful of all. The man said he never sold a stallion. I showed him money. I promised more. Much more. But it was useless. He offered me others. He said stallions were not for ladies. This one, he said, was scarcely broken to the saddle yet and even he could hardly ride him. I said I could. Then he laughed and said that if I could ride this one once round the field he would give him to me but more likely I would get a broken neck. I said, "Saddle him." While he was being saddled I let him smell me, and I talked. I told him his name was Jamil and that he belonged to me. Then I rode round the field three times. The man called upon his God to strike him dead, but that did not happen. Instead he *cried*. That big strong man, he wept. Then he made me promise never to mate Jamil to any mare except one of his own, at that place. I swore by the sun. And I left all my money on the gatepost.'

'No wonder Tom Thoroughgood cried. He was breaking a rule that his family has kept for longer than man can remember,' Sir Godfrey said. Then a thought struck him. 'Did you speak in English to the stable boy and to Thoroughgood?'

'How else would they understand?' She made this admission without shame. 'I know what you think, Godfree. But the Arabic we speak together is all that we can share. It is precious to me.'

'Well, in future you can speak English to Ursula.'

'Then I should only see you when you come to supper with me. And to do that too often would not look well.'

To herself she thought that if her plan worked this evening he would come of his own accord.

'You are always welcome at my table,' he said.

'Thank you. I think that now I shall give Jamil his head a little.' Horse and rider disappeared around a bend in the lane. He followed as fast as he could, but both the Knight's Acre horses had covered ground already that day and he did not sight Tana again until he was through the water splash and entering the tunnel of trees where it was almost twilight. Then he saw the pale horse standing, without a rider on the verge of the lane and Tana huddled on a heap of beechleaves at the wood's edge. The brute had thrown her! Tom Thoroughgood had spoken of breaking her neck.

He dropped the leading rein and kicked his horse to a gallop.

65

Then, throwing himself out of the saddle he ran to her, 'Tana! Are you hurt?'

'Only tired,' she said in a soft, languorous voice. 'I have not ridden for so long. Now in one day, to Bywater and to Nettleton, and three times round that field . . . I must rest a little.'

'It's no distance now. We'll walk.' What with one thing and another they'd be late, not early as he had promised.

'I am so stiff. Help me up,' she said and held out her left hand. He took it. Her right arm went round his neck and pulled him close.

A man being tempted — and aware of the temptation — but determined to resist, does not cut an admirable figure. Among a medley of feelings he was aware of seeming ridiculous, longing for what he must repulse. Her kisses, the murmured endearments, the very scent of her hair stirred memories of the joy they had once known, even as he grappled to reach and control her caressing hands. The Devil whispered that Sybilla would never know; that he had lived like a monk since June . . . He said, short of breath, 'Tana . . . no. You promised . . . to behave . . . We must behave . . .'

'You promised that I should be *with* you. For me there is only one way to be with. It is this, heart of my heart.'

He had her hands now and could free himself, get to his feet. He jerked her to hers and still holding her at arms' length said,

'You must understand. I will *not*. Never, never do this to me again.'

'Then how can I live? And who would be hurt?' There was no real answer to that, unless he spoke stark truth and said — I should; in my own eyes; Sybilla and I made mutual vows; she held to hers for more than eight years, lonely years. I broke mine, but she understood and forgave me and treats our bastard exactly as she treats her own.

'And you do love me, Godfree. I could tell by your voice when you thought Jamil had thrown me. It was like that time in Seville . . .'

'I love you, but in a different way. Come, we must get along.'

Final touch to a ridiculous situation, was to find both his horses gone. They were within easy reach of their own stable, their own manger and at an easy pace had set out for home, the one which had carried Tana that morning, now and again tripping over the long leading rein.

'God in Heaven,' Sir Godfrey said, 'if they get home before us . . .'

He started to run.

Tana untethered Jamil and stood for a moment leaning against him, her face buried in his silky mane. 'At least I have you, my beautiful one.' But the resignation was not real. She had just suffered another defeat, but not, she felt, the final one. She had underestimated the strength of Sybilla's hold on him. She would not make that mistake again.

CHAPTER THIRTEEN

Sir William Barbury, having read his uncle's letter, gave them the gist of it. Bywater was no longer of any importance; the French were not coming, had never intended to come. The final confrontation between York and Lancaster would be in the North. The Queen's forces were mustering and Lord Thorsdale wanted every fighting man who owed him any allegiance to move immediately.

Only one man failed to respond. An archer, sweating and raving in one of Master Johnson's outlying barns. Genuinely ill, Sir Godfrey saw with his experienced eye. The others were rounded up and sent on their way and Sir Godfrey went hastily to his home to take leave of Sybilla who said, 'My love, I thought we were done with all this . . . And you not yet home a year.' But she was trained; a knight owed his allegiance to his lord. So she put on a resolutely cheerful face, hastily gathered a change of clothing and some food that would be edible for a month, kissed him, said as she had said so many times before, 'God keep you and bring you back to me, my dearest dear.'

Afterwards he could not remember where exactly he began to feel ill and had no appetite for supper, but forced it down and then went out to be sick. In the morning he mounted and rode alongside the others; and then his throat became so sore that even bread sopped in broth was hard to swallow, yet he must eat in order to be strong and keep up with the others. He was not conscious of the fact that he talked what sounded like nonsense — 'What happened to that donkey? But for it Arcol would never have gone aboard ... Oh yes, I can swim. It was the new armour, everything in the wrong place ... And I will not do it. Every sworn knight in Christendom is my blood brother. Tell him no ...'

They left him at an inn at a crossroad. A miserable place, but they had no choice; in the saddle he sagged, on ground he reeled about, calling Sir William Sir Robert. Useless. The landlady, Sir William noted had a mean face, eyes like pebbles, a mouth like a trap, but she was susceptible to money. Sir William had noticed that Sir Godfrey's pouch was thin. As usual when he went on campaign, Sir Godfrey had left almost all that he had with Sybilla, taking only just enough for bare necessities. Sir William therefore dived into his own purse and pressed into the hand a sum sufficient to keep a man for six months, and said, 'Good dame, tend him well.'

'He shall have the best that this poor house can offer, sir.'

She was afraid of infection, and left the work of caring for the sick man to the young maid of all work whose position was practically that of a slave. Upon her Sir Godfrey made a strange impression. At first she thought that he resembled a stone man who lay in the near-by church with his legs crossed and a little dog by his side. Then, as his illness ravaged him, he came more to resemble Christ, just taken down from the Cross, in a wall-picture in the same church. Also he had a beautiful voice, and although much of his talk was disorderly raving, he never said anything offensive.

There was nothing even remotely sexual in Griselda's attitude; she disliked men. She had been raped in a ditch when she was six. Shortly after that she had been taken into a convent orphanage, and from there thrust into the hurly-burly of life in a low-class inn; and there, despite her tangled hair and poor clothing, some men had used her. It was a case of comply or be beaten. She would have run away, but she had nowhere to go and she had vivid, painful memories of life on the roads as a beggar-girl.

On the third day the landlady was sure that Sir Godfrey would not recover; and his room was needed, for a steady stream of men, knights, archers, pikemen, were going through to the north. So she said to the man who was her only other assistant, and to Griselda. 'Put him in the barn. He will die in any case.'

After that Griselda's behaviour was dictated partly by her almost mystical feeling towards the sick man, and partly by a hatred of her mistress. He shouldn't die if she could prevent it.

She was supposed to look in on him twice a day, to see whether he were alive or dead. She went far more often, usually under cover of darkness. She smuggled out broth, and milk, and propping him against her bony little shoulder, spooned the stuff into him. Once when a customer left wine in a jug, she took that, too. Now and again, mannerliness, ground into him from childhood, broke through the haze of delirium and he would say, 'Thank you'. Sometimes he called her Sybilla, and sometimes, Tana.

When the frost clenched down she took him an extra blanket, snatched from the bed of a customer whose face she did not like. Keeping him clean was easier here than it had been in the proper bed. He lay upon straw and all that was needed was to pull away that which was soiled and push clean under him.

Sir Godfrey became fully conscious, after what seemed like years of wandering in strange places, to find himself in a real, but equally strange place. The barn at The Swan was a rickety building with gaps in its walls, and the light that came through the gaps was the curiously chill light of sunlight on snow.

No pain; just an overwhelming weakness which prevented him from getting up and investigating. He could remember nothing and lying there could only conclude that he had gone to do battle and been hit on the head. And reached, or been carried to, the sanctuary of a barn. Yet he had no wound.

One of the chinks widened, admitting so much of the bleak light that he was obliged to close his eyes. Then, opening them, he saw a tatterdemalion figure, rough edged against the light. A lot of hair, skirt. Female. She carried a jug in her hand. He asked the natural question — 'Where am I?'

She said, 'Ah, you are back in yourself. But nobody must know. Drink this and then lie still. I will come when I can. We're busy.'

Busier even than they had been with the surge to the north. The tide had turned, now the move was to the south, or to the east. Not the gay, free-spending men of the wave which had landed Sir Godfrey at the cross-road inn, but desperate, defeated men, fleeing. Staying just long enough to snatch a bite of bread and cheese, to water and bait their horses. But of this Sir Godfrey knew nothing. All he knew was that he seemed somehow to have survived whatever it was that had stricken him down, that he was weak as a new-born kitten and that lying still would only further weaken him. What the young woman, whoever she was, had brought him in the jug, tasted of beef and onion and barley. Oxtail soup? Fortified by it he set himself to crawl, like a baby to the nearest wall and there, pulling himself up by its struts and beams, try his legs. The broth-bringer had said nobody must know that he was back in himself and as he stumbled, legs, arms, hands as flaccid as half-melted candles, his mind was alert and he was ready at any moment to drop down, to pretend to be asleep.

Before the last blue-white light faded he had made the circuit of the barn three times and was glad to lie still, in the straw, as she had told him to do.

Then it was dark and when, at last, she did come, she carried a lantern and in the crook of her arm some bread, some cheese. Welcome, for he was hungry now.

Wolfing down the first solid food he had had for a long while, regarding her as a friend, he asked, 'How did the day go?'

'What day?'

'The battle.'

About that she was informed. 'Badly for the White Rose. The Queen, or so they say, is terrible spiteful. She put the Duke of York's head on the city walls. With a paper crown on it.'

Then, click, click, click, things began to fall into place. He had come north, rallying to Lord Thorsdale's call to arms for all good men and true.

The girl said, 'If you was for the White Rose, sir, you was lucky not to be there. And you should move as soon as you can. Where do you come from?'

'Suffolk.'

'Is it far?' He tried to think back, but the last stages of his journey were still hard to recall.

'Several days' ride.'

70

'You'd want a horse, then.'

'Did I not arrive on a horse?'

'Yes. She sold that to a gentleman whose own went lame.'

'Who did?'

'My mistress. The landlady. You're at The Swan, at the crossroads, near Tadminster.'

'In the barn, why?'

'So's you should die and not know about the horse and your money. She took that, too. And you would of been dead, 'cept for me. I been looking after you as well as I could.'

'I am deeply grateful.' He finished the bread and cheese and lay back. Badly for the White Rose, the girl had said; a defeat always meant heavy casualties, so the chances were that Sir William and the others were dead. God rest their souls in peace.

The girl gnawed on her thumb, meditatively.

'If I got you a horse, could you ride?'

'I'd make shift to.'

'And take me with you? Find me a place? I'm a good worker and I don't eat much.'

'I owe you my life,' he said. 'While I have a roof and bread on my table, you shall share them.'

'That'll do for me,' she said. 'I'll fetch the horse while you dress. I brought your clothes to make you a pillow. I'll leave you the lantern. It's a moonlight night.'

He found his outer clothes and fumbled his way into them. The effort was exhausting and when the girl led the horse — its hoof-falls muted by snow, to the barn entry, he thought, weakly, 'What a tall horse!' And nothing, nobody to help him to mount, with his shaky, tremulous legs, he, whose pride it had once been to get astride Arcol with a single, smooth movement. The girl crouched, offering her shoulder. She said in a low voice, 'Heave on me, sir. I'm strong as a donkey.' Agile, too. She had no sooner thrust him into the saddle than she was up herself, her skinny little arms clasped around him, less to suport herself than to support him.

They rode through a night, sharply black and white. Now and again waves of weakness washed over him and the black and white mingled into a grey blur. He would not yield to it. Nor would he think about the ethics of his situation; riding a stolen horse, absconding with a girl. Presently, after endless years the sun came up, unfriendly, a pale lemon yellow. But it was to his left, the East, so he was riding South. Sheer luck since he'd been too weak and confused to consider his road.

A village of grey stone, such as he remembered from his first ride to Yorkshire.

'Go straight through,' the girl said. 'The Queen's men may be looking for people like you. I'll look out for a haystack.'

When she sighted one she thought suitable she said, 'Go to its far side,' and jumped down, ready to help him to alight. As soon as he was on his feet he stumbled and she said, 'I'll have a bed for you in a minute.' She dragged hay from the base of the stack, making a slight hollow. He was asleep, or unconscious as soon as he was prone. She stood for a moment looking at him dubiously. He wasn't fit to travel, but she hadn't dared delay. She'd always been aware of the risk that the landlady might think he was taking too long to die and order the yardman to pull enough straw over his face to suffocate him. That danger, at least was over, but he seemed to be a White Rose man; and between them they'd stolen a horse! Griselda turned her attention to that animal, placidly eating hay. When it had had its fill who could guarantee that it wouldn't wander off while she took a little nap? She made herself a little niche in the hay, higher up the stack, level with the horse's head, so that she could keep her arm through the rein. It was not very comfortable, but she slept. She had been awake and busy since dawn on the previous day.

A jerk on the rein woke her and looking down she saw a large shaggy dog sniffing suspiciously at the horse's heels. Then, on the farthest rim of the white expanse there was movement; a man, some sheep, coming this way. The little haystack had in fact been pitched in this isolated spot so that sheep could be fed when the ground was snow-covered.

She was down on a flash, shaking Sir Godfrey with rough urgency. Not knowing his name she could not use it, but she shouted, 'Wake up. Get up. We must go. Somebody's coming.' Weak as he was, he still had the old soldier's trick of being instantly awake and active. The dog was trained to work silently with sheep, to bark only in emergencies. Satisfied that this was one, it gave tongue. It followed them, barking, as far as the road which was outside its territory. Its master who had intended to give it a good hiding for running off ahead, gave it a pat instead. Plainly somebody had been at the hay. Would have done more damage except for Old Rough.

'Do you feel better, sir?'

'Vastly better,' he said, though he had not taken stock of his state. He had noted the place of the sun however. It was westering, its cold lemon-yellow mellowed to pale gold and pink. He must have slept for hours.

'What we need now is something to eat. Presently I'll do a bit of begging. I used to be good at it.'

She was not in fact very hungry, having learned early in life to do with little. She had, as she said, been good at begging, a stick-thin little girl, but usually one of the adult members of her band had taken the biggest share. Then there had been the convent where the meals, though regular, had been sparse, unless you were a favourite. After that The Swan where everything depended upon whether the place were busy or not, and even at the busiest times she'd lived largely on what people left on their plates. In slack times she had subsisted mainly on Tinker's Broth; bread crusts and crumbs soused with hot water and if you were lucky a little salt, if very lucky a sprinkling of pepper. But he was different. He was a man, accustomed to eating well: and for days he had had nothing but slops.

It was almost sunset when a cluster of houses and a church tower came in sight.

'This'll do,' she said. 'Set me down here. I mustn't be seen on a horse. You ride straight through and wait for me, well on the other side.'

Despite his sleep he was exhausted again, glad to halt the horse and lean forward sagging, half-dozing. Yet it seemed a long wait. Once when he roused himelf it was deep dusk; next time the moon was bright. He tried to make allowance for the fact that she had had to approach the village on foot, and had perhaps been turned away from several doors. He had a vague idea that some places had rules about begging and punished it as a crime. Of that level of life he had no experience at all. He'd always been rather poor and from time to time hungry, but the net of privilege had always been there. And no doubt, not so far away from this place there was some house where Sir Godfrey Tallboys would be welcomed. Unless the owner were a Red

Rose man. But he did not know where he was; on his ride North he had ceased to be observant. This might be Yorkshire, or Lincolnshire . . . All he could do was sit and wait for a good-hearted little kitchen slut to bring him food that she had begged — that is if anybody had given.

She came at last, pattering along over the snow. She was breathless and vociferous. 'Mean old bitch,' she said. 'Made me work for it. But I got it. Enough for a day. *And* found a place for the night. No, not worth getting up. It ain't far. Back this way. Follow me.'

She led the way on the road back to the village and stopped by a broken wall. 'In here,' she said, and there was a derelict house, its roof sagged, one wall was gone, but it offered shelter of a kind. And to its side a pond, greyly glimmering under a thin covering of ice.

'Ah yes,' Sir Godfrey said. 'The horse needs water.'

They had eased their thirst by scooping up snow and sucking it. The horse, offered a handful, had turned his head disdainfully.

'I'll see to him later. I want you settled first. I got a loaf and a pie. But I had to scrub out a bakehouse. Funny thing, soon as anybody sees me they think about scrubbing! I tried the priest first. Sometimes they're good. This one wasn't but he sent me along to what he called a good charitable woman and she said scrub the place out and she'd give me a loaf.'

'And a pie.'

'No. I took that.' This confession she regretted immediately as she remembered her company. Not like the old days when such an act would have been applauded. 'I earned it,' she said, defensively. 'I shouldn't think that floor had been swept, leave alone scrubbed, for about a year.'

She insisted upon his eating the pie while she contented herself with a small portion of bread.

'You have been ill,' she said, when he protested. 'You gotta build up your strength.'

There was much in this escapade — the makeshift food, the makeshift shelter, that recalled those days in the mountains with Tana. Curious, he thought; this makes the second time I have been saved by a woman. Their attitudes were very different, nothing seductive here, simply a brisk, businesslike motherliness.

74

'Now you lay and rest, and I'll have a look round for something that'll hold water.'

He fell asleep immediately and woke to faint morning light. The girl was not in sight, but she came in almost immediately, holding her raggy skirt in a pouch.

'We're in luck,' she said with a grin that completely altered her sombre little face. 'Look what I found.' She displayed her treasure, a lapful of bright red apples. 'Nobody's been this way for a year I should think. These was still on the tree. Some on the ground, too. I gave them to the horse.'

Munching the cold, crisp fruit he said, 'I don't even know your name.'

'They called me Griselda at the covent.'

'It's a pretty name.'

'Is it? I almost forgot the sound of it. At The Swan it was always *girl*, or *you there*. What's your name?'

'Sir Godfrey Tallboys.'

'I reckoned you was somebody important.' Cracking the last pip of her apple between sound white teeth, she went on. 'We'll stow these about us and be on our way. That woman may have missed the pie. You'd hardly believe what a fuss people'll make about nearly nothing. I have watered the horse.'

'Did you find a bucket.'

'No. Nothing. So I took him to the pond and jumped on the ice.'

The horse was still bridled and saddled and Sir Godfrey thought — tonight I must do better, not go straight to sleep, neglectful.

He felt better this morning, clearer in his mind, stronger on his legs. They were still moving south, the snow covering grew thinner; here and there dark patches of earth and winter-bleached grass could be seen. Griselda did no begging that day; they finished the loaf and the apples, dismounting only to perform natural functions, about which Griselda showed a surprising delicacy — until one remembered that she had spoken of a convent. From one of her modest errands she returned with an armful of hay. And after all, Sir Godfrey thought, such petty thieving, except that it was so petty, was no different from the process known to all fighting men — living off the country, gathering loot.

There was very little traffic on the road, and they attracted

75

no attention; why should they? A man with a half-grown beard taking a girl to a new situation. Towards evening that day he recognised the inn where he had forced his dinner down and been sick — the onset of his illness. So now he knew where he was, and was back — so he thought — in a place where his credit would be good. The net of privilege tautened beneath him, and turning his head slightly, he said to Griselda, 'We may find a welcome here. And proper beds.'

He was disappointed. The first wave of refugees, fleeing to the coast to take ship to the Netherlands, had carried news of the terrible vengeance that Queen Margaret was taking upon all the supporters of the White Rose. Innkeepers had never been able to afford partisan sympathies, but they could at least be careful. And this one was. Yes, indeed, he remembered Sir Godfrey Tallboys, even though this gaunt unshaven man bore only a slight resemblance to the man who had been one of a number who took their dinner here on their way to Thorsdale — and to defeat at the Battle of Wakefield, fought while Sir Godfrey lay raving in the straw. 'But, sir, I can do nothing. The Queen's men ...' And it was strange, Sir Godfrey thought, that the King, Henry VI should now be so utterly discounted — not savage enough; he, the gentle scholar would never have ordered that mockery of a severed head, crowned with paper.

'They are widening their search. If you were found here ... But on the other hand, if I did not *know* ... If you rested in one of my outbuildings and your horse took what he could find. In the pasture. That is all I can do. I am sorry, Sir Godfrey.'

The horse, free of saddle and bridle after so many hours, cast himself down and rolled in the bit of pasture, easing his hide. Sir Godfrey and Griselda slept warmly, in hay again. And woke hungry.

But at least he now knew where he was.

And next day, hour by hour, the countryside became more familiar ...

Unlike Sybilla who had thought Knight's Acre too large and unwelcoming; unlike Tana who had thought it mean and small, to Griselda the house looked wonderful. Just the solid, sturdy kind of place which in her dreams had always meant home. Some image, imprinted upon an infant mind, too young to have conscious memory, had been with her, through the beggar days, through the convent days. She had a distinct feeling that at last she was coming home. She had in fact spent her first two years in such a house. Then the owner — an oldish man had died and his heir had made what he called a clean sweep ... The impression had remained, however.

CHAPTER FOURTEEN

Once again Sybilla said, 'Darling, darling,' and flung herself, weeping into his arms. 'I have been so worried. Not about the battle, I knew you were not there, but about your sickness.'

He said, after endearments and embracings, 'How did *you* hear about the battle, sweeting?' It was a reasonable question, for as he and Griselda had moved south knowledge of the great Lancastrian victory at Wakefield had faded away. Nobody knew; nobody cared.

Sybilla said, 'Sir William Barbury is here. He escaped. He needs help, more than I could give.'

'Here?'

'Here. In our hall. He was hurt, but not seriously.'

All the jauntiness and confidence had leached out of Sir William together with the blood he had lost. He made light of his wound, which was in his shoulder, a well-directed arrow having pierced the joint in his armour, but he was grave about his predicament.

'The Queen is rooting out all known Yorkists, Sir Godfrey. I am the last of the Barbury family. My uncle, my cousin who was his heir, and my brother died at Wakefield. I am Lord Thorsdale now and I am safe nowhere in England.'

'We must get you out,' Sir Godfrey said. Something in his mind said — Tomorrow! In the eyes of the Queen, in the eyes of every Lancastrian, all Yorkists were rebels, and to harbour a rebel was as bad as being one. He thought — and was not proud of the thought — that apart from harbouring Sir William, his own record was fairly clear. All the preparations for holding Bywater against the French had been, as Lord Thorsdale had ordered, secret; he himself had not been within miles of the battle; neither he nor his brother James had ever taken a stand for Red Rose or White.

Money! The essential thing which for many years he had taken so lightly.

'You will need money, Sir William.'

'I know. That is why I came. I have none. One does not ride to battle with a pouchful of money. All my friends in the north were dead or in flight. I could only hope that you had recovered and reached home. And would help me.'

'And so I will. To the utmost,' Sir Godfrey said staunchly, though the thought occurred that now there would be no more regular payments.

'It will not be for long,' the new Lord Thorsdale said. 'Edward of York will avenge his father.'

'I will arrange money, and a passage for you. Rest easy now.' Suddenly he remembered Griselda. 'My love, I brought a girl home with me. She saved my life.'

'You make a habit of it,' Sybilla said, laughing rather shakily. 'Does this one plan a pavilion?'

The most obvious person to make a loan was the wool-merchant, Master Johnson who had had so many dealings with Lord Thorsdale in the past. But he was a cautious man and without sentiment. He had been accommodating over the secret defence of Bywater — but he had been paid for it. He was willing to make a loan, but he must have some security.

'I have a small flock,' Sir Godfrey said. 'I'll pledge them, hoof and hide.'

'Unreliable,' Master Johnson said. 'The bloody flux or the liver rot can wipe out a flock in no time at all.'

Sir Godfrey thought of his brother James and of Tana and quickly dismissed them both. James was not only careful with his money, but with his politics as well; and to borrow from Tana would commit him further.

'I have a good house,' he said, 'and three fields.' And even as he spoke he thought — the house is Sybilla's, and the fields are Henry's. However, in the eyes of the law they were his, and he pledged them at a crippling rate of interest. About that he dared hardly think. Instead he thought that Sir William — so like Sir Robert — need not beg or starve in Amsterdam, to which city there was, most fortunately, a ship about to sail.

Sybilla took charge of Griselda in whom she saw the possibilities of the kind of nursemaid she had never been able to find when the other children were young. Griselda's hair, well-washed, proved to be the colour of straw and naturally curly. It was her best feature; her eyes were greenish, but small and seemed lashless, the lashes were so fair; her nose was snub, her mouth thin-lipped. Not pretty, but in one of Sybilla's made-over dresses, she was a neat trim figure. She was anxious to please, and in the convent orphanage had learned something about the care of children. She began to model herself, voice, manner, posture upon Sybilla who, for her, was compact of every virtue, every grace.

Jill and Eddy and Ursula across the yard who had seen her when she first arrived and thought that here was somebody to be put upon, given all the unpleasant tasks, were envious of her status, cruelly mocking about what they called her fine airs. Generally she ignored them but occasionally she would show them something of her other side. She had a vicious tongue and where abuse was concerned a vocabulary that vastly exceeded theirs.

For the first time in her memory she was consciously happy; pleasant easy work in a clean, orderly house, a kind mistress to be copied and adored. Her feeling of homecoming at the sight of the house had been fully justified.

In the shuttered room where Sir James now spent most of his time, Sir Godfrey said, 'I'm sorry James, that I did not take your advice a year ago. I've come to it now. My employment has ceased — and I have incurred a debt.'

Sir James' wits were still sharp enough to enable him not to ask about the debt. Godfrey, apart from the one period of prosperity which had had so short a run, had always been more or less in a financial muddle. And over the eviction of tenants with no unalienable rights at Intake he had been definitely wilful.

'You mean you are about to tidy up your estate?'

'Short of causing any great hardship, yes. It was never an estate, James. The rents fixed by that old parchment were ridiculous, even in Father's day. I cannot exactly remember how many of the people are protected by it.'

'Less than half, if I remember rightly,' Sir James said. 'But

Joycelyn will know. He looked into the matter for you and he remembers everything. Poor fellow he grows very stiff.'

Curious the pleasure ageing and afflicted people took in the ageing and affliction of those who were their contemporaries. Sir Godfrey had seen it. before without reflecting upon it much. Now he did, thinking it not unlike a game of cards; one man slapping down his stiff joints, another his gout, a third his failing sight. Pray God, he should not end in such decrepitude, suffering infirmities and taking comfort in the infirmities of others. God, let me die in battle, my spirit high, my blood hot, my end sudden.

Yet Sir James had his comfort. Richard's wife was pregnant and Richard was happy. He and his wife walked about hand in hand; a pair of turtle doves. And Emma — choking back her doubts and fears, spoke cheerfully, admitting that Richard was not quite what one could have wished, but that could be explained by the fact that he was so late born. Margaret was, in her opinion, just a silly girl, made sillier by Sybilla's mismanagement. 'She spoiled all her boys until they were intolerable. She spoiled Margaret until she was stupid. There is *no* reason why the child should not have all his wits about him.' If prayers were answered, he would, for Lady Emma constantly added to her ordinary prayers an urgent plea that the child should be all right and that James should live to handle his grandchild.

At Intake there were no evictions, for most of the vulnerable tenants, warned by the inquisition in the previous year had money ready for the increased rents. There was a good deal of grumbling, many sullen looks, but at least Sir Godfrey was able to pay the interest on Master Johnson's loan, due on Lady Day.

At Moyidan, on that same day, Margaret, who had no clear idea about her state, said, 'Margaret has a pain.' Within an hour Margaret had a baby, in such a state of profound indifference as not to bother to ask, girl or boy? Richard seemed almost equally unconcerned. Lady Emma was cautiously delighted. It was a boy, a good compact child with a lot of black hair. That meant nothing; birth hair almost always wore off and grew again. It was too early to tell whether the baby's wits were in good order; it would take six months. Lady

Emma remembered the moment when she realised that Richard, at six months — the son so long awaited, so much desired — had seemed so inert and un-noticing compared with what his sister had been. But then Richard had been frail from the first. This was a lusty child; and Margaret, however stupid and indifferent should feed him, Emma decided, even if she had to take her by the neck and force her to it.

The family cradle had been brought back from Knight's Acre and thoroughly refurbished. The family emblem had been reprinted by a good craftsman; the hare brown, the leveret buff, the grass green. Lady Emma had seen to the stuffing of the little mattress and the pillow with the finest goosedown, and with her own hand had quilted the cover. The carter's son lay soft and warm.

'Of course I wish to see him,' Sybilla said when the message came. 'And of course I can still ride ...' It seemed a long time since she had threatened, if Sir Godfrey couldn't rouse himself to do it, to exercise the great warhorse, Arcol. 'I am not so nimble as I was, but I shall manage.' The years reduced one's nimbleness; and her fall had left her lame and slightly lop-sided and then Robert's birth had taken toll. Also just lately, she had been subject to sudden attacks, about which the less said the better. Quite disgusting. She thanked God for Griselda, so capable, so reliable, and so understanding. 'Griselda, say that it is just a head-ache. No need to mention ... the rest. My head does ache.'

During the attacks she ached everywhere and was sick, forced to the stool-room five times in an hour, afflicted with pins and needles in her hands and feet. But the attacks always passed and she was well again — until next time. It was her age; she accepted it. Some women grew grossly fat or violently ill-tempered ... She had seen it happen to others and thought that on the whole she was getting off lightly. On the day of the visit of Moyidan she felt very well and was able to say to Emma, on the other side of the cradle, 'Well, here we are, Emma. Grandmothers. God send that his wits are as sound as his limbs.'

'God send it should be so. We can only wait ... Sybilla, what have you been putting on your face? Allow me to say that it does not become you at all.'

In the old days, before Knight's Acre was built, when she had no home of her own and was forced to accept the increasingly grudging hospitality of Moyidan, Sybilla had become accustomed to criticism. She had always done her best with re-made, even re-turned dresses and the latest hair style, and she could make a fashionable head-dress out of almost nothing. All the little secrets and the little tricks she had been most willing to share with Emma who had very seldom accepted the humble offering in the right spirit. But this accusation of putting something on her face was quite unjustified.

'What do you mean, Emma: Nothing but water has touched my face today. As you should know, such frivolity I gave up years ago.'

'That may be. But come to the light. Yes, I am not mistaken. Your skin is a most peculiar colour. Less yellow than jaundice . . . Not sun tan — not that there has been much sun so far. Did you wash in muddy water?'

'No. Our well, even in high summer gives good clear water.'

'Well, all I can say is that you have a dusky look. Almost bronze. And you had such a pretty complexion . . .'

'We grow old, Emma.'

'That is true.' But, turning from the window to the cradle, Emma thought — I must not! My son is a fool, his wife is a fool, James is failing; there is something wrong with Sybilla and Godfrey, if a bugle blew ten miles away would ride off on one of his fruitless errands. On me and me alone this child depends.

Gallant to the end Sybilla said, 'No. I do not want a doctor. He would only bleed me and give me calomel. The one thing I do *not* need. I will try the Lamarsh cure. Dame Agnes there, when I was going through my training in the infirmary always said "Give them nothing to be sick *with*". It often worked.'

It worked — or seemed to for her illness receded when she took nothing but water and a bite or two of bread. Not a diet, Sir Godfrey pointed out, upon which one could live for ever. 'There never was much of you, darling, and now you seem to be wasting away.' It pained him that he could no longer afford the good red wine which was so heartening — however, Tana was generous with hers, and also with various dainty dishes which Ursula had at last been taught to make.

Without telling Sybilla Sir Godfrey fetched the physician

from Baildon. He spoke portentously about a bilious humour, bled her from the third finger of the left hand, advised a light diet and prescribed, not calomel, but opium pills which did something to alleviate the stomach cramps.

Henry worried, too. Their manner of life during his father's absence had bonded mother and son very closely not only because of the raid, Walter's death, and the plague, but in the shared work and the business of making ends meet. The cure for worry was hard labour, and of that the boy had sufficient to keep his mind occupied during the day; it was in the evening, coming into the house — perhaps to find Mother in her place at the supper table, assuring them all that she was better, but eating almost nothing and looking ghastly; perhaps to be told that she was having another attack, then misery smote. On one such evening he remembered her flowers, and went around to the garden and gathered a few of the first rosebuds and a stem or two of the lilies on which the flowers were just breaking. There was something infinitely touching in the way his big, toil-worn hands carried the fragrant, fragile offering. And he was so like his father ... though Godfrey had been some years older when she saw him first. She was obliged to force back the tears. She thanked him for the flowers, and for the thought and then turned to practical things. 'You started the hay today, did you not? Is the crop good?'

She was ten times more conversant with the farm work than Father, who, now that his wonderful appointment had ended, did his best to help about the place, but so ignorantly and clumsily that it made Henry impatient to watch him. And suppose he'd been fool enough to heed Father's suggestion about leaving the farm!

They talked for a little. John had been Idle Jack, as usual; Tom Robinson had had to lie down for a bit; they'd caught two rabbits. 'Not as big as harvest ones, but they'll make a meal,' Henry said. He was again the provider — this time for more mouths.

'I must wash,' he said, and gave her one of his rare, but singularly sweet smiles, as though sharing a joke. She had always been so insistent upon the washing of hands before meals and upon other small niceties. She'd said, 'Poor we certainly are, but good behaviour costs nothing.'

'I hope you will feel better tomorrow.'

'I am sure I shall.' Dame Agnes' stringent cure had been again effective, and although she felt weak, she was better. But as Henry turned towards the door, Sybilla wondered for the first time, about the certainty of that betterment. Fasting did cure, but it also weakened. She said, 'Henry I pray that you may be happy and successful all your life. Choose your wife with care. A good wife is the best thing a man can have.'

'Is Mother dying?' the brutal, brusque question brought Sir Godfrey's own hidden fear to the surface and he rebuffed it.

'No, of course not! The doctor did not take that view at all. What made you think that?'

'Something she said. It sounded as though . . . as though she were taking leave of me . . .'

'She did not speak so to me when I carried up her supper and lit the candle. But I will see . . .'

'When was that?'

'Just before supper. I took her a few flowers.'

'But I've seen her since then . . . She said she . . .'

Abandoning his supper Sir Godfrey rushed upstairs, two at a time, stood at the top and drew a steadying breath and then, forcing a casual manner, entered the sick room.

'That was a very short supper,' Sybilla said.

Yes, he thought, she sounded weaker, farther away. He sat on the bed and took her hand. It felt cold and clammy. So little time ago it had been hot.

'You feel worse, darling?'

'Weaker . . . I think, perhaps, Father Ambrose . . .'

It was as much as he could do to call from the stair head.

The old priest was now so blind that except in his house or in the church, where he could feel his way about, he needed guidance or made slow progress by sweeping a stick in front of him to make sure that his path was not obstructed. With mounting impatience Henry saw him collect his little basket, guided him into the church and out again. Then he said, 'Father, with your permission, I will carry you.' The age-withered body was not very heavy and Henry was able to break into a trot. Not, Father Ambrose thought, quite the proper dignified way for

the Host to travel, but so long as they reached the poor lady in
time ...

They were too late.

CHAPTER FIFTEEN

It took Tana some little time to understand that in disposing of
Sybilla she had cleared her way to nothing. She was hardy,
ruthless and young. She thought it natural enough that in this
strange country — one woman to one man — when that one
woman died there should be a little time of mourning. A few
months ... during which she must be patient, tactful. She
absolutely refused to see that Sybilla's death had been, in a
way, Godfree's too.

There was the small matter of the place where Sybilla lay.
Henry explained that. 'My father grieves that my mother lies
under plain stone. He wished for marble.'

'And where, in this country, is marble to be found?'

'How can I know?' In fact Henry was not quite certain what
marble really was. Some kind of stone, he supposed, having
regard to its purpose — a floor over the dead. 'There is a stone-
mason in Baildon. I could ask him.'

The stonemason in Baildon did not usually stock such costly
stuff, but he had, in the early summer, laid a floor in an ornate
little side chapel of the Abbey, and due to a slight mis-
calculation, had a bit of black marble left over from that job.
Four feet by two and a half. Henry found it, brought it home
in the wagon. Tana paid for it.

It made no difference. Sybilla under marble was just as dead
and lost as Sybilla under stone. Tana was not warned by that,
not by something that happened late in November, momentous
as it was. What had been taking place in the outer world had
concerned this bit of Suffolk very little. But here was Lord
Thorsdale, with three friends, apologising for delay in
coming — he'd had to take possession of his Yorkshire estates,
attend upon Edward IV who had indeed avenged his father.

Faced with this invasion of young, and very happy men, Sir
Godfrey had asked Tana to come and preside at his table. But

when assured of his re-appointment, and of the paying back, ten times over of the loan, that harassing debt, he had simply said, 'It is too late. Sybilla never had anything . . .' and hurried from the table to hide his tears.

Henry said, diffidently yet firmly, 'Father, you now have money . . .' That was the odd thing, the boy thought; work from dawn till dusk, contrive, make do, and all you had was a bare livelihood. Do nothing useful, make no plans, and money simply fell into your hand. In his heart the son resented his father's extremity of grief and the way in which he had given way to it. *He* was sorrowful, too, but he had no time to droop about and nurse his feelings.

'Yes,' Sir Godfrey said mildly. 'Lord Thorsdale repaid the sum I lent him, with a very generous gift. And he re-appointed me as his agent. But . . .' And Henry knew that he was about to hear yet again, the cry that prosperity had come too late. He forestalled it.

'I should like to clear some more land. Walter and I did what we could and the three fields kept us. The household has grown since then . . .'

'*And* diminished . . .'

'Mother is dead,' Henry said, harshly because pain stabbed. 'And we miss her good management. That is one reason why we must do better. Also, with due respect, sir, this see-saw between York and Lancaster is not ended. It may tip the other way. It has before. The best guard against disaster is a field yielding food, and a well-filled stockyard.'

'Do what you think best,' Sir Godfrey said. He thought, with a slight resentment: Yes, the young recover and forget the dead, make plans, think about money. He forgot that he had, with equal resilience, survived the death of both his parents.

Tree-fellers came, and after them the ox teams, straining and pulling away the trunks of the cut-down trees. Then came the grubbers, men and women and children who, with the most unlikely tools, and with their hands, grubbed out the tree roots, carried them away and cut them up to be hawked as firewood. Henry, helping them all, hurrying them all because he wanted the newly cleared land ploughed and seeded, gained himself an unenviable reputation as a slave-driver.

Late in November of that year he looked out over the newly

86

cleared land and said to Tom Robinson, 'It's more than we can manage, Tom. Is there nobody in the village to be hired?'

'I'll go down and see,' Tom said. His real roots in the village had been severed in the time of the plague when he had lain sick, almost to death at Knight's Acre, and been tended by the lady and by Master Henry. Since then his loyalty had been absolute and his reputation in the place of his birth very low. The people of Intake — rebels to begin with, had never looked on Knight's Acre with any great favour. Walter had been hated, with his scarred face and arrogant manner — and there was the Wade girl, who had fled because — she said — he had assaulted her ... But Tom Robinson had, when he cared to exercise it, a glib and persuasive tongue. Nobody was asking, he said, that men should live in the house, as he did himself, and apparently quite comfortably, if you didn't mind the servility which living in implied. Day labour was different; set times, set wages. Two of the families who had none of those 'inalienable rights', and who were now paying extra rent, decided that they could spare a boy. To be paid by the week and given a mid-day meal.

Tom, walking back at the slow pace which since the plague he had found most suitable to his state, just missed Father Ambrose who, clearing the way with his stick made his way from the church to Knight's Acre. He knew, only too well that he was almost blind and often forgetful. He also knew that what he had just experienced was unusual, if not unique.

'I was,' he told Sir Godfrey, 'changing the candles. The good lady, as you must know, gave the church a supply of good candles as soon as she could afford. I took no light ... I work well, in the dark ... by touch. So I was in the dark. Then I smelt lilies. She always brought them you know ... for the altar. I smelt them and forgetful of time, of everything, I turned to thank her ... I forgot — old men do, you know — that it was winter and she in her grave. There was a faint light, visible even to me, over her tomb and a strong scent of lilies. I am not a man to make judgments ... and about what awaits us all, after death, I must only believe what the Church teaches. But ... Would it be too fanciful to think that she knew how grieved I was ... not to be in time to administer ... while she was conscious, and could respond . . . and perhaps asked, or was given, leave to return . . . To re-assure me that all was well and that she was happy, with the flowers she loved?'

Hitherto Sir Godfrey's religion had been almost a military exercise. There were orders and rules which must be obeyed; rites to be observed, or, if disregarded, done penance for. Now and again, in a desperate situation he had called upon God; God help me; God save me . . . but always as a man might call upon his liege lord. Of mysticism there was not a trace in his nature. Even when God had seemed to fail him — in that narrow, balconied street with his scorched fingers trying in vain to release Lord Robert; under the lash of the whip in the mine, and more lately when he prayed for Sybilla's recovery; a disciplined soldier did not query his overlord's decisions. Now, however, something hitherto unknown sparked in his mind and what Father Ambrose said about the possible reason for the manifestation was absolutely in accord. If Sybilla wished to re-assure the old man who had not failed in his duty but had simply been too late, how much more would she wish to assure him?

That night he knelt on the cold stone, just inside the church door, with Sybilla's grave between him and the altar. He had kept a similar vigil, in the chapel at Beauclaire on the night before he received his knighthood. He did not think of that now, he was concentrating too fiercely upon his petitions, partly to God, partly to Sybilla's spirit, for some sign of her presence, of her awareness of him. No infatuated young lover ever craved more avidly for some glance or gesture of favour. In the chilly, damp-smelling church on this winter's night he sweated with fervour.

He saw nothing, smelt no lilies.

In the reluctant dawn, the sense of failure and rejection heavy upon him, he examined the cause of failure. Then he remembered that other vigil so carefully prepared for; the ritual bath, the clean clothing, the confession and the absolution, so that the would-be knight came to the altar as clean and pure, both in body and soul as mortal man could be. For this one he had made no preparation at all.

Henry, if asked, within his own mind, would have said that his father was irresponsible, but in fact his own deep feeling of

88

responsibility was inherited from Sir Godfrey; they merely moved in different worlds. Sir Godfrey, as the light crept in through the unglazed window, was prepared to acknowledge that the failure was due to fault in him.

Father Ambrose came as always to perform the morning office. Between his house and the church he had no need to bother with his stick; he could feel his way along the walls. So he walked into, and stumbled over Sir Godfrey, and they fell together, in an ungainly heap upon the floor. Sir Godfrey scrambled to his feet and lifted the old man, apologised, asked was any damage done.

'No. No. I fell upon you, Sir Godfrey . . .' He recognised the man by his voice. 'Are you hurt?'

'No.'

'Why are you here so early?'

Sir Godfrey, never good at explaining, tried to explain. The priest with long experience with inarticulate people in this rural and not very friendly parish understood. Then, abruptly assuming clerical authority, as a man might don a cloak, he said,

'My son, that was a very wrong thing to do. Such an experience cannot be demanded. It came to me — the *last* thing in my mind. I was thinking about the candles, pure wax, and so thick. Her gift.'

'I was ill-prepared,' Sir Godfrey said, and he spoke as though he had, in his own sphere, neglected his armour or his horse. 'Father, will you take my confession now?'

It was rambling and incoherent, and with one exception, not concerned with anything that the Church regarded as sin.

'I neglected her . . . Not wantonly. Not for other women. But I was careless with money . . . Had I been more careful . . . I once gave her a ring, with a blue stone. It was no sooner on her finger than it was off again, because I needed a new horse. She always wanted a house — and that I did at last provide. And I spoilt her joy in it, coming home as I did, in evil temper . . .'

'My son, these are not *sins*.'

'They are to me, now. I only realised . . . when she was dead.'

The old priest in his way as rigid and disciplined as Sir Godfrey thought — if every man who bore hard on his wife and gave way to temper, came to confess, the line would stretch from here to the water splash! And what possible penance could I order?

Sir Godfrey said, 'And I did sin. I . . . I committed adultery.'

So! Father Ambrose thought — now we come to the nub.

'Did you confess, at the time?'

'I did. To the first priest I could find.'

'And performed your penance?'

'Yes, Father.'

'Took notice of the order to avoid the occasion?'

'To the best of my ability.' Sir Godfrey looked back; how many times? All confessed, all absolved. There had been that moment in the lane, and that he realised was more than a year ago. He *had* avoided the occasion for further sin. But in his mind something still weighed heavy. He said, bringing the words out with difficulty. 'My wife knew . . . and forgave me. What she did not know and what I could not tell her was that it was not only the flesh — as she thought . . . There was a time when my mind, my heart were corrupted, too.'

'And would that knowledge have given her happiness?'

'No.'

The old priest had met this condition before. Bereavement bringing remorse. Even the most earthy people would say, 'And I spoke sharply to him on Wednesday for forgetting my new needle,' or 'Only the day before last I fetched her a clout, as my dinner wasn't ready.'

Father Ambrose brought to the forefront of his mind a thought which had been nibbling behind the attention he had been giving. He could not see what was taking place at Knight's Acre, but he could hear gossip. The flock of sheep enlarged, more land being cleared. Bert Edgar and Jem Watson hired as day labourers. It all smelt of prosperity.

He said, 'It is best to put such thoughts away. The Lady Sybilla was a good wooman, and is now in Heaven where there is neither marriage nor giving in marriage . . . I cannot claim to have had a vision, but there was something . . . It is possible that there was a purpose behind it all. She loved this church. She brought her flowers, always. She gave the candles. She deplored, with me, the state of decay into which it has fallen. I am sure that, given the means, she would have repaired the roof.' He let the hint fall gently upon the contrite heart. The effect was immediate. Once Sir Godfrey was enlisted to a cause he was with it, heart and soul.

'I will do it,' he said. And he meant not the roof only; the walls upon which the painted pictures were almost indecipherable; the Virgin in her little niche, all should be restored. And the altar properly furnished. A fitting memorial to Sybilla.

It did not bring the comfort which had been a fraction of Father Ambrose's intention. Considering how small a part of their married life had been spent together, he missed Sybilla disproportionately. They had not always been together, but she had always been in his mind, his mental lodestar and there were times when, seeing some progress in the work, or a hitch, he would think — I must tell Sybilla and then realise . . .

Henry thought the whole thing a sad waste of money that could have been far better employed. Certainly mend the roof, which had been thatched; thatch could be patched; no need to strip it all and cover it with stone slabs, brought down from the north at vast expense; no need for the window behind the altar to be filled in with coloured glass, little leaded panes which when assembled formed the letters, S and T and some flowers. Pretty, but Mother, Henry was sure, would have preferred to see the money spent on practical things.

Tana watched. This, she believed, was Godfree's final tribute to his first wife. Men did such things. About a day's journey from her father's fortress, southwards, into the desert there was an oasis, a whole flourishing village which one of her forebears had established as a memorial to a dead woman; Mahbuub, beloved.

Once this was over Godfree would be himself again.

The villagers of Intake, knowing nothing of the debt which Sir Godfrey had incurred and which had been paid back, grudged every penny, assuming that it was their money, the extra rents, being so recklessly squandered. They were interested none the less and curious and for several weeks Father Ambrose had the kind of congregation formerly only seen at Christmas and Easter.

The year pulled itself out of the slough of winter and advanced steadily towards summer.

CHAPTER SIXTEEN

Sir Godfrey was not as his son thought him, a mere idler, a fritterer away of money, nursing his grief. He had been re-appointed to his post at Bywater and went there regularly to oversee matters. But every visit darkened his mood. There was the jetty from which Arcol would not move unless preceded by the old donkey. He remembered the clatter and clamour of that day and must think — I am the only one left alive. Then there was the house in which the knights had lived, making merry while guarding against an invasion from the French. There, God forgave him, he had enjoyed a taste of bachelor life, away from women and babies. He was not the only one left of that merry company, for William Barbury was now Lord Thorsdale; he sent kind messages and gifts from time to time.

In Bywater he had nothing to *do*. His post was a sinecure and everybody treated him as though he were old. All very respectful — 'A keen wind this morning, Sir Godfrey. Don't stand about. Everything goes well.'

'All that is needed is your signature, sir.'

He loathed it, being treated like a dotard. He was forty-six and he knew that given a chance he could still outride, outfast any of these bustling, careful, kind little men, appointed by Lord Thorsdale to make his post a sinecure. Curiously, his inner breakdown, his hopeless misery had affected his outer appearance very little. He'd lost weight all to the good in a man of middle-age. The silvery streaks in his hair had multiplied, but he had been fair once, and the paler hairs, mingling with the fawn of his later years made him look, if anything more youthful.

He made regular visits to Moyidan, and they did little to cheer him; James was now bedridden, his legs swollen to im-mense size, the rest of his body shrunken. Emma still cared for him competently but it was plain that the focus of her at-tention and emotions had shifted to the child; in her opinion the most wonderful child ever born. Certainly little Richard seemed to have inherited none of the weakness of mind and body which had afflicted his parents. Nor was he at all like a normal Tallboys child; he was thick set, black-haired, dark-eyed, and to Sir Godfrey's eye lacked the charm which his own sons had had, even at their naughtiest moments. A man should take pleasure in his grandchildren, but watching little Richard or listening to Emma's infatuated account of his latest show of precocity, strength and intelligence, Sir Godfrey felt nothing except, now and again, a vague wonder that the child should seem so different. Emma accounted for his colouring by saying that he resembled her side of the family. She had always accused Sybilla of spoiling her children, but no child had ever been so spoiled as this one.

Visits to his own nursery — established in what should have been Sybilla's solar — brought him little joy, though both children there were charming, lovely to look at, and — firmly ruled by Griselda — well-behaved. The thought was unavoidable, Sybilla had never fully recovered from that premature birth, and until Griselda's arrival, had worn herself out caring for both children. Joanna in no way resembled her mother but to look at her was to be reminded of the infidelity which Father Ambrose had dismissed so lightly. Easy enough for an old man who had lived all his life in celibacy. Also there was something about Griselda herself at times which was disquieting until he spotted the reason for it — a vagrant likeness to Sybilla, a mocking likeness. He decided that it was the dress and asked if it was one from the chest upstairs.

'Yes, sir. But I didn't *take* it,' Griselda said, instantly defensive. 'My lady and I were patching it just before . . .'

She was perhaps the one person who, given the slightest encouragement, could have offered him genuine sympathy and understanding, for she shared his sense of loss. Sybilla had been, as well as mistress and mentor, a mother to her — the mother she had never known. Without her Griselda felt stranded, there was nobody at Knight's Acre whose advice she could ask — or would have taken; and it was sad that the lady could not see how Robert's health had improved and the difference between the two children was growing slighter. A pity, too, that the lady could not see how well Griselda was managing, remembering all the rules, the gentle hints. Of all this the girl showed nothing; life had early robbed her of the capacity to show the gentler emotions.

'If it is already patched you'll soon need a new one,' Sir Godfrey said. 'I will bring you some stuff.'

Another painful reminder came when John discovered Sybilla's lute and soon developed an ability to play it. The lute having a limited range it was inevitable that he should make some sounds that evoked memories. To some men the sight and sound of Sybilla's son playing Sybilla's lute might have brought some sentimental consolation, to Sir Godfrey it merely rasped a raw nerve and one evening he said, 'Go and play elsewhere.'

Henry, who regarded the lute-playing as effeminate, and a waste of time, grinned and said, 'That's right. Go play to Young Shep. He spends half his day making pipes.'

In all this time Tana had behaved impeccably. She had never obtruded on his grief; Sybilla had been dead a full three months before she issued a supper invitation and that included Henry and John. She looked in at the nursery from time to time and occasionally drifted into the kitchen to spur Jill and Eddy into some show of activity and to see that the larder was kept supplied. Jill was no manager and would use the last handful of salt or flour without asking Henry to bring some from Baildon, or Sir Godfrey to buy in Bywater. Nobody seemed to mark that with Sybilla's death the ability to speak fluent, rather prettily accented English, had come upon Tana suddenly.

Apart from an exchange of suppers, at which there was never a glance or word amiss, Sir Godfrey and Tana met most often in the stable, for, useless at other work about the farm, Sir Godfrey could care for horses and Jamil was just as arbitrary as Arcol had been. He *just* tolerated Sir Godfrey who was not afraid of him, but preferred Tana. Everybody else was scared to death of him — not without reason.

The stable had been enlarged with the resurgence of prosperity. The newly cleared field had provided the timber. Henry now had two proper plough-horses, sturdy beasts, who under Sir Godfrey's care were glossy as war-horses. There was a lighter, leggier animal which was suitable for riding, or pulling a not too heavily laden wagon. There was also the tall black horse upon which Sir Godfrey and Griselda had ridden from

Tadminster. About his ownership of that animal Sir Godfrey, scrupulous man, had no scruples at all. Because inn-keepers so often had surreptitious dealings with horse-thieves there was a law that inn-keepers were responsible for animals stolen from their premises; the landlady of The Swan had robbed him of a horse, of the money in his pouch, of the money which William Barbury had left with her. But for Griselda's intervention, she would have robbed him of his life. So he hoped that the owner of the black horse had claimed his legal right.

For stable work Tana wore a kind of smock, anything but seductive, and had her head — the hair about which she was always so careful, wrapped in a turban of linen. She never talked to Jamil in English; she claimed that he had understood Arabic from the moment that she had told him that he was beautiful; and often, as he groomed all the horses, Sir Godfrey heard Arabic terms of endearment coming from the far stall. Words she had used to him — now as empty as a nut-shell eaten out by maggots who having consumed what fed them, died.

In a farmer's year there was a space, just before haycutting began, when a man could take a little time for himself; or, if he were industrious and ambitious do things about his house and yard, chop wood for the winter, mend his roof, slap clay on cracks in the wall. Henry, this year, had leisure to go riding with Tana — at her invitation. 'To ride alone is lonely, Henree.' That she should actually seek his company he took as proof of his adulthood; they were roughly of an age but she had always treated him as though he were much younger, lumping him and John together. Her change of attitude changed his whole world. He had been in love with her from the moment of her arrival when he had thought her the loveliest thing he had ever seen, but there had for a long time been the barrier of language; she was rich, he was poor; she had been married and borne a child, he had never even kissed a girl. He'd been obliged to adore her from afar, without hope. Now she was noticing him at least!

He was anxious to impress. And he had one thing which she had not, or at least not in England, family.

'We'll go to Moyidan,' he said.

This was a breaking away from Walter's standards. Walter had been scornful about ancestry. He said that come to think of it we were all descended from Adam and John Ball was right with his jingle; When Adam delved and Eve span, who was then the gentleman? At other times, however, Walter would say that Henry's mother would have been a lady if she'd been a goose-girl.

Of Moyidan Castle Tana said, 'It is very big,' and it pleased Henry to be able to say that he was born there.

'At least, not there, the castle is no longer used. The house is to the rear.' And that was impressive, too; much in the style of Knight's Acre but larger and with more stone about it, the family emblem carved in a massive block over the main doorway.

Lady Emma was entertaining guests for dinner. She entertained more than usual nowadays and with good reason. She wanted to show off her wonderful grandson and any guest worth his salt would step upstairs and talk to poor James for a little while.

In no time at all Henry realised that he had chosen his day badly. His aunt welcomed him and Tana most genially, and the table was at its best, stiff white linen over scarlet cloth, all the silver gleaming, the waiting boys neat and nimble — very different from Eddy who since Sybilla's death had grown slovenly. But one of the three other guests was a man whom Henry's instinct immediately recognised as a rival. Not young, almost as old as Father; not handsome really, but a well-dressed man, with exaggeratedly good manners and a kind of *look*. Something sparked in his eyes as soon as Lady Emma made the introductions. Had he been a dog Henry would have raised his hackles, bared his teeth. As it was he could only sit rather glumly through the excellent meal and hear the man — Sir Francis Lassiter was his name — talking about himself; how he had recently inherited Muchanger from an old uncle, rather miserly who had let the place fall into disrepair, how much in the way of re-building and decorating there was to do; how in these affairs a woman's hand and eye mattered so much, and how he, being unmarried, must rely upon the Lady Emma who in some complicated way was a relative.

Lady Emma whose whole life had altered when little Richard proved to be strong and sensible, smiled and said, 'Francis, as you well know, I can be relied upon for nothing but advice these days. What with poor James and this little rogue . . .'

(The little rogue, fourteen months old, knew his power. He ate heartily, but choosily, demanding and getting the choicest bit of every dish.)

'Ah well,' Sir Francis said, with one of those eloquent glances at Tana, 'perhaps some other kind lady will take pity on me.'

To Henry's intense disgust Tana said that she knew little about English houses, but she had built herself a pavilion with which she was delighted; perhaps Sir Francis would care to view it one day.

Little Richard allowed his doting grandmother no time to sit and digest her meal peacefully.

'Ducks, Umma. Ducks!' he cried, pulling at her hand with astonishing strength. She rose at once, excusing herself and explaining that every day after dinner they went to feed the ducks on the moat. As she allowed herself to be tugged away she looked backward at Henry and said, 'You will have a few words with your Uncle James, Henry.'

Outside, on the bridge which had long ago replaced the old drawbridge, Lady Emma thought— I daresay they think I am an old fool to pander so, but let them think what they like! Nobody knew the pleasure she derived from this little boy, so unlike her own son. Watching him throw some of the meal's debris with an aim singularly purposeful and accurate for one so young, she prayed, as she often did; God, grant me length of days so that I may leave Moyidan in his charge.

Henry mounted the stairs unwillingly, meaning to stay with Sir James the minimum of time permitted by civility, but the old man, bedridden by the gross swelling of his legs, and obliged by his sore eyes to live in semi-darkness, was avid for company and asked questions which must be answered. What did Henry think of little Dick? Henry who had been too much preoccupied to notice his nephew much, except to think that he made a nuisance of himself, replied, 'He's a splendid fellow.'

'In this dusky room I cannot see him so well as I should like. When he was smaller your aunt would place him beside me and I judged him a good solid child. He is too big and active for that now. With my legs as they are. Is he tall enough, do you think?'

'He looks to me to be almost as tall as my brother Robert who is— what? — nine months older.'

'Good! Good! I know that our name does not mean tall, being a corruption of Taillebois; but we have always been tall and it would come hard on a squat fellow to be called Tallboys.'

No subject in the world could have interested Henry less at any time and now he was anxious to get back to Tana, to remove her from the company of that leering old goat.

'Nothing to worry about there, Uncle James,' he said heartily. 'Well, I . . .'

Sir James recognised the about-to-take-leave sound. Nobody stayed long. A greeting, an enquiry as to his health, an expression of good wishes, and gone.

'Tell me, how are your sheep doing?'

It was not a subject upon which Henry could expound much. He was not trained to sheep; Walter had been against them, holding that they needed more open country than Intake could offer.

'We have some new ones.'

'Yes. So your father told me. Black-faced, I believe.'

'Some have black faces.'

'Not a breed I favour. They don't yield the wool. Some people hold that they're sweeter eating, but I never thought so. How does the flock look? On the whole?'

'All right.'

'They should. Young Shep knows his job. He was practically born in a lambing pen himself.'

Henry, knowing nothing of the rhythm of a shepherd's year; the periods of immense activity interspersed with times when little but watchfulness was needed, privately thought that Young Shep was an idle fellow, but he did not pursue the subject. He said firmly that he must be going.

The dining hall was deserted so was the smaller room beyond it. From the window he could see Emma and little Richard on the bridge, still feeding the ducks. A horrid thought occurred. Tana had gone off with that abominable man, either to see his hateful house or to show him her pretty pavilion. He rushed out and said, 'What's happened to everybody?' The two other guests had left, she explained; Richard and Margaret had wandered off — 'They make wreaths for one another all day long.' She could say such a thing without bitterness now. 'Your Lady Serriff took Sir Francis to the stable yard. She could not convince him that she rode a Thoroughbred stallion.

It was all right. They were not even standing close together; Jamil would not let Sir Francis near him. And they were not alone. From various points around the yard men with awed faces were watching the beautiful animal whom only this young lady could approach.

'All the same,' Sir Francis was saying, 'I would like to try him.' His face set in cruel lines. Tana, leaning against the horse whose silky mane, only a few shades darker than his cream hide, made a perfect background for her, laughed and said, in her pretty English.

'If ever I am wishing, Sir Francis, to see your neck broken, that day you shall try Jamil.'

'That,' he said, 'would be too high a price.' Then he laughed too.

It was the kind of exchange of words of which Henry was ignorant. In his world people said exactly what they meant, and a broken neck was nothing to joke about.

He was a little silent on the way home, answering when spoken to but offering nothing. His first venture into social life had been a dismal failure, and that part of him which Walter had shaped and tempered said — and serve you right! Trying to show off!

Where the road forked, one to Baildon, the other to Intake, Tana, well aware of what was happening, halted and said, 'Henree, would you like to try Jamil?'

'Do you wish to see *my* neck broken?'

'I will speak to him,' she said. She leaned forward and seemed to whisper. The horse's ears moved. Henry watched and wished, absurdly for a moment, that he were Jamil. Straightening up she said, 'He understands. You are his master. Until the stable.'

Up the lane, through the water-splash, past the priest's house and the church on the one side of the track and the sheeprun on the other, Henry rode not on one of the best horses in England, but on air. She had granted him a favour denied to Sir Francis. What she could do for one man she could as easily have done for the other. But she had chosen to do it for *him*.

When feeding the ducks palled because they were so full fed that they no longer competed for a crust, little Dick was ready with another occupation. He said, 'Umma, swarbwerries!' It was too early. Strawberries came with the hay and the shearing in June. But on a well-tended bed, like that at Moyidan, sloping slightly to the south and with every plant upheld to the sun by a collar of straw, one or two berries reddened early. And the boy had sharp eyes and a strong stomach. Only two days before he had found a few pinkish on their upper sides, green underneath and gobbled them down with none of the sorry results which might have been expected. Anything that little Richard could swallow he could digest, Lady Emma thought, with joy and while he searched, she could sit down. Never, never would she admit that just occasionally she found little Richard slightly exhausting. Never, never would she hand him over to hirelings.

She had barely seated herself before she heard hoof-beats on the trail that led from Moyidan to the road. It was Godfrey whom she was always nowadays glad to see; he at least did not grudge poor James a half-hour's chat. Not that he could be called cheerful company, but perhaps for that reason his visits seemed to benefit his brother who had even been known to take his eye off his own affliction long enough to say, 'Poor Godfrey.'

From her seat on the wall she could watch Sir Godfrey approach. The bright May sunshine shone on his hair, now much more silver than fawn, on his slightly hollowed cheeks and the lines that ran from nostrils to mouth. He had always been the handsome one, she reflected, and even misery had not ruined his looks. He was still good-looking in a melancholy way; and only about forty-five or six — not old for a man.

He rode without looking about him and did not notice her until she called his name. Then he halted and dismounted. He made what was a visible effort to cast off gloom and be pleasant, asking after her health and James', glancing at little Richard and saying, 'No need to ask about *him*.'

The gift of this sturdy child with all his wits about him had sweetened the Lady Emma's disposition; happy herself, she wished others to be happy, and even in her brusque days she had had a soft spot for Godfrey, while regarding him as a fool. The thought she now entertained was not new to her, but now she had a peg for her argument.

'Your young people were here for dinner,' she began.

'What young people?'

'Henry and the lady from Spain.'

'Oh. Something new for Henry to give himself a holiday. I'm glad.'

'If I am not very much mistaken they intend to make a match of it.'

'Well, I suppose they are much of an age.' In years, he thought; but Henry is an untried boy and she is older than Eve.

'Have you ever considered, Godfrey, how that would affect *you*?'

He gave her that singularly candid, very blue stare and said, 'How could it affect me?'

'That young woman has a mind of her own, and for a time at least, Henry will be wax in her hands. You would be pushed aside. You'd have no say in the ordering of the household. You'd find yourself in the second-best bed.'

'Where I sleep is of no importance.' (I sleep alone. In the biggest bed, half of it empty and cold; sometimes I wake and forget for a moment, and reach out — to nothing.)

Some of Lady Emma's acerbity returned. She could have shaken him.

'It should,' she said. 'I have thought this before and now I say it. You should marry again.'

'Never.'

'Why not? Sybilla, God rest her, has been dead almost a year. Would she — ask yourself — wish you to go about for ever grieving. And your clothes as they are.'

In the irritating way he had of muddling the important with the non-important, he said, 'What is wrong with my clothes?'

Lady Emma could have said — everything, and not been far wrong. His doublet had fitted him once, before he grew thin; now it was too big, it was faded, its sleeves were frayed and spotted with tallow; one hole in his hose had been patched, another gaped. With a sharp eye and a pointing finger she detailed the faults.

Griselda is good,' he said, 'but the children keep her busy.'

'Exactly. What you need is a competent, comfortable wife whose first care would be for *you*. And I know . . .'

'Spare yourself!' he gave her another look, just as blue and just as straight, but with something fierce in it. 'Emma, if you ever mention this matter to me again, I shall not come here any more . . .'

Well, she had done her best, she thought, and turned back to the child.

CHAPTER SEVENTEEN

After May came June. Still carefully emulating Sybilla, Griselda carried roses and lilies to the church. The shearers came, and despite his apparent idleness, Young Shep had kept the fleeces free of maggots and when the wool merchant's agent came to inspect and to haggle, he rejected none. The hay crop was heavy and the harvest promised well. So why was Henry so glum?

Sir Godfrey knew the answer. From the pangs of unrequited love, either real or pretended, he had escaped entirely, but he had spent a good deal of his youth with young men who had suffered, or pretended to. He'd been fortunate; in the chill convent parlour he'd seen Sybilla and known — that is the woman for me; and when he and Sybilla had married, she had told him that at first sight of him she had felt the same, had known instantly why she had resisted all attempts to make her take vows, take the veil. Happiness long past, and in a way he was paying for it now, but he understood and felt pity for the boy.

One evening, at the risk of being thought interfering, he said, 'Son, what's wrong? Is it Tana?'

'Yes. She blows hot and cold. It is all very well for her to say that now I employ men. So I do. But that does not free me. Tom works whether I'm there or not, but he's frail and cannot command. Bert and Jem work while I am there, setting the pace . . . She does not understand. She says come riding and when I say not until evening, she goes off. And where? To

Muchanger. Or he is here. Francis Lassiter. Have you not noticed his grey horse? How often . . .?'

No, locked in his grief Sir Godfrey had noticed little. Now he could remember that in what seemed another life, when he had thought of bringing Tana back to England with him, he had thought of protecting her from fortune hunters. Sir Francis was not that. He was a rich man, well-connected, distantly related to Aunt Emma. Not young, and Sir Godfrey dimly remembered that he had a reputation as a womaniser. All the better. His wild oats were sown and he was probably prepared to settle down and become a model husband and father. An ideal match, in fact. Very different from the proposed one with poor Moyidan Richard which Sir Godfrey admitted he had been reluctant to encourage.

'And yet,' Henry said in a puzzled way, 'sometimes she is so amiable to me. She even allows me to ride Jamil.'

'You ride him?'

'Quite often.'

Surprising and disquieting. Sir Godfrey considered himself a good judge of horses and considered the beautiful animal to be dangerous; even to Tana who managed him so well. He had warned her more than once that stallions as they grew older became unreliable, especially when denied the natural outlet for their energy.

'That is what I mean by blowing hot and cold,' Henry said. 'I never know where I am. Sweet as pie one day, prickly as a nettle the next.'

'You love her?'

The dark tan on the boy's face deepened as he blushed. Almost defiantly, he said, 'Yes, I do. With all my heart. She's the only girl I ever cared for — or ever shall.'

Coming from one so young, so entirely inexperienced that was an extremely pathetic statement.

'It's early days for such a decision,' Sir Godfrey said, rather awkwardly. 'Young women are notoriously fickle.' Not that most of them had much chance to be, before marriage, since their parents chose for them; it was later on that the fickleness showed and they switched lovers as they might switch horses; but he had known a case or two where a girl in great demand, and with indulgent parents had kept as many as four suitors on a string. He could even remember wagers being laid.

He brooded over the business for a day or two and then decided to take action. After all, Henry was Sybilla's son, he must not be made miserable for lack of a hint or two. It occurred to him that Tana might be playing one of the oldest games in the world, deliberately provoking jealousy in order to bring one man — in this case almost certainly Sir Francis — to the sticking point.

Walking through the scent of roses from his own hall door to Tana's, Sir Godfrey gave no thought to the risk to which he was exposing himself. Grief had purged him. And just as he had told Lady Emma that where he slept had no importance, so people had become unimportant; shadowy figures. Henry had for a little time emerged from the shadows, a real person, with a real problem; but Tana existed now only because of Henry. Also, since he had rebuffed her in the lane, on the day when she bought Jamil, Tana had withdrawn herself. Certainly during Sybilla's illness she had been kind, sending wine and tempting little dishes. Afterwards she had made no attempt to obtrude herself, even to offer comfort.

So here he was, exactly as she had foreseen when she designed her pavilion; he came, uninvited, to her door.

Perhaps in this strange country where a man could have only one wife there was another rule — that the old one must be a year dead before a man could approach another woman.

She said, 'Godfree, you are most welcome.'

Ursula, gossiping with Jill had once said that Spanish clothes were funny, not much sewing and very little cover, either. On this warm summer evening Tana wore what Ursula believed to be Spanish clothes, and which were in fact the very reverse, all gauzy folds, half revealing, half concealing.

She busied herself pouring wine, offering the cup prettily; and Sir Godfrey accepted it. He could afford wine now and could have drunk to excess had he been so minded; but it dulled his grief, he had discovered and thus seemed in a way which his simple mind could not even explain to itself, a betrayal of Sybilla. So, unlike many sad men, he had not become a drunkard.

Tana arranged herself to best advantage on one of the divans; he sat on the other, politely raised his wine cup towards her, took a sip and set it down. He said, 'Tana, I want to talk to you about Henry.'

'Henree? What of Henree?'

Getting the order wrong, Sir Godfrey said, 'I don't want his neck broken. Or his heart.'

'His neck? Jamil? Hee is no danger, Godfree. Always I am telling him — behave well and always he does. His heart?' Abruptly she slipped into Arabic, so much easier, more intimate, more given to aphorisms. 'The heart is its own keeper.'

Sticking stolidly to English, Sir Godfrey said, 'That may be. But Henry is young, easily hurt. I came to ask you not to play with him. Not to encourage him unless ... unless you have some fondness for him.'

'Fondness,' she repeated the word in English. 'As for dogs or a food or a colour. What way to talk!' She slid into Arabic again. 'The heart once given is a slave for ever.'

Sudden and sinuous as a snake she was across the angle where the two divans met and he was enveloped in the gauze, the scent, the soft desirous flesh.

In the lane, tempted, and responsive, he had repelled her. Now it was different. He sat like a dead man. Harem trained, she knew every trick, every word and movement calculated to stimulate a satiated appetite. And he sat like a dead man, feeling nothing, not even pity for a girl so wrong-headed and so set in her ways.

She soon understood and stood off, gathering the gauze and the dignity about her. 'Better you had let me drown,' she said.

Out in the garden among Sybilla's flowers, he suffered feelings which his unhandiness with words prevented him from expressing, even to himself. There was shame, but he knew that had he acted otherwise he would have been more deeply shamed. His mind produced a phrase — impotent as a mule! And that, which he should have minded, he did not. He thought how little he was wanted. Useless here, un-needed at Bywater. Get away! Get away! Throw off this life which was no life.

Into his muddled mind some words slid, as gently and naturally as the lily scent came to his nose. *The Knights Hospitallers of the Order of St. John of Jerusalem.*

And where had he heard of them? Fighting his way back into the past, he remembered. Aboard the *Four Fleeces,* outward bound for Spain, all those years ago; Sir Ralph Overbury who had been everywhere and knew everything, discoursing about his Order, men who were monks but also knights, banded together in the first place to guard the path of pilgrims to the Holy Land, and now devoted to repelling the Turks on their inroads into Eastern and Southern Europe. He hadn't paid much attention at the time. Sir Ralph had been a great talker. And even now he was not sure about the Hospitallers' headquarters. Malta? Rhodes?

Nor was he sure about his eligibility. He had been married, had fathered children; but he did not expect to be accepted as a member in the full sense; he was a trained knight, he could train others; at the lowest level he could tend horses.

The idea slid into his mind at a vulnerable moment and he did not recognise it for what it was — a logical step in his life pattern. Always since he was knighted — except for those years of slavery — he had been on the move, always hoping for something.

He set about the business in his usual single-minded way. He spoke to Henry; 'I am useless here; I am too old to become a farmer.' And that even Henry, though wishing to be civil, could not contradict. He regarded it as a favourable sign that his father had sufficiently recovered as to be making plans.

His next step was to seek information about the Order, its rules and the conditions of enlistment; the most likely source was the Dominican Priory at Bywater, so he went there and ran into a fog of deliberate ignorance. The knightly Orders had never been well regarded by those purely religious, too rich, too powerful, too worldly and the Templars — very similar to the Hospitallers — had been forcibly disbanded in most scandalous circumstances; they had been accused of homosexuality, human sacrifice and Devil worship. Doubtless the Hospitallers were much the same. The Prior did not say these things openly, he simply denied all knowledge, except that the Hospitallers' headquarters were in Rhodes. He found a map and pointed out the position of that island. Bent on escape, Sir Godfrey noted with satisfaction how far distant the place was.

The next problem was money and that, except for the briefest periods, had beset him all his life and he soon saw a way of solving it without bothering anyone very much. He went to Moyidan and asked Lady Emma to be good enough to write a letter for him. She agreed willingly and then, learning what he wished written, expressed her strongest disapproval. 'This is the most hare-brained scheme I ever heard of,' she said. 'When you went to Spain you had some hope of remuneration and the expedition was properly organised. Of these knights you know nothing — not even that they still exist. A tale told on ship-board twelve years ago! If they exist what guarantee have you that they will accept you. Forty-six years old and out of train-ing! And what about those poor children?'

'Griselda sees to them well. Joanna has her mother and Henry will see to Robert.'

'Henry will get married and have children of his own. How can you so shirk your responsibilities? You have a comfortable home — at least it could be, with a little money spent on it. You have a salaried post . . .'

She went on and on, until he said, 'Will you write the letter for me, or not?'

'If you ask me to write, how can I refuse? I warn you it will be useless. Lord Thorsdale will take the same view of this madcap notion as I, as any sensible person would do.'

'I think not. He is my friend. Also he owes me a favour.'

'Gratitude is a plant of short life.'

But he was stubborn; all Tallboys were stubborn, she thought. Then she remembered that he could not read, so dip-ping her pen into the ink she set herself to write a letter far less final than the one he had outlined to her. She did not write that he wished to *join* only that he wished to *visit*. She did not write that John Burgess, the overseer, was an honest man and capable of taking full charge of his lordship's Bywater affairs; she wrote *temporary charge during my absence*. Instead of requesting two years' salary as a gift, she asked for it as an advance to be deducted from future earnings.

Innocently, Sir Godfrey wrote his name and thanked her. She thought: You little know how much you have to thank me for; I have left a way of retreat open for you.

The letter despatched, all that was left to do was to make his will. He gave this matter deep consideration. Margaret needed nothing, but some provision must be made for John and Robert. A younger son himself he was sensitive to the position of younger sons and grateful to his own father to leaving him Intake.

Of the money which he had no doubt Lord Thorsdale would send, he intended to take just enough to keep him in the most meagre fashion on his journey. This time when he embarked he would take no armour, no great horse. Even if he could have afforded to do so he felt that to present himself fully accoutred and mounted would appear to be an assumption that he would be accepted. He intended to travel whenever possible as a pilgrim. Rhodes lay astride the pilgrims' route, and most pilgrims travelled humbly. Sir Ralph Overbury, who knew everything, had once said that ship-masters and inn-keepers did well out of pilgrims though they charged them less than ordinary people; it was the numbers which brought the profit; four to a bed in inns, crowded like cattle aboard ship. This prospect did not deter Sir Godfrey who was intent upon leaving all worldly things, including comfort behind him.

He had, he thought, every detail of his will clear-cut in his mind when he entered the ground floor room of the house in Cook's Row which Master Turnbull, the lawyer, kept as his office.

Master Turnbull was all in favour of people making proper wills; when a man died, murmuring — *All to Edmund,* he was robbing a lawyer of his livelihood.

On his table Master Turnbull had a pile of scraps of parchment, some clean, bits economically snipped off finished documents, some grey and grubby from having been used, well-scrubbed, and used again. On one of the latter kind, its surface almost fluffy from scrubbing, he began to jot down salient points.

'Henry must have his rights,' Sir Godfrey said. 'Intake is mine — as you know, having drawn my father's will . . .' Do I really, the lawyer wondered, look so old? It was my *father* who dealt with Sir Godfrey's. But the fact was not worth mention.

'You wish, Sir Godfrey, to leave Intake to Henry Tallboys. Your first-born son.'

'No. I mean, yes, Henry is my oldest son, but he cannot have all. I must consider the others.' He had remembered that his brother William had found the ladder of promotion eased by a legacy from that same just father. In the same way he must think of Richard — his son whom he would not have recognised had he met him in the road. Richard had taken to the Church, and to the Law, had done his time at Cambridge, was, by the latest bit of information, drifting through, through the new Bishop, through Moyidan, now on the staff of the Bishop of Winchester.

'Richard must have his portion. The house is mine, I built it. Henry made the fields, that is the Knight's Acre fields not those of Intake.'

'They are readily distinguishable, Sir Godfrey?'

'Oh yes. Intake was never a three field manor. There are twelve holdings, none large.'

'Rented?'

'Yes. Different rents.'

'And you wish these holdings to be left to your second son, Richard?'

'No, divided fairly between Richard and John.'

Master Turnbull's quill scratched as he made his jottings.

'Then there's my flock. I should like that divided between Richard and John and Robert. My youngest,' he explained.

'And the land?'

'What land?'

'A flock pre-supposes a sheep run, Sir Godfrey.'

'That had better be Henry's. Oh, and I think that to be fair to Henry, if the others wish to sell the sheep, he should have first offer.'

He fell silent, sweating slightly. What else? 'Oh, two other things. I am expecting to receive a sum of money. I'd like Robert . . .'

'Sir Godfrey, a man can only bequeath what he possesses. Shall we say that any money of which you die possessed?'

'That is what I meant. Then there's a lady . . .' He did his best to make the situation clear.

The lawyer thought, what a muddle-minded fellow! Having just bequeathed his house to his first born son he now wants to leave part of it to another person.

Clearing his quill of the fluff it had collected from the rough surface of the old parchment, Master Turnbull said, 'In such circumstances it is as well to be precise. These apartments are part of the main house?'

'Yes. At least, no. They're at the back, but separate.'

'They do not adjoin?'

'Oh yes. Up to a point.'

And what might that mean?

'They share a common roof?'

'No. At least, yes. Perhaps if I might borrow . . .'

Master Turnbull handed over the quill and the greyest of the grey scraps and pushed the ink-pot across the table.

Better at laying things out than at expressing himself, Sir Godfrey proceeded to draw a lawyer's nightmare. Master Turnbull could see that, even looking at it upside down.

'And there is access to these apartments?'

'Oh yes. Lady Serriff's main door is here — on the garden side. And her kitchen opens into the yard.'

'Both of which constitute part of Knight's Acre?'

'That is so. As you see,' Sir Godfrey handed across his diagram — curiously well and firmly drawn for a man whose talk was so contradictory. The lawyer saw that this was a right-of-way case. He'd been pestered with them since enclosures began. When people shuffled land about, a well, common to all, could end up in the centre of one man's fenced field; a path, used by everybody through the generations could be brought up short at a newly planted quickthorn hedge.

'It would appear that this lady occupies an island in the centre of your property.'

Glad that he had at last made himself clear, Sir Godfrey said, 'Yes, that's just it. I was thinking ahead. When she wanted to build I said, of course she could; but we didn't bother then with any deed of gift. It *is* her house; she built it, but it looks like part of the house. I thought I should mention it.'

'You were right, Sir Godfrey. We must now assure her right of way. Otherwise she might be denied access.'

'Henry would never do that.'

You would be surprised, Master Turnbull thought, at what people will do where property is concerned. A death seemed to change ordinary, decent people into a lot of carrion crows.

'We must indeed think ahead. This will, properly drawn up,

will apply to your heirs, and to the lady's. They might well be inimical.'

He took his ruler and drew two parallel lines from the yard entry to Tana's kitchen door, dog legging it so that it should include access to the well which Sir Godfrey had indicated by a circle, remembering as he did so, how Sybilla had stood there, drawing water, her white hair blowing, when he and Tana rode into the yard.

There seemed nothing more to be done — except perhaps to make a search into the relative values of the Intake land, small holdings, rented differently. But when he suggested that Sir Godfrey became impatient and said that that had all been gone into. Everybody knew where he stood.

'Write it out on one piece and I'll sign it,' he said.

'It will take a little time, Sir Godfrey,' Master Turnbull said, thinking of the new parchment; the formal opening, 'In the name of God, Amen! I, Godfrey Tallboys, Knight, of Intake in the Country of Suffolk . . .'

'I'll give you an hour,' Sir Godfrey said. And still in a society based on a code of chivalry, a lay lawyer, however clever, took lower place than a knight, however poor and muddle-minded.

'I have no wish to hurry you, Master Turnbull. But it is urgent. I may be away, perhaps even tomorrow.' He gave the lawyer his singularly sweet smile.

'It will be ready, Sir Godfrey.'

Turning back to the business, Master Turnbull reflected upon how much better off his one son would be. The boy was studying law at this moment, but he would never, if things went right, need to apply his knowledge except where his own property was concerned. Master Turnbull had invested very carefully; he owned several houses in Baildon, small but steady paying, some shares in several mercantile adventures, bits of land to the north of the town, dry and scrubby, but excellent for sheep when the time came; other bits to the south, splendid building ground when building began again as soon as things settled. Not yet; this tug-of-war between York and Lancaster wasn't over yet: London and the south was Yorkist completely. The north was different and Master Turnbull had a shrewd idea of where Sir Godfrey might be going, in such a hurry. He had never heard of the Knight's Hospitallers, and he did not know that there was an island called Rhodes.

Over the will he did his hurried best. And because Sir God-frey seemed to have so little, to be divided between so many, charged the minimum price.

Now there was nothing to do except wait for the money from Yorkshire. It might come by land, through Master Johnson, or by one of the coal-cobs. In either case it would come to Bywater, so Sir Godfrey went there every day. And the days shortened relentlessly. August; September. Layer Wood began to blaze again. Evenings and mornings grew chilly. He began to think that Emma's cynical remark about gratitude was justified.

At last a coal-cob put in. Its master, explaining that he had been delayed by bad weather, handed over a paper, folded and sealed.

'And is this all?'

'All I was asked to carry, sir.'

The dismay and disappointment lasted only a minute. Sir Godfrey remembered the complicated way in which money changed hands. This might be a money order which Master Johnson would cash for him. He broke the seals and stared at the meaningless words. There were nine of them. His own name, which he could recognise, was not among them. And there were no figures.

John Burgess, whom he had nominated to take charge was able to read but Sir Godfrey hesitated to carry the paper to him. The very brevity seemed ominous. It might be a curt dismissal; in which case he preferred Burgess not to know. He would resign and thus save a little dignity.

Lady Emma seemed hardly to glance at the words.

'It says, "Come at once. I have work for you here." '

'Just that? No signature?'

'No signature.' She turned the paper about. 'Nor is your name between the seals, Godfrey. It seems,' she frowned at the message, 'as though should the message have miscarried there would be nothing to show who wrote it, or to whom it was sent.'

'It could only come from Lord Thorsdale. It came on a coal-cob. And that was belated! Thank you Emma. I must go at once.'

Well, she thought, it was better than haring off to the world's end. Later she was to think that it was fitting that a man who had gone on so many wild-goose chases, should have gone on this one in response to a summons so carefully anony-mous.

Leave-taking was brief and painless. He was back at Knight's Acre in time for dinner. He looked in upon the nur-sery, kissed the children and pleased Griselda by saying that he left them in her care with all confidence. Only to Henry did he say some valedictory words.

'My plans have changed. I was thinking of a longer journey, a longer absence, Henry. You spoke once of Lancaster and York being at one another's throats again — I think it is about to happen and that Lord Thorsdale is mustering men, secretly.'

Henry remembered Walter saying about knights that they were like hunting hounds, blow a horn ten miles away and they'd all come at the gallop. But Sybilla, as well as Walter, had had a hand in Henry's upbringing and he said all the correct things, including that myth, so often proved wrong but still held — It would all be over by Christmas.

'If anything should happen to me, my will is lodged with Master Turnbull. I leave you in full charge. Look after them all.'

'I will do my best, sir,' Henry said, little knowing the weight of the load he was accepting. After all, what had Father ever done about looking after anybody. 'When do you leave?'

'Now.'

About saying goodbye to Tana he was of divided mind. Since that June evening they had sedulously avoided one another. Even their stable work had been re-timed. He hated the idea of facing her — their shared failure heavy between them — but he was still grateful and he knew that he was going away for ever. Even if he survived the coming battles, he would not come back here. Perhaps he should just say farewell . . .

It was not his to decide. Kitchen spoke to kitchen and while he was saddling the black horse — the stolen one, the best of the lot — she came around the end of her pavilion and into the yard. Nothing now seductive about her dress or her posture, or her speech.

'I am understanding,' she said, 'that you go a long journey. If you wish you may have Jamil.'

A noble, magnanimous offer indeed. Akin, in its way to Sybilla's in accepting Tana and her unborn child. My God, what have I ever done to deserve . . .?

'It wouldn't do,' he said. 'Much as I appreciate it. Jamil just tolerates me, but only just . . . In inns and such places, he would be . . . an embarrassment, biting stable-boys. And if you would take heed . . . You should take him back to Tom Thoroughgood and make an exchange before . . .'

'Yes, you have said it many times. I am not agreeing . . .' Her voice changed slightly, 'It is to war that you go?'

'I think so.'

'May your dead enemies equal the number of stars in the sky.'

Sybilla had always said, 'God go with you and bring you safely back to me.' He had never before left on any campaign without a change of clothing and some food of the long-lasting kind; smoked or salted meat that was practically imperishable, bread baked once, sliced and baked again so that it was impervious to mould.

Late as it was, on one of the rose trees there was a half-opened bud. A latecomer, slightly discouraged by the morning and evening chill. Still, it was a rose, one of those that Sybilla had loved. He broke it off, carried it into the church and laid it on the black slab under which she lay. Then he knelt and said to Sybilla in his mind. 'You never come to me, but I shall come to you. Soon.' He could hear the steady thud of his heart — every beat brings me nearer. God grant me clean swift death in battle.

CHAPTER EIGHTEEN

Manuring the land — known as muck-spreading — was routine in the farmer's year; an unpleasant but necessary job. John who was fastidious always tried to evade it and since the flock was installed had always had the excuse that he must help the shepherd.

Sir Godfrey had never actually interfered with the farm work, but now and again, when Henry said bitter things about idleness, he had said mildly that John was still young. Henry replied angrily that John was fourteen, just about the age that he had been himself when he assumed full responsibility. Sir Godfrey would then point out, still mildly, that Henry had always had a taste for general farmwork, whereas John tended more towards sheep.

Two or three days after Sir Godfrey's departure, Henry said, 'You come and shovel muck today. Young Shep needs no help, and we do.'

'He has a name, you know,' John said coldly. 'It is Nicholas. How would you like it if people called you Young Ploughman?'

Henry's astonishment was genuine. 'How could they? Everybody knows that I am Master Tallboys of Knight's Acre.' That was true. There was something about Henry which forbade any familiarity, even in the market. Never any hob-nobbing, or back-slapping. 'Anyway, if I say you shovel muck, you shovel it.'

'It is not a job I care for.'

There had never been between Henry and John the urgent rivalry that had existed between Henry and Richard, the differences in age had prevented that, but Henry had always thought John idle and frivolous; now insubordination threatened. In earlier days when John had shown any sign of defiance a good cuff had sufficed, but now the boy was too big. Like most of the Tallboys family, at fourteen he was practically full-grown.

'Very well,' Henry said. 'You tend the sheep and *Nicholas*,' he brought out the name with sardonic emphasis, 'can come and help with the muck-spreading.'

Henry was far too lacking in sophistication to see anything sinister in the relationship between the two boys — if Young Shep at eighteen or so, could be called a boy. The link between them he saw as a mutual liking for making musical noises, and their mutual wish to loll about and avoid what Henry considered as *real* work. He did not notice the look of sheer hatred which John shot at him as he delivered his edict; and he missed entirely the significance of John's reply.

'I'll do it. I'm stronger than he is.'

The self-sacrifice contained in that remark passed unnoticed.

On the surface it was true enough. Young Shep was not very sturdy, but he looked healthy, always a good colour in his cheeks ...

'Right enough,' Henry said, the incipient rebellion quelled.

Shovelling muck himself he gave thought to another matter with which he could deal in a similarly masterful manner, now that he was in full charge. Tana.

Sir Francis Lassiter's grey, though most often in the yard or stable, was not the only one. Tana, who towards Henry had blown hot and cold, was plainly playing fast and loose with other men.

Not that he cared. With Walter's death, and Sybilla's he had learned that hard work could cure almost anything. Give your whole mind to the job in hand and there was no time to think; go to bed tired out and you slept. Henry believed that he had done with Tana. His father had said something about women being fickle; very well, she could be fickle with others. Not with *him*, not with Henry Tallboys who now, left in full charge, had at least the right to say what horses should stand in his yard or stable. He sincerely believed that he had outgrown his boyish infatuation and was his own man again.

January; a clear frosty night, sparkling with stars and the moon bright. In the hall the fire was heaped high and John said, 'Eddy and Jill let the kitchen fire die as soon as supper is served. I am going to ask Nicholas to bring his pipe in here. We have a new song to try.'

'Not here,' Henry said. 'The hall is no place for hired hands.'

'This is my *home*,' John said stubbornly. 'Half the fireside is mine. I have a right to bring my friend to share it.'

'This is father's house. And you would never have dared make such a suggestion to him.'

'Father was not fond of music.'

'If you call that music! Squealing and scratching!'

'We make very beautiful songs. As you will realise one day.'

'In the meantime, I am in charge here and I want no argument.'

John flung out, slamming the door, and Henry settled down to work, re-lining a worn horse collar. The words, *I am in charge here,* went on echoing through his mind. He was in charge here; he was responsible; and about what he had to say to Tana there could be no argument.

He got up and went into the yard. There was no strange horse, grey, brown or bay here tonight. He regarded the sky with a countryman's eye and was glad that the muck was spread, for it served a dual purpose, it protected as well as nourished. He walked round to Tana's door, knocked once and entered.

It was the first time he had ever set foot in the pavilion in his working clothes. Standards had lowered a little since Sybilla's death; hands were still washed before meals, muddy or mucky footwear left at the kitchen door. Otherwise he was just as he had come from the field and in this luxurious, scented bower he made an incongruous figure.

She had begun to blow cold to him for the last time somewhere back in the summer. On the Eve of the Midsummer Fair to be exact. He had actually offered to take a day's holiday in order to show her the Fair. They must go in daylight for after dusk rowdiness prevailed, but the Fair began as an immense market to which people brought useful things and beautiful things from great distances, some even from overseas. The Hawk in Hand put out an awning in its forecourt, a guard against too much sun, or a shower, and under it served strawberries and cream all day long. Still poor by most standards, and very poor by those which he had set himself to attain, Henry was yet prepared to spend money in order to give Tana a treat. He would even — unless her fancy was taken by something quite impossible, like amber — buy her a fairing . . .

She had rejected his invitation with cold scorn. The tone of her voice, the look she gave him, cut to the quick. After that he had made no overtures; nor had she, and it was a long time since he had been close enough to her to observe that she had changed. After that last encounter with Sir Godfrey she had despaired and turned to the wine cup for comfort; and to other men, lechery being one of Despair's jackals.

The room was bright; there were two four-branched candlesticks; it was warm; two charcoal braziers which exuded not only warmth but sweet odours. Between the flicker and the glow Henry saw her plainly for the first time since summer and saw that her beauty had begun to fade and blur, like those paintings on the church wall, before they were restored. For months she had lived just on the border of intoxication. Only Francis Lassiter had really observed this and decided that attractive, seductive as she was, he would be a fool to marry a woman who had to be half-drunk before she was any good in bed.

As Henry entered, and rudely sat down before being invited to be seated, Tana said, 'Oh. Henree. You have news?'

What had existed between her and Sir Godfrey was dead and done with. But now and then she found herself caring.

'No; if you mean Father. But I have something to say to you.' He drew a breath, deeper than he realised. 'In my father's absence I am master here and I will not have the place turned into a brothel.'

It was surprising that he knew the word, living here, isolated, jogging into market once a month or so, to sell and to buy. Already — this would be a lonely evening — she was wine-flown.

'Do you know what you speak of, Henree? A brothel is a place open to all. And men pay.'

'We won't split hairs. What I came to say . . . I will not have Sir Francis's grey, or any other horse in *my* yard. If you must play the whore, do it elsewhere.'

The easy anger of the half tipsy flared in her. This clod, this loutish boy whom she had toyed with, in the hope of making his father jealous, to make him see that she was desirable. A boy upon whose innocence she had never trespassed . . . Saying such things. Sitting there, so self-righteous . . . A bubble formed in her head and burst. With the same swift, snake-like action with which, months ago, she had flung herself upon Godfree, she crossed the space between them and hit Henry twice across the face, forehand to one cheek, backhand to the other. He flung up an arm to restrain, to control, and for all her anger she was no more than a butterfly . . . When, defending himself, he grabbed her by the arms, she fell, half across the divan, half across his knees.

It was, for both of them, a new experience. Henry had never possessed a woman before and Tana in all her time had never had a virgin love. She had given herself to many men, working her way up to the position of first favourite in the Zagela harem, always with purpose, to free the man she loved, the man who had been hers for so little time . . . those wonderful nights in the mountains as they made their escape, never sure of what the next day might bring; a few times in Spain. Then nothing, even after the old wife, the first wife was poisoned and dead.

Henry she found herself hating because in shape and size, in the way his hair was so crisp to the touch, in his body odour — a thing only recognisable by lovers and enemies — he was so like his father. The likeness should have endeared him to her, but it did not. It infuriated her. When the moment of frenzy was spent she eased herself away and said, cruelly. 'You must go. Henree. Or there will be more talk.'

'There will not,' he said. 'First thing in the morning I shall go to Father Ambrose and tell him. Banns can be called on other days than Sunday if the priest is agreeable. Darling, my darling, we can be married within a week. He will do as I say.'

She looked down the reaches of the years — married to Henry, a constant reminder by night and by day. And cold sober! Because how and when could she do her drinking? He had caught her this evening about halfway; she would need much more wine before she could sleep.

'I cannot marry you,' she said.

He had his father's single-mindedness, his full share of the Tallboys' obstinacy, and all the egoism of youth. He took no notice; this was probably fresh evidence of fickleness.

'Of course you can. You must. After tonight. And my dearest dear . . .' He took her hands and kissed them, pressed them against his face and vowed to love and serve her and honour her to the end of his days. He poured out promises and all his hopes; he would not always be poor; he'd set himself to prosper, and he would. With more money and more leisure they could cultivate acquaintances, entertain: she mustn't judge by what he was now, but consider what he would be . . .

On and on, with every nerve in her body screaming for the only relief she knew; wine and more wine.

From kissing her hands and talking he proceeded to give signs of wishing to make love again. Just to be rid of him she said, 'You must go now, Henree. All this can be talked about tomorrow.'

'Yes, tomorrow,' he said. The beginning of a new life. Dazed with happiness, he stumbled away.

Left alone she poured wine and swallowed it without tasting. More, and still more. Tonight no merciful blunting of mind and memory. The whole of her past, as it related to Sir Godfrey, was lived again as she walked up and down. Two women dead, the favourite of the harem by intrigue and Sybilla by poison. No remorse about that, only bitterness that with all her striving and taking of risks the end had been nothing.

She twitched aside the curtain and saw the world, bright with frosty moonlight. A gallop, she thought, might calm her. She went swiftly to the stable where the work horses sagged and drowsed and Jamil welcomed her eagerly.

The cold air cleared her mind and she could think again. She knew what she must do. Get away from Knight's Acre and the pavilion with had never served the purpose for which it was built. Get away from Henree and the men in whose embraces she had sought, and failed to find, consolation. She would go to the north, where the fighting was. Not in pursuit of Sir Godfrey, to invite further shame. She would go to the side of the Red Rose. The fierce Lancastrian Queen, Margaret, a fighting woman herself, would welcome a woman who could ride and handle a sword. Another memory from the past! Fighting alongside her father and brothers in that last disastrous battle.

But for the fact that she was unsuitably clad, and that her treasure lay in the chest in her bedroom, she would have ridden on and never seen Knight's Acre again. She would have ridden straight through Baildon, Jamil's hoofs on the cobbles disturbing the respectable men, each in bed with his one wife! But she must go back, so on the outskirts of the town she turned the horse.

On one or two former occasions she had had difficulty with Jamil in two places, both near the house; one in front where the trail ran between the rose-trees before curving towards the rear of the house, the other at the entry to the yard. She had attributed his jibbing and prancing to his intelligence — he realised that the outing was over and was reluctant to return to his dull stable. She'd always steadied him and forced him on, telling him in Arabic, 'Do not be lunatic.' Tonight there was no trouble near the roses, but at the yard entry he was more lunatic than ever. He stopped abruptly and then tried to turn. She fought him, keeping his head towards the opening between the end of the house and the ruined cottage. It lay in shadow, but for a moment she seemed to see a wavering light such as a carried lantern might give. Unperturbed she spoke into Jamil's ear, 'Steady, my love.' Then she called sharply towards whoever carried the lantern. 'Out of my way!'

Jamil reared and turned, swivelling round on his hind legs. Tana's left arm and knee came into sharp contact with the house wall; she lost balance and control. Even as she fell, she kept her head, let go, get your feet out of the stirrups so as not to be dragged ... As she hit the ground she could smell lilies ...

Henry came, stretching and yawning, out into the frosty morning. He stood for a second and stared at Tana's pavilion which presented a blank, windowless wall to the yard. Sensuous thoughts moved through him as he imagined her sleeping, all scented and silken. He could still hardly believe that what had happened had happened and that he had at last attained his heart's desire. But work would not wait. Success and prosperity had always been his aim and now, after all the promises he had made, they were more important than ever. He kicked up a clod with his heel and was pleased to see that although the night had been frosty the frost had not penetrated below the surface. At least, not here in the yard, where it was sheltered; it might be different in the open field. Just as well to make sure before harnessing the plough-horses. As he walked — with Walter's gait — towards the yard entry he planned for the evening. He'd go straight from the field to the priest's house and arrange for the wedding; then he'd wash, most thoroughly, and don his best clothes. And then ...

With that thought he came upon her, broken and dead, her head at a curious angle and a faint rime of hoar-frost on her black hair.

The shock stunned him into something like insensibility. He was like a wounded man who at first feels no pain however mortal the blow. Somebody — not Henry Tallboys — went back into the yard where the others were awaiting his verdict, to plough or not to plough, and a voice — not his — said from a vast distance, 'Lady Serriff is dead. She has met with an accident. Carry her in.'

So now here he was in the priest's low room arranging not for a wedding, but for a funeral. And Father Ambrose was making difficulties.

'Young sir, at a burial the Christian soul is committed to God. There was never any sign that the dead lady was a Christian. She never once attended Mass, never knelt at the altar, never made a confession . . .'

Henry said harshly, 'How could she? She was Spanish. In what language could she have confessed to *you*? And how, unconfessed and unabsolved could she have taken Christ on her tongue?'

Father Ambrose said humbly, 'That is a question I never thought to ask. I have been rash in judgment, forgetting that she was a stranger within our gates.' He gave Henry a stricken look. 'I should have bestirred myself. In the Dominican Priory there are those with the gift of tongues . . . I have failed in my duty.' He did not excuse himself because he was old, frail, blind. There and then he set himself a penance — no meat for a month. 'Of course I will bury her,' he said.

Rest in peace, the woman who, before she was fully-grown, had conceived an inordinate passion for one man and to gratify it had stopped at nothing. Rest in peace, also, the promise of happiness for Henry Tallboys whose childhood had been cut short by the need to work like a man, whose youth had ended with a night of joy and a morning of sorrow.

Tana's pavilion stood deserted. It had never been part of the main house and of those now living at Knight's Acre, Henry was the only one upon whose consciousness it had impinged. Setting himself to forget Tana, as he had forgotten other griefs, meant ignoring the place in which she had lived, never even glancing towards the windowless wall which bordered the yard. On the side overlooking the garden, spiders wove their webs between curtains and glass at the windows; a rosemary bush by the side of the door grew large and encroached, honeysuckle and ivy threw out exploratory fingers. Soon the door was almost hidden and quite inaccessible. Not until the children were old enough to be curious was the pavilion ever noticed. To them it offered the fascination of mystery; a house where no one ever went, a house no one ever mentioned, a house without a door.

CHAPTER NINETEEN

News came, slowly but surely. The Lancastrians had met with success early in the campaign, and then been defeated — surely for the last time. Sir Godfrey Tallboys had been killed in the re-taking of Bamborough Castle and lay buried in York, near his friend and patron, Lord Thorsdale. When this report had been twice confirmed, Henry ordered and paid for six Masses to be said for his soul and then turned to practical things. He remembered his father's mention of a will and in leisurely fashion, not making a special errand of it, called upon the lawyer who said that in his opinion Richard should come home; the last will and testament of Sir Godfrey Tallboys — God rest him — being far more complicated than it seemed.

'I don't know exactly where my brother is,' Henry said. 'When my mother died, my aunt, Lady Emma of Moyidan, did write to inform him; but she had no reply.'

'Where was he when last heard of, Master Tallboys?'

Henry, who had never given Richard a thought for years, said, 'He'd finished his Cambridge studies — we did hear that, and was something, chaplain or secretary to the Bishop of Winchester.'

'He should not be difficult to find. It is your wish that I should write a letter?'

'I should be much obliged. I can write my name and no more.'

He said this without a trace of shame and the lawyer thought that the perfect, orderly world could never come about until everybody was literate. When he eventually met Richard Tallboys, he changed his opinion. With his Master's degree from Cambridge, his ordination — he was now a deacon — and entitled to the courtesy of Sir, the young man was obnoxious. He criticised the form of his father's will in terms that were fully legal, and even justified. 'Hurriedly and badly made,' he said. He denounced the division of the Intake farms, with their differing rents, their differing terms of tenure, as 'most ambivalent. Are we supposed to draw lots, Master Turnbull?'

'Your honoured father — God rest him — had no time, Sir Richard. I did in fact suggest . . . but he over-ruled me. The whole thing was drafted, signed and witnessed, in a single afternoon.'

'That is quite obvious! Never mind, Master Turnbull. I have no doubt that my brother and I will come to some amicable arrangement.'

'Ah,' Richard said, 'here I perceive a flaw of which John and I can take advantage.'

He had gone to Moyidan and borrowed that old, crackling parchment, with its mention of inalienable rights. At ridiculous rents. No word about what happened should the land be sold. This was the kind of loophole which his training and present occupation rendered him capable of dealing with. He and John would have some ready money soon. But it was not enough for Richard who knew that profitable appointments could be bought.

'I propose,' he said, in a most amicable way, 'to sell my share of the flock immediately.'

Henry was not much interested in sheep, but his common-sense made him exclaim, 'The very worst time! The lambs are not all down yet, some of the ewes couldn't travel. Then you'd lose the wool money. People sell sheep in June, after shearing.'

'If you buy now, you'll get both lambs and wool.'

'I can't afford to buy.'

'How unfortunate. I am afraid that I cannot afford to wait until June.'

'I want to sell mine, too,' said John. He had a plan in mind; he also relished a chance of getting his own back on Henry whose treatment of Nicholas had rankled.

'I'm not sure that at your age you can make such decisions.'

John looked to Richard for support and found it. 'Father made no mention of guardianship. Strickly speaking, Henry, even you are not of full age. John has as much right to sell his sheep as you have to inherit Knight's Acre.'

'Maybe Robert would like a say too,' Henry said sourly.

Resolutely amiable — imperturbable good temper, outwardly, at least was one of the qualities he had cultivated, Richard said, 'I see no difficulty. You have security, Henry. You could borrow money and buy us out.'

'I'm not borrowing money,' Henry said. 'Father did that once and hung a loan round his neck. Very well, if you are set on this absurd behaviour, sell — if you can find a buyer. Meantime, remember, they are your sheep now, running on my land. I shall charge rent . . .'

As Master Turnbull knew, only too well, no will was ever settled amicably.

John at least was happy.

'Our hut' to which he and Nicholas had resorted when Henry had been so disobliging, was a straw structure in the corner of the sheep run, that one-time common, now known to the villagers as Grabber's Green. It differed from a lambing pen only in that it was thatched while lambing pens were open to the sky. It was built of closely bound bundles of straw, made into walls, about four feet high, with branches laid across them, and more straw as thatch. Such huts were intended for a shepherd to take refuge in bad weather, and to live in, day and night, during the lambing season. The one to which John sped, hot-foot, was snug and cosy, with only one disadvantage, one could not have a fire in it or even very near it; but a fire six feet away gave heat and light enough.

Tonight the fire burned brightly, for with lambing imminent, Young Shep had taken up permanent residence in the hut, and the iron tar-bucket, full of black, viscous liquid stood near-by. There were two seasons for tar, summer, when flies laid their eggs which unless promptly dealt with grew into maggots, and lambing time when about one lamb in ten developed navel trouble.

Crouching to pass the low entry, John seated himself on a bundle of straw and said, 'Nicky. We can do it now. I'm going to have some money. We can *go.*'

They'd talked about it often enough, fashioning their tunes, making their songs which the outer world had only to hear to acknowledge and admire, they had talked endlessly. One day they would make music in great halls, in castles, in palaces. But neither of them was prepared to starve or beg while awaiting the recognition to which their genius entitled them. Knight's Acre did not appreciate them, but it offered bread and beds. So they had stayed, scorning the present, looking to the future and saying always, 'One day,' without the slightest idea when that day would dawn.

Now it had come.

'They're going to sell the flock,' John said, 'and a third is mine.'

Young Shep said, 'Sell. Now? With the ewes in pod? That'd be bad business. That old black-face is there now ...' He jerked his head towards the nearest lambing pen. 'Grunting. By the size of her, it'll be twins. Maybe I should take a look.'

He was gone for quite a time and when he came back he said, rubbing hands on a bit of sheep's wool, 'She's all right. It was twins. Bit small, but lively.'

'You won't be bothered with such things in future, Nicky. We'll be on our way ... I'd reckon that selling the flock, and the farms will take a bit of time. But my brother Richard is clever — and impatient. I'd say that by May Day ...'

'Yes. All right in summer. But there's the winter to think of.'

'I'd have enough money ...' delicacy of feeling made John change the words, 'We'd have earned enough, Nicky, to see us through the winter, somewhere cosy.'

'It'd be all right, time we're young. But Johnny, you ain't always young.'

It occurred to John that Nicky had accepted this glittering future with less enthusiasm than it merited. He failed to make allowance for the differing strain of character and behaviour which their ancestors had bequeathed them. John's forebears had been riding, as Walter termed it, helter-skelter, all over the face of Christendom. Even to Jerusalem. Griselda's recognition of the resemblance between the man cast out to die in a barn and the crusader, with his legs crossed, had been no accident. Young Shep's forebears had lived and worked at Moyidan since the first field had been scratched there; Briton, Roman, Angle, Dane, Norman — all in turn had overrun the place, and Old Shep had always been there. Even the move from Moyidan to Intake had caused Young Shep pangs of homesickness which his association with John, their mutual interest in music, had done something to assuage, something, not all.

'Don't you *want* to get away, Nicky? We've talked about it often enough.'

'There's a difference between talking and doing. Thing like that should be thought over.'

'Thinking won't help much if they sell the flock. You'll have to move then.'

'Some might go to Moyidan. There'd be a job for me there if so. My father's got all he can handle. Getting stiff, too.'

'If that's what you meant by getting away, we weren't talking about the same thing. I shall go whether you come or not.'

It was their first dispute. The first time they had ever sat in a silence which neither found easy to break.

Young Shep said, at last, 'Made a new song today, Johnny. Like to hear it?'

John gave a grunt of assent.

'I'll tell you the words first, then you'll see how the tune fits.' A lute-player could sing and play at the same time; with a pipe this was impossible.

Young Shep began.

> Pray God the summer cometh soon
> That I no more must be alone . . .

John struck the bale of straw that served him as a seat and said, 'Another of your whines about love; with a tune like the bellyache! And I know who it is. That red-haired trollop who came with the shearers.'

Most shearing gangs had a woman with them — old enough not to be a cause of trouble, active enough to keep up with the swift pace at which the men moved between jobs. Such women did a bit of washing and mending, prepared food at irregular hours, tied up a nicked finger. Last year's gang had been accompanied by a girl thin as a thread, berry brown, with flaming hair. She'd pretended to like music, and Nicholas had made a pipe for her. The shearers had moved on to other flocks, but twice while they were still in the neighbourhood, within running distance, she'd come back on some excuse or another. John had thought nothing of it at the time, but now he realised that lately all Nicholas's songs had been about love — as indeed was the fashion, so he had not been warned by that. Now he said, 'I know what *you* meant about getting away! You want a live-out job in a clod cottage, with a wife and a baby every year! You're welcome. Think of me — playing before the King!'

Rather more than half of Young Shep did want exactly that — but in Moyidan, if possible, and perhaps not a baby *every* year. He did want the clod cottage and the son who would be Young Shep when he was Old Shep. The other, a smaller part of him knew that in such a life his music and his songs would be wasted, never finding the audience they deserved.

Pull Devil, pull Baker!

'Maybe you're right,' Young Shep said.

John walked back to the house knowing that he fitted nowhere, except in the world of his own imagination. A dream he had tried to share. From this time on, he decided everything he planned would be secret to himself. *Secret to myself, my secret, my secret* — a good song theme.

CHAPTER TWENTY

Henry now faced the need to make some economies. He had expanded while his father was receiving a regular income and was responsible for the household expenses; but he had been allowed no time to consolidate. He was short of money because it had seemed sensible to buy a portion of the flock. He felt bound to keep Robert's third of the sheep and husband them carefully — they were all the poor child had inherited. 'All money of which I die possessed' meant nothing. Father had had no money. Still ignorant about shepherd's work, Henry had decided that since Robert's sheep were there, and the sheep-run was there, he might as well have a few of his own and for them his brothers demanded instant payment. His own animals were distinguished by a cross of red ochre. Henry intended to hoard every penny gained by the sale of wool, or sheep from Robert's flock, so that by the time the boy needed money it would be there.

Looking around his household, Henry decided that Young Shep and Eddy were dispensable; he and Tom between them could look after the flock, and if he himself took his meals in the kitchen, as most farmers did, there would be nothing for Eddy to do. Young Shep did not make the move to Moyidan — as he had hoped — but to Clevely, which at least was a place served by the same gang of shearers, and where he did not live in. When the berry-brown girl, whose name was Beth — rhyming with nothing except breath and death — came back in June, and if she still wished to settle down, as she had told him she longed to, he would have something to offer. Eddy, making a venturesome move, found a job as pot-boy at The Hawk In Hand at Baildon.

Henry had overlooked the fact that in his muddly way, Eddy had also waited upon the nursery, a service which Jill was not prepared to undertake in her present dejected mood. She missed Eddy, who, idle as he had appeared to be in Henry's eyes, had been good company. She also missed Ursula. Ursula, shedding ten years for her mistress and a hundred for herself had left before Tana was committed to the grave. She could never, never, she declared, go into *that* part of the house again; even to think of it sent icicles down her back: and she thought that Sir Edmund, over at Nettleton might give her a place.

Ursula gone, Sir Richard gone, Master John gone, Eddy gone, and Young Shep who so often obliged with a merry tune on his pipe, or with a song. Four men, the master, Tom, Jem Watson, Bert Edgar to cook for every mid-day as well as that upstart, Griselda, and the two children. And then, in the evening, everything was so glum, Jem and Bert went stumping home to Intake, Griselda was with the children, Tom, hoarding his remnant of strength, went to bed early; so did the master. So there was nothing left for Jill to do except to go to bed, too. Very dismal.

One morning, Henry rather early or Griselda slightly late, they met in the kitchen where Griselda and Jill had just had a dispute about the apportioning of fat and lean. Robert, though no longer weakly, could not stomach much fat and though in her inmost heart Griselda had small patience with foibles, a sick child was a sick child, something to be cleared up after. So she had put up a fight for a bit more lean.

She had grown since coming to Knight's Acre, but she was

still small, and a meal for three on a tray appeared to be a load for her.

Henry opened the door into the hall for her and said, 'Surely there is no need for this. They are old enough now to come to where the food is.'

Next day they were all in place. Henry sat at the top of the white-scrubbed table, to his left the two children, brought to table level by cushions from the settle in the hall; between them, Griselda. On his right, back to the hearth for convenience in serving, Jill and beyond her Tom; and at the far end Jem and Bert, consuming the mid-day meal that was part of their wage.

Sybilla lay under the black marble slab, yet something of her hovered about this table at which she had once presided and there was a marked difference between those who had come under her influence and those who had not.

Children tended to copy.

'Slosh your food like that,' Griselda said, addressing Robert, but with her eye on Jem and Bert, 'and you can go eat with pigs.'

Robert was slightly afraid of pigs and ceased what Griselda denounced as sloshing.

'Ask, don't grab,' Griselda told Joanna. 'You can say, *Please, the bread.* Come along, let me hear you.'

Joanna was less easily subdued. 'Bert grabbed,' she said.

There was the matter of the salt. It was contained in a bowl of wood and it had a spoon, also of wood, its handle nicely carved — one of Walter's whittling jobs, not an apostle as so many spoon handles were made to represent, because Walter had not been pious, but an oak leaf and an acorn. Those at the table who had come under Sybilla's influence used the spoon. Jem and Bert, asserting their rights did as they did at home, dug their knives, dribbling in drops of grease and gravy. One day, catching a look of pain on Griselda's face, Tom said sharply, 'There is a spoon, Bert.'

'Why so there is!' Bert said with simulated, sardonic surprise. 'Such a little tiddly bit of a thing. Never noticed it. Did you, Jem?'

Tom was not allowed to forget that spoon. It came up with heavy-handed humour again and again. 'Try a *spoon*, Tom,' one or the other would say as Tom struggled doggedly with some job just beyond his strength. 'Old Granfer Robinson used to wet the bed. They cleaned him up with a *spoon*.' 'Ah, thass how Tom got so handy with a *spoon*.'

The rough teasing covered something deeper and darker. Tom belonged at Knight's Acre, had lived there ever since the plague time. Jem and Bert worked there but they belonged to Intake, a community which held a grudge against the big house and the Tallboys family. First Sir Godfrey had raised some people's rent — and frittered the money away on the church; and then Sir Richard had done worse, found some legal way to cheat them out of their rights so that he could say, 'Buy or get out.' The fact that by pooling their resources every family had managed to buy, did not lessen the ill-feeling; and when Tom behaved in a mannerly way, he was siding with Them and being a sort of traitor to Us.

Also to be held against Tom was the fact that when he had recruited them to work at Knight's Acre he had promised them a sound good dinner every day. That had held for a while; now the food grew steadily poorer and the sight of Henry eating the same stuff didn't deceive them for a minute. They were being fobbed off at mid-day, and then, when they had trudged home this same table was spread with very different stuff.

Tom, though he could not match Walter's carving, could whittle quite handily, and out of a bit of birch wood he made another salt bowl into which Jem and Bert could drop gravy or bits of meat if they wished.

Griselda said, 'That was thoughtful of you, Tom,' and gave him one of her rare smiles.

'Can't do with this, can we Bert bor? No *spoon*!'

Usually Henry took little notice either of the lack of manners or the conversation at the far end of the table. This was a way of life forced upon him — temporarily; just a set-back — and he must bear with it. But presently it was borne in upon his self-absorbed isolation that Tom was being teased in a not-altogether pleasant way, and from the head of the table he said, 'That'll do.'

It was enough. They didn't like him, but they heeded him. He never had been particularly good-humoured and of late had been positively surly. Also, not to be overlooked was the fact that slave-driver as he was he drove himself even harder.

Up and about in the morning when they arrived; at it all day, and often when it was time to knock off, doing that little bit extra; or saying, 'Leave it. I'll mend it after supper.' How this repair of tools or harness accorded with those vast suppers which they imagined, they did not bother to think.

Tom Robinson decided that Spring that he was in love with Griselda. He had always been aware of her, seen her tripping about, neat and *nice*-looking, if not actually pretty. But he had never had an opportunity to know her until the household was re-organised. Now, the more he saw of her, the more he liked and admired her and the more he felt that she was the girl for him. He knew that he could never be content with a village girl — a female counterpart of Jem or Bert; and there were many things about Griselda which reminded him of the Lady Sybilla.

Tom owned nothing, not an inch of land, no roof. Down in Intake there was a holding called Robin's Acre, but Tom, younger son of a younger son had no claim to it. And he wasn't very strong; ever since the plague he had been subject to fits of weakness and dizziness, quickly passed, though liable to strike at the most inconvenient moments. However, he had taken responsibility for the sheep and Master Henry valued him; had indeed once said, 'Tom, you worth two other men.' He was reasonably sure that if Griselda agreed to marry him, the master would make no objection.

Tom had his eye on a more or less separate establishment — there it was, just across the yard. He'd never been into Tana's pavilion, but he knew from Ursula that there were two rooms and a kitchen.

All such things must be done in orderly fashion. It was May, and Layer Wood was a lake of bluebells; the perfect place for that preliminary walking-out during which a girl could give indication of whether she liked you or not.

He asked her as nicely as he could; he said, 'It's a fine evening, Griselda. And the bluebells are a sight to see. How about taking a walk when you've settled the children?'

Nothing wrong about that, was there? To Tom's amazement Griselda looked offended. Her green eyes seemed to glitter; her lips clamped down together before she spoke. Then they parted and she said, 'No thank you, Tom Robinson,' and closed them again, in a formidable line.

Griselda knew what went on in woods, in bluebell season, or out: and she wanted nothing to do with it.

Like Tom she had been looking to the future and it did not include *him*! One day, and that not so distant, when Robert and Joanna were three years old, independent, she was going to propose to Master Henry that she should take over the cooking and the management of the household; she *knew* that she could do it better than Jill, that idler, that sloven.

Tom accepted the rebuff. If she didn't like him there was nothing he could do about it.

Before the last bluebell had faded in Layer Wood, there was an incident at Intake. At Edgar's Acre.

Bert's father, making ready for cutting hay, sharpening his scythe, nicked his thumb as he had done at least ten times before. He took no notice, but it went bad on him and presently, his jaws clamped together and, his body arched in convulsion, he died. Nobody mourned him; he'd been a heavy-handed man.

He left two sons, Peter, first-born, Bert the younger. But Bert had contributed all he had, all he had earned, first to the raised rent and then to the outright purchase of the little holding.

The two brothers had a furious quarrel, ending in a tragedy which Bert's mother, bereft of husband and son within a few days, convincingly explained. They'd both, both her boys, been hot and sweaty from haymaking, the one in his own field, the other up at Knight's Acre; so they'd gone to the river to take a splash, and Peter had drowned. Of the shouting and the blows, of Bert carrying Peter's body to the river she said nothing; she needed Bert now . . .

There were hired labourers who in Bert's position would still be under compulsion to work to the end of a stipulated period, but in his case there was no such contract and he was free to go.

'You see how it is, sir. I got my own hay to see to.'

Henry saw how it was. That big extra field; hay and harvest to be got in by himself, by Jem and Tom. It'd mean neglecting the sheep a bit.

'Is there anybody down there who'd come and take your place?'

'There ain't the spare men there used to be,' Bert said, a

133

nasty undertone in his voice. 'Buying the land all of a sudden ... lot of families had to put boys out to work. Girls, too.'

Henry had had nothing to do with that transaction but he was not going to excuse himself to his hired man. Nor did he bother to say that if Bert hoped to make a success of Edgar's Acre he'd have to work a good bit harder than he had ever done here.

'Very well,' he said.

'I'll have a word with Griselda fore I go.'

Griselda was in the garden, doing her best to make up for a year's neglect. The lady had loved her plants and it was still Griselda's wish to be as much like her as possible, but last year the children had been too young to allow her to divert much attention from them. Now, nearing their third birthday they could play about and amuse each other while Griselda did vigorous and ignorant things which would have made Lady Randle who had supplied most of the plants, turn in her grave.

Bert came and stood in front of her.

'Want a word with you.'

'I'm listening.'

'How about us getting married?'

For several seconds surprise held her dumb. Then she said, 'No, thank you, Bert Edgar.' Her lips closed in a thin line.

'You ain't thought about it. You think. The place is mine now. Don't you want to be missus in your own house?'

'Not in *yours* ' Her green eyes sparkled even more frostily than they had done when she refused to take a walk with Tom.

'Whass wrong with it then? 'S'tidy little house. Look to me you'd be better off there, looking arter your own children ...'

'Do you think I want to spend my life watching you gobble like a pig? Blowing your nose on your fingers? Sneezing without so much as a hand up? Spitting all over the floor?'

The stolid East Anglian stood his ground.

'You could do a lot worse. Lot of men in my position'd look for a wife with a bit to bring him. Or pretty, which you ain't, let me tell you.' He jerked his thumb at the two children, busily disinterring lily bulbs and calling them onions. 'They'll grow up. Who'll want you then?'

'Get out of my sight!'

'Shan't arst you agen.'

She turned and vented her wrath and disgust upon the children, scolding Robert and slapping Joanna. It was always safe to blame Joanna for any mischief that went on.

Busy as he was just then, Henry was aware of the bad housekeeping. Jill seemed to grow more lethargic, more careless. He thought of his mother, how well she had managed, making the best of even poorer materials than Jill had to hand.

Jem, now aware of his indispensability, complained audibly, 'Cold bacon agen! This ain't what I call a dinner. My owd mother could put me up something as good as this, in a poke.'

'I was expecting roast mutton myself,' Henry said. 'What happened to the meat?'

'I let the fire get low, master. Time I mended it, it was too late to start roasting. *Eddy allus used to see to the fire.*'

Jill had not taken on any of Eddy's work.

'I suppose Eddy used to scrub this table, too.'

It had been clean once, now it was disgusting.

What, in fact, did Jill do? Griselda looked after the children entirely, washed and mended for everybody. She now did the garden, flung scraps to the fowls, helped by the children, gathered eggs, and from the wood's fringe the twigs which served for the kindling of the fire. Once Henry had even seen her carrying the swill bucket from just outside the kitchen door and tipping it into the pig-trough, doing it daintily, holding her skirts clear.

One evening Henry said, 'There is no salt.'

Jill said, 'No master. We ain't got none. I forgot.'

'I asked you especially, before I went to market for the last time for maybe a month, to think ahead and tell me what was needed.'

'*Eddy allus used to remind me about such things.*'

'Maybe you should have gone with him,' Henry said. He was irritable. Angry with nature which had ordained that haymaking and sheep shearing should coincide. You had either to be a farmer or a sheep man and Walter had been right in recognising the distinction. As each sheep, shorn of the wool which in this warmer weather had been more of an encumbrance than a comfort, jumped up from the shearer's hand it had to be marked anew if it belonged to Henry. The stick which applied the blob of red ochre, the stick which dabbed tar on the little wounds made by the shears were both kept busy and there were times when Henry was prepared to admit that Young Shep had earned his keep.

As soon as the shearing was finished one of Master Johnson's buyers arrived with pack ponies and a pair of scales. Over the selling, as over the shearing, Henry was careful to distinguish between his own and Robert's, and on his next visit to Baildon he took Robert's share — the larger part of the money — to Master Turnbull.

'I want this to be legal and in good order,' he said. 'So if you'd lock it away.'

Master Turnbull counted the money and wrote a receipt. Then he said, 'Money locked away earns nothing, Master Tallboys. This is not a large sum, but carefully invested it could increase.'

'Loaned out?' Henry could remember his father had once borrowed money — and been hard put to it to find the interest. 'I should not like Robert's money to be at risk. Suppose the borrower could not pay back, or died.'

'In my experience money invested in property is seldom lost. A plot of land or a house cannot get up and run away. One may wait to see returns but the demand is certain to come.'

'That,' Henry said, nodding towards the money, 'wouldn't buy much in the property line.'

'Not in itself, but added to other, similar sums. I have organised many such transactions for people who have only small sums to invest.'

Henry thought for a moment and said, 'You know best. Anything that could profit the boy. He'll have little enough.'

'You may rely upon me.'

Master Turnbull thought it strange that two brothers, quite similar in appearance, should be so different; Henry so honest; Richard so almost shifty, within the strict letter of the law. Young Robert Tallboys was lucky to have been entrusted to Henry.

This act of providing, in however small a fashion, for Robert's future, seemed to set Henry thinking about his own.

He thought in a mercenary way. They'd done well with the wool this year, the hay-crop was good and once again a good harvest promised. He had survived the set-back of having to buy, cash on the nail, what sheep he had and should this year end on the right side of the balance. His ambition and his determination to succeed were two things which had not succumbed to the shock of the catastrophe which had killed so much else within him. And when Knight's Acre was what he intended to make of it, it would need an heir.

Therefore he needed a wife.

He thought of marriage in a cold-blooded way. He wanted a decent woman, amiable, capable of child-bearing, capable of running his house. He would not love her, or even be fond — all that was over.

He never nowadays thought of Tana in his waking moments, with his will in control. Very occasionally he dreamed, sometimes dreadfully, sometimes blissfully, but as soon as he had splashed his face with cold water, and put on his working clothes, the horror or the delight were banished.

In finding himself a likely wife he intended to enlist his Aunt Emma's aid; a woman should be the best judge of a woman, and she knew a lot of people. Where the road forked he actually hesitated, thinking that he might as well go to Moyidan while he was tidily dressed. Then he remembered that he had done some marketing in Baildon and that flour was among the necessities he had bought. Jill might be waiting for it; she was a hopeless manager who never had anything in reserve. And nowadays every visit to Moyidan meant having a word with his Uncle James whose one idea seemed to be to detain anyone who called upon him. The business of marriage was not urgent. So he swung his horse into the lane that led to Intake.

Tom held a head of oats in his hand and said, 'Smut!' in a doleful voice. Henry in all the years that he had been farming had never had a case of smut, or 'black blight' as it was sometimes called. But there it was, the field of oats, so pretty a few days ago, now looked as though soot had blown over it; just as it was ready for the scythe.

'What's to be done, Tom?'

'Nothing. Save keep it off the wheat. If we can. It's as catching as the plague.'

'We cut it?'

'Take too long. Burn it. Fire's the cleanser. God send we're in time. Otherwise it's ruination. I've seen this afore. When I was a tiddler. Seeing a whole field aflame I hopped about. Excited. Till my father fetched me a clout . . .'

Between the fields there were no hedges, just the headlands of unploughed land, the space left for the turning of the ploughs, at this season all full of wild flowers. Weeds. Poppies, cornflowers, cranesbill. And this field was the one known as Middle Field. Every field had its name, bearing some relationship to the house. Near Field. Middle Field. Far Field.

Henry visualised Middle Field all ablaze, the flames and sparks crossing the banks into Near Field, growing barley, or Far Field, growing wheat.

'Tom, if we fire this, can we contain it?'

'Beat the bounds sharp enough, yes. We want branches. And they're handy. Cut three good branches. I'll go fetch the fire.'

Henry stood there, staring at the blackened crop, appalled. It was a cash crop. Oats were always marketable. Rich men fed oats to their horses, poor men ate oatmeal as a dish by itself, or used it to thicken broth.

Jem arrived and corroborated everything that Tom had said. The black blight had struck Wade's place yesterday and Wade had fired his oats and reckoned he'd saved his wheat and maybe his two bullocks.

'Bullocks?'

'They're all connected, Master Tallboys. Smut on oats, black blight on wheat and the murrain in cattle. A sickness and a curse.'

'Now, mark my words,' Griselda said. 'You stay on this side of the bank and watch, or do whatever you like. But if you set a foot over it, you'll get a good spanking.' She addressed herself to Joanna; Robert was not venturesome. He would never do anything unless Joanna led the way. Having disposed of the children, Griselda broke herself a branch and joined in the tricky operation. The blighted oats must burn just long enough for the blight to die with those nodding fern-like heads, but not long enough to set the neighbouring fields afire.

In the middle of this battle, Tom had one of his weak spells and was obliged to lie prone for a while, but he recovered quickly.

By mid-day the stricken field lay blackened and flat and they all went into the house where Jill had not even had foresight enough to realise that four people, fighting fire needed hot water for washing. Even the children, safe on the far side of the flowery bank, had been smuttied. And they all deserved a better dinner than that provided. Jill had spent most of the morning watching the fire from an upper window.

As usual, Jem was the one to make open complaint, and Henry who had been about to issue a reprimand himself, changed course and snapped.

'If things go on this way, we may think ourselves lucky to have bread and bacon by this time next year.'

Tom said with as much cheer as he could muster, 'We may have saved the wheat.'

Griselda sat and wished that she could cook. It was an art in which she had no experience; the orphans' food had been prepared in the convent kitchen and the landlady at The Swan had done the cooking, relegating the rougher, dirtier work to Griselda.

Towards the end of the disagreeable meal Henry jerked himself out of gloom long enough to say, 'Thanks for lending a hand, Griselda.' It sounded a bit brusque so he added, 'And the children were good, too.' She took that as a compliment on her handling of them, and thought to herself — There isn't much I can't do, if I set me mind to it; I'll learn to cook.

Jill, however, was unwilling to teach; unwilling even to be watched. 'You fidget me,' she said, or 'Hadn't you better see what they're up to?' When she cared to Jill could cook, liked to make a mystery of her art and was certain that in a household a cook ranked higher than a nursemaid — despite all her fancy airs — whose charges were rapidly outgrowing the need for her ministrations.

The wheat had been saved from the smut, but at least half of the barley was affected by another plague, the rust. Henry's hope of a good year, financially, receded and his general air exuded gloom.

It was with no lightening of the gloom that he said one evening, at the end of supper, 'Griselda, I have something to say to you. Will you come into the hall?'

Everything within her dropped to knee-level. In one flickering second she remembered Bert Edgar's words about the children not needing her for ever. And Henry's words on the day of the oat-burning, about the children having been good.

She was about to be dismissed, as Eddy had been — a useless mouth. Well, there were other children in the world! But she loved Knight's Acre, the first place where she had ever been happy. She loved the house, and the garden in which by hit-and-miss methods she was learning management; she liked the little church — and even the embracing woods.

That Henry held the door for her to pass into the hall, meant nothing to her. He was surly and short-spoken, but the lady, his mother had drilled him to mannerliness. Passing through the doorway, Griselda set her lips together. She would give no sign of dismay. He was a fool if he thought that in retaining Jill and dismissing *her*, he was doing himself a service.

With a gesture, Henry invited her to a seat on the settle. Then, standing at a distance, he pulled his fingers, so that the knuckles cracked. He was finding the words of dismissal hard to say. And so you should, you great fool, she thought angrily. I'm worth ten of Jill.

Awkwardly, because however one approached the business, there should be some trimmings to conceal the harsh reality, he said, 'Would you consider marrying me?'

Griselda, the tough survivor of various vicissitudes had never swooned in her life. Now suddenly the hall tilted and darkened. She put out a hand and grabbed the side of the settle, and by that movement steadied both herself and her surroundings. She was capable of thought, and her thoughts were rapid and concise.

It would mean what she always thought of as *that*. But he was clean, different from men in ditches, men half-drunk at The Swan. And she would have Knight's Acre, for the rest of her life. Well worth it!

'Oh yes,' she said. 'Most gladly.'

With the burning of the oats, the threat to the wheat, Henry had realised that he was no longer what his Aunt Emma would consider eligible, except perhaps for some woman, well past her prime, and he was thankful that he had not, in an optimistic moment, turned towards Moyidan. He might well have found himself landed with a woman who had every right to expect more than Griselda ever would.

He moved forward, kissed her — on the forehead — and said, 'I shall do my utmost to be a good husband, Griselda.'

On an upsurge of confidence, she said, 'I will be a good wife to you.'

Nothing more to be said. And after all this betrothal was different from the majority only because the two people directly involved had struck the bargain between themselves. No parents hovering about and doing the haggling.

'I'll go across and speak to Father Ambrose,' Henry said.

When he had gone Griselda walked about the house, soon to be hers. By the best bed, in the biggest chamber — the bed in which the lady had died, she stood still, thought of *that* and knew that she could bear it. She made a promise — half to herself, half to Sybilla whom she had truly loved. *I will look after them all.*

After that she went downstairs, just looking about, planning changes, thinking, 'All mine. Mine.'

Jill said, 'You looking for something, Griselda?'

'No.'

In three weeks' time you will be calling me *Mistress*. And mistress I shall be. I shall watch you cook. You will never drive me from this kitchen again. And when I can cook, you will go.

CHAPTER TWENTY-ONE

Tom Robinson, the person most nearly concerned because he loved Griselda, took the news calmly. It seemed to him natural enough that a girl should prefer the master to the man, the healthy to the sickly. He was still grateful for what Henry had done for him during the plague time. He was able to wish them well with all his heart.

Lady Emma, the person next most nearly concerned was furious. It was a disgrace to the family. And fearful waste! Henry — she could bring herslf to admit this now that she no longer had to deceive herself about her own son — was a good-looking, well-set-up young man who owned a good house and some land; he was a Tallboys, too. Had she been consulted, as she should have been, she could have found him a wife ten times over; some with a little money; all with breeding. And without a word to anybody he had gone and married a kitchen slut, whose children would be little Richard's cousins! How disgusting!

The third person concerned was Jill. It was bad enough to have a nursemaid elevated to mistress, more irritating was the standard of cleanliness imposed . . .

Griselda's own experience of cleanliness was chequered; as a beggar-child she had been filthy and lousy. In the convent orphanage the standard of cleanliness had been so high that the children's heads were shaven. The inn was filthy, and she had reverted; and then she had come to Knight's Acre and been reclaimed by Sybilla. Now in full control, she was for ever saying — Scrub this table, scour this pot, wash your hands before handling dough. There was also the constant watchfulness — Let me see how that is done, Jill; and the questions — Why do you do that?

Jill was denied even the relief of a good grumble. Against Griselda Tom Robinson would hear no word of criticism, and she had little opportunity of seeing Jem alone. Once she did catch him and began to list all that she now had to put up with, he simply said the food was better nowadays. That was all he cared about.

One day Jem happened to mention that Bert Edgar's old mother had fretted herself to a skeleton and got so useless that Bert had sent her to his married sister in Nettleton.

'Who do for Bert, then,' Jill asked.

'He do for hisself mostly. Some days he get a dinner at Wade's. They're sorta related.'

Next day, as soon as dinner was over and the dishes washed — This plate is still very greasy; take some ashes to it! — Jill slipped away, washed herself with unusual thoroughness and put on the better of her two summer dresses and went down to the village. It was almost the end of harvest and in some of the brown stubble fields women and children were gleaning. Bert Edgar, single-handed on a holding which had kept two men busy, was still scything. He stopped when he saw Jill and wiped his sweaty brow with his sweaty forearm.

'What you want?' he asked ungraciously. She had never endeared herself to him, lazy fat cow.

'I hear you got nobody to do for you, Bert.'

'Thass right.'

'I'd come. I can't do with things up there any longer. Come

into the house all rags and filth and now lording it over all.'
Here she could at least air her grievances.

As she talked Bert looked her over. Lazy fat cow, but given a
bit of stick behind her, she could be made to move; one or two
bad dinners chucked at her head would learn her! She was
strong, and if not actually young, not old, not past bearing a
child. One. That was what he wanted. A boy.

'When could you come?'

'Any time. Eddy and me wasn't bonded. We was just sent
over from Moyidan.' Wives *were* bonded, for life! And she'd
soon learn not to talk about Eddy. A clout on the jaw worked
wonders!

'I'll marry you. That is if you start in right now.'

She was almost as overcome as Griselda had been, some
weeks earlier in the hall. By the rough and ready reckoning of a
peasant family she was thirty-five years old, and nobody had
ever shown the slightest desire to walk out with her, take her to
the Midsummer Fair, leave alone marry her. She'd been fond
of Eddy, but he was years too young and he'd always be poor.
Married to Bert she'd be mistress of Edgar's Acre; the equal of
that upstart little bitch.

'All right,' she said. 'What'll I start on?'

'Making sheaves and stooking them,' Bert said. 'Then,
back at the house there's a rabbit I clumped. We could hev a
pie. . .'

He dealt fairly gently with her until they were actually married; it wouldn't do to frighten her off before she had committed herself. And in fact Jill, during that time exerted herself
to please. It wouldn't do to frighten him off until she was
legally his wife. Mistress of Edgar's Acre. After that she'd
show him.

Two loveless marriages, made for convenience, as most
were. The one at Knight's Acre was, apparently, the more successful. Henry and Griselda remained civil, mannerly and of
one mind. But the spark which bed-intimacy so often kindled,
even in loveless marriages, remained dead for them, two people
rippled by experience; the one in a ditch, the other in a silk-
hung pavilion. Griselda still, in a marital embrace, set her teeth
and endured and Henry thought that he must not compare;
this was something that he had let himself in for, something he

had deliberately undertaken. It suited him. Griselda made no demands, was capable, energetic and thrifty.

Thrift was of importance, because although the penury of the early part of that year had passed — never, Henry hoped, to be repeated — and the price of wool remained steady and the harvest not a complete disaster; taxes had risen out of all proportion. There was even a new one, grotesquely called 'a Benevolence' the proceeds of which were supposed to go to renewing the war with France. This form of direct taxation could not be evaded — tax on wines and other luxuries could be; you simply didn't buy. But by whatever standard the tax-assessors used — number of rooms, or windows, or hearths, or acres, Knight's Acre was a substantial property, to be taxed accordingly. Unless you paid, and paid promptly, an order for distraint was issued, and you lost your stock or any other movable.

To make matters even more difficult for a man just struggling to his feet, was the tinkering about with the coinage. Edward IV, ruling without a Parliament, which meant that he was out of touch with ordinary country people, while still in close contact with London, that centre of commerce, decided to abolish the noble and issued a new coin, the ryal, of greater face value, but less purchasing power. The result was raging inflation. And the result of that was cautious buying. Families who had eaten meat twice or even three times a week, now ate it once; those who had eaten white bread — priding themselves upon it — reverted to the dark brown bread of the poor. The market sagged.

Knight's Acre, so largely self-supporting, benefited in a way; it still had food, good food, and thanks to Griselda, well-cooked, but Henry's dream of prosperity, like the rainbow's end, receded and the silver, the hangings for walls and all the other things which he had promised, first to his mother, and then to Tana were as far out of reach as ever. He had never promised Griselda anything and she seemed to be happy and content with what she had. Good manager. Good wife.

They had been married rather less than two years when on a Saturday afternoon, Griselda went to the church with an armful of flowers. Robert and Joanna went with her. She was bringing them up to be useful and they could now be trusted with such small duties as filling the altar vases from a bucket of water which Father Ambrose's housekeeper kept ready just inside the door. Less for flowers than against an accident. Fumbling about with candles the old man might well set fire to something. To himself.

Father Ambrose knelt by the altar and Griselda, putting a finger to her lips, hushed the children's chatter. Then she whispered, 'We will wait a minute. We must not disturb him.'

They waited for what seemed a long time, both to the restive children, and to the woman who had left a ham simmering in a pot over a fire which would die unless attended.

Presently Joanna said in something louder than a whisper, 'He's gone to sleep!' She giggled and so did Robert; to go to sleep in the afternoon, and in such a position, seemed comic to them. Griselda took a step or two into the church and looked more attentively. His posture was strange, she now saw, his head on the altar's edge and his arms stretched out on either side. She went forward and placed her hand lightly on his shoulder, and said, 'Father Ambrose.' At the touch he lurched sideways and she saw that he was dead.

Some women would have sent the five-year-olds away, told them to go and play. But death was death, they'd come up against it sooner or later.

'Father Ambrose is dead. God rest him,' she said, and crossed herself. The children solemnly copied her action. Griselda dropped the flowers alongside the body and said, 'We must tell Henry.'

Outside in the sunshine, solemnity fell away and Joanna shouted, 'I'll tell him,' and began to run to the hayfield.

'Me too,' Robert shouted and followed her. She could still outpace and outjump him, so she reached the field first, calling, in a kind of rhythm, 'Father *Am*brose is *dead*! Father *Am*brose is *dead*,' as though announcing glad tidings.

'I suppose it was only to be expected,' Henry said when Griselda joined them. 'But he'd lasted so long somehow it seemed as though he'd go on for ever. Well, that'll be the end of work for today. I'd hoped to get this finished. Tom. Jem. You heard? Go and take him up and put him on his bed. I'll have to go to Moyidan.'

'Why?' Griselda asked. So far as she could remember he had

been to Moyidan only once since their marriage — and that was for his uncle's funeral.

'Well, for one thing Father Ambrose must be buried. Also, because my great-grandmother built and endowed the church, Moyidan has some say in appointing the priest. Thank God for Aunt Emma. Richard would have sent us a deaf mute!'

Lady Emma received him more amiably than their last parting warranted. When Sir James died Henry had behaved correctly and offered his help with any affairs which the widow did not wish to deal with herself. She had replied sharply that she needed no help, and if she did, would not look to him who had so mismanaged his own. That was not only ungrateful but rude, and misguided for within his own limited sphere Henry managed well and had the reputation for being a shrewd though honest bargainer.

'I don't see that I've managed so badly,' he said.

'I am referring to your marriage. Most ill-advised. And a disgrace to the family!'

Had he married for love and been infatuated with his wife, Henry could hardly have been more deeply offended.

Now he stated his business bluntly and she dealt with it in her usual efficient way. 'I will inform Father Thomas today and he will see to everything. As for the future — I believe he has a nephew, recently ordained who would be quite suitable. I believe one should consult the Bishop, but how can one, when he is so seldom in residence? You can leave it all to me, Henry.'

He would have left then, but she urged him to take some cool wine. When he hesitated, she did a thing most unusual with her; she apologised.

'At our last meeting I believe that I offended you, Henry. You must not bear me a grudge. I was not myself that day.'

Actually she had been very much herself; her grief merely a bow to convention. Poor James had been dying by such gradual stages for so long a time, and had suffered so much that his death had roused little emotion but relief.

'We'll leave it at that,' Henry said.

The wine came with a dish of little saffron cakes. Hard after came little Richard.

Without greeting Henry, he said, 'I thought something was going on.' He snatched two of the cakes, and stuffing one into his mouth, spoke through it. 'Umma, you said pony as soon as it was cooler.'

'Yes, darling. Go tell Jacky to saddle him and then *walk* — mind what I say — walk to the bridge and wait for me. I have something to discuss with your Uncle Henry.'

She had decided when he was four years old — and big for his age — that he must have a pony and that no one should teach him to ride but herself. She was not a horse-woman, but she knew the rules and was willing to trot alongside, issuing instructions. The exercise exacerbated the stitch in her side, but it did not cause it. It was always there and sometimes kept her awake at night.

'I'm worried to death about that boy,' she said, when little Richard, with yet a third cake, had stumped away.

'There's nothing wrong with him that a good smack on the behind wouldn't cure.' Lady Emma had always accused Sybilla of spoiling her boys and had once administered to Henry the correction which he now mentioned. He thought — Mother would never allow us to behave in that oafish way!

'I mean his *future*. When . . . if . . . anything should happen to me. Two parents with not a ha'p'orth of sense between them. They think of nothing but themselves. Two good meals a day and a bed to sprawl on. Once I'm gone the nearest unscrupulous person who offers them that much could rule Moyidan and ruin it. And I want it kept intact for him.'

She was not acting upon what might appear to be a sudden decision but which was in fact the result of long cogitation in the night hours when her mind would go round and round the circle of relatives and friends, suggesting and rejecting, and always coming back to Henry; honest, solid, and apart from his stupid marriage, sensible.

Sometimes her night thoughts would end with the idea of approaching Henry and making a proposition to him. But she had offended him, and would have to apologise, and night thoughts were unreliable, everyone knew. There was no hurry. A stitch in the side never killed anyone; she might have many years yet. So she had never moved in the matter.

To her the death of old Father Ambrose seemed opportune and here was Henry, looking exactly as he sometimes appeared to her in the night; honest, solid and sensible.

'What I need,' she said, 'is somebody reliable to assume control of everything. Naturally, in the eyes of the law, Richard will be heir, but I strongly doubt if he would even realise the fact. He would certainly never oppose any arrangement that kept him comfortable. I have thought about this very carefully, Henry and I know that there are provisions, in law, for the administration of the estates of those who are incompetent — but as I see it, that would be like hiring a pack of wolves to guard a sheep-fold. What I want is somebody honest and reliable — preferably a relative — to take charge and hold the place together until little Richard is old enough to take over.'

Henry sat there looking honest and solid, and sensible and reliable — but quite unhelpful. Had her apology not been humble enough?

'Would you do it, Henry? You shouldn't lose by it, I assure you. I have a little property of my own. I would leave it to you in return for your promise to look after Moyidan and keep it intact for the boy.'

'I couldn't do it. I couldn't spare the time. My own place keeps me busy from dawn to dusk. And I haven't the learning . . .'

'Clerks are ten a penny.'

'Maybe. But they need overlooking. No, I am sorry, but I could not undertake it. I have all I can handle.'

The stitch in her side tightened and she put her hand to it with a gesture that was now almost a habit.

'Would Richard?'

'How could I say? I know nothing about him — except that he went off with enough money to buy himself a bishopric, and took John with him.'

'Is he still in Winchester?'

'Even that I do not know.' Richard's behaviour and John's was still a matter of rancourous thought. If Richard, if John, encouraged by Richard, had not insisted on the break up of the flock . . . 'No,' Henry said, 'I know nothing. But surely there are people nearer. On *your* side of the family.'

They had all been sorted through during those wakeful nights.

'The old are too old; the young, too frivolous . . .'

From the bridge beyond the window Little Richard called imperiously, 'Umma. I'm ready! Umma!'

Lady Emma rose with a good pretence of her old briskness.

Naughty little boy! He had not heeded her order to walk; there he was, mounted.

She took short leave of Henry and went out. Impossible to scold this child who was so exactly what she had hoped her own son to be. Bold and able. She used the word *naughty*, almost as a caress, and then said that they must go into the village because she must talk to Father Thomas.

'I wanted to go the other way.'

Indomitable, she said, 'There is time for both.'

Time to go to the priest's house, along a path where, what with geese, dogs, goats and children all asprawl, Little Richard could have no real ride. His pleasure, she thought, must not be curtailed simply because another old man, due for death, had died. So, all arranged and the daylight lasting, they came out into the other way, the long straight way that led from Moyidan to the highway.

'You may go on your own,' Lady Emma said. 'As far as that big tree. Turn there and come back. We will then gather strawberries for supper.' She gave in to weakness and having shot out a few last instructions about the position of elbows and heels, and not making the jerks that hardened a pony's mouth, she sat down and once more placed her hand against the pain in her side, and for the first time felt the lump. Incredible! It had not been there earlier in the day. She remembered that her mother had suffered from what was called a growth, never complained of until it was too large to be concealed. Was it possible that for years her mother had suffered in silence? If so, how many years? There was no answer to that. No means of knowing how long . . . Dear God and the boy only four!

Obedient for once, he turned at the big tree she had indicated and came back at the fastest pace the pony could manage. As he neared her he called, 'Up, Umma! Up.' She rose, put her hand to her side. Nothing! Imagination, pure and simple. In any case, when her mother had died the growth was as large as a blown-up pig's bladder. What *she* had imagined . . . No, carefully probing, she found it again, no bigger than a walnut. So there was time. No need to write hastily to Knight's Acre Richard. Give Henry time to think it over. Not that she considered it likely that he would change his mind. Looking back she could hardly find an instance of a Tallboys changing his mind, once it was made up.

CHAPTER TWENTY TWO

When, at last, warned by a symptom even more sinister than the growing lump, Lady Emma wrote to her nephew Richard, the time was exactly right. The longed for, the schemed for, the *paid* for promotion had never come. Always promises that were never kept. Disappointment and disillusion, time after time.

Of the real barrier across his path he knew nothing. The truth was that His Grace of Winchester found Richard too good a servant to be spared. He never said so; even a hint to that effect would soon have reached the ears of the young man who had quite sufficient self-esteem. But in such a closed community as the Church no positive statement was needed; a silence, a shrug, the suggestion of another candidate ... Time after time Richard had had the embittering experience of seeing lucrative and authoritative posts go to men of less ability. He had just suffered another disappointment when his aunt's letter reached him. He gave himself leave of absence and rode to Moyidan to spy out the land.

Had he been capable of pity he would have felt sorry for Emma, aged so much since the last time he saw her, when he was in this neighbourhood to help settle his father's will. But why be sorry for her? She'd had her life; more years than most people, more power than most women, ever knew.

Weak as she was, she insisted upon showing him the land which was indubitably hers. And she explained.

'There was a time, Richard, when I feared that your uncle might die and my Richard might marry a strong-minded woman who would rule him and oust me. So I asked for this piece of land. I had then some intention of building a house, but it was never needed.'

Richard stared about him. The land was a sheep-run, and even at that, not very valuable. Too difficult of access. But that meant little; the real pickings would be at Moyidan; an old sick woman, two idiots and a boy of five.

'Well?' she asked anxiously.

If he accepted this job he would never become a Bishop — but he could live like one! He'd be done with dancing attendance on ungrateful men and be not only his own master but the master of others.

He asked a few cautious questions. Suppose Moyidan Richard and Margaret had no more children, and something unforeseen happened to little Dick, who would then be the heir?

'Your brother Henry.'

'And when would you wish me to take over?'

'As soon as possible. Not ...' she said, and put her hand to her side, to the lump which her unfashionable loose gown concealed, 'that I am in imminent danger of death. I think you should come while I am still active and able to show you how an estate like this is administered.'

A comic statement since his work, ever since he left Cambridge, had been concerned with the administration of estates. Thinking of that work all done for other people, and no pickings, jerked him to a decision.

His Grace of Winchester was dismayed when Richard tendered his resignation because he had inherited a small property in Suffolk.

'But my dear fellow, that is a barbarous place. Only the other day the Bishop of Bywater was telling me that two months at a time is as long as he can stay there and remain sane. Hardly a literate person within miles. That would not suit *you*! No, you must appoint a steward and stay here and pursue your career.'

What career?

'I am sorry, Your Grace. It is not so simple. Family responsibilities are involved. *My* property adjoins that of some relatives — an elderly aunt and her grandson, a boy of five. I shall be able to care for all.'

'It is a thousand pities. I was planning to take you in my entourage on my next visit to Court.'

That might or might not be true; but no matter. Any man of sense, given sufficient resources, could hold Court on his own; and that was what he would do at Moyidan.

Within a week of his arrival — high summer of the year 1466, Lady Emma was giving thanks to God that Henry had refused her offer. Richard was charming to her, listened with attention and apparent respect as she instructed him, entertaining her with gossip, not only from Baildon and Bywater, but from the wider world in which he had moved. He did not criticise little Richard's behaviour — as Henry by implication had done. He constantly re-assured her that nothing should be changed; Richard and Margaret could be certain of comfort to the end of their aimless, useless days, and Moyidan should be most carefully preserved, handed over intact to little Richard when the time came.

She need no longer be busy or bothered. All was in good hands. Hitherto she had avoided as far as possible, the medicines which eased the pain, but dulled the mind. Now she could make free with them because all was in Richard's capable hands. She drifted towards death in a haze of opium, self-satisfaction at having managed so well, and gratitude towards God and Richard.

It was fitting to anyone who knew her well that the last clearly articulated word she spoke should have been 'Money'.

On the last day of September when Richard came in to wish her goodnight — she had taken to rising late and retiring early — she said, her voice muted and blurred, 'Richard . . . the money . . .' She and James had always lived well, but at the same time had been thrifty, sparing where they could, never thinking in Master Turnbull's terms that money laid away was unprofitable. They had, in fact, not wanted their gold to be earning, they wanted it to be safe; safe from robbers, and from the tax collectors. And from the ups and downs of a war which was no concern of theirs. They had lived in a time when a gold coin was worth its weight in gold — unless it had been clipped, and there was *no* clipped coin in their hoard.

'What money, Aunt Emma?'

She gave him no answer. Weakness and peace flooded in like the tide. She moved in the bed and arranged herself in the exact posture which, years ago, she had occupied in her mother's womb; knees drawn up, head tucked down. And so, in the night, died.

In the days immediately following, Richard sometimes wondered whether, on the threshold of death she had wanted to tell him something about money, stored and hoarded. For in the iron-bound strong boxes there was less, far less than might have been expected. Moyidan had always been well ordered, prosperous. When rigorous search revealed nothing more, Richard decided that enough was enough and that his plans should not be interfered with, he sent for Master Hobson and gave him such a job as came only once in a lifetime. Not merely an expensive job, but all indoor work, a consideration with winter at hand. And not merely that, but the kind of job to give a man prestige in the eyes of his fellows. Some of the work involved was a kind outside Master Hobson's experience, but he had his Guild to fall back upon. Guild members wherever they lived were sworn to brotherhood and in due time Master Hobson was in possession of plans and sketches, and of advice, written and verbal, all concerned with rendering a virtually uninhabitable place habitable. And splendid.

'And when can I expect the work to be finished?' Richard asked.

'Aah,' Master Hobson said, holding to his rule never to make an over-optimistic promise. 'All being well, sometime between Christmas and Easter. Say Easter to be on the safe side, Sir Richard.'

Nobody questioned Sir Richard's assumption of complete control. Even those of Lady Emma's distant relatives who felt a flicker of envy took comfort in the question — Who wanted to live with a pair of idiots and a spoilt child?

Richard had no intention of doing so. His work in Winchester had brought him into contact with a good many 'failed men', clerks of the kind Lady Emma meant when she said they came ten a penny. One of these was a man named Jankyn, a good scholar whose failure was due to a physical cause. He suffered from incapacitating headaches, accompanied by a rain of spots before the eyes. In the ordinary way their onset was unpredictable, but one thing was sure; before an examination or an interview an attack would lay him low for two days. Failure and ill health had soured his temper — just the man to deal with Little Richard! Sir Richard sent for him.

'It is not the easiest post in the world, Master Jankyn,' he said in the easy way which endeared him to underlings. 'The boy is well over five and has never been curbed. I have no doubt that you will know how to deal with him. But I should wish you also to have an eye to my cousin and his wife. They will give you no trouble. They are children too, but amenable. They need a certain amount of overseeing. In effect, you would have three charges.'

Master Jankyn would also have a rewarding post. A bedroom to himself — at Winchester he slept with two other men in a kind of cupboard; there was here a good, well-lighted room, school-room and dining parlour during the day, in the evening, his study; good, regular meals, servants to wait upon him and the princely salary of forty ryals a year. For a man who could only claim that he was a *failed* BA of Cambridge it was a wonderful job and he was duly grateful.

Nobody, Richard thought, could fault his arrangement. The boy who would eventually inherit Moyidan did need a tutor who could instil not only the elements of learning, but manners. And a pair of idiots needed a keeper.

He also brought from Winchester another man whom his sharp eye had noticed; a very good cook; another ill-done-by man who made beautiful things for which the master-cook took all credit.

To him Richard said, 'This is a very primitive kitchen, Matt, but I plan to have a new one. Made to suit *you*. I am not well-informed about ovens and stoves and spits. Hobson's men will take your orders.'

'You mean, sir . . . Sir, that I may *design my own oven*? In brick? And hooded?'

'If that is what you wish. Once the work here is done I intend to entertain a good deal. Meanwhile, if you would do your best . . .'

Do his best! Matt was an artist whose beautiful work had never been recognised, attributed to another. To Sir Richard who had given him his chance, Matt, like Master Jankyn was deeply grateful.

While Lady Emma lived Richard had made one visit to Knight's Acre. He had heard about the most unfortunate marriage and Griselda was a surprise to him — so neat, clean and almost well-spoken. At first sight he considered that a man in Henry's circumstances could have done much worse for himself. She could cook and everything about the place, including the two children offered evidence of good management.

However, Richard was more of a connoisseur of women than a priest without a parish might be expected to be; mouths were an indication of temperament and about Griselda's there was nothing inviting at all; the thin lips firmly pressed together hinted at a cold nature and possible bad temper, though there was no other sign of ill-humour. Her manner towards the children was firm, but kindly. Richard, eager to ingratiate himself, addressed her as 'madam' and gathered from the look in her eyes that the term of respect pleased her.

He observed — as Tom Robinson had observed from the first — a curious lack of *anything* between Henry and his wife. A stranger, uninformed, would never have guessed that they were married; they never exchanged a meaningful glance, a shortened name, a nick-name, an endearment or a smile. Married for just over two years — and no children.

It was on his first visit that Henry asked, 'By the way, what is John doing?'

Once the property had been divided, John had coaxed Richard to take him to Winchester with him, and Richard had consented, saying that without doubt he could find him some kind of employment in the musical line. Now Richard was obliged to say,

'I don't know. He gave me the slip at Colchester.'

Henry scowled. 'Gave you the slip? How could he do that? He was riding pillion!'

'I know. But we stopped for a meal. He excused himself, left the table and did not return.'

'Did you ask around?'

'Naturally. Nobody seemed to have noticed him.'

'Did you search? Raise the hue-and-cry?'

Here it was again, Richard thought, that elder-brother business which he had always so deeply resented. But he must keep in with Henry who, after that frail looking Moyidan Richard, and a child with most of childhood's ills to face, was heir to Moyidan.

'The hue-and-cry, no! He had stolen nothing. He could hardly be looked upon as a lost child or a horse gone astray. I search, yes, and waited . . . Henry, have you ever been to Colchester:'

'No, What has that to do with it?' Henry had never had any particular fondness for John but he had a strong sense of responsibility.

'Colchester is at least ten times the size of Baildon. It is a very busy place, too. John knew where I was. As I say, I waited . . . He had his money — and his own ideas.'

'He could have been murdered for his money.'

'Unlikely. He is as big as most men; he wore homespun and carried a lute. He's safe enough, wherever he is — and no doubt doing well. Otherwise we should have heard.'

'Oh well ... I hope you are right. After all,' Henry said, shrugging off responsibility, 'I'd had him from a pup and never gained any real control. You could hardly have been expected ...'

The brothers next met at Lady Emma's funeral and Richard took the opportunity of having a private word with Henry. He had, he said, already looked into sundry matters, including the venery rights. 'From what I read, Uncle James gave you permission to take a deer or two.'

'Me? That was so long ago, I could hardly bring down a hare. Permission was granted to Walter. I always assumed that what was granted to him would not be denied me. Was I wrong? Because if so,' Henry said with a slight grin, 'I took a young buck only yesterday. Clean through the throat.' It was as good a shot as he had ever made — except when he shot his friend Walter, by mistake — and the carcass hung in the larder awaiting dressing. Griselda was probably even at this moment making an umble pie of the entrails, liver, heart, kidneys.

'I just wanted to confirm your right,' Richard said.

Henry said, 'Many thanks!' but he didn't *look* grateful. One day, Richard thought — he would do him a favour which could not be accepted in such lunatic fashion. He went on to say that he planned considerable improvements to Moyidan and Henry did not even bother to ask what they were.

'Old property needs to be kept in repair,' he agreed. 'Thank God, Knight's Acre is new. Even the thatch should be good for another twenty years.'

'If you ever are short of money, you know where to come.'

'I take that kindly,' Henry said with a straight look, 'but as you know, I don't like borrowing.'

It did not strike him as strange that Richard should be in a position to lend; Lady Emma might well have had a secret hoard and left it as well as her bit of land to the nephew who had taken on a pretty thankless task.

'As soon as I have the place habitable,' Richard said, 'you and your wife shall be my first guests.'

156

And even with that Henry was far less impressed than he should have been.

Nor did he notice that the invitation was long in coming. Winter set in, short days and miry roads. People bent on a long visit might venture forth but it was not the season for making journeys in order to share a meal. Then it was spring, with primroses on every bank and hazel catkins dancing in the wood; and if Richard knew anything at all he'd know that the lambing season was no time for gallivanting.

The invitation came, late in March; brought by a boy, dressed in very fine cloth, buff-coloured. On his breast he wore an oval badge, embroidered with the family emblem. Sir Richard wished Master Tallboys to name a day in the following week when it would be convenient for him and Madam to come to supper and spend the night: and did Master Tallboys wish the wagon sent? The boy's hair, cut level with his ear-lobes and curling slightly inwards, matched the buff of his doublet. He rode a sturdy pony — just the mount which Henry had yearned for when he was young, and would now dearly have loved to afford for Robert, but could not. Quite apart from the initial cost, ponies, though able to fend for themselves in summer, needed hay in winter ... It may have been this thought that made Henry decide that the boy's manner was pert, and dictated his answer. Mistress Tallboys and he would come to supper at Moyidan on Tuesday; they would not stay the night; they did not need the wagon.

Now, for the first time in her life, Griselda faced the age-old feminine problem — what to wear? She was always neat and clean but her wardrobe consisted of the clothes which Sybilla had given her and those she had made herself from the stuff which Sir Godfrey had brought her. Nothing suitable.

Sybilla had had few clothes; what she had owned still lay at the bottom of the clothes chest in the biggest bedroom. They were well-cared for. Griselda, standing in this room had made a promise to the dead lady — I will take care of them all; and she had fulfilled that promise, even to the point of taking these unused garments out now and again, exposing them to the sun and air, returning them, with fresh lavender and rosemary sprigs to deter moths.

Now she stood hesitant. Women often bequeathed their

clothes, she knew that because in the orphanage she and the others had sometimes benefited by such bequests. In this chest there was one silk gown, very beautiful, or so it had seemed to Griselda when Sybilla wore it. Surely the lady would not mind ... She took out and shook the dove's neck coloured gown and held it against herself. Just the right size. But the stout sensible shoes would not do. She rummaged in the depths of the chest and found a pair of dainty shoes; too short and too narrow, but the pain could be borne for one evening. And what about a head-dress? Delving even deeper she came across things she had never bothered about, moths had no taste for gauze and wire. She did not know that many of these crushed, pitiable things were older than Knight's Acre itself, remnant of Sybilla's other life when appearances must be kept up on a shoe-string, and an eye to the latest fashion and nimble fingers and a bit of ingenuity went a long way.

Fully dressed, fully armed, Griselda came to the top of the stairs, just as Henry, hurrying was halfway up. He stopped and reached for the banister rail.

Old Father Ambrose had never mentioned to anybody except Sir Godfrey, his curious experience in the church. Sir Godfrey had never spoken of it. Yet the idea that there was something not quite canny about Knight's Acre had taken hold, part prejudice, and the need to excuse it, part communal consciousness. The place was regarded as haunted, by whom, or why nobody knew but in such matters vagueness simply lent credulity and Henry, recovering said,

'God's teeth! Just for a second I thought you were my mother!'

Natural enough; with the light behind her, in that gown, and in that head-dress.

In a way it was a compliment, however little intended, but under his hard carapace of not caring for anything or anybody any more, Henry was sensitive enough to realise, in a flash, that to mistake your wife for your mother might be hurtful. He amended it to, 'You look very grand.'

At Moyidan everything was very grand indeed. The bleak, high hall of the castle had been ceiled in, the ceiling coffered and painted. The windows were glazed, one with coloured glass, the tiny leaded panes making the family emblem. There were many wall-hangings, all gay and the benches that flanked the vast table were padded with scarlet velvet. Silver glittered on the court cupboards and side tables.

Griselda was awed. Henry only said, 'A bit different from when we used to play here. It must have cost a fortune!' Not quite the response that Richard had desired.

'The improvement of property is always an investment. The boy will be grateful to me, one day.'

At the moment little Richard was anything but grateful. 'Umma used to let me ride in there when it rained,' he said as soon as the workmen moved in.

'What happened to the stairs?'

'They were removed. They were so worn as to be dangerous. The new ones are here.' He opened a door in the screen which now ran across the far end of the hall, and displayed a fine flight of stairs, wide, level and with shallow treads. 'Roofing in the hall gave three extra bed-chambers, which will be needed when I begin to entertain,' Richard said. All were well, even luxuriously furnished.

'Not unlike Beauclaire,' Henry said. Irritating man! Not a word about the care and the taste that had been lavished.

At the foot of the stairs and still on the far side of the screen, Richard pointed to a new door. '*My* kitchen is there.' Some savoury scents were perceptible and Henry realised that he was hungry. In the great hall, however there was no sign of any preparation for a meal.

'This is too large for a small company,' Richard said and opened a door which Henry could not remember; the room beyond he did, changed as it was. It was the main room of the new part of the house, the one in which Lady Emma had entertained. Here the table was set. More silver, a centre-piece, candlesticks, salt bowls and three wine cups. A buff-clad boy stood ready to serve the wine.

'If you will sit here, upon my right, Madam,' Richard said. Griselda sank down thankfully. The shoes were pinching cruelly, and for some reason she felt low-spirited. So much splendour over-awed her, so much space made her ill-at-ease. Even this room which Sir Richard deemed suitable for a small company was far too large. At Knight's Acre she had felt instantly at home; here she was out of place. She lacked the ability to *chatter*, that was it, she thought, pin-pointing a shortcoming. She could remember, during that happy time, before Sybilla became ill, chattering lightly about nothing, being amusing, making pretty gestures. Often in those days the door between the hall and the nursery stood open and although keen wits and a desire to learn had enabled her to catch pronounciation, inflexion, even a certain amount of grammar, the art of conversation had eluded her.

Richard did his best to include her now and again. It was of her that he enquired after the children; but when she had said they were both very well and growing fast, she had said her say, and it was Henry, not usually talkative who added, 'And wicked. At least Joanna is.' He managed to make quite an amusing tale — though he had been anything but amused at the time — of how he had come upon them, yelling with laughter, playing a competitive game; who could get nearest to the target — a patch of mud slapped on the barn door; the missiles eggs, straight from the nest. 'I gave them both a sound good slap. To teach Joanna never to do such a thing again; and to teach Robert not to be so easily led.'

I could have said all that, Griselda reflected; but why should something the very reverse of funny at Knight's Acre, be amusing here?

She eased the shoes off a little, not much, she did not intend to be caught barefoot. Barefoot! The thought occurred to her that if Henry and Sir Richard and she were all suddenly cast out on the roads with *nothing* she'd be the one to survive. Then she gave attention to the food, which was unlike any she had ever seen, far less tasted. In his new kitchen the cook from Winchester had done his best. The new kitchen had a doorway — newly made — which communicated with this room. Through that doorway came dish after dish, mostly contrived to look like something other than it was. Richard explained that what he called the other end of the house was still served from the original kitchen. 'It seemed easier,' he said. 'Richard and Margaret care so little what they eat, elaborate dishes are wasted on them. Children fare best on plain food — and so does Master Jankyn. A dish made with cream or butter provokes nausea with him.'

Abruptly, Griselda, her mouth full of some creamy concoction, felt sick. The ultimate humiliation. She gripped the velvet padded arms of the wide chair and fought back. All right, she thought; now I know! All being well, I shall have a child of my own by . . . by November . . .

'It was a blow,' Henry was saying. 'Less for myself than for Robert. But that is what Johnson said himself, to me, last time we met in Baildon. He asked me how the lambing had gone and I said, badly. He then said that what with men asking higher wages and ponies costing more to keep, he could no longer afford to collect from such an outlying place, and in such small quantity. You see what that means? Hauling the damned stuff to market and selling to miserable little men who pay almost nothing because most of what they buy is maggot riddled or full of burrs.'

A chance for Richard to do Henry a *real* favour.

'No need to let that worry you, Henry. The solution is simple. Get your clip here. Market it with mine . . . with Moyidan's.'

'A good offer,' Henry said with just a spark of what Richard had always wanted from him. Immediately quenched as Henry added, 'And after all, Robert is your brother too.'

Oh how could one deal with this mentally flat-footed fellow and his dumb-seeming wife?

'It'll mean marking my own fleeces, too,' Henry said. 'Robert's are done in red ochre; mine had better be black. I'll see to it.'

Time they were moving Henry thought; at Knight's Acre, as the mornings lightened, they were early astir.

At Knight's Acre, where Tom had been left in charge of the children, the kitchen fire died down to a red glow and Robert leaned sleepily against Joanna's shoulder.

'Time for bed,' Tom said. He liked to retire early, carefully husbanding reserves of strength which lessened all the time.

'Just one last story, Tom,' Joanna said, shifting to make Robert more comfortable.

Tom had a vast store of stories, most of them handed down from generation to generation, muddled and mangled in the process, but still good; most of them with a touch of eeriness about them, capable of sending a pleasurable shiver down the spine when you were indoors, in company, in firelight and candlelight. What he usually lacked was a receptive audience, for living close as they did, he might start to tell a story and be checked halfway through by Master Henry saying not to fill young heads with old rubbish or Griselda saying that it was bed time for children. Now and again both Joanna and Robert would come up to the sheep-fold where Tom spent much time these days and there he would tell tales which sometimes seemed a little less believable in the open daylight. Even so Robert would sometimes turn pale and put his hands over his ears; 'I don't want to hear it! I don't like it.' Joanna had stronger nerves, nothing upset her, but she was considerate and would often halt Tom at the crux of the story which she herself wished to hear. 'Better stop, Tom, if it's what I *think* it is. Robert wouldn't like it.'

The flow of narrative was often interrupted by questions — 'What is a grandmother, Tom?'

'Well, your father's mother or your mother's mother. We'll say an old woman . . .'

Wolf was to them an abstract term, quite familiar because mentioned in connection with greedy eating, but neither child had ever seen one. 'What's a wolf like, Tom?'

'Well, a bit like Wade's dog, only grey and savager.'

That story was the ultimate in horror for Robert. Suppose, just suppose, that he looked across at the other bed one night and saw, not Joanna but something like Wade's dog — frightening enough as it was. Or suppose the dreadful change should come when he and Joanna were alone gathering sticks in the wood.

Joanna's reaction was entirely different. If she'd been that little girl carrying food to an old woman and found something like Wade's dog in the bed, she'd have hit it with her basket, or the poker, and the more it bared its teeth and snarled, the harder she'd hit it.

'You wouldn't turn into a wolf, would you, Joanna?'

'Of course not. How could I? It's just one of Tom's tales. You're safe enough with me, Robert.'

They were deeply devoted to one another but they used no terms of affection. No endearments, except perhaps Sybilla's, lost to memory, had ever reached their ears.

That summer, as Griselda grew heavier and slower, she kept them busy. They were seven years old — a year older than she had been when in the orphanage she had been told to earn her keep. Imperceptibly as her own child grew within her, her attitude towards Joanna and Robert changed. So did her attitude towards Henry, who in her view had behaved badly on two occasions. Once when she broke the news to him and he said, 'Good. Let's hope it's a boy,' and again when, the wool sold, she asked him to bring flannel and linen from Baildon, so that she could begin making baby clothes. Angered that at this of all times, economy must be considered, Henry said, 'What happened to what they wore? Robert and Joanna. I remember Mother stitching away. The clothes must be somewhere in the house.'

They were. Nothing here had ever been lightly discarded; but there were stains on the linen which no amount of washing and bleaching in the sunshine had ever completely removed — or ever would; and the flannel was hard as board. Not what Griselda wanted for her son — she was sure that it would be a boy . . .

One August morning Jem said, 'I've had enough rabbit to last me a year.' Henry promised him roast fowl tomorrow and told Tom to catch and kill a young cockerel first thing in the morning.

Joanna wished to watch because people often said, 'Running about like a hen with its head off', she wanted to see for herself whether a cockerel — not so much unlike a hen, actually would. It was just another old tale; helped by her Tom cornered the rooster, and with one swift stroke severed its head. It did not then get up and run about the yard. Robert had not watched. And he seemed only slightly consoled by Joanna's assurance that the rooster had died instantly.

Griselda said, 'Pluck it.'
Robert looked at the blood smeared on the bright neck feathers.
'I can't,' he said. 'I couldn't touch it.'
'You will when it's cooked,' Griselda said.
'I think not,' Robert said. Curiously, despite his timidity, his willingness to be led, the boy had something, a kind of dignity and a short way with words.
Joanna plucked the bird, nimbly, quickly, separated the edible from the inedible of its insides, tipped the inedible into

the swill bucket and carried it along to the pigs. About the swill pail, the water, Henry had shown some consideration, saying, 'Don't heave anything, Griselda.' She knew it for what it was — care for the child; not for her. In a primitive kind of way she reasoned; Henry had married her in order to get a good housekeeper and a brood animal. Fair enough by her measure, because she had married him to get Knight's Acre. A fair bargain, but bleak . . .

Joanna said, 'Now we have done our duty. We've emptied the swill pail, gathered eggs and sticks and brought water. Shall we *do it* — what we always said — now?'

What they had always said was that they would look into that mysterious, unused part of the house; something not much different from one of Tom's stories about a girl, ill-wished by bad god-mother, who had pricked her finger with a needle and gone to sleep for a hundred years.

'Tom, what is a hundred?'

'Spread your hands,' Tom said; 'thass ten. Do it ten times and there's your hundred.'

Asked about that disused part of the house Henry had said, 'Just some empty rooms, Joanna,' and Griselda had said almost the same thing. 'Rooms we don't need. We have enough to see to. Go give the hall a good dusting.'

Despite these rebuffs the place enquired about held its fascination. It seemed to have no door, for a vigorous rosemary bush had spread upwards and outwards, and a self-sown honeysuckle had grown downwards. But there were windows; two of them, the drawn curtains within sealed to the glass by cobwebs.

'Is somebody asleep in there?'

'Robert, of course not. How could anybody . . .? That is just another of Tom's old tales. But we always said we would *look* in, didn't we: Just to see? I'll go first.' She took off her shoe and hammered a pane which splintered. She reached in and worked, not without difficulty, the latch which held the casement. She clambered in, pushed aside the sun-rotted silk of the curtains and the cobwebs, and leaning out, stretching her hands to Robert, said, 'Up you come. Isn't it *pretty*?'

Apart from flowers and trees their lives so far had held little of beauty and nothing at all of magnificence. Despite the dust and the cobwebs which had collected in five years the silk of the walls and the ceilings, the divan covers and cushions, still shone bright. So much colour excited the children who ran from room to room, and bounched on the divans. They opened the chest that stood by the bed. Tana's outdoor wear in winter had been of fine woollen cloth and fur which moths had ruined but a soft leather pounch, its neck closely drawn, lay intact among the wreckage. Joanna lifted it out and spilled the contents upon the bed which had been her mother's. More and more exciting colours; red stones, and blue and green, and some like the rainbow, and some, strung together, colourless but with a pleasing sheen.

The children who had once shared a cradle and never been apart for more than five minutes at a stretch throughout their lives, often shared a thought; they shared one now though they spoke differing words.

Joanna said, 'Better than pebbles,' and simultaneously Robert said, 'How Many Birds In A Bush?'

'And Five Stones.' Joanna named the other traditional game of poor children. Tom had taught them, with little stones. 'We must get them loose first.'

The experienced Jew who had bought a necklet from this collection had seen that the setting had not been worked west of Damascus. It was too delicate. Eager little fingers made short work of the filigree settings that had been wrought with such care. Joanna's sharp teeth severed the silk thread that held the pearls together. They divided the stones between them and Joanna said, 'You can start, Robert.' It was a simple game, but it held an element of deceit. You kept your main store hidden. Robert rummaged about in his and then presented what looked like a fist strained to the utmost to cover what it contained, 'How Many Birds In A Bush?' he demanded. 'Eight.' With a grin of delight he spread his hand and revealed a single pearl. She solemnly counted seven from her own hoard and paid her debt. Then it was her turn to ask the question.

The new playthings made the old game even more entrancing than usual and they played on until a change in the light reminded them of the time. 'We must go or there'll be questions. We haven't time even to count, but it looks as though you've won.' They hastily pushed the tangled gold and then the pretty things into the pouch and Joanna carefully closed the bedroom curtains. It was hardly necessary to say, 'We shan't tell anybody.' Robert was just about to say, 'This is our secret place, isn't it?' She helped him through the open window, went out herself, drew the curtains, closed the window and reached through the broken pane to latch it. The empty pane showed, but there was ivy on the wall near by. Two long trails, re-directed would conceal the hole. 'It's our very own place, Robert and we can come here whenever we can get away without anybody seeing us.'

CHAPTER TWENTY-THREE

Henry was less casual than he seemed and just before the Michaelmas Hiring Fair he suggested that he should hire a good strong woman for half a year.

Griselda scoffed. Feed and pay a woman for six months just because you were going to be laid up for a few years. She had seen two child-birthings, one a beggar woman by the road side — she'd been up and walking next day; the other a lady on her way home to her mother for the great event, taken short and obliged to use the inn. It had taken her almost a week to recover sufficiently to make the rest of her journey in a litter, but then she'd been one of the soft kind.

'All I need is a sensible woman to be with me at the time. I shall leave plenty of food. A village like Intake must have a midwife.'

A stinging little sentence formed in her mind. *No new clothes for the baby, but a woman hired for half a year; does that make sense?* The words were not spoken, for although she and Henry did not exchange endearments they were resolutely civil.

Tom Robinson did not hear this conversation, but watching Griselda's growing bulk and knowing what lay in wait for her at the end of road he wished — for the first time — that his old granny were still alive. Many of her brews had been horrible but she had one for easing birth pains. He should have taken more notice.

By mid-October Griselda learned that pregnancy was not simply a matter of growing heavier and slower and at the end displaying fortitude. (The beggar woman had shown fortitude; just a few grunts. What the child Griselda, watching, did not know was that this was the twelfth confinement the woman had faced in as many years. The lady, a soft one, had screamed horribly.)

Griselda's ankles swelled first, then her legs. Too late, she admitted that she had been wrong; a woman was needed. But by this time the hiring season was over; everybody was settled in until Christmas, at least. Jem *said* he would ask around Intake, and did indeed do so. He liked a good dinner and could see that Griselda was past it. But Intake was suffering still under a sense of grievance against Knight's Acre.

Tom, mistrusting Jem, went down himself and was treated like a stranger. One of *Them*.

Henry said he would ask about Baildon and if that failed, try Moyidan. He did ask of everybody with whom he came in contact, even the old woman at whose stall he refreshed himself on market days, always as cheaply as possible. She, like everybody else said, 'I'll bear you in mind. If I hear...' Not unfriendly, not very promising either. Well, he must try Moyidan; Jill and Eddy had come from there — and Young Shep; all, he now realised in a disspirited moment, too lightly cast off.

He heaved a sack of flour into the back of the wagon, and turned to confront whoever it was who had said, 'Master Tallboys...' in an urgent voice.

It was the saddler at whose shop in Cook's Row, Henry had been a rare, a reluctant and most unprofitable customer.

'Could I have a word with you, Master Tallboys? It has come to my ears that you need a bit of help in the house.'

'That is so.'

'Would you try my niece? She's a good girl, well trained. An orphan, my wife's sister's child. We took her, reared her as our own, but now ... Well, they no longer hit it off, Master Tallboys. Two women in one house ... You know ...'

The secret guilt, the memory of that dreadful moment brought a flush, unevenly disposed to the saddler's sallow face.

'How old?

'Oh, well-grown. Over seventeen. And very skilled. There is

nothing in the way of managing a household that Leonora does not know."

Henry knew the shop, obviously prosperous; three apprentices working away in the background; the window full of ready-made leather goods. It struck him as strange that a man with such a business should not be seeking for his niece, not a good marriage, but a job in an outlying place like Knights Acre.

A possible explanation occurred to him — a girl of seventeen, and an apprentice.

'Look,' he said, 'my wife will have a baby in November and is lame. We need help; not trouble.'

'Oh, I assure you, there would be none.' The flushed patches darkened and the pale ones grew paler as the saddler remembered his wife's edict, 'Out of my house . . .' It was her house; the saddler had married above his station and although there was a general rule that a wife's property became that of her husband there were all kinds of tricks, played by careful fathers.

'What wage?'

'Oh, nothing . . .' But that did not sound right, and despite his shattering experience the saddler had not completely lost his head. 'Nothing much. Pin money. Five or six ryals a year.'

'And she could come today?'

'Oh yes.' His wife's fully justified wrath had ended in the ultimatum. By tomorrow!

'Well,' Henry said, still dubious. 'You know where my wagon stands. Bring her along and I'll take a look and decide.' The saddler had just time to think, resentfully — They're all alike; even this one, poor as a church mouse. All tarred with the same brush! Then Henry, with one of those singularly honest looks, said, 'I'd hoped for an older woman. And strong.'

'Leonora is far stronger than she looks,' the saddler said, remembering the clasp of those long, slender arms on the dark, supposedly deserted landing.

The girl's baggage — the neat, leather-covered, bright-nailed chest such as a saddler's niece might be expected to own was in the back of the wagon and the girl herself, well dressed, stood by the horse's head. She had removed the nose bag and unhooked the tether from the railings. It showed sense — but also the assumption that she was hired. Henry felt two conflicting emotions, exasperation and relief. The decision appeared to have been taken for him. The saddler — or whoever had carried the chest for her — had vanished, the market place was emptying, the daylight waning; he could hardly tip out her baggage and leave her standing there. He was further confused by not being able to see much of her; the cloak she wore was bulky, thickly furred, and the hood of it was drawn well forward over her face. What had the man meant by saying that she was stronger than she looked? What did the whole situation mean? And why was he himself not more elated? After all he'd obtained what he had asked for — somebody to help about the house.

'You'd better get in,' he said. 'I'm afraid I don't know your name.'

'Leonora Fitzwilliam.'

The wind was from the east and they drove into it.

'If I'd known I'd have brought a rug.'

'I am well-clad, thank you.' She was; she even had gloves.

At least, he thought, she was a quiet girl. Shy perhaps, though her voice when she replied to his few halting remarks, was clear and assured, and in the one statement that she volunteered — 'I am grateful to you, Master Tallboys, for offering me a place at such short notice,' bitter and mocking. She was consumed with rage, at her aunt, at her uncle, at fate itself. So small a slip to be punished so savagely and the stupid man whining — 'She says that if you're not out of the house by tonight, she'll have me out, too. And then where would the business be? Honey, it's only for a short spell. I'll make other arrangements as soon as I can . . .'

In the kitchen, when she had shed her cloak, Henry understood the remark about being stronger than she looked. She looked anything but strong or workmanlike; very slender, an exceptionally long neck, elegant hands. There was something doe-like about her, in shape and in colouring. Her hair — worn short, just a cap of curls, and her eyes — very large and lustrous, were both chestnut in colour, but muted. Her nose, short but straight and wide nostrilled and a mouth rather too big for her face, added to the doe-like look. She wore a close-fitting dress of cloth so fine that it had the sheen of silk, with some darker velvet about it, and a string of amber beads. She was about the last kind of female creature to be a welcome sight to a woman in the final few weeks of pregnancy — and with swollen legs.

'It remains to be seen,' Griselda said, withholding judgment, 'whether she can cook.'

She could, when she liked. Extravagant of course. Cream, butter, eggs, all the things of which Griselda had been sparing. In the comfortable rooms behind and over the saddler's shop nothing had been stinted; the saddler lived far better than many of his customers, and Leonora's aunt had always, until that shocking evening, visualised her niece taking charge of a solid, prosperous household. She herself had married beneath her, just as her sister, Leonora's mother, had married above; but things levelled out and until that truly shocking evening, the saddler's wife had thought that for Leonora, Master Turnbull's son at least . . .

Exiled to Knight's Acre, anger died down — all her moods were shortlived — Leonora was conscious of one advantage. Freedom. A thing she had never enjoyed before. Even when — as had happened lately — she had been entrusted to do the marketing, the little kitchen maid, or one of the apprentice boys had followed, to carry the basket of purchases. Here she was free, and, the cold wind veered and the weather mild, had all the woods to roam in, with just the children for company. One day, in a sheltered clearing they found mushrooms.

Tom said, 'Here let's take a look at them. We don't want to go poisoning ourselves, do we?' He examined each one and was satisfied. 'They're late, but they're wholesome,' he said. And fried with bacon, very tasty. Leonora and the children gathered hazelnuts, too and a few late ripening blackberries. Of them Tom took a sterner view.

'No good after Michaelmas! Michaelmas Day the Devil fly over and after that they're *his*.'

Leonara said, 'Superstitious nonsense, Tom.'

'Well you wouldn't catch me eating one. Not after Michaelmas.'

Robert, who had eaten several during the gathering, and who greatly feared the Devil, blanched.

Joanna said, in all haste, 'It doesn't matter, Tom, does it, until you're *twelve*.' She fixed him with her cold, ice-blue stare; a *compelling* look. Torn between the beliefs in which he had been reared and his desire not to upset anybody, Tom said, 'Well, so they say.' He sounded dubious and Griselda by the fire took charge, 'Throw them to the fowls.'

'Next day Richard made a visit; just in time for dinner. He brought two men with him, but they rode straight into the wood.

'It is this business about boundaries,' Richard explained. 'So vague as to be misunderstood. There was always some mark, a bank, a line of trees plainly planted, or some stones. They know what to look for.'

Leonora, busy at the hearth, wearing an apron of sacking, hitched high to protect her good dress — one of several — from the spitting and spluttering of the leg of mutton, spiked with rosemary, did not turn her head, but directed her voice over her shoulder. She said, 'I think the Three Pools mark a boundary. They were dug, probably for defence, long ago. They are not natural, the banks are too sharp cut and precipitate.'

Richard's attention was arrested by the clarity and assurance of her voice and by the knowledgeability of the statement, and when, having dished up and divested herself of her apron she took her place at table, he eyed her covertly. Better than beautiful; extraordinarily attractive.

After the mutton there was blackberry pudding.

'I thought,' Griselda said with cold anger, 'that I told you to throw those things to the fowls.'

'It seemed such waste,' Leonora said. 'And now we are all to be saved. Sir, you are a priest and have power to exorcise. Please be so kind as to dismiss the Devil from this inoffensive dish.'

Richard laughed. 'The rite of exorcism requires the permission of the Bishop. By the time that was obtained the dish would be cold. I will show my faith in its inoffensiveness by eating it.'

Nothing actually flirtatious in this exchange of words, and yet there was something — intangible as a scent.

Griselda's temper smouldered. The girl simply didn't know her place! The moment Griselda was on her feet again, Henry could return her to Baildon.

'The children can amuse themselves this afternoon. This table needs a thorough scrubbing.'

This order, inspired by spite, pleased Robert and Joanna because it allowed them to visit the secret place. They quite liked Leonora who in a good mood was companionable. She'd shown them the test for real amber — rubbed between the palms until it was warm it could attract a feather from a hand-span's distance. She had a fund of stories, different from Tom's but quite entertaining; she could sing and play the lute. (She had brought the instrument with her, a fact that roused resentment in Griselda, just as the fine clothes, the elegant manners and the ability to make sprightly conversation did.) Leonora in a bad mood was a different creature, silent and sullen, inclined to say, 'Be quiet,' or 'Behave yourselves.'

Leonora had never scrubbed anything; the kitchen behind the shop housed two stout maids and she had only entered it in order to learn to cook, an art her aunt believed should be learned by every girl, and one she herself practised with pleasure.

Griselda sat by the fire, her feet on a stool and watched the unhandy process with malice. 'Don't scrub across. Go with the grain of the wood,' she said. 'Put some weight behind it!'

This on what might well be one of the last sunny afternoons of the season. I'll show her, Leonora thought, expending fury on the table, leaning heavily on her left hand all the while.

By supper time her left wrist was extremely swollen. Henry noticed, asked what was wrong. 'Let me see,' he said. His long brown fingers probed the joint. 'Nothing broken. Just a sprain,' he said. 'Tom, fetch the liniment.'

It was still made to Walter's recipe and was powerful stuff which brought tears to the eyes of the one who applied it, and unless used with great care, took the skin off, being intended primarily for horses who had tough hides. Henry dabbed it on lightly and Tom said, 'A bit of a bandage wouldn't hurt.'

What Griselda felt was not the flare of sexual jealousy which was one aspect of love; she loved neither man. It was the colder feeling of envy for the solicitude being shown.

Henry said, 'Go easy with it for a while. Maybe Tom could scrub the table next time. We're not all that busy just now.' He thought, in a purely selfish and practical way, what a good thing I didn't marry a bird-boned woman!

Early in November there were some foggy days, then a spell of bright, sharp weather. On a Wednesday morning Henry set out for market with three squealing young pigs under a net in the wagon's body. This would be the last time he attended the market before Christmas, the season for which the pigs had been fattened. He had a good many things to buy and his horse needed new shoes. He was not particularly pleased to see the saddler, eager and at the same time, shame-faced. He dealt with the questions briskly. Yes, Leonora had settled down well, and was good with the children. Happy? Well, yes, she seemed happy enough. Henry felt slightly ashamed of himself because he had never taken the girl's happiness into much consideration; nor — fearing to worsen matters — had he intervened when Griselda was unpleasant. 'Anyway,' he said, 'she'll have a bit of excitement today. There's a hunt in the woods near my place and she's taken the children to watch. From a safe distance, of course.'

'She'll like that. She always was one for a bit of a show. I got a little gift for her. For Christmas. With my best wishes, if you'll be so good, Master Tallboys. And tell her . . . tell her everything's quietened down nicely here.'

Tom came into Griselda's bedroom, carefully carring a tray which held some dainty slices of chicken breast and a piece of fresh bread.

'Where's that girl? I've been calling and calling . . .'

'I thought I heard . . . She's gone to watch the hunt.'

'What!' The absolute dismay in Griselda's voice, the look of horror on her face halted Tom as he advanced towards the bed.

'Is it . . .?' He knew that it was and for one terrible moment feared that he was going to have one of his falling spells. But his desire to be a source of strength and comfort to her rallied him.

'How far?'

A pang wrenched her, she set her teeth and waited. When she could speak she said, 'Nearly here.'

'Then that look as though you'll have to make do with me. However fast Jem went running . . . Horns and hounds sounded well beyond the Three Pools . . . Now don't you worry. I know just what to do. I helped my old granny a time or two. You're safe with me.'

Griselda realised that she was better off than she would have been as she had planned to be — in charge herself and giving directions to an ignorant girl. Tom did know — and there were times when, for all her fortitude, she was incapable of issuing an order. And Tom was very comforting and calm. 'Just bear down, my dearie. Don't fight it. Bear down, and yell if you want to.'

This was nothing like the birth she had watched by the roadside, and presently Griselda knew that the lady at the inn hadn't screamed just because she was soft. She was yelling herself and pulling on Tom's horny hands. The afternoon was darkening when Tom said, 'I'll try a good tug . . .' Awkward little bugger, coming into the world feet first! There was pain unbelievable, a moment of blackness and then Tom saying, 'You've got a boy, my dearie. It's over. Take your rest.'

'Is he . . . all right?'

'Couldn't be better.'

What she needed now was wine. His old granny had always said wine was a great heartener. A statement not without self interest, since midwives needed heartening, too. No wine at Knight's Acre, unless . . . Tom was visited by sheer inspiration. That kitchen across the yard . . . Lady Serriff was always well supplied, and nobody had set foot in the place since the coffin was carried out. Worth a look, Tom thought, setting out with a jug. He found a cask full of the sweet red wine which age improved and ripened.

As he fed her the new bread sopped in wine, Griselda said, 'Thank you, Tom. Thank you for everything. You're too good to me.' For a moment the memory of those unvisited bluebells hovered — for Tom tinged with a gentle wistfulness, for Griselda with a new, bitter self-knowledge. Assuming that she could never be fond of any man in *that* way, she'd taken the man with most to offer. And now that she knew how different, how lovable Tom was, it was too late.

Even so the baby's coming might have been a turning point in the marriage. Henry was astonished at the emotions which filled him when he looked upon his son for the first time. Some of the warmth and tenderness might have spilled over on to the

174

woman who had borne the child, but Griselda gave it no chance; even when every allowance was made for the ordeal she had been through, for the natural touchiness of the newly delivered, there was now something so cantankerous, so sharp and hard about her behaviour that it made fondness unthinkable.

It centred first upon Leonora.

'I won't have her near me. She deliberately went off and left me to die. But for Tom I should have died, and the baby with me.'

'She didn't know,' Henry said, making the mistake of trying to reason with an unreasonable woman. '*I* didn't know or I should not have gone to Baildon . . .'

'We none of us *knew*! But I told her several days ago to stay within call if she *must* go out. If that isn't downright disobedience, I don't know what is. Did she ask leave to go?'

'Not exactly. I only knew that she'd promised to take the children to watch the next hunt and I met the first brace of hounds at the end of the lane, so I reckoned . . .'

'You know how you left me, bedridden for the last week. You knew what she'd promised the children. Couldn't you have turned back and warned her not to go galloping off?'

'I suppose I could, but it didn't occur to me.' He had been at fault there, but he'd been thinking of the pigs for sale, the stuff to buy and getting the horse shod, all in one short winter's day.

'I shall be about by Friday,' Griselda said. The swelling in her feet and legs had lessened within an hour of the baby's birth. 'And on Saturday you can take her back to wherever she came from.'

'That I can't do.'

'Why not?'

'Well, for one thing I can't go to market twice in a week. For another I'd more or less agreed to keep her till after Christmas, at the very least.' He had tacitly promised that by accepting the gift. 'And in any case, you mustn't hurry things. You have a good rest.'

'I shouldn't know how to,' Griselda said tartly.

It made you glad to get out of the room.

It was on to Tom that the spare ripple of Henry's emotion spilled over. He actually had tears in his eyes as he wrung Tom's hand and thanked him.

175

'It was nothing, Master. You saved my life for me. I only thank God I was here and knew what I was about.' And didn't have a weak spell.

'She's talking about getting up on Friday. Should she?'

'No. My old granny always said that where it could be managed — a week in bed.'

'You tell her that, Tom. She might take it from you.'

About the child's name there was no argument; Griselda had no male relatives to be remembered and flattered. The little boy would be Godfrey Tallboys. (And Sir, too, if I have anything to do with it, Henry thought, for once abandoning Walter's standards and those he had considered to be his own.) Over the question of god-parents there was conflict. Sir Richard was an obvious choice, a blood relative, competent in worldly affairs, and celibate. No children of his own to care for.

'And Tom,' Griselda said.

'Tom Robinson!'

'Who has more right? But for Tom there wouldn't be a baby to *be* baptised.'

'I know. But it would look odd. After all, he is only a hired man.'

'I wasn't even hired, and I am the child's mother.' By some curious quirk Griselda had become glib.

'There's a difference,' Henry said. He knew the answer — a wife took her husband's status and by marrying her he had made her a knight's daughter-in-law. But in no circumstances would he have said it — his mother had taught him the elements of courtesy. 'It is the question of looking to the future,' he said, rather lamely. 'God parents should be chosen for the child's benefit. Tom could never . . . advance him in any way.'

The new glib tongue said, 'And who were yours? And how did *they* advance *you*?'

A sharp question. Henry knew that one of his god-fathers had been his Uncle William, Bishop of Bywater who, if he had shown the slightest sign of wishing to be a scholar would have done his best for him. Of his other god-father and his god-mother he could remember nothing.

'Nothing,' he said, 'and that is why I wish him to be better served.'

'So we'll have Tom,' Griselda said. And a woman feeding a

baby must not be crossed. There was always a risk that the milk might turn sour and the baby have colic.

The relatively minor question — for a boy — the choice of god-mother, was easy. Father Benedict, who at Intake would be the 'new priest' just as the man who had taken the Good Bishop's place would be the 'new Bishop' until a whole generation of people with long memories had gone to their graves, had an aunt who kept his house and kept it well.

She was a widow; Mistress Captoft, and although rather young and sprightly to be aunt to a man so little her junior, her status and authority had never been questioned. Nobody now could count, as people had done in old days, on instant attention, in the worst of weather; in the middle of the night. Mistress Captoft answered the knock on the door and almost always said that Father Benedict was at his prayers, or at his studies and could not be disturbed. Sometimes she would ask what ailed the person who needed the priest in such haste and quite often she would say, 'Wait here,' and close the door, presently to open it again and offer a draught; 'Try this.' Her medicaments were frequently effective, but usually so horrible that people thought twice before sending for the priest.

Her manner towards Henry was different; he might work like a hired hand and live little better than a peasant, but he was well-connected, his great-grandmother had built the church, his father had repaired and embellished it. She greeted him with respect, congratulated him upon the birth of a son, and upon learning that Sir Richard of Moyidan was to be one god-father, Tom Robinson the other, enquired tentatively as to the god-mother.

Over that question Henry had realised, for the first time, how thoroughly he had cut himself off from his own kind; he simply didn't know a suitable woman — except Leonora, and to suggest her was useless, dangerous, too, likely to throw Griselda into a fit. What he intended to do was ask Richard who knew many people. He told Mistress Captoft so, and she said brightly, 'If there is the *slightest* difficulty, you can always count upon me, Master Tallboys.' He accepted the offer willingly. She would be on the spot, able to do what god-mothers were supposed to do.

Even that didn't suit Griselda. 'She might have waited to be *asked*.' She had nothing personal against Mistress Captoft, except that she was grand and threatened to usurp the place which had been the lady's and was now by rights, Griselda's. Mistress Captoft appeared to have money; she was always finely clad, had practically re-built the priest's house and made a garden to the side of it, so that Knight's Acre was not now the only source of flowers for the altar.

'Whom would you suggest instead?' Henry asked. It was the first really ill-natured thing he had ever said to her.

On the day before the christening, Richard sent gifts. A quarter of fresh beef, well hung, ready for the spit, the kind of meat which only the very rich ate in winter, a cask of wine, and a good supply of his cook's specialities, all coloured and twisted into fantastic shapes. Watching the gifts being unloaded, Henry thought — very generous! But he wished he had known earlier, before he had killed a young pig or spent money on wine which he could ill-afford. Then, out of the wagon came the family cradle — not quite so splendid as it had been when Lady Emma made it ready for her grandson, but far more impressive than it had been when it was last loaned to Knight's Acre. More than generous, it showed a sensitive thoughtfulness. And seeing his son, laid in the ancestral cradle with the family badge above his head, Henry felt again a resurgence of sentiments which he thought he had done with.

The day of the christening dawned bright and clear. Sir Richard arrived early, accompanied by little Richard who was told to go and play with the other children. 'But not anything that will make you dirty,' Griselda reminded them. They approached each other with the cautious inquisitiveness of strange dogs, but were soon playing noisily in the garden.

Henry thanked Richard for all the gifts, but particularly the loan of the cradle.

'It was not in use. The idiots couple enough, God knows, but I am inclined to think that they fired their bolt with little Richard.'

Griselda said that it would be a great convenience to have two cradles, one upstairs and one down. 'But after today this one must go upstairs, the plain one is more suitable for the kitchen.

A sensible, thrifty statement but Richard raised his eyebrows.

'The kitchen? I had imagined a nursery, Madam, with Leonora in charge.'

'That girl! She goes immediately after Christmas. She would not be in my house now but for Henry being so tenderhearted! Even if she stayed, she is the last person in the world to be left in charge of a child — or any other thing.' Griselda bustled into the kitchen where Leonora had been left in charge of the roast.

'What happened there? I thought the girl suitable and settled.'

'They never got on really well. And then there was an unfortunate incident.' He related, briefly, the circumstances of Godfrey's birth. It helped to explain the choice of a labourer as sponsor. 'Sheer mischance. The girl couldn't foresee ... And she is not utterly useless. She can cook; she's good with the children. And she sets a pretty table.'

The long table in the hall had been polished to a glitter and along its centre, like a spine, ran a bank of green stuff and berries; holly, spindleberry, candleberry and ivy. At intervals candles, their makeshft holders hidden, raised their heads and the pretty trifles from Moyidan were so arranged that when the candles were lighted their shapes and colours would show to advantage.

'And even that didn't suit. Griselda holds that to bring holly indoors before Christmas Eve is to invite bad luck. It was too late to dismantle it.'

Richard changed the subject. 'I have been thinking about Robert. He's my brother, too. I feel I should do something ... He won't have much money. A little learning is often a good substitute. How would you feel about sending him to Moyidan to share Dick's lessons?' (Little Richard had recently decided that he was now too big for the diminutive.)

'I'd welcome the idea. I have wondered, from time to time what best to do for him.'

On this amicable note the christening day began and it continued well. The baby screamed as the touch of holy water drove out the Devil. Leonora had done nothing to ruin the beef and everyone ate heartily. Mistress Captoft made the slight, but understandable error of congratulating Griselda upon the decoration of the table and was answered rather curtly. Father Benedict addressed a remark in Latin to Sir Richard and was answered in the same tongue — a satifactory display of learning, proof that the new priest was not one of those who knew only the Latin of the rubric. Tom Robinson produced his godfatherly contribution to the feast, wine so excellent that even Sir Richard remarked on it and asked where it had been obtained.

'I got it where Samson got his foxes, sir.' In rustic talk — I'm not telling you!

To Henry it did not seem remarkable that Tom should produce such good wine. His wage was small, but he had no expenses, apart from his clothes. He did not frequent fairs, or buy from pedlars, gifts for girls.

The candles, lighted not from necessity for the day remained bright, but to give an air of festivity, shed their kind light; on Griselda's dove-grey dress, now retucked and re-seamed so that the darker stripes did not show; on Leonora's glossy hair and string of amber beads — a gift that had been the start of the trouble. The slight bump, darkening to a bruise on Robert's forehead and the even bigger and darker one on Dick's cheek, were not noticeable.

'It gets dark early,' Richard said. 'Before I go, Henry, I'd like a word with you.'

Father Benedict and his aunt were sensitive to the note of dismissal. Griselda lifted the baby and went away to feed him. Tom Robinson said he would bring the horses round. Leonora said, 'I have duties, too . . .'

'Could Griselda be persuaded to change her mind, Henry? About the girl?'

'I doubt it. It took me all my time to persuade her to stay her hand, until after the christening — for the use she could be today and over Christmas, when nobody should be homeless.'

Why? What does it matter to you?

'She took my eye. But I do not wish for scandal. Here she would be under a respectable roof and my visits, however frequent would raise no comment.'

(No shame must come upon this *respectable* house! After all these years of forgetfulness, deliberate and stubborn forgetfulness, Tana's mocking voice echoed.)

Henry was not shocked. Men did, he knew, find vows of celibacy hard to keep. At the same time, in the core of his mind, he thought that any kind of vow should be observed, any promise kept, any debt paid.

'It wouldn't do,' he said slowly. 'Griselda is determined to be rid of her.'

'But you are master here, Henry. Do I scent disapproval? Look at it from my point of view for a moment. They catch us young. You could always count upon Knight's Acre . . . I had nothing; and there are hundreds like me. Nothing to hope for outside the Church. If it demanded an arm or a leg we'd have given it. How much easier to foreswear the love of women? Something we did not know — as we knew our arms and legs. Also, there is more to it. Clerical celibacy is comparatively a recent thing. Our Lord made no such rule. Nor did St. Paul. In times not *so* remote the definition of a Bishop was a man with only one wife . . .'

'It isn't that,' Henry said. 'I'm no judge. Griselda wants the girl out of the house.'

'I can't have her at Moyidan. Nobody would believe she was my aunt! What about the part of the house that is empty? Would you allow me to set her . . .?'

Henry said, 'No!' very loudly. Such instant refusal seemed to call for explanation. 'Even there, Griselda would know. And disapprove. She *is* pious.'

'No more to be said then.' Richard was angered, but he had learned to control his temper. He went quickly to the door where Tom, Leonora and the children and the horse and pony waited.

Dick had refused Joanna's request to have just a short ride. Round from the stable to the front of the house.

'No. I hate you. You hit me.'

'You hit Robert first.'

As he passed Leonora, Richard said something to her and she smiled.

Joanna knew some impolite words which Jem used freely but which were forbidden to her. They were all meaningless and she chose one at random. Going close to Dick she said loudly, 'Bastard!'

Dick recognised it as a term of abuse, freely applied to

animate and inanimate things; even the weather could be a bastard. Nobody had ever called him that before and his interest was roused.

'What *is* a bastard, Uncle Richard?'

'A child born out of wedlock.'

'Why should she say that to me?'

'Hold your tongue. I have thinking to do.'

Quick-thinking too. So little time. He was going to keep Christmas in great style; every bed in the house occupied and day guests coming for dinner; it all took some arranging. He had counted upon Henry's co-operation. Now he must act; because that trap-mouthed woman would do what she said — have Leonora out of the house after Christmas.

Henry also had thinking to do. He had offended Richard who would very likely now withdraw his offer to have Robert schooled. Poor boy, I've ruined your future. And why? For a bit of sentiment that had sneaked in and caught him unprepared. Tana was dead; the whole thing forgotten. Let the rosemary and the other growing stuff obscure the door which had for one evening been the gateway to Heaven; let the roof fall in upon that divan . . . Decay might come, but the place should not be *desecrated*.

It had all been sealed away. Even the memory of Jamil, rampaging about and utterly unapproachable, so that Henry had been obliged to send for Tom Thoroughgood, who came and did clever things with bits of rope, with little leaden weights at their ends and cast enough of them to catch the horse, as in a net.

Five years ago. Why rake the ashes now? Just the casual mention of those empty rooms.

CHAPTER TWENTY-FOUR

There appeared to be no house to rent in Baildon, and only one for sale. It was far too large, but had the advantage of being private, standing at the farthest end of the street called Saltgate, behind a high flint wall. It had its own stables and orchard. Richard knew better than to appear eager, but his impatience showed and the owner, who had recently inherited it and did not wish to live in it, seized the opportunity to make a sharp bargain. He named a sum fully twice the worth of the house and when Richard agreed to it without visibly flinching, proceeded to raise it by a simple strategem. 'That's for the house, sir. The yard and the orchard come separately.'

'I shall not require *them*.'

'But they go with the house. Can't split 'em, sir.'

Richard knew that he was being fleeced, but he had no time. He still had furniture to find — and a decent, middle-aged woman to act as Leonora's companion and give the establishment an air of respectability.

The house was furnished, and its owner, exploring this gold-mine a little further, asked, 'What about furniture, sir?' Richard said he could use some of it, and the man said, 'I'm afraid it's all or nothing, sir.'

The only one of his cronies to whom Richard had confided his plans was Sir Francis Lassiter who fully approved and said he knew just the woman for the post; a widow, a remote relative of his own, very respectable, the soul of discretion. As for the place being far too large, the old roué said, 'All the better. Since I inherited this place I have given marriage my serious consideration — I shall need an heir, after all. But I tire easily and might well be glad to keep another little lamb in another little pen.'

On the third day of Christmas the letter which Sir Richard had promised, arrived for Leonora. She read it with brightness flooding her face. Some of its contents she relayed. Tomorrow Sir Richard was sending the wagon to fetch her and Robert . . .

Henry, assuming that he had irretrievably offended Richard had said nothing of Robert's going to Moyidan. Griselda snatched upon a chance to scold. 'You should have told me. How can I have the boy's clothes ready by tomorrow?'

'I couldn't tell you what I didn't know myself.'

'My new post sounds pleasant,' Leonora said. 'I am to live with an elderly lady, bear her company and see that her servants do not cheat her.'

'Poor soul,' Griselda said. 'She should pray that *she* is never bed-ridden!'

Nobody noticed then, that the two young faces, so curiously alike, had turned sickly green.

Born on the same day they had never known an hour's separation. They'd shared a bed until Griselda married Henry and went to another room. Even after that, when they had a bed each, whenever the night was very cold, or the wind howled dolefully, or thunder rolled. Robert had gone across the room and found shelter and comfort with Joanna. They had worked together — Joanna always taking the heavier work; they had shared their food, each offering the other the preferred little tit-bit. They were one.

Robert — once away from the others, cried. Joanna could have cried, too; the lump in her throat ordered tears, and then, somewhere in her head, rage dried them before they could be shed. She took the positive action of appealing to Henry.

'Why must Robert go? What good will it do? That boy Dick is horrible. He hit Robert, for no reason, that day he was here and would have hit him again, but for me.'

Henry tried to explain; it was for Robert's own good. It was a chance in a thousand. At Moyidan there was a tutor who would see that Dick did not hit Robert, too often or too hard. Here again Henry fell back on tradition — *A boy must learn to stand up for himself.* He had avoided the hurly-burly of the pages' table and sleeping quarters at Beauclaire, but he had contended against other, more demanding things, working with Walter through wind and weather, striving to learn, to match, to excel.

'Dick will be cruel to him. I know he will.'

'Robert is almost a year older than Dick. He'll learn to stick up for himself — all the sooner when you're not there to do it for him.'

'Robert isn't so thick as that boy. Or so rough. Please Henry, *please* don't make him go.'

'That'll do, Joanna.' Henry was out of patience. Griselda was completely without sympathy and at suppertime even kind Tom Robinson said, 'Come on now, eat up. You couldn't look to spend the rest of your lives together, could you?'

In bed together — for the last time; terrible thought! — Robert cried again and Joanna said, 'I shall think about you, every minute.'

'I don't want to go. I want to stay here with you.'

'I shall miss you. I shall be worst off, Robert. You'll have Uncle Richard and this tutor man and Dick . . .'

'I hate him. He hit me.'

'He won't if you hit him back a few times. He'll see that you can stick up for yourself.' She tried to sound confident, though she knew that Robert, so amiable and gentle, would never learn that lesson. Her own helplessness racked her. 'One thing, Robert. Don't cry whatever he does. He'd *like* to make you cry.'

Morning came, inevitable as death, and the wagon came, and with it, on his pony, Dick.

The christening feast had given him a false idea of food at Knight's Acre and he hoped to be asked to stay for dinner. The guests had gone from Moyidan, Uncle Richard with them: dinner there would be left-overs. Master Jankyn was in bed with a head-ache, so Dick was free. And although Joanna had hit him and called him an ugly name, he was fascinated by her. Riding, now before, now beside and now behind the wagon he'd wondered whether to arrange things so that he had a chance to hit her, as she had hit him; or whether to offer her a ride on his pony.

In the dinner he was disappointed. From Joanna he got more than he had bargained for. At the sight of him her feeling of helplessness vanished to be replaced with such an upsurge of power that she was for a moment dizzied. All the stories that Tom had ever told melted into one . . .

'I want to tell you something,' she said, before he could even offer the pony for a short ride. The man who drove the wagon was bringing down Leonora's clothes chest. Robert was fetching his own smaller bundle, and Dick and Joanna were alone in the yard. 'You may *think*,' she said, 'That you can be unkind to Robert. *But you are mistaken*. I shall be watching. All the time and I shall know.'

'How?'

'I shall drink a brew that makes me invisible. And if you are unkind to him, even *once*, I shall turn myself into a wolf and come in the night and tear you to bits.'

Dick had seen only one wolf in his life and that a dead one; caught in a trap, it had died snarling and the cold had fixed the grimace. All suddenly, as she said the last words, this pretty girl looked like that wolf. Shocking to a boy in whose veins ran the blood of the carter who believed that he had spent an afternoon with one of the Little People, a boy who had also listened to fireside tales.

'I swear,' he said. 'I won't lay a finger on him. I swear.'

'I think it will be all right,' Joanna whispered as she parted with half of herself. 'Remember me.'

'Till I die,' Robert said.

She knew that her threat, though it had had an instant and desirable effect, was only a hollow boast. She could not make herself invisible, or turn herself into a wolf. The only true thing was — *I shall know*. She knew with deadly certainty that Robert was bitterly unhappy. As she was herself; everything they had ever done together, like gathering sticks, or eggs, or drawing water was now misery; her misery and five miles away, his, communicating itself with her. Sometimes when the misery struck she would stand still, stiffened, her head at a listening angle and her gaze blank. 'Stop looking like a moon-calf,' Griselda snapped. Do this, do that, run and fetch . . .

'Tom, tell me that story about the wolf again. The one about the old woman the man shot when she was a wolf and she was lame in the morning.'

Tom obligingly repeated this tale — no Robert now to say he didn't like it.'

'*How* did she do it?'

'Magic brews.'

'What were they made of?'

'I don't know. The only brews I ever see were my old granny's.'

'What did *she* use?'

'Herbs and such.'

Tom remembered how the worst of his suffering during the plague had been concerned with the thought of his granny's hideous brews. He'd shrunk away from the lady's harmless ones.

'I never took much heed. Just bits of green and such.'

There was a suitable receptacle to hand — the silver christening cup which Uncle Richard had given Godfrey. It stood alone on the cupboard in the hall, was never used, would not be missed. There was an abundance of green stuff available too, for Leonora's table decoration had been thrown into the yard.

The first dose tasted just like water and had no effect. Perhaps like cream which must be allowed to ripen before it could be made into butter, a brew needed time. It grew nastier, but she sipped it determinedly. Then Griselda missed the cup.

'I only borrowed it,' Joanna said when questioned.

'Where is it now?'

'Under my bed.'

'Fetch it, at once.'

It hadn't worked yet; maybe it was only pretend, but it had been a slight comfort; at least it proved that she was *trying*.

'How dare you?' Griselda demanded. 'How dare you take Godfrey's cup and make such a filthy mess in it?'

It *was* a filthy mess; the clear water had grown murky as the bits of greenstuff and the berries rotted; on the surface bloated berries red, white, pink and black floated, amidst a few bubbles. The last few doses had been very nasty indeed.

None the less, had Griselda said, 'Empty it,' Joanna would have tried to preserve it; but she did not. She took the precious brew and threw it into the yard.

'Now wash it well, inside and out. Then pound up some ashes and polish it. And never, never, touch it again until I tell you to.'

It was now early February and the days, though cold, brought that little lengthening of daylight; preparations for supper could be made without a candle.

'Chop that onion,' Griselda said, and bustled into the larder to fetch the flour, the pig lard and the dried herbs which went to the making of a savoury dumpling. When she returned the onion lay there, unchopped and Joanna was nowhere to be seen. Angrily, Griselda chopped it herself, made the dumpling, lighted a candle and thought that while it cooked she could feed the baby.

The cradle was empty.

She did not immediately fall into panic. Perhaps Godfrey had wakened and cried and Joanna had taken him up to give him a soothing walk up and down the hall.

Not there. Nowhere in the house.

Stoic fortitude, bred by hard circumstance, gave way completely: Griselda ran into the yard screaming. Henry and Tom came running and found her in such a state that time was wasted in the attempt to get an even moderately coherent statement out of her. When they understood, they acted.

'I'll try the wood,' Tom said. 'I know all the paths.'

Henry said, 'She may have gone to Moyidan.'

Running and calling, Henry rounded the church and reached the lane. Darker here, and in the dark a darker shadow. Father Benedict on his good grey mule. (The new priest — or his aunt — had money of their own.)

'Our little girl,' Henry gasped, before Father Benedict could ask what was amiss. Haste and anxiety had not competely overset him. He was the son of a man, the descendant of many men, trained and tempered to a cool head in crisis. 'She has gone astray.'

'Not in this direction, Master Tallboys. All the way from Moyidan where I have been visiting my uncle, I have seen nothing on the road.'

'You are sure?'

'Not so much as a rabbit. What about the village? Children tend . . . Some family, with children may have asked her to stay for supper. If you wish, I will enquire. I will knock on every door.'

The mule, prodded by a kick from its owner's heel, trotted off towards the village. Henry ran back to Knight's Acre, and being on foot, took the shortest way in, through the main door, across the hall. As he opened the door between hall and kitchen, Joanna opened the other, between kitchen and yard and walked in, jaunty as the Devil.

Griselda cried, 'Where is my baby?'

'Safe and warm,' Joanna said. 'But you'll never find him. He'll stay where he is *until Robert is brought home.*'

Infuriated, Henry snatched a stick from the hearth and held it aloft, threatening. 'Where is he? Tell me at once, or I'll beat you.'

'Kill me,' Joanna said. 'And you'll never know.'

Henry had never beaten anybody or anything. Men did beat their wives, their children, their dogs, their working animals, but he had not, and in the midst of all this confusion, stick in hand, he felt ridiculous. What was there here to hit? Compared with Robert, Joanna had always seemed big, sturdy, now she was slight, nothing much but some bird-bones and a pair of ice-blue eyes with defiant fire behind them.

But now he was near enough to *smell*. That fox lair odour which years ago, had clung to his clothes and his hair.

'I know where he is,' Henry said. He was gone before Griselda could ask, 'Where?'

'You are the most wicked . . .' Words of abuse poured from Griselda, but they were not enough. She was beside herself. She snatched up the stick. She knew what a beating was and she applied that knowledge. But she was inflicting pain and hurt on the daughter of a man who under the *khurbash* had prayed God not to let him scream, and of a woman whose forebears, for uncounted generations had regarded resistance to pain as a point of honour. Just as Tana, in the marble quarry had tried to wrench away the overseer's stinging cane, her daughter tried to wrench away the stick, almost succeeded, failed, kicked, dodged behind the table, threw things. And with every act of resistance, every glare from those defiant eyes, Griselda's fury grew.

Only Tom Robinson's arrival saved Joanna.

He ran forward, seized the stick and gasped, 'You could've killed her. Then what'd happen to you, my dearie?'

The kitchen was a shambles. At least two of Griselda's blows had split Joanna's scalp, and head wounds bled freely.

'Master knew where to look,' Tom said. 'Somewhere I'd missed. He sent me back . . . Joanna, dowse your head in the bucket. You and me,' he said, turning to Griselda, 'got a bit of clearing up to do . . .'

The bucket of cold well water stood behind the door. Dizzily Joanna made towards it and knelt, hanging her head forward.

Denied the outlet of violence, Griselda's emotion turned to tears.

'There, there,' Tom said. He put one arm around her and with his hand patted her shoulder. 'He'll be all right. He's well-wrapped . . .'

'Suppose he isn't where Henry . . . Oh, my poor baby! That wicked . . .'

She began to repeat the words of abuse she had flung at Joanna.

'Now, now,' Tom said, 'You mustn't carry on like that. He'll be all right, my dearie . . .'

Henry flung the door open so hastily that Joanna keeled over and the bucket rocked. Cold air and the smell of foxes came into the kitchen.

'Here he is, safe and sound.' Griselda flung herself on the baby, snugly wrapped in his two blankets and sleeping soundly.

'Oh, thank God. Thank God.'

'A mite overcome,' Tom said in an attempt to explain a position which Henry, entering the lighted kitchen had not even observed.

'No wonder!' Henry had had presence of mind not to blurt out the whole truth to Father Benedict, but now that the crisis was over he could admit that it had shaken him. He'd have something to say to Joanna! He turned to close the door, and here she lay, on the floor. Dead? No, breathing, and still bleeding.

'Hold the candle, Tom.'

Among all that hair, water drenched, blood soaked, the wounds were hard to find. One was superficial, one deep.

'I'll make a plaster,' Tom said.

A thick paste of flour and water and salt, spread on a bit of flannel checked the bleeding, but Joanna did not regain consciousness.

'Burnt feathers,' Tom said. There were plenty in the yard where the chickens clucked and pecked all day. But even the stench of burning feathers failed. Joanna remained limp, deathly pale, infinitely pathetic. Not unlike . . . Hurriedly Henry thrust that thought aside.

'She'd be better in bed,' he said. 'And she's cold. Griselda . . .'

No help from that quarter. While the men had clumsily applied the plaster and waved stinking feathers about, Griselda sat by the fire and placidly fed the baby who had wakened and made the noise which to a mother indicated hunger.

'I'll heat a couple of bricks,' Tom said.

Henry carried her up and placed her, fully dressed as she

was, under the bedcovers. The candle with which he had lighted his way, holding it in his left hand, his right supporting Joanna, thrown across his right shoulder, like an empty sack, had lurched and was burning crookedly. As he straightened it she came to herself. A bit muddled; something about Robert and a wolf and then, less muddled — 'I didn't mean any harm. I would — have looked after — the baby . . .' She murmured a few more words and changed from the position in which Henry had laid her and passed from a swoon, if swoon it was, to natural sleep. He put his hard, work-worn hand to her cheek and felt the warmth of returning life. Let her sleep.

He was hardly downstairs again and in the kitchen when there came the sound of hoofs and a rap on the door. Father Benedict, his breath steaming, his mule's breath steaming on the frosty air.

'All is well, Father. The child was lost for a while; but she is safe home and in bed.'

'I am glad to hear it. I rode all round the village.'

'I am indeed much obliged to you, Father. She had simply lost her way.'

'I do not understand Knight's Acre or its master,' Father Benedict said to his aunt. 'I did him good service. I knocked on every door ... And he thanked me as though I had been searching for a button.'

'Ah,' said Mistress Captoft who had a taste for gossip. 'If that little girl has disappeared she wouldn't be the first — not from Knight's Acre. The house has a bad name.' As he ate his somewhat belated supper, she entertained him with a patched-up version of what she had gathered from those in the village who had benefited from her medications. She had never mentioned the subject before for tactical reasons. If a foot into Knight's Acre meant a foot upwards she did not care how many scullery boys, drunken archers or even steady — though detested — men like Walter had vanished over the years. But now with a blank between the christening and what she had hoped for, she let herself go. And Ben — she called him that in their intimate moments — said, 'We must keep watch for that child . . . If within a few days nothing is seen or heard of her, we must look into it.'

Henry said, quite mildly, 'There was no need to hit her quite so hard, Griselda.'

'Hard? I didn't hit her nearly hard enough. Putting the baby's life in danger and frightening me out of my wits.'

'You laid her head open to the bone and knocked her senseless.'

'You did that, when you opened the door.'

A false accusation. Joanna's fall might have toppled her over and account for one of the many bruises on her face; it could not account for the wounds on top of her head, or for the bucket of what looked like blood.

Henry did not argue, however. While he put Joanna to bed, Tom had cleared the kitchen while Griselda sat clutching the baby. Even when it had drunk its fill she did not, as usual, lay it back in the cradle; and now she made no move to serve up the dumpling.

'Come on, Tom. If you're not hungry, I am.' Two bouts of acute anxiety in so short a time had left Henry ravenous.

'I'll dish up,' Tom said. Out of doors few men were handier than Henry, making and mending and contriving, indoors he was far less handy than Tom.

Cutting into the savoury-smelling dumpling, Henry said, since Griselda showed no sign of coming to table, 'You going to eat yours there?'

'I'm far too upset to eat. And when I think of what happened while I just went to the larder ... I shall never make that sort of dumpling again.' It was a reaction as natural as Henry's hunger, but it made him impatient.

'Come on, Mistress,' Tom said. 'If you don't eat, you can't feed *him*. I wonder, now ...' Lighting one candle from another he went into the larder into which, just before the christening, he had carried that cask of Lady Serriff's red wine. It was still there and not yet empty.

'That'll do the trick,' he said, coming back with a jugful. 'Do us all good after such a conflopption.' In many ways Tom's speech, like Griselda's, had been influenced by the lady, but there were some words, acquired in childhood which had no match among those learned later.

Contrasting the behaviour of the two men — greatly to Henry's disadvantage — Griselda accepted the wine, and then, mainly because what Tom had said about feeding the baby was true, but also because Tom had thoughtfully placed a portion of dumpling on the hearth to stay warm for her, she ate it. Then she spoke.

'After this, she goes!'

'Where?'

'I don't care. I only know that I shall never have a minute's peace with her around. She's an orphan, isn't she. Put her in an orphanage.'

'I can't do that. My father owed his life, his freedom to her mother. She is my charge. And part of this place belongs to her. Under my father's will.'

'What part?'

'Nothing much,' Henry said, shying away from the hurt. He intended, when the time came, when he was prosperous, to buy back that part of the house, and the right of way; it would, he thought provide just a small dowry.

'I shall *never*,' Griselda said, 'have her in the house again without somebody to *watch*. And how can I do my work with Godfrey on my hip?'

'I'll make her promise . . .'

'Much good that would be!'

'She was thinking of Robert. Holding us to ransom. And she failed. She won't try that again.' His mind slipped away to his own attempt to hold somebody to ransom — his own mother. Using that same foxhole. The only difference was that he had used himself, and won. Joanna had used the baby and failed. The memory gave him some sympathy with the naughty little girl. And he thought — Funny how things work out, if I hadn't been a naughty boy, well-deserving a beating, I should not have known where to look.

'You'll feel different about it in the morning,' he said.

In the morning Griselda felt no differently and Joanna was banished from the house.

Pale and frail at first, but growing stronger every day, she plodded about with the men, anxious to be useful and prove her worth. And although the brew had failed and the desperate action of stealing the baby had failed, the link between her and Robert had tightened, and she had a sharper awareness of what was happening to him. When she stopped, seemed to listen, and looked as Griselda had once said, 'like a moon calf', what she seemed to hear or to see was more real. Though it was not actually seeing or hearing . . .

Henry and Tom were kinder than Griselda and did not call her sharply to attention; but one cold morning, when she and Tom were building the lambing pens, Tom did say, 'You stand about like that, Joanna, you'll freeze.' Caught off guard she said, 'It's the pony. He's so scared . . .'

In that bitter weather both Henry and Tom made attempts to change Griselda's mind. Separate and private attempts.

Henry said, 'Let her stay in by the fire today, Griselda. The wind is cruel.'

'So it was when she took my baby! I've told you, and I meant it — I will not have her in the house, unless somebody else is here.'

Tom said, 'Can't you find it in your heart to forgive her?'

'So now *you're* siding with her!'

CHAPTER TWENTY-FIVE

Early March, and despite the cold the wild daffodils in Layer Wood were breaking, and in the sheep fold the ewes were dropping their lambs. The shelter which John and Young Shep had called 'our hut' was occupied, day and night. There was no great differences in temperature between the hours of daylight and those of darkness, no great difference in the demands on the shepherd's care but night watches seemed longer and more exacting, so Henry took those.

As soon as the lambing began he had worried about Joanna. Of course, wherever you went you found women and girls working alongside men and boys . . . dressed so much alike that they were almost indistinguishable. But Henry had been reared in another tradition.

One bright morning — red sky in the morning, shepherd's warning — Tom and Joanna came along in the rosy light and Henry said, 'I always knew sheep were witless, Tom. That black-face had a dead lamb, the whiteface in the same pen died, but had a live one. I tried to put the two together but it didn't work.'

'We could trick her maybe. It's an old trick, sometimes it works.' Tom took his knife and skinned the dead lamb, clamped its curly hide over the living one and shoved it in beside the black-face, who, after a cautious sniff or two accepted it. Allowed it to suckle.

Steady to his resolve to do his best for Robert, Henry said, 'Put the red mark on it, Tom.' The little skinned corpse lay there. And Joanna stood there, staring.

Not a sight for a little girl. And Griselda had grown crankier during this lambing time. A man sound asleep was no guard, she said.

Henry, yawning widely said, 'Joanna, I shall be up and about by dinner time. You go and gather some daffodils . . .'

She came out of her trance with a shudder and a stare and said,

'All right, Henry. Sleep well.'

She appeared to enter the wood just behind the church. Mistress Captoft saw her and thought, not for the first time, how deplorable it was to see a little girl of good family dressed like a peasant boy. When Henry realised that Griselda was not going to give in and that Joanna must be out in all weathers, he decided that she must be warmly clad, and suitably clad; he had bought a hooded sheepskin coat, too large, but it was the smallest size he could find; below it Joanna wore a thick woollen bodice, and hose. Over the hose were the woollen leg wrappings that were peasant's winter wear, and her slender feet were shod with heavy shoes that reached above the ankle — a necessity when walking through mud.

At Moyidan the servant who commanded the door which had recently opened to admit the Bishop, took one look and said, 'Go to the back!'

The five-mile trudge had given time for thought and planning.

'I have a message for Sir Richard from his brother, Master Tallboys of Knight's Acre.'

Neither her voice nor her manner was that of a peasant, and from inside the shadow of the hood her ice-blue eyes glittered, unabashed. The servant, however, held to the rule.

'Go to the back and deliver it properly.'

By that time she was inside, slippery as an eel and shouting, 'Uncle Richard!' at the top of her voice.

Inside the smaller dining hall the Bishop said, 'Another nephew, Richard?' Among the clergy the word was often used with a peculiar intonation of sceptical amusement because since paternity could not be admitted an avuncular relationship was claimed. Not that there was any doubt about Dick's being a nephew.

'It sounds more like ...' Richard was about to say that it sounded more like his young brother; that whining, complaining boy.

The door opened, roughly; a peasant boy darted in. Behind him the servant said, 'I did my best to stop him, sir ...'

They were then regaled by the sight of a boy making two curtsies, one to each man at the table. The edge of the heavy coat struck the floor and made balancing difficult. But she managed it. Just then she could have managed anything.

'It's Joanna,' she said, and in proof pushed back the hood. Above the no-colour wool her head rose like a flower; the dark-gold curls, flattened by confinement, clinging close to the neat, shapely skull, the profile cameo clear. His Grace of Bywater thought — What a beautiful child; in ten years' time ...

'And what are you doing here? Disguised as a plough-boy?' Richard asked.

'I wanted to see Robert. May I?'

'Of course you may. How did you get here?'

'I walked.' Her manner was slightly cool — Uncle Richard had not stuck up for Robert as he should have done.

'Have you had your dinner?'

'I was walking.' In as much as he remembered her at all, Richard remembered her as a lively, merry, spirited child. Now, though they were both smiling at her, there was no answering smile.

'Come and eat now,' said the Bishop, making room for her beside him on the bench. Immediately he regretted it. She smelt strongly of sheep, and although His Grace was the shepherd of his flock and on the right occasions carried a crook, that was completely symbolic. The table was littered with what

Henry called kickshaws. Joanna took one, but before biting into it, she said, 'May I see Robert? Please.'

To the next boy who stood waiting Richard gave an order. Joanna then bit into a mutton pasty, shaped to look like a shell. His Grace of Bywater observed that her eye-teeth were very pronounced and sharp. Not entirely unattractive.

The inner door opened and Robert came in. Changed — but she was prepared for that; he looked sullen and cowed — he who had been so merry — and he had been crying not so long ago.

Joanna jumped up from what she did not know was a very favoured place indeed — a seat next a Bishop and on the right hand, and flung her arms around her other half . . .

'Quite touching,' the Bishop said, watching the two young creatures merge, clutch, cling, kiss. 'Are they twins?'

Richard had never said much about Knight's Acre to his new friends, and never taken one of them there. At a distance it was a reliable background — my father's house. Closer to, it had flaws. Henry could be mannerly when he chose, but he did not always choose; Madam did her best but it was not quite good enough.

'Curiously, they are not related at all . . .' While Richard explained, Joanna hissed into Robert's ear, 'Make some excuse to get us alone.'

He understood instantly. He always had.

'Sir, I would like to show Joanna my pony.'

It was the first time that he had ever used the word *my* about that innocent animal and Richard regarded it as a good sign.

'Off you go . . . But you've had your dinner. Joanna had none. Take some food. And tell William to have the wagon ready to take Joanna home.'

In that same hissing whisper Joanna said, 'Take a lot!' Robert obeyed, and she took a lot herself.

In the courtyard and around the stables the after-dinner relaxation lay. The two children slipped away, unobserved. Layer Wood which had sheltered so many fugitives engulfed them. Once within its shelter they sat down on a fallen tree trunk, ate what they had brought and talked. And talked.

Robert spoke of his miseries. Dick had never touched him. So that threat had worked! But he had managed cunningly so that for ink spilt, or ruined quills, for anything blameable on a boy, Robert had been blamed, and beaten. And the pony — 'I was frightened at first, but as soon as I got over that, they did things ... All the serving people are Dick's friends. They played tricks on me — and the pony.'

'I knew,' Joanna said. 'That is why I came to take you away.'

'Where?'

'Our secret place. I'll bring you food. We can play all our old games. It will be pleasant for me too, now that Griselda won't have me in the house.' She explained how that had come about.'

'How brave you are,' Robert said, thinking of venturing into the wood alone, at dusk. The red dawn's promise of bad weather was being kept and dark, sagging clouds were cutting off the daylight. As Robert glanced nervously around the distances between the trees filled with shadows. Moving? Prowling? Watchful? He gave a shiver and Joanna, instantly self-reproachful, realised that he had come out in indoor dress. She wriggled out of the coat and tried to make him put it on.

'No,' he said, 'we'll share.'

'And be on our way.'

Huddled together, their inner arms wrapped around each other, their outer hands holding the sleeves of the jacket, they set off.

Joanna was certain of the way. In the morning she had simply cut through the wood behind the church and reached the lane. Now — because Robert might be missed — she avoided the lane, keeping to a course which she thought was parallel to it. The east wind, sharp with sleet, blew on the jacket that sheltered them both, helping them along. Soon, soon they would come out behind the church, skirt it and be in the Knight's Acre garden. Robert would climb through the window of the secret place and she would go in, pretending that she had forgotten the time, lost her way; that would explain her absence from the dinner table and perhaps gain her an extra large supper portion; most of which she would secrete and save for Robert.

She knew where she was. She had a sense of direction, so innate and strong that she was certain that if her arm were only long enough, she could reach out and touch the church, the priest's house, Knight's Acre. The trouble was that in a wood, with darkness and a blizzard coming on, one could not keep to a direct path. There were thickets of brambles, more fallen trees, a pool, all to be circumvented. Presently she knew that either she had lost her way, or the wind had changed. The sleet was now striking from the left. They skirted another thicket, another pool, almost indiscernible in the gathering darkness, and now the wind blew in their faces.

Joanna did not say 'we are lost'. To do so would frighten Robert and perhaps make him cry. She said, 'I think we should rest a little, when I find a sheltered place.'

'I *am* tired.' He could confess it now that she had suggested rest. 'But, oh! So happy.'

What she needed was a hollow similar to that in which she had hidden the baby, but she had left it too late. Had such a shelter been near at hand the darkness and the driving sleet would have hidden it from her. They almost walked into the next obstacle, a fallen tree. It must serve. Crouched on the side of it away from the wind, they would have some protection.

Robert sank down with a sigh and a shiver and with another pang of self-reproach she thought — his feet! I let him come out in those flimsy shoes! Inside her own ugly footwear — stout, well-greased leather, lined with felt — her feet were dry and warm. She removed his soaked shoes and pushed his cold wet feet into hers, still warm from her body. He was too sleepy to protest.

'We'll play the grunting game,' he said, in a voice that indicated that tonight he would win it. It was one of their old games — who could be asleep first. One would make a little grunting sound which the other, if awake, was in honour bound, forced to answer. Tonight, after one exchange of grunts, Robert slept. A beating in the morning, the excitement of reunion and a long walk had exhausted him.

Joanna intended to stay awake, on guard; for in one of her angry tirades Griselda had spoken of wolves in the wood.

However, on the lee side of the fallen tree it was not uncomfortable; Robert lay with his back to her; her body fitted about him, her arm held him and the sheepskin coat covered them both. Despite all the mistakes she had made, she had done what she set out to do — a good thought upon which to fall asleep.

When she woke it was morning. The blizzard had blown itself out. It was clear, and cold. The sheepskin coat crackled as she moved and sat up and took her bearings. She had been right to halt when she did, for she could tell from the direction of the light that they had been walking due east, away from Knight's Acre.

Robert was sleeping so peacefully that it seemed a shame to wake him, yet. She must re-plan for it had been her intention to smuggle him into the secret place under cover of dusk. Now they must be far more careful, stay in the wood, *just* inside, until they were beyond the back of the church and the priest's house and directly in line with Knight's Acre with only a strip of garden between them and the secret place. She would then help Robert in through the window and go to the sheep fold. Henry would be gone to his bed, and asleep; it would be to Tom that she must explain that hunting for daffodils she had lost her way and been overtaken by darkness and the storm. Tom would have food . . . Joanna's sharp eyes had not failed to notice that these days Griselda took better care of Tom than she did of Henry. Henry could watch through the night with no more than a bit of bread and cheese for company; Tom had stew or broth in a jar, placed inside another, bigger one, lined with hay to keep the inner jar warm. The significance of this behaviour was lost on the child who only thought that Tom was less hardy than Henry, just as she was more hardy than Robert.

She gave Robert a gentle nudge. He went on sleeping. She spoke in his ear. 'Robert! Time to wake up. Time to go.' When he did not respond to that, she shook him and called his name more loudly.

Deeply devoted and attached as they were, they had never used loving words to one another. It was an unknown language which both their mothers had used, but Sybilla had died before it could be communicated and Tana had reserved hers . . . So in this extremity all Joanna could say was 'Robert.' When the name, repeated with increasing force and urgency brought no response, she realised that he had gone, beyond recall.

He was dead. Like old Father Ambrose in the church.

At Knight's Acre she had not been missed until dusk when Henry went to change places with Tom. 'I thought maybe she'd come back to you here.'

'Haven't had sight of her since morning.'

'You'll have to stay here, Tom, while I take a look. She may even be in the house; if so I shan't be long . . .'

She was not in the house and a blizzard was blowing up. Carrying a lantern Henry went to the fox-hole. Not there. He shouted, the sound torn to shreds by the howling wind. He went back to the house, hoping.

'No,' Griselda said in answer to his anxious question. She was sewing and gently rocking the cradle with her foot. Her complete indifference infuriated him.

'God damn it, you might show a little concern!' To that she did not bother to reply.

Fighting his way back to the fold, Henry thought — as once before — of Moyidan. If Joanna had run way, and who could blame her? it was for Moyidan that she would make, and if she had set out for Moyidan in the morning she'd be safe now.

'All right, Tom; off you go.'

It was a bad, busy night. Lambs were supposed to come into the world with their noses pressed close to their forefeet, that way they slid out easily. If for some reason unknown to man, they presented themselves with heads thrown back, feet showing but no nose, then a shepherd had to get busy, pushing and re-arranging. Ewes always knew when they were in trouble and cried for help with voices that sounded almost human. Four called for help that night.

In the morning, all soiled as he was, and gritty eyed for need of sleep, Henry saddled his horse and went to Moyidan. Richard was not there — he had gone to Baildon. Only the door servant knew anything; a girl, looking like a boy, had pushed her way in and been well-received, not only by Sir Richard but by the Bishop . . . Henry assumed that unwanted in the house, unwanted in the sheep fold, Joanna had run way, told a piteous tale and been taken care of.

The story she told would, he realised be slanted to his disfavour. Unfair, because as far as he could he had always done the best he could for this child — no kin of his. The thought, however did not unduly perturb him; if Joanna were safe, in some place where she stood a chance of being reasonably happy, he would be content. But he needed to be *sure*. He felt that he could not spare the time to go to Bywater, or to search for Richard in Baildon; so he left an urgent message — Would

Sir Richard let him know immediately exactly what had happened to the little girl ...

He then rode home, and there she was, with Tom in the sheep fold.

He could have shaken her; but she seemed to be in such a poor way; her face deathly white and swollen from crying; it bore scratches, too. She appeared to be calm, though now and again a shudder shook her.

'Tom told me how worried you were, Henry. I am sorry. I went to Moyidan to see Robert.' That much was known; she had been seen. 'Then coming home I lost myself in the wood. There was a storm ...'

'If you'd only shown a little sense, and waited. I intended to *take* you to visit Robert as soon as he'd had time to settle — and this was over.' He waved his hand around the fold. 'You're a very head-strong, inconsiderate little girl.'

Part of his anger was directed against Richard. God's teeth, couldn't he have sent her home by wagon, or Pillion. She was mired to the knees and her boots were so caked with mud that standing there she seemed anchored to the ground.

'Come on,' he said, reaching down from the saddle. 'The sooner you're in bed the better.'

On the short canter from the fold to the stable he relented; even inside the bulky clothes she seemed so frail. In a kinder voice, he asked, 'Well, and how did you find Robert?'

'He was lonely at first. But not now. In fact one of the last things he said to me was that he was happy.'

'There you are, you see. A lot of fuss and anxiety all about nothing.'

She shuddered again and Henry said, 'God send you haven't taken a chill.'

She had not, though the night in the open had changed her in some indefinable way. Since Robert's going she had been quiet and unhappy; you'd have thought, Henry reflected that having seen him and learned that he was happy at Moyidan, some of her old spirit would have returned. It had not; she still seemed to be quiet and unhappy, though she no longer stopped and stared and listened. It was possible, he thought, that seeing Robert living in comfort had made her compare his lot with her own. He wished very much that there was somewhere where she could go, away from this unnatural life, outdoor work all day and the evenings made wretched by Griselda's unrelenting hostility. But there was nothing he could do, except be as kind to her as he could.

Since she was home he expected no message from Moyidan as to her whereabouts, but on the third morning after the escapade Richard arrived, looking slightly less sleek and composed than usual. He halted his horse by the sheepfold and said, 'Is Robert here?'

'Robert! No Why should he be?'

'He's vanished. Is the girl here?'

'Vanished? How could . . .? Yes, she's here. In the shelter. Joanna!'

This was a moment which she had known was bound to come and she was prepared for it.

Richard, lawyer as well as priest, knew the value of attack. 'Where's Robert?'

'Robert? I don't know.' That was strictly true. She knew where the body lay, but the all-important part, the gentleness and merriment and affection — where were they? She'd knelt and prayed — God, let his time in Purgatory be short; he never did anything bad. He never did anything but I led him into it.

'So far as I can make out you were the last person to see him.'

'I saw him. You said I could.'

Young as she was she had the known feminine way of going off on a side track.

'Yes. I said you could see him and he said he wanted to show you his pony. What happened then?'

'He showed me his pony.'

'And after that?'

'I came home and lost myself in the wood . . .'

Henry said, 'And spent the night there. In a blizzard. I think you could at least . . .'

'I did. As they went out together I told Robert to tell William to get the wagon ready. By the time it was ready they'd both disappeared. Joanna, did Robert say anything to you about running away?

'Not a word.' I was the one who thought of that.

'You say you lost yourself in the wood. Could he have followed you?'

'He didn't follow me. I am sure about that.'

'Could he have gone into the wood by himself?'

'He would never do that. He was frightened of the wood.' Always, even on the fringe of it, gathering sticks or flowers. Now he — or at least his body, lay there alone for ever, under the bracken and leaves she had heaped over it. All her determination could not prevent a shudder. Henry noticed.

'Go and help Tom with the feeding,' Henry said. Once she had gone he asked, 'Have you dragged the moat?'

'The moat?'

'I was thinking ...' Actually he was remembering how nearly Griselda had come to killing Joanna. 'You were away. Suppose that tutor struck an unlucky blow.'

'Most unlikely. He is not at all the kind. When boys need correction he punishes them, in the proper place, with a thin leather strap. And God in Glory, Henry, a corpse is not so easily disposed of.'

No? Walter, with pigs as accomplices, had disposed of more than one; Henry had disposed of Walter's — with some help from Sybilla.

'I will have the moat dragged, of course. He may have *fallen* in.'

'Set up the hue-and-cry, too. I'll set it to work in the Baildon area, you take Bywater.'

'If we must,' Richard said unwillingly. 'It will not *sound* well. Children of that age do not run away from happy homes. And I still think ...' He looked broodingly at Joanna who was distributing hay. 'She showed no surprise or distress.'

'She's not one to make much display of her feelings.'

'All the same, I'd like another word. Call her over.'

Reluctant witnesses must be pressed.

As she scattered the hay Joanna had been thinking about not knowing where Robert's soul was; and how Masses were said for the quick delivery from Purgatory. And she had no money to buy one. Henry would provide — if he knew. But he could only know if she confessed. And if she did ... Griselda had often said that there were places for mad, bad people. Stealing the baby had been bad, and snatching Robert away in his indoor clothes had been mad. Somehow, somehow she must manage to buy a Mass without committing herself to being chained to a post and regularly whipped.

'Now, Joanna,' Richard said. 'You know what the truth is. I want you to swear, on the Cross, to tell the truth.'

'I swear, on the Cross, to tell the truth.'

'Do you know *anything* about Robert that you have not told us.'

Inwardly the wild blood that was her heritage took control. Outwardly she might have been reciting the Credo.

'Yes. I know a great deal. And all your fault. You didn't look after him properly. You let that man beat him for things Dick had done. That man dared not beat Dick because all the servants are his friends and if he beat Dick the man's food came cold to table or some such thing. Then there was the pony. Robert was frightened at first, but it was a nice pony and he liked it. Then Dick would arrange — with servants — that it should be harnessed badly, or hit suddenly before he was properly in the saddle. Robert was always given fat, which made him sick. When Robert complained to you, *you* said he was whining. And that man beat him for tale-bearing. I hate you all, that man, and Dick and you. I hope God will punish you for what you did to Robert. And I shall never call you Uncle again.'

Small, ridiculously clad, a wisp of hay in her wind-chapped hands and sheep's dung clogging her half boots, she flung her challenge to the man on the horse — from time immemorial the symbol of superiority and authority. That her final sentence was the ultimate in bathos only Richard knew. He was in any case not her uncle. It would have been comic, had Henry not been listening, and had Richard not craved Henry's approval.

'I'll try Bywater and the moat,' Richard said, swinging his horse round. 'I'll let you know. As soon as I know anything.'

Henry said, 'Joanna, your stories don't fit. You said that Robert said he was happy.'

'So he was. Happy to see me. Happy to be able to tell all his woes.'

'Poor little boy! If only I had known . . .'

'I tried to tell you. You took no notice . . . If you had believed me, what would you have done?'

'Fetched him home.' That was the hardest blow of all. She wept.

Henry, who had been up all night and about to go to bed, having handed over to Tom, when Richard appeared, said,

'Sweeting *don't*. Boys can't just *disappear*. I'm going to Baildon now. We'll have the criers out in no time.'

Cry his name, his description in every street, along every lane, at every crossroad in the whole world. Robert would never answer . . .

CHAPTER TWENTY-SIX

Richard had been right in assuming that a public search for Robert would draw undesirable attention. A young boy vanished without trace — and not from some humble home. Servants talked, giving Master Jankyn a reputation as a savage flogger of the kind disapproved even by people who believed in a cuff of the ear, or good hammering occasionally. The story became garbled as all stories were, and was confused by the fact that the Moyidan door-keeper said that he knew that a girl was missing, as well as a boy. He'd seen the girl himself and next morning Master Tallboys of Knight's Acre had come asking about her. So some versions mentioned two lost children — done away with the more lurid stories ran, by a wicked uncle who wanted their property.

In the flippant way which made him such good company, Richard said to the Bishop, 'Had I been minded to do away with a boy it would not have been Robert — who, incidentally was my brother, not my nephew, but with Dick who will inherit this place. Not that it would benefit me; it would do my brother Henry some service. He's next in line.'

During the weeks of fruitless search and busy rumour, Richard had often wished that it had been Dick who had vanished without trace.

'Next, that is, after your cousin, the present owner,' said the Bishop, who liked to get things clear. 'I must say, my dear Richard, yours is a very *complicated* family.'

'In more ways than one. And I am the steward — just or unjust as you care to regard it. It is often a thankless office.'

But not unrewarding, His Grace thought, looking about him.

'You have never seen my cousin, or his wife, who — just to make matters more complicated, is my sister. Or their son. One is not inclined to make a display of what is dismal. But if you would care to see . . .'

The Bishop saw two obvious idiots, blank-eyed except when they looked at each other. Both fair and frail-looking, both wearing faded garlands of wild roses — for it was summer now. Neither took the slightest notice of him or of Sir Richard. The boy, their son, did glance up and then returned to gobbling his supper; the man in charge stood up and bowed. Then, in response to a whispered request, he gave, in a quiet voice the kind of report about his remaining pupil which schoolmasters landed with the unteachable must always give. Not good enough to promise anything and not bad enough to decry themselves. Dick could do better if he attended more. Dick was improving, but slowly. Dick would do better in time.

Back in the cosy, intimate atmosphere of the small dining parlour, with fresh wine, Richard said, 'You see what I have to contend with?'

'I do indeed. Breed idiot to idiot and what can one expect but an idiot? The Church has always been against . . . Did they have a dispensation?'

'I cannot say. I was in Winchester at the time.'

At Knight's Acre, too, the wild roses had bloomed and then faded. After them came the big moon-eyed daisies. The shearers came and went, the wool went to Moyidan for sale and Henry conscientiously deposited Robert's share with Master Turnbull. After all the boy had been lost only for three months, it was too soon to despair.

Then it was harvest again; Jem and Henry scything, Joanna and Tom making the sheaves and stocking them.

'Take it easy, Tom,' Henry said. 'She doesn't like to be outpaced.'

Actually he was concerned for Tom, whose attacks of weakness and dizziness came with increasing frequency. Nothing much was made of them, least of all by Tom who usually blamed the weather, the sun was too hot, or the wind too sharp; sometimes he blamed himself, he'd eaten too much, or he'd hurried.

This harvest was hardly under way before he suffered an affliction of which even he could not make light. He stooped to gather an armful of corn, tried to straighten up and gave a yell. Henry put down his scythe and came back across the stubble.

'Jinked your back, Tom?' He knew what to do because it had happened to him several times in his growing days and Walter had put it right in a blink. He took Tom by the shoulders, put his knee into the small of his back and gave a sharp jerk. Tom yelled even more loudly.

'No good, Master,' he gasped. 'It's the Witch's Strike.'

Jem, always ready to waste a minute said, 'Somebody bin ill-wishing you, Tom:'

This sudden, agonising, crippling pain in the back was called Witch's Strike because its onset was so sudden, and so seemingly without cause. The only things to be said of it — small comfort to the sufferer — were that it was never fatal, lasted only a few days and disappeared as suddenly as it came.

'Help Tom into the house, Joanna. Tell Griselda to give him a dab of liniment — not too hard. You'll find it in the stable.'

Fortunately they were working in the field nearest the house.

Griselda was delighted to have a chance to cosset Tom. She installed him on the settle in the hall and wedged him with pillows. He said he was all right so long as he didn't try to straighten out or move. Away from the communal table, she could slip him little tit-bits, presenting them with love and wishing that she could do better.

Apart from the absolutely necessary excursions out of doors, Tom stayed, rigid and bent over, on the settle for three days. Then at a stroke he was restored and out in the field again. A less modest man would have observed with pleasure that he had been missed; things had got a bit behindhand because one girl, however willing and nimble, couldn't sheaf and stook the corn cut by two reapers and from time to time during the three days either Henry or Jem had been obliged to cease scything and make sheaves and stook them. Corn left lying flat tended to sprout, forerunning its season.

'We've got a bit of lee-way to make up,' Tom said.

He had never seen the sea, but like most of his fellow East Anglians he was descended from a sea-faring race who had inherited, with their blood, some ancient terms of speech. Any woman, having clinched an argument would say, 'And that took the wind out of her sails'; any man rebuking a busy-body, would say, 'Now don't you go shoving your oar in.'

So Tom said 'lee-way', and when it was partially made up Joanna said, 'Tom, what did Jem mean by saying somebody had ill-wished you?'

'Oh, just another old tale.'

'I like your tales, Tom. Tell me.'

It was not the ideal situation for the telling of any tale, least of all one concerned with magic rites; they parted to gather up the corn, make the twist of about seven strands which bound for the sheaf, and then met again, stooking the sheaves into a tent-like structure. Just a few words, and another few. But by the end of the morning Joanna had learned what she needed to know about ill-wishing. About the making of what Tom called 'mommets'.

They could be made of anything, mud, tallow, dough. There must be a mockery of baptism — the Cross made the wrong way. Once named they could be subjected to ill-treatment, stuck with pins, set to waste by the fire. One most intriguing thing about this account, so broken and interrupted — 'Go on, Tom, what next?' — was that Tom himself was neither quite a believer nor quite a disbeliever. He said, 'Well, they say ...' and 'My old granny always held ...' He said, 'It's all an old tale, but I remember something funny ...'

As Henry had said she was not one to show her feelings; but they were there. And to Tom's half-reluctant account she added a few imaginative touches of her own. Surely a mock baptism would be more effective if the water was taken from the font. A little cup, hidden in the sleeve.

One by one she made the little figures, named them, mutilated them. Sir Richard Tallboys; Master Jankyn; Dick.

And it all was, as Tom said, just an old story, like the brews that made you invisible, or turned you into a wolf. It just did not work.

Sir Richard was extremely happy, despite a few things that he could have wished otherwise. Leonora was all that, and more than, a man could expect from a mistress. Her moods, her behaviour, were so unpredictable that in possessing her a man possessed a dozen women at least. He never entered that gateway in the grey wall without a sense of keen anticipation; never left it, going the other way, without a sense of satisfaction, and self-congratulation. And even though Sir Francis' poor relation, Mistress Neville, was not exactly what he had expected, perhaps she served his purpose better than a woman he would have chosen himself.

The words 'poor relation' envisaged somebody meek, accustomed to sitting overlooked in corners, sombrely clad, undemanding, grateful for a good home. Mistress Neville was in all ways the reverse of this. She was poorly clad when she arrived, but that was swiftly remedied — at Richard's expense; of gratitude she showed no sign, always acting as though she were doing him and Leonora a favour, which in a manner she was. She was masterful, shrewd and worldly. For a woman in her forties she was not unhandsome; one could only think that the reason she had not married again was that she was penniless — and possibly rather choosy.

She took control from the first. Richard had imagined the two women living quietly together, himself their only visitor.

'But, Sir Richard, that is precisely the way to draw attention to yourself and give rise to gossip. We must entertain frequently. Nothing is less noticed than a straw in a strawstack.' They entertained frequently, and royally. Moyidan supplied meat and various other essentials as well as luxuries such as asparagus and fruit in due season, nevertheless the expenses of the household were staggering.

The furniture and the fittings of the house which Richard had taken over so unwillingly — and at such cost, were, Mistress Neville said entirely unsuitable for the position which she and Leonora must *appear* to occupy. 'No widow of good family and adequate means would live in such squalor,' she said. But he need not bother, she would see to it. That she was herself of good family there could be no dispute and her husband, though he died poor, had been a member of the family whose head was the great Earl of Warwick. Sir Francis called her Aunt Alyson, and again with the air of doing a favour, she proposed that Richard and Leonora should address her similarly. Sir Francis was a very frequent visitor and often stayed overnight — as did other gentlemen though less regularly. 'It will prevent servants' talk.' For of course, they must have servants; three the very minimum.

Towards the world and towards all those they entertained the two women presented a united front. In private a good deal of rivalry smouldered. Who was mistress of this house? Leonora who made its existence necessary, or Aunt Alyson who made it possible? Disputes of that kind usually ended in a victory for Mistress Neville, not because Leonora was incapable of standing up for herself but because she was fundamentally idle.

Unfortunately for Richard this rivalry, took an expensive form. Like any lover, he delighted in giving things to Leonora and did not think it strange that she should want such a number of dresses — most of them with a jewel to match; what was annoying — and eventually alarming — was that Aunt Alyson would support any demand Leonora made, and then, as soon as it was met, begin to throw out broad hints on her own behalf. 'Leonora's new tawny velvet makes everything I own look positively *shabby* by comparison.' Or, even more sinister, 'Leonora's *beautiful* emerald does make one wonder about the wages of *sin*! That *virtue* is its own reward is only too evident.'

Sometimes Richard wondered whether Aunt Alyson was quite as virtuous as she pretended to be. Quite early on she had said, 'Francis, I know you call me *Aunt*. I am in some confusion, when I come to think about it, as to what our exact relationship is.' They had spent a pleasant half hour scrambling about far flung branches of their family trees and reached the conclusion that there was no blood kinship between them at all. And whenever Sir Francis spent the night at the Saltgate House, Mistress Neville would lead him off to her own little parlour with a proprietary air. It was tactful, it was exactly what her position required of her but . . .

The setting up of such an establishment had naturally not escaped notice in so small a town.

First of all Master Turnbull was angered to learn that the house in Saltgate had been sold so quickly, so quietly, behind his back one might say. He'd had an eye on it for a long time. A good solid house, big enough to make two, or even three of the sort and size which let so easily; and a big yard and some other ground, a neglected orchard, most suitable as building ground. Peevishly he asked who had acquired it and when told Sir Richard Tallboys, felt an astonishment that he did not betray.

He had been concerned with Sir Godfrey's will — and with Lady Emma's. Neither of them, so far as he could remember conferred upon Sir Richard the kind of wealth that would justify the purchase of a town house by a man already well-housed at Moyidan. It was a thing which justified some looking in to; and the most superficial enquiries revealed that Sir Richard had not sold that remote, not very valuable bit of land bequeathed to him by his aunt. So how?

The next people to be concerned were the saddler and his wife. Mistress Neville, far from pious, regarded attendance at church as a social obligation and one Sunday morning Leonora's real aunt, the saddler's wife saw the viper she had nourished in her bosom, most splendidly clad . . .

'I thought,' she said to her husband, 'that you told me you had found that girl a menial post. In the country.'

'And so I did. With Master Tallboys. Out at Intake.'

'Then I would be glad if you could explain to me how it has come about that she was in church this very morning with more miniver about her than a dog has fleas.'

How could he explain? He knew nothing of it. He could only say, 'I know nothing. It is none of my doing.' How could it possibly be when his wife, being the one who could read and write and reckon overlooked the finances of the business. It had taken him a deal of scheming to buy the ear-bobs as a Christmas present.

'I shall make it my business to find out exactly what is going on,' Leonora's real aunt said.

I, too, the saddler decided in his mind. He was anxious.

Her way was devious and took a little time; his was abrupt; he looked out for Henry's wagon and put the point-blank question which Henry answered shortly, 'I can tell you what I was *told*. She left us to take a post as help and company to an old lady.'

'Well,' said the saddler's wife when she knew what there was to be known. 'What I should like to know is that if the girl had an aunt, named Neville, so well-connected and rich, why she didn't come forward and offer when my poor sister, God rest her, died? *We* had all the trouble and expense of rearing the creature.'

It was a question that she would have liked to put to

Mistress Neville herself, 'but that was the worst of being in business. Mistress Neville was related to Sir Francis Lassiter at Muchanger and so to half a dozen other families, kin to him, and all potential customers. It would not do to offend ... So, on various Sundays and Holy Days for the next eighteen months, the saddler's wife suffered the exasperation of seeing the ingrate come with that peculiar grace of manner, into church; velvet and furs, silk — thick and ribbed, then fine and almost flimsy for high summer; heavy silk again, velvet and fur. Beautiful headdresses always.

At Knight's Acre Joanna gave up the making of mommets. So far as she could see nothing had come either of ill-wishing or well-wishing. The last had been a device of her own. Little images, named Henry, named Tom, lay cradled in sheep's wool and flower petals; if ill-wishing worked, why not well-wishing? But in fact none of it worked. The year 1469 began badly for Henry — the worst lambing on record, and footrot, due to the wet weather, and liver flux, due to nothing certain.

And Tom became weaker and weaker.

Two weak dizzy spells, long-lasting, in one day.

Henry said, 'You stay in bed tomorrow, Tom, and take a good rest. We can manage.'

'I shall be all right tomorrow,' Tom said; but he knew now. Hitherto his funny spells had been something of a mystery, something left over from the plague, now from the way his heart was behaving, he knew what ailed him. And thanks to his old granny he knew a cure.

'You and me,' he said to Joanna, 'we've talked about brews in our time. Mostly old tales, but *some* good. And I need one now. Mostly foxgloves are past flowering, but no matter, it's the leaves do the good. If you'd go gather a good handful ...'

The foxglove leaves, eagerly gathered, well pounded and infused, were curative at first, spurring the sluggish heart. Tom was able to help with that late harvesting, half a day here, half a day there, but he knew it would be his last. There was a point past which a dying horse could not be flogged. Or a dying heart. Facing up to death much as he had faced his life, outwardly so bleak and unrewarding, Tom took stock of the situation he would leave behind and was saddened. For some reason beyond his comprehension Griselda and Henry were at odds, even over the child. And Griselda was at odds with Joanna, such a good girl if only Griselda could bring herself to see it. Tom loved Griselda, respected and was grateful to Henry, was fond of Joanna. He wished, with all his heart, that they should be happy.

No field work for him that autumn; he doddered about, doing little jobs about the yard, stopping when the labouring heart seemed to choke his breath and everything went black. He helped in the kitchen, sparing Griselda the most distasteful tasks, skinning pigeons, flaying and de-gutting a hare, but he knew — having earned his keep since he was about four years old — that he no longer earned it and lately, whenever he prayed he added a little piece — God, don't let me be a burden.

One morning, he was skinning pigeons and Griselda was making the dough for the pudding casing that was to enclose them, he said, 'I want you to be happy.'

Taken by surprise she used the voice that she used to others now, but never to Tom.

'What do you mean?'

'More contented, like. Happier. Take Joanna ...' Best to start on the lesser matter. 'I know how much she upset you. But you can't go on bearing a grudge *for ever*.'

'Oh, can't I.'

'Not if you're going to be happy and comfortable. After all, we pray, don't we, to be forgiven, as we forgive.'

'Don't you think I have tried? Tom, I can't. Just to look at her gives a cold grue.'

'Dearie, she's only a child.'

'I know. *What will she be like when she's full-grown.*'

'None the worse for a bit of friendliness now.'

'You talk like a priest,' Griselda said, giving the dough a mauling that promised ill in terms of edibility. Across it she looked at him and saw how greatly he had changed. The weather tan had faded from his face, leaving it the colour of tallow and his lips had a bluish tint. His big hands which had worked about her, gently as a woman's, had softened and paled; dark veins stood out like whipcord.

'There's the master, too.' Tom persisted. 'You're out with him.'

Out indeed!

Henry had compounded all his other faults by never once giving her a chance to repel a sexual approach. Ever since the baby was born all *that* had ceased. Henry got into bed, said, 'Goodnight,' blew out the candle and turned on his side. He was far too much all-of-a-piece to wish to bed with somebody who railed and scolded all day. Griselda, who had always been obliged to set her teeth in order to accept him was now perversely offended. All he'd ever wanted was somebody to keep his house and bear his child.

Her hands motionless on the dough, she said,

'There's no help for the way we are, Tom. I made a mistake, and must live with it. I didn't know it was a mistake, till that day . . .' She glanced at Godfrey, capering about on the hobbyhorse that Tom had made for him. 'Till then all men were alike to me. Too late to do anything about it.'

'I know. But it ain't all loss, my dearie. You got as good a man as ever wore shore-leather; you've got the boy. You've got the house.'

'The house! Oh Tom . . .' Her green eyes filled with tears and she put her floury, dough-patched hands to her face.

He rose and went over to her, put his arms around her, comfortingly, without desire — he was past it. She could hear and feel the heavy, irregular labouring of his heart.

'Make the best of it, honey sweet. Try a little kindness. It'll oil the wheels.' She made no promise, no reply and after a pause he said, 'They'll be wanting their dinners.'

'Mumma cried,' Godfrey informed Henry.

'Don't be so silly,' Griselda said. 'Anybody'd cry, peeling that lot of onions.'

The morning came when the weakness attacked as soon as Tom stood on his feet. The floor dropped away. Heaving himself into bed again Tom thought —— I will *not* lie in bed useless and rotting, like my old Granfer. I will not add to *her* load.

That evening when Joanna looked in to ask how he was — she had offered to carry up his supper but Griselda said *she* could see to Tom — he gave her an exact description of henbane, where to find it, what to do.

'The foxglove worked for a bit; now I need something

stronger. And I wouldn't say anything to Griselda. She took over making the foxglove and it might put her out.'

Of Tom's death Henry said, 'It's a loss. But it's the way he would have chosen for himself.'

Richard's thoughts as he rode into Baildon were as glum as the November afternoon. He had always enjoyed financial juggling, but those who juggled with money, like those who juggled with plates, needed a sound footing, and he had never had that. His was more like a morass, every floundering step took him deeper. He'd made two mistakes — he'd overestimated Moyidan's recuperative power, and underestimated the cost of the Saltgate establishment — now just under two years old.

As he turned in at the gate in the wall, his spirits lifted. He thought — After all, given time . . . and he thought — It is well worth it.

The good smell of roasting venison had penetrated even to the yard. He'd sent in a well-hung haunch, and a hamper of Moyidan's special late-ripening red apples and brown pears and he imagined that Aunt Alyson's hospitable instinct would have been aroused and there would be company for supper. But the stable yard was empty and when he went in he found Leonora alone.

'Aunt Alyson has gone to bed. With a headache.'

She'd never looked lovelier, he thought. She could wear any colour, but always looked best in the various brownish ones which emphasised her fawn-like quality. The dress was new, pale buff velvet, the sleeves lined with cream-coloured lace; with it she wore exactly the right ornament, a necklace of yellow rock crystal and pearls, and the gauzy headdress, cream coloured was held by a band, almost a coronet, that matched. In his pocket he had a ring of the same yellow crystal — a present to celebrate the second anniversary of their real meeting in Layer Wood after the hunt was over and they had reached an understanding.

It was not only the clothes; she was in one of her elusive moods, seeming to melt and slip away from his ardent embrace. And some inner excitement seemed to light her from within. Her eyes shone and her full-lipped mouth, one of the first things he had noticed about her seemed now and then to harbour a smile. Devil take the cost and the danger, he thought; this was a woman in a million. Almost two years and never a dull moment or a regret.

Over the meal — the first they had ever taken alone together he said, 'I have a surprise for you.'

'I have one for you, too, Richard.'

Like a blast of icy air suspicion struck. A baby! That would account for the radiant, excited look.

It was not that he did not wish — as all men did — for living proof of his virility. And he would have welcomed, or at least accepted a child if only he'd been as rich as he seemed, as Leonora believed him to be. Or even had he been successful in his career so that he had influence enough to promote the interests of his 'nephew'.

And how typical of women — even of Leonora, the most exceptional of her kind, to be pleased, to have put on all her finery in order to tell him about the last thing he wished at this moment to hear. Fools, fools, all of them, even the best of them!

She said, 'Bring your wine to the fire, Richard. I have something to tell you.' He saw then that under the excitement, the female complacency, she was nervous, and because he loved her, determined to be kind, pretend to be pleased, not mar her joy by any mention of practical considerations.

The wine in her cup slopped a little; his own was steady.

She said, 'I am going to be married.'

It was an explosion; deafening; reverberating.

'Who?' he asked when he had mastered himself enough to speak.

'Francis Lassiter.'

Another explosion.

'That old man!'

'He is no longer *young*,' she said, steady now that what had to be said *had* been said. 'But not so old either. And he offers marriage, a name, a place in the world.'

'And you . . . you,' he said, filled with fury. 'Where'll you be after a fortnight of his futile fumbling? In bed with the nearest ploughboy!'

It seemed a long time ago since Sir Francis had spoken of settling down, getting himself an heir to Muchanger. And he'd done nothing about it except a bit of posturing flirtation with Mistress Neville — and even that had come to nothing. Roués bought early impotence!

'You wrong me,' Leonora said. 'And him!'

'Have you ever tried him?'

'Of course not. One does not *give* what is of value.'

That simple, cynical statement was not to Richard offensive — simply proof of her worth.

'You are a whore, a born whore,' he said. 'But . . . damn all to hell. If you *must* be married, I'll marry you myself. Vows take a bit of time to cancel out, but it can be done. I'll get myself unfrocked.'

'And that would be ruin for us both. Dear Richard, you may not know this . . .' She looked at him gravely 'In the town there is talk — of money raised by dubious means. I think it is only because you *are* a priest that things are not worse . . .'

And who is to blame, he asked himself. Two rapacious women and a household, costly out of all proportion to its size. Infatuation whirled and showed its reverse face, hatred. And when she stretched out the slender, long fingered hand upon which the yellow crystal would never glimmer — though other rings would, and said, 'Come to bed. It may be for the last time,' he could hardly speak for the nausea which shock and disgust, and dismay had engendered in him.

The entry was dark for nobody was expected to come and go, and Mistress Neville, extravagant in many ways, was sparing over such small items as candles. Richard was fumbling his way to the door when some faint illumination fell downward from the stairs and Mistress Neville said, 'Sir Richard . . .' The light of the candle she held in her hand lit her face in a grotesque way, throwing such shadows that she looked like a gargoyle.

She must have connived, he thought furiously; the skilled deceiver, the paid procuress, open-handed for any bribe.

'How much did *he* pay you?' he asked brutally.

'Nothing. I had no suspicion . . .' Now that she had descended and stood level with him, the light between them, he could see that the change in her face was not an illusion. She was not actually crying *now* but her puffy eyes and swollen nose told of tears shed not long ago. In addition her whole face seemed to have collapsed, from within, just as Leonora's had seemed to be lighted.

'It was a great shock to me,' she said. He believed her, and he understood; for her also Sir Francis and Muchanger would have been a great prize. He did not feel sorry for her; self-pity was the only kind known to him. He thought of her exactions and pretensions and said brutally, 'Then you must be very blind or very stupid. What were you paid for except to watch?'

He made towards the outer door, but she reached out and caught his sleeve.

'What now? Will you keep on the house?'

'Is that likely?'

'Why not? There are other young women.'

'You make me sick! Let go!' But her hold tightened.

'What about me?'

'Go back where you came from.'

'That is impossible. I left in what the family considered to be ungrateful haste. And I cannot go to Muchanger, or to any place where I should be likely to encounter *them*.'

'Then go to the devil!'

'I should prefer the Bishop ...' No need to pull his sleeve now; he stood rigid.

'What do you mean?'

'Clerical gentlemen often employ housekeepers. I am a good manager. I am sure that if you gave me a hearty recommendation ...'

She spoke quietly but the threat rang loud.

'You'd better come to Moyidan.'

'Not,' she said, in her old manner, 'the most *gracious* of invitations. But I accept. One thing more. It would be wise to keep a good face on things. I am disgusted with Leonora — so unfair to you! But we must appear to be on good terms until she is married. Then, if you wish, I will stay and dispose of everything; getting the best price I can.'

'Do that,' he said, and let himself out into the night.

Riding home he had time to think. First of his loss. But he was a man of reason, rather than of emotions; he had loved the false little bitch so far as he was capable of loving anyone, yet he was not heart-broken. Affronted, disgusted, robbed, not broken, or bereft. That was proved by the fact that soon his thoughts centred upon what she had said when he had made her that rash offer of marriage.

'Already there is talk in the town — of money raised by dubious means . . .' Richard did not believe it. The only person who could have the faintest glimmer of knowledge about what he had been up to in the way of raising money 'by dubious means' was that false friend, that Judas, Francis Lassiter who had once, during a particularly tricky piece of juggling, helped, to the extent of writing his name which had all the solidity of Muchanger behind it. And that only for a temporary loan, a bridging operation.

What Leonora knew, Francis had told her; probably using it as an argument; *The time will soon come when Richard will not be able to keep you*. Yes, that would explain much. And not an entirely displeasing thought to wounded vanity.

In reasoning thus, Richard deceived himself. The rumours stemmed from other sources.

Three weeks to the wedding; a fortnight to clear the house and by the time Mistress Neville arrived at Moyidan, she had a perfect excuse for the best prices obtainable being so very low. The sweating sickness had struck Baildon and with the uncertainty of life being thus thrust under their noses people lost interest in acquiring material things.

A life containing many vicissitudes had made her resilient and she had largely recovered from disappointment. She had a home — and she would see to it that it was a comfortable one; she had clothes, beautiful clothes, enough to serve her for the rest of her days. She had her trinkets and she had money. She had saved on the housekeeping bills while appearing to provide lavishly, and on everything she had bought in the early days or sold at the end she had made profit. So she arrived in a cheerful mood which survived even the discovery that she had been relegated to what was known as 'the other side' and would take her meals with the idiots, the tutor and the boy. She'd soon alter that, when she felt more energetic. The fact that she was here at all proved that Richard feared her. But she did not feel disposed to exert herself immediately; there had been the shock, the pre-wedding strain, and then all those bargains to be driven. She needed rest.

On the third day she knew that with all the other things she had brought to Moyidan was the sweating sickness.

This was slightly — not much — less feared than the plague and offered more chance of recovery with careful nursing. But fear made people keep their distance. A devoted spouse, relative or friend could mean the difference between life and death. Also in crowded hovels or tenements where many people lived closely together and contagion was unavoidable, a sufferer could expect attention. Mistress Neville lay alone. Nobody loved her; nobody went near her. She died.

Margaret was more fortunate, and should have recovered. Her husband never left the bedside except on the most urgent errands, and to fetch food and water which nervous servants placed at some distance from the sickroom door. He sat by the bed, holding her hand. When the sweating from which the disease took its name soaked the blankets, he wrapped her in fresh ones. When she was in pain he held her, smoothing back the damp hair and saying, 'Better soon.' But Margaret had never been strong — though she had survived the plague — and she died, too.

There were no other cases, though Master Jankyn was suspicious of himself. He had always been subject to terrible headaches which began with spots before the eyes, moving spots, travelling slowly from left — the side where the worst headache was, to the right. A headache began on the day of Margaret's funeral; it lasted the usual two days; the pain vanished and his appetite returned, but the spots remained. It made reading — his one pleasure — difficult and he was far much too concerned with himself and his affliction to notice, or care that the bereaved husband was eating nothing. Dick noticed and had a characteristic thought — all the more for me.

Moyidan Richard couldn't sleep, either. Any bed was abhorrent to him now; he spent his nights stretched on the cold stone under which his beloved lay; and his days in a futile search for flowers. Margaret had loved flowers.

He outlived her by eight days. Dick was heir to Moyidan.

CHAPTER TWENTY-SEVEN

The invitation to go to the Bishop's Palace at Bywater, to dine and sup and spend the night was somewhat sudden, but quite understandable — and definitely flattering. A Papal Legate, the note explained had just landed at Bywater, after a terrible journey and the Bishop wished to entertain him suitably.

So much, Richard thought, riding out on a frigid February morning, for the Bishop of Winchester's warning that in Suffolk he would find himself relegated to the company of unlettered men.

For some time now His Grace of Bywater and Sir Richard of Moyidan, had, in private, been on Christian name terms while sedulously observing formality in public; the conventional modes of address did nothing to detract from the good fellowship of the occasion. The Papal Legate whose English was adequate, but somewhat inflexible, gladly relapsed into Latin, the language which more than any other lent itself to the witty aside. There was a good deal of merriment and in the morning, the Papal Legate, about to mount his horse to continue his journey to London, where he faced an errand which to put it most mildly, would be difficult, said he was glad that his ship had been blown off course and obliged to put in at Bywater. He only hoped that everywhere in England he would meet such a welcome and such good company.

'Sir Richard,' John Faulkner, Bishop of Bywater said, when the little cavalcade had set off, 'There is a matter I wish to discuss with you.'

He led the way, not back to the comfortable, luxurious place which he had made out of old Bishop William's dismal place, but along a passage to some part of the building which Richard had never seen before; the series of rather bleak rooms where business was done; men making lists, men doing sums; the backwater to which Richard had once thought himself doomed for life. In the farthest room, comfortably but austerely furnished, the Bishop seated himself behind a wide table on which papers and parchments lay in neat piles. He had shed all his geniality and was no longer the hunting, drinking and feasting companion of the last few years. Richard sensed the change and did not, as he would otherwise have done, take a seat until invited by a gesture to do so. The Bishop pulled one of the small piles towards him and said,

'I have received a letter from a man who calls himself a lawyer. His name is Turnbull. Is he known to you?'

'Very slightly. He *is* a lawyer. He drew my father's will. And that of my aunt.'

'Is there any reason why he should bring unfounded allegations against you?'

'None that I know of, Your Grace.'

'Then I find myself in a most difficult position.'

Richard thought — Leonora! But the liaison had ended in November and this was February; it was not a thing about which either Sir Francis or his wife was likely to speak, and Mistress Neville was in her grave. And how was Turnbull concerned?

'Perhaps you would care to examine these.' The Bishop handed over three papers. Two of them represented Master Turnbull's unpaid work for two years — his hobby. The other was a covering letter, couched in the most humble and respectful terms. Master Turnbull begged permission to draw His Grace's attention to certain irregularities which had come to his notice regarding the administration of the Manor of Moyidan. Since the perpetrator of the malpractices was a man in Holy Orders, Master Turnbull thought it fitting to refer his findings to His Grace. He enclosed a copy of the transactions which a preliminary investigation, necessarily superficial had revealed to him and begged leave to point out that the present heir to the estate was a child of tender years.

With one of those sour twists of humour which judges allowed themselves, His Grace said, 'If this is the result of his *preliminary* investigations one rather dreads to think what thorough ones would reveal.'

Taken as a whole it was damning and as he read Richard paled a little; but he did not lack courage — he was Sir Godfrey's son, Sybilla's son: he was also a trained lawyer, well versed in the art of disputation and the even subtler one of picking a case to pieces.

'He was right to say *superficial*, my lord. Much of this is superficially true, lifted out of context. Take this — "That he did waste his ward's substance upon the restoring and embellishing a derelict building to make for himself a grand dwelling." It was not a derelict building; all it needed was to be made comfortable, and that I did — for the benefit of others — eventually. And the term *ward* is completely misleading. Neither my poor dim-wit cousin, or his son was ever committed to my guardianship ... Or take this — "That on divers occasions he did commit forgery." Is it *forgery* to write your own name, Richard Tallboys, when dealing with the affairs of an idiot who never learned even to spell his own name, identical with your own?'

The Bishop listened — not without admiration. But his first casual perusal of Master Turnbull's accusations had revealed what he thought to be the real object — a challenge to the Church. Act and thus expose a scandal; do nothing and provoke one even worse. The open enemies of the Church — the Lollards, had been driven by persecution and the bad odour adhering to their followers, underground, but something remained, critical, obstinate among the middle sort of people, like this man Turnbull. Laymen with some education, a danger to everybody.

Richard Tallboys was clever; but John Faulkner, Bishop of Bywater was clever too and presently he said, almost in his old, amiable way, 'Very well, Richard, we need not chase every word. But this I must ask. Was the buying of a house in Baildon, with money raised by a mortgage on Moyidan, a profitable investment?'

'No. At least, not yet. It could prove to be.'

'It is in your name?'

'Yes. One of my worse ventures. In fact an act of charity. To put a roof over the heads of two women. One is now married to Sir Francis Lassiter of Muchanger; the other, the older, is dead. The house is now for sale.'

'In your name? What else is indisputably your property?'

'The piece of outlying land, difficult of access, a remote sheep-run, willed to me by my aunt in a return for a promise to care for them all. Which I have done. And intend to do. This homespun lawyer, counting pence, bandying words ...'

'How old is the boy?'

'Dick? Nine. Nine next month. And despite whatever Turnbull may have to say about my management, by the time he is of age, he will have much to thank me for.'

'No, my dear fellow. Not you. The Church. This is what we must do. And if this Master Turnbull had no malice towards you, only against the Church, this will make him gnash his teeth. Listen ...'

Despite the more friendly manner it was plain that the

Bishop was sitting in judgment and had indeed reached his verdict before even discussing the matter; his plan was already so well-thought out. The last bit of hope and confidence drained out of Richard as he listened. The man whom he had regarded as friend bore heavily on the charges over which he himself had chosen to skip lightly — the word 'embezzlement' was several times repeated. 'There may be some more esoteric term for it. There may be mitigating circumstances. And of explanation, I am sure, no lack. But to the ordinary man it is embezzlement. You appear to have milked this estate for purposes of your own.'

'It may seem so, Your Grace, but I assure you that given time ...'

'The *one* thing we cannot afford. All this reflects upon Holy Church and requires swift action.'

Having outlined his plan which would leave Richard penniless, and almost demolished his self-esteem — not quite, Richard was still too proud to ask mercy, His Grace relented. He remembered the hours he had spent in Richard's company, the splendid hospitality he had received from him. Richard might retain his Thoroughgood horse, one servant and a horse for him; he could choose a bed with all its appurtenances, so that wherever he lodged he would sleep snug, a little silver to uphold his prestige ... Richard, reduced as he was, could not resist a quip.

'That is generous, my lord. All, except the servant, saleable or pawnable!'

'It will not come to that. I have a very good friend who holds high office in the Treasury. I shall commend you to him in the warmest possible terms.' He allowed himself to smile. 'With your aptitude for financial juggling, who knows, you may end as Chancellor.'

'Is this a sudden decision?' Henry asked.

'Not really. I soon reached the conclusion that I had sacrificed my career for very little substance. Aunt Emma's property was so near worthless. On the other hand I could not very well ask the Church to take charge of Richard and Margaret without the danger of exposing their lunacy. So I was tied ...'

'And the boy? Where does he go?'

'Oh, he stays at Moyidan, with his tutor. The Bishop proposes to use the Castle quite often and will keep some staff there. Dick will hardly notice the difference. Except when there are a few monks about.'

'Monks?' Richard explained.

Actually it was one of the Bishop's more cunning touches. In the present climate of opinion, with so much criticism of the Church about, especially in East Anglia, it might not look *completely* well for Moyidan to be used merely as His Grace's country residence; so he had visited the Abbot of Baildon and offered some rooms to be set aside for the use of monks who had been sick and needed convalescence in clean country air, or for ones who were to be rusticated for some offence. And that, when Master Turnbull learned of it would make him gnash his teeth even more, for the ordinary layman's resentment he bore secular Church was as nothing to the resentment he bore towards the religious houses, regarded as being full of fat, idle, lecherous fellows.

Having explained about monks Richard proceeded to the real reason for his visit.

'I want you to store some stuff for me, Henry. A few things at Moyidan are mine. The Commissioners will arrive any day now, noting down every salt spoon. I should not care to have confusion; once anything of mine was entered on their lists, I should never get it off again.'

Unsuspecting, Henry said, 'Send it along. It can go in the barn.'

Richard's few things proved to be almost a wagonful of bales, wrapped in canvas, neatly corded. The man who drove the wagon was one whom Richard had called from Winchester and now chose to take with him to London, a most welcome move.

'Sir Richard said, sir, not to unload. He'll be bringing a few personal things later.' The man trudged back to Moyidan and the wagon, snug under a piece of sailcloth, stood in the yard.

It was not stealing as Richard saw it. *Nobody* was being robbed. And although he had not actually paid out of his own pocket for these wall hangings, bed hangings and other luxurious bits and pieces, he had used his taste and judgment in choosing them, and spent valuable time in acquiring them. He should — in a just world — have enjoyed them for many years; until Dick reached his majority. His plans had been wrecked — but most wrecks washed up a bit of salvage.

Some days later Richard on his Thoroughgood horse, the servant on the ordinary one, arrived, bringing smaller bales. They were tucked under the sailcloth. The horse which had drawn the wagon and which in the interval had stood in the stable, eating its head off, was hitched between the shafts, the horse the servant rode was tied to the wagon tail, and Richard once again, moved out of Henry's life. As John had done. As Robert had done.

In explaining the new arrangement Richard had said that Dick would hardly notice the difference. That was untrue. Fond of his fare to the point of being actually greedy, Dick soon noticed that his food, hitherto plain but plentiful was now becoming meagre. While Uncle Richard had been in control, entertaining, living in style, there had often been oddments, things left over, eagerly consumed. None of that now. Somebody in the Bishop's office had reckoned with parsimonious exactitude what was needed to keep a boy, an inactive man and three servants. The clever cook had been taken into the Bishop's household, the one who had hitherto cooked for this side of the house had found another post, a new man ruled the kitchen and helped with the cleaning of the house as well, for although the Bishop intended to use Moyidan chiefly as a summer residence, and a place from which to hunt in autumn, dust and cobwebs must not be allowed to gather, nor beds allowed to get damp. When, in the early days of the new regime, Master Jankyn who also liked his food, ventured a complaint, Wat answered him curtly and said it was impossible to do two jobs with only one pair of hands. Since Master Jankyn did not carry the complaint further, grumbling to one of the Bishop's men that food was bad and Wat was rude, the tutor ceased to count.

Master Jankyn in fact dare not call much attention to himself. The spots before his eyes — particularly the left one — grew worse rather than better, and rubbing his eyes, which he did constantly, though knowing the uselessness of it, had inflamed the lids. He was so conscious of his affliction that he felt it might be noticeable to everyone and who wanted to employ a tutor with poor sight? So whenever the commissionary men came — bright young clerks, especially chosen because they had country backgrounds — Master Jankyn was careful to stay out of their way, engrossed in reading or writing, with the spots dancing between him and the page.

Dick's friend Jacky had been kept on but he no longer spent his whole time in the stable; he worked in the garden, too. The third servant whose name was Joseph acted as yardman, helped in the house, helped in the garden, and should by all ordinary standards have occupied the lowest place in the hierarchy of the kitchen. But he was soon in the ascendant. He had a vile temper, a foul tongue, a vast amount of general knowledge and as much cunning as Wat and Jacky put together.

Moyidan was being used as a larder for Bywater. 'Robbing you right and left my boy,' Joseph told Dick. 'And nothing you can do about it. A minor can't go to law on his own account; only through his parent or guardian and the bloody Bish ain't going to take hisself to court is he?'

When summer came with its gifts, green peas, asparagus, strawberries, raspberries, the Bishop came too, with the clever cook, serving men and a horde of guests.

Dick was introduced — not without some ceremony which should have elated but actually humiliated him. He was growing rapidly now and his clothes no longer fitted well. In addition to being greedy, he was very vain. Sleeves that now did not reach his wristbones made his hands look clumsy; trunk-hose too tight made a bow dangerous exercise. But there he was, heir to Moyidan, a well-grown, well-fed boy.

'Come and gone like a lot of locusts,' Joseph said when this invasion was over. Jacky and Wat and Dick, who now spent more and more time with the servants — he had even managed to ingratiate himself with Joseph — didn't know exactly what locusts were. Joseph explained. Devourers who passed over and left nothing behind. 'Only these is worse because they don't really *go*. I reckon the regular buggers know every bloody fowl by name.' They almost did; the fat capon with the black tail was missed when Joseph had wrung its neck, Wat had cooked it, and the three servants and Dick had enjoyed a secret feast.

Autumn came and the 'grease season' when the deer were sleek and fat. The Bishop and his friends came for hunting and momentarily everybody ate well though Joseph was critical. 'Ignorant sods,' he said. 'Killed a couple of does that could have bred in the spring! This go on, Dick boy and you'll end up in a poor way. Keep taking out of the well and put nothing in and one day there's nowt to *take*.'

Weather grew cooler and appetites sharpened. One day a sow farrowed and produced four piglets. Joseph saw his chance. He removed one, wrapped it warmly and placed it under his bed. The locusts were always gone by nightfall, so every evening this special little pig was carried out to the sty, his siblings were pulled away and he took his fill. Thus privileged he soon grew fat.

'Piglets 3,' the locusts wrote at their next visit. They would make a dish for Christmas; each roasted whole, restored by the clever cook's art to semblance of life, and holding a red apple in its mouth.

Handicapped as he was, Master Jankyn still adhered to the outer forms of professional conduct. 'Show me your exercise before we sup.' A page of scribble or a page of figures, with the moving spots intervening. After supper, he intended to read, his left hand cupped over his left eye, until the spots, as though aware of this ruse, began to invade the right. He really could not waste his eyesight by closely scrutinising what this unpromising pupil had to show. 'It is not well done. Repeat the exercise tomorrow.' Dick now had several pages, all of which had been submitted several times and would be again, since his master either couldn't see, or had ceased to care.

Supper was thin, onion-flavoured broth and dark bread. The fire was growing low and Master Jankyn knew without looking that the wood which should be piled on the hearth would not be there.

'When you go to the kitchen . . .' not 'if' for Dick spent every evening in the kitchen where the company was more to his taste and the fire good, 'tell Wat I need logs.' The likelihood of their coming was remote and as a precaution Master Jankyn had brought down a blanket from his bed. Wrapped in it he covered his left eye and read until the spots transferred themselves. His right eye often benefited from a short rest so he closed both his eyes and waited, musing as he often did over the injustice of a world where a man of considerable learning and honest reputation should be reduced to such a pass. He was not aware of falling asleep, but he must have done because he dreamed. A beautiful dream of fresh roast pork; he could taste it and smell it. And when he was awake, he could still smell it, the most appetising scent in the world. After a minute he realised that he had not been asleep and dreaming. The scent was real and it was coming from the kitchen. He took up his candle and went into the little lobby which separated the schoolroom from the kitchen, and off which the stairs serving this part of the house led. Also in the lobby was the door to the parlour where the idiots had lived.

He had never entered the kitchen, regarding it as beneath his dignity to do so: blinking and peering he stepped in now. A different world, very bright; there was a huge fire and three candles. Before the fire a sucking pig turned slowly on the spit. Fat and juices fell into a dripping pan set to catch them.

Dick and the three servants sat on stools near the fireside end of the table, and they were drinking ale. The ale allowance at Moyidan had lately been as meagre as everything else, but for some days — ever since the date of the piglet's death had been decided, the men had saved theirs — and Dick's and Master Jankyn's. The first time ale had failed to appear on the school-room table Master Jankyn said, 'You have forgotten the ale, Wat,' and Wat had replied, 'There ain't none.' Now there were two large jugs.

The tutor's entrance was not immediately noticed.

Wat said, 'Wind it up, bor.'

Dick rose and wound up the spit which worked on a wheel and a weighted string.

'Time thass run out, he'll be done,' Jacky said.

'Better drink up then! Come fill the cup. Death and damnation to all locusts and all bloody bishes.'

'If they could on'y see us now!'

'Sod all. Thass the boy's pig, reared on his place,' Joseph said. 'He had his rights he'd hev sucking pig whenever he fancied.'

'Thass right,' the others agreed.

'And if the bloody bish walked in this minute I'd tell him so to his face.' As Joseph said that he looked towards the inner door — the only one by which anybody was likely to walk in. 'Look who's here! What d'you want?'

'I have come to join you.'

'The devil you hev! We'd wanted you, we'd hev arst you. Sling your hook,' Wat said.

Joseph then spoke in such a low voice that Master Jankyn could not catch the words. Joseph was the quickest witted of them all — he had planned this affair — and there was reason in what he said — if the tutor shared the feast he couldn't very well report it. On the other hand his company was not welcome.

Dick had the last word. As roughly and disrespectfully as the others, he said, 'You can hev some if you promise not to tell. *And to ask about my shoes.*'

Short sleeves and tight hose were not actually painful, outgrown shoes cramped the toes. Dick had himself tried to draw the attention of the Bishop's men to his need for new shoes, but they had pushed him aside. It was not their business. Dick had then urged Master Jankyn to write to the Bishop, but he had not yet done so.

Swallowing his dignity and his pride, Master Jankyn said, 'I promise,' advanced to the table and pulled up a stool, stared hungrily at the pig, and thirstily at the ale jug. Jacky, the best natured of the four, reached for a mug and filled it.

Wat rose, plunged a knife into the carcase and hit bone.

'Thass done,' he said.

Here there were no niceties of serving. The sizzling meat was lowered into the pan and the pan set on the table and they set about the meat with their knives. They had bread which from time to time they dipped into the greasy gravy.

At first there was little talk; then, when the edge of appetite blunted, there was a good deal and a lot of laughter. Much of the talk and many of the jokes — he supposed they must be jokes to rouse such merriment — were beyond the tutor's comprehension. He was not a Suffolk man and, keeping himself to himself, had never learned the dialect. Also they all talked with their mouths full and grew tipsier as the second jug went round. Master Jankyn had never before eaten in such uncivilised company; and he had never enjoyed a meal more.

Throughout its course he had only one uncomfortable thought and that provoked by the reflection that his pupil was completely indistinguishable from the servants. Master Jankyn had resigned himself to the fact that Dick would always be a poor scholar and do him little credit so far as learning was concerned; but he *had* insisted upon a certain standard of manners, and of speech ... He blamed himself for allowing the boy to consort so much with servants, but he had been glad to be rid of his company — who could read with a boy fidgeting about? Tomorrow he would deal with this problem — how exactly he did not know, but sufficient unto the day was the evil thereof. Food and ale had made him comfortably soporific. It was time for bed. The travelling spots had increased in size, speed and scope. Master Jankyn rubbed both eyes furiously.

'I think I will retire now.'

They had all except himself who had come late to the drinking and Dick — given small portions of ale because he was young — reached that stage of tipsiness where good humour tipped over to bad. Left alone they would probably have squabbled among themselves over some triviality, a drunken quarrel, easily patched up. As it was here was the alien, the one who did not belong; a ready target, saying 'retire' when ordinary people said 'go to bed'. And by merely mentioning time reminding them that the feast was over.

'You ain't emptied your mug,' Wat said. 'Wasting good ale! Come on, down with it!'

He lifted the mug and held it to Master Jankyn's mouth, forcing the rim between his lips.

It was a mistake, the tutor realised, to have come. He had lowered himself, because he was meat hungry. But he had courage of a sort and gulped down the unwanted draught, lest it should spill on his clothes.

Dick, seeing his master thus reduced said, 'And don't forget what you promised, *sir*!'

'I will write to His Grace at the first opportunity.'

Dick at least knew that asking and writing could mean the same thing. The others did not.

'There you are,' Wat said, 'breaking his word as soon as he got a bellyful!'

They all entertained the illiterate man's distrust of the literate man.

'Break one promise, break both,' Jacky said. 'Poor little bastard with no shoes to his feet!'

It was the one word which sent Dick's temper flaring.

'Don't you call me bastard or I'll crack your skull.'

'Let's see you do it, bastard yourself!' They fell into a grapple, relatively harmless, though both had bruises and hacked shins next day. Wat looked at the almost but not quite stripped skeleton of the little pig, bedded in congealed fat — pork dripping best of all, frilled round the edges and with the gravy set solid beneath it, and thought that he must think of a hiding place for it, because the locusts did not come at regular times. They were tricky and could well be here tomorrow.

The coolest if not the most sober mind in the kitchen was Joseph's. He knew that the pig had been stolen, so to speak; and what Jacky had said about broken promises had meaning. They could be accused.

He said, 'This way, Master. I'll light your way.'

What with the noise and the spots Master Jankyn was grateful for the small civility and the guidance. Joseph opened the door which gave upon the moat, the door through which kitchen refuse was thrown. It took only a slight push; the bit of stone pavement between house and water was here very narrow. Master Jankyn went to his death surrounded by such bits of the little pig as Wat had judged to be uneatable.

Nobody missed Master Jankyn. Except for seeing that it had its allotted ration of food the schoolroom was no concern of the Bishop's men and the tutor had always avoided them. Nobody had pangs of conscience or sought to apportion blame; they'd all been a bit merry and there'd been an accident. Dick was glad to have done with lessons and moved in with the servants happy about everything except his shoes. When he mentioned them Wat said, 'Give 'em here. I know a way out of that!' He took a sharp knife and cut away the upper at the toe part of the shoe, leaving the sole like a platform upon which Dick's toes lay comfortably.

After some days Master Jankyn's body, swollen and buoyant with gases rose to the surface. It was an unpleasant sight, but no one who saw it was squeamish. Wat suggested hauling the corpse out, weighting it well with stones and returning it to the water. But Jacky remembered the dredging of the moat in the hunt for Robert. 'Do we do that and he was ever found there'd be trouble. Better tell the priest and make out it was accident.'

'He couldn't see very well,' Dick said, and told about the same exercises being handed in again and again.

Father Thomas remembered how of late Master Jankyn had always come to the altar, looking as though he had been crying; he made no demur about burial. Nor did he feel under any obligation to report the sad accident. Since Moyidan had been taken over by the Church Father Thomas had carefully avoided anything that might give the impression that he was interfering. For that reason he ignored Dick's request that *he* should write to the Bishop concerning shoes. That would be interfering indeed!

After Christmas the cold weather came and Dick's unprotected toes developed chilblains. He thought Wat and Joseph, even Jacky very lacking in sympathy; they had not spent their early years as pampered little boys. Everybody had chilblains some time or another; they all knew of an infallible cure — a good thrashing with nettles — but not one of them had actually tried it, and Dick did not feel disposed to. *Some* people, they reminded him, went barefoot all the year round. If he wanted new shoes he should ask the locusts when next they came.

'But I did! And nothing happened.'

'Try again, bor.'

He had a feeling of being let down, of seeing, for the first time, something false in their friendliness. In genial moments they were happy enough to point out that all Moyidan was his, that he was being cheated, done out of his rights, poor little bastard, poor little sod. But when he suggested that on the locusts' next visit they should all line up with him and back his request ... 'They took no notice of me, maybe because I am young. They brushed me aside; but they couldn't brush four ...' Joseph said, 'Use your wits. We did that the first thing they'd ask is where's that teacher man and afore you could blink, you'd hev another. Maybe worse.'

It was plain to Dick that if he were ever going to be properly clothed again, he must depend upon himself.

The locusts, although similar in appearance and behaviour, were not always the same and the pair whom Dick accosted were not the ones to whom he had entrusted his former, and unanswered plea. They were surprised to find themselves confronted by a raw-boned peasant boy, clad in garments, far too small for him, obviously handed down to him by some charitable person. His manner surprised them, too; it accorded so ill with his appearance. Arrogant?

'I want you to carry a message from me, to the Bishop. I sent one before but it was never delivered. I am in great need of clothes, particularly shoes. Tell him that as soon as you get back.'

How ignorant he was. They saw their master but rarely, and then only from a distance. Whatever they collected from Moyidan was turned over to the head of the kitchen staff, their meticulous accounts went to some secretary. The world was full of boys who needed clothing; this one must be mad!

No answer. No clothing. No shoes. Plainly verbal messages were ignored. Faint and far away, from the grave, came Master Jankyn's voice. 'You must learn to write, boy. The word spoken lasts as long as the breath that bore it. The written word lasts as long as the paper or parchment.'

The schoolroom was deserted now. No one had kindled a fire on its hearth or dusted the table. But it was not disused. In a corner, snug in straw lay another purloined piglet. Joseph did not mind harbouring one under his bed in the earliest days of its life, but little pigs growing stronger, did as he said, 'tend to root about a bit'. Also a little pig, fattening in a satisfactory way grew heavier to haul upstairs and downstairs. So the schoolroom was the obvious place.

The little pig, associating the opening of the door with the prospect of feeding, ran to welcome Dick with squeals. He silenced it with a kick.

The ink bottle, left unstopped had either dried out or frozen and Dick spat into it and stirred vigorously, and with the uneven mixture thus produced he wrote, wishing, *wishing* that he had paid more attention. Something of what had apparently drifted unobserved, because uncared for over his head, came to help now.

My Lawd Bishop of Bywater, I have sent messages by yor servats but they were not headed i nead noo close shoose most. My Toes is frosen this is not rite or fare if yoo new wot yor servats wil not tel yoo yoo wood ackt.

On the whole, looking it over, he was not ill-pleased with his effort. It said what he needed to say. He signed it with his proper name, scorning the diminutive, for it was all his now. And that he could write well. Richard Tallboys. Master Jankyn had once made him write it twenty times. With a little less skill, but no decline of confidence, he added — 'of moidan'.

Nothing came of this great effort.

CHAPTER TWENTY-EIGHT

By the time he was three little Godfrey Tallboys was suffering the boredom of the overfussed, over-protected child. He was a strong, active boy, full of curiosity and he must never be for more than a minute out of Mumma's sight. If he played in the yard it must be within view of the kitchen door. He mustn't go near the sty — pigs might bite him; he was forbidden to go into the stable — horses kicked; there was a cat in the barn, but he was not allowed to play with it — cats scratched and had fleas. If he got a speck of mud on his hands or his clothes he was immediately washed and changed.

He had two outings. Griselda went often to church, holding his hand all the way; in church he must be very quiet. He preferred the stick-gathering errands to the edge of the wood, where with both hands busy, Griselda could not hold him; but even there she never took her eye off him. 'Don't wander away, dearie.' 'Show me what you have in your hand.'

On the fringe of his life were other people who because they came and went, occupying a different world most of the time, were interesting. There was Farder who gave him rides on his knee, with pretend falls that made him squeal with delight and say, 'More!' or held him under the arms and swung him round until he was pleasantly dizzy. Such games almost always ended with 'Don't'. 'Don't, you make him so wild that there's no doing anything with him.'

There was somebody called Janna who must be watched from a distance. Godfrey was not allowed to go near her, for some reason that he could not understand; she seemed unlikely to bite or kick or scratch. Once, when she sat, as she often did, very quietly, making fascinating patterns with a piece of string between her fingers, he went close to watch. Mumma said, in a voice that threatened another wash — though he had just had one, 'Come here, Godfrey.' Mumma then said to Janna, 'It's a pity you can't find something more useful to do than playing Cat's Cradle.' Farder said, 'For God's sake. She's done a full day's work today.'

Perhaps Farder was interested in what could be done with ten fingers and a piece of string, for he said he'd like to see how it was done. Janna went and stood on one side of Farder and gave directions. Godfrey went to the other, but Farder was soon in a tangle, at which they both laughed, and Godfrey joined in. 'Now me! Now me!' His tangle was even worse, and they all laughed again. Mumma did not even smile. She had on what her son called her sewing face.

That expression was the outcome of sharp observation.

Nowadays when Griselda sewed she scowled and pressed her lips together. At no time was her poverty more sharply brought home to her than when she was trying to make certain that Godfrey was as well clad as any little boy for miles around — and with nothing to do it on. When he was a baby he would wear clothes which Robert and Joanna had worn, shrunken and stained as they were. By the time they were the size Godfrey now was, they had begun to *wear* their clothes, so that mended, patched and outgrown, they had been not discarded, but put to other uses; kitchen clothes, cleaning cloths.

And despite all the hard work, a profitable year in yard and in field, Henry still had no money to spare for non-essentials; so Griselda cut up and worked angrily upon what remained of Sybilla's clothes. Even the dove-grey silk.

Interest in her own appearance had ceased with Tom's death. Griselda no longer bothered to do her hair in a becoming style. She had neither the impetus nor the time to spare. It was washed — her standard of cleanliness had not lowered — straightly combed back and done in a little tight knob at the nape of her neck. She never even noticed that its colour was fading from the bright colour of new straw to that of old straw and that the little light knob was gradually, but steadily becoming smaller.

One thing which made her angry with Henry was his stupid

behaviour over what he called Robert's money. It was still being meticulously, conscientiously put away.

'But he's dead,' Griselda said.

'Of that we have had no proof. Not a shred.' So every lamb dropped by an ochre-marked ewe was promptly marked with ochre. Fleeces or the sale of an animal 'on the hoof' as the slaughterhouse was called, religiously reckoned.

Joanna who was well aware that although the money being set aside for Robert was not very much, it could make all the difference, one day said, 'Henry, I am sure that Robert *is* dead.'

'How could you know, sweeting?'

'Because ... because while he was alive I always knew what was happening to him. Now there is nothing.'

It was not the kind of statement that Henry was prepared to regard as evidence.

Dick's letter brought no response because it had never reached His grace of Bywater who employed men to sift the important from the unimportant, and who were in any case unlikely to pass on a complaint about 'yor servats'. By February Dick was desperate and bethought himself of his Uncle Henry. Somebody must do something!

With Tom dead, despite all the well-wishing, and Henry just as overworked and worried, and the evil-doers, Richard particularly, seeming to flourish, Joanna had abandoned dabbling in spells, deciding that they were what Tom had always said — just old tales. However, when Dick arrived one bleak February morning, neither he nor his pony looked quite as they had done on their earlier visits. The pony was on the Moyidan list, but fodder as well as food was rationed there; and Jacky said, rightly, that nowadays he had more to do than groom ponies. Dick had never sufficiently adjusted himself to his new way of life to undertake the work himself, so the animal had been neglected. As for Dick ... Velvet was beautiful material for gentle wear, given rough treatment it was less resistant than homespun and Dick, despite plain and sometimes scanty feeding — interspersed by illicit feasts — had grown so enormously that his sleeves now ended just below his elbows; his feet were wrapped in sacking.

Surprised as he was by the boy's appearance, Henry was

kind as Dick had somehow expected that he would be. Griselda was horrid. 'What now? Another pauper?'

It was a difficult meal. As soon as Dick started on his tale, Henry, aware of Jem's presence said, 'We'll talk about it later, boy.' Griselda banged the pots and pans about as she always did when she was displeased and Joanna sat watching, her fingers linked to prop her chin. Outside a thin sleety rain began to fall.

Henry said, 'All right, Jem, go on with the baling. There's nothing much more to be done on such a day. Now, Dick, let's hear the whole of it.'

Joanna listened. Of the three most hateful and blameworthy people, the three who had made Robert so unhappy and had been ill-wished with the whole of her violent nature, only Richard had seemed to escape. Master Jankyn who had beaten Robert without cause had stumbled into the Moyidan moat and drowned; Dick, who had been to blame for most of those beatings was here, saying, 'Look!' and unwinding the sacking wrappings exposing his toes, with their broken, festering chilblains. Good. Oh, good!

Margaret as a person had never meant anything to Henry, but he was sensible to the fact that her son was his kin and that injustice had been done. He must take some action, what exactly he could not immediately decide. What he could do at once was something practical about these chilblains. A good soak in warm water, an application of goose grease.

Griselda had whisked Godfrey away as soon as the meal had ended; Dick looked so dirty, was likely to be lousy, far from fit to associate with her son. Henry found a bucket and from the pot on the fire tipped in hot water, then cold. 'Put your feet in there, Dick. Joanna, look in the larder and see if there's any goose grease.'

Joanna sat still, her eyes sparkling. After a perceptible pause she said, 'If I do, it's because *you* asked me to, Henry. Not for *him*! I wish his toes would rot clean away and drop off.'

Dick, whose whole tone had been whining, began to blubber.

'Cry baby!' Joanna said with infinite contempt.

'That'll do. Fetch what I want. Come on, Dick, pull yourself together. Nobody ever died of chilblains yet.'

Joanna, working as she did had enough experience of small cuts and abrasions to know that salt could sting where the skin

239

was broken, so she poured a lot of salt into the soft, viscous grease and stirred it well. The result was most gratifying. Henry privately thought that his nephew was a poor-spirited fellow, but that was no excuse for the way he had been treated.

'There you are,' he said, when he had wrapped Dick's feet in clean linen, and shod them in his own church-going shoes. 'And tomorrow I'll go down to Bywater and try to set things straight.'

The Bishop knew of Henry's existence, had indeed seen him, but always at a distance, Henry at work in the fields, the Bishop on his way to the hunt. Richard had often spoken of his brother with a mixture of affection and mockery; Henry, who had refused to go to Beauclaire, Henry, who had refused the position and the legacy which had thus come to himself; Henry, who had chosen a yokel's life, and married a servant. He made his brother sound mildly eccentric. Not enough so to be interesting.

It was a surprise to be confronted by a man of considerable dignity and presence whose manners and speech were at odds with his humble dress, and who seemed perfectly at ease in these palatial surroundings. The palace had undergone changes but to Henry it was still the place where he and Richard had romped and quarrelled and always been slightly hungry.

Henry wasted no words. His Grace listened, genuinely shocked.

'I take it that you have proof of all this, Master Tallboys?' The question was a mere formality; this was not the kind of man to concoct or exaggerate a tale.

'I only know what the boy told me, Your Grace. I have seen his clothes, and his feet. He must have been practically barefoot for months.'

'I am appalled,' the Bishop said, and began to make excuses to this fellow who followed the plough and had married a serving wench. 'Of course, I am not always here; I have in fact only just returned from an absence of some duration. I left the boy in good hands. Your brother himself appointed Master Jankyn and I thought it right to retain him. Two of my staff make regular visits to Moyidan. Why did nobody see fit to inform me — or in my absence, the chaplain whom I leave in charge?'

'That, my lord, I cannot answer. The boy says that he has sent messages, both by word and in writing.'

'Not one of which ever reached me, I assure you. I was not even informed of the tutor's death.'

'Well, you know now. The question is, what happens next?'

Smoothly the cunning, experienced mind went to work. Here, unless promptly checked was material for another scandalous story about the avarice, the callousness of the Church. Fodder for Master Turnbull and his ilk, should they ever hear a whisper of it. Another tutor — who might go mad or deaf; an unreliable breed, all failed men. Keeping the house serviced for the benefit of a boy and his master? Or the grand gesture, which would shed the responsibility and silence all criticism?

'I often think a little wine lubricates difficult discussions, Master Tallboys. You will take a cup?'

'I thank you,' Henry said, oblivious to the honour being done him.

Over the wine, which came promptly, the Bishop said,
'You are the boy's natural uncle?'

'Yes. His mother was my sister.'

'Would you be prepared to take charge of him?'

That needed thinking over. Although he had never loved Griselda, and now occasionally hated her, Henry was still considerate. Establish Dick and a tutor and that would add to Griselda's burden; bring in a woman to help and there would be conflict; Griselda had quarrelled with Ursula, with Leonora and towards Joanna her hostility was rock hard.

'Only on my own terms,' this extraordinary fellow said, giving His Grace a straight look from eyes very blue and candid.

'And they are?'

'No nonsense. He said he *wrote* you a letter. If he could do that — more, I admit, than I could do myself, he has enough of learning. On the other hand, when he comes into his inheritance, some sound practical knowledge might be to his good. I *know* that. I learn as I go. When I employed a shepherd I considered him an idle fellow. Since I have had charge of a flock — smaller — I know otherwise.'

'You would be willing to take and train him?'

'I could at least see that he was fed, and had shoes on his feet.'

That stung and the Bishop said, 'Master Tallboys, there is one aspect of this whole affair which you do not know about. I admit that there has been negligence. But I will take you into my confidence and tell you *why* Moyidan has been so meagrely run . . .'

He spoke — and it was for the first time openly, for he was a man who preferred not to let his left hand know what the right was doing — about Richard's depredations; about how long it would take for Moyidan to recuperate. 'That bit of outlying land, the one thing that was definitely his own was virtually unsaleable to any outsider; there is no access, except through Moyidan. I managed, since the whole manor was being taken over into a kind of guardianship, to buy and incorporate it. That and the house in Baildon which he had brought in his own name, but with money illicitly raised from mortgages on Moyidan, were all that Sir Richard owned, even in the most tenuous way . . . In a most difficult situation I did the best I could. You understand? I *liked* your brother.'

'So did I,' Henry said; shocked in his turn by these unexpected revelations. 'We never spent an hour together without quarrelling. But I liked him. I apologise for the mess he left. I thank you for dealing with it so — discreetly.' Had the Bishop not been so discreet Henry knew that he himself would have been committed, pledging Knight's Acre and the hard-won fields in order to save the Tallboys name.

'Naturally,' the Bishop said, 'there would be an allowance. For clothes and keep.'

'Clothes, yes, my Lord. He'll earn his keep.'

It was not the up-turn in fortune which Dick had expected as soon as attention was drawn to his plight. True he now had clothes and sound footwear but he had to *work*. Uncle Henry was kind enough until he saw signs of slackness or carelessness, then he could be nasty. Aunt Griselda was nasty all the time and Joanna was horrid. Dick made overtures. 'You can have a ride on my pony if you like.'

'I wouldn't ride your pony if I was walking all the way from Baildon in the rain!'

'Why not?'

'The way you treated Robert!'

'Me? I never did nothing to Robert.'

'You saw to it that that man did. I hate the sight of you. I don't want to talk to you.'

The servants at Moyidan had failed him over the appeal for new shoes, but they had been company and had given lip-service at least to his ownership of Moyidan. Here he had no company and of his inheritance no mention was ever made. He missed even those secret feasts. The food here was bad. The only fowls ever seen on this table were old hens, past laying, that had to be boiled to tastelessness before they could be eaten. Birds fit for roasting, sucking pigs, even eggs were destined for market. Godfrey occasionally had little treats; Godfrey was indeed treated much as Dick had been in Umma's day.

Ever since his grandmother's death Dick had gravitated towards servants and felt at home in their company but here even Jem was unfriendly, turning a deaf ear to Dick's blunt hints that he might ask him home to supper with him.

Nor was this new, bleak way of life, free as it might have been expected to be, of correction concerning speech and manners. Henry could be as strict as Master Jankyn, often saying to Dick what had been said to him — it was just as easy to say *my* as *moy*, *old* as *owd*. Griselda was equally strict about table manners and washing. 'Don't think,' she said once, 'that you are coming to church with those dirty ears. What would people behind us think? If you can't wash yourself I'll do them for you.' A positive threat of discomfort.

Dick was far from being as miserable as Robert had been at Moyidan but he was miserable enough until he discovered the significance of those days when Uncle Henry and Joanna came down in the morning more tidily clad than usual and then drove off in the wagon.

It was now April, and he had been at Knight's Acre for almost two months and he had seen it happen twice. On the third time he asked,

'Where're you off to?'

'Market,' Henry said. Since he did not regard going to market as an outing it did not occur to him to ask Dick to accompany them. Joanna had been going ever since she was banned from the house.

'Can I come?'

Joanna said, 'No!' in a ferocious tone.

'Not in the wagon,' Henry said, 'we've a full load. But you could ride your pony. Go and make yourself tidy.'

Dick scampered off to don the better of the two outfits which the tailor at Nettleton had made for him — allowing for growth. Joanna said bleakly, 'Now my day is ruined. Completely and absolutely *ruined*.'

'You're carrying this a bit far, honey. Maybe he was a bit cruel and thoughtless, boys often are. But he's young and pretty stupid.'

'You don't know half of what Robert told me *before he died*.'

It shot out in anger. For a second her anger was transferred to herself and she used in her mind all the words that were forbidden.

'What did you say?' Henry asked.

She had made an instant recovery. 'I told you that I *knew* Robert was dead, didn't I? I should have said what Robert told me the last time I saw him . . . Dick had been vile. And if *he* is coming to our booth today, I'd sooner stay here and work with Jem.'

'Don't be so *silly*,' Henry said. 'Who'd take the eggs to the inn? or buy the red flannel?' Griselda had been insistent upon red flannel. Red guarded against small-pox.*

'Is he coming to our booth?'

'No. I'll give him a farthing and tell him to spend it elsewhere. Come on, get in.'

'You promise?'

'I promise, sweeting.'

He was unaware that he had slipped into the habit of using towards Joanna, terms which were the right of the sweetheart or the wife. Griselda had not at first invited, or latterly deserved any terms of affection, and almost every day, by some show of willingness, or hardihood, or a glint of humour, the child endeared herself to him. He sometimes worried about her future and wished he could do more for her. His youthful dreams of prosperity were receding now. This year had begun badly with the worst lambing season he had yet known and towards the end of March there had been winds so fierce that in places the topsoil, with wheat and barley grains already rooted and sprouting, had been whisked away.

The drive into Baildon, with nothing to do but sit and ride,

* An old superstition, now partly justified by modern science.

gave them an opportunity for talk. Often Joanna regaled Henry with tales — either those she had heard from Tom or ones she had made up and in return Henry raked his memory for anecdotes told him by Walter or things he remembered from his own past. She loved to hear about Beauclaire and all its glories and his Aunt Alyson who was so beautiful. He found that he remembered more than he realised. He spoke without sentiment, however, and when he said, 'It's ruined now. The war put an end to it,' the regret in his voice was for Joanna, not for the place; had Beauclaire still existed he would, by hook or by crook have persuaded his Aunt Alyson to take Joanna into her household.

When they reached the market Henry tied his horse to the church railings and indicated an empty space near by for Dick's pony.

'Don't forget what you promised,' Joanna said.

Henry took out the farthing. 'Get yourself something to eat. There's plenty of choice. You'll hear the the church bell at mid-day and again at Nones. We shall be here, ready to start back then.'

Joanna realised with a sigh of relief that the little ritual which was the high-light of her life was not to be spoilt by the presence of the horrible boy.

Dick had never before been into Baildon and the market entranced him, such a noise and a bustle, so many things to see. Not only the people and the stalls, but the entertainers; a man juggling six plates; a man with a dog which danced, and answered questions, one bark for yes and two for no; a man who appeared to swallow a knife; a man so seemingly boneless that he could wrap his legs around his neck and roll about like a ball. Unfortunately each entertainer had an attendant who moved among the watchers, cap in hand. A failure to contribute led to rough speech, 'Get outa the way, then.' 'Don't stand there blocking the view.' He was pushed and jostled; the ragged little girl collecting for the knife swallower actually spat at him and he spat back at her.

He turned his attention to find something to eat. He had never actually *bought* anything in his life and had no idea of the value of money. He decided against pies, sausages, brawn, slices of cold pease pudding, for although Knight's Acre was poor by his standards, dull and flavourless, it was plentiful enough and he wasn't hungry in quite that way. He craved something really tasty; and presently found it; a comparatively small stall, covered with a white cloth and set out with things he had not seen since delicacies from Uncle Richard's table had sometimes been passed on to the schoolroom. Sweetmeats. He took his time making his choice. Had he looked hungry or ragged the woman behind the spread board would have ordered him off; but by Baildon standards he was well-dressed. A likely customer. So she waited and presently Dick pointed to the three things of his choice and tendered his farthing.

'Trying to be funny?' the woman asked, quite amiably. 'Come on, out with it! You know everything here is a penny — except them,' she pointed to the little squares of marzipan. 'Them's twopence!'

'This is all I have,' said the indisputable heir to Moyidan.

'Be off with you then,' she said, seeing from his expression of real disappointment that what he said was true.

As Dick moved away, disconsolate, the woman said to her neighbour who sold new pots and mended old ones, 'Did you see that? A farthing: For fourpennorth of stuff! Must be a idiot though he didn't look it.'

When he had satisfied himself that no other stall offered sweetmeats, Dick decided to buy a pie. Behind this stall a girl of about his own age was temporarily in charge and when, having made his choice, though the pies varied little in size, he pointed and again held out his farthing, youth responded to youth.

'That all you got? Pies is a ha-penny. You could hev a sausage.'

'I wanted a pie.'

The little girl took a quick glance to see whether her mother was in the offing. She was not. 'All right, then,' she said. 'Hev a pie. But don't tell nobody or I'll get my ears boxed.'

Not at that pie-stall, but another, Henry and Joanna kept their tryst; sharing something *very* special. Eating together at leisure and alone. They sometimes took food to the field or the lambing pen, but such mouthfuls were always hasty. Here, the day's business done, there was a kind of cosiness, for the pie-stall not only stood near the church wall — one of the reasons Henry had chosen it since it was so near the rails where the wagon was, but this pie-seller, a matriarch of seventy, liked a bit of sail-cloth between her and the wind, and over a charcoal brazier she kept pies and sausages in an iron pan. By now she knew them, and knew that they always had the farthing thing, a sausage poised on a wedge of bread.

'Did you get all you were told to?' Henry asked. To forget one of Griselda's errands would provoke a tirade that would last until the next market day — and beyond.

'Yes. And all wrong. As usual. The flannel is *red* but the weight will be wrong, too light or too heavy. As for the thread ...' She laughed a little and took a bite of her food. It was perfectly true, Henry knew; every shopping expedition ended with a scolding; but it was not the kind of talk to encourage. So he said nothing and Joanna dismissed Griselda and gave herself to the joy of standing with Henry in this little enclosed space, a buttress of the church wall on one side, the stall on the other; isolated, in the market but not part of it; almost like being in a tiny house of their own.

Dick, circling the market inevitably arrived again at the sweetmeat stall. It was almost bare now for the woman who kept it knew almost to the last bit of sticky gingerbread what she could sell in a day. The marzipan which needed real sugar and was cheap at twopence a small square, was all gone, God be thanked, so had the saffron cakes. So she could turn away and enjoy another little gossip with the tinker. Dick's hand shot out and closed on the nearest piece of gingerbread. Nobody noticed and it tasted all the better for not costing him anything.

The disastrous year went on. Rain in April was good; but in showers, not in the steady downpour which rotted the seeds so painfully and carefully planted to replace those which the wind had uprooted. Wet weather, too long continued, made the sheep-run soggy and the sheep developed footrot. Henry remembered, bitterly, that Walter had said at the beginning that Knight's Acre, lying between the wood and the river was not suitable for sheep. The men of Intake had recognised this truth generations ago and on their holdings kept only a sheep or two, tethered and moved about every day and in exceptional conditions taken indoors.

May brought a few dry sunny days, but towards the end of the month the rain came again. Good for the hay, Henry told himself in despair, for it would plainly be a poor harvest the fields were patchy looking. Even June was wet and the shearing was done in the rain, by disgruntled men whose leader and spokesman said that a day and a half's work wasn't worth the trudge. That was unpleasant news, linking in as it did with the wool-merchant's decision that such a small crop of wool was not worth collecting. About that Richard had been helpful but Richard had now been gone for more than a year and last summer Henry had sold his wool — and Robert's — on that bad, casual market. And must do the same this year.

Intending not to work here again, the shearers were slipshod, making more nicks in the hides than usual so that Henry was kept busy with the tar-stick and not troubling to keep the black marked fleeces and the ochre-marked ones in separate piles, that duty fell to Joanna. The gang's woman attendant this year was a stringy, middle-aged woman with a brown face and very red hair; she seemed faintly familiar though at first Henry could not place her. Her manner was markedly hostile, even when Henry handed over the food which, as the employer he was bound to provide. It was good food, too; fresh pork and newly baked bread. She took it without a word, but her manner said — *Thank you for nothing!*

His memory worked. 'I've seen you before. You married Young Shep, didn't you?'

Hostility deepened. 'Worst day's work I ever did.'

Henry had thought Young Shep an idler, then changed his mind but that remark and the fact that she was back in this rough way of life indicated that as a husband and a provider Young Shep had been a disappointment.

'Why was that?'

'Due to that young brother of yours! We hadn't been married more'n a year when he came along, all fancy clothes and fancy talk about music and where he'd bin and where he was going. Turned Shep's head. He up and left.'

This was the first word that Henry had heard about John since he'd given Richard the slip, seven years earlier and he was anxious to hear more.

'Do you ever hear anything of your husband?'

'I used to at first. He'd send money. So he should — I'd got a baby to keep. But money don't make up for being left and made a laughing stock of. And I ain't even had money for a long time now.'

Greatly against his will Henry felt the nag of responsibility. It was John, his brother, who had robbed this woman of her husband. He wished that he could afford a generous gesture, give her some money and say, 'Buy something for the child.' But it was impossible. All he could do was to say, 'I am sorry.' She did not answer, except with a look which said very plainly — *So you damn well should be!*

Afterwards, thinking it over, Henry reflected that if for some time Young Shep had sent money home the pair of strolling musicians had not been doing badly. That the money had ceased to arrive did not necessarily indicate that they had ceased to prosper. Young Shep might have thought that the child's dependent days were over. Henry hoped that was the explanation. John had been idle, defiant, sly, but nobody liked to think of a brother fallen on evil days. Soon, however, Henry was too busy to have much time for thought.

Fleeces cut in the rain and heaped together while still damp quickly deteriorated, felted together and lost weight. So Henry made primitive racks upon which the wool, well squeezed, was hung out. When the sun shone the racks were carried out of the barn to the yard; when rain threatened or fell, they were hastily carried back under cover. It was a constant anxiety. So was the hay. It could, it must be cut whatever the weather, but it was hard work. When hay was ripe and stood straight the scythe went through it sweetly, each swishing stroke cutting a wide swathe. In weather like this, the hay beaten down by the rain it was often a sickle job, slow, done by the handful, the left hand holding the grass upright, the right hand wielding the smaller tool. Nor was the cutting all. Pile damp hay into the ordinary haycocks and it went mouldy before you could blink. It must be left as it fell and regularly tossed; on the rare, sunny day, turned about as often as three times.

'When are we going to market again, Uncle Henry?'

'That depends upon the weather. As soon as the wool is dry. And the hay in.'

'*I* could go,' Dick said, 'and do Aunt Griselda's errands.'

'Yes, I suppose you could.' Dick's services could be dispensed with. Utterly unlike his Uncle John in appearance and in character, Dick resembled him closely in his attitude towards work. Henry had always been obliged to goad John into activity and it was the same with Dick.

Dick had several most enjoyable days in the market. He was shrewd enough to perform any errand entrusted to him scrupulously and to keep the money apart. He had his farthing to spend and he always spent it at the pie-stall where the coin bought him a ha-penny pie while the friendly girl was in charge, as he always made certain that she was before approaching. Once, taking his priced-down pie he gave her a length of red ribbon for her hair. She was pleased, even though at the back of her mind she wondered how a boy who had only a farthing to spend, could have bought such a gay and expensive thing. Her mother, coming back from a very necessary errand in the churchyard where the mounded heaps of the dead provided a little privacy for the relief of bladders and bowels, wondered, too. 'Who give you that?'

'A boy.'

'And heven't I towd you time and again, not to hev nothing to do with boys?' The box on the ears was duly delivered.

Of that Dick knew nothing. What he did know was that a similar offering, blue this time, was completely rejected by Joanna whose goodwill he still craved.

'Go hang yourself with it!' she said. And Uncle Henry asked, 'How did you come by it, Dick?'

'I spent my farthing on it.' Moving between schoolroom and kitchen at Moyidan the boy had become a glib, convincing liar. Around Baildon market place he had become a slick thief.

CHAPTER TWENTY-NINE

In early July when the sun shone it had power. The wool was at last saleable. Henry mounded the wagon high, loaded bales on to the other horse, even called Dick's pony into service. Joanna, who weighed light and did not take up much room, was to drive the wagon; Henry, leading the horse would walk. So they made an early start.

Overnight there had been a squabble. Griselda said that now that the time for selling the wool had come, something must be done about Godfrey's clothes. Those she had contrived for him were now outgrown or washed and worn into shreds. She needed this and that. Henry said, 'I'll see how the wool sells.'

'Do you realise,' she asked, becoming shrill, 'that apart from a bit of red flannel your son has never had anything *new* in his life? For myself I ask nothing. I never did. I never shall . . .'

She was infuriated to think that some of the wool money was set aside for the benefit of a dead boy. Robert *must* be dead or there would have been news of him long before this. She was also infuriated by the fact that out of the money entrusted to Henry for Dick's clothing the stupid fellow had not squeezed out something for his *own* son . . . All the stored-up anger poring out, the voice as grating as an ill-tuned saw until Henry who usually bore her tirades with patience, said, 'Be quiet! Can't you see that I'm doing the best I can for you all?'

'And a fine best it is! Best for everybody except your own.' She grew almost tipsy with the delight of denunciation. 'Work yourself into the grave,' she said, 'work me into the grave. And for what? Ask yourself *that*.'

It was a cogent question and one that had now and again occurred to Henry himself. The struggle did sometimes seem to be hopeless. What he had to sell seemed to loose value, what he must buy seemed to increase in prices. And there were taxes, more exorbitant with every assessment. Old sheep with foot rot, lambs dead with navel trouble, despite all his care. And for what? He knew the answer to that; simple; to go my own way.

He always had, and though the way he had chosen was hard and unrewarding, he had managed so far to hold his own. And honestly.

The Baildon market was less happy-go-lucky than it seemed to be. It was in fact, strictly ruled. There were inspectors of weights and measures, any offender was liable to a spell in the stocks, arms and legs thrust through holes, head exposed and likely to be pelted with sticks and stones, and filth. There was also the market overseer who saw to it that no stall encroached upon its neighbour. His authority straight down from the time when the market had been the province of the monks in the Abbey. There was also the constable whose power was derived from an even older time. Long before abbeys. Thieves, people who caused a disturbance, or made an obstruction on a public highway must be dealt with by the constable — the caretaker.

Both men were there to protect the public, and the public was markedly ungrateful. Even the testing of weights and measures and the tasting for the quality of ale, all designed for the public's protection, was not popular. And although every-body hated thieves few were ever handed over in the proper fashion. For one thing the punishments were so ferocious, for another the whole thing took so long. It was seldom sufficient to say — 'This boy stole from me; I caught him in the act.' You had to produce at least one witness, invariably unwilling because it meant a waste of time. So the market people had devised their own system, completely illegal since it involved taking the law into their own hands.

They kept one another informed. The whisper would go round — 'Look out for such-and-such a person; he or she is a thief, or a cheat, or a passer of bad coins.' Thus everyone was on the alert and punishment was prompt since almost every-body carried a stout stick.

There had for some time now been a dubious character around the market, a biggish boy with black hair and tidy clothes. He had two methods. Turn your back for a second and he had whipped something away; or have a crowd near your booth and he would join it, as though waiting to be served, due to his clothes he looked a likely customer, then when you were serving a customer, he'd slip away — and something had gone with him. This had happened twice to the man who sold ribbon and tape and such things.

This morning there was a new stall on the market — new at least to Richard. It was filled with small trinkets; the man who owned it had come to Baildon for the Midsummer Fair and done rather poor trade, so he had stayed on for a bit.

Dick was not actually caught in the act; he stood staring at the pretty, gaudy things trying to decide what to take as an offering for the friendly little girl who had already let him have a ha'penny pie for a farthing. There were beads of all colours, ornaments for hair and for hats, thimbles that looked like silver, rings that looked like gold. He decided upon beads, red ones to match the ribbon he had given her. The stall-holder who, being an outsider, had not been warned by the whisper, saw nothing suspicious, but the ribbon-seller said, 'Thass him!' and somebody else said 'Clubs!'

Such punishments, slam! slam! were administered with the minumum of noise and fuss because the constable resented such usurpation of his legal office; and most offenders had the sense not to yell, since to draw attention was to invite official punishemnt later. Dick yelled lustily and the market overseer and the constable came running. Within two seconds all the people who had been hammering Dick were back behind their stalls, their sticks concealed, only the trinket seller who had now guessed what it was all about, and Dick, bearing marks of punishment, still stood there.

'Whass all this about?' the constable enquired.

The trinket seller was a quick-witted man.

'Lazy little sod,' he said, giving Dick a warning glance which was not understood. 'Fine thing, I must say, if a man can't give his own son a wallop or two to teach him not to go forgetting.'

Through the blood and tears streaking down his face, Dick said, 'I ain't his son.'

Nobody heeded that. Stepson perhaps; adopted; or an apprentice. Satisfied that no law had been broken, no disturbance caused the two men strolled away.

'You're a thick-headed young fool,' the trinket-seller said. 'But for me you'd be on your way to the Bridewell.'

'My name is Richard Tallboys,' Dick sobbed.

This piece of information quickly went the rounds. Tallboys was a well-known and honoured name. Henry was not popular, too stand-offish, and too close-spending, but he was respected. And if this snivelling little sneak thief were his son, he was also the grandson of Sir Godfrey, the good knight in whom the neighbourhood had taken a vicarious pride, and who had come back from the dead! Oh, what a disgrace! Shame enough for any decent family to have a thief among its members; but a Tallboys!

But these were people not ruled by sentiment. Alongside the story on its rounds, ran a certainty. If Master Tallboys knew what his son had been up to he'd give compensation, good honest man that he was. All the stallholders would have been shamed to have a son caught stealing, but a bit of sharp practice was quite another thing. Almost everybody except the seller of pots and pans, suddenly remembered missing something lately, and multiplied its value by ten at least.

Henry was at that moment closeted with Master Turnbull, handing over Robert's share of the wool money. An act of faith, the lawyer thought, making a meticulous entry and mildly regretting that the sum had decreased again.

'And you still have no news of the boy?'

'None. I heard of the other young one — John — only the other day. And that after seven years. And my father; as you may remember, was gone even longer.' Master Turnbull supposed that his family history accounted for Henry's stubborn refusal to accept that Robert was dead. Though there *was* a difference between a full grown man, a boy in his teens and a child! However, it was none of his business.

Henry crossed the sunny market place, making for the pie-stall where Joanna would be waiting. He was not a self-conscious man and did not notice the stares. Today, he decided, Joanna should have a pie, a twopenny one if she liked, and also a glass of the sweet cider which the old woman added to her wares in summer. Not that the wool price justified extravagance, but Joanna's exertions did. He only wished that he could buy her something really expensive and pretty and useful.

She was waiting, as he expected her to be, for his business with Master Turnbull had delayed him. But surely, he thought, as he approached, a little waiting could not account for her expression of acute distress. She never, even in the finest summer acquired much sun tan; in this almost sunless season she had not tanned at all; so now she looked very pale, blanched, her very lips white. He saw her before she saw him, he was taller. When she did see him, threading his way through the crowd, she ran and seized his arm in a frenzied grip.

'It's awful, Henry! But don't pay! Don't pay. They can't make you. Even *she* says you can't.' She jerked her head towards the pie-seller who was not looking very cheerful.

Everybody knew where Master Tallboys took his dinner,

and the pie-woman had been deputed to speak for all. And she rather liked Henry; not a good spender, but regular; he didn't come every week, but whenever he came — and she knew because she could see his wagon, what he had to spend was spent with her; and he was always civil. So she broke the news to him without taking any pleasure in the task, and without claiming, as she could easily have done, that Dick had robbed her.

Henry was furious. Furious with Dick; greedy little bastard! Hadn't he always had his farthing, exactly the amount that Henry spent on himself: Furious, too with the exaggerated claim for compensation. If the little swine had come to every market and eaten himself silly each time he couldn't possibly have consumed what he was said to have consumed. And if only he'd been rich! Rich enough to throw money in front of these money-grubbing liars and watch them grovel for it! A silly way to think for a man who had in his purse only the price — disappointing at that — of his own share of the wool; which must last until after harvest.

He said to the pie-woman. 'They shall all be paid. Now we want two twopenny pies and two mugs of your good cider.' He and Joanna then retreated to their little nook and he said, 'Cheer up, sweetheart. Don't let it spoil your appetite.'

'But how can you? Pay I mean? I told you not to. And it's a lot of money.'

'I know how to get it,' Henry said. *I'm going to sell his pony!*

For a second they looked at each other with eyes which despite their differing colouring, were exactly alike, dancing with mischief and with malice. The expression made Henry look *young*.

'What a wonderful idea,' Joanna said, biting happily into her pie.

Henry thought — Practical, too! It would punish Dick; it would restrict his movements; and it would be saving. For when Henry had undertaken to supply Dick with his keep he had not taken the pony into consideration. A pony could share the sheep-run in summer; in winter it needed hay, and soon it would need to be shod.

Dick had taken refuge in the wagon. Henry dragged him out, made sure that he was not hurt, bruised and battered but with no wound in any way comparable to the one Griselda had inflicted on Joanna because several sticks aimed at the same target clashed and defeated one another's purpose.

'Now you walk,' Henry said, remembering how, long ago, he and Richard had quarrelled in the wagon bringing them from Beauclaire to Knight's Acre and Walter had told them to get out and walk.

For those who had gone to market an eventful day; and not less so for Griselda who had stayed at home.

About clothes for the child whom she now regarded as far more Tom's than Henry's, Henry had been evasive, promising nothing, saying I must see how the wool sells. An evasive and unpromising answer. So Griselda sought about in her mind for some other way, and presently was visited by much the kind of inspiration as had touched Henry when he thought of selling the pony.

Those empty rooms on the other side of the house!

She had been into Tana's pavilion on various occasions, but once the two babies were weaned she had no reason to go there, and with Lady Serriff dead that part of the house was of no importance. Knight's Acre was quite big enough to manage single-handed. Now, all of a sudden, some memory stirred. A lot of silk! Griselda had not asked Henry for silk — only for good linen and some sound homespun.

She entered as the children had done, hauling Godfrey in after her. The place smelt of dust and neglect and of something which she did not recognise though it reminded her sharply of the loft at the Swan. Bats found their way in through the pane Joanna had broken.

'I don't like it here, Mumma.'

'We shall not be long,' Griselda said. She was amazed to think that she had not thought of this treasure-house before. Silk everywhere! Godfrey could be silk-clad for the rest of his life — even in winter, for a tunic and hood made double and stuffed with sheep's wool and quilted would keep out the coldest winds.

Then, staring, she thought silver! Enormous, four branched candlesticks, several wine cups, and a bowl; all black with tarnish, but that was proof that they were silver.

'I don't like it here, Mumma.'

She hushed him with an impatience unusual in her dealings with him. She thought — Oh Tom, if only I'd used my sense! You could have had wine and manchet bread . . . All the luxuries in the world.

Then she thought that if she had been stupid, Henry had been even more so. He should have remembered.

She investigated further, entered the inner room, opened the chest. She had never owned a trinket in her life, but she had seen precious stones. The image of Our Lady in the Convent chapel had worn a crown of them, and now and again travellers of a better sort had lodged at The Swan because it was handy. God in Heaven! Here she and Henry had been all these years, working their fingers to the bone, counting pennies, with wealth unimaginable waiting just across the yard.

'Can we go *now*?' Godfrey demanded with all the imperiousness of a spoilt child. There was nobody to notice the resemblance but very often his manner towards his mother closely matched that of Dick's to Lady Emma.

'Yes. We can go now. You hold this.' She whipped off her apron and into it piled the emeralds, sapphires, diamonds and pearls, rubies and the tangled mass of gold setting out of which they had been broken. About them she twisted the apron as she would have twisted the cloth about a bag pudding. 'Hold it tight,' she said, and lifted him out of the window. The silver things she dropped out, one by one on to the soft soil and then clambered out herself.

She spent the rest of her afternoon polishing the silver things. She'd have something to show and even more to say to Henry when he came home!

Joanna and Henry walked into the kitchen together, bringing their frugal purchases. Through the west facing window of the kitchen the lowering sun sent its rays, winking upon the glittering silver and waking the fiery colours in the stones, precious things brought from the world's farthest end, now spread out on a well-scrubbed kitchen table.

At the sight they both stopped as though the floor had dropped just before their feet. Then Joanna ran forward and spread her hands over the coloured stones with which she and Robert had played five-stones and How Many Birds In A Bush.

The silver things, the tangled mass of gold she ignored. Only the stones mattered.

'They are ours,' she cried. And then, realising that she alone was left, 'Mine. They are mine.'

Henry said, 'She is right. They belonged to her mother...'

The shoes which Dick wore on Sundays and market days were not yet softened by use; soon he had a blister on his heel and began to limp. The old woman pedlar overtook him easily and then slowed her stride, glad of company on what she always thought of as the nasty bit of road. She was not much frightened of being robbed, though all her wordly wealth was contained in the pack she carried. Her father had been in this trade and he had made for himself a very cunning box. Opened out, and held forward on her solid bosom it made a splendid tray for display; folded up, it was compact and easily carried on her back; it had a secret drawer in which gold coins, well wadded with sheep's wool so that they did not rattle, lay hidden. As often as she could she changed the small currency of her earnings into gold, reserving just enough to meet her day-by-day expenses. So she reckoned that the most she could lose was her stock and a few pence. She fell into step with the limping, snivelling boy because they were nearing the point where Layer Wood ran alongside the road, and some very funny tales were told of that wood.

She had been in the market that day and recognised him instantly as the boy who had received a well-deserved hiding. She had no sympathy with thieves and her amiable manner towards him was entirely false.

'Did they hurt you bad?'

'They nearly killed me.'

'What made you do it? Take stuff I mean.'

'I was hungry.'

'Don't your father give you enough to eat.'

'I ain't got no father...'

He had no friend, either. No friend in all the world except the little girl for whom he had intended the red beads. At the thought of his friendless state the snivelling changed to real crying for a while. This old woman seemed interested at least and into her ears he poured out the story of his woes and his wrongs, not failing to mention that really Moyidan belonged to him; the Bishop had taken Moyidan and kept him without shoes; his Uncle Henry made him work like a labourer and only today had sold his pony and made him walk home.

A lurid story, the old woman knew, was as good as stock. Everybody liked a story and women at kitchen doors, unwilling to buy, would stand and listen and decide that after all they could do with a reel of thread. So she clicked her tongue sympathetically and now and again said, 'You poor boy!' while her mind took note of every detail and improvised embellishments. And didn't this tale of cheating and ill-treatment link up with another? Two children deliberately lost in this very wood and left to die? By a wicked uncle?

'You hungry now?'

Dick said, 'Yes.' And that was true. A swollen jaw and a tooth loose on that side where a stick had reached its mark was no hindrance to eating; misery had never lessened his appetite. So presently, to her highly coloured tale the old woman could add with some truth, 'I was that sorry for him, I give him my own bite of supper and he ett like a starving dog.' In fact she had shared her bit of supper — bread and cheese with a careful eye to her own interest.

'Your Grace,' said the young clerk, about the only one who would ever get anywhere, being the only one with a spark of spirit, 'when the Moyidan boy was found to be without shoes, you complained, if I may say so, quite rightly, that you had not been informed.'

'That is so.'

'Would Your Grace welcome more information about the same boy? A singular story is going around.'

'Tell me.'

The Bishop listened with some consternation, but even more disappointment. He remembered the impression that Henry Tallboys had made upon him and how he had thought — as Master Turnbull thought from time to time — how unlike his brother Richard; so honest and forthright and short-spoken. Even now His Grace found it rather hard to believe that Henry Tallboys over-worked, underfed and regularly beat his nephew. Had sold his pony and left him to walk home from Baildon in shoes so ill-fitting that the boy could hardly hobble.

And so hungry that a pedlar woman had felt obliged to give him her own meagre supper.

'Where did you get this tale, Jonathan?'

'Your Grace, from the inn on the waterfront. The landlady there is second cousin to my mother — and she is growing old. I feel it my duty to look in upon her from time to time.'

'Most admirable,' the Bishop said. Deplorable, too, because if Jonathan, a bright boy, played his cards rightly, the Church would lose and the Welcome To Mariners would gain.

'You were right to inform me. I will look into the matter myself.'

Henry and Jem were scything, Joanna and Dick working behind them. At the sight of a mounted man Henry came towards the edge of the field and when his visitor was recognisable, looked pleased. With that incongruous grace of his, he bowed, spoke words of greeting, laid his hand on the horse's bridle and led the way to the front of the house, steadied the stirrup.

'It was in my mind to come to see you, my lord, but once harvest starts . . .' He threw open the door and stood aside.

A very poor place, His Grace thought, looking around the hall of Knight's Acre for the first time and accepting the only comfortable seat, its cushions now much the worse for wear.

'About the boy?' It seemed incredible, but it was just possible that living in such near isolation, Master Tallboys did not know what tales were being told of him.

'No, the girl . . . I wish I could offer you wine. All I have is ale.' And that only because there was an understood agreement that hired men, at harvest time, should have ale.

'Ale would be very acceptable,' the Bishop said graciously. Henry fetched it himself. Not good ale; very thin and sour.

'You wish to speak to me about young Richard,' Henry asked.

'Some story regarding him, his welfare, has reached my notice.'

'Rightly so. He behaved very badly and had he not been soundly thrashed in the market, I should have thrashed him myself. But it was taken out of my hands; the people he had stolen from beat him much harder than I could have brought myself to do; they then claimed extortionate compensation, which I managed to meet by selling his pony. So he will not trouble Baildon market any more.'

Short and to the point.

'As it was reported to me, he stole because he was hungry. When I heard that I felt inclined to blame myself for accepting your offer not to charge for his board . . .'

'Greedy,' Henry said. 'All boys are. He has eaten alongside me ever since he came here, and in the market he had to spend exactly what I spend on myself. Would you care, my lord to see him and assure yourself that he is well nourished? I'd like you to see Joanna, too. *Her* future is what I am concerned about.'

He went out and gave a clear piercing whistle.

His Grace remembered thinking, years ago, at Moyidan, that given ten years this girl would be beautiful and he did not retract his opinion now though all the childish beauty had gone and she was angular, the youthful curves not yet replaced by those of budding maturity. All arms and legs, eyes and mouth. But her hair was the colour of a well-kept saddle, her eyes the colour of aquamarines and her profile, if anything, more clear cut than ever. The boy looked well-fed enough; indeed beside the girl he looked thick and sullen. The marks of the beating he had received in the market had vanished and he bore no resemblance at all to the ill-fed, ill-treated boy of the story which the pedlar woman had hawked around with her wares.

'All right,' Henry said, dismissing them. 'It's hardly worth going back to the field before dinner.'

As soon as they had gone, he went to the court cupboard, with its solitary silver cup and reached up to its top for something hidden behind the carved pediment. A bundle wrapped in a piece of old cloth.

'I wanted your advice about these, my lord.' Out on the table tumbled a wealth of jewels and a tangled mass of gold.

'Great God in Heaven! Where did they come from?'

'They belong to the girl. They were her mother's.' Whatever it had been which had forbidden Henry to speak, or even think of Tana, which had made him ignore that part of the house, and which had prevented him from ever regarding Joanna as Tana's daughter, had now lost power. He was able to say in a natural manner, 'I suppose you know the story? No? Well, my father went to Spain, to fight against the Moors. He was captured and was enslaved for almost nine years. A Spanish lady — Lady Serriff — contrived his escape, and he brought her back with him to England. She was pregnant and Joanna was born some months later. The lady had an unruly horse which eventually threw her and she died. It did not occur to anyone to go through what she left and these were discovered only a few weeks ago.'

'What a story!' From the tumbled, flashing heap of colour one thing stood out, a ruby of exceptional size and darkness. He picked it up and held it against the light. What a thumb ring it would make! 'Who broke the stones from their settings?'

'The children. Joanna and my youngest brother — the little boy who was lost. They found things and regarded them as playthings, prettier than pebbles, so they pried them loose ... What I wanted to ask Your Grace was advice upon how to deal with them.'

Extraordinary man! A small fortune within reach of his hand, and drinking this poor ale.

'These represent a small fortune, Master Tallboys.'

'So I hoped, for the child's sake. My father once, through my aunt, Lady Astallon of Beauclaire, disposed of a few similar things. I have no such outlet. I have no knowledge. I do however remember another thing. When my sister — that boy's mother — was younger, my parents wished her to go to Lamarsh, but they would only accept girls with money behind them. I have been wondering — you are the only person I know who could advise upon such matters — if you, my lord would help me, both about the disposal of the trinkets and about getting the girl accepted there.'

The Bishop frowned. All this for Lamarsh; so rich already! The old breach between the secular clergy and the religious houses opened and yawned in this ill-furnished hall where an honest man sat, asking advice.

In theory all the religious houses; the abbeys and the convents were ruled by the Bishop of the diocese, subject to regular visitations; always excepting such places as that decayed house at Clevely where a few old women rotted under a rotting roof, the blind propped up by the lame, the lame guided the blind. He had never visited Clevely, but he knew Lamarsh. Its financial arrangements solidly founded by a former Abbess — ah yes! Another member of this very curious family? Now it was full of women, the widows and spinsters whom every war threw up, more boarders, with little pet dogs in their sleeves or in their laps. They defied all discipline and by their bad, indeed loose, behaviour, they brought convents into disrepute.

'That,' His Grace said, after cogitations which had lasted only a few seconds, though wide in scope. 'I should not advise.'

Not only the waste of a small fortune, but a waste of a girl who was going to be beautiful.

'Then what would you suggest, my lord?'

'Placing her with a family of repute, with daughters of its own. Somewhere where she could learn all the . . .' he hesitated for a second, 'accomplishments necessary for a gentlewoman. All this does not make her a *great* heiress, but properly handled it could make a not inconsiderable dowry. How old is she?'

'Eleven years and some months.'

Six or seven years then for the handling.

'So long as she's safe,' Henry said. 'And happy . . .'

'If you care to leave this to me. Offhand I cannot name a family such as I envisage. But I have no doubt . . . I am shortly going to London. A tiresome conference. I could, at the same time dispose of all this and make arrangements . . .' In these troubled times dozens of men, not actually poor, and some with power, would welcome ready money, and what it could earn in seven years. His Grace's eye looked again at the tangle of gold and saw what he was almost sure was the setting from which the big ruby had been pried. He thought — Any competent goldsmith . . . Like Lady Astallon he considered that the middleman was worthy of his hire. *This* would be his!

Henry bundled the whole treasure into a cloth and handed it over; glad to be rid of it. He had been obliged to take it and hide it in a place which neither Griselda nor Joanna knew about — or could reach, for the discovery had brought their simmering hostility to a head and *he* acknowledging Joanna's claim, refuting Griselda's strident, 'Findings keepings!' had fallen into even deeper disfavour. A bad father!

'Oh,' he now said, remembering, 'there was more. Some silver things.' He stooped and opened the enclosed part of the cupboard. Candlesticks, four-branched, fit for any altar; cups; a bowl. Gathering tarnish again for since Griselda's claim to ownership had been denied she had not bothered and Joanna had had no time.

'Of considerable value,' the Bishop said. 'I cannot well take them with me, but I will send.' He had come alone because if what he found at Knight's Acre should correspond in any way with the rumour, the fewer people who knew about it, the better. Always, everywhere, there were eyes watching, tongues wagging and ill-informed minds all too ready to think the worst.

Henry felt as though a load had been lifted from his shoulders. What he had always wanted for Joanna now seemed likely to come about. Safe and happy — that was his wish for her. Thus relieved, he remembered his manners. 'If you would care to eat with us, Your Grace . . .' It was only rabbit, but rabbit in harvest time was as good meat as one could wish for. Henry had derived from his mother not only his manners, his way of speech, but something deeper, not an ignoring of class distinction but the capacity to over-ride it. Sybilla, poorly dressed, ill-provided for, had never failed to preside graciously over her table, even when that table was in the kitchen, and one she had just scrubbed with her own hands.

'I thank you. But I have guests awaiting me at Moyidan.'

Outside the house, between the roses, again overgrown because Griselda had lost interest, the two men took civil leave of one another. The Bishop mounted, and remembering his waiting guests, set off at a swift trot. Henry turned back into his house.

Just beyond the church where the track turned into the lane, something hurtled out of hiding and in the most reckless manner grabbed the horse's bridle and swung on it. His Grace was almost unseated. Recovering himself he said, 'What the Devil . . .' and then recognised the boy.

'What do you think you're about? You could have caused a serious accident! What do you want?'

Dick said, 'I sent you messages. I writ you a letter. And you took Moyidan and sent me here. I hate it here. And it ain't right that I should be.'

The Bishop said, 'So far as I can see you have no cause for complaint. Let go of my horse. You make him restive.'

'Then you'd ride off! You gotta listen to me.' And uncouth, ill-spoken boy! 'Umma always said Moyidan belonged to me. I was a *rich* boy and I'd be a rich man. Here I work like a

264

labourer — but unpaid. I have horrible food and Griselda grudges every mouthful I chaw. Something oughta be done about me. Umma'd turn in her grave . . .'

'Who was Umma?'

'My grandmother. Lady Emma. She always said . . .'

'She would certainly turn in her grave could she know how wicked, how *ungrateful* you are.'

'What hev I got to be grateful about?'

It was curious — the boy did not look like a Tallboys, but he had something, quite indefinable that linked him with Richard who at his lowest moment would make a jest about the un= pawnability of a servant, and with Henry who had just tipped out — and handed over a collection of jewels, as though they were hazel nuts; what exactly this quality was . . . there was no word.

'You should be grateful,' His Grace said sternly, 'that your property is in safe hands, being properly admin . . . looked after, until you attain your majority. You should be grateful to your uncle.'

'He sold my pony!'

'Quite rightly. You had stolen in the market.'

'Because I was so poor. If I had my rights I wouldn't have to steal, would I? I'd be at Moyidan, with all I wanted. And servants. Like when Umma was alive.'

'Your grandmother is dead. Your father and mother also. You have a good home . . .' Strange to have come here this morning in order to scold the uncle and now to be scolding the nephew. 'Many boys in your position — especially trouble-some boys such as you are — find themselves in orphanages, or schools.'

'If they're *poor*,' Dick said stubbornly. 'I'm rich. Moyidan is mine . . .'

His Grace thought quickly. The boy was obviously not starved or ill-treated as rumour held; he was a liar. But liars could be dangerous. Doubly so when mingling with the lies there was an element of truth. As in this case.

With a change of manner he said, 'If you are not happy here some other arrangement must be made. Would you like to come with me to London?'

'What for?' Suspicious as a peasant.

'To enjoy yourself and see something of the world.'

What an absurd situation, he Bishop of Bywater, actually coaxing this young oaf who still kept firm hold on the bridle.

'I druther go to Moyidan, if I could hev proper food and shoes when I wanted. I don't know about London only what Joseph said — all right if you was rich, like living on a muck-heap if you was poor. And I *ain't* poor. Moyidan . . .'

'I think you would enjoy London.'

'Would I hev my pony back?'

For the animal *as* an animal Dick had been little concerned, but it had been a possession, something poor little boys didn't have.

'Naturally. You would need one in order to ride to London.'

'All right, then. I'll go.'

Alongside the faint warning bell about the danger of lies mixed with some truth, the word 'school' had run in the Bishop's mind.

There was one, already famous. It was called The King's College of Our Lady of Eton beside Windsor. It had been founded by Henry VI some twenty years earlier for the benefit of twenty-five indigent boys; now it housed over seventy — and not all indigent, for even the rich and the noble were beginning to see some value in learning. Places there were eagerly sought but the Bishop had no doubt that with his contacts and his influence he could contrive for this boy to be squeezed in. It would look well; what more could the Church do for an orphan who had fallen into its hands than administer his property to the best advantage and send him to the best school in England?

And there the blabbermouth boy could go about saying, 'Moyidan,' and nobody would even know where the place was.

It was slightly ironic that the Bishop of Bywater who, if he had ever indulged in amorous ventures had done so with the utmost discretion, should appear seeking at the same time a place at Eton for a loutish boy and a place in a good household for a girl. The boy, when he became of age would inherit a flourishing estate; the girl — said to be pretty — had a considerable dowry, in ready money, money that could be invested now and begin to earn.

His reputation was not damaged. Obviously he was clever, a

good manager. A great ruby of exceptional size and quality shone on his thumb . . .

CHAPTER THIRTY

Joanna had watched Dick's departure with mixed feelings. It was pleasant to think that she would never have to sit at table with him again. But he had left somewhat grandly, mounted on a new pony, bigger than the other. When he arrived, almost barefoot, when he had been beaten in the market and lost his pony she had almost thought . . . almost . . . that ill-wishing was not entirely futile. Now, seeing him ride off, all cock-a-hoop, she had a feeling of defeat. There was no one to tell her and that extra sense which she had possessed where Robert was concerned did not operate where Dick was concerned — that Dick's ultimate destination was the reverse of joyful. Tutors far more strict and more powerful than Master Jankyn had ever been; dozens of rules, and to break one meant a real beating; no ponies allowed and food intended for pauper boys, every half year lagging a little behind what was absolutely necessary because the Bursar always reckoned backwards; so much meal, so much bread, so much fat coarse meat had sufficed so many boys for the last half year; it would serve for this; time enough to think about the extra mouths next year.

At Knight's Acre it was a bad and troublesome harvest. Far too much rain. A *sickle harvest*, a vast amount of labour and small reward.

One day, coming in because the rain made work impossible, sharing an old sack to protect them from the downpour, Joanna said, 'Henry, if those things of mine are so valuable, this wouldn't matter so much. We could give her half, to stop her mouth and buy things for ourselves. A cow *with* a calf and some more of the black-faced sheep. They do better. Don't they?'

They did, with their longer legs and lighter fleeces.

'Honey, I don't know what the things were worth. I expect to hear any day. But whatever it amounts to it must belong to you, not spent on Knight's Acre.'

'Why not? It is my home.'

And what a home, Henry thought. Griselda, hostile and spiteful ever since the baby episode, had become ten times more so since the finding of the treasure and Joanna's claim, and his backing it.

You couldn't say that she had gone mad — she had sense enough never to mention the subject in front of Jem at midday; sense enough to provide food then. It was the evenings that were horrible. Rave, rant, scold, denounce and deride. Sometimes it seemed as though she was talking to herself — as indeed she might well have been. Henry and Joanna had learnt to take refuge in silence and anybody looking through the window, seeing the trap-like mouth open and shut, open and shut, would have been justified in thinking that Griselda was addressing two dumb mutes. Anything could start her off; nothing ... On and on, and much of it so unfounded as to sound insane. She'd linked, somehow, the finding of the treasure with Dick's going to London. 'Riding off like a lord and your own son dressed in bits and pieces. No doubt you'll do the same for *her* one day. Here am I working my fingers to the bone — ' That was one of her favourite expressions, for all the tasks in which she had once taken pride and pleasure now seemed to be heavy impositions — 'and what do I get? I *found* the things after all.'

So, when Joanna made the remark about Knight's Acre being her home, Henry said, 'Not much of one, lately, I'm afraid. Still let's hope ...' He left it there, having heard nothing from the Bishop.

'It suits me,' Joanna said. She seized his hand and swung on it, taking a few hopping steps. 'Outdoors, that is,' she added in the voice she used when referring, however indirectly, to Griselda.

Henry gave her a sideways glance. True enough; she seemed happy, seemed to have forgotten Robert. And even indoors, with Griselda at her worst, she would occasionally catch his eye and flash him a glance of wry amusement; or make an almost imperceptible movement of the shoulders. He'd miss her, indoors and out if the plan came to anything. And for the first time he wondered how she would take to a new way of life, so utterly different from the one she now led. Easily, he assured himself; children were very adaptable.

'Up! Up the Maiden,' Jem cried, heaving the last sheaf of this prolonged harvest on to the wagon. 'Oughta hev a bitta ribbon on her. For luck.' He said it every year. He was inclined to think that Henry's disregard for such old customs was responsible for the way in which things seemed to go against him. Not that anybody could help the weather of course; a bad season hit the careful and the neglectful alike. But look at the way he'd got married, no jollifications, nobody to wish him luck, drink his health or throw an old shoe; and how had that turned out?

Joanna had been prepared for this moment and with glee whipped out a length of blue ribbon. 'Dick left it behind,' she said. 'I found it when I had to clean his room.'

'That should work miracles,' Henry said dryly. 'It cost enough.'

She began to scramble into the wagon which was not loaded high; then she dropped back and stood rigid and staring in exactly the way she had done soon after Robert's departure to Moyidan.

'There's a man coming. Henry, don't see him. Don't talk to him. Send him away. It will do us no good!'

He turned to look. This, the last field to be cleared, was called Far Field, the one farthest from the house and very slightly higher than the others. He had a clear view of the track which led from the house between the sheepfold and the church and the priest's house, where it curved to join the lane. Nothing moved on it. Nor was there anyone on the narrow footpath beyond the sheepfold, the path which since the common had been enclosed had linked the village to the church.

'There's nobody there,' Henry said. But even as he spoke a mounted man came out of the lane, rounded the church and the priest's house and came towards Knight's Acre.

'Please, Henry. Please. Don't listen. I know it is bad. I always knew . . .'

'Don't be silly. Of course I must see the man. Up you get. Tie the pretty bow on and wish next harvest better luck.'

He lifted her into the wagon. Her bright brown hair brushed his face and revived something which he had no time to recognise.

His Grace of Bywater was still in London, but he had

written a lengthy letter to one of his secretaries at Bywater and directed him to go immediately and convey the gist of it to Master Tallboys.

Richard's fate was easily disposed of — a place for him had been found at Eton, the best school in England.

Joanna's could be enlarged upon. Her small fortune had not yet been entirely converted into currency — such things took time. Also time-consuming had been the Bishop's meticulous search for a completely suitable home for her; but one had been found in the household of Sir Barnabas Grey in Hertfordshire. Sir Barnabas was a knight of the highest possible reputation, extremely well-connected, a remote relative of the Queen's first husband. He had two daughters, one aged twelve, the other nine, and his lady who was extremely accomplished was educating her own daughters and was willing for Joanna to join the household. About monetary arrangements the Bishop thought it only necessary to say that a satisfactory arrangement had been reached. Sir Barnabas was scrupulously honest and would invest wisely what was available now and what was to come when the rest of the goods were sold. He would use the income from it in return for treating Joanna as his own — even to the point of finding her a suitable husband when the time came.

'Would you like me to repeat, Master Tallboys?'

'Thank you, no. I think I have it.'

'His Grace also wished me to tell you that a suitable escort will be arranged if we are notified.'

It was exactly what he had wanted for her. A suitable home, suitable company, in due time a suitable marriage — all the things which he could not provide. He should have felt elated, but he did not.

'It is always the same,' Griselda said, slapping the only-just-belated meal on to the table. 'As soon as the food is ready somebody comes and you talk and talk. What did the fellow want?'

'Nothing that concerns you.'

Such a downright snub was unusual. Henry's tone of voice, the expression on his face convinced Joanna that she had been right. The man had brought bad news. What? There were curious limits to her flashes of knowing and seeing and although she had seen the man, before he rounded the corner, and known that the news was bad, she could only guess at its nature. She wanted to say — 'Never mind, Henry, we shall manage.' Such a statement would merely provoke Griselda who had a tendency to pick on one word and overwork it and was likely now to say — *manage*. How do we manage? We *manage* by scrimping and scraping and working harder than labourers; but we *manage* to provide well for other people, never for our own . . .

Jem had not stayed for dinner. It was an unwritten rule that as soon as the last sheaf was carried the rest of the day was given over to merry-making, eating, drinking, singing, dancing. There was none of that at Knight's Acre, but if he hurried down to the village, with any luck, he'd find somebody celebrating the end of harvest properly. And everybody welcome.

Henry quickly finished his meal and stood up. Joanna bolted her last mouthful and stood, too. With the last field cleared, gleaning could begin; and she and Henry would be alone. He'd tell her what the man had said, and she'd do her best to make light of it. Though it was bad! She knew by the way he stood in the yard, irresolute. Quite unlike him!

He said, 'We'll take a holiday. We'll go blackberrying.'

She had never known him waste an hour. She thought, 'This is supposed to be a treat for me; because the bad news concerns me.' Then she knew. The pretty pebbles *were* only pebbles, not the jewels Henry had thought them.

'We'll need a basket. I'll get one.'

She ran back into the house.

'What *now*?' Griselda asked as though this were the twentieth interruption.

'I want a basket. For blackberries.'

There were two on the larder floor. One was broken; she took the other.

'Not that one,' Griselda said.

'The other has a hole.'

'Use a dock leaf.'

Joanna changed baskets and ran. Godfrey's wistful stare followed her. He longed to be free to join in all the exciting things that Farder and Janna did outside the house, and more and

271

more often lately he'd said, 'Can't I come, too?' Sometimes he sensed that Farder would have taken him, but Mumma always said, 'No,' and gave some silly reason. Once not long ago Farder had said, 'Not today, my boy. But you're big enough now to help with the gleaning.'

'When?'

'I'll tell you.'

Mumma had been angry — not with Godfrey, but with everything else, he knew by the way she banged things about and muttered. (Indeed Henry's promise to take Godfrey to the field with him was the result of a realisation that the boy couldn't spend his life tied to his mother's apron strings. And Griselda had simultaneously realised it. Then what would she have left?)

Joanna, now that she knew what the trouble was, and how trivial compared with what it might have been — something about taxes! — decided not to open the subject but to let Henry tell her. She set herself to cheer his mood, as she had often done after a bad market day. She was not very successful because Henry was preoccupied with the problem of how to make the proposition sound attractive and then wondering why it must be made to sound so. Surely any girl . . . Surely just to get away, out of reach of Griselda's tongue . . .

It was the third week in September; under the trees it was cool, but in the clearings, where blackberry bushes grew the sun was warm and the air was scented by the ripe fruit. Joanna's chatter moved from the superstition about blackberries being cursed after Michaelmas to such beliefs in general. 'Like tying a ribbon on The Maiden', she said. 'You don't believe in such things, do you, Henry?'

'Not much. I may be wrong. I spent most of my time with Walter, you see; and he wasn't superstitious. I remember what he once said about salt and it being unlucky to spill it. He said it was concocted to make people careful.'

'Well,' she said, 'we shall see if Dick's blue ribbon and the good wish bring a better harvest next year.'

Dear child, you won't be here to see; you'll have forgotten such things.

He began to look around for a fallen tree on which to sit. Light talk could go on across a blackberry bush but it did not seem a suitable way to conduct a serious conversation. Presently he saw what he wanted and said, 'Let's sit down. Sweetheart, I've got something to tell you.'

She waited, but he looked so bothered and took so long to get started that she said,

'I'll tell *you*. Those jewels weren't worth anything.'

'On the contrary, they were worth a great deal of money. It is being handled for your welfare. Listen . . .'

She sat quite still, her hands, work-roughened, blackberry-stained, yet elegant, clasped together. Her crystal blue gaze fixed on his face discomfited him by its intentness and some of the sentences he had prepared forsook him. When he had blundered his way to the end she asked, in a thoughtful way,

'This money is mine? It really belongs to me?'

'Oh, beyond any shadow of doubt.'

'Then I should have some say in how it is spent. And that won't be on learning to embroider, or play the lute!' Something, amusement? derision? flashed in her eyes.

'Darling, it is for your good.'

'How do you know? I should hate it. Wasting time on such nonsense. I told you what we would do with the money.'

'You're too young to have any say. Too young to understand that the way you live . . .'

'And what is wrong with the way I live?'

'Everything. It may seem all right to you now but . . . It's the future we must think of. It always has bothered me, Joanna. I'd always hoped to be able . . .' Oh, why pursue that thought of failure? 'This is exactly what I hoped for you, and by sheer lucky chance . . . It is a wonderful opportunity and you must take advantage of it.'

'Must? Who says so?'

'I do sweeting. You must trust me to decide what is best for you.'

'Is it best for me? First I have nothing — more than once Griselda has called me a pauper, but I tried to earn what I ate — more than Dick ever did — and I am happy. Then *she* must go prying and suddenly I am rich. So *because* I am rich I must go away and live with strangers and break my heart. That is nonsense. Unless . . .'

Suddenly, with the widening of the pupils of her eyes, they darkened and she said in a less reasonable voice,

'Is it because of *her*; would she be nicer to you; would you be happier with me away? I know I did a silly thing. Two silly things. And both times you were kind and that angered her. Is *that* why you wish to be rid of me?'

'No. Griselda has nothing to do with this — except that she stumbled upon the jewels that made the whole thing possible. And I don't want to be *rid of you*. That is wrong. I shall miss you, your help with the work, your company. But it is for your good.' He flung off all of Walter's egalitarianism and spoke of her mother having been a lady and therefore it was only right and proper that she should be reared to be a lady too.

Convinced?

It seemed so, as he talked, dredging up things he had forgotten, the ladies' bower at Beauclaire; ladies bright as butterflies, doing their stitching, making their music.

Again she seemed to be listening.

She sat planning desperate things. Refuse to go. Be forcibly handled. Get there. Refuse to eat. Who would care? Run away. Where to? No welcome back here at Knight's Acre. Cast on to the scant charity of the roads and market places and every step taking her farther from Henry.

She said, 'You really *mean* this?'

'Yes, sweeting. For your good.'

'I see.' She did, in one blinding, emotion-intoxicated flash. She jumped up, skipped lightly over the tree trunk and began to run in the wrong direction, into the wood, towards the Three Pools.

She was light and nimble; he, though lean and hard, was more accustomed to plodding than running. She outdistanced him easily.

Neither of them could know that this was an inexact re-enactment of a scene in Spain played out between the mother of one of them and the father of them both. Tana had flung herself over a rotting balcony into a great river, sullied by the refuse of a great city. Joanna flung herself into a quiet pool, where the last of the water-lilies, yellow, pretty but stinking, floated on their pads above a surface green with duckweed. Sir Godfrey had been able to swim after a fashion, past the swollen carcase of a dead dog and a lot of kitchen rubbish; his son could only wallow through sucking mud towards the place where the lily pads were disturbed and some bubbles rising.

Dead?

Dead. And I killed her.

But in fact he had never really forgotten anything that Walter had ever told him, and one of Walter's most spectacular stories had concerned the bringing back to life of a man seemingly drowned dead. *He laid him over his knee,* Walter said, *and gave him a good bang. And that brought the water out. Then he put mouth to mouth and breathed in. That got the air back.*

He did it all, just as though Walter were standing behind him, giving directions. It worked. Not immediately; there was time enough for pity. So young, so frail: and for remorse — my fault! Then she gasped, once, twice.

Her first conscious act was to twist aside and vomit up the water that had reached not her lungs but her stomach. Henry held her as she retched.

'Better now?'

'Yes.'

'A fine fright you gave me. God! I thought you were dead.'

'I wanted to be. Rather than go away. Oh, Henry . . .'

As swiftly as she had turned from him, she turned towards him, her mouth smelling of muddy water, of blackberries and bile, pressed against his. Against his mouth, his eyes, his hair. She murmured endearments between the kisses. Things she could never have heard.

His seemingly uneventful life had held terrible moments but this was the worst. So stark, so shaming. Utterly shaming. A child, of eleven! It was unthinkable. But there it was.

He mastered himself, and her. He pulled himself free of her hands and stood up and said in a voice so hoarse that it growled, 'Come on. We're both soaked.'

Ignore it. Forget it. He began to walk back along the path and although she could outrun him his long loping stride gave him an advantage so that she had to take a running step now and then in order to stay level.

'Are you angry with me, Henry?'

'Yes, I am. Who wouldn't be? Such a daft thing to do.'

'The only thing. I couldn't live away from you, darling. And if you are angry I don't want to live.' He heard the threat and countered it.

'Walk ahead of me.'

As she passed him to obey she gave him a look, not shame-faced, not apologetic. Incredibly, a look of triumph, explained by her next words which she spoke without turning.

'*If* you were so angry, why did you pull me out?'

'Step out,' he said. 'We shall both catch our death of cold.'

'You love me, too, or you wouldn't have bothered. And I shall love you for ever and for ever, with all my heart and my soul and my strength.'

'Rubbish. If you were even mildly fond of me — or grateful — you'd do what I say.'

'Go away? And die of grief?'

'You don't know what you're talking about. Step out.'

They always knew, damn them, he thought. Tana had known that he loved her even as he was denouncing her. Griselda had known that he did not love her even as he was getting her with child.

The leaf-lined basket full of berries waited by the tree trunk. Neither noticed it.

Henry, hithero not over-troubled by imagination, now considered the future with dismay. There had always been casual physical contact between them, as innocent on his part as on hers. She'd swing on his hand and say, 'What a lovely morning.' Between the church and the end of the pie-stall they'd stood close together with their sausages, and often, in the wagon she'd lean against him or snuggle close. No more of that! But how would he manage?

He could see where he'd made this error this afternoon. He should have said, 'Yes, with you away, things will improve between Griselda and me.' She'd have gone then, and within a week forgotten him and been happy as a lark. Not that he doubted the sincerity of her fondness for him. Since Robert's going who else had there been? Poor child.

A child of eleven, he thought, with another wave of self-disgust. He was far too ignorant of the world to know that races differed in the age of reaching maturity. Half Joanna's blood was that of a tribe where girls were nubile at eleven, often married before they were twelve. Tana had been only just over twelve when she gave her heart, once and for ever to Sir Godfrey.

While Henry walked in miserable self-abasement, Joanna went lightly, too happy and elated to be aware of the chilly touch of the drenched linen smock. Ordinarily she was susceptible to cold. She viewed the future with joy. Henry might be angry now because she had given him a fright, but he'd come round. She'd make him come round. She knew exactly what she wanted, and what it would be like when attained. She was even capable of distinguishing between the love she had felt for Robert and what she felt for Henry — so different that it was silly to use the same word! And there would be added zest in deceiving Griselda!

Griselda!

Joanna stopped dead and turned, her hand to her mouth.

'Holy Mother! We forgot the blackberries! Shall I run back?'

'No. We've got to get home and into dry clothes.'

She gave him one of her merry, companionable looks. 'Well then, the Devil can have them without bothering to fly over. And Griselda will have enough to scold about — the state we are in! What shall we tell her?'

'Accident.'

'Yes. I over-reached for water-lilies and fell in. You pulled me out.'

The deceiving of Griselda had begun, the logical outcome of those half-amused glances, a lifted shoulder, the change of voice when she was referred to, either as Griselda or the more significant *she*. All, up to this moment innocent enough, the natural allegiance of two people suffering the same affliction. Now, suddenly, it had a deeper significance, smacking of connivance. Ugly and dangerous.

They had now reached the fringe of the wood, more frequented, more threaded with tracks, for even Sir Richard had not thought of withholding from the Intake men the right of appanage, a right which allowed them to drive their pigs, in autumn to eat the acorns which the oak-trees dropped. Nor had any ban been laid upon the gathering of hazel nuts and blackberries. So there were several beaten paths and Henry said, 'All right, that's settled! Take the shortest way. To the yard . . .'

CHAPTER THIRTY-ONE

The yard was flooded with the mellow, pre-sunset light against which, emerging from the shade they both squinted their eyes and squinting, saw in the entry, between the end of the house and the ruin of what had been Walter's cottage, a black, moving mass, at first sight neither human nor animal.

Henry said, 'What the Devil?' and lengthened his stride. The mass resolved itself: two men and a donkey. All three skeletonally thin and in the last stages of exhaustion.

Beggars.

One man sat astride the donkey, sagging forward. The other man, on his feet, was engaged in the almost impossible task of supporting his fellow with one hand and with the other urging the animal to take its few last steps. Both men wore rags which fluttered in the little breeze; the one on his feet wore shoes, badly broken; the one on the donkey was barefoot.

Beggars.

The man on the donkey coughed, sagging lower and spitting. The other steadied him and said, 'Bear up, Nick. We're *home*!' With his free hand he flailed the donkey.

John and Young Shep! No time to think. Henry knew enough about animals to see that the donkey was about to fall. He leapt forward and caught Young Shep just as it did so.

John said, 'Henry! Thank God! He can't walk . . .' Then he coughed too, a cough less shattering, less prolonged, but bad enough. Recovering from it, he said with a pitiable imitation of his old jauntiness, 'I'm afraid we're in rather a poor way.'

'Let's get in,' Henry said. Young Shep, though reduced to skin and bone was an awkward burden. Unyielding, all arms and legs, quite different from old Father Ambrose who once lifted, had accommodated himself. By the feel of Young Shep Henry thought he might be dead, and as he staggered around the end of the house and towards the kitchen door he reflected that it might be just as well. John circled round, getting in the way, saying, 'We're home, Nick! We did it. We're home!'

Joanna followed; interested, but wary. She did not recognise either man.

Griselda was giving Godfrey one of his special little meals, a treat to make up for his lack of freedom. It was not exactly surreptitious, even she, at her worst, could not persuade her self that Henry would grudge his own child a couple of coddled eggs! But it was private, something between herself and her son. It could be made into quite a performance — hunting the eggs, letting him choose between white shell or brown, letting him crack the shells. She never shared these little repasts; she no longer cared what she ate. Just enough to keep alive, and she knew from experience that she could keep alive on very little. She no longer took any care over supper; dinner yes, or there would be complaints from Jem. More often than not, nowadays Henry and Joanna fetched the loaf, the bit of hard cheese, or cold bacon. And it delighted Griselda to say, 'He's had his supper.' In equal measure it annoyed her when Godfrey persisted in standing by his father and accepting, with obvious relish, something from his platter. 'That's right,' she would say. 'Make him sick. I told you, he's had his supper.'

Once Henry had said, 'But he's hungry. Anybody who can eat this must be sharp set.' And once he had said, 'At his age I could have eaten an old woman on a horse, harness and all.'

Now Godfrey, spoon poised, turned his head in a listening attitude. 'Farder,' he said, his face lighting up.

The door was flung open and Henry staggered in.

Just for once Griselda was rendered speechless. Henry and Joanna, all muddied and slimed with green, and two strangers; one dead; the other mustering a kind of smile on his death's head face and saying, 'Ah, Griselda! Still here.'

As Henry had done, she recognised John by his voice. Dumbfounded at first by surprise she was now rendered speechless by rage. Her mouth opened and shut without sound. Two more paupers! Joanna, Dick, Robert — worse than a pauper because, alive or dead he was a drain on the frail resources of Knight's Acre. And now this!

Henry lowered the dead-looking man into the chair which had been Tom's — specially provided for him as he grew more feeble. Seated, he began to cough, and John coughed too. Then Griselda recognised the lung-rot. It had been endemic in the orphanage, a slow killer for which there was no cure. And the nuns had believed that it was spread by coughing, sufferers had been ordered to turn their heads away when they coughed.

Still without speaking, she seized Godfrey by the hand and hustled him towards the door of the hall. He protested.

'I wanted to *see*. And I hadn't finished my supper.' She pushed him through the doorway, turned back, snatched up the bowl and the spoon, went into the hall and slammed the door behind her.

Here she could speak. 'Now mark my words. You are *never* to go near those men. Never!'

'Why not?'

'They have a sickness on them and if you go near them you will catch it and die.' Godfrey had never seen a dead person — only dead animals and birds. The thought that *people* could die was appalling. He stared at her wide-eyed and with something of the repulsion that attached itself to those who gave unwelcome information.

'Like rabbits?' he asked in a stricken voice.

'Yes. Just like that.'

He pushed the bowl away. 'I don't want any more.'

'Don't be silly. If you don't eat you will be sick, too.'

'And die?'

'Yes. People who don't eat do die.' Oh, why hadn't that pair died before they got here? Reluctantly Godfrey took up his spoon and began to eat, but with less than his normal gusto. As he ate Griselda repeated her warning, never, never to go near those men. She thought — God alone knows what else they have brought with them; other illnesses probably; lice almost certainly. And how could life be so organised as to avoid all contact?

The black pot used for broth stood on the hearth. It was seldom empty. Lumps of meat or stringy fowls were boiled in it, taken out and eaten. To the liquor onions, dried peas and beans were added, bones were returned to it. From time to time bones and other solids were scooped out and the process begun again. When the broth was often set like glue.

Henry lifted the pot and hung it on the hook over the dying fire. Without being told to Joanna added dry sticks, one by one until the fire revived. She put four bowls and four spoons on the table. John knelt by Young Shep and said, over and over again, 'We did it, Nick. We got here. I told you. Get some food inside you and you'll feel better.'

280

Henry said, 'Joanna, go and get out of those wet clothes.'

'What about you?'

'I'm all right.'

John turned on his knees. 'A little wine would help.'

'There's not a drop in the house.' As he went to fetch bread, Henry thought sourly that if John had been content to leave his share of the flock in the field, and buckled down to hard work, things might have been different here.

Young Shep had another coughing spell, and John held him, pressed to his mouth a piece of old linen, already horribly stained.

Henry's knowledge of the disease was less intimate than Griselda's, but he had seen people coughing and spitting in the market. To spit red, as people said, was a sure sign that the end was not far off.

'Lung-rot,' Henry said.

'It is *not*!' For a man in so weak, emaciated a state John spoke with astonishing vehemence. 'He caught a cold. In Italy — it can be very cold there, in winter — and it settled on his chest. I caught it, too, but more mildly.' He coughed. 'You can't sing or make music with a chest cold. So we began to go hungry — the very worst thing. A little good food and a rest will set him right. Won't it, Nick?'

Joanna came back. She had cleaned herself a bit, though green duckweed still clung to her damp hair. She had on the clothes she wore to church or market and she carried Henry's winter coat, a rough sheepskin.

'It'll warm you,' she said. Henry, that independent, strong-minded man, entertained for a moment an extraordinary thought. Nobody, since Mother died, has ever given my comfort or welfare any consideration. Even in the early days of their marriage Griselda had done her duty, but as a duty, no more. He thought — I have been nothing but a provider; the workhorse of the place. And things would be worse now; more to provide for. And so unfair. John could say, with justification, that this was his home. It was not Young Shep's!

The black pot bubbled. Joanna swung the hook so that the base of the pot was no longer over the fire. 'I'll do it,' she said, seizing the ladle, 'you cut the bread, Henry.' Having filled the bowls she lighted a candle.

John left his broth to cool while he fed little bits of sopped bread and spoonfuls of broth to Young Shep, encouraging him, as a fond mother would a child. It was ridiculous, Henry thought — two grown men! But it was touching too. Abruptly, Henry remembered a day when John had shovelled muck in order to spare Young Shep the distasteful job.

Something in Young Shep revived. He spoke for the first time. 'I never thought ... we'd do it ... Johnny boy.'

'I knew we could — because we must. And we did. There now, you sit back and rest.'

He came to the table and began on his own broth, cooling, slightly scummed with congealing fat. Between spoonfuls and great chunks of bread — he was plainly starving — he talked, bragging, bringing into this candle-lighted kitchen in a remote corner of England a tale of far places, of palaces, success and acclaim beyond any comprehension. His playing of the lute, the songs Nick made — even when translated — had been recognised, applauded. One great lord had commended them to another ... They'd had a wonderful life, until ...

'We were in Padua,' he said, 'and bound for Venice. The Doge had expressed a wish that we should sing and play before him. We had a new — a wonderful song all about an old custom they have. They call Venice the Bride of the Sea, you know and every year ...' Coughing interrupted him.

'Better not talk,' Henry said. 'It'll keep.'

Yes, it would keep, the long sad story of the chest cold which would not budge; the attempt to earn a living and look after a sick man; falling sick himself; the decision to try to reach home; begging a way across Europe — and even the charitable feared the cough; the final act of despair — the sale of the lute and Nick's silver pipe to buy a passage from Calais to Bywater and the acquisition of the old donkey which had been abandoned as worthless.

'Yes,' John said, 'and Nick should be abed. Even if we could have paid, innkeepers don't like customers who cough. I can't remember where or when we last slept in a bed.'

'Shall I get it ready?' Joanna asked. Henry was about to say yes when the door opened and there was Griselda. She had taken a decision and nothing would move her. She had no fear for herself — had she been likely to catch the lung-sickness she'd have taken it long ago in the orphanage, but she had the child to consider.

Addressing Henry, ignoring everyone else she said, 'I'm not having them here. Let that be understood!'

'It's *my* house. And John's *home*,' Henry said. Young Shep had a coughing spell and she raised her voice. 'Listen to that! It may be your house, Henry Tallboys, but it's mine too. Hard earned if ever anything was and I will not have them under my roof. If they must stay, let them go in the barn.'

She was not aware of speaking and acting very much as the landlady of The Swan had done, all those years before. And it did not occur to her to explain the reason for banning them. Fear and fury, mingling with long cherished resentment had intoxicated her. The light of the one candle on the table, the fire dying down again to a glimmer, did not give light enough to show the crazy determination in her eyes.

Henry said, 'The barn isn't suitable.' It was in fact a ramshackle building, hastily built from odds and ends of timber, a thing he meant to replace; one day; when he had money and time.

'Go make that bed, honey,' he said to Joanna.

'Don't you dare,' Griselda said. She stopped by the hearth and thrust a dry twig into the embers; it blazed and holding it high she said, 'I'll set fire to the bed first. I'll fire the whole place. If I'm to have no say, I'll burn it down.'

Joanna watched. What would Henry do?

Henry went towards his wife and took hold of the wrist of the hand that held the burning twig. In a flash she transferred it to her other hand and jabbed it at him. Had his hair been dry it would have flared, but it was damp. He seized her other hand, threw the stick towards the hearth, took Griselda by the scruff of her neck and propelled her into the hall. But it was — and he knew it — only a temporary victory. There would be tomorrow . . . and tomorrow. Fire always accessible to her.

The smoke that the blazing brand had given off had set both the coughs going. Mastering his attack, John said, 'Actually a barn would be welcome, Henry.' Across his ravaged face there flitted the ghost of his old cheeky smile. 'I take it you married her.'

'Never mind that now.' Henry looked at Young Shep, his long limp limbs asprawl in the chair. 'It'd be easier if I could get him on my back and he'd put his arms round my neck and hold on.'

Young Shep had not spoken since he'd said, 'I never thought we'd do it, Johnny boy,' and now John answered for him, as a mother would do for a child. 'Oh, Nick'll hold on, won't you, Nick? Just one more effort, my dear, then you can rest and get better.'

Young Shep still said nothing, but his sunken, over-bright eyes looked at John with adoration, and he nodded.

Well, Henry thought, love comes in all shapes and sizes. He slipped off the cumbersome coat and went towards the chair.

Joanna said, 'Henry!'

'Well?'

'Wouldn't the rooms across the yard be better?'

'Of course! Why didn't I think?'

'But the door is blocked . . .' She was already busy with the lantern, lighting its candle from the one on the table. 'I'll help,' she said. 'You chop the rosemary and I'll pull away the other stuff.'

Outside Henry found a hatchet and together they went around the end of the pavilion to the door of the pavilion which had figured so largely in both their lives — old lives, over and done with, like a cast snake-skin.

The rosemary, overgrown as it was, offered little resistance and as Henry hacked at it and Joanna ripped down the honeysuckle trails, he had time to think. He thought of John's reply to Young Shep's one remark. 'I knew we could — because we must.' That was the voice of the survivor — of all survivors; and he was one. Because he must he could; because he could he must . . .

He could and must disregard utterly what had happened by the pool that afternoon. Any man worthy of the name should be able to rule himself. He must, because he could, now assume responsibility for supporting two sick men — one perhaps not for long. John, not yet spitting red, might linger for years.

'That'll do,' he said. 'Stand clear.' He put his shoulder to the door which briefly resisted and then slowly creaked open. It was impossible not to remember that night when, entering in anger, he had found Paradise, but he thought of it, and of the morning that followed in a distant kind of way, just one more thing that he had survived — like Walter's death, and Sybilla's, and his joyless marriage which had this evening revealed itself for what it was.

Joanna was remembering, too. Those few happy times when she and Robert, entering by the window had played pebble games with jewels; and the plan she had made to hide him here, and of what had come of that. All past now; not exactly forgotten, but pushed aside. *Lived through.* That was the answer. It wouldn't do, she realised, to make any open display of her love. It simply made Henry uncomfortable and therefore angry. He was married to Griselda, who, by her behaviour this evening had surely forfeited any claim to consideration. Griselda had threatened her with places where mad people were confined, chained, whipped. And surely any woman who threatened to set her own house on fire was mad. And bad.

Rounding the house again, Joanna said, 'Shall we go gleaning tomorrow? If we do I think Godfrey should come. You did promise . . .'

'So I did.'

With instinctive feminine wisdom Joanna knew better than to swing on his hand, clutch his arm or press against him. She said, conversationally, 'I want to hear more of John's stories, when his cough is better. Don't you?'

'Yes. But there'll be time for that. The thing is now to get them both to bed.'

Back in the kitchen, Henry went straight to what had always been regarded as Tom's chair, stooped to a level at which Young Shep, urged by John, helped by John, could clamber on to his back. Upon shoulders, braced to take the load . . .

Book Three

THE LONELY FURROW

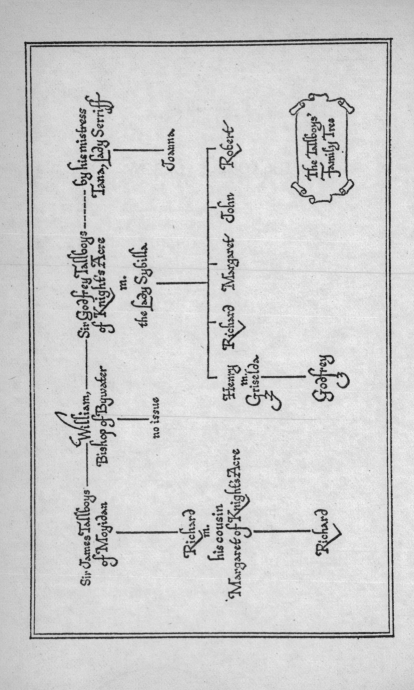

The Tallboys' Family Tree

Sir James Tallboys of Mayidan

William, Bishop of Bywater — Sir Godfrey Tallboys of Knight's Acre ------ by his mistress Iana, Lady Serriff

m. the Lady Sybilla

no issue

Richard m. his cousin Margaret of Knight's Acre

Joanna

Henry m. Griselda   Richard   Margaret   John   Robert

Richard

Godfrey

At the end of the last furrow Henry Tallboys halted the plough and looked about him with grim satisfaction. Some way behind him in the field, Jem Watson, his hired man, was spreading the wheat grain – less evenly and rhythmically than Henry himself would have done, but no man could plough and sow at the same time. Behind Jem was the girl, Joanna, dragging the branch which pulled soil over the seed to protect it from weather and the ravages of winter-hungered birds.

Henry was tall. It was a family characteristic, but the name had nothing to do with stature; it was a corruption of the Norman–French Taillebois. Most men of more than average height, at the end of a day at the plough's tail would have needed to straighten up; at the end of years of ploughing, would have acquired a ploughman's stoop, but Henry had adapted his plough to himself, not himself to his plough. He had fitted it with long, high handles, like a deer's antlers. So, on this October morning, with the wind from the north telling of winter's onset, he stood straight and flat shouldered, more like the knight that his father had been – as he might have been – than the farmer he had chosen to be. Even in his homespun hose and jerkin, in heavy ankle shoes and the cloth leg wrappings of the working man, Henry Tallboys was an impressive figure; hard manual work since the age of seven, some of it, like shovelling manure, dirty work, had done nothing to impair his dignity. His looks he had inherited from his father, Sir Godfrey – in his time a knight of renown but of no great intelligence, of a curiously childlike simplicity. From his mother, the Lady Sybilla, Henry had inherited fortitude, self-will and impregnable dignity; but he owed even more to a man who was no kin at all, a sardonic, sceptical, ex-archer named Walter who had taught him the valuable lesson of ingenuity, the art of survival in a hostile world.

Unaware of all the things that had gone to his making, Henry looked around, taking stock of the situation. He could now take the seed tray from Jem's neck and say, 'I'll finish. You take the horse in.' If he did that the last furrows would be more evenly sown, in Walter's way, but it would leave Henry alone in the field with Joanna, the girl, the child, dressed like a ploughboy, eleven and a half years old, but precocious beyond belief. So he called to Jem and to Joanna, 'That's the end. I'll take the horse away. You should be finished by dinnertime.'

Everywhere else oxen, not horses, were plough animals, but twenty years earlier, with no ox and no money to buy one, Walter had hitched a makeshift plough to a decrepit horse, and Henry, willing pupil, had stuck to Walter's ways.

On this October, winter-threatening morning, he led the horse to the stable, unharnessed it, gave it a friendly thump and saw that the manger was full. Then, out in the wind again, he hesitated slightly. He could go to the right, enter his own kitchen door, or left, round the end of the shorter wing of his peculiar house. He chose the latter, thinking— Better get it over and done with! He hoped that Griselda was not glancing from the kitchen window. She herself did so many things from sheer perversity that she took his daily, necessary visit to two sick men, one his own brother, as a deliberately provoking action on his part. In fact the visit was a penance to him; partly because of the memories which this part of the house evoked, and partly because of the worry which the present occupants represented.

It cost him an effort to say, with some semblance of heartiness, 'Well, how are you today?'

'I'm better,' John Tallboys said. 'I told you I ailed nothing that rest and good food couldn't cure. Not that the food has been all that good!' As he made this criticism the young man grimaced, half a smile, half something else, a sly, conniving we're-all-in-the-same-boat look which should have taken the sting from the remark, but did not.

'You've had the best the place afforded,' Henry said. It was true; milk straight from the cow, eggs, fresh meat when

8

the pig was killed a fortnight ago, fowls which could be ill-spared. Not only that, John, who was able to move about had been provided with new clothes to replace his rags, and the one physician in Baildon had been brought out to confirm, or deny, Griselda's hasty, damning verdict of lung-rot and to offer what palliatives he could. He had confirmed it; both young men would be dead by Christmas, he said, and all that Master Tallboys could do was to see that they were as comfortable, as happy as possible during the interim. For this gloomy verdict and a few cough-relieving medic-aments, the doctor had charged two nobles – the better part of a pound and while he was tapping chests and listening as though chests were doors to be answered, his horse had claimed a guest's privilege and gobbled down what was in the manger.

That was almost a month ago and John had said at the time that the old mutt-head was wrong; he and Nick were simply suffering from colds that had settled on their chests, aggravated by exposure and near starvation. Maybe in his own case he was right, for here he was, chirpy as a sparrow, gathering flesh on his bones. But from the inner room, the bedroom, Henry heard the rattling, doomed cough.

'And how is he?'

'Better, too, thank you, Henry. One must remember that he is older and caught the cold before I did. I kept him in bed today because I was clearing this room up a bit and there was dust. Tomorrow he will lie on one of these divans and I shall beat about in there.'

The two rooms had been furnished by a woman from a far country who had lined ceiling and walls with silk, pleated, in imitation of her father's temporary pavilions, put up, taken down, well shaken at each move. Shut away, deliberately ignored for years the two rooms had accumulated dust and cobwebs and could certainly do with a cleaning.

Henry said, 'I'm glad you feel up to it. I'll go get your dinner ... No, I'm full early ... John I have something to ask of you.'

'Yes?' John said, in a non-committal voice. 'What is it?'

'It concerns Joanna.'

'Yes?' John said. He was not being helpful; but then, Henry remembered, he never had been, even when he lived here. He'd always shirked work as much as possible and gone running off to the sheep-fold to play his lute and make songs with the young shepherd who shared his frivolous taste.

'Her mother,' Henry said, avoiding as usual the use of Tana's name, 'left her a small fortune – in jewels.' He saw John's eyes brighten, interested at last. 'The Bishop of Bywater took charge of them, and converted some, at least, into cash. At the same time he found a place for her in the household of a man with daughters of his own; a place where she would have an upbringing suitable to one of her birth and the chance of a good marriage. She absolutely refused to go.'

'I always thought Tana was not quite right in the head. Her daughter takes after her.'

Without knowing it Henry clenched his fist.

'You could help. You have seen the world; how people live; the comforts and pleasures people enjoy ... Joanna dotes on stories ... I think that if you tried, you could make another way of life sound attractive enough to make her change her mind. It's no sort of life for her here. Griselda has taken against her. She works and dresses like ploughboy ... I'm worried about her.'

'I could certainly spin a yarn or two,' John said, recalling wistfully those glorious days when he and Nick had been in much demand with their new songs and catchy tunes; welcome in great halls, in palaces; no village green audiences, no market squares for them! They'd been on their way to Venice, by request from the Doge himself, when this cursed illness had struck, and ruined them. But the good days would come again. He himself was better, and Nick would be, given time. They'd need money at first. They'd had some on the former occasion – John's share of his father's estate.

'I'll do my best to persuade her.' He said, smugly, 'I'm supposed to have rather a way with women.' Which was, he thought, something of an irony, since he had no liking for them. 'If I do succeed, I shall expect something for my trouble.'

'You shall have it.' Henry had the excellent memory of the illiterate man. 'His Grace sent word that some of the jewels had been sold and the money deposited with Sir Barnabas Grey who had a use for it, and who was willing to take the child. No doubt everybody would be so glad to have the whole thing tied up, they'd be willing to pay.'

In the bedroom the man whom Henry still thought of as Young Shep, coughed again.

'I'll start this evening,' John promised, 'when she brings our supper across. As you say, she is interested in the outer world. She's always asking questions.'

'Give her the right answers ... You're better, and I'm glad of it. But I think she'd better not go too near him. Griselda may be right.'

'Your pardon, Brother. Griselda is a bitch – and a mad bitch at that!'

'And my wife. So mind your tongue!'

Ignoring the rebuke, John said, 'Speaking of supper, what's for dinner?'

'I'll go and see.'

For the first time in Henry's memory – apart from the time when the plague struck and he was trying to get the harvest in, single-handed, and Sybilla, his mother, was nursing three desperately ill people, there was no sign of a meal being prepared in the kitchen. A good fire blazed in the hearth, but neither spit nor black pot were in use, and the faggot that should have been used to fire the oven – for this was bread-baking day, Henry remembered – lay there untouched. The table was clean and completely bare.

Griselda and Godfrey were by the fire playing cat's cradle. As Henry entered, Griselda said, 'Godfrey, go play in the hall. Run about to keep warm. Give your hobby horse a good gallop.'

The boy was now four, with the Tallboys' precocity, tired of his restricted, mother-ruled life, and on the verge of rebellion. But Griselda had ways of dealing with even incipient rebellion. She could change in an instant, as Godfrey well knew, from fond, doting mother to something quite frightening. She did so now because he did not move quickly towards the door between kitchen and hall. She said in her nasty voice, 'Get along with you. Do as I say!' and speeded him with a push and the smack on the bottom.

One day I shall hit her back!

*

'What about dinner?' Henry asked.

'There will be no dinner. Not today, nor any other day so long as this goes on. I've come to the end of my tether. I'm not going to work my fingers to the bone to keep a couple of vagabonds with the lung-rot! I've told you and told you. I might as well talk to the wind. You went there this morning and dared to come straight in here, with the cough in your hair; on your clothes. I told you that first time; I've said the same every day since and that's more than a month. I arranged things as well as I could, no comings and goings, I said. This is *my* home, and God knows it cost me dear enough! I'd had other offers – did you know that? If it'd only been a clod cottage, I'd have been mistress of it, not the slave I am here, working my fingers to the bone and no say in who comes or goes. That wicked, wicked girl. You sided with *her* against *me*, even when she'd nearly killed your own child! There's never any money for anything. When did I have a new gown? When did Godfrey have anything except shoes? Pinch and scrape, pinch and scrape. Then along come two rogues and the best is hardly good enough . . .'

Henry was accustomed to her railing, skilled at turning a deaf ear, but this morning John had used the word 'mad', so now he looked at her with more attention than usual. Her eyes, greenish and rather small, glittered, but with malice rather than madness, or so it seemed to him. He swung round and went towards the larder. Four pigeons, unplucked, lay on a shelf. Dinner today should have been pigeon pie! The thought reminded him that he was hungry. Jem must be fed – a good dinner was part of his wage and anything less provoked grumbling; Joanna was still growing and had done a hard morning's work, she needed food, too. And there were two men across the courtyard. Waiting. For what? Henry seldom entered the larder but it struck him that today it was singularly bare, even for Knight's Acre in the middle of an unprosperous spell. Most of the pig, killed the week before last was now either salted down in a cask, or being smoked in the chimney, but surely, surely there had been the better half of a side of bacon from the pig before that, enough to tide them over until the new side was ready. All that was left was enough to make four or five rashers, cut very thin. Two for Jem who would grumble even at that preferential treatment, one each for Joanna, John and Young Shep. Henry himself would make do with bread and cheese. He lifted the lid of the bread crock, which was not a crock at all, but a wooden container made by Tom Robinson who had liked to be useful even when he couldn't work. It was a huge log, hollowed out, chip by chip, and fitted with a lid, with some airholes and a knob. It was quite empty because in any ordinary week this was the time when the fresh new bread should have come, sweet-smelling from the oven. The butter crock – which was a crock – was almost empty. And where was the cheese? He remembered it from last night, suppertime; a good new cheese which would as days passed get harder and less palatable, but still nourishing. No sign of it anywhere. Beside the poor bit of bacon the only thing the shelf offered him was yeast, of which, aware that winter was at hand, he had bought a good jugful on his last visit to Baildon. Griselda had dealt with it properly, spreading a little on a board, letting it dry, spreading another layer, and so on. The cake was now about three inches thick, nine wide, ten long. Enough to last through the bad weather when marketing was impossible. Also there was a sack of flour.

Henry stood there, utterly defeated. He'd taken some blows in his life, faced some peculiar and puzzling situations, but the problem of how to feed five hungry people – he included himself but excluded his wife and his son for Griselda often fed Godfrey apart and ate little herself – on a few scraps of bacon, some yeast and flour, made him despair. It couldn't be done. Nobody could do it. Even Walter – and years after Walter was dead, Henry was accustomed to ask himself – in any crisis – what would Walter do? Even the Lady Sybilla, his mother, a marvel at managing and contriving couldn't have done it.

He stood there with the north wind cutting through the slatted window of the larder and thought how ridiculous! After all I have borne to be defeated and shamed now by a woman's refusal to cook or keep house.

The girl, Joanna, came padding in. She had remembered, as he had not, the house rule of shedding muddy footwear. She said, 'Henry, Griselda has gone moonstruck. I will make dinner.'

'Out of what?'

He pointed to the remnant of bacon, the empty bread crock the bare shelf where the cheese should have been.

'But ...' Joanna said. 'Only yesterday ... where can it have gone?' Determination replaced the puzzlement on her face. 'I'll make pancakes. Brighten the fire, Henry.'

That a girl child, eleven and a half years old, should be able to cook was nothing marvellous, but ever since Joanna had offended Griselda four years earlier, she had been banished from the kitchen, from all the sheltered, domestic side of life, driven away from the hearthside into the fields or the fold.

'Can I do anything else to help, Sw ...' Henry chopped off the endearment, formerly in frequent use and still coming easily to his tongue, reaching back as it did to the days when he had regarded her as a child, as his ward.

'Yes. You can chop this bacon into tiny pieces while I beat the batter.'

Griselda was not in the kitchen, but Jem Watson was, hungry for his food, and watchful for anything which might be related afterwards, down in the village where what happened up at Knight's Acre was always news and he, firsthand gossip, welcome to a place by the fire, a mug of ale and a ready audience.

'Missus took ill, Master?' Not unlikely, with the lung-rot about the place. And Master Tallboys chopping some scrag ends of bacon, the little girl whipping batter.

'Not quite herself,' Henry said evasively and was immediately contradicted by a burst of laughter from the hall where Griselda, to make up for the smack and the push was playing with her son. He astride his hobby horse was the hunter, she, down on all fours, the quarry.

Joanna made five pancakes.

Henry said, 'I'll take theirs across.'

'No. You sit down and eat yours, Henry. This is one of my jobs.'

One of those which Griselda had assigned, rather more than a month ago when the two men had arrived, ragged, coughing, dying. Griselda had refused to have them in the house, and it was Joanna who had remembered the empty rooms on the other side of the yard. Rooms which had for her as poignant memories as they held for Henry, but different.

Griselda had accepted the need to provide food for the ailing men, but she had done it grudgingly, and ordered Joanna to do the carrying. The other side of the house had a kitchen of its own; its kitchen door faced, almost exactly, that of the main house. But for good reasons of her own – which nobody knew about – Joanna's mother, Tana who had built the new wing, had built it with a kitchen accessible to the yard, but not to the two rooms which made up the dwelling place. Even when that kitchen had been in use anything cooked in it must have been carried out, round the end of the building, and in by the door on the garden side.

Accepting the dinner – surely the best anybody could have produced in such short time, with so little, John said, 'Is this all?'

Joanna said, 'For now. There will be pigeon pie for supper, I promise you.' The words sounded placating, but the glance she gave him was not. Her feelings towards him and towards Young Shep were not much unlike Griselda's, though stemming from a different cause. The two men, too ill to be useful, not ill enough to die, were part of Henry's burden and loving Henry as she did, she could only resent them and regret that she had suggested housing them here, in comfort, instead of letting them go, as Griselda had shouted, to sleep in the barn. She'd acted on impulse, wishing to help Henry when Griselda turned so awkward.

'You know, Joanna, properly dressed, you'd be very pretty.' John was beginning to exercise his charm. Too late. Hitherto he had taken little notice of her, answered her questions brusquely and often seemed ungrateful for what she brought.

Now she said, 'I know,' and hurried back to her pancake.

In the kitchen Jem Watson was displeased with his meal – a bloody pancake, like the beginning of Lent! and displeased, also, by Henry's uncommunicativeness. He'd have liked to know what ailed a woman who was unable to make a dinner, but, to judge by the noise, was capable of romping about in the hall. It could be mere bad temper. Jem knew that the Missus was a nagger and a scold, but never before had she failed to provide, and he would have liked to know *why*.

Spearing up the last crumb of pancake on his knife, chewing thoughtfully and then speaking before he had emptied his mouth, Jem said, 'Would it suit better if I brought my bit of docky with me in future?'

'Your *what*?' That was infuriating, too. Master Tallboys wasn't Suffolk-born, but he'd lived here long enough to know the language.

'My docky, my dinner, my nosebag. I mean, if it suited better, my owd mother could put me up a bit of dinner in a poke. Then I'd hev to ask another fivepence a week.'

Henry gave a sour smile. 'I'm glad you think that your usual dinner here is worth that much!' It was a third of Jem's weekly wage.

One of the reasons why a good dinner was so often part of the bargain between master and man was that in most places cash money was in short supply; even now the system of barter ruled many transactions. Between Henry and the miller who turned his wheat into flour, or the smith who shod his horse, no coin ever changed hands. The miller paid himself by withholding so much flour, the smith would accept a dozen eggs, a pint of butter, a goose ready for the oven.

Thinking of this, Henry Tallboys cast a backward look upon two things which, because they had involved him in cash transactions, had kept him poor. His brother John, seven years ago, had insisted upon taking his share of Sir Godfrey's estate out in cash: and to buy in John's share of the flock, Henry had been forced to borrow and pay interest. And then there had been the question of his other, much younger brother, Robert, who had simply disappeared. Joanna insisted that he was dead, but of that there was no proof. Until there was Henry would go on taking Robert's share of the dwindling profits from the flock into the office of the lawyer, Master Turnbull of Baildon. Henry was well versed in the lesson that people could disappear and then, after years, turn up. Hadn't his own father, Sir Godfrey, vanished into Spain, been deemed dead, and then turned up after eight years of slavery with the Moors? Five years ago his brother Robert had disappeared, a child, six years old; possibly stolen; he'd been a pretty boy . . . Roaming bands of people, half entertainers, half beggars, did recruit attractive children – or steal them . . . Anyway, if Robert ever came home, he would find his bit of patrimony safe and ready; in cash, safely invested by Master Turnbull.

It took Henry only a second to recall these things, which with bad weather and bad luck had contributed to his present state. He also had time to think that so far, although he had taken heavy knocks, he'd never yet been floored. So he said, 'Please yourself, Jem. But twopence is the limit. And mind this – if you can find another job, better paid, better fed, within walking distance, go to it. Never mind about our Michaelmas bargain.'

Jem said, 'I was only thinking, Master Tallboys . . .' Thinking – Jesus and Holy Mary, where would I find a job between Michaelmas and Candlemas Day? Within walking distance, at fifteen pence a week and a good dinner?

'I was only thinking,' he said again. And an explanation occurred to him. The Missus had just started up another baby!

Women often went funny at such times, took against their husbands and against rounded, bulging things, like cooking pots. Not the first time so much, the first time they were in pod they were glad . . . If they got a boy and managed to rear him out of the cradle, they reckoned their job was done. Men often felt the same.

Down in the village Jem knew of a couple – and it was odd, they'd both worked up here at Knight's Acre at one time. Bert Edgar, when he inherited Edgarsacre had married a woman called Jill. He'd wanted *one* son, and got him; and in every following year, every time Jill came into pod again he'd given her such a thrashing!

Had such a thing happened here? Was Mistress Tallboys away there in the hall, hiding a bruised face?

'Henry, you don't *pluck* pigeons,' Joanna said in reply to his offer to help. 'Is that water hot yet? Good, then I will show you.' She plunged in the little bodies, heads and feet chopped off, disembowelled, but still wearing their feathers. Count a hundred and there they were, dredged out, feathers stuck together, ready, with the skin that held them to come off like the shell of a hard-boiled egg.

'That's a trick I didn't know,' Henry said. 'Where'd you learn it?'

'When I was young,' she said, speaking as though youth were a far distant thing, 'I used to watch Griselda. There, now I have only the pastry and the bread to make. Thank you for firing the oven for me.'

'Call me when you want it opened. I shall be nearby, shovelling muck.'

The oven had an iron door, placed at a height in the wall suitable for a grown woman; a little too high for Joanna, though she was tall for her age; and far too heavy, hardy as she had proved herself to be at field work, ever since her banishment from the kitchen. Anxious to prove herself, anxious indeed to excel, she had often succeeded in seeming to be what she looked like – a small, but willing and capable ploughboy. Henry had always been aware that she was in the wrong place, leading a highly unsuitable life; wished he could do something about it. Had finally been able to. And to what end? He still shuddered away from the memory of that unbelievable, fantastic scene in the wood after he'd told her what plans he had made for her; but he did remember the extreme lightness, the seeming frailty of the body he'd dragged from the pool.

'Thank you, Henry. I'll call if I need you.'

She was, she thought, behaving very well; giving no sign of the jubilation which shot through her – stimulating as wine – as she thought; he never offered to do that for Griselda!

Thumping the dough and setting it on the hearth to rise, turning her attention to the pastry, Joanna thought about Griselda and hoped that this latest queer mood would last for ever. She knew in her bones – had known it for a long time – that she fitted Henry far better than Griselda did. They could share jokes, not only outright jokes but the unspoken things, the lift of a shoulder, the twitch of one corner of the mouth which said: Funny! He'd always stood up for her, even when, in desperation, she'd stolen Godfrey. She'd done him no harm, he was warm and snug and safe and the bargain could be struck in a minute – Promise to bring

18

Robert home from Moyidan, where he is so unhappy, and you can have your baby back. It hadn't worked. She'd had to try other, even more desperate means – and Robert had died because of what she had done. But that was all long ago, and far away. Her attachment to Robert, motherly and protective, had transferred itself to Henry and was altogether different.

Now, if only Griselda could remain moonstruck, she could prove to Henry that she was as useful inside the house as without. That done she could surely coax him into using some of *her* money to buy new animals, hire more help. Beyond that her view of the future was hazy, but it included fine clothes and good horses, and living in the hall which she could just remember, so splendid with candles when Godfrey was christened.

Joanna did not visualise marriage; her emotional experience was already wider than that of most adult women, but her knowledge of the world was very limited; and half her blood was Tana's, wild and free, not concerned with monogamy. Joanna was unaware of this, except in instinct, in her bone marrow. What she did know was that it would be to her advantage to manage the oven without calling Henry from his work.

The faggot which he had placed in it and fired, had burnt out now. Standing on a stool she grappled with the heavy door, felt the full blast of the heat which the bricks had absorbed and were about to give off; raked the ashes to one side, pushed the bread to the back of the hot cavity and placed the pie in the front. Slamming the heavy door, she thought of the words with which she would produce it – Henry, not the four and twenty blackbirds, baked in a pie, but the best I could do. He'd understand, and smile, at least.

Griselda had shot her bolt, made her stand. And so far nobody had taken any notice. What they'd done about dinner she didn't know. When Godfrey tired of the hunting game and turned querulous she had said, 'All right then, we'll go for a walk.'

'Not to church, if you please.'

Quite suddenly he'd begun to grow away from her, could speak properly, watch, ask questions; soon he would be hers no longer; and he was the only person, the only thing she had ever fully possessed in all her life – except Tom Robinson's devotion, the value of which she had realised too late.

'No. We'll walk in the wood.'

'And gather sticks?'

'Yes, darling. And nuts if there are any left.' She sounded like herself again and her son reflected with childish complacency that she was never angry with him for long. He did not notice that she was unusually quiet or that she gathered sticks and hunted for nuts with less energy than usual.

He was never allowed to venture into the wood by himself, so he had developed no sense of direction and was displeased to find that as they emerged from the trees they were near the church and the priest's house.

'I said *not* church. Did you forget?' He spoke with the arrogance of a pampered child.

'Not to go in. Just to go past,' Griselda said.

That was all right then. The little boy did not know that he led an unusually boring life every day, but he did know that he hated those long sessions alone in the church with his mother, who knelt down, covered her face with her hands, and seemed to go away. When he had studied the pictures on the walls and they were all too familiar by now, there was nothing to do; he mustn't speak, and if he moved must go on tip-toe. By contrast he liked church on Sunday morning, with more people there, when Father Benedict did mysterious things at the altar, and you knelt, or stood and were allowed to say things at times, even if you hadn't yet fully mastered the words.

He hoped that Mistress Captoft would come out of the house by the church and perhaps invite them in and give him a honey cake. Quite apart from her offerings, he liked her; she had a smiling face – for him, at least – her clothes were pretty and she smelt sweet.

Mistress Captoft spent a good deal of her spare time looking out of the window; not that there was anything to see, except the sheep-fold across the track, and beyond it just a glimpse of the roofs of the highest standing village houses; but looking out of the window was a habit she had formed when she lived at Dunwich, a busy, bustling place.

Now she looked out and saw Mistress Tallboys standing

stock still and staring into the graveyard, as she often did. Rather a puzzling habit, for only the dead of Intake lay under the mounds there, and Mistress Tallboys was not a native of the village. The only grave in which she might be presumed to take an interest was inside the church, where Lady Sybilla slept under a rather short slab of black marble. Lady Sybilla had employed the girl as a nursemaid. Later, after his mother's death, Master Tallboys had married her, so there was a relationship, although a posthumous one. (All this, and some other things, Mistress Captoft had learned, not from village gossip — that she sedulously avoided, but from the old woman who had kept house for the former priest, and who now shuffled up to do the roughest work.)

Mistress Captoft took a honey cake, lifted her cloak from the peg inside the door and went out. She wouldn't ask them in this afternoon, for Father Benedict was in the parlour, busy with his studies, and the other little room, having no hearth, was cold.

'Good day, Mistress Tallboys,' she said brightly. 'And how is my god-son today?'

It was true that she had sponsored the little boy at the font, and as she placed the honey cake into the eager hand she had a piercing memory of that occasion, of all that it had seemed to promise and the nothingness that had resulted. Master Tallboys' brother, Sir Richard, had been there, one of the child's godfathers; a Cambridge man, himself ordained and a great friend of the Bishop of Bywater. Hearing him and Benedict exchanging Latin quips across the well-lighted, well-spread table, Mistress Captoft had cherished high hopes that Sir Richard would report to the Bishop that a man so learned was wasted on a place like Intake and should be offered a post. Sir Richard was then in charge of the real Tallboys estate, at Moyidan, acting as guardian to its heir; but something — nobody knew what — had happened. Sir Richard had vanished from the scene and the manor and the boy had been taken over by the Church.

All this could be remembered in the time that it took for Mistress Tallboys to come out of what seemed almost a half-trance and mumble a greeting. It struck Mistress Captoft that the woman was not quite like herself; a heavy scowl

21

knotted her eyebrows together and her mouth was like a trap.

'Growing like a willow,' Mistress Captoft said, attempting the right note, 'and his hair even prettier.' This was the kind of thing Godfrey liked to hear and he gave a puppy-like wriggle. It was also the kind of thing mothers like to hear, but this afternoon Mistress Tallboys made no response. *Then* Mistress Captoft remembered the situation at Knight's Acre; two men, one Master Tallboys' young brother and his friend, come home to die of the lung-rot. No wonder the woman looked distraught.

In a less hearty voice Mistress Captoft asked, 'And how are the invalids?'

'I don't know and I don't care,' Griselda said, roughly, coarsely. Again unlike herself, for though, railing against Joanna, against Henry, against things in general, she had both in voice and manner reverted to her origins she had so far held, with outsiders, such as Mistress Captoft, to the gentle speech and the courteous manner which she had so resolutely copied from Lady Sybilla herself.

In his clear treble, Godfrey said, 'We don't go near them. They live on the other side of the house.'

Mistress Captoft knew that, for Jem Watson had carried the news to the village and by way of the old woman who came to scrub and wash, it had seeped through. Mistress Captoft had behaved as a neighbour should; she made good brews – some deliberately designed to be unpalatable – one should not encourage malingerers. But the one she had made and carried to Knight's Acre had been one of her best; the root of a plant brought from abroad – glycyrrhiza, commonly known as liquorice, she had brought several plants of it when she was making her garden; it had flourished fairly well; then there was horehound and honey; an excellent concoction. Master Tallboys, happening to be near the door, had opened it, received her offering and thanked her most courteously – but had not invited her in to view the sufferers; nor had he told her anything that she did not already know. A very aloof man.

'My Uncle John is better,' the child gossip said. 'He can walk about now. But they still have the best of *everything*, don't they, Mumma?'

22

He had never gone without, Griselda had seen to that, but what delicacies the impoverished household could afford were no longer strictly reserved for him. That was one of the things Griselda greatly resented. The last of a mounting list of grievances.

'You talk too much,' Griselda said in a voice harsher than Mistress Captoft had ever heard her use to the child before. In fact there was about her whole manner this afternoon something different, coarser. Mistress Captoft was acutely class conscious and knowing that Mistress Tallboys was of lowly birth, had often wondered that her speech and manner should be so very ladylike. She now thought with a touch of malice – truth will out! Masks fall in times of strain. Then her better nature came uppermost. She was even willing to forget Master Tallboys' civil but chilly reception of her cough-cure.

'You must have your hands full,' she said sympathetically. 'If there is anything I can do ... I have experience; my husband ailed for several years.'

Griselda, in response to this truly noble offer, turned upon Mistress Captoft a glance that was at once dull and wild.

'They can manage,' she said. She took Godfrey by the upper arm and turned him away. He twisted himself free, stepped back to face Mistress Captoft and made a little bow.

'Good day, Mistress Captoft. Thank you for the cake.'

'Really, her manner was most *peculiar*,' Mistress Captoft said to Father Benedict, whose aunt and housekeeper she was held to be by all but the lewd-minded who thought she was too young, too gaily dressed for the role. 'She was quite abrupt to the child. I always thought her over-doting. And to me she was rude. Then, after hurrying away, without so much as a good-day, she stopped and stood staring. As she sometimes stares at the graveyard.'

Father Benedict, born to be a scholar, had never been much interested in his parishioners, and finding the Intake people on the whole faintly hostile and curiously evasive had lost what little interest he had ever had. But he liked suppertable talk, however trivial. Mattie had a soft dovelike voice, very soothing; and sometimes her comments were sound and shrewd. An unusual and very pleasant combination.

Halfway along the single track which led past the church and the priest's house to Knight's Acre, Griselda had stopped and stared.

There it is; the place I sold myself for. Sir Godfrey brought me here. He saved me from that horrible inn where I knew nothing but squalor, and hardship and degradation. I saved his life there, because he looked so much like the carved saint in the church and I couldn't bear to see him dragged into the barn to die. I saved him while he lay in the barn, and afterwards on the long road back from the north. He could never have managed. So I came here riding pillion on the horse I stole for him and Knight's Acre was heaven to me, with Lady Sybilla so kind. I knew nothing about love then – I'd never met it in any form . . . In all my life I only met it once, and that was too late. I married Henry Tallboys because I wanted to stay at Knight's Acre; the one place where I had been happy and felt secure. He married me because the place was in such a muddle that only the firm hand of an indisputable mistress could get it on the right lines again. It suited us both until the day when Henry was at market, that flipperty girl, hired to help me, out watching the hunt, and only Tom . . . Tom Robinson to help to deliver the baby. Then I knew how wrong I had been; refusing Tom's shy offer to take a walk amongst the bluebells; accepting Henry's offer of marriage which was in reality no marriage at all. Always, always, if he could side against me, he did. I was never first with him; never in all my life have I been first with anybody – except Tom, who is dead.

The extreme climax of self-pity, everybody against her, everything gone wrong, might have lifted had Griselda walked into the kitchen and found it as bare as she had left it. Earlier in the day she had hidden most of the available food, left them to starve, to come to their senses and to a realisation of how important she was. The slightest evidence that she mattered, was, however little loved, indispensable, would have steadied her tottering mind.

What faced her as she entered the kitchen was – like

everything else in life – wrong. Warmth and the smell of freshly baked bread; and that little bitch, that little bastard who had once stolen Godfrey and tried to hold the family to ransom, taking a pie from the oven and saying something silly about blackbirds.

Suddenly something happened inside Griselda's head, inside her bones. She was tough, she had survived life as a beggar girl, raped in a ditch at the age of six; she had survived the austere life in a convent orphanage, and after that worse, maid of all work, unpaid prostitute, at an inn. She could bear this, though she felt weak and had to hold on to the table while she tried to explain, did to the hearing within her own mind, explain that this was her kitchen, and though she had deserted it at midday, as a protest against the various wrongs she had suffered, she had come back to cook now, that Joanna had no right to be wearing her apron.

They – Henry and Joanna – pretended not to hear, or not to understand. She spoke more loudly, forcing herself to ignore the weakness, the dizziness, the incipient nausea. Well, if they wouldn't listen or understand, they must be *shown*. Leaning heavily on her left hand she managed to move her right, pushing the new loaves to the floor. This is my kitchen! I do the baking here! How dare you take my place? Away with your rubbish! Give me my apron, you little slut . . .

It came out as babble, the slurred words running into one another. Don't stand there staring, pretending not to understand.

They stood and stared. Only Godfrey moved, sidling away to take shelter behind Henry. Then with another wordless roar, Griselda bore down upon Joanna, meaning to snatch the apron. Henry remembered that other time when Griselda had become violent and attacked Joanna with such ferocity that she had almost killed her. He acted swiftly, seized both his wife's workworn hands in one of his own and with the other grasped enough of her clothing to lift her from her feet. She struggled wildly and screamed. Godfrey began to scream too and Joanna turned to comfort him, saying the first thing that came into her head.

'Mumma is just being funny, Godfrey. You should laugh, not cry.'

Griselda was borne away to the accompaniment of the hysterical laughter of her son.

Henry carried her to the room which she had chosen when she decided not to sleep with him any more. It happened to be the one in which many years earlier, his sister Margaret, merely dim-witted and harmless except for her obsession about men, had been confined. He pushed her inside, backed away, snatched the key from inside the door, inserted it into the lock on the outside and locked her in. He was surprised and a little ashamed to find his hands unsteady. He'd lived through many things far worse than an incoherent display of temper. Here on this very stairway he had stood, taking careful aim – taught him by Walter, with the bow and arrow made for him by Walter – and Walter, unrecognisable in his new blue jerkin, and behaving in an incredible way, had fallen dead. The hardening process which, now completed, made him seem aloof, imperturbable, unfriendly, had begun then. But it was something imposed upon him from the outside, a suit of armour donned as defence against the world; it was not part of his true nature and in many ways he was far more vulnerable than he appeared to be.

He was not surprised to find himself very hungry – every major crisis in his life had been followed by fierce appetite. He tackled his pigeon pie with zest, admonishing Godfrey, still precariously balanced between tears and laughter, to eat up. 'She'll be better in the morning,' he said.

'What about her supper?' Joanna asked, without solicitude, but as though referring to the feeding of an animal. She hated Griselda, less on account of her behaviour to herself than because of the way she treated Henry, doing her best to make him miserable.

'It can wait. Give her time to calm down.'

'I'll take her something presently.' Again not because she cared whether Griselda ate or not, but to show Henry that she was not frightened. She'd been six when Griselda had set about her with murderous rage, and even then she'd hit back as savagely as she could. Since then she had grown a lot!

'No!' Henry said sharply. 'You're not to go near her. Neither of you. Mind that. We'll see how things turn out.'

How would they? In his mind he tried over various phrases: temporarily distraught; demented; possessed of the Devil.

He was an illiterate man. Sybilla, convent bred to the age of sixteen, and an apt scholar, had tried to teach him to read and write, but the business had bored him and he had been content when he could sign his name. But she had read to him, and told him stories; his vocabulary far exceeded the range of the words he used every day.

He was not sure that Griselda was merely temporarily distraught. Looking back he thought that he could see signs of a mind gone sick and getting worse, on the lines of a physical illness.

It had begun on the day of Godfrey's birth. She'd turned against Henry then, and with even more rancour, against the girl – Leonora – who had, quite unintentionally, been absent at the critical moment. It was unreasonable. So had her behaviour towards Joanna been. The poor child had done the baby Godfrey no harm; she'd simply taken him, snugly wrapped, and hidden him and made a piteous attempt at blackmail – they could have their baby back if Robert could come from Moyidan where everybody was so unkind and he was so wretched. There'd been some inexplicable link between Joanna, Tana's daughter, and Robert, Sybilla's son, born on the same day, but Henry had treated lightly then Joanna's claim to see, to know what was going on at Moyidan. She had been proved right. In the end Robert had run away – and never been heard of since. Back to Griselda; though Henry had gone straight to the hiding place – one he had used in his time – and brought back the baby, who had not even woken, Griselda had again been unreasonable in holding an undying grudge. Silly, too, about Godfrey as he grew and wished to explore, to share in the life of farm and yard. He must never go beyond that part of the yard well within view of the kitchen; he must never have dirty hands or clothes, or ruffled hair. Maybe, Henry thought indulging for once in the self-examination which his busy life, the mere struggle for survival, ordinarily forbade, I have been at fault there; let her have her own way too much. But, self-consolatory, he thought that over bigger issues, like taking in his brother John and Young Shep, he had been firm. And by being firm, had perhaps turned Griselda's brain for good and all. But could a man turn from his door, his own brother, ill and fallen on evil days. Merely to humour an ill-tempered wife?

Joanna moved about, with none of the bustle or noise with which Griselda had performed such tasks. She had already lifted the scattered loaves and given them a perfunctory brush with her apron. All loaves had a smearing of the faggot ash on their undersides; these were no different; Griselda, working her fingers to the bone – dismal expression – kept a clean kitchen floor. Now the meal over and the platters clean, she lighted one candle from another and said, 'Godfrey should go to bed.'

'Where?' For as long as he remembered the little boy had slept with his mother.

'You can share my bed, son,' Henry said.

That was good. A possible forerunner of a new way of life. Something to be immediately exploited.

'Then tomorrow may I go out with you? To the field?'

Henry said, 'Yes,' well knowing that if tomorrow Griselda had recovered, there would be argument, dispute, another row.

Upstairs, in the room that darkened from dusk to night with the steady inexorable progress of the first heartbeat towards the last, Griselda sat on the bed and knew that her every action, her every word had been sensible. Henry, Joanna and even Godfrey were all in a plot against her. Pretending not to understand what she said, or why she acted as she did. Picking her up as though she were a wild cat. Locking her in as though she were mad. And she the only one in the place with a grain of sense! That thought spurred a further burst of rage: she beat on the door and screamed: took off her shoe and hammered the floor. Knowing all the time that it was useless. If they pretended not to understand they could pretend not to hear. Ah, but wait until tomorrow, she thought, cunningly. Tomorrow, dinnertime, when Jem Watson would be in for his dinner. He'd hear and ask what was amiss: he was one of the noseyest people in the world. Henry would be forced to act then; release her, make up some plausible tale –

to which she would give full backing. Otherwise there'd be such a tale round the village by suppertime. Griselda knew how proud Henry was, in a quiet way, of his good name and his reputation. He wouldn't want a scandal. Come to that, nor did she. A few good thumps tomorrow, a scream or two, easily explained if she and Henry told the same tale, and she'd be out of this. She thought: I must save my strength for tomorrow. Fully dressed except for one shoe, she went to the bed, huddled the blankets around her and soon fell asleep, completely exhausted.

Downstairs, Henry said, 'You'd better get to bed, Joanna. I'm going across to the other side. There are some questions I want to ask Young Shep, while he can still talk.'

'He isn't going to get better, is he?'

'I'm afraid not. Good-night, Joanna.'

He was now as cool and aloof to her as he was to other people, and for that, she thought, as she raked the fire low and left the pot of breakfast oatmeal not to cook but to ripen in the lingering warmth, she was to blame. It was a month now, since that scene in the wood. When she thought of it she could still smell the ripe warm scent of blackberries.

Henry had explained that he had arranged for her to go to Stordford, a grand house where she would learn all that a lady needed to and she'd said she'd sooner die, and had given proof of it by running to one of the three pools and throwing herself in. It had not been just a dramatic gesture; she would rather die than leave Henry and Knight's Acre. They were her life.

Henry had plunged in after her, dragged her out, revived her and when she was herself again his mouth was on hers. All in a muddle, she'd mistaken this last resort of the resuscitation of the drowned for love. She had responded, embracing him ardently using endearments that she hardly knew that she knew. He'd been shocked? disgusted? Anyway, different, ever since then. Formerly he had called her my Sweet, or Sweeting, even Darling, terms more properly applied to one's wife, but who could possibly use them to somebody as waspish and scolding and nagging as Griselda?

Now he didn't use such words at all. He called her Joanna; in the last month he had been to market twice, but

29

he had not asked her to go with him. Such a pity; they'd had such fun, such a closeness on market days. Even when what Henry had to sell brought in less money than he had expected, and all that was to be bought cost more, she'd been able to cheer him, make him laugh.

And of course, Joanna thought, resolutely hopeful, time would tell. She'd counted on that before Griselda finally went so mad that even Henry was bound to take notice. In her opinion Griselda had been demented for years. Now she was locked up; would probably pine and die. And even if she lived on it wouldn't matter, so long as she was out of the way, leaving Henry and Joanna together. That was all Joanna asked at the moment; her dream of happiness did not reach to having a ring on her finger and being able to call herself Mistress Tallboys.

And one thing was certain, she thought, comfortably as she climbed the stairs; Henry was now dependent upon her to cook and keep house. There'd be no more idiot talk about exiling her to Stordford to learn how to play the lute and do embroidery.

Henry went heavily and thoughtfully across the yard towards the other part of his house. He, too, recalled that scene in the wood. The trouble was that every time he was obliged to be brusque and off-hand with the child, it was a reminder. He'd believed her dead, driven to suicide at the thought of being sent to Stordford. Desperately he'd set about restoring her in a way he had once heard described by Walter and like everything Walter had ever advised, it had worked. Under the pressure of his hands, the breathing of his mouth, Joanna had come back to life and changed from a woebegone child to an ardent woman, caressing him, using such expresions of love – heart of my heart, and similar terms, that he was shocked. The disgust was for himself, for the instant response of his body. Quickly mastered; never repeated, but a shaming memory. To a child, not yet twelve years old; a child he had always regarded and treated as a much younger sister, tried to protect from Griselda's hostility. He'd always found her company congenial, too. He was anything but a jovial man and she was far from being a gay, prattling child, but they had in common a keen sense of the ridiculous; sometimes, with no word spoken, a look, a lift of the eyebrow, shrug of the shoulder, small movement of the hand was enough.

Poor little girl; upon a few careless words, a few acts of protectiveness and many a good laugh, she'd reared a shining fantasy, spun herself a fairy tale. She was fond of tales.

Think about sheep, he told himself sternly.

It was true that ever since Young Shep had gone off, years ago, the Knight's Acre flock had not flourished; foot-rot, liver-rot, and scab – most injurious to the fleeces. Henry had tried to be a good shepherd, and once upon a time, he'd had the help of Tom Robinson who was good at everything he undertook: but he was dead now. He'd survived the plague, but it had left him weak and ailing; finally he'd ended so frail that he could only give Griselda a bit of help in the kitchen; and when he was past that and took to his bed, she'd been very kind and tolerant; very different from the way she had been towards anybody else who lived at Knight's Acre and did not pull their weight.

Henry stepped into the silk-hung room and saw that John had indeed been busy. The dust and the cobwebs were gone and the room bore more resemblance to the one which Henry Tallboys had once regarded as the most beautiful room in the world.

Young Shep – but I must remember not to say that! Years and years ago, in the lost mists of youth, Henry had said 'Young Shep,' and John had rebuked him, saying, 'He has a name you know.'

Young Shep lay on one of the divans, propped up on pillows, purple, scarlet, rose pink, primrose yellow. He looked ghastly, skin the colour of tallow except where, just under the eyes, there was a flush. Not of health, of fever.

Aware of the falsity, Henry said, 'Good evening, Nick. I am glad to see you out of bed.'

John, hovering, slightly aggressive, said. 'I told you he was better.'

Better? A man plainly dying, but making a great effort to hide the fact from his friend.

'I hoped I could pick your brains a bit – about sheep.' Again that false heartiness.

'Anything I know,' Young Shep said. He produced a smile

31

which might have emphasised the death's head look, but strangely did not; it was a sweet and genuinely grateful smile.

It was necessary for Henry to keep his attention on sheep and refuse to remember.

On that divan where the dying shepherd lay he had known one night of love – his first and his last, but such, he was sure as few men ever knew; the consummation of years of boyish adoration of the beautiful lady from a far land, exotic, mysterious with whom he had fallen in love at first sight. It was Tana who had saved his father, Sir Godfrey, from slavery in some heathen country called Zagela, and done so at such risk to her own life that she had been obliged to flee too. She'd been pregnant when she arrived, and six months later had given birth to the girl Joanna, child of a Spanish knight, now dead. Nothing, widowhood, pregnancy, motherhood, had detracted a whit from the fascination which she held for Henry. And in the end he had possessed her; with absolutely no idea that she had once been his father's lover; that Joanna was in fact his half sister. Tana was so young and the father-come-back-from-the-dead had seemed so old.

Henry had risen from the divan where he had lost his virginity and begun to plan; immediate marriage, a lifetime of happiness. Tana, for some inexplicable reason of her own, had gone riding on her only half-broken stallion which had thrown her, as everybody had predicted. Henry had found her, dead, just at the yard's entry.

Think about; ask about sheep!

Willing as he was to be helpful, Young Shep was vague; what he knew about sheep had either been inherited from his shepherd father, or acquired at such an early age as to be almost incommunicable. He said: Well, that'd depend on the weather; or: I'd know, just by taking a look.

His cough was not troublesome, but he sounded weak and breathless and at one point asked, 'Could you prop me a bit higher?'

John forestalled Henry's move, re-arranged the pillows and settled Young Shep on them with hands as gentle as a woman's. Then he said, softly, secretly, menacingly, 'Don't tire him!' And in a loud, rallying, fate-defying voice, 'Do the questions matter? In a week or two Nick will be up and about, and can *show* you!'

In a week or two Young Shep would be dead. He knew it; Henry knew it. Only John refused to face the truth. But then, he never had. He'd always been, in Henry's opinion, idle, frivolous, dodging work when he could and sneaking off to consort with the shepherd boy, slightly his elder, a maker of songs and a player of pipes.

In fact even at this moment, when Henry, seemingly so stolid and insensitive, could feel the throb of conflicting emotions in the room, he was also thinking that between them John and Young Shep had been largely to blame for his present poor financial position. If John hadn't insisted upon taking the value of his share of his father's inheritance out in cash – money Henry had been obliged to borrow at an exorbitant rate of interest; if he'd settled down, and worked, as a younger brother should; if Young Shep had remained in charge of the whole flock . . .

No good thinking of that, either. What was past was past. Ask about scab!

John fidgeted about, pulled a curtain closer, added a little charcoal to the brazier. Tana had made these apartments as much like one of her father's pavilions, which had neither been in Moorish Spain nor Christian Spain, but in North Africa, as possible; she had called this part of the house her pavilion and had no hearths; just charcoal braziers. Providing the charcoal had been easy for her; she was rich. For Henry it was an extra burden, borne without grudge.

Abruptly, John interrupted: 'Did you bring the milk, Henry? We've had none today.'

'No. I'm sorry. We've had a bit of an upset in the house today. I'll fetch it.'

He wanted to get away from this place with its bittersweet memories of the past and its present sad little drama; but in the time it took him to get up from the low, soft divan, not designed for sitting upon, and to think of what he had called a bit of an upset – Griselda violent and incoherent, he saw Young Shep's eyes fixed on him in dumb appeal.

'There's more I can tell you, John can fetch the milk.'

Henry thought: what now? He said in his imperturbable

33

way, 'There's a candle in the kitchen, John. And the milk is in the dairy. In a brown jug.'

'You get it, Johnny,' Young Shep said and his skeletal hand made a gesture, commanding, dismissing. Something flashed through Henry's mind, a recognition of something out of order. After all, his father, and John's, had been Sir Godfrey, at one time the premier knight in England. Young Shep's father had been Old Shep. And when John and Young Shep had failed in their venture, it was to Knight's Acre that John had come home, dragging Young Shep with him.

Henry had risen to his feet, and the door had hardly closed behind John, going obediently to fetch the milk, before Young Shep moved his hand again, this time to grip Henry's wrist in a weak, yet urgent clasp of thin, burning hot fingers.

'Master,' he said, reverting to the old mode of address and the rustic way of speech. 'You been here ... All along. Please, did you ever see or hear tell owt of Beth?'

Beth? Complete blank. The name meant nothing; conjured up no mental ... wait a minute ...

'She used to come with the shearers, she was their gang woman,' Young Shep said, helpfully.

Then Henry remembered – not the berry-brown girl with a mouth as red as a rose-hip, but the fierce, bitter, resentful woman, who, after some years of absence, had appeared again, a deserted wife, sole support of her child and hating the very name of Tallboys because John Tallboys had lured her husband away.

Was this something to tell a dying man?

Henry thought not. He said, 'Only indirectly. But she was well.'

'I did wrong by her. Thass hard to explain. I married her and sort of settled down.' His fever bright eyes looked flinchingly towards the door by which John had gone out and at any minute might come back. 'He never did understand ... That a man could be sort of divided, neither one way nor t'other. I used to send her money. Sometimes easy. Sometimes a pinch. There was allust a row. Proper owd mess I made of things, Master. I'd've liked her to know I was sorry.'

Henry was aware of something being demanded of him:

34

aware too, of being at a loss. Ought he to speak with false cheer, pretend as John was pretending? Tell Young Shep that he'd be up and about in no time and able to talk to his wife himself?

'If I ever see her, as I well may, I'll tell her. And now ... Would you like the priest to come?'

'Thass a kind thought, Master. I would. But it'd upset *him*. And he've been so good to me.' His voice trailed away and he loosened his clasp on Henry's wrist.

Ever since the lung sickness had come upon him he'd thought of it as a judgment on himself. For being neither one thing nor the other. To die young, with all those songs unmade, unsung. He'd always been the song maker; a tune on his pipe first, then the words to go with it. John's quick ear had picked up the tune and the words and the combination of voice, lute and pipe had been just that little bit out of the ordinary that made for popularity. They'd had wonderful times, welcome wherever they went, treated like princes.

Now that the good times had gone and the end near, Young Shep sometimes remembered that shepherds usually lived to be old, saw their children learn their craft, getting a bit stiff in the joints but able to hobble out on the first mild day of sunshine, see the lambs skipping and the primroses in flower ... None of that for him. And to be honest he had to admit to himself that during his spell of married life he'd been restless, discontented. It had taken very little persuasion from John to coax him away from Beth. Bad husband, and never really wholeheartedly the other thing, either. A lot of pretence. And now he must pretend absolutely, even forego the consolation of the last rites, say each day, as he felt worse, that he felt better.

'I'm glad we got here. He'll hev you to turn to,' he said.

Henry thought: and that won't be much comfort to him!

'I'll do my best, Nick,' he said simply.

Going back towards his own part of the house, Henry looked up at the window of the room into which he had locked Griselda. She *might* be better tomorrow, but somehow he doubted it.

*

35

When Griselda woke she was a little confused, not instantly remembering what had happened. She came out of sleep unwillingly, as she always did, facing another hard-working, thankless day. She stirred and felt more than the usual morning heaviness, especially down her left side. Then her mind cleared and it all came back. Not merely the events of yesterday, but all that had led up to that complete loss of temper. That was all it was, just being tried beyond endurance.

Nobody knows what I have borne. Everything against me. Still, that was small excuse for throwing good bread on the floor! That was crazy! In future I must be more careful.

She went, a bit lopsidedly, to the door. As she expected, it was locked. So she couldn't get to the stool room and must use the chamber pot. She found and replaced the shoe she had taken off, but her preparations for facing the world, for facing Henry, stopped there and she did not, as on other mornings, run the comb through her hair. Instead she sat and thought how silly she had been to hammer on the floor and scream: and to think of doing it again. Very foolish.

Presently the lock clicked and there was Henry, looking wary, edging in, carrying a tray, clumsily as all men did.

Now, be humble, placating, apologetic; the only way out of this.

She said, and it sounded just as it should: Henry, I am sorry about yesterday. Something came over me and I gave way. It will not happen again, I promise you.

Henry thought: No better! Meaningless babble. The room faced east and the merciless morning light showed him what had happened to her face, and her hair was all rough and tumbling down. Her face looked as though invisible fingers were pinching it, pulling the corner of the left eye down, the mouth on that side upwards. No better; rather worse.

He felt sorry for her. He'd never loved her, but until she changed, little by little into a nag and a scold, he had respected her, decent, amiable, industrious woman, just what he and Knight's Acre needed. But the years, the oddities of behaviour, the spurts of violence had eroded even that amount of feeling for her and now he was able to regard her

36

dispassionately; a pitiable creature, rather like cripples and beggars with sores, seen on Baildon Market Place.

The only difference was that for her he was responsible. Because she could be violent, he must restrain her; he must feed her, keep her clean, empty the chamber pot.

Griselda said, deliberately controlling her voice: Henry *why* do you pretend not to understand? How can it serve you? What more can I say than that I am sorry? What can you gain? What harm did I ever do you that you should treat me so?

For years she had complained of having too much to do; now she had nothing. Absolutely nothing to do and that in itself was torture. And what was happening to her child?

Against her better judgment – and yet what did judgment count for in such a lunatic situation, she screamed.

Downstairs Jem Watson, all agog with curiosity, cocked his ear to the ceiling.

'Missis took bad?'

'She has some pain,' Henry said. 'Tomorrow when I go to market, I shall consult with the doctor.'

The doctor who had already been once to Knight's Acre and there given the best advice possible in such hopeless cases, greeted Henry with a certain reserve but warmed to the business when told the real situation.

'How old is Mistress Tallboys?'

Who knew?

Henry could remember her arriving at Knight's Acre, a pitiable waif, who'd made a lot of growth, fed properly. She couldn't have been very old.

'Twenty-six, or thereabouts.'

So it was not the menopause, that most common cause of mental disturbance in women.

'Is she pregnant?'

'No.'

'Master Tallboys, forgive me. How can you be certain? Women are often secretive – in the early stages.'

'I am certain. I have one son and shortly after his birth my wife said that she wanted no more children. I respected her wishes. We sleep apart.'

Very odd. But then the man himself was an oddity, wearing homespun as though it were cloth of silver.

He considered the possibility of fits, the ancient, known disease of epilepsy. And Henry who had seen, in Baildon, men writhing, frothing at the mouth, said, 'No. She is ... at times ... violent.' That very morning, Griselda, despairing, had sprung at Henry and tried by force to get to the door.

This stripping away of all reserve, to a man so naturally self-contained was a painful business.

The doctor said, with the air of one propounding an original theory, 'Violence must be controlled.'

He was not eager to go jogging out to Intake again. On the previous occasion it had proved a longer ride than he had envisaged, and the days were shorter now, the roads more miry. And seeing the poor woman would tell him little that he had not been told already. So he said a few things about diet for the demented; nothing heating, no spices, no wine, a low diet, in fact, and said he would provide some soothing drops.

He then remembered the two young men with lung-rot and asked about them.

'My brother is making a good recovery; his friend is dying.'

There was no recovery once the lungs began to fail; there were intermissions. This he did not say. He offered a little general advice. John must avoid physical exertion, exposure to the weather, any kind of coarse food. He handed over the little leather bottle of soothing drops and once again said that his fee was two nobles. Secretly Henry was appalled; so much of his scanty ready money, and so little for it; the man had made no journey, spent no time on examination. In this he underestimated the cost of the bottle's contents; its chief ingredient came, like spices, from far away.

Riding home he suffered a bout of the lowness of spirit which often attacked him on this road. He never fully realised to what extent sheer hard work had protected him from melancholy. With nothing to do – even the horse knew its way and needed no guidance – he was ready prey.

He thought of the failure of all his youthful hopes.

Twenty-seven years old and if anything worse off than ever. The last year had been calamitous.

Griselda to be controlled, cared for.

John to be coddled and fed special food.

Joanna to be by some means persuaded to go to Stordford and take her proper place in life.

Into the lane towards Intake; through the water-splash at its lowest point: on to the track which led only to the church, the priest's house and Knight's Acre. There it stood, his good solid house, with the rose-trees in front, the garden to one side and the fields on the other. The newly ploughed, newly seeded furrows lay ridged, dark brown on one side and in this dying light a curious, muted purple, almost a shimmer, on the other. At the sight strength and determination flowed back into him. I have my house and my land: I shall manage . . .

He made a mistake in the administration of the drowsy syrup. There was only one handsome drinking vessel in the house – the silver christening cup given by Sir Richard, then apparently rich and in control of the family manor at Moyidan, to his god-son, young Godfrey.

With an equal amount of warm water, or milk, and well stirred, the doctor had directed.

'It's doctor's stuff,' Henry said, holding out the cup. Griselda stretched out her hand as though to take it and then struck his wrist upwards, so that the dark, sticky stuff shot in an arc, soiling his best, market-going jerkin.

You can't fool me! It's some filthy brew that little slut made. I remember her doing it once before. In that same cup. Don't look at me like that! You know very well what I'm saying. I suppose you thought that locking me in here with nothing to do, would drive me mad. But that wasn't quick enough. So now it's poison!

The noise was angry, but meaningless.

'We could try it in broth,' Joanna suggested.

Griselda could resist broth; and bread and milk, well sweetened with honey; and a coddled egg, done just as she had so often prepared one for Godfrey. She had learned,

39

early in life, to stay alive on very little. She could keep alive on little sips of water, until they came to their senses and stopped the silly pretence that they couldn't understand her. That she was mad!

Mad! The word had more meaning for her than to most people, for the convent which had taken her in – a beggar child, also stretched its limited resources to offer asylum to the mad. There was no traffic between the orphanage side and the bedlam, the whole convent building and the chapel lay between, but from part of the garden where able-bodied orphans worked and regarded themselves as specially favoured, the iron grille in the far wall was visible and behind it, sometimes faces. Some terrible faces which, if not behind bars, would have been frightening. Safely locked away, they were amusing. Sometimes there were cries from the building too.

Griselda did not realise that her own face had slipped into a grotesque mask, or that the extremely sensible things she said emerged as nonsense. Her link with real life had not actually snapped, but it was like a frayed rope, some strands had given way. She did not ask herself *why* Henry and everybody else should be in a plot against her; she only knew that everybody was.

She still tried to reason with Henry.

Henry, I know I offended you. All those jewels which I found in those rooms that had been shut up for years. I thought that finding them made them mine – ours – and that we should be safe and comfortable for ever. *You* said they were Joanna's because they belonged to her mother. All right. I was angry at the time, but I accept it now. Let her have them. And I offended again when John and Young Shep arrived, all in rags and nearly dead. Yes, I said then that I'd burn the house down sooner than have them in. But Henry, I knew it was lung-rot; I knew what it could do ... Henry please, I must see my son, I must have something to do. Shut away here like this, I shall go mad.

He went on pretending not to hear, or not to understand. It was all babble. And apart from that, would any woman in her right mind go on rejecting food; or take a thread from a blanket and try to play cat's cradle with it – a game which after two moves needed another player?

*

Griselda lost count of time, but she knew that even she could not live without eating. Not for ever. What she must do to save herself was to get away, find somebody who was not in the plot and explain.

The only way to do that was through the window and it would be difficult; very difficult, for it was a barred window.

Who now living remembered why that already narrow window should have been barred?

Henry had had a sister, Margaret, pretty as an angel but dim-witted beyond belief. There was this weak streak in the Tallboys family; most of the children they bred were big and strong, precocious. But now and again, as though in compensation, the family produced a simpleton.

That Knight's Acre should include a dim-wit girl was a pity, but not a tragedy. That the head of the family, Sir James Tallboys, and his formidable wife, Lady Emma, should, at Moyidan, the real centre of the family, have another dim-wit as heir was a catastrophe which neither would acknowledge. Their Richard was slow to learn, was delicate, was shy; all the usual parental excuses. Then the day came when, the Moyidan family visiting at Knight's Acre, Richard of Moyidan and his cousin Margaret of Knight's Acre had each recognised in the other the perfect mate. Found, in the hay, no real harm yet done, they had been torn apart and Margaret locked in her room. This was not her first escapade, but everybody intended that it should be her last.

She'd gone out by the window, on a summer day, making for Moyidan, but easily diverted by the sight of a carter, resting himself and his horse by the water-splash in the lane. To the end of his days the carter believed that he had spent a summer afternoon with one of the Little People, the fairies who lived in Layer Wood. Margaret had been found, brought back and the window barred. At Moyidan, Richard had used one of his tried weapons – he would not eat a crumb until his parents agreed that he should marry his cousin Margaret. And at Knight's Acre, the Lady Sybilla, pious, knowing that marriage of cousins, even sound healthy ones was against canon law and needed a special dispensation, had discovered that Margaret was pregnant; only

41

just; a week, ten days. The marriage had been quickly and cunningly arranged, and its outcome had given everybody a delightful surprise; a lusty boy, a real Tallboys in everything but colour of hair and eyes ...

Of all this Griselda knew nothing; she saw the window barred and was discouraged; then hopeful. Despite the dragging feeling in her left side she thought that if only she could squeeze through the narrow opening she would be free. Free to speak to somebody who did not pretend to be deaf, or not to understand, somebody not in this senseless plot.

It was not easy, but then nothing had ever been easy for her. Now carrying her left side as a load – but in her time she had carried heavier and more awkward ones, Griselda forced herself through and saw that the drop was negligible; just on to the roof of the new part, the other part, single-storied. From there to the ground.

The nearest house was the priest's and moving a bit crab-wise, Griselda made for it. She could remember being a bit gruff to Mistress Captoft on that terrible day; but she knew how to apologise. For a long time, in fact before everything became too much for her, Griselda had copied Lady Sybilla in every way; and Lady Sybilla had once said that only a well-bred person could apologise gracefully. That piece of information Griselda had tucked away and now, dragging that side of her which seemed not to belong, she planned her apology and her appeal for help.

Mistress Captoft, as everybody knew, had money and she had spent some on the priest's house. There was now a tiny room, just to the right of the door where parishioners, needing spiritual or physical comfort could wait; shielded from the weather, and yet not disturbing Father Benedict in the parlour. It was very difficult to get access to him; even calls to deathbeds were obstructed by Mistress Captoft who would suggest trying a good dose first. She made very potent brews.

The day was already darkening when Griselda knocked urgently on the door of the priest's house. The light was behind her and Mistress Captoft did not notice anything strange in her appearance except that her hair was in disorder. Her errand could be guessed; one of the sick men was about to die.

Good afternoon. I have come to apologise for being brusque the other day. I need help. Mistress Captoft, you and Father Benedict must help me. I am in danger. It is a matter of life or death.

Poor woman, completely incoherent. Mistress Captoft reached back and opened the door of the little room.

'Come in, Mistress Tallboys. There, sit down. Now tell . . .'

Here the angle of light was different, revealing the distortion of Griselda's face, the wildness of her eyes.

Mistress Captoft prided herself upon being level-headed. Once when she lived in Dunwich she had been called upon to deal with a little boy, so badly bitten by a dog that one side of his nose was hanging by a mere thread of flesh. She had kept her head, clapped the loose flesh back into place, secured it – and stopped the bleeding – with a stiff plaster of flour and water, and administered a good dose of febrifuge. Later she had the pleasure of seeing the boy as good as new except for a slight lumpiness on one side of the nose; and even that, she had thought complacently, would be less noticeable when his face attained full growth.

She was calm now, though a little taken aback.

'Sit down,' she said. Griselda, anxious to prove that she was not mad, sat down as bidden. The room was so small that it contained only one chair and a stool. 'Take a deep breath,' Mistress Captoft ordered. 'Now, try to tell me, quietly.'

Another burst of gibberish; not merely words mispronounced or slurred in a way for which the distortion of the mouth could account; sheer nonsense, accompanied with wild gestures.

The woman was mad; and madness was more a priest's business.

'Wait here. I will fetch Father Benedict,' Mistress Captoft said. She went nimbly away, but keeping her head, remembering to pull the latch string through so that the door could not be opened from inside the little room.

She said from pure habit, 'I am sorry to disturb you. It is Mistress Tallboys. I think she has gone mad.'

Father Benedict looked up from his writing and went through the process, familiar to her, of coming back to everyday life.

'In what way?'

'Talking nonsense. And looking horrible.'

He thought; Poor Mattie! She made a great sacrifice in coming with me to this barbarous place where there is no one of her kind with whom to associate, no shops, nothing to see from the window except a sheep-fold. Small wonder that she tends to exaggerate! But even as he discounted something of what she said, he observed that some of her bright colour had drained away, and that she had lost some of her self possession.

'Drink this,' he said, pouring wine from the jug which invariably stood ready to refresh and strengthen him as he pursued his studies. 'I will go to her.'

'I think better not. In addition to the nonsense and the wild look . . . I have just remembered' There is a smell. Like a wild animal. Somebody once told me that such a smell went with madness. I will run to the house and fetch her husband. It is for him to deal with.'

An indirect and unintentional reflection upon his manhood. People so often made that mistake about priests – though Mattie should have known better.

'My dear, if he could have dealt with her, why is she here? Subjected to strain, or shock, women often become incoherent.'

Alone in the tiny room, seated on the stool, Griselda thought that so far she had not done badly. Mistress Captoft had listened, and seemed to understand; had said that she would fetch Father Benedict. The right thing to say, since he was the one with authority. She waited.

'I think I should come with you,' Mistress Captoft said. 'She looks very frail, but the mad often have more than natural strength. She could be dangerous.'

'To me?' He gave her a look, half humorous, half rebuking. 'No meddling!'

She accepted it. But she remembered to say, 'I pulled the latch-string. Put it back as you go in.'

It was this adjustment of the latch-string as the priest entered which made Griselda suspicious. Here without realising it, she had also been locked in. Why? Because Mistress Captoft was in the plot, too?

Father Benedict appeared not to be. Having adjusted the string of the latch and closed the door, he stood for a second or two, a big solid man, reliable and authoritative, greeting her as a priest should greet a parishioner: God bless you, my child.

Griselda, remembering her manners, slipped from the stool and made the bob due to his office. Then she sat again. I must remember not to raise my voice or wave my good arm about. The other, the left, was too heavy and she held it by the elbow, supporting it, somewhat in the manner of a woman with a baby.

'Now, Mistress Tallboys; take your time. Something has upset you. Tell me.' He sat in the chair, folded his hands and seemed prepared to listen.

Not one intelligible word. Urgent, emphatic, fluent. Had this been his first encounter with her he would have taken it for her native tongue, one unknown to him. But he had known her for years; knew that she was as English as he was himself. Also before he had immured himself here as parish priest at Intake, he had been clerk, and general amanuensis to a merchant in Dunwich and had, of necessity, acquired not merely a smattering of various languages but also the sensitive ear which must make a bridge between people who could not allow differing languages to impede business.

But what Mistress Tallboys was now saying fitted in nowhere; not French or any of the varieties of German; not even Spanish or Italian. A language apart; the tongue of the mad. He was rather less credulous and fearful than the average man but a little shiver ran over him as he remembered that to speak in strange tongues was one sign of being possessed by devils. Such a state would be in keeping with her looks, so haggard, so distraught. Perhaps, poor creature she knew what ailed her. He shivered again as he considered the possibility that she had come to him trusting him to act as exorcist.

In theory it was within the power of any properly ordained man to cast out devils: Christ had left such power with His Apostles, and through ordination, the touch of a Bishop's hand, the humblest parish priest was directly linked with St. Peter, the Apostle chosen to be the founder of the Church; in actuality exorcism was a dangerous, tricky business, not to be lightly undertaken. Never by one man alone. Never without consent from one's Bishop.

I am over-fanciful, he told himself. But he did move his right hand and made the sign of the Cross in the air between them. Then he said, 'Mistress Captoft, I did not understand you. Perhaps if you spoke more slowly...' It was a frail hope, but all he had.

So! Griselda thought; they are in the plot, too! He understood; she understood. Now he is keeping me here, telling me to say it all again, but more slowly, while she runs off to fetch Henry.

Father Benedict sat in the chair between her and the door. A big solid man in a chair which though not large was solid. Her glance, frenzied, sly, went to the window; not a casement, just a few panes set in the wall. No escape. Trapped again.

We'll see! Nothing to be lost be trying.

Swiftly, despite the heaviness of her left side, she jumped up, lifted the three-legged stool and drove it at him. One leg hit him in the mouth, another in the chest; the third just missed his shoulder and struck the back of the chair. The onslaught, made with all her remaining strength, inspired by desperation and fully in accord with the streak of violence which was part of her nature, toppled him. Griselda stepped over his legs and opened the door and ran straight into Mistress Captoft who stood in the narrow entry, a freshly lighted candle in her hand.

Mistress Captoft had gone through one of those periods when a minute was an hour of anxiety. Without words he had told her not to meddle; he was priest, he had authority; he was a man of good physique, but he was not, especially when just roused from work, very alert and he was, at any time, slow at summing up a situation. And there he was, alone with a mad woman. And now she had, as the day darkened, a perfectly good excuse for going in and satisfying at once her curiosity and her protective instinct. She was taking a candle to set on the shelf which, jutting out between

46

the chair and the stool, served as a table in a room too small to accommodate such a thing. By its light, when the door flew open, she saw Benedict on the floor, tangled with the fallen chair. She hardly noticed Griselda, pushing past, making for the outer door. She did not know, or knowing, would have cared, that the mad woman's hair had flicked across the candle and begun to blaze and sizzle.

'My dearest,' Mistress Captoft said, speaking and behaving in a manner forbidden by man – but not, she was certain by God, 'she hurt you.'

She helped him up and took him into the warmer room. He was bleeding from the mouth, but that, thank God, was not the deadly symptom that it sometimes could be. A bad enough injury, but superficial; both lips split. Water, ice cold from the well. Alum, the drying powder. Even as she ministered to him the broken lips swelled and when he spoke his words were blurred, too; but at least they made sense. He said, 'They must be warned. She attacked me, unprovoked. There are children there.'

He was showing courage, a virtue he greatly admired and had seldom been called upon to exercise. He did not even mention the other, worse hurt which the other leg of the stool had inflicted.

'You must tell Master Tallboys. She is *dangerous*.'

'I can't leave you, my darling.'

'Of course you can. I'm all right now. Run along, tell them to beware. Please, Mattie, do as I say.'

'If you are sure . . .' But then, he had always been sure, of himself, of her. 'Very well. I shall be back in no time.' She put a log on the fire, lighted another candle.

Left alone, Father Benedict tried to probe his hurt and thought it curious that though from the outside it was so widespread that he could not determine whether it was in his belly or his chest, it was worse inside. A full breath was like the stab of a knife. It was nothing, and to say anything would simply worry Mattie. Leaning himself in the attitude which seemed less painful, and taking only shallow breaths, he returned to his work.

Mistress Captoft went briskly to Knight's Acre. There was no light in the front, so she went around into the yard. The

47

kitchen window was golden and through it she saw something not unlike a scene in one of the morality plays which in Dunwich she had so much enjoyed. The girl, Joanna, dishing something out of the black pot, the little boy, already served, in the act of lifting his spoon, Master Tallboys holding a tray. Caught in a timeless moment ... And God be thanked, so far unharmed.

What with haste and lack of breath, she sounded slightly incoherent at first, and Henry said, 'But how could she? The door ...' Then he set down the tray, snatched up a candle and hurried away. Across the hall in a few long strides and up the stairs, two at a time. The door was locked. The room empty, the window open, but offering so small an exit. Was it possible? Not only possible, but fact.

Downstairs again he said, 'Which way did she go?'

'I do not know. My concern was with Father Benedict, injured, bleeding ...'

'I hope not seriously,' Henry said, but he was already busy with his lantern and his lack of real concern confirmed Mistress Captoft's opinion of him as an unfeeling fellow.

'A stool wielded by a maniac can be a dangerous weapon,' she said, rather reprovingly, making for the door; anxious to get back.

'Wait,' Henry said. 'I can light you home. Joanna, bolt both doors, and on no account open until you hear my voice.'

He had no idea of where to search. He'd start with the track and the lane into which it led – as far as the watersplash – in her weakened state Griselda was unlikely to have gone farther than that. He'd shout and wave the lantern on the edge of the wood. Then – and with reluctance, he would try the village. A fine lot of talk *that* would cause.

Bursting out of the priest's house, Griselda had turned left, towards the lane, towards Baildon. The mere act of running, with one side so heavy, demanded so much attention that for a little time she was not aware that her hair was blazing. (One old woman in Intake, closing her shutters for the night, saw what she thought was a ball of fire, travelling slowly along the far edge of Grabber's Green – the villagers still called it that, convinced that by turning his own land into a sheep-fold, Sir Godfrey Tallboys had cruelly wronged them. She was alone at the time and crossed herself, muttering 'Lord preserve us!' for anything unusual was a portent, usually of evil. Nobody else seemed to have seen it and she did not mention the strange sight, for since portents were uncanny, those who brought news of them were unpopular.)

Griselda, like any woman who cooked, knew the two ways of extinguishing flames, by water, or by smothering. She tried to smother her burning hair by pulling her skirt over her head. The stuff was old and thin and since she had for a long time lost interest in her appearance, splashed with grease. It flared up like timber. Her last conscious thought was that she must get to the water-splash.

Candles used in lanterns were thicker than ordinary ones, but through the panes of thin horn which shielded them from the wind and from movement, gave little light. Henry held his high to make it more visible from the wood's edge, and as he walked called Griselda by name. Before he reached the dip in the lane where the water ran he thought he could smell something like meat roasting. Vagrants, he thought, somewhere just inside the wood's cover, cooking a rabbit. He could see no fire though. He halted and called at the top of his voice, 'Where are you? I mean you no harm. I need help.' The last word seemed to hang in the silence, which otherwise remained absolute.

He almost walked into Griselda's body. Recognisable only by a piece of petticoat, charred all round, from which the flame had been extinguished when she fell. He knew it, for it had been one of his mother's dresses. Griselda had taken over Lady Sybilla's scanty wardrobe and made the best use of it, both for herself and her child. When any garment was too worn for outward wear, she'd made it into shifts and petticoats. A bit of silk, the colour of a dove's neck, sorry remnant of a length which Sir Godfrey had been so pleased to find, so proud to pay for, on one of the few occasions when he had money in his pouch, now identified something half charred stick, half meat on a neglected spit.

For some reason Henry found himself unable to touch it. He'd managed to drag Walter's corpse to its secret, unhallowed grave; and Tana, with her neck broken, he had

49

lifted up tenderly. With this he should have been able to deal, but could not; there was no sorrow or grief to mitigate the nauseating repulsion.

He must have a blanket and to go home for one would mean questions.

Questions were already there in the kitchen. In the precise, rather delicate diction which Griselda had learned from Lady Sybilla and – except when angry, had always used towards her child, Godfrey said, 'What was that all about, Janna?'

'Nothing for you to bother about, my dear.'

'Who hit somebody with a stool?'

'I didn't understand either,' she said, untruthfully. 'Your father is seeing to it. Everything will be all right. Finish your stew and have an apple. They're the last we shall see this year.'

Thank God he was easily distracted. Pray God Griselda had run away from Knight's Acre, and from the priest's house, and would be found dead. She'd eaten nothing for days – and Robert, whom Joanna could now remember in a dispassionate way, had eaten well – and yet died from one night's exposure. It could happen again.

'Why did father say bar the doors?'

'It is safer so.'

In the priest's house Mistress Captoft said, 'I blame myself for leaving you. But you sent me.' He seemed rather more ill than split lips warranted. Shock, and a fall.

'You must go to bed,' she said. She offered her arm, her shoulder, since he moved so slowly and so feebly.

'I can walk, my dear,' he said. He could. The fall had not injured him; but every breath was a pang.

Two hot bricks, wrapped in flannel, one at his feet, one at his back. Now a wine sop; red wine, because he had lost blood. Not much, thanks to her prompt action.

She had the wine, warmed and sweetened – but no spice, no pepper to sting his hurt mouth – and was cutting the best, whitest, manchet bread into tiny cubes when another knock sounded on the door. The mad woman again? Mistress Cap-

50

toft snatched up the heaviest ladle she owned, went to the door and opened it just enough to enable her to strike. Tit for tat. Mistress Tallboys had attacked, unprovoked . . .

It was Master Tallboys.

'May I borrow a blanket?'

'You found her?'

'Yes. I need a blanket – if you would be so kind.'

Understandable, it was a night of frost, and so far as Mistress Captoft remembered the mad woman had come out with no cloak. She hurried upstairs and snatched a blanket from the chest which held several. Then she hurried back to the kitchen and was enraged to find that during her brief absence, the red wine had boiled; which meant that it had lost all virtue. She had to start again.

In bed Father Benedict was comfortable if he did not take a full breath or shift about. Mattie put another pillow in place to raise his head and spooned in the sops-in-wine.

She talked as she did so. 'Master Tallboys found his wife. Where I did not stop to ask. It is a curious thing; I was always against the cruel treatment of lunatics . . . Now I hope he locks her in, gives her bread and water and beats her when she is obstropulous.'

'I was to blame. For not heeding you.'

He thought: Most women would elaborate upon that theme, say Didn't I tell you? or: Serves you right. But not Mattie. She combined good sense with good nature, a sweet disposition with a talent for management. It was a pity . . . He did not pursue that line of thought.

What had been Griselda, bundled into a blanket made a lighter and more manageable load than many that Henry had shouldered, but it was horrible and he tried to divert his mind by thinking about the future, how decent privacy could be maintained. He wanted nobody to know the truth; it was so shocking. Some kind of stigma attached to madness, while ordinary illness, and death were accepted as commonplace. What Jem Watson knew, Intake knew, and all that Jem knew was that Griselda had been ill, screaming with pain on Tuesday and that Henry had fetched her some

51

medicine from the doctor on Wednesday. Everything, so far, in good order; even to Griselda having grown quiet. But would Father Benedict, would Mistress Captoft talk? Would Godfrey grow up and one day hear, from some long stored up tale, that his mother had gone mad, attacked a priest with a stool and then set herself on fire? A taint like that could cling through generations!

For a moment his thoughts veered. How had Griselda set herself on fire? A fire was not so easy to kindle. Had she carried a lighted candle, or flint and tinder? No time to bother about that; he must get this *thing* indoors, on to a bed, get it coffined, with nobody knowing. He must send Joanna to bed. What to tell *her*?

He laid his burden down, somewhat short of the kitchen door, and rapped and called. The door opened immediately and there was Joanna.

'Did you find her?'

'Yes. Dead. Where's the boy?'

'I coaxed him to bed. Where was she?'

For years, suffering under the lash of Griselda's tongue they had shared a mildly joking resignation, saying *she*, saying *her*.

'The less you know, the better,' Henry said.

Joanna's ruthless spirit spiralled upwards. Griselda, Henry's wife, her enemy, dead. Her joy would have been complete, had Henry not seemed so stunned and so stricken.

'She was mad, Henry. Had been for a long time. I knew years ago. Not only by the way she behaved to me . . . Other things. Look, I have kept your supper warm. I only wish I had wine.'

And why should she not have wine? She had inherited a small fortune in jewels; bright stones which she and Robert had found in one of the rooms on the other side. Pretty pebbles, playthings, a childish secret until Griselda found them and Henry had said that if they were valuable they were Joanna's, and must be used to her advantage. Some part of this fortune was already invested, with somebody called Sir Barnabas Grey, at Stordford, the place to which she had refused to go. The the rest was presumably still in the Bishop's hands and could be used to advantage *here*, if only Henry would agree.

For the first time that he could remember Henry had no appetite. Through every other extremity or exertion in his life, so long as he could remember, he had emerged hungry. But not tonight. Some of the sickening, charred meat odour clung to his jerkin. The kitchen was warm, so he removed the garment, seeing as he did so the three-cornered tear, called for some reason a hedge tear, which Griselda had mended. Neatly, expertly, but grumbling all the time; the eye of the needle too small, or the thread too thick, the wrong colour; and why if he must do something that tore his clothes, couldn't he wear his leather coat? And how could one woman, with one pair of hands, worn to the bone, be expected to deal with everything? Only last week. It seemed a long time ago. And now she lay, silenced for ever, by the house wall.

'Save it for tomorrow,' he said, practically, rejecting the stew. 'And go to bed. Forget all about it. Nothing to do with you.'

She said, 'Henry, you must not grieve. She was mad and would never have been better.' It struck her that his stricken look and his refusal to eat might indicate sorrow. Perhaps once, before Griselda turned so sour and nasty, there had been a kind of fondness. Nothing much; nothing at all like what their marriage would be, once attained. On the thought of marriage her mind halted. There might, for all she knew, be some law about the age at which one could be married. But betrothals were different; a betrothal could take place at any time; she knew that from Tom Robinson's talk. Mere babies could be betrothed, and were, especially where property was involved. And a betrothal was practically as good as a marriage.

Tom Robinson. Her mind halted again. To him Griselda had been quite different, gentle and tender. He was a sick man, towards the end bed-ridden; yet never once had Griselda called *him* a pauper, never once had she complained about the extra work *he* made. Enlightenment burst in upon her. Griselda had loved Tom Robinson! Then why had she married Henry? The answer was simple; Tom had nothing, no home, no money, not even health. Poor Henry, Joanna thought; how I will make it up to him. Once we are married, as we must be, will be.

She was so engrossed in her own thoughts that she did not even wonder where the dead woman was.

Henry waited, fidgeting about uneasily, until enough time had elapsed for Joanna to be in bed, and asleep, then he opened the door quietly and stepped out. He was halfway towards the body when he heard crying, wild, unrestrained, on a womanish note. He went rigid and cold sweat burst from every pore in his body. Oh God, it could not be! It was unbelievable that the faintest spark of life remained in that burnt out body.

Then he felt rather than saw some movement across the yard, near the outjutting part of the other side of the house. It could only be John. He called and the desolate noise increased. John, weeping like a woman, stumbled towards the kitchen lights. He just managed to say, 'Nick's dead!'

'He was dying when he arrived, John.' The statement sounded blunt and unsympathetic, but it was true. John must have known, must have seen ...

'I kept – hoping. And he was – better. He was taking his food. He coughed without blood. Only this evening ... We were talking about setting out. In the spring.'

You were, Henry thought; Young Shep knew he was dying. But then you always could believe what you wanted to. Did what you wanted to.

He tried to muster some sympathy, but there was something distasteful in the sight of a man weeping like a woman. Sybilla's death had broken Sir Godfrey in mind and spirit, but so far as Henry could remember his father had never cried.

He wished he had wine; or good strong ale. He did what he could, helped John to a bench by the hearth and stirred the dying fire. Involuntarily, he remembered his own bereavements; Walter; the mother whom he had loved; and Tana. There were words of comfort, he supposed – the life everlasting, the resurrection of the body, but he had never been able to understand how that could be, and the words would sound hollowly, coming from him. They were for the priest to say.

He said, awkwardly, 'You did your best for him, while he

54

lived, John. You brought him home. Even when you were ill yourself, you nursed him.'

'I owed him that,' John said. Suddenly he stopped crying, wiped his wet face on his sleeve. 'I took him to his death.'

'That is nonsense.'

'It is not! Nick didn't come with me at first. Did you know that? He got himself married, settled down. He'd have stayed, making his beautiful songs – with only sheep to hear. And I knew – I'd seen for myself – what could be done, the rewards, the favours. I loved him, Henry. I wanted him to share. So I persuaded him. And he took this cold in Padua.'

'That is nonsense,' Henry said again. 'He didn't *have* to go with you. He wasn't a slave. He could have stayed where he was – and caught a cold tending sheep.'

'Hard as stone,' John said. 'You always were.'

Henry accepted that in silence. He waited a little, conscious of all he had still to do. Then he said, 'You'd better try to get some sleep, John.'

'Not there,' John said, with a nervous start – like a woman again. 'I couldn't sleep across there! You ... You haven't seen him.'

Henry thought of what he *had* seen. But he seized the chance of getting John out of the way. He took up the candle and said, 'Come along, then. You can sleep here. Come quietly, the boy sleeps lightly.'

Waiting again, to give John time to settle. Then he conpleted his grim journey, laid the blanket-wrapped bundle on the bed, locked the door again. From the far room came the sound of John, sobbing. Henry thought, without sentimentality— No tears for Griselda! But then what purpose did tears ever serve?

Next day was Sunday and Henry was early at the priest's house. He wanted to arrange things as well as he could, before it was time for Mass.

Father Benedict was down, but not dressed yet. Wearing a voluminous woollen wrap, he sat at the table, carefully easing tiny spoonfuls of bread and milk between his broken lips. He looked very pale.

'I've come, partly, to apologise,' Henry said. 'I am indeed

55

very sorry that my wife should have injured you, Father. But she was out of her mind.'

'I know. Poor woman,' the priest said, speaking carefully from the uninjured corner of his mouth. 'I shall pray God to heal her.'

'She is dead.'

'God rest her in peace.'

'God rest her,' Mistress Captoft echoed. 'But *how*, Master Tallboys? I thought when you asked for a blanket ...'

In as few words as possible, but well-chosen, as was customary with him, Henry explained.

Shocked out of being cautious, Mistress Captoft said, 'Oh! How terrible. She must have brushed against the candle as she pushed past me. But how was I to mark *that*, with Father Benedict on the floor, and bleeding?'

Cautious, as he always was about any fortunate chance, Henry said, 'Nobody in his right mind would dream of blaming you, Mistress Captoft.'

As he spoke he looked straight at her. He had inherited his father's singularly candid eyes, but whereas in Sir Godfrey the candid look had had nothing behind it but candour – often to his own detriment – Henry's clear look was less simple. Mistress Captoft thought – I should not have said that: *qui s'excuse, s'accuse*; for she had seen that the straight blue gaze also said— But I would! Unless ...

'I should wish,' Henry said, 'that this should not be bruited abroad. I have my son to consider. People talk and exaggerate. I do not wish my son to be told one day that his mother was a madwoman who attacked a priest, before setting fire to herself. If there were an enquiry ...'

Sudden or violent deaths were enquired into, by a Coroner. And unless violence had been seen to be done, or poison suspected, the process depended upon the priest's willingness to bury. If he had doubts he was in duty bound to refuse and await the result of the enquiry.

Father Benedict deserved the high opinion, the high hopes which Mistress Captoft had once entertained for him. He had a subtle mind, which, allied to his unquestioned abilities, would have taken him far, had he been born into another class, or chanced to meet up with a powerful patron. Speaking with difficulty, not only because of his mouth, but because talk demanded breath and to take a full breath still drove a sharp knife somewhere between his ribs and his stomach, he said, 'I understand, Master Tallboys. So far as an enquiry is concerned ... Even suicide will never be suggested. The act of self-destruction must be deliberate and a person even temporarily deranged cannot take such a decision. Of this,' he touched his mouth, 'I shall say nothing. A man of my size, knocked down by so small a woman.' He had his pride, too.

Henry had achieved – more easily than he had dared hope – exactly what he had come for.

'There has been another death, too. The friend of my brother. He died, last night, of the lung-rot, in his bed.'

'Both shall be buried with proper rites. On Wednesday.'

He named the day, not utterly at random. Time was needed, not only for the shrouding and the coffining – for those who could afford it – and the grave-digging, but to allow this inner hurt to heal. As it must. Concealing this hurt from Mattie, who would have fussed, made plasters, made him stay in bed with a bag of hot salt applied to his side, was simply to spare her. And it could only be a bruise, gone inward.

Ironically, the one person in Intake who could have helped Father Benedict at that moment was Young Shep who lay stiff and cold with the blood of his last violent cough, stiffening on the silk.

Shepherds knew more about bones and bodies than any physician, or any surgeon. Had Father Benedict been a sheep in Young Shep's care and met with an accident, jostled against a fence or a gateway, and then – showing no outward injury – began to ail and take little gasping breaths, Young Shep would have out with his knife, tripped the animal over; once on their backs sheep were helpless, and he would have slit it open, found the bit of broken rib bone which had pierced the spongy mass of the lungs and plucked it out. No such surgery was available to human beings: only crude amputations.

'About the laying out,' Mistress Captoft said, seeing Henry to the door. 'The old woman who once served Father Ambrose and now does my heavy wash and scrubs floors, does, I think, earn a few pence by such services. She will certainly be in church this morning; she is one who never misses. Shall I send her?'

'That would be kind,' Henry said, thinking that if this thing were to be secret . . . well, while the old woman busied herself with Young Shep, he must do something about Griselda.

'He shouldn't be up and about,' Mistress Captoft said. 'I told him. I urged that he should stay in bed. But he is very stubborn.'

The old woman took her threepence and muttered, with an air of grievance, 'Mistress Captoft said *two*.' It mattered to her. She had always been poor, but while Father Ambrose was alive she had been sure of a roof over her head – leaky as it had been. She had been sure of food, too, scanty and plain, but willingly shared, in fact when one portion was better than another, the old priest had insisted that she had it, pointing out that she worked harder than he did. Now all was changed. Father Benedict, having Mistress Captoft to serve him, had not wanted her, and she lived on sufferance with a nephew-by-marriage, whose wife took all her meagre earnings and grudged her every bite. Sixpence would have been very welcome.

'My wife's body has already been dealt with,' Henry said. 'Are the coffins spoke for?'

'Not yet.' It sounded mean – even to Henry himself – to think about what coffins cost; but the four nobles paid out to the doctor had left him very short of ready money. Griselda – mistress of Knight's Acre, a Tallboys by marriage, must have a coffin by right, but surely Young Shep could have gone to his grave wrapped in a shroud, as the poor generally did. But John, who never gave a thought to other people's problems and evidently regarded Henry's pocket as bottomless, had said that he wanted Nick properly buried, coffin and all.

'Shall I tell Sawyer, then, Master?' There might be a ha'penny to be gained in that way. It was a good order.

All the men of Intake were skilled at woodwork and could make spoons, bowls, buckets as well as keeping houses and out-buildings in repair, but over the years a certain amount of specialisation had developed. Sawyer made coffins, and Gurth made most of the high-soled clogs in which people clumped about in very bad weather.

'I should be much obliged to you,' Henry said.

'At the moment of the elevation,' Mistress Captoft said, 'I saw you wince with pain. You must have hurt yourself when you fell. Where?'

'It is nothing,' Father Benedict said, courageously. 'Nothing to worry about.'

But she was insistent and by now he was actually longing for the comfort of a hot salt bag to press to the hurt, or one of her willow-bark plasters to draw out the bruise. And some of her pain-killing draughts.

'It was not the fall, my dear. It was the other leg of the stool. It hit me here.'

'Let me see.'

'There is nothing to see. I looked myself, before I dressed.'

But she must see, and he was right; there was nothing to see. Also the site of the pain was ill-defined. 'Here,' he said, and then after a deeper breath, moved his hand slightly higher. 'No, here.'

An inward bruise. Worse than an outer one; but she knew exactly what to do.

He lay flat in his bed, that position was most comfortable; the warmth of the salt bag was soothing, and so were the opiate drops, with which, for once Mistress Captoft had been generous.

'You should sleep now,' she had said, taking away the cup which had contained not only the drops but a good measure of the best wine.

He drifted, up to the very border of sleep and there stayed, floating somewhere high, not in the little Intake room but from a point where he could see his whole life, the whole world, like a map, with people moving in it, unrolled before him.

A clever boy, not one of the poorest, a second son whose labour was not needed on the family holding. He'd gone to the monks' school at Norwich. The Church offered the best road – perhaps the only one, to an ambitious boy. Not that he had ever been inordinately ambitious. During his studies, and at the time he took orders, the most he had wanted and hoped for was a pleasant, quiet post, something to do with books and a chance of associating with men of like mind. He had never seen himself as a parish priest, possibly the only man in the community who could read. And he knew that he had no talent for dealing with people. An undemanding post on the staff, or in the library of some important cleric would have suited him well. It had never come his way. No particular reason except that there were more candidates than jobs of that kind, and some young men, whose families had closer connections with a manorial lord than his had, often benefited by a slight push from behind; the right word spoken at the right time into the right ear.

Still there was always a market – not highly paid, but steady, for men who could read and write and count without making notches in tally sticks. It was an anomalous position; respected as priest, regarded as a hireling and sometimes despised – a mere clerk. He had had a variety of jobs – hours spent in cold, ill-lit rooms, by the time he had drifted to Dunwich and become general amenuensis to a prosperous man who not only shipped wool out to Low Countries, but shipped in the finished cloth. There, in the course of his work, he had met Mistress Captoft, acting in a similar capacity for her aged, ailing husband. This situation had come about because she was young, had a smattering of education and a managing way with her; a habit of saying: I will see to it all. She could ride, she could count, she could manage.

Mutually, and violently attracted, they had been, up to a point, scrupulous. Benedict had never cuckolded the old man, Mattie had never committed adultery. Then the old man died, leaving her well provided for and she had hired a house in Dunwich and invited him to live with her. 'I could at least see that you were well fed and your clothes kept in order.' The outcome was inevitable.

In Dunwich there were neighbours who thought it queer that a widow, with a decent income, should take a lodger. There was also Benedict's employer who refused to add a penny to his wage. 'You had bed and board here. You made the change; you can't expect me to pay for it. I can get another man, half a dozen of them, on the old terms.'

Benedict had an uncle, Father Thomas at Moyidan, and when he knew that his nephew was anxious for a living, in however poor or remote a place, he was willing to help. Intake, poor and remote indeed, fell vacant and Lady Emma Tallboys, then in complete control of Moyidan and of the Intake church and house and living, since another Tallboys lady, long ago, had built the church and endowed it, had accepted Father Thomas's plea.

There was one small falsity. By implication, rather than definite statement, Lady Emma had been given to understand that Father Benedict was recently ordained.

So they had come here; parish priest, with his aunt as housekeeper; and they had been happy. He was no longer the hired clerk, bound to given hours. Mattie had acted as a bulwark between him and the trivialities of parochial work. There were no neighbours.

From his point of view it could hardly have been better.

What about hers?

So splendid, so admirable, so lovable a woman surely deserved something better than this furtive relationship. Sinful? But sinful only because some men, dead to all human feeling, had sat at Westminster, years ago, and decreed that the clergy must be celibate. Before that clerics had had wives, and when the new rule was made, so many had threatened to resign rather than abandon them that some slight mitigation was made, those already married and determined to remain so, could continue to hold their posts and offices. Future candidates for ordination must forswear the joys of matrimony – and of children. It was a stupid, cruel law, made by stupid men; for what had it resulted in? Every kind of squalid subterfuge, endless pretence, and the dearth of good children.

He thought of Amsterdam. He had never seen the place, though on his employer's behalf he had written letters to, and received letters from it. He had gathered – again rather by implication than by positive evidence – that learning was respected there.

Now, even nearer the verge of drugged sleep, he thought that there were ways of renouncing vows, of getting oneself defrocked; but they took time and had the inevitable consequences of commotion and scandal. He could do better.

61

Mattie peeped in and saw him, asleep, thank God. She tiptoed away, busied herself with the willow bark plaster and another posset. When the dusk crept in she mended the fire, lighted candles, wondered whether perhaps she had over-done the drowsy drops. Heated another salt bag to place outside the plaster. Sleep, like Time, was a healer, but he needed nourishment. The night and the day had now gone their full round and he'd only taken a few sops. Far less than a full-sized body needed in good health; how much more so a body trying to heal itself from within?

Finally she ventured, carrying the wooden tray; salt bag, plaster, posset and candle.

He was awake.

He said, 'My love, I have been thinking. We will go to Amsterdam and get married.'

Afterwards she was ashamed of the way she had behaved, priding herself, as she did, upon being level-headed, able to deal . . .

She gave a cry and dropped everything.

'No great harm done,' she said. The candle had rolled, but was still burning; the salt bag and the plaster were just as they had been, only the posset was spilled. Setting things to rights gave her time to regain her composure; time to think that perhaps this astounding proposal was due to the drops. They were known to have a curious effect upon some people. Perhaps Benny had been dreaming and was not yet fully conscious of where he was, of who he was. Marriage had never once been mentioned between them even by so little as – If only . . . He was a priest before he became her lover, and inconsistent as it might seem, she had respect for his office. Enough respect, in the early days, to make her feel guilty since she could not distinguish so clearly as he seemed to do, between the law of God and the rule made by some men at Westminster. In fact, her conscience was so uneasy in these early days that once a month, deeply hooded, she would steal out to some church where she was not known, and confess and ask absolution. There were plenty to choose from, for, although the sea had begun its relentless erosion, of the forty-two churches in Dunwich only one or two had col-lapsed or been abandoned as dangerous. The sin to which she confessed was fornication. One was under no compulsion to name one's partner in sin. Now and again a conscientious confessor would ask did she mean adultery? So many people seemed to be unable to distinguish between the two. Mistress Captoft could truly say no. She was a widow. And the man? Unmarried. Usually the penance was light, almost derisory. Usually it was accompanied by the order to avoid the occasion for sin – a thing she had no intention of doing; and gradually, her good sense saw that such half-confessions were worthless and had ceased to bother. But she still thought of herself as a pious woman and was careful about most outward forms.

Father Benedict said, 'Did I take too much for granted?? Should I have *asked*, first?'

'I dared not answer. For fear I had not heard aright. For fear that the drops had made you – not quite yourself.'

'I'm myself. And I meant it. As soon as I'm on my feet again.'

He was disturbed to discover, as soon as he moved, or took a real breath, that despite everything, the pain was still there.

He could, lying very still, taking little breaths, forget it as they made their plans; all the more urgent and delicious for having been non-existent yesterday.

She would leave her property, two good farms with houses, and her sheep-run, in the hands of the honest attorney who now collected her rents. But she would instruct him to sell when the time was right. She would then take passage to Amsterdam on a wool-carrying vessel. Mistress Captoft, intrepid, venturesome woman, making a visit to some relative who had settled there. Exchanges between the Low Countries and England were not confined entirely to wool and cloth; people, and language made traffic to and fro. She would find a suitable house. And she would wait. He would finish here, give up what was called a living – really no living at all, and make for London where it was easy for a man to lose himself and change his identity. He would allow his tonsure to grow out – priests were for some reason as unwelcome aboard ship as corpses or donkeys. Then as Master Freebody, an apt name and one to which he had some tenuous claim since it had been his mother's maiden name, he would go to Amsterdam. There he and Mistress Captoft would meet and get married.

Joy would be complete. There might even be a child.

Ever since her marriage at the age of fifteen and a half, Mistress Captoft had longed for a baby, completely hers, completely dependent; but Master Captoft had been too old and in her illicit relationship with Benny pregnancy must be guarded against with little bits of lambs' wool soaked with vinegar. Now, though rather late, it was not too late.

Of this hope she did not speak, but as she busied herself, tending the sick man and beginning to sort and pack what she intended to take with her, or what Benny should bring with him, she could at last confess how dull she had found life at Intake. Imagine, she said, the joy of being within reach of shops; of being able to look out of the window and see people in the street; of having neighbours and proper servants from whom nothing need be hidden.

The only cloud on those few halcyon days was Benny's condition. If only the bruise would come out! He insisted upon getting up, kept saying that he was better, but she knew by the way he looked and moved that he was still in pain. The position of it was still uncertain, it shifted, he said, and she continue to regard that as a hopeful sign; but his breathing was still careful and shallow, and once, coming on him unawares, she saw him press his hand against his heart. Just a pang in another place he said when she asked about it; only momentary. In fact the pain seemed to have taken possession of the whole of his rib-cage. But he would not give in. On Tuesday afternoon Mistress Captoft said, 'My dearest you are not well enough to officiate tomorrow. I will ride to Moyidan and ask your uncle to come and act for you.'

'That would be absurd. Tomorrow I shall be better.'

Talk reverted to Amsterdam, the golden city of their dreams.

At Knight's Acre things had gone more easily than Henry had dared to hope. The fact that there were two corpses had distracted from the one. What remained of Griselda, heavily shrouded, was coffined without question. John's behaviour was a distraction, too. Sawyer and his assistant agreed that if you hadn't known different you'd have thought he was the one who'd lost his wife.

Indefatigable in her efforts to earn an extra penny or so, the old woman, Ethel, cheated of one laying out, turned up again offering her services in another capacity.

'You'll need a sin-eater, Master Tallboys; the more so since they both died so sudden.'

It was a very old custom, already dying out in many places, but lingering on amongst the ignorant. It was simple. A man or woman stood at the foot of the bed where the corpse lay and ate a piece of bread which had been sprinkled with salt in the form of a Cross and called upon God and all those present to witness that by this act the sins of the dead were transferred to the sin-eater. The sin-eater then, as quickly as possible sought absolution for all sins committed and all sins assumed.

Henry, still, after all these years, influenced by Walter, that complete sceptic, said, 'No.' He had three good reasons for his refusal; the ritual was barbarous and silly; it cost money, sin-eaters rated their mystical service highly, probably sixpence; and although Griselda had died suddenly and unabsolved, she had always been pious. Certainly striking Father Benedict had, even in Henry's lax view, been an act of impiety, but she was mad, and the mad were not, could not be, held responsible.

John was of another opinion; he was sodden, almost senseless from grief, remorse and sheer sentimentality. Just as he had wanted Nick properly coffined, so he wanted him to go to his grave accompanied by all the ritual, all the panoply.

'Our Mother was laid to rest without such antics,' Henry said harshly. He thought of other deaths, too. Walter had not even had a shroud or a Mass; he lay in unhallowed ground, under what was now no more than a weed-covered hump which marked the one side of the entrance to the yard.

'I'd like it done,' John said; and in Henry a thought of which he was instantly ashamed, took form: *Then you pay for it!* But he knew that John did not possess a penny. And if sixpence, however hardly spared, grudged, wasted because it could have been put to so much better use did anything to stem the tears, the lugubrious self-reproaches, it would be well spent.

Old Ethel ate Young Shep's sins whatever they were, took her sixpence, and then, avoiding the path which Sir Godfrey had thoughtfully left when he made his sheep-run, the shortest way between church and village, she went to the priest's house where earlier that day she had, as usual, done heavy, menial jobs. She wanted to rid herself at the first possible moment of the sins she had, for sixpence, assumed.

'No, you *cannot*,' Mistress Captoft said in reply to Ethel's request to see Father Benedict. She had always stood, a firm, bristling barrier between him and parochial claims. 'Father Benedict is unwell. As you well know! He is abed now, and I hope asleep. He must gather strength for tomorrow.' Ethel went, resentful, away.

Lying flat, a wide mustard plaster covering his lower ribs and part of his stomach, a bag of hot salt cuddled against him and one of Mattie's brews soothing the pain and blurring his mind, Father Benedict did feel better; felt inclined to think that he had made altogether too much of what, after all, was a trivial accident. The fact that his split lips had healed so rapidly was a sure sign of the health of his body. The fact that the pain had shifted, upwards and inwards, towards his heart, he, like Mattie, regarded as a favourable sign. Tomorrow he would be fully restored, and his last thought, as he drifted off into a drugged dose, was of Amsterdam.

'I must tell him something,' Henry said, referring to Godfrey.

The strange thing was that the little boy had never once asked about or shown any concern for Griselda who had loved him, cosseted him, given him little secret meals, and never let him out of her sight. He was intoxicated by his sudden new freedom.

'The truth,' Joanna said. 'He's bound to know sooner or later and death means nothing to the young.' She spoke with the authority of first-hand experience. 'You remember, Henry, that day when Robert and I went to church with Griselda and found old Father Ambrose dead. We came racing to tell you, quite excited.'

The death of a very old, almost totally blind priest had left no mark at all; but there had been another death which had cut her to the heart; but there again, she had been

66

young and had survived. The fact that she could now say Robert's name in such a casual way, proved that.

She and Robert had been twins in all but fact; born on the same day but to different mothers; the Lady Sybilla's boy baby, prematurely born, unlikely to survive, and Tana's daughter, Joanna. They'd shared a cradle. Lady Sybilla, worn and old for child-bearing had been ill, had in fact never fully recovered. Tana had suckled them both until she grew bored with the business.

Joanna and Robert had never spent a day, had a meal apart until Henry's absurd idea of what was fitting – not for himself, but for others – had got the better of him, and he had arranged for his young brother to go and live at Moyidan and share lessons and a tutor with Young Richard; by that time in the charge of Henry's brother who, because he was a priest and also a Master of Arts at Cambridge, was known as Sir Richard.

The parting had been agonising, but what was worse was that Joanna, over a distance of five miles away, had known that Robert was bitterly unhappy. His misery flowed out and she was receptive to it. So one day, unable to bear any more – or to think of Robert bearing any more, she'd set out, dressed like a miniature ploughboy, to rescue him from Young Richard's sly persecution, from the tutor's deliberate, cruel ignoring of facts, and from Sir Richard's complete carelessness of what was going on under his nose.

It had been, in part, a very successful operation. She'd forced her way in, charmed the Bishop of Bywater who was dining with Sir Richard that day, and got Robert away. But only for a little time. In the blizzard which had spoiled her whole plan, which was to smuggle Robert into the empty rooms on the other side of the house, Robert, despite all her care, had died in the poor shelter she had found. She'd covered him with leaves and bracken and come home and never said a word. For quite a long time she had avoided the use of Robert's name; but there it was; she'd been young then; the wound had healed and her hungry love had fastened upon Henry. To the young death was something to be survived.

And Henry was thinking: Suppose when I was Godfrey's age, romping through the Long Gallery, the Gardens, the

Maze at Beauclaire, my aunt Astallon's palatial home, somebody had come up to me and said, 'Your mother is dead.' Not a pleasant thought but one to be faced with honesty; it would have meant very little. It was only later when, two against the world, he and his mother had come together, bonded by common misfortune, allies in the fight against poverty and disaster.

'You may well be right,' Henry said. And she was; for informed that his mother was dead, that he would never see her again, Godfrey said, 'Oh!' and then, with hardly a pause, 'Next time you go to market, can I come?'

'We'll see,' Henry said; on the whole relieved that Godfrey had made so little fuss; for John was making fuss enough for a dozen. Crying, making self-recriminatory statements, most of which Henry did not understand, and refusing to eat.

That at least, Henry did understand and losing patience, he said, 'Look. Starving yourself can't help Young Shep and could hurt you. It was lack of food that brought you to such a low state as you were in when you arrived here. You'll make yourself ill again.'

'I only wish I could die.'

Henry could only wish that John might pull himself together and be, feel, better once the funeral was over.

Mistress Captoft was also concerned about the funeral. She had suggested – sensibly, she thought – that the one committal service might serve for both. Stubborn as rock, Father Benedict said that except in times of pestilence, or war, mass committals to the grave were wrong. In ordinary times each soul must be regarded as individual, coming at birth to house in a separate body, and when the corporal frame broke down, by accident or disease, still a separate entity, to be committed, as such, into the hand of God.

Interments took place after nightfall; Mistress Captoft was glad that at this time of the year dusk came early, so that he need not spend a long evening in waiting about. He yielded to her plea that he should stay in bed until dinnertime, and afterwards he rested. He said he felt much better and well able to perform the double task that awaited him.

He had never been an assiduous parish priest; he had never, as old Father Ambrose had done, gone visiting houses in the village, or stood after Mass by the door of the church asking after the health of the absentees – a habit which the people, mistaking the old man's motives, had resented – but he was a conscientious man, and thorough, and he missed no word nor movement as he performed the two identical ceremonies.

When he came in he seemed none the worse. A heaped fire and a cup of warm, spiced wine awaited him.

'Get me the Parish Book, my love.' She brought him the rudimentary parish record, sometimes called the Kin Book because the original purpose in keeping it had been the prevention of incestuous marriages. Father Ambrose's predecessor had been so careless about it that it seemed as though during his twenty years in charge there had been few marriages, fewer baptisms and no interments at all. Father Ambrose had been far more scrupulous and had recorded everything in any way to do with the parish; but as his sight had deteriorated, so had his writing; his last entries were practically illegible, sometimes written across each other.

Father Benedict wrote a clear, scholarly hand and now he entered the date, and recorded that he had buried Griselda Tallboys, wife of Henry Tallboys of Knight's Acre, and Nicholas Shepherd from the same house. He wrote firmly, allowed time for the ink to dry and then closed the book.

'This may be the last entry I shall make,' he said. And smiled. After that he ate, with more appetite than he had shown lately, two coddled eggs.

He went, comfortably, to bed; bag of hot salt, mustard plaster, soothing drops. Until they took effect Father Benedict and Mistress Captoft chatted cheerfully. She would leave in two days time. During the following week he would resign his living, which meant going not to Moyidan, but all the way to Bywater because the Bishop of Bywater now had complete, if only temporary, control of that rich family manor.

Since Father Benedict's uncle, Father Thomas, had lived through all the changes there, Father Benedict and Mistress Captoft had a rough kind of knowledge of what had happened.

Sir James Tallboys, indisputable head of the family, had died, leaving his wife, Lady Emma in full charge of the land and of the grandson, the heir. Aware that she was carrying about within her a disease incurable, she had sent for a nephew, Sir Richard, brother to Master Tallboys at Knight's acre. And he'd spent lavishly, lived like a lord, and come to grief. The Bishop had stepped in, settled the debts, taken charge of the manor, and of the heir – now at Eton College. So when Father Benedict resigned his living he would have to approach not a member of the Tallboys family, an ancestress of whom had founded and endowed the church, but the Bishop, who might show some curiosity as to the cause of the resignation.

'And if he does,' Mistress Captoft said with some asperity, 'it will be the first sign of interest he has evinced in all the time you have been here.' She had fiercely resented the Bishop's negligence, having been certain all along that he had only to spend a few minutes in Benny's company to realise how wasted he was in this remote, barbarous place.

However, it was all over now. Stooping over the bed to kiss him good-night she thought that one of the first things she would buy in Amsterdam would be a fine big double bed. Always, up to now, they had been careful to preserve all the outward forms of convention; separate rooms, small single beds.

He was dead in the morning. Lying just as she had left him. Afterwards she found comfort in the thought that he had died in his sleep without pain, but that was no comfort at the moment.

Ah, Intake said, when it heard the news, everything goes in threes. That was so rooted a superstition that when a man or woman broke something useful, two useless things, even two twigs, would be broken to ward off the curse.

Old Ethel, first with the news and for once the centre of interest, said with spite, 'Carrying on like crazy, she is. You'd think she was widowed. Take me. I was with the good old Father more years than you could reckon – and he was took sudden, too. Did I wail and weep? Though I lost my home and my job, too, and was cast on charity.' She threw an ungrateful look at the relatives who had given her grudging shelter.

Old Hodgson, a village Elder, and one of those who had reason to be grateful to Mistress Captoft for one of her doses, said, 'Mark you! She *was* related to him.'

A woman said, 'Only nephew. Take me. My brother over at Muchanger lost three boys at a go. Smallpox. I never acted crazy.'

There was much interest, but little sympathy. Mistress Captoft, with money of her own, her fine clothes, her head-dresses, her grey mule, had incurred deadly envy in women who never had a penny of their own. They earned; yes! Work like an ox in the fields, in the yard, in the house; cook, mend, spin, bear and rear children: all unpaid labour. There were good husbands and bad, sons kind or unkind, but one and all they held on to the purse strings. If you were lucky you might get a present now and again, but some man chose it and paid for it, and wanted thanks for it. And if it was stuff for a gown it was always the wrong colour. The women of Intake envied Mistress Captoft; and the men did not like her. Far too masterful, starting with the men she'd hired to add to and improve the priest's house. She'd hired them from outside, a fact which with grand inconsistency, had been resented. Asked to do a bit of building work on the little low house, or to dig enough of the long neglected glebe to make a garden, the men of Intake would have asserted their independence in a variety of ways, choosing their own time, their own pace, demanding extortionate wages. Mistress Captoft brought in hirelings, slaves, landless men who could be harried about. And the jobs had been done in no time.

Curiously, the one person in Intake who came to offer real sympathy, and, more, help was Master Tallboys whom Mistress Captoft had never much liked, thinking him cold and aloof and utterly unhelpful to Benny's career as she had once planned it.

But now here he was, grave, stolid, kind. For when in her agony of loss she screamed at him: If only you had kept your mad wife under control, none of this . . . he showed nothing but a desire to help. He'd ride to Moyidan, he said, and tell Father Thomas and ask him to come and conduct the funeral; he'd send a message to Sawyer about the coffin; he'd see to everything.

And she needed support now. Proud and independent as she might appear to be she had never, so far in her life, faced any serious challenge; fond parents, doting old husband; a period when, if a woman could be said to have a career, she had had one; after that, Benny and all the little subterfuges, the good management, the self-control upon which she had prided herself. Always, somewhere in the background, a man. Now nobody.

A strong stone tower in collapse left more of a ruin than a wattle hut, Henry reflected. And Mistress Captoft's collapse was absolute.

There was not a place in the little house which had not a fresh blow to strike as soon as she entered; here he sat at his books; here I cooked his meals; in this room, my bedchamber he came to me; in the other he died. And perhaps most painful of all the little narrow room where the mad woman had struck the lethal blow, and in which now lay, so carefully and hopefully packed, what she had planned to take with her to Amsterdam; the silver cups and plates, wadded with the fine linen in a leather bag. More linen and a few clothes bundled into a kind of sausage, enclosed in sailcloth. Meant for Amsterdam! Unbearable.

'And I do not know where to go,' she said to Henry.

'I always understood that you owned property, Mistress Captoft.'

'So I do. But leased. And I could not live . . .' The two farms, with houses which her kind old husband had bequeathed her were, if anything, more isolated than Intake; and the sheep-run had no proper house at all.

'Well,' Henry said in his practical way, 'there is no immediate hurry. If I remember rightly it takes a little time to instal a new priest. And there are houses for sale or hire in Baildon. I have to go to market next week. Would you like me to look around?'

'I don't know. I cannot decide, or plan. I just do not know.' All her talent for management, her ability to organise had gone, no more substantial than the whipped cream on top of a custard pie.

72

Full responsibility for her Henry was prepared to shuffle off. After all, Father Thomas at Moyidan had been Father Benedict's uncle, and Mistress Captoft had been Father Benedict's aunt; so they were, if only by marriage, related and families must hold together.

As he was holding to John, irritation weaving its way through concern. There was an expression – nursing one's grief, and that was exactly what John was doing; sitting about, hands idle, eyes vacant, taking a bite of this, a bite of that, never a whole meal, though Joanna was doing her best.

It was true that he must go to market on the Wednesday; he had two pigs ready for slaughter; one for sale; one for house use.

'Come with me, John. It'd take you out of yourself.'

Nothing could do that. All very well for Henry. What had he lost? A scold; a shrew, a mad woman. Whereas I . . .

'I couldn't,' John said, tears welling up again. 'Just the sight of people, alive while Nick is . . .' He went, choking and stumbling out of the kitchen.

Godfrey said, 'You promised, Father, that next time you went to market, you'd take me.'

Rasped by his failure with John, Henry said, 'I made no such promise. You're old enough now to get things straight.' That was the way Walter had talked to him; and what was wrong with it? Yet he felt compunction, looking at his son's wide blue eyes, hurt.

I must not take out on this poor little boy, this motherless little boy, my exasperation with these two people who cry so easily.

'Of course you can come,' he said.

Baildon market was really three, the big general market, a wide space dominated by the church and the inn; the beast market with the shambles adjoining it, and, at a little distance, the horse market. In the big market Henry halted to let Godfrey out of the waggon. As he did so he had a sharp memory of the days when his nephew, Richard of Moyidan, had come to market with him. There'd been a time, just after the church took possession of Moyidan, when the boy had been sadly neglected; his loving godmother dead, his idiot parents dead, his unofficial guardian, Sir Richard, gone back to London. Henry had taken him in, against Griselda's loud protests and much against Joanna's wishes. And he'd been badly rewarded! So now, presenting his son with a farthing, he said solemnly, 'This is for you to spend. You can buy yourself a cake or pie. You can *look* at things, but you are not to touch. Do you understand me? You can have whatever your farthing will buy, and nothing else.' Young Richard had gone around pilfering for quite a long time before he was caught, thus disgracing the family name. 'I'll pick you up by the church,' Henry said, and drove on to sell his pig.

On his way he passed what he and Joanna always referred to as the rubbish stall, kept by a man with so glib a tongue that Joanna once said, 'He'd sell you Knight's Acre, Henry, if you stood there long enough.' Amongst the jumble of broken or inadequately mended things there was sometimes an article of which a handy man like Henry could make use, and Henry decided that on his way back from the beast market, he'd see what was on offer.

'Is that a lute?' His mother had had one and played it beautifully; she'd tried to teach all her children, only John had taken to it, and Sybilla's lute had gone with him when he left home.

'Right you are, sir! Beautiful thing and in splendid condition. Not a broken string. Untuned of course. I have no ear. Try it, sir.' The battle was half won if a customer could be persuaded to handle any article. He pushed the lute into Henry's hand and turned to persuade a woman that a cooking pot, properly tinkered, was as good as, even better than, a new one. 'Where it's mended it's thicker, you see. Last a lifetime.'

To Henry, never enamoured of any lute, this one was anything but beautiful, shabby, chipped and dirty. But with a clumsy stroke of his thumb he assured himself that some sound could be produced and he thought of John who had been obliged to sell his own beloved instrument somewhere on that long hungry journey home. A lute might cheer him a bit, rouse a spark of interest.

'How much?'

'Well, to anybody else, it'd be seven shillings, sir. But I can

74

see you've taken a fancy to it, and I like to see a thing like that go where it'll be appreciated. Say three, and at that I'm robbing myself.'

Most customers enjoyed a haggle. Henry, despite his perpetual lack of money and need to exercise the utmost thrift, thought haggling undignified. The price was extortionate, but he paid.

Godfrey was waiting. As he clambered into the waggon, Henry asked, 'Did you enjoy yourself?'

'Oh yes. Except for the dog. It danced, but the man was *rough* to it. I didn't like that. So when he came round with his cap I didn't put my farthing – you did say it was a farthing? – in.'

Rough was about the most derogatory word in Godfrey's vocabulary. Drilled into him by Griselda who, so far as her son was concerned, had only two standards of behaviour, rough and otherwise.

'So what did you spend it on?'

'I bought something for you, Father. I don't know what it is, but the woman said it was nice. And more than a farthing, but I was a pretty little boy and could have it.'

Shyly he produced an orange.

Such a luxury that Henry had not been within arm's reach of one since, at about the age his own son was now, he had left Beauclaire that rich place where luxury was commonplace. Oranges came from Spain. Henry could remember his father saying that there they were common as apples in England and grew on peculiar trees which bore sweet-scented flowers and golden fruits at the same time. In England oranges were rare and very costly because picked when unripe and hard they shrivelled; picked ripe and luscious, unless the ship that carried them had a favourable passage, the wind behind her all the way, they rotted. Not a cargo to appeal to the ordinary ship's captain who preferred to carry the oranges in preserved form. Rendered incorruptible' because saturated with sugar, this concoction was an even more costly luxury. But Henry had known it, and short of a miracle, his son never would.

Henry's thought teetered. Beauclaire, so rich and splendid, had, despite all his uncle's endeavours to be neutral in the war between York and Lancaster, been utterly destroyed; whereas Knight's Acre, bare, humble, poor, had survived.

One could think a lot in almost no time at all and Godfrey had not been aware of any lapse.

'The woman said it was nice to eat.'

'No doubt about that. We'll share it with Joanna.' Then a rush of feeling came over him. That his son should have spent his poor farthing . . .

'You're my boy,' he said.

Godfrey said, in exactly the manner with which he had accepted the news of his mother's death, 'I always was. Wasn't I?'

John recoiled from the lute.

'As though I could . . .' Another proof of Henry's complete lack of understanding.

Disappointed, but now skilled in concealing any emotion, Henry said, 'It'll serve as firewood!' Inside him something cried— Three shillings for what could be gathered, for nothing, at the wood's edge.

But though John had repudiated it, he kept looking at the lute. Poor thing; derelict, like me! It had once been beautiful; not unlike the one he had been obliged to sell. It had been inlaid, either with silver or mother-of-pearl; ill-used, exposed to the damp, it had lost most of its decoration; but it still had its strings. Finally he put out a hand, reluctantly, tentatively, and retrieved the poor thing.

Wrecks, both of us, he thought, but still . . .

The time between supper and bedtime he spent in cleaning and retuning it. Under the dirt even some bits of the decorative inlay came up shining. A good lute, full bodied. He thought of all those songs that Nick had made; the words conveyed by word of mouth, the tunes translated from the rather thin, though pleasing sound that a hazelwood pipe could produce into lute music.

Nick would never make another song; but those he had made were all there, stored away in John's memory.

And while John remembered, played and sang them, passed them on, so that even grooms whistled them as they tended to horses, and young gallants who could sing or strum a little, used them for serenading – then something of Nick would remain. All suddenly his shattered life began to mend, acquired aim and purpose.

For a similar restoration, Mistress Captoft had to wait a little, suffering meanwhile another blow. Master Tallboys had been mistaken in saying that there was no hurry, that it took some time to instal a new priest. Father Thomas could see very plainly that while this living remained vacant he would be expected to be at least partly responsible for it; and since Moyidan was his parish and hardly a day passed without some servant of the Bishop coming to see that all was in order there, he was in a good position to expedite matters. A word in the right ear . . .

Henry was in his sheep-fold, gloomily unloading the hay which would soon be needed to keep this wretched flock alive through the winter. His father's decision, taken years ago, to rear sheep at all had been a mistake – Walter, never yet proved wrong, had said Intake was no place for sheep; and his own decision to be his own shepherd had been an even worse mistake.

And there, at the door of the priest's house, was Mistress Captoft, laying in wait for him. Oh, God give me patience! I've only just got John on the mend. And she is none of mine. But in the time that it took for him to make the hay enclosure safe against greedy sheep who would have gobbled it down in a day and all swollen up as though they were pregnant, and to lead the horse and waggon on to the trail and close the gate of the fold, he had been given, if not patience, an inspiration. John had stopped mourning as soon as he had something to do – something acceptable; and plainly what this poor grieving woman needed was employment.

'I was coming to see you, Mistress Captoft. To ask a favour. Very shortly I must kill a pig and I am ignorant of how to preserve and cure pigmeat. I wondered whether you would be so kind as to come and give advice. There would be no heaving and hauling. I could do all that, Joanna and I simply need guidance.'

Something within Mistress Captoft sprang to life. She knew all that there was to know about casking and curing and smoking, though she had never actually seen a pig killed. In her father's house, and in her husband's when it was pig-killing time, she'd always shut herself away or taken a walk. Pigs did squeal so, with an almost human sound. Once it was dead it was meat and, though she had never been obliged to dabble her hands in brine or expose herself to the smoke in the chimney where hams and sides of bacon were cured, she knew all about the processes.

'Have you salt, Master Tallboys? Saltpetre? Honey?'

'Salt, yes. For the other things I cannot answer.'

Helpless man, with nobody in charge of his kitchen but a mere child.

'I think,' Mistress Captoft said, 'that I had better come straightaway and take stock.'

She was needed again; active again.

Joanna watched, with hatred, the gradual encroachment. She was not jealous, female to female, Mistress Captoft was far too old; well over thirty and fat. And Henry's manner towards her was never more than polite. But inch by inch she was edging Joanna out of the position which she had hoped would have been strong enough to save her from any more talk about going to Stordford. For a few days they worked together, Mistress Captoft cheerful, Joanna sullen. A newly killed pig meant some meat, at least, fresh roasted on the spit, naturally Miss Captoft must be asked to share it. And baking day came round. Joanna did not take kindly to the idea that every loaf should be marked with a Cross. 'They rise better,' Mistress Captoft said. And she'd brought from her home a little packet of spice and dried fruit, and gently suggested that *one* loaf, given this stuff, and some melted butter would make a cake loaf. Much enjoyed.

The sharpest blow fell when Joanna said, in her joking way, 'Henry, unless we take care, she will move in.'

'I have already suggested it. The new priest will be here any day now, and she has as yet made no arrangements.'

Rage almost choked the girl. But she must not, would not behave like Griselda. Lest her face should betray her she turned quickly to the hearth and prodded the sausages in the pan. She did so with exaggerated gentleness, again not to resemble Griselda who when angered banged things about.

Unaware of the feeling he had roused, Henry said, 'The rooms on the other side will hardly accommodate all her furniture, but it is only a stop-gap arrangement. Some of her things can stand in our hall.'

But those rooms are mine! I only lent them to John and Young Shep because Griselda said she'd burn this house down sooner than take in two vagabonds with the lung-rot. You had no right!

It was a slight shock to discover that it was possible to be so angry with the person you loved. And that simply because he was doing a kindness. Instantly penitent, she said, 'Or, if Mistress Captoft preferred, we could move some of those divans into the hall.'

'No! I wouldn't want ... I mean they would be quite unsuitable there.'

Planning for Amsterdam, Mistress Captoft had been ready to abandon her furniture since the cost of transport and shipping would be so vast. She'd thought, quite happily, how comfortable and well-furnished the in-coming priest would find the little house. But she had had Benny then and material things had mattered less. Now they mattered a great deal, so when Henry's waggon made its last creaking journey between the two houses all that remained in the empty one was what Mistress Captoft had found there, old Father Ambrose's poor stuff which she had banished to a shed. However, taking a last look round, she made a kindly resolution. If the new priest – Father Matthew – proved to be a pleasant person, she would bring back, as gifts, certain things to make the place more habitable. Then he would be grateful. And he would be grateful, too, when she requested a Mass every day for a year for the benefit of Benny's soul. She knew how totally inadequate the stipend was. She would be generous in other ways later on.

Her court cupboard, tough not so beautifully carved as the one Walter had managed to find for Sybilla, looked well in the Knight's Acre hall, and her well-padded settee made the one already there look small and shabby. She unpacked her silver and distributed it between both cupboards. For the first time in its life the hall lost its half-empty, ill-furnished look.

Joanna had half hoped that since the rooms across the yard had their own kitchen, inconveniently as it was placed,

Mistress Captoft would busy herself there and cease to meddle. It was a vain hope. Mistress Captoft was a born meddler, and had a convivial nature, long denied outlet. She was in and out all day, every day, generally with an excuse to which no reasonable person could take objection. Her own furniture must be dusted regularly, and polished occasionally; her silver must be kept bright. She included Henry's furniture in her ministrations. She came bearing gifts; she'd made some of the honey cakes of which she knew Godfrey was so fond; she'd just opened a barrel of pickled herrings which, though small, was more than she could possibly eat by herself: she had some wine, better than average, which she thought she must share.

As the weather grew colder the question of fires arose. The only hearth across the yard was in the kitchen; and a brazier though it gave a good steady heat wasn't the same as a fire, was it? And for the sake of the furniture and the fabric of the hall itself, it was advisable to have a fire there at least once a week.

If Henry ever thought her intrusive or meddlesome, he gave no sign; he was always courteous. Poor woman, she was lonely. Godfrey was always pleased to see her, and John was almost effusively welcoming. He said how pleasant it was to try a tune with a listener who could tell a lyric from a dirge. Actually he was employing his winning ways with women with a sharp eye of self-interest. He intended to make his second assault on the wider world the moment the weather improved with the coming of spring, and he needed money to start off with. If Henry couldn't or wouldn't help, Mistress Captoft might. She was obviously well-to-do and open-handed.

Only Joanna remained unfriendly, sullen – though she was glad enough, Mistress Captoft noticed, to hand over the making and mending. And Mistress Captoft was glad to do it, for she had received another little shock from which her mind must be diverted.

Father Matthew had arrived and she had disliked him at first sight. She had not, of course, ever imagined that Benny's successor should be even half worthy; but this man was an oaf. Ill-spoken, mannerless.

Mistress Captoft had suddenly remembered that a mild

day in early November was the ideal time for moving plants. Accompanied by Godfrey who claimed that he could push the flat, two-wheeled, long-handled barrow and that he could also dig, she'd gone up to the empty house to fetch away the best of the things which she had cherished over the years. She had four rose-trees which because they had been pruned and fed on the grey mule's dung, were in far better condition than the six at Knight's Acre, lately sadly neglected. She had the usual garden bushes, rosemary, lavender, southernwood, barberry; and also, because she had lived in Dunwich, a port in close contact with the Continent, a number of imported, rather bare bulbous plants.

They must all be lifted and transplanted, because though Henry regarded the present arrangement as a stop-gap measure, Mistress Captoft did not. She had been so eager to get away from Intake, but now it was different; the place where Benny had spent his last, happy days, and though he was not an outdoor man, had often lifted his eyes from his books to comment on the beauty of Layer Wood as the changing seasons touched it; and the place where he lay buried. Lifting the rosemary bush she thought of breaking off a piece and placing it on his grave. Because rosemary remained not only green but fragrant even in winter it had come to be regarded as the symbol of remembrance.

A coarse voice said, 'Who're you? And what d'you think you're doing?'

Mistress Captoft straightened up. She was a woman who had always been, and would always be, acutely conscious of her appearance; at the same time sensible enough to match clothes to the occasion. This, being a workaday occasion, she wore, not a head-dress, but a plain linen hood and her skirts were hitched up a good six inches above the stout shoes needed for digging.

'I am Mistress Captoft. I am removing a few plants. My own. And you are Father Matthew.' She managed to poise these words between question and statement, while her glance reminded him that he had not shaved for two days.

He had no tact at all. 'If they're yours,' he indicated the plants, and somehow managed to sound as though he doubted her word, 'then you lived here. Was it always the way it is now?'

81

'In what way?'

'So bare.' And that he managed to make sound as an accusation; as though she had stripped it.

'I had my own furniture,' she said crisply. 'And indeed you find the place in far better fettle than I did on my arrival. There was not even an oven, then.'

She was angry with him because his unmannerliness had made her unmannerly. Naturally she had a high standard of what behaviour to priests should be. But then such an oaf had no right to be a priest at all.

This hasty decision was justified by the way he said Mass, mispronouncing several words. The thought of him in Benny's place was so hurtful that she decided to attend Nettleton church in future, and it was to the priest there that she entrusted the duty of saying a Mass each day for a year.

With her plants transferred, she was ready to throw herself into preparations for Christmas. It could not be merry this year with bereavements so recent, but Joanna learned with some surprise, that Christmas must not go unmarked; there must be a bag-pudding, and something called mincemeat, things she had never seen and knew nothing about. No matter, Mistress Captoft would see to it all. And just as she had suggested the lighting of the fire in the hall now and then, so she now suggested that Henry should coop and fatten a goose. She knew — and possessed just the wine that went best with goose. The modest feast, it was tacitly assumed, would be communal.

It was difficult for Joanna to have a word with Henry alone these days. But the chance came. Godfrey in bed, Mistress Captoft gone to her own place, escorted by John, who had taken his lute which meant that he would be away for a while.

Joanna went straight to the point.

'Henry this is something I have been wanting to say. That day in the wood . . .' Never before referred to, and now hastily skirted around. Cool; quick. 'You said that *some* of my money had been placed with Sir Barnabas Grey at Stordford, but that there was more to come. I said I wanted it used *here*. You refused. Please, Henry, think again.'

'I said what I meant, Joanna. I hold to it.'

'Then you would rather be beholden to *her* than to *me*?'

'It has always been my wish, my intention, to be beholden to nobody.'

'You drink her wine.'

'Very little. John is the one with the ready mouth. Set against it, I stable and feed her mule.'

'You will eat her pudding and her mincemeat.'

'And she will eat our goose.'

'But Henry, surely you see . . .' She changed, gave one of those closely observed, rather cruel imitations. 'Oh, Master Tallboys, you must just *taste* this wine. Master Tallboys, my saffron cakes turned out *exceptionally* well. Master Tallboys, I have a self-winding spit, too wide for my own hearth, but it would just fit . . .' She dropped the mimicry which had not been exaggerated, and said, in her own voice and almost fiercely, 'Is that how it is to be for ever? When your jerkin is past mending, she'll buy cloth and make you a new one. Godfrey will outgrow his clothes, she will provide. Can your pride bear it? Even if her mule had five meals a day?'

That was what she hated, even more virulently than the meddling, the subtle reduction of Henry.

'It will not come to that, dar – Joanna. It just happens that we are at low ebb now. The tide must turn.'

'But why wait? With my money there to be used? Why is it all right for Sir Barnabas Grey to use some of my money and not for you to use the rest?'

'There is a world of difference. You see, it is a question of *how* the money is used; what return it will bring. I might take your money, buy stock that'd sicken, clear a field that took three years to come to fertility. Then where should we be? As I understand it, Sir Barnabas is a man of business. He would not put the money entrusted to him into a farm, only just holding its own. And nor will I.'

'Not just *a* farm, Henry. It is my *home*.'

A true, perfectly natural thing to say, but that was not the way he wished her to think. His desire to get her away, into a different life, was genuine and of long standing.

'It is your home, in that you were born here. And of course you will always be sure of a welcome.' For some reason that sounded pompous. He hurried on: 'But it isn't suitable. First working like a farmhand, now like a servant. I want you at least to see, to try, something different.'

'Like Stordford?'

'Yes.'

The matter had never been long absent from his mind, and now that Mistress Captoft seemed to have settled in and certainly seemed prepared to stay until after Christmas, he had given his own circumstances some thought. He could manage, he thought, with the cheapest possible kind of kitchen labour, possibly an orphan girl, just glad of a home. To her Mistress Captoft would gladly give such elementary instruction as was necessary and all would be well. Henry had never done any cooking, had only seen it done and was inclined to underestimate the skill required.

Joanna closed her eyes for a second; the lashes, some shades darker than her hair, lay in crescents against the warm pallor of her cheeks. Pretty, pretty little thing, Henry thought; she must not be wasted here!

She was trying to visualise what her next remark would mean in terms of homesickness and misery. She was deliberately inviting the kind of seeing forward, or seeing into the distance which had afflicted her sometimes in the past. Now nothing came; she'd lost that kind of eye. All she could see was the immediate situation; Mistress Captoft encroaching, inch by inch; Henry's pride and independence being worn away and herself reduced to servant status. There was a world of difference between doing hard, even rough and dirty work, in your own place, of your own choice, and being ordered about, even when the orderer was punctilious about saying, 'my dear'.

Her eyes which could change so rapidly through many shades of blue and blue-green, were bright aquamarine when she opened them and said, 'Very well, then, Henry. I will go. On certain conditions.'

'Well?' He was eager. Willing to comply.

'First, three years, not the four you mentioned.'

He was certain that six months would suffice. Six months of the kind of life he could remember his aunt Astallon's ladies living at Beauclaire, and she'd forget all about Knight's Acre.

'I agree.'

'And what remains of my money to come here and be used.'

'Joanna, I have tried to explain. It would not be right. No, to that I cannot agree.'

Stubbornness was a recognised Tallboys characteristic. Sir Godfrey amiable – some said stupid – had had his full share; the Lady Sybilla and Tana had both been resolute characters.

Deadlock across the kitchen table.

Joanna said, 'Then I must get John to marry me and use my money. He would, you know!'

With a jolt everything inside Henry, heart, breath, came to a standstill; and then with another jolt went on again. John would!

Ever since the shabby old lute had restored him to life John had been talking about setting out again in the spring, and the absolute necessity of having some money to start out with. Unless a musician, however good, had something to fall back upon, so that he could pick and choose, he ended on market squares or village greens, singing, literally, for his supper. He knew, he'd seen it happen. He'd aimed such remarks about equally between his brother and Mistress Captoft and neither had responded immediately. Henry had thought that he would do what he could, when the time came, and Mistress Captoft had realised that to make any promise prematurely would be unwise. While he was still unsure John would continue to be attentive, escort her across the yard and stay for a while, mitigating the loneliness.

'Yes; he *would*,' Henry said almost viciously. 'He'd take whatever was yours that he could get his hands on and then leave you – like Young Shep left his wife; shamed and deserted. You don't know what you're talking about.'

'I know enough to know that that would suit me splendidly! He's not a person I should wish to live with.'

She spoke lightly but she was watching Henry with narrowed, hard eyes. Behind them some compunction stirred; poor Henry, to be so forced! But it was for his own good.

Henry thought: She's capable of it! There had always been a wild, reckless streak in Tana. And John, of course, wouldn't hesitate for an instant.

A feeling of helplessness added itself to his anger. He could do nothing; she was not his ward; she was not a member of the family of which he was the head. If she put this preposterous suggestion to John ... Henry was not accustomed to feeling helpless. Within the limits imposed by lack of money he'd always been master in his own small world. True, Griselda had nagged and scolded but he'd soon learned to ignore what was a mere fretful noise. Nothing vital; nothing like this.

'God damn it all! You leave me no choice! All right. Sooner than see you ruin your life, I'll take what money the Bishop still holds for you, and use it here. Putting what is due to you away, as I put Robert's.'

'There is one other thing,' she said.

Somebody had spilt a little water on the table and she dabbled her finger in it, making a pattern. Watching, Henry thought how strange it was that neither work out-of-doors nor indoors had affected her hands at all; slim, smooth, cream-coloured. Beautiful hands. Her mother's hands.

Stop that!

'Well?'

'Nothing difficult. Just a promise. *If* I go to Stordford, for three years and learn *all* there is to be learned, and behave like a *saint*; and if you haven't found someone you prefer – and I haven't either – you'll marry me. At least, *think* about it. Seriously.'

Nothing to be lost by promising that. The bargain with Sir Barnabas and his lady – made through the Bishop of Bywater – included the arrangement for a *suitable* marriage. And just as Henry visualised Joanna being one of the gay, butterfly ladies of Beauclaire, so he imagined suitors, very much like the young knight who, during Sir Godfrey's absence, had visited Knight's Acre from time to time. Young, handsome, rich. Once installed at Stordford, she'd forget Knight's Acre and presently, wooed by somebody young, handsome, rich ... Nevertheless, something about that wild threat to marry John had rung a warning bell.

'In return for that,' he said, 'I must exact a promise, too. Nobody expects you to behave like a saint, but you are not to do anything secret. Try no madcap scheme or trick.'

'How could I? You have my promise, Henry, and I have

86

yours. I regard it as betrothal. Tom Robinson once told me about betrothals. As near as nothing to marriages, he said, unless one or the other didn't agree when the time came.'

Three years of exile; but she'd got what she wanted. Her mother had borne a longer servitude; but nobody knew that.

Mistress Captoft, asked to help and advise in this new direction, was in her element; sensible enough to know that she was herself out of date in the matter of fashion. Of course the girl must have some new clothes, but the minimum; Lady Grey would know and decide what was needed apart from two decent dresses, one of woollen cloth, one of velvet; and, of course, a hooded cloak.

Mistress Captoft was, secretly, so delighted to know that the unfriendly girl was about to depart that if required she would have stitched sail-cloth.

Joanna's going would not only remove something hostile, it would leave a bedchamber vacant. Mistress Captoft would not admit it, even to herself, but she never felt comfortable, really comfortable in the beautiful, silk hung rooms which, only so short a time ago had seemed like a haven of refuge. She knew and John constantly reminded her that Young Shep had died in the bedchamber; that meant nothing to her; it would indeed be very difficult to find a house, or part of a house in which somebody had not died. It was just she felt out of place, uneasy, as though – this was the way she expressed it to herself – as though her skin didn't fit. Once – and it was a moment she remembered with self shame, she'd heard something, a kind of tap and a fumbling at one of the windows. Just a spray of ivy, moved by the wind, she realised, but not before she had cried out, sharply, 'Who's there?' She looked forward to moving into the main house, and to being in full control.

Stitching away, she said, 'I really think, my dear, that you should master *plain* sewing. Far more exacting forms of needlework will be expected of you at Stordford.'

'Embroidery!' Joanna said with supreme contempt: hurtful to a woman who prided herself on her skill in that art.

'It is one of the things that a lady needs to know,' Mistress Captoft said tartly.

'I have no need to learn how to be a lady. My mother was a lady of Spain.'

A plain statement of fact, innocent of malice, yet it hurt, too. Annoyance deepened the colour in Mistress Captoft's cheeks. She was herself a member of the emergent middle class, daughter of a prosperous merchant, wife to another. In manners and style of living they were as good as any in the land, in learning and in morals superior to those who regarded themselves as more well-bred. To have such a remark made to her by an unlettered girl who could not even sew a seam! And yet, and yet . . . It was something, Mistress Captoft reflected, about the way the girl held her head.

'Unfortunately, she did not live long enough for you to benefit either by her precept or her example.' That should even the score.

His Grace of Bywater had a liking for Henry Tallboys with whom he had come in contact over the business of Moyidan's young heir, who, by some extraordinary oversight, a failure in communications, had, in the winter after the Church had assumed control of the estate, suffered a little privation; grossly exaggerated by the boy himself. He'd gone running to his Uncle Henry and Henry had offered to be responsible for him, with no profit to himself. The fact that the boy was a born liar was proved later when he'd been caught stealing in the market and given as his excuse that he was hungry. A boy born to make trouble, born discontented; as he had vilified the Bishop when he lived at Moyidan, and his Uncle Henry when he lived at Knight's Acre, now he was vilifying Eton, where – at some little trouble to himself – the Bishop had secured him a place.

As proof of his approval, the Bishop had Henry admitted immediately and greeted him affably.

'This is most timely, Master Tallboys. I was about to ask you to call upon me. I have been away for a while, and a letter from Lady Grey awaited me here. She and her husband are anxious about the child.'

'Naturally, my Lord.' Henry had no intention of explaining the delay. It would sound absurd to say that Joanna had defied him. 'I have been unable to give my full attention to the business.' He could have listed the distractions, spoken of Griselda's death; but he wanted no formal expressions of sympathy for a grief that was no grief. 'She is ready to go now and I think it would be well if she could be there by Christmas.'

'An excellent time. She will enjoy the merrymaking.'

Henry had thought of that, too.

It was twenty years since he with his mother, with Richard and Margaret, and John, a baby in arms, and, of course, Walter, had set out from Beauclaire, just missing the Christmas festivities; but he remembered the Christmas before that. Everything topsy-turvy, the Lord of Misrule in control for the Twelve Days, enormous feasts and open house for all. At such a time, he thought, a stranger would not feel strange, and by the time the season was over, Joanna would have settled.

Now, he thought, in order to keep his bargain – and he'd never failed yet in that respect, he must raise the question of the rest of Joanna's dowry. Hateful. Not begging exactly, since he intended to make the money work, but something that went against the grain. His father, Sir Godfrey, had always had a curious, almost ambivalent attitude towards money; it was necessary, something to be pursued at the risk of life and limb; once obtained – by honourable means – to be spent, given away, lent. As a result he had stumbled from crisis to crisis and died poor. Henry had, of sheer necessity, taken a more practical view of money, but he never haggled even on the market. (Unknown to him, that attitude – take it or leave it – had on occasions served him well.)

Now he was spared. The Bishop's hands moved amongst his papers. On one smooth plump finger he wore the amethyst of his office; on the other the great glowing red ruby which, out of all Tana's hoard, his covetous and knowledgeable eye had fixed upon. Now he had it; fair commission for his efforts.

'Then that is settled,' he said. 'But I needed to talk to you, Master Tallboys, about the child's inheritance. You entrusted me with her jewel hoard and of some I disposed easily. As you were informed, wealth enough to secure her a place in Sir Barnabas Grey's family and a modest, but adequate dowry. Some of the stones I held in reserve. As you know, these are troublous times, everything in a state of flux.

But the market will recover and my agent in London will be the first to take advantage of it.'

'Nothing here and now?'

'I am afraid not.'

'That's all right, then,' Henry said. He looked, the Bishop observed, as though he had just received good, not bad, news. Very odd.

The jewelled fingers moved again amongst the heaped, but orderly papers.

'I have here another letter which may interest you. The boy, your nephew. He has written before, always the same strain. He is ill-housed, ill-fed, ill-treated.' His Grace listed young Richard's grievances in a light, mocking voice, inviting Henry's amusement. Not instantly forthcoming. Inside Henry the sense of family responsibility moved a little. He'd never really liked Young Richard, knew him to be dishonest and a liar; but there were excuses, he'd been so spoiled from the first, and then suddenly no longer spoiled.

'Is there any truth in it?'

'None at all,' His Grace said with conviction. 'The demand for places in Eton College is now so high that the one schoolroom will presently no longer serve. Men of substance – and rank – Master Tallboys, are not over-anxious to have their sons starved! And certainly, I perceive a great improvement in his writing.'

Never once had Joanna had cause to doubt Henry's word; but now suddenly she did. He'd been from the first so averse to using her money, except for what he so wrongly thought was to her advantage, that she believed that, forced to it, he had concocted this tale about the rest of her mother's jewels being unsaleable. She could not hold that against him; he was fiercely independent, he was pig-headed, he was Henry, altogether admirable in all his works and ways. But he was wrong to think she could be so easily fooled.

Between himself and unwanted visitors the Bishop had the great man's usual defences; servants, secretaries, chaplains, all skilled in the art of diversion, and not a few of them open to bribery.

Joanna had seen only one building – except for the church

at Baildon – more imposing than Knight's Acre, and that was Moyidan; years ago. There she had not accepted a rebuff; nor did she here.

'Tell His Grace that I am Joanna Serriff. He will understand. He will see me.' Told to wait, she said, 'No, I cannot wait. The days are short now.' As though in contradiction of this statement she sat down and seemed prepared to wait for ever. There was some scurrying about and then she was admitted into the presence.

The Bishop had seen her once before, at Moyidan where he had been dining with Sir Richard, when, dressed like a little ploughboy, she'd burst in, demanding to see Robert. Her curtsey, and when she flung back her hood, her hair and face, had revealed her sex and His Grace of Bywater had thought then— Give her ten years and she'll be a beauty.

It had taken a shorter time. To her, flowering had come early. Vaguely, His Grace remembered some mention of her foreign origin. Spanish? Yes. Spanish. And he remembered his pilgrimage to Rome. In the South girls ripened early; nubile at eleven, married, often mothers at twelve. He had always conducted his secret affairs with the utmost discretion, but he had great knowledge of, was a specialist in the subject of women, and as he greeted her with great cordiality two saddening thoughts flashed through his mind. He, alas, was growing old: and early ripening of beauty all too often meant early decline.

Joanna gave her best curtsey, combining it with a down sweep of long lashes. Her eyelids, her lips, were luminous with youth. An attraction older women strove – sometimes without success – to recover by the use of salves. When she lifted the lashes, her eyes, blue as cornflowers, were fixed on him in a look of appeal.

'My Lord, I was obliged to come to you. Only you can help me.'

'You did rightly. Rest assured that I shall do all that is possible. Sit here. Loosen your cloak. This room is warm.'

His mind worked quickly. She had come about the rest of the jewels; and he must explain again about the sluggish market. With the Yorkist cause completely triumphant most of those who had supported the Lancastrian side had lost their lands. Lancastrian ladies had sold their ornaments in order to buy necessities; and though there still was, and would always be, a demand for stones of exceptional quality, such as Lady Serriff's diamonds and emeralds, there was a glut of more mediocre jewels.

And yes, he had been right. That well-shaped head, so elegantly poised on the slender neck; the way the hair grew from the forehead. The hair itself, such a warm brown as to be almost russet, lending warmth to what might have been a rather cold and austere beauty. Nose, perhaps a trifle high at the bridge. As she aged she would probably become sharp-featured. In the meantime, delectable.

'It is about my mother's jewels – the rest of them. Henry said they couldn't be sold.'

By accident or intent her glance shifted to the great ruby. She recognised it. She and Robert, finding the hoard in the long-empty rooms had pried the pretty pebbles loose and used them in their childish games. They had agreed that the big red one was best of all. It had been the prize pebble.

Once more the Bishop explained.

Joanna said, 'Oh. Then I wronged Henry. In my mind.' The thought that she had suspected Henry – Henry! – of deceiving her was horrible. And the truth made her errand here seem foolish.

Mistaking her look of dejection, His Grace said, kindly, 'It will not affect you, my dear. Enough of the best stones were sold to ensure your future. And the others will be sold, at the right moment.'

'That,' she said, making a gesture with one beautiful hand, 'doesn't matter. It is Henry, and Knight's Acre. Henry needs money *now*. And all mine is with Sir Barnabas . . . Can it be recovered?'

'Not without much inconvenience – and possibly some offence to Sir Barnabas.'

'I did so want to help Henry. He has been so *kind* to me. I was an orphan, you know; and until Griselda found those jewels, I was a pauper, too. Henry was always kind and once or twice, when I did silly things, he stood up for me.'

Who wouldn't?

She looked down at her hands; and then up again. Her eyes had changed, grown paler, harder.

'Master Turnbull might help.'

The name of that meddlesome, anti-clerical lawyer jabbed His Grace like a knife. Joanna regarded Master Turnbull with great respect.

Ordinarily when she and Henry went to market together they'd gone their separate ways to meet at the pie-stall. But one day Henry had taken her along with him to Master Turnbull's office and there Master Turnbull had made one more attempt to persuade Henry that saving money for Robert was not very sensible. Joanna had thought: I could prove that. I could tell you something about Robert. He's dead! She did not speak, of course, because to have done so would be to reveal herself as a cunning and stubborn liar and disgust Henry. So she sat silent while Master Turnbull talked about money, what could be done with it; what he was doing with it; and she had thought him very clever, and a friend to Henry.

So she thought of him now.

'Master Turnbull?'

'Yes. At Baildon. He's very clever about money, Henry says. Perhaps he could think of a way of getting some of mine back. Some would do. Henry doesn't need much; but some he must have.'

His Grace looked at her with close attention and decided that she was innocent of all malice. Had she been less appealing to the eye he would not have reached this decision so readily.

Over the matter of the jewels, the arrangement with Sir Barnabas Grey, there was nothing to be feared from Master Turnbull. All open and above-board, except perhaps a slight overestimation of the value of his negotiations in assigning himself the ruby. Moyidan was another matter. The meddling, near-heretic lawyer was the one who had first drawn attention to Sir Richard Tallboys' mal-administration of that estate, and was doubtless enraged by the outcome, the taking over by the Church; the use of the Castle as a summer residence by the Bishop. No legal questions had been asked, but they could have been. Still could be. Set a really good hound on a hare's trail and he might start bigger game.

'I do not think that Master Turnbull need be involved. Or Sir Barnabas put to inconvenience. There must be some simpler solution . . .'

It flashed upon him. Neat. Obvious. But he pretended to be thinking deeply.

'Suppose I bought what remains of your legacy. I can afford to wait until the market improves.'

'Would you? Oh, that would be wonderful.' Every line of her vivid little face expressed gratitude, and then, abruptly, dismay. 'I have just thought, my Lord, Henry might think it his duty to put most of it away for me. He is such a stubborn man. And what he really needs is stock. A little money perhaps, but mostly animals. He couldn't go hurrying them off to Master Turnbull, could he?' She gave him a dancing look of amusement.

'It is difficult to tell what a really stubborn man may do. We can but try. What, in your opinion, does he need?'

The question was only half serious. Newly clad through Mistress Captoft's efforts and of such ethereal appearance, she looked unlikely to know much about stock animals.

'Sheep,' she said with assurance. 'Two hundred. And the long-legged, black-faced kind. They do better on our land.' And with a larger flock, Henry would need a shepherd. Talk about that later. 'Store cattle . . .' It was her turn to doubt. Would this kindly old man know anything about them? 'Young bullocks. They have to be fed through the winter, but we did save our hay crop. Then in the spring they can eat grass and fatten up before going to the Shambles. Oh, and pigs. A few young and an in-pig sow. And . . .'

They watched one another across the polished table. Was she asking too much? She had no idea what the remaining jewels were worth, or the cost of what she listed. Her experience of money was limited to meagre shopping with coins of the smallest denominations; had she gone too far? Apparently not.

He was watching her, completely fascinated by the combination of delicate beauty – look at those hands – and downright, earthly commonsense. How fortunate some unknown fellow was to be! And if circumstances had been a little different, if the Tallboys–Grey connection had not been made, he would, God forgive him, have risked just one more amorous venture.

He did not flinch when she spoke of two cows. A bull.

'Henry,' she said, 'would welcome a bull of his own. There

is one in the village, but nobody there likes Henry and we do not like them.'

Still no protest, so she said, 'And a horse. It must be young. Heavy enough to pull the waggon, light enough to ride. Then. Just a small sum of money. Because I shall not be there to help, with the flock, in the field.'

The house, she judged rightly, could be left in Mistress Captoft's busy-body hands.

Then she remembered her manners. Handed on to her through Griselda who had learned from the Lady Sybilla; who had been in fact an unlikely pipeline, conveying courtesy from one generation to another.

'It is much to ask of you my Lord, but I shall be grateful for ever.'

Tears rose and stood in her eyes. The ageing man, with experience, knew how those tears would fall. To this girl had been granted one of the rarest assets that a woman could possess, the ability to weep without disfiguring herself. The tears would spill, dewdrops on a rosebud. He waited, but she blinked rapidly and banished the tears.

Another doubt had assailed her. He had noted down Henry's needs, but who would do the buying? Somebody ignorant, or careless.

'I should like Henry to have the best beasts, my Lord.'

'He shall. I have experienced men on my staff. They will understand that they are buying for *me*.'

'Thank you.' She was thoughtful for a moment, and then appealed again. 'I know it is a *great* favour to ask, but would it be possible to allow Henry to understand that this arrangement came from you, not from me? That might not be quite ... straightforward, but it would make it easier for him to accept.'

Here she was not quite sure of her ground; the kind old man was a churchman and she was asking him, practically, to act a lie. It did not trouble her at all although she knew the rules that supposedly governed Christian behaviour. She could not know that half her blood stemmed from a pagan, sunworshipping race who had moved from Persia to North Africa long before the birth of Christ. They'd carried their own religion with them, and even when overtaken by the wave of Islamic invasion, they had conformed only in minor ways. Tana, captured and enslaved, had lived in Moorish Spain for years, in Christian Spain for as long as it took to ride across it; and then, for a longer time, in Christian England, but she had never been converted. To her, Christianity had been the ridiculous rule that allowed a man only one wife. She had held to her tribe's code, very simple, the sun the giver of all, master of all, and a rough kind of ethic; one never forgave an enemy, never betrayed a friend.

Joanna only knew that the cold little church, the three-in-one God, and the Virgin Mother in her niche, were for her meaningless.

'I have no doubt it could be managed,' His Grace of Bywater said.

And he wondered what she could possibly learn at Stordford, or anywhere else. She'd been born, knowing it all.

'I must get back before, I hope, Mistress Captoft misses her mule.'

'Borrowed? Without permission?'

'It was necessary,' she said, and gathered her cloak about her, hiding the long slim arms in the tight sleeves and the small but fully shaped breasts, and with the pulling into place of the hood, careless, charming gesture, covering her beautiful hair.

All he could do was to say that he hoped she would be happy at Stordford. After all he had found the place for her; another swimming glance of gratitude was no more than his due.

'I think I shall be very unhappy. But three years is not long.'

No. Not to the young. When he was young what had three years been? Mere steps on the ladder, aims, ambitions, achievements. And now? In a way even less, as time counted, the days filled with business, speeding by, the nights – he slept rather badly, seemingly endless.

'I chose the place with an eye to your happiness,' he said, a slight repreach in his voice. 'Sir Barnabas has daughters of about your age.' Even as he said it he thought: How ridiculous! She is older than Eve!

She was on her feet now, and he rose, too, intending to pay her the courtesy of seeing her out himself.

She said, 'My Lord, I am most grateful for *all* that you have done. Most of all for this.' Then something flashed into her eyes and she said, in a different voice, 'I am even thankful to you for finding an *unhappy* place for Richard of Moyidan.'

He thought that a strange thing to say. Certainly he had no liking for the boy himself, and Master Tallboys had not pursued the subject of the complaints.

'Why do you say that? Did he ever . . . affront you in any way?'

If he had, Heaven help him! His last complaining letter would go to the Provost of Eton with a little admonitory note suggesting that the writer of it needed another flogging.

'Me? No! He would not have dared. But he was very cruel, in a horrible, sly way to a gentle little boy who could not stand up for himself. For that I wished him ill – and always shall.'

Now His Grace saw another flaw in her beauty; her eye-teeth were too prominent, wolfish. And her eyes were as green as her mother's readily saleable emeralds.

Into the over-heated, well-furnished room something alien crept. Something cold, old, evil. The Bishop entertained a thought inconsistent both with his calling and his sophistication – I would rather she wished me well than ill.

Absolute nonsense!

And yet, was there not, in the Bible, as well as in heathen mythology, some hint of god-like creatures consorting with the daughters of men and breeding, begetting, something out of the common rut? 'There were giants in the earth in those days.' Size, naturally, the masculine ideal; what of the feminine? Discount the looks, extraordinary as they were. How, isolated out there at Knight's Acre, just a farm with a better-than-average house, had she acquired such manners? Such style?

A puzzle to anyone who knew nothing of Griselda, faithfully aping the Lady Sybilla to a point where even Henry had once been deceived. A pipe, which before it broke had conveyed courtesy, airs and graces between two generations.

A puzzle. Nonsense. Rubbish, His Grace of Bywater thought and sharply rang his silver bell; sternly began to dictate – Item: two hundred black-faced sheep of the best quality.

'But you told me ... I was prepared for ... a child of between eleven and twelve. She is fourteen at least. She makes Maude look like a dwarf!'

Lady Grey's protest came from the heart and her husband made haste to soothe her.

'My dear, Maude still has growth to make. This girl has probably completed hers and in a year's time Maude will overtop her.'

Just the kind of remark that Barnabas, with his resolute over-optimism *would* make!

'Had you ever *seen* her?

'No. How could I? This was all arranged in London. I told you at the time. My good friend, Shefton, told me that the Bishop of Bywater was anxious to place a girl of good family and moderate fortune in a respectable household, with other children of her age, and with a view to a suitable marriage. I owed Shefton money at the time; he was doing himself an immediate service, and me a long-term one. I volunteered immediately. It isn't every day that three thousand marks, free of interest for five years drops into one's lap.'

Lady Grey took a long look at the two men, inside the same skin, to whom she had been married for fifteen years. Perhaps she should think herself fortunate that his double personality operated only in the financial field; he'd never taken a mistress that she knew of, never caused even the merest whisper of scandal in *that* way. Remembering what other women suffered – she'd seen them sitting frozen-faced in the stands around a tiltyard, while in the dust and clash of the mêlée, their men wore favours given to them by other women: a sleeve, a glove, a flower even. It was, in a way, a kind of secret language, not words, signs; and she, thanks be to God, had never been compelled to endure that humiliation. But what she had borne was Barnabas's attitude towards money. One Barnabas was shrewd, hard-headed, business-like; the other was a gambler of the utmost recklessness. What one Barnabas could *make* in a week, by diligence and attention to business and no small physical effort, riding hither and thither, the other could lose in an evening, over a card game, or throwing dice. She was resigned to it now, knowing that he was capable of making a sharp good deal with the Hanseatic League at the Steelyard in the morning, and then making some senseless bet upon which fly could clamber up a window pane faster than the other.

He had a good reputation, for he had never dodged a debt; what one Barnabas lost, the other would repay. And living in style was a help. So perhaps was this tenuous relationship to the Queen. There had been ups and downs, but Stordford had never gone short of anything, partly because Lady Grey was so excellent a manager. When money was available, the estate came first; more acres, more stock. All under her immediate, personal supervision. She went to London very seldom, preferring country life and country activities, and preferring to entertain in her own home, where as hostess and lady of the manor she could not be overlooked, as had so often happened when she had ventured into wider and more glittering circles. Even as a girl she had not been pretty, and then only with the bloom of healthy youth and she had not been born with, nor bothered to acquire the vivacious manner, the witty tongue, the avid attention to fashion and cosmetics with which many plain women compensated for their lack of looks. In addition to this, as the youngest of a large family, three boys and five girls, her dowry was small. She was twenty before any man showed any interest in her. Yet of all the Tetlow girls she had made the best marriage. Everybody was astounded when Sir Barnabas Grey, gay, handsome and popular and experienced, chose to marry plain, dull Gertrude Tetlow. What could he possibly see in her? He was twenty-seven, and much sought after. What he saw and recognised almost instantly, was the balance, the ballast that he lacked himself.

It had been a successful marriage. Within a year she had presented him with a son, Roger, now serving his time as page – soon to be squire – in the household of Lord Bowdegrave at Abhurst. A second son had died in infancy. Then had come Maude, and after three years, Beatrice.

It was a common belief that sons resembled their mothers in looks, daughters, their fathers. in this case, regrettably, the rule was reversed; Roger was handsome and the girls even

99

plainer than their mother. Maude *was* squat, in or out of Joanna Serriff's company; she had sallow skin, hair and eyes the colour of mud; Beatrice was fairer, in fact, too fair, almost bleached looking.

Lady Grey, who had borne her own lack of beauty with a kind of defiant fortitude, and then made mock of the whole thing by marrying well, was truly concerned by her daughters' lack of comeliness. Baffled, too – at least in her youth she had carried a good colour! Still had it, in fact, the one agreeable thing about a face too heavy featured, too square. And even to her loving maternal eye, other flaws were visible. Maude was lethargic, Beatrice frivolous. What would their future hold? Such sheer good fortune as she had met, with Barnabas, was unlikely ever to come their way. They would, of course, have dowries far more substantial than hers had been, but curiously, inside this solid, stolid woman, a romantic streak lurked, assuring her that marrriages made entirely for money were not, on the whole, happy. That was what accounted for those signs of infidelity on the tourney ground – and for the number of children, the results of secret intrigues, whom men accepted as their own, rather than wear the horns of a cuckold. (The dull, plain girl, always overlooked, had been sharply observant.) She was working and scheming so that her daughters should have good dowries, but she did not wish them to make what she called money marriages.

So the régime into which Joanna now stepped was rigorous. Exercise in the open air – good for the complexion; a spell in the covered tennis court – good for the figure. A dinner, meagre, when Sir Barnabas was away, as he often was, but luxurious by Knight's Acre standards. Immediately after, the day being fine, a spell at the butts. Archery was not regarded as a feminine pastime, but Lady Grey believed that it straightened shoulders. After that lessons. Reading, writing and reckoning. Lady Grey knew that her learning, acquired in lonely moments, when the mainstream of life had appeared to pass her by, had stood her in good stead.

After the lessons came supper; a very different meal from that at Knight's Acre, where people ate because they were hungry and needed sustenance, and went briskly to bed in order to sleep and be ready for another day's work. Suppertime at Stordford was a long, leisurely meal, taken in what seemed to Joanna circumstances of confusion. Almost invariably there were guests, for the house stood near the point where the road to London, the road to the east and the road to the north met, and it was known for its hospitality. Anyone with even a nodding acquaintance with Sir Barnabas was welcome to break his journey there. Minstrels, mummers, men with performing dogs or bears would appear, uninvited, but welcome. Sir Barnabas thought nothing of coming back from London with a riotous company of five or six other men. Neighbours came to supper and stayed overnight; members of the Grey or Tetlow families came and stayed for a week, a month; one indeed, an aged woman known as Aunt Agnes, had come to stay, taken a fall and remained ever since. In the midst of all this noise and bustle and apparent disorder, Lady Grey ruled, unruffled; the spider in the centre of a web of her own weaving, its strands reaching out from kitchen to attic, by way of delegated authority, rules rigid and constant watchfulness. Hospitality might appear to be prodigal, but the lady of the manor knew exactly how much of the best manchet bread, should be served and to whom; how much was left of the great joints, brought hissing from the spit into the hall; to whom the best wine should be offered or not.

On the rare, quiet evenings, or when the company in the hall became too riotous, the ladies retired to the solar, and even there Lady Grey continued to be indefatigable. Out with the embroidery; try a tune on the lute; practise some steps of a dance, so that next time that there was dancing in the hall, there should be no clumsiness.

Joanna was, from the first, aware that this was exactly the life, the education and training which Henry had desired for her, and that, in order to keep her part of the bargain, she must endure it for three years. But she hated it, all of it, and would continue to hate it. She missed Knight's acre, the brooding quiet of the woods. Here there was no quiet, no privacy at all; she shared a sleeping chamber, half a staircase above the hall, with Maude and Beatrice who prattled. She had never been idle, but at Knight's Acre even the most laborious jobs had proceeded at an even pace. Here all was hurly-burly, with Lady Grey, rather like a well-trained sheepdog, making no obvious fuss or noise, constantly rounding up a flock. Do this; do that; go here, go there.

Joanna had never before been ordered about. Banned by Griselda from the house, she had gone into the fields, the yards, the market, and worked hard – but always because she wanted to, not because she must.

She had immediately sensed that Lady Grey disliked her, though so far as she knew she had done nothing to offend. And even, disliked, she was more fortunate than Maude and Beatrice, who often suffered chastisement, slaps on the hands or face, cuffs on the ear. Nothing unusual, Joanna learned. Some ladies behaved very violently to their daughters and dealt blows that broke their heads. Lady Grey never so much as laid a finger on Joanna, perhaps because she was not her daughter, or because she did not entirely lack sensibility and knew that, struck, the girl would strike back. Her disfavour showed itself in other ways. Cutting little speeches: Of course coming so late to learning ... Any child who has not mastered a needle by the age of six ...

There was also the question of clothes. Mistress Captoft had very sensibly said that Lady Grey would know what was needed beyond the one good woollen gown and the velvet. Winter ebbed away and the warmer weather came. Maude and Beatrice had pretty new dresses, two or three of them; Joanna had one of indeterminate colour and hideous shape.

Never mind! Six months of the three-year sentence already served, and at the end of it Knight's Acre and Henry.

The Knight's Acre about which Joanna dreamed – and was to continue to dream – was being changed, both within and without.

Soon after Christmas one of the Bishop's officials arrived with a message. After all, his Grace had succeeded in disposing of the rest of Joanna Serriff's property, but not for cash money, for stock, of which his Lordship assumed that Master Tallboys would wish to take charge.

Henry was first astonished and then angry.

'What do you mean by stock?'

'Animals, Master Tallboys. Sheep, pigs, cows, steers. Oh yes, and a young horse.'

Of all the stupid, clumsy arrangements, this was surely the worst! Mid-winter, after a disastrous summer, with both hay and corn harvests well below standard.

'And what am I supposed to feed them on?'

'May I continue? A proportion of the property was sold for money. I have it here.'

He was plainly accustomed to dealing with vast sums, for he shot, out of a leather bag, more coined money than Henry had ever seen at one time before as though offering a sample of beans. Enough to buy fodder for many animals for a long time. But *what* animals? Surely to God, if he had to take charge of them, regard them as part of Joanna's heritage, keep them, rear them, breed them, he should have had some say in their choosing. He could just imagine what he would get; the wrong kind of sheep; cows with only two working teats, steers which somebody had hoped to keep alive through the winter and then found an unprofitable business. And a horse, young, but already ruined by ill-handling.

Oh, if only he had learned to write! Left with nothing but the spoken words which might be garbled, Henry said. 'You may tell his Grace that I regard this as a most *unsatisfactory* arrangement. Say that. Word for word. That is an order.'

From time to time, without intention, and without knowring it, Henry could pluck a word or a phrase out of the past. Nothing to do with what he appeared to be, a farmer, clad in homespun, illiterate, so that messages must be carried by word of mouth. Walter, long ago, had noted this oddity in Henry who, trained by him to disregard chivalry as an outworn thing, sometimes came up with phrases like 'Upon my honour'; 'I pledge my troth'. It was another language, almost.

'They are all good beasts,' the Bishop's messenger said placatingly.

Unplacated Henry said, 'That remains to be seen.'

Astonishingly they were good. The first to arrive was a flock of sheep, all of the right kind. Henry could not have chosen better himself. Black-faced, long-legged. And with them came what Henry knew he needed, a shepherd, knowledgeable, single-minded; a gnarled-looking old man, but spry, accompanied by a shaggy, sly-eyed, slinking dog called, very rightly, Nip. But for the old shepherd's gruff, incomprehensible order the dog would have nipped Henry.

'I'd like to stay with them,' the man said. 'I don't hold with flocks you can't count. I know all these and if agreeable to you, Master, I'll stop with them. I can build a shack for myself...' He had already looked about and seen what Intake offered; down by the river, willows in plenty, and willow boughs, being supple, made the best foundations for a shack. 'I'd like my dinner regular, and say ... a shilling a week...'

He could have earned more, but on uplands, vast wide places from which people had been driven to make room for sheep. He thought that Knight's Acre looked cosy, enclosed, more what sheep-folds had been before everybody went mad and began to look on sheep as so much wool, so much mutton. He knew it must be so; they were wool and mutton, or breeding ewes and rams, that was the way it went. But somehow, for no reason at all, this place seemed to offer a chance of something a little more human. He did not crave the company of his fellows, his sheep and his dog sufficed, but he liked to be within sight of dwellings. Here only the width of the track separated the fold from the church and the adjoining house; Knight's Acre was in full view, and some of the roofs of Intake were visible. He had a feeling of having come home.

Other animals arrived and Henry realised that the Bishop had done him a singular service. Months of searching markets at Baildon or Bywater, or visiting farms and manors could not have produced so many first-class beasts. Faintly below the surface imposed by repeated disillusionments, some of the old ambition woke and stirred. He might yet attain a moderate prosperity.

Within doors it looked as though prosperity had already arrived. Mistress Captoft moved into the main house as soon as Joanna left, and proceeded to reorganise everything, and to spread comfort, even a certain elegance around her.

She could have servants, now! Throughout her association with Benny it had been wise to manage with casual help – like old Ethel who came, did the roughest work and departed. Servants pried and listened, were prone to gossip, inclined to invent what they did not know.

She decided against seeking servants from Intake – not because it would be useless; she was unaware of the enmity that existed between the village and the house; but because she knew from experience that servants within walking, or even running, distance of their homes were for ever wanting to visit; my mother is ill, madam; my sister is having a baby, I must go. And if it wasn't going it was coming, relatives of every degree dropping in for a chat, a good warm up by the fire, and a bite of whatever was going. And there were smugglings out from the larder. All this Mistress Captoft knew from ruling her husband's comfortable house. She would seek servants in Bywater, a good mule-ride away.

She handed over her mule to a stable-boy in the yard of The Welcome To Mariners, and then went into the inn. The morning, though sunny, was cold and a glass of mulled wine would be welcome. Also inns were centres of information.

In this inn something quite extraordinary had happened, a fortnight ago but not forgotten – never to be forgotten, because of the gross ingratitude. And the shock. And the giving a well-conducted house a bad name ...

Katharine Dowley; age uncertain, neither young nor old; entered service at The Welcome To Mariners, in the most humble capacity; worked herself up, became cook, very good.

Dozens of customers, all expecting the best, and each to be served as though he were the one person in the world. Offer a perfectly spitted roast and what about the fresh fish for which Bywater was so famous? Have the fish ready and the brutes had already had fish earlier in the day, or yesterday; what about a change, grilled lamb?

And no limit to the hours. Travellers on land in the ordinary way timed their journeys more or less; but a ship depended on the wind, could come in at almost any time.

Subject a woman, conscientious by nature and very slightly hysterical at times, to this kind of régime, year after year, and something was bound to go, to give way.

It had given way very late on an evening when a customer asked for roast duckling and Katharine Dowley, whimpering and howling – 'like a dog locked out, or locked in', the land-lady said – had brought the duckling in, not on a dish, on the practically red-hot spit and flung the whole thing in the customer's face.

Fortunately no great damage had been done; but naturally Katharine Dowley had been summarily dismissed. She had gone back to the Lanes from which she had come.

The Lanes were a feature of Bywater about which little was known. Towards the sea the little port showed a pleasant face. The inn, some solid, respectable houses, occupied by solid, respectable citizens. And there were the shops, in streets running off at right angles, shops which offered, in more plenty, and at cheaper prices, some goods from abroad. The Lanes, as Mistress Captoft realised with a flashback memory towards Dunwich, were a different thing altogether. Hovels, crowded together, upheld by one another, in which lived the poor, not poor as country people were, with a cabbage patch, and onions, often a pig, sometimes a goat. Here no such palliatives to poverty were available. Young men, or tough older men could go down to the harbour and offer their arms, shoulders, legs to the business of bringing a weighty cargo ashore. And women, ages ranging from the too young to the too old, offered the services of *their* bodies in a different way.

It was a sinister district and malodorous, but Mistress Captoft entered it without shrinking and without trepidation. She found Katharine Dowley, still, after a fortnight in such a filthy place, looking clean, and though miserable, calm.

'Suddenly, it was all too much. Thae's the long and short of it, Mistress. Never a proper night's sleep. And now ... Twenty years,' she said, 'twenty years' hard work, all wiped out and forgotten. That one time remembered and handed about so's nobody'll ever want me again.'

Except in one way, which she didn't fancy, the thing she had tried to avoid, preferring work at the inn, kitchen slut, cook's assistant, cook. And no chance to save; always on her heels the clamorous, growing family, which when she was chucked out had not been welcoming, but had indicated, in the most deadly way, how she could, and must earn enough to make a contribution – if she wanted to stay here. To Katherine Dowley Mistress Captoft appeared like a shining angel; a deliverer.

Thus fortuitously provided with a woman who could cook, Mistress Captoft thought wistfully of a serving boy, neat and nimble like the ones her own family and Master Captoft had employed. She visualised him in tawny hose and jerkin; a well-scrubbed boy between eleven and fourteen years old, waiting upon her and Master Tallboys in the hall and making himself generally useful. There were, no doubt, boys of that age in the Lanes who would have been glad of a good bed and two meals a day but she was wise enough to know that in such a district any boy by the time he was eleven would have acquired bad habits. She decided to wait a bit, until she chanced upon a boy, poor but of decent family, whom she could train in her own ways.

She walked back to the inn where she intended to dine upon fresh fish, a luxury now unknown at Intake, though Master Tallboys said he could remember the time when an old woman, with a donkey, had occasionally brought fresh fish as well as the salted or dried kind. Apparently she had brought the plague, too; and died of it herself, just in the lane. Nobody had replaced her.

Mistress Captoft would dine upon fish straight from the sea – probably herring with a smear of mustard sauce; then she would go out on to the quay and buy fresh fish, hurry the mule home and give Master Tallboys and the child a delicious supper.

Somebody at the corner of the inn's forcourt said, 'Mistress, of your charity . . .'

She turned about and confronted a beggar who did not look like a beggar. Young; not a day over thirty, poorly clad, but clean and tidy, and with no obvious disability. Thin, certainly, her rapid assessing look informed her, all the face bones prominent under the taut skin, sea-blue eyes rather sunken.

She was not an indiscriminate giver-of-alms. She had lived in Dunwich which was infested by beggars and she had learned to harden her heart, except where children were concerned and even that kindly attitude had shifted a little when she learned that beggars often borrowed, hired, bought or actually stole children in order to appeal to the soft-hearted.

She knew that there were genuine cases of men unemployed because sheep-runs were proliferating and that acres where many men had once ploughed and sown and reaped were now in the charge of one man and a dog. There were the partially blind, cripples, people who had fits, but alongside them were those who were merely idle. Face to face with this man, who did look hungry, she said, briskly, 'Surely an able-bodied man like you could find some better way of making a living.'

One of her beliefs, oddly at variance with her sheltered upbringing and her inherited income, was that, cast out upon the world, with nothing, she would not have been reduced to beggary. She would have made brews, baked bread, checked talleys, done miles of stitching, dug and hawked cockles, scrubbed floors . . . Anything.

The man re-acted to her astringent remark. He said, 'Tell me one, Lady. Tell me where a lame man is wanted – and I'll be there. Ready and willing.'

'In what way are you lamed?'

She was prepared for some horrible sight; a self-inflicted sore; some trivial cut or blister kept open by diligent irritation by sand or woodash. And sometimes the so-called 'sturdy beggars' would stop by a shambles where animals were butchered and daub themselves with blood or stick bits of completely inedible offal on to their arms, legs, faces.

None of that trickery here. As the man bared his leg Mistress Captoft immediately saw how lame he was, and why. The bone of his left leg, mid-way between knee and ankle had been broken and not set even by some unskilled but sensible woman like herself. Nobody had known enough, or cared enough, to lash the broken leg to a broomstick! As a result it had knit in its own way, at a slight angle and his left leg was some two inches shorter than his right. The man had done his poor best to remedy the fault by tacking a wedge of wood to his left shoe.

She saw instantly what was wrong with that. Not flexible and not graduated. In any shoe there should be a difference between heel and toe.

'What happened?'

'A cask broke loose. In a storm.'

'You are a sailor?'

'I was. Since I was about seven. I know no other trade.'

'Could you learn?'

'Learn what? It was all too plain that he was not going to get anything from *her*, though she'd looked likely, good for a farthing, so he allowed his anger with life to sound in his voice. 'Who'd take a man of my age as an apprentice? Who'd lay down the premium for me? Everything's tied up, either with the damned Guilds, or some family.'

For a second his eyes showed some animation, then reverted to their expression of dull despair. 'Once you're beached, you might as well be dead,' he said.

Keeping her dignity and her calm — unusual as it was for a beggar to swear until finally turned away — Mistress Captoft said, 'Walk ahead of me to the inn door.'

'Even *that* I can't do,' he said angrily. 'The landlady warned me off. She didn't like her customers being accosted.'

'You are about to *be* one,' Mistress Captoft said. She was a woman of impulse and had decided that having seen him walk, whether or not she considered him likely to be useful, she would buy him a good dinner.

He was lame would always be lame, but a properly made shoe would mitigate his disability.

He ate hungrily, but not grossly and refused a second helping.

'Mustn't overdo it after a long fast,' he said.

She then told him of the job she had to offer. A boy's job really but there was no reason why it should not be done by a man; waiting at table, mending fires, keeping silver bright, that kind of thing. A good home and a shilling a week.

Somewhat to her consternation — for this was, after all, a public place, his face twisted, his jaw began to tremble and his eyes filled with tears, two of which escaped and ran slowly down his hollow cheeks.

'There, there!' she said kindly. 'Don't upset yourself, David. If you perform your duties — none of them heavy — to my satisfaction, I shall have done myself a service, too.'

Knuckling the tears away, he said in a broken voice, 'I'll serve you to the death, Madam.'

She began to issue instructions. He was to find a cobbler

and have his shoe built up with leather. Two and a half inches on the heel, one and a half on the sole.

It would no more have occurred to her to provide transport for a maid-servant within walking distance, than it would have done to anyone else. But it was a long walk for a lame man. So, as soon as his shoe was improved, David was to go round to Tanner's Lane, to the cottage next the tanyard and tell Katharine Dowley not to start walking first thing tomorrow morning, but to come to the inn yard and join him. He was to hire a carter to bring them to Intake. She explained where that was; on the road to Baildon. There was a turn-off to the left, avoid it, it led to Moyidan only. Eventually there was a turn-off to the right; avoid that, too. It was the Basildon road; keep straight on, along a narrow lane with trees on each side and there was Intake. The house itself could not be missed.

She handed over money for the cobbler, but not for the carter. That she would pay, she said, at the end of the journey. It was the general rule, for carters were notoriously tricky; paid in advance they got drunk and either did not turn up at all, or were days late, with some excuse that the horse had fallen down, or a wheel had come off the waggon.

Riding home, with enough fresh fish for two days in a rush basket, Mistress Captoft thought with some complacency about her hirings. Neither quite ideal; a woman of uncertain temper, a man with a lame leg. But both so *grateful*.

'I never take that road,' said the first carter whom David approached.

David misinterpreted this as an admission of ignorance of the way.

'I can direct you,' he said, and oblivious to the change which had come over the carter's hard, weathered face at the mention of Intake, he repeated what Mistress Captoft had told him. And surely it was a journey any carter would gladly undertake; such a light load. One woman with a small bundle, a man with nothing at all. No strain on the horse, no weight on the waggon.

'I never travel that road.'

'Why not?'

'Thass my business. Find somebody else.' The carter had

never told anybody what had happened to him on a mid-summer day, ten, eleven years ago. He'd never forgotten it either; it had profoundly affected his life.

Taking his ease, lolling on the sun-bathed bank of a little stream, with a dock-leaf full of wild strawberries as an end to his dinner, he'd been visited by one of the Little People, wreathed with flowers, and so loving that no mortal woman had ever since been of any use to him. To this day the sight of the big white daisies which she had worn, a crown on her head, a garland about her neck, or the smell of strawberries could take him straight back to that enchanted afternoon, the delight, then the fright, he had trodden on forbidden ground; and then the way she had run after him, crying: Take me with you.

He did not know that his son was now at Eton, being flogged into shape.

What he did know was that never again would he travel that road. So he said, Find somebody else. Which David did without difficulty.

Now Mistress Captoft wallowed in gratitude, a thing she needed as a plant needed water. It was a weakness in a competent, self-assured woman – the desire to serve and to have her service recognised. One of the things which had alienated her from the people of Intake had been their marked ingratitude. She was clear-headed enough to admit that many of her doses had been provided for a double purpose – to protect Benny from going out to administer the last rites to somebody with a belly ache. Try this first. Very often it worked, but what thanks did she get? Yes, the patient was better. The dose was all right. It did the job. One of the most poignant stories in the New Testament – something with which Mistress Captoft was more familiar than most because Benny's life work had been an attempt to dovetail the four Gospels – was the one about Christ healing ten lepers; one came back to thank Him; and He had said, 'Where are the nine?' If the Son of God would ask such a question, be so sensible of man's lack of gratitude, why not mere Mattie Captoft?

However, now in the kitchen were two intensely grateful people; both wrecks, both saved. By her. She was reasonably sure that Katharine, wakened in the dead of the night, would rise and without so much as a secret feeling of resentment, do whatever was asked of her. As for David, his devotion was dog-like.

About Master Tallboys she was not so sure. She'd come back, hot-foot from Bywater with fresh fish for supper and the news that she had found two servants. He'd seemed a bit dubious.

'I fully realise that you could not be expected ... I intended to look around, ask around Baildon, next time I went in.'

'Well, now you will have no need to do that.'

Personally he thought the engagement of two fully adult people, one of them an experienced cook, was somewhat in excess of their needs, but to say so would sound mean.

'What wage did you agree upon?'

'Now, now, Master Tallboys, you must not give that a thought! Both Katharine and David are *my* servants – not more than I should have had had I set up house on my own. Any small service they do you, is paid for by your providing bed and board.'

'We'll see,' Henry said. He had money now, but not to squander. He had fodder to buy until sheep-fold and pasture sprang green in mid-April. And when John left, as he fully intended to do at winter's end, he must be provided for. And when the day came for Joanna's dowry to be handed over, he was determined that the money invested in Knight's Acre should be seen to have been as well invested as that entrusted to Sir Barnabas.

No friendliness had ever existed between Knight's Acre and Intake, but interest in Knight's Acre was keen in the village where most people were interrelated and anybody's business was known to everybody. Anything to do with the big house was news; and Jem Watson was the one who carried it.

Lacking more accurate information he attributed all the signs of new prosperity to Mistress Captoft.

'Ah, she proper rule the roost there and no mistake. And they don't eat alongside us now. No! Fire in the big room now and the table set – you'd think the King was coming. Silver all over the place. Him at one end of the table, her at the other, Master John and the little boy between. Still, give the new woman her due, the grub is better nowadays.'

'And what do the new man do?'

What didn't he do? With a few good meals behind him, every mouthful a strengthener, the adjusted shoe on his foot and burning desire to serve in his heart, there was practically nothing that David couldn't do. He had told Mistress Captoft that he knew no trade but the sea, and that was true in a way, but sailors knew almost everything. Many ships carried live-stock, to be cherished and coddled until the death blow came; so he could feed bullocks and pigs; he could milk a cow. Given space and the right tools he could make butter, and cheese. Any sailor worth his salt knew how to deal with wood and in no time at all David had built a proper bullock yard. With every bit of outside work he did something of his manhood, so sadly humiliated, sprang to life again; and his gratitude to Mistress Captoft who had made this re-habilitation possible, deepened.

'Hop about like a flea, he do,' Jem said, with the lazy man's disapproval of one less sparing of himself.

There was time to gossip, the winter days so short, and now around the shared firesides was a new listener, an en-couragement to the dragging out of old tales. The new priest, Father Matthew, had done what Father Ambrose, trying hard, and Father Benedict, not trying at all, had failed to do: he had become one with his parishioners. He came of the same stock, knew about animals, especially pigs, he had a hearty manner and an earthy sense of humour. And although he never actually said so, they sensed that he was no fonder of Knight's Acre than they were themselves; his lack of fondness showed itself in the avidity with which he listened to the hostility-tinged talk. His dislike, if so strong a word could apply to a feeling so shadowy, was based on the fact he hadn't taken to Henry, cold, aloof, superior and that, thick-hided as he could be in certain areas, he had sensed Mistress Captoft's scornful disapproval.

The Intake people's hostility was older, deeper rooted. It went back to the time when Sir Godfrey, taking only what was indisputably his own, had come and built his house there. On a site which had once been a farm but long left derelict, ever since an outbreak of the sweating sickness, so long ago that no one had even a memory of it. What most did remember was that the untilled ground and especially the great oak-tree around which the house was built, had provided space, and food for pigs and a few goats. Pigs thrived on acorns, goats liked the self-sown saplings.

The building of Knight's Acre had put an end to that. The grievance had begun there and presently found other things to feed upon.

Take the common land. Sir Godfrey had pastured his great horse there – as was his right, common land was common land, but a thing of that size ate a lot, and was in addition very dangerous. Once when Gurth went to fetch in his donkey, the warhorse had as good as attacked him. Great yellow teeth, up-lifted iron-shod hooves.

Then Sir Godfrey, and his dangerous horse, had took off to some war somewhere and stayed away for years and years.

The whole place had been ruled and run by a man called Walter, a horrible fellow.

Ah. Hadn't he one time tried to rape Bessie Wade – then a servant in the house, and hadn't the Lady Sybilla stood up for him, when the Elders went to complain. Lady Sybilla had said nonsense, she had been there all the time; she didn't believe a word.

And what happened to Walter?

To that there was no answer. Nobody knew anything more about Walter, dead, than of Walter alive. He'd just gone off, they said.

What they did all know and remembered with hatred was that after all those years Sir Godfrey had come home and taken three quarters of their common land to make his sheep-fold.

No credit was given him for the fact that he had left them a quarter of it.

Then he'd died, got killed fighting up in the north somewhere and one of his boys – no, not Master Tallboys up at Knightacre, his brother, Sir Richard, had swooped down and upset everything. A priest – Father Matthew was aware of some sidelong glances; yes a priest, but a lawyer too, and he'd found flaws in the parchment which his great-grand-father – or his great-great-grandfather had given them.

Ah; that had been a proper old confluffle; you had to

trace your family back and then either buy or get out. The fact that their status had gone up a notch, that they now owned the land they tilled and were entitled to call themselves yeomen, affected the Intake people very little.

Now and again, during these most interesting talks, Father Matthew tried to bring up the question of his glebe. Glebe was the ten acres of land which was, by custom, attached to every church.

His was wilderness, neglected for many years, and since he could see that serving a church so poorly endowed, he and the ugly, rather dim-witted boy whom he had brought with him as his servant, would be largely dependent on the produce of the glebe, he was anxious to get it ploughed. It was when he mentioned the glebe that the Intake men tended to remember that it was time for bed, or that some job awaited them elsewhere. An ox was lame, a plough needed repair.

Father Matthew did not press the matter; he had a peasant's patience. One day, when they knew and liked him better, they would volunteer. Meanwhile he managed to buy a pig and on the bit of the glebe which Mistress Captoft had made into a garden, though she had taken away as many of the roots as she could, the ugly boy was growing onions, cabbages, peas, beans. They'd survive. Anything rather than widen the gulf between priest and people which had plainly existed in former times. More people attended Mass, and observed their other religious duties than ever before.

'I can't pretend to favour this,' Henry said. 'You'd be better off here, with a warm bed and sound food – and doing light work about the place.'

'And going mad?' John asked. Light jobs about the place, and Nick's songs lost for ever. He knew, with a knowledge not of the head but of the heart, the lungs or the bowels, that restored as he might seem to be, he had no time to waste.

'Mind this,' Henry said, 'wherever you are, if that cough comes on again, make for home. Don't wait till you're on your last legs.'

When that time came, John thought, he would simply creep into a corner and die; it was only his determination to get Nick back to England, back to some kind of comfort, that had kept him going all the way from Padua to Knight's Acre.

He thought Henry's parting present – ten nobles – miserly. Henry felt that he was stretching generosity and brotherly responsibility to the extreme limit. When the Bishop's man had tipped out all that shining money on the table one of his first thoughts had been that now he could clear another field, hiring the labour; now he would do it himself, so every penny he gave John represented an incalculable outlay in toil and sweat.

He felt the need for more land because he had a belief, inculcated by Walter, that arable ground was more reliable than live-stock, so subject to disease. A dead animal was a dead loss whereas even the worst harvest left the fields waiting for next year's, which might be better.

At Stordford Lady Agnes had finally and reluctantly taken to her bed. So long as she could hobble, with the assistance of a sturdy servant, down the stairs, she had done so, eager for the life and bustle in the great hall, or the spiteful talk in the solar, but now she needed assistance on both sides, and the stairs, originally built with the idea of defence, were too narrow. Lady Grey could have made room for her on the ground floor but had no intention of doing so – old, ailing, and often irritable, relatives were best at a distance.

On the other hand, Aunt Agnes must not be allowed to feel neglected; for she was wealthy and had no children of her own. There was always the possibility that she might will her money to the Church. So each morning and each evening Maude and Beatrice were required to make a short routine visit, with a curtsey and a greeting and a little conversation. Their great-aunt considered Maude very dull and Beatrice insipid – partly, no doubt, due to their being over-rigidly disciplined by their mother. Lady Agnes was one of the many who could never see why her gay, pleasure-loving nephew should have married such a dour, charmless woman.

Joanna was under no obligation to make these visits, but, at first urged by Maude who liked and admired, almost *loved* her, she had gone and somehow, just by being there, had lightened the whole atmosphere. She had a way of saying things, of seeing the comic side, nothing much that you could put a finger on, or a name to, just different and refreshing. Also, she was lovely to look at, and like many old women who had once been pretty, and then with age grown wrinkled and grey, Lady Anges liked girls to be comely – myself when young! Presently, if Joanna failed to appear on one of these twice-daily occasions. Lady Agnes would ask why; what was she doing; where was she? Be sure to bring her next time.

She regarded the summer-weight dress which Lady Grey had provided for Joanna with a mixture of disapproval and bewilderment. What exactly was wrong with it? In her day the old lady had been devoted to clothes, had cut and stitched many of her own dresses. The answer she gave herself was: Everything, but in a subtle way. Granted the stuff, though of no quality, had not been skimped, there was plenty of it, but in all the wrong places; where it should have taken on a smooth, flowing line it looked – constricted. A dress deliberately designed . . .

'It looks like a sack,' Lady Agnes said.

'So I thought, at first sight. It made me feel that at any moment I might be put on the scales and weighed and my quality tested between a miller's teeth.'

'About the colour nothing can be done; but the shape could be altered to great advantage. Bring me my basket.' Every lady of quality had such a basket, a pair of scissors, a fat cushion stuffed with sawdust and a little pounded beeswax to save needles and pins from rusting even in the dampest weather; skeins of wool, spun very fine, and silks.

I am old; I am lame; but I still have my eyesight and the use of my hands. I can make something of this sack!

And after this another. No girl could manage with only one dress. What was Gertrude thinking of?

The girl was useless with a needle – she'd have been handier with a hay fork, Lady Agnes concluded, little guessing how near she was to the truth. But when the no-colour dress was re-shaped and made gay with embroidery, she remembered that she had many dresses – never to be worn again. But before she parted with one of them she must know that it was necessary, that the object of such charity *was* an object of charity.

'Are you so poor?'

'I am not at all poor, Lady Agnes. My mother, a lady of Spain, left me a considerable fortune, part of which Sir Banabas is handling; and part – in another place.'

Oh, and the green grass springing on the pasture and the sheep-fold at Knight's Acre; Layer Wood, a haze of green and a flood of bluebels. In the fields the young corn, stroked by the young wind. The violent homesickness which she thought she had mastered surged up. She had overcome it before, and could again, could now. Obediently, but without much enthusiasm she opened the chest where the old woman's dresses lay, smelling of lavender and rosemary and thyme – and age. Sad.

'Red,' said Lady Agnes, 'is for the very young – or married women. Yellow? No. You would look as sallow as Maude. Tawny would suit you well, but that is a winter colour. Ah, that is what I had in mind. Hold it against you.' It was midway between the young green and the blue-bells.

Lady Grey was not particularly pleased that her intention to make Joanna more ordinary-looking should have been frustrated by an old woman's whim. On the other hand she was not displeased that Joanna, wearing the sea-green silk and looking far from ordinary, should catch Lord Shefton's eye. *He* was not what she wanted for either of her daughters, rich though he was. She still cherished the hope that both her girls, plain, but well-trained and well-dowered would make happy marriages. Lord Shefton was far too old. There was something to be said, in some cases, for marrying a rich old man who would die and leave you a widow, wealthy, and still young enough to re-marry. But this particular old man had a son, by his first marriage which had been to a very young girl; too young perhaps; she'd died in childbed. His second wife, again young, but slightly older than the first, had borne a son and a daughter before she met with an accident, strange enough to warrant an inquest. Left, unaccountably, alone in one of his more remote houses, she'd fallen downstairs and cracked her skull; without disarranging her head-dress or her skirt. Death by misadventure ... But there were rumours that the second Lady Shefton had been on the point of running away. One story said back to her own family; another said with a lover. Un-named;

possibly Scottish. Gertrude Tetlow, sitting, neglected in corners, Lady Grey, ruling in her own house, had not missed much, and though she was prepared to entertain Lord Shefton, one of Barnabas's *business* associates, she certainly did not wish him to take a fancy to either of *her* girls whom she loved in her own fashion. Far too much to hand them over to old men with rotten teeth and stinking breath ... Really so bad that, when, as was his due, he sat on her right at the upper table, and with courtesy – his manners could not be faulted – helped her first to the dish proffered by a page down on one knee, she felt slightly nauseated. She told herself, as sternly as she would have told a child or servant – Tainted breath cannot affect food. But the feeling was there, a repulsion, and she was glad that the rheumy old eyes focused on Joanna.

Time plodded on. Or raced. And presently Joanna had served three-quarters of her sentence.

'A bit near the river, and all shut in,' Joseph, the old shepherd said. 'What we need is a bit of drainage.' A lifetime ago, Walter had said almost the same thing. Intake was not the place for sheep.

'Then we'll drain.' And that was hard work, too. But it fitted in with the clearing of the other field; an abundance of twigs and small branches. Dig the trench, and another and another, across the sheep-fold, lay in the bundles of twigs and small branches, end to end so that they carried off surplus water towards the river.

'There'll be less foot-rot now,' Joseph said.

With the house running so smoothly, Mistress Captoft could turn her attention to the garden, to giving some elementary lessons to Godfrey, and to the completion of a remarkable piece of embroidery which had occupied two generations of Captoft women. In the early days of her marriage, before she became so busy with Master Captoft's affairs, she had worked on it herself. Then it had been rolled up and forgotten, though she had taken it with her to Dunwich and then to Intake. Whoever had planned it had been artistic and ambitious – and no prude. It had been designed to hang on a sizeable wall, and even had Mistress Captoft, in Dunwich or Intake made time to work upon it – servantless as she was, it would have been difficult in such small rooms, with Benny's books always on the table. It depicted the Garden of Eden, with Adam and Eve, almost life-size, standing under the Tree of Knowledge – every apple and every leaf in place. There were other trees, too, and every known flower, every known animal.

Possibly some Captoft long ago, had gone on a pilgrimage to the Holy Land and remembered what he had seen, come back and given descriptions, which had been handed down and fired some woman's lively imagination. Some of the beasts were very strange indeed.

Adam and Eve were naked, except for, in his case, the figleaf, and in hers – symbolic touch – one coil of the Snake which she appeared to be fondling.

When Master Captoft's household was broken up, nobody wanted this article. Two of his daughters said they had spent so many tedious hours on it in childhood that they never wanted to see it again – in fact just to look at the tiny forget-me-nots and pansies made their eyes ache; the third had an aversion to snakes. One of his sons thought so much naked flesh indecent, and the other said he had hangings enough. Their stepmother was more than welcome to it.

Very little work remained to be done on it, and now Mistress Captoft realised how useful a seemingly useless thing could be. It would look splendid on the unbroken stretch of wall over the hearth. And it fitted as though made for it. Jem Watson was called in to help Henry and David with the hanging of it, for it was so long that it needed two men to hold it level and taut while a third drove in the nails. Everybody then stood back to study the effect.

Since when not being worked upon it had been kept rolled, the colours were as bright and clear as ever, and the glowing, crowded panorama altered not only that one wall, but the whole hall.

Mistress Captoft was enchanted with it – so beautiful in itself and another contribution to Knight's Acre. David was under the misapprehension that she had stitched it unaided and was dum-struck with admiration. Henry said, practically, that they must never in future put a smoky log on the fire for fear of dimming it. Jem reserved his opinion, until he was back in the village.

'You never seen such a thing in all your born days.'

'Tell us about it.'

'You wouldn't believe me if I towd you,' but he proceeded to tell. A man and a woman, stark naked, not so much as a clout between them, standing together under a tree. Close together? Yes, hand in hand. And all around such beasts as never went on four legs. Things with stripes, with spots, with humps; one with a single horn in the middle of its head, and one like a dog, but with a face like ... 'not unlike your Timmy, Father.' That was a most accurate piece of observation.

It could be, thought Father Matthew, who was one of the gathering in Bert Edgar's kitchen that evening, a picture of the Garden of Eden.

'Is there a snake?' he asked.

'Is there a snake? Thundering great thing as thick as my arm. And the woman a-nursing it, like it was a baby.'

That brought a gasp of horror from all the women in his audience. All women had an inborn horror of snakes. And was not a snake as much the representative of the Devil as a dove was of the Holy Ghost?

'Suckling Old Scrat, eh? And she stitched that into a picture! Well, you don't surprise *me*.' That was Old Ethel, still venomous against Mistress Captoft who had, she felt, usurped her place as priest's housekeeper, then employed her in a very menial capacity, and seen to it strictly that the humble jobs were properly done – and then, crowning injury, not employed her at all after the move to Knight's Acre. A born gossip, Ethel could always give the impression that she knew more than she chose to say. In fact she knew nothing of the relationship that had existed between Father Benedict and Mistress Captoft, for until the shutters were closed and the door barred they had acted their parts to perfection. Father Benedict, priest of this parish, and Mistress Captoft, his housekeeper and his aunt.

Jill Edgar, hostess for this evening; in winter the people of Intake saved firewood by taking it in turns; letting the fire die on three or four hearths, gathering around another – had no specific grudge against Mistress Captoft but she hated

Knight's Acre, and Master Tallboys because she'd once had an easy job there. Then Master Tallboys had chosen to marry Griselda, a fellow servant of Jill's; jumped up, pernickety, unbearable. So Jill had married Bert Edgar. A plain case of out of the frying pan into the fire; with Bert such a *beast*. Worse. Beasts at least knew whether a female wanted it or not; Bert took no notice of her wishes, and then when what couldn't be helped happened, beat her. As though a woman deliberately made a baby; on her own. Out of her own deep misery Jill Edgar was prepared to take some slight comfort by criticising another woman, apparently more fortunate. So she said, 'You mean to tell, Jem Watson, that him and her sit there together and take food with naked people looking down from the wall?'

'Ain't that what I been saying? Anyway, they're as good as married. Leastways they oughta be.'

Many of these evening gatherings ended up with a bit of bawdy talk. It was the thing everybody understood and found amusing. Father Matthew in spite of a little learning, was one of them, earthy and coarse humoured. He was capable of understanding why nine out of ten brides coming up to the altar to ask God's blessing on their marriage, were pregnant. He understood that any working man needed to know that a woman was capable of bearing a child before he committed himself for life – till death do us part. Jokes about children born seven, six, five or even four months after their begetters had been united in Holy Matrimony did not bother him at all. But, plodding home, Father Matthew recognised that he was a priest and responsible for what went on in his parish – not in the ditches and hedgerows, or under the shelter of haystacks, but openly, in the only big house, occupied by the very people who should be setting a good example.

He was unaware – or unwilling to face the fact – that he liked neither Master Tallboys nor Mistress Captoft. He considered the Master of Knight's Acre to be mean; he never proffered the invitation to share a meal or a mug of ale, leave alone a glass of wine, as the better-off parishioners should do; and his manner, though invariably civil, struck the priest as cold and unfriendly; Mistress Captoft he had sensed, criticised and despised him: she'd taken herself – and her order for Masses – to Nettleton.

These personal feelings, combined with a sense of duty which was not lacking in him, to assure himself that a rebuke, a warning would be in order.

Mistress Captoft opened the heavy front door herself. Of two servants only so much could be expected; Katharine was in the kitchen and David busy with one of the many jobs he had taken on.

'Oh! Good morning, Father,' she said, her tone betraying the surprise she felt. She was no longer of his congregation and Master Tallboys was not a man who needed to be rounded up and reminded of his religious obligations. Although he never gave any other sign of piety, he never missed a Sunday Mass, or a Holy Day.

Now that he was in her presence, Father Matthew realised the awkwardness of his mission.

Mistress Captoft knew how a priest should be received. She indicated a seat on the most comfortable settle, near the bright fire, and bustled about, producing wine, and silver cups, and small saffron buns from one of the cupboards. She made an affable remark or two about the seasonal weather, and how the leaves were falling.

Father Matthew seated himself, clumsily, perching on the edge of his seat, spreading his knees wide and placing his coarse hands upon them. A peasant's stance. For a second the contrast with Benny sprang to mind again, but it no longer pained her. Pouring the wine she thought, in a way unusual to her, that some people had quick-healing flesh, and in the same way some people had quick-healing spirits. While he was alive she had given Benny all she had to give; when he died she had given him deep grief, misery that had driven her almost distraught – and Masses for a year to shorten his time in Purgatory. So the wound had healed, not festered.

She seated herself on the other, less comfortable settle, the one that Walter had somehow procured for the Lady Sybilla, and waited for Father Matthew to state his business – if he had any.

123

She thought it might concern the glebe. For, despite his hob-nobbing with the people of Intake, his – in her view – lowering attempt to be one of them, he hadn't got his glebe ploughed. And never would at this rate. Though she had held herself aloof from the village, she knew the people of Intake. With one exception, ingrates.

And if, having failed with them and their oxen, he'd now come to ask aid from Master Tallboys, and his horse-drawn plough, she had her answer ready; Master Tallboys had all he could deal with; offer the men of Intake eleven pence and the job would be done. She was willing to give the money; for she, of all people, knew how utterly inadequate the living was.

Since she was thinking such fundamentally kind and charitable thoughts, it was all the more shock to her when the clumsy man, after some false starts, some mumbling, managed to say what he had come about.

Unpleasant talk about her and Master Tallboys down there in the village!

She always carried good colour in her face; now it darkened until it matched the crimson velvet of her new winter gown, brought into use only two days earlier when the wind changed and the leaves began to blow about.

Unless I control myself, master this rage, I shall be taken with a fit.

And she was schooled in self-control. No protest, or sullenness when she was informed that the husband her parents had chosen for her was an old man, with children older than she was. And after that, when she was running the old husband's business for him, patience and calm had been demanded of her; and after that the years of secretive, rigidly controlled life with Benny, every word to be watched, and the little vinegar-soaked sponge between her and what she most wanted – a child.

Draw in, hold, count to twenty before releasing that breath. It worked. She felt the hot flush subside; knew that she was again in command of herself, and of the situation.

'I wonder at you, Father Matthew, giving an ear to village gossip.'

The contempt in her voice was a spur to him and he said, 'You live close.'

'Certainly we eat together, at this table. Would the people of Intake prefer that I ate with servants in the kitchen? As for sleeping ... Between my bedchamber and Master Tallboys' are two others; one occupied by a maid-servant; the other by a child – except when he chooses to sleep in his father's room.' And she thought; the irony of it! All those years with Benny, being careful, dreading this very thing, and now to be accused of it with Master Tallboys! Good-night, Mistress Captoft. Good-night, Master Tallboys. And each to a lonely bed. 'I daresay,' she said, keeping her temper, but feeling the worse for it, 'your village cronies may find it difficult to believe that a man and a woman can share board but not bed. If so, you have my permission to question my cook-woman about any comings and goings in the night.' Suppressed anger made her vicious, willing to wound and knowing exactly where to strike. 'When tongues cease to wag about Master Tallboys and I living close as you call it, they may turn on *you* and accuse you of sodomy with that ugly boy.'

It was a word that most people understood but seldom used, except in its shortened form, silly sod, poor sod, terms of derision or pity. Never, never used by decent women.

Father Matthew did not know – and had he known, would have discounted – the fact that Mistress Captoft had for years lived close with a scholar who had used words as words. He was therefore shocked and appalled. He stood up, clumsily and said, 'That is an insult, to me; to my office; to Christ Himself.'

'It was not so meant. A mere warning.' Mistress Captoft rose, too and faced him. 'Who started this scurrilous talk? It is someone to beware of.'

Being ushered in he had caught only a glancing look at the picture; sitting below it, he had had no view of it at all. Now, backing away, he saw that it was all and worse than Jem Watson had said. Thought the serpent was not actually being suckled; its head lay on the woman's arm, its lidless eyes staring with defiant malevolence.

Confused; shocked; an evil woman and an evil picture, Father Matthew said, 'I do not know. The kitchen at Edgarsacre was crowded.'

With that he made for the door.

The ugly word rang in his mind all day, the more clangingly when he looked at Tim, so like the strange beast in the evil picture. An object for charity if ever there was one. And the priest had been charitable. It was so unjust. Such a terrible insult. Grown man as he was, Father Matthew could have wept from sheer mortification. At one point he seriously considered finding a lodging for the boy in the village – for what that evil woman had *said*, others might be *thinking*. He rejected the idea; nobody would lodge the boy for nothing, and he simply could not afford to pay even the smallest charge. Besides, it would expose the poor creature to the harsh cruel world from which he had been rescued.

In addition to that most repulsive word the wicked woman had used others. Village gossip. Your village cronies. In a lonely parish like this with whom could a priest consort except with the villagers? With whom had Christ consorted during His earthly sojourn? Humble men! It was all very well for her to be so scornful; when her nephew occupied this living he'd had a mule and could ride around making visits to his own kind. Moyidan was five miles away; Nettleton as far if not farther. Besides, hadn't friendliness with the villagers borne good results? More people came to Mass now than ever before. A nasty voice – not unlike Mistress Captoft's, spoke in his mind, stating the fact that the ultimate sign of friendship had not yet shown itself. His glebe was still unploughed. Father Matthew spent a miserable day. He was an earnest, conscientious, practising Christian; but he lacked the mysticism that had kept old Father Ambrose going; nor could he, like Father Benedict, seek consolation in books.

Mistress Captoft, finishing off the wine, was thoughtful, too. If such things were being *said* ... Why not? But this time no subterfuge. Marriage – and perhaps, after all, a child.

She was not skilled in the art of cajolery. Her marriage had been arranged by her parents, and the attraction between her and Benny had been mutual, both in a way fighting against it but caught in a net. Now she faced the task of attracting a man somewhat her junior, a grave, courteous reserved man and one with whom, as Father Matthew had said, she had lived close for over a year without the slightest sign of familiarity.

Her glass – just large enough to show her face, assured her that though youth had gone, the years had treated her kindly; fresh complexion, firm flesh, bright eyes, hair fading a little but still plentiful. Her figure had lasted well, too, though thickening slightly around the waist. Something could and should be done about that.

She had other assets. She was capable, level-headed. She had money of her own.

She had the affection of her god-son who had taken to calling her Mamma-Captoft. At first he had resented being taught, but a little bribery – a cake or a sweetmeat or a ride on the mule, worked wonders, and Henry had used his influence. 'When I was your age, son, I had the chance to learn and didn't take it. I've often been sorry.'

'It is never too late,' Mistress Captoft remarked. 'I could teach you at the same time.'

There was something not quite acceptable to his pride in that suggestion; to attempt to remedy a defect was to admit its existence.

'That is a kind offer. I'm too old a dog to learn new tricks.'

'What nonsense, Master Tallboys. You are in the prime of life.'

'For doing things that I know, maybe. Not for learning.'

That was before Father Matthew's visit. Now she could see that this lack of learning might be to her advantage. She began to make frequent references to the great service she had been to her first husband.

'He was old and infirm, you see, when we were married– his children were all older than I was myself. Quite soon he became house-bound and relied upon me absolutely. I assure you, Master Tallboys, that if at any time I can be of assistance to you, in any way, you have only to ask.'

Thank you; but I do little business in that sense of the word. And I have a fair head for figures.'

She spoke of the child. 'I have come to look upon him as my own. I have always felt that a child does better with *two* parents.'

'Most of my youth we made do with one. Our father was so often absent.'

'Ah! I see that you are looking at my new gown, Master Tallboys. Do you think the colour too garish? I hesitated myself between this and crimson.'

'Poppy colour is cheerful on a dull day, Mistress Captoft.'

'One of the sad things about growing older – away from the place where one was young – is that there is nobody to use one's given name any more. Mine is Martha, but I was always known as Mattie.'

'It has occurred to me, from time to time,' Henry said, 'that you live rather a lonely life, Mistress Captoft. But I thought you would know that any friend of yours would have a welcome here.'

A snub direct? Inside herself she re-acted with spirit and why not indeed? Who provides the wine, the silver, the spices, the servants, everything which lifts this house above the level of an ordinary farm?

Impervious, that was the word to describe him. Deaf to all hints; blind to new bright dresses and a waist rendered more shapely by the cruel clench of iron-braced stays.

She tried other approaches; an appeal to self-interest. Under pretence of consulting him as to whether this was or was not a good time to sell, she let him know exactly what she owned. Henry listened, pondered, asked a few cogent questions about lease terms and rents and then said that so far as he could see land was the one thing that had real value. It didn't go sick; it couldn't get up and run away.

There was one trick left. Withdrawal. And that she tried.

She had, she said, sometimes considered buying or hiring a house in Baildon or in Bywater. Which did he advise?

Again that careful consideration.

'Bywater is livelier, all the year round. When my Uncle William was Bishop there, we used to look forward to our stay with him, though he supported so many charities that his guests were half-starved. And there is the east wind to bear in mind. It is tempered a bit by the time it reaches

Baildon, but having lived in Dunwich you know about the east wind.'

He was impervious. He'd lost his heart, and presently, his virginity to such a different woman – a cloud of black hair, great black eyes, and bones like a bird's – and as easily broken. He had then married; sensibly, prosaically, as most men did, and that – except for Godfrey – had been a disaster. He had finished with that side of life. He'd known a moment of weakness – and not a pleasant memory at all. Anyway, Joanna was safe at Stordford, and by degrees he was paying off his debt to her. He'd never sold a calf or a fattened steer without going along to Master Turnbull's office and putting half the money into trust; he paid in all that came from the sale of her wool, or any sheep marketed. His obligations to his brother Robert, so mysteriously vanished – and his obligations to Joanna, kept him poor. And though everybody thought he was stupid to go on saving up for a lost child, Henry could always fall back upon his own experience. His father had vanished, been deemed dead, and come back.

Lady Grey said, 'I never *quite* believed that she was short of twelve when she came here. So very mature. And with such assurance. Well, that means that she will be at *least* fourteen in the June of next year. I see nothing against a betrothal.'

She wanted Joanna out of the house, or at least firmly spoken for. Maude, who had developed tardily, was now marriageable – and who would look at Maude, except to make unfavourable comparisons?

Sir Barnabas's usually cheerful face had a troubled look and she attributed this to his feeling about the discrepancy in the ages. Men could be very sentimental – where a pretty face was concerned.

'Not perhaps an ideal match,' she said with the air of one conceding a point. 'Not what I should wish for Maude or Beatrice. But compare their families! You were told that she was a girl of good family; she says that her mother was a lady and her father a knight, of Spain. There has never been the slightest evidence of the truth of such a claim.'

'I'm concerned about the dowry, my dear.'

'What about it?'

'I'd counted on it until she became sixteen. Shefton has an

eye to money, for all his wealth. And to hand it over now would put me in a muddle.'

'Oh,' Lady Grey said and became thoughtful. She understood the running of a household, the management of the estate, but of higher finance, dealings in London and such like she knew nothing. For some reason they never seemed real to her. 'Leave this to me,' she said. 'Tell Lord Shefton that I do not favour the match.'

'But you just said you did.'

'Tell him otherwise – but that I am willing to discuss it with him.'

Well, Sir Barnabas thought, he'd never known Gertrude to make a muddle yet, while he seemed to blunder from one to another, and to a man of his nature the words: Leave it to me, were welcome, particularly when they concerned a matter which threatened to be troublesome.

Resolutely, Lady Grey raised every possible objection. Far too young she said; not fourteen until next June and as yet quite unfitted to occupy the position that she would hold as Countess of Shefton. In another two years, perhaps. She flattered his failing virility by a discreet reference to the inadvisability of girls bearing children too young. There were other aspects of the matter. In the course of Nature, barring some catastrophe, the expectation of life in a girl of fourteen exceeded that of a man in his sixties. 'You have other children, my lord, with prior claims. The poor girl might find herself a widow in straitened circumstances.' And after all she had been consigned to the Greys' care with a view to her making a *suitable* marriage. She hoped his lordship would not take offence at her plain-spokenness, but she had never been one to take responsibility lightly.

It was an impressive performance, but the mention of the girl's prospects as a widow, seemed to offer a shred of hope that if a satisfactory financial settlement could be reached Lady Grey might be less obdurate over the matter of age. He was a mean man, but he was also enormously wealthy, cost meant nothing and he was infatuated by the girl, not only with her looks, which were remarkable enough but by something else quite undefinable; the nearest he could get to it was a hidden promise; and the thought that even with a sack over her head she'd still be attractive. He proceeded to make promises so lavish – including asking no dowry – that Lady Grey had a wistful thought about Maude; if only he weren't quite so old; if only his teeth were better . . .

Outwardly she kept up a pretence at reluctance. All these promises must be set down in proper legal form. And the nearest thing Joanna had in the way of a guardian was the Bishop of Bywater, who must of course, be consulted. It would all take a little time. Perhaps if his lordship cared to keep Christmas at Stordford, and came prepared . . She herself would do her best to prepare the girl for the high destiny that awaited her.

At Intake, though at a ploughman's pace, things went forward inexorably.

Father Matthew could not forgive – never would forgive the dreadful insult. He knew that he should; it was a Christian's duty to forgive, 'seventy times seven'. And in every Pater Noster one prayed that God should forgive as man forgave man. It was impossible. Every time he looked at Tim, so ugly. No bridge to his nose, wide, almost lipless mouth, eyes with red rims and no lashes, he was reminded of that shocking word. That anybody could possibly *think* . . . And since the boy cooked, served, cleaned, tended the pig and the bit of garden he was constantly within view, keeping the wound open like a beggar's sore. And since one of any man's needs is self-justification, Father Matthew moved from the effort to forgive the unforgivable to question: Should one forgive evil?

Christ on the Cross had said, 'Father, forgive them, they know not what they do.' A plea for forgiveness for the ignorant. But Mistress Captoft was far from ignorant – the very use of the word proved that. Christ on the Cross had promised the dying thief, 'This day thou shalt be with Me in Paradise.' But that man was simply a thief, paying for his crime by dying a dreadful death. There was a difference.

'As you said, Jem Watson, it is an evil picture. One no decent woman would have stitched upon, no decent man hang upon his wall. And she is an evil woman.' Having made this statement he felt better, more justified.

Now some idle thoughts – less than that, mere speculations, came drifting up. Put into words for the first time because nobody in Intake was prepared to risk being thought fanciful. A bit of embroidery on an old, accepted tale, a bit of exaggeration here and there was perfectly in order. Any kind of fancy was likely to be dismissed with laughter. But now ... What about?

Ah! What about Mistress Tallboys; a young woman, in the best of health one day, in screaming agony the next, and dead in a week.

What about Father Benedict; standing up there one day, burying two, and dead the next day.

What about the brews Mistress Captoft made? Bitter and horrible. Bitter as gall, sour as a crab-apple.

One dissident voice. Old Hodgson, really so old that he should be dead now, but alive and hearty – apart from a bit of stiffness in the joints – a common affliction with all over forty.

'She make a good brew,' he said. 'But for her I'd be dead now. Five days I hadn't been to the privy and I'd got a lump the size of a millstone, just here.' He struck the lower part of his belly. 'I reckoned my time had come and I said to Ted – Go fetch the priest; my last hour is come. So off went Ted, at the trot and Mistress Captoft she sent a dose and said try that first. So I did and it shifted. Afore morning light. In the dead dark I got myself to the privy and was there till dawn. Give them all a surprise when I walked into the kitchen, cleared out and as good as new.'

It had given them a surprise, and not a welcome one. His son, Ted, and his wife, Bet, would have been only too glad to have him out of the way; he knew that. Ted wanted Hodgacre for his own and Bet wanted the extra room. Mistress Captoft's dose had saved his life, for which he was thankful; it had also thwarted their little schemes; almost as important and decidedly more amusing.

Old Ethel said, 'Them that make good brews can make bad ones too.'

The talk swung round again to the suddenness with which Mistress Tallboys and Father Benedict had died, and the haste with which Mistress Captoft had moved in and begun to rule Knight's Acre. This time Father Matthew asked his question aloud. What then prevented them from marrying?

'Could be the money,' somebody said. 'Left to her so long as she didn't marry again. Lotta men put that in their wills.'

It fitted, the priest thought. Living in sin for the sake of money. What one would expect of a woman who had stitched that picture, and used such language. One day he'd borrow Johnson's horse and ride to Moyidan and ask Father Thomas what he knew about Mistress Captoft's circumstances. That errand was delayed; it was almost as difficult to borrow Johnson's horse as it was to get the glebe ploughed.

Father Thomas said, 'I really know very little about Mistress Captoft. In fact I never heard of her, or saw her, until my nephew – your predecessor – came to Intake. She called herself his aunt, but I could never trace a direct kinship. Relationship by marriage possibly. I never bothered. Why do you ask?' Why come to Moyidan on a borrowed horse and disturb an afternoon's rest? Father Thomas felt rather peevish.

'I wondered about her money. Whether it is hers or only hers on conditions?'

Father Thomas blinked the sleepiness from his eyes. Widows with money were the Church's best friends and maybe Mistress Captoft was making a will in favour of the church at Intake, which, God knew, needed such an endowment.

'That I can tell you – at least what Benedict – God rest his soul! – once told me. And I have no reason to doubt his word. He said . . . Yes, I remember almost his exact words. I ventured to say that I thought she was frivolous and worldly, and he said, on the contrary, she was a near saint, burying herself in so remote a place and keeping his house, when she was well-to-do, in her own right. What her first husband left to her, he left absolutely, without conditions. Had she stayed in Dunwich she could doubtless have married again.'

(Even then, years ago, while Father Benedict was grateful to his uncle for having procured him a living – though a poor one – he had not been able to accept even the most glancing criticisms of Mattie, his love.)

Jogging home on his borrowed horse, Father Matthew

thought – Then there is no impediment; except the will of a wicked woman.

There was one bull in Intake – apart from the one at Knight's Acre – and it belonged to Bert Edgar who, because his father died and his elder brother met with an accident, had inherited all. This bull, a black and very savage beast, served the cows of Intake, Clevely, Nettleton and Much-anger, and occasionally those from further afield, since he was known as a good sire. Every year in autumn – cows varied in their seasons, it could be September or October – men would come, leading the meek yet suddenly frisky cows. While the bull was taking the only exercise in his cruelly restricted life, the cow's owner and Bert Edgar struck the bargain. So much down now, either in cash or kind, and so much more when the cow was visibly in calf. After that Bert had no responsibility; the cow could slip her calf or the calf could be born rump first. None of his business.

This year, instead of bringing the second payments, man after man came with complaints. The Edgarsacre bull had failed.

At first Bert was truculent: 'You gotta a barren cow, you gotta a barren cow, no good coming here whining to me.'

At the best of times Bert was as ill-tempered as his bull. He'd married Jill, knowing her to be lazy, but convinced that given enough stick, she'd improve. He'd wanted *one* child – a boy to inherit; and he'd got him; but he'd got more. Every year, regular as the changing seasons, pregnant again, grow-ing heavy and useless. Every time, after the first, he'd given her a thorough good thrashing, but she wouldn't learn. Five gaping mouths to feed now. And no second fees to come. And the whole thing a bit of a mystery. Everybody knew that bulls, like all other animals, like people, grew old, grew tame, went unresisting to the butcher, or to the bull-ring.

But the black bull was not all that old. Eight years at most, but useless.

Like a witch's strike!

Everybody in Intake *knew* about witches and what they could do. Some remembered, handed-along stories, some less remote. All but the very young could remember Granny Robinson who had lived in their midst and been tolerated, partly because she was one of them, partly because in the main her activities had been harmless. She made love potions, brews that got rid of an unwanted pregnancy, and she could charm away warts. People had been very careful how they behaved or spoke to her, however, because she could turn very nasty if provoked. Ah! What about her granddaughter who'd married against the old woman's wishes, or advice, and remembering some sharp words, did not invite her grandmother to the wedding.

'No. I ain't going,' Granny Robinson said. 'And *he* might as well not go hisself!' People remembered that remark when the marriage proved to be childless, and the girl confided to her mother, in the strictest secrecy, that her husband was useless in bed. In strict confidence meant telling somebody else, after swearing her to secrecy; soon all the village knew. And naturally pleas, even bribes failed to persuade the old woman to lift the spell, for to do so would have been to admit that she had put it on in the first place. 'Nothing to do with *me*,' she said.

Impotent was not a word used in the village; Bert's bull was useless; past it; not up to his job.

There was a perfectly good bull, young and of surprisingly mild temper, so Jem Watson said, up at Knight's Acre, but to use him would mean doing business with Master Tallboys and that would go against the grain. Added to the tradition of unfriendliness between the village and house, there was a dislike for Henry personally. He worked just as they did; he wore much the same clothes, but he was different. Even in the market. Did he ever greet a man who'd made a specially good bargain, with a hearty slap on the shoulders? Did he ever drink a mug of ale in The Hawk In Hand?

The Elders of the village held a meeting to discuss the question of the bull, and after much talk decided upon a practical arrangement. Every landowner in Intake, whether he kept a cow or not, would subscribe to the cost of a new animal which would be kept at Edgarsacre because Bert had the experience. Any Intake cow would be served free of charge; those brought from outside would pay fees as usual — the charge to be slightly higher than in the past, and to be paid in money. One fifth of this money was to go to Bert

Edgar for feeding and managing the bull, the rest was to be divided between the men who kept no cow. A just and sensible arrangement and one which would not be questioned, for in village affairs the Elders' word was law. Intake had never had a lord of the manor to rule from above, but since some order must be maintained, the men who had hacked their acres out of the forest, had reverted, unwittingly, to the fashion of a far older day, of the free settlements of Danish origin. They had chosen seven, the oldest, presumably wisest men to settle domestic matters. When one died, or grew senile, the six remaining chose someone to take his place. Such choice, never openly disputed, had on occasion led to ill-feeling between families; but on the whole it worked.

Old Hodgson, a good hand with a tally stick, was chosen to keep the accounts.

The new bull was bought and installed, but a season had been lost; next year there'd be no calves in April or May to romp on the Common or in the meadows; and cheese and butter would have to be bought. Still, the future was provided for.

Then a new disaster struck, beginning at Edgarsacre, but threatening the whole community. Jill Edgar, pregnant again, and with another black eye, went to feed the pigs; a sow and six young, one destined for home consumption, five for market just before Christmas when young porkers were in great demand. Ordinarily the sow came pushing and grunting at the sight of the swill-bucket, but this morning she lay in the corner and did not stir. Jill thought bitterly that there were mornings when she felt like that herself! She took a stick and prodded the animal, alive though listless, with measured ferocity. The sow did not move, and emptying the bucket into the trough, at which the young began to guzzle, Jill went back to the house. She said nothing to Bert; he was not a man who would take a bit of bad news without venting his wrath on the bringer of it; so let him see for himself.

He saw, later in the day and recognised, in the reddened eyes, the dripping nose, the quick, panting breaths, that curse of all who reared pigs; the dreaded swine fever, as deadly as the plague or the sweating fever was to human beings. And as catching. The last outbreak had occurred before Bert inherited when, second son, he had no expectations but was working as a hired man, up at Knight's Acre. Then every pig in Intake had died and the year was still remembered – the year we had to buy bacon. Bert remembered it well and presently saw that this disease was different. The sow did not develop the rash of spots around the ears or on the belly; instead she coughed, more like a cow or a steer with the husk than any pig suffering from swine fever. And instead of her innards – and those of the young who promptly sickened – turning to water, this went the other way. Stopped up, blocked up. No mess at all.

He asked advice and his neighbours came, looked, standing well away, and said they had never seen anything like it.

No other pig was afflicted.

Once again the all-stand-together spirit triumphed over old feuds and personal disagreements and the village combined to provide Bert with the start of a new styful. Jem Watson's father sold an in-pig sow for a trifle less than market price. Father Matthew contributed a halfpenny and gave the procedure a decorative touch – in helping an unfortunate neighbour, he said, they were offering thanks to God for sparing their own animals. Most of the men felt sorry for Bert – no bull fees this autumn, no porkers ready for Christmas; five children at table and another on the way! A few women thought it was judgment on him for illtreating his wife. Though when you came to think of it, it was a queer kind of judgment, for she was being punished too. It had long been the custom at Intake to share when a pig was killed; you have a piece of mine now, and I'll have the same from you, when you kill yours. Jill's new sow wouldn't farrow until after Christmas, and she'd have nothing to share until well after Easter, but you couldn't stand by the rules at a time like this. They'd share, and wait.

But the Watson sow lay down in the Edgarsacre sty and died in the same mysterious manner as the others had done.

Three blows, coming as fast and furious as those Bert dealt out to his wife and the unwanted children.

'Somebody put the evil eye on me, no doubt about that,' Bert said.

But who? But why? The only person with an obvious

grudge against him was his wife, and even *she*, senseless as she was, must know that his ruin was hers.

Father Matthew was present at many of these fireside talks, and suddenly, one evening, inside his mind, something flared, like a dry old log on a dying fire. Mistress Captoft!

He remembered exactly what she had said, after dealing him the wound that never healed. Who started this scurrilous talk about me? And he had mentioned Edgarsacre.

Apart from a bit of desultory schooling, aimed at a single end, he was exactly like the Intake people, which was why he had become part of the village so easily. He was just as superstitious, and with a smear of learning to prop up beliefs not openly accepted by educated men nowadays; but lurking in the background. Our Lord had admitted the existence of evil; during His forty days in the wilderness. He had actually talked to the Devil: Get thee hence, Satan. He had also said: Go, to two evil spirits which possessed two men, and so banished them into a herd of swine. The Gadarene swine.

And he, humble parish priest, had recognised evil; in the picture, in the woman, in the word she had used.

Just about a year ago.

Yes; October had come round again, and last year's October ale was ripe for drinking. The brown jug went round and tongues loosened. Bert Edgar's mention of the evil eye seemed to have unlatched a door. Somebody recalled and recounted the spell Granny Robinson had put upon that poor man. Somebody else raked up an older tale. But that had happened at Nettleton.

The October wind rattled the shutters, howled at the door. Make up the fire, draw closer, pass the jug ...

Well, there was this old woman at Nettleton who was a witch and could turn herself into a wolf. As a wolf, at night, she went round robbing hen roosts and lambing pens. Everybody knew, but nothing could be proved until a man, three times robbed, set a trap. It didn't go off quite as it should, and in the morning all he found was a bit of a paw, and some hair, all bloody. But that was enough; taking some neighbours with him he'd gone to the old woman's cottage and there she was, with her left hand wrapped in a cloth. The top joint of her first finger chopped off. *She* said she'd done it chopping wood, meaning to spit a fowl. Ah, but what fowl?

One of her own, she said; but hers were all speckled, and the feathers of the one she was about too cook were white – just like the ones which the man had set the trap to protect.

Old Sawyer, father to the coffin maker, and Old Hodgson's senior by just eighteen months, could vouch for the truth of this story.

'She went afore the Justices, all fair and square, and she was burnt for a witch on Baildon Market Place. My grandfather journeyed in to see it done. And he towd me hisself Time she roasted, he said, the smell wasn't like meat cooking. More like burnt hair, same's you'd get burning a wolf.'

Except as the eldest of the Elders, Old Sawyer no longer counted for much; his son had taken over his trade and his holding, and his memory for anything recent was so faulty that, as his daughter-in-law complained, you couldn't even trust him with a message, send him to borrow a little salt and as like as not he'd come back with a spoon. But for bygone things his memory was as good as ever. Most of his tales – including this one – had been told and re-told so many times that nobody listened any more. Tonight they did, and he enjoyed being the centre of attention for a change.

'She confessed, in the end. It was done by brews.'

Father Matthew thought; Mistress Captoft wouldn't turn herself into a wolf; no, it'd be a snake. The snake in the picture was marked green and red; and he now remembered that the woman had worn a gown which in some way combined those two colours.

The October ale was potent, and he could see, in his mind, a snake slithering through the night, striking a bull with impotence, bringing disease to the pigs. And leaving no trace.

They were talking about brews now; about Granny Robinson who had carried the secret of hers to the grave with her, so that nobody in Intake could make such things nowadays.

'Except Mistress Captoft,' Ethel said. Still relentless.

Well, suppose then, just suppose that Mistress Captoft could cast a spell, as well as make brews, *why Bert Edgar*? What had *he* ever done to offend her?

'I never even spoke to the woman. Never even seen her, except across the church, two-three times.'

139

'I may be to blame,' Father Matthew said, hatred and ale combining to make him incautious. 'I went,' he gave a loud hiccup 'to speak to her about her way of life. She insulted me. And she asked who started the gossip. I couldn't say who. I did tell her where.'

'My place?'

'Yes. I'm sorry. Very sorry, if I brought all this on you.' (So you should be, damn you! I'll get even with you, you blabber-mouthed bastard!)

When Bert Edgar was angry with Jill or the younger children, he struck them with his belt, or anything that was handy. On men he used his fists and his feet. But he couldn't very well set about a priest, especially one so popular. And at this moment Father Matthew, by proving how thoroughly he was one with them, sharing their belief in magic, was very popular indeed. But just let him wait! This year the men of Intake were actually on the verge of ploughing up his glebe. It wouldn't be done if Bert Edgar had any say in the matter. He wasn't an Elder; he was no longer even one of the prosperous, but he still had his fists, and most men were a bit scared of him.

This was the time of year, middays still warm, chill coming with sunset, when foggy nights were known at Intake. The people believed that it came in from the sea, blowing up along the river and trapped by the encircling woods. Carrying his lantern – almost worse than useless on such a night – Father Matthew blundered his way home.

So far as he could tell no snake crossed his path, but in the morning he woke with no voice. A croaking, a hoarseness would follow, he knew, upon an ordinary cold – but he had had no cold; he'd simply lost his voice. And that confirmed – had confirmation been needed – that Mistress Captoft could cast spells. Because he had joined in the talk against her, she'd struck him dumb. And what good was a dumb priest? Intake was a poor living, but it sufficed; once his glebe was under cultivation – and some of the Intake men had practically promised that this year, their own ploughing done, they'd spare a little time for *his*, things would be better. But dumbstruck, what future awaited him? He hadn't learning enough to be a clerk, or a professional scribe. He had no powerful friends, no family. And the shocking fact was that if you couldn't speak, you were regarded as idiotic.

He faced this dismal prospect for three days and then, as suddenly as it had gone, his voice came back and he was able to tell Timmy that he had been a good boy. As indeed he had. Timmy knew all about bodily afflictions; his face for a start, and as though that weren't bad enough, a fit now and then, everything lost, a whirling darkness and then the long, slow climb back to life. Timmy owed Father Matthew more than any amount of faithful service could ever repay.

Speech restored, conviction hardened, Father Matthew borrowed Johnson's horse again and this time rode down to Bywater and with peasant patience, under which lay peasant doggedness, waited, this room, another room, men who had done better in life, flitting in and out, telling him that His Grace was busy, but would see him presently. And presently he was admitted to the presence, knelt, kissed the amethyst ring, sat when invited to do so, on the very edge of the chair. Ungainly, as Mistress Captoft had judged; knees apart, coarse hands planted on the knees. But His Grace was a realist and knew that it was upon just such men as this one that the Church depended. The complicated, glittering structure had, like all others, to have foundations, roots. St. Peter, the humble fisherman – *'Upon this rock I will build my church.'* He was prepared to listen patiently to what he sensed would be a rambling, trivial story, to advise if he could, reprimand if he must. What he was not prepared to do, and that appeared to be what Father Matthew was asking of him, was to take action against a so-called witch.

Enlightened men no longer believed in such things. That French girl, Joan of Arc had been burned as a witch and by the very manner of her death – she had asked for a cross and an English soldier had hastily made one, two sticks tied together – she had brought the whole business of witchcraft and magic-making under fresh examination in which intelligence over-rode prejudice. Most reasonable, modern-minded men – and the Bishop of Bywater was one – were now of the opinion that she had been the victim of political strife, condemned by judges who were biased – or bribed. Simply by dying as she did she had brought witch-hunting into disrepute. So although His Grace listened with some semblance of patience, he listened sceptically to this tale of bulls rendered impotent, pigs dead of swine fever that was no swine fever, pictures of nude people and snakes that struck men dumb, the whole thing protracted, in true rustic style by what he said, what she said, what I said. At the end of the jumbled tale, Father Matthew said, 'So I thought, Your Grace, I'd best come and ask your advice. What should I do?'

'Nothing.'

'Nothing? But Your Grace ... What I have been saying ...'

'A hotch-potch of out-worn superstition, some co-incidence and, I suspect, even more spite. I think that you will find, Father Matthew, that when you look into the matter more dispassionately, you will find that somebody – possibly more than one person – has a real or an imagined grievance against this poor woman, and failing other means of redress, concocted this charge against her. Such an easy charge to bring; so difficult to refute.' He saw it all, he thought. Intake, that remote place, backward, and Father Matthew, lonely, consorting with peasants, his own kind, except for a little, a very little education. But even so, a priest was an ordained man; he should maintain a certain dignity and not get himself so entangled with bulls and pigs and gossip.

He gave Father Matthew a little homily on the subject; gentle, because he was not an ill-natured man, and because he could, in a vague way, see the man's predicament. At the end of it, sensing something stubborn and resentful in the man, to whom he had – look at the measured glass where the sand dropping, marked the hours, and their halves and quarters – already devoted more time than he could really spare, he said, 'You came for advice and I have given it. Do nothing. Above all do not go running to the secular authority. Take this tale to the Sheriff and you will bring not only yourself but the Church into ridicule.'

Father Matthew rode home in a curious state of mind. Angered, yes. He was furiously angered; he'd gone to seek support which had not been forthcoming. He'd been given a lecture; told to be friendly but not familiar, to lead rather than follow. All very well, but hadn't he, by being familiar as well as friendly, got far more people to Mass? However there was another side to it. Spite had been mentioned and in all honesty he was bound to admit that he had not only felt spite against Mistress Captoft himself, but encouraged it in others.

Johnson, at Johnsacre was waiting for his horse. There were a few men; waiting. No women, they were busy with the last meal of the day.

So, what had the Bishop to say?

Do nothing.

Just the sort of bloody silly thing somebody sitting down there in Bywater *would* say! But they'd always been independent, acting on their own, sticking together when the occasion demanded it. This was a job for the Elders.

Now Old Hodgson faced a predicament. To speak up for Mistress Captoft, as gratitude demanded he should do, would be useless. It'd do her no good; one voice carried no weight against six; and it would do him harm. Sticking up for a witch. Who wanted that to be said about him? Especially just at a time like this when Old Sawyer was failing, mumbling about, making no sense of what was happening around him. Any day now he'd be asked to stand down, and Old Hodgson would be eldest of the Elders. So he sat quietly, making no suggestions of his own, but with nods and sounds of agreement going along with it all.

Having dismissed Father Matthew, the Bishop turned to correspondence, writing two letters in his own hand. One to Lady Grey, expressing his hearty approval of the proposed match and conveying his congratulations on the splendid management which had produced such a satisfactory result. The second letter was to Lord Shefton, slightly sycophantic and deftly calling to his Lordship's attention the fact that to some degree he had himself been instrumental ... The Earl was not only very rich, but very powerful, too.

'He's off to market tomorrow,' Jem reported.

'You sure?'

'Certain. He was altering the waggon this afternoon.'

Most fattened bullocks walked to market, spending two days on the journey if necessary, and being beaten all the way, not only by their drover but by any casual person who cared to take a whack – the blows were supposed to make the meat more tender. Henry, though not unduly sentimental about animals – no farmer could afford to be – thought it a barbarous custom as well as quite useless. So he conveyed his in the waggon, and since a well-fed beast was too much of a load for one horse, he had made a contraption consisting of one shaft, so that the two horses could pull side by side. Even so, with one horse getting old it was a slow journey and he left home early, and disregarded Godfrey's pleas to be taken, too. 'You'd add to the weight. You shall come next time.' It didn't do to let boys have their own way all the time.

'Perhaps even on my mule,' Mistress Captoft said. 'That is if you try really hard with your sums.'

The lesson was going on in the hall, on the side of the table nearest the fire, for it was a cold day; Katharine was making bread and David busy in the dairy when the iron ring on the main door – serving both as handle and knocker – banged. Mistress Captoft went to the door herself. Opening it upon two Intake men in their working clothes, she thought it insolent of them to have come to this door and was about to send them round to the back, when she became aware of a kind of urgency in their manner.

'What is it?'

'Can you come, Mistress?'

'What is wrong?' Her thoughts went at once to her store of curatives. The people of Intake had done nothing to endear themselves to her, had indeed grossly offended her but she was not the woman to deny help to an individual in order to punish a whole community. Also she half recognised one of the men – he had come for the priest and been sent off with a dose, which had worked, and the father, restored to health, had actually thanked her.

'Thass what we don't know. Thass why we come for you.'

Possibly an accident, requiring prompt attention.

'I'll just get my cloak,' she said. She left the door open and in the half minute that it took her to run upstairs and down again. Ted Hodgson and Bert Edgar made the most of their

144

chance to study the picture stretched across the wall, over the blazing hearth. The only other pictures they had ever seen were those painted on the walls of the church; once so faded and peeling from damp as to be almost meaningless, then restored by Sir Godfrey. And those pictures had been painted in the then contemporary fashion, so that Mary, and the other Mary at the foot of the Cross, wore nun's garb; and even the figure on the Cross wore a decent breech clout. The almost life-size nude figures were quite shocking, and the snake was horrible.

'Can I come, Mamma-Captoft?' Godfrey asked as she ran down the stairs. Anything to avoid sums, which he could do, but hated.

Expecting blood, or somebody in a fit, choking on his own tongue, or a breech-birth, Mistress Captoft said, 'No,' in a voice sharper than that she usually used to him.

They took the shortest way to the village. Sir Godfrey, remembered only as a grabber and a tyrant, had had a sharp eye for terrain, and had realised that unless he planned well the people of Intake would have to trudge around the perimeter of an irregular oblong in order to get to church; so he had left them, in addition to a good part of the common, a path which skirted his sheep-fold on its shorter side, emerged practically in front of his house, and so to the church.

It was not a wide path. People used it when they came to church; Jem Watson used it every day, coming and going to work; it was well trodden, but not very wide. Was there, however, the need to jostle? As they were doing, almost as though ... as though she were a wrong-doer being hustled along to the lock-up.

Put them into place, she thought. After all, they had sought her aid, they could at least be respectful.

'What is it? An accident?'

The man she did not recognise – Bert Edgar had said himself that he had never spoken to her, only seen her across the church a few times ... he was not much of church-goer, just Christmas and Easter; he'd never ailed himself, and nor had his first boy; for Jill, and the other unwanted children he would certainly never have gone plodding along asking for aid – said, 'You'll see when you get there.'

And then she sensed something wrong. Sinister.

She was not a timid woman; she said, in the face of something wrong, wrong in a way she could not account for, 'I refuse to take another step until you have explained your errand.'

'You'll see,' Bert Edgar said, speaking as roughly as he did to his down-trodden wife. The most tricky part of the business was over now. He put out a big, work-hardened hand and took Mistress Captoft by the upper arm.

Godfrey Tallboys, curious as all children were, wanted to know what was happening. If he opened the door Mamma-Captoft might look back, see that he had left his task and hold it against him when it came to lending of the mule. But he could look out of the window. He was tall for his age, all Tallboys were, but not yet quite tall enough to have much of a view from a window which Master Hobson who had built the house had deliberately set high and narrow. But Godfrey dragged up a stool and attained a wider, longer view and saw Mamma-Captoft being manhandled. One man on each side.

There was no thought about it. He came of fighting stock – belligerence could be diverted, as it had been with Henry, fighting the weather, fighting circumstance, fighting himself. But in the boy, softly reared, pampered, spoilt, the old tough spirit sprang up. He took the poker from the hearth and ran out.

Something warned him not to shout, not to give any warning. Take the enemy by surprise! Hit where you can hit hardest. Both hands!

He hit Ted Hodgson on the side of the knee; a really crippling blow. The man let go of Mamma-Captoft and clasped his leg in both hands, yelping. Mamma-Captoft, thus released on one side, twisted around, but still held by the left hand of the other man who also swung round, still grabbing Mamma-Captoft with one hand, his other ready to snatch the poker. Which he did. The boy's strength and fury was no match for a full grown man's. Bert Edgar's left hand, hurt, but not much weakened, thrust the poker back, straight into the face of the fierce little cub who fell backwards into the brambles that edged the path, and lay still.

Mistress Captoft, truly alarmed now, struggled frenziedly

and flailed about with her free hand. Bert Edgar said, 'Lay ahold of the bitch on the other side, Ted. Never mind your knee.' He had little sensitivity to pain himself and no sympathy for it in others. 'If you must hobble, lean on her,' he said.

Once, in Dunwich, Mistress Captoft had seen a woman of known bad character, dragged out of town on a hurdle. Every sea-port had women who lived – and often supported families – on their immoral earnings. Now and again some almost symbolic action was taken against them, and that woman had been the victim of one of the brief purges. Banned for ever from the town itself, and from the 'hundred' of which the town was the centre. Mistress Captoft knew that the term hundred dated from long ago, when each hundred families was regarded as a responsible unit, answerable in law for the behaviour of its members and thus eager to expel anyone really recalcitrant.

Much the same thing, she imagined, was about to happen to her. The way she had been treated; the bigger man's use of the word *bitch*: all pointed that way. As she was hustled roughly across a yard and into a kitchen, she prayed urgently if incoherently; God save me, Jesu help me, Holy Mother of God let them leave me my skirt ... And all in a muddle her mind was still capable of thinking: How ironic; I lived in sin as they would call it, with Benny; and no stone cast; now, after two years with Master Tallboys and not even a fond word ...

But it was not that.

Six Elders sat around the kitchen table. Old Hodgson was suffering one of his fairly frequent bouts of stiffness of the joints and was confined to his bed. The unwritten rules demanded an odd number, seven or five, so that on any vital question there should be a casting vote, but this morning that rule could be ignored, for Old Sawyer no longer counted, babbling away about things long ago. Ignore him and that left five, all good men and true – and all violently prejudiced.

They used curiously formal terms, brought out of some remote past. They said: You are accused ... They said: You are charged ... They asked: How do you plead; guilty or not guilty? All was in order. She was invited, given the opportunity, to defend herself. But against something that she had never, even in nightmare, imagined.

Witchcraft.

The Bishop had described it exactly, a charge easy to bring, difficult to refute. Had the charge been of immorality she could have demanded that they sent for Katharine Dowley to swear on the Bible that though her room lay between she had never seen or heard any comings or goings, that she made both beds and never seen any evidence. David Fuller who waited at table and mended the fire could have sworn that no fond word or even glance, had ever passed between Master Tallboys and Mistress Captoft. Also, distasteful as it would be to drag in a child, Godfrey could have been asked: Where do you sleep? and the answer would have been: often in the little bed in my father's room. Oh, that would have been easy.

Also – and this was a thought to chill the heart – even had such defence failed, she would still be alive; publicly whipped perhaps, and wearing nothing but her petticoat, run out of Intake on a hurdle. But alive. A so-called witch had no chance at all. Procedures varied. Sometimes she was stripped and searched for any unusual mark, a mole or a wart by which she was supposed to suckle her familiar; or she was pricked with pins to discover an insensitive part – held to serve the same purpose. She could be starved, denied sleep, forced to walk up and down until her feet were bloody rags and she made a confession simply to escape further torments. Death was certain. Burn the witch! There was another way, ironically called a test. Throw a witch into water; if she floated she was a witch and could be taken out and burned; if she sank, she drowned and was regarded as innocent. Then everybody said what a pity and gave her Christian burial.

Oh God, I have sinned, grievously, but grant me, of Thy mercy, death by drowning.

Except for prayer there was nothing she could do except deny all charges which she did stoutly, though without hope. She said that she knew nothing of Bert Edgar, had never spoken to him; did not even know that he had a bull. She asked why should she wish to harm him?

Ah, they knew the answer to that. From the mouth of the priest himself. They could have called him in and confronted her with him, but Father Matthew, though informed of what was planned, had excused himself from taking any part in it. A priest, they must understand, could not disobey a direct order from his Bishop. His Grace had told him to do nothing; therefore he must do nothing.

What was planned was a swimming; it was the showiest way and provided most entertainment for the ordinary people.

Outside Bert Edgar said to Ted Hodgson, 'Come on, walk about, else it'll stiffen on you.' That was, in Intake, the rough-and-ready method of dealing with most injuries, short of a broken bone. Bert had a suspicion that his thumb was broken – and for that Ted Hodgson was to blame. Hit on the knee by a brat no older or bigger than Bert's own firstborn. and dancing about as though his feet were on fire. If Ted hadn't let go the woman's arm so that he'd been left to deal with her *and* with the young rascal, he'd have given him something to remember.

Hobbling, forced to walk about the yard, each step more painful, Ted Hodgson said, 'Wait a bit, Bert,' and propped himself against the rails of the empty pig-sty. 'You ever known a young 'un behave that way?'

'No, I never. It'd be leather'd out of them, afore they was that size.' Even his own wanted, eldest son, always privileged in the matter of food and general treatment, knew the limits of paternal indulgence and never over-stepped the limit.

'Come up without a sound,' Ted Hodgson said, anxious to explain why he had been taken unawares. 'And struck with the strength of ten. And then, when I looked round, he wasn't there. I'm beginning to wonder ... Bert, some of *them* have cats and toads and such things.'

'Never mind about that. She's as good as done for. Come on, walk. Don't you 'o'n't get down to see her swum.'

'I reckon my leg's broke.'

'Don't talk so daft. Broke bones grate. Listen to this!'

He gave audible evidence of his own broken bone, and was too ignorant to know that a knee-cap, without being broken, could shift.

*

Godfrey Tallboys disentangled himself from the brambles. He couldn't breathe through his nose, which hurt when he put up an experimental finger, and seemed to be lopsided. There was nobody on the path now. And, his blow struck, he knew that he was no match for two grown men. He thought of David and dismissed the thought, lame. But there was Father. And there was the mule, which now he did not need permission to use. He began to run, breathing heavily through his mouth.

Many people had hung about Bert Edgar's yard while the trial went on in the kitchen – his premises were used because he was the injured party and the Elders had no settled meeting place – but some had already gone down to the riverside, to get a good place for the show.

There was one main dipping place from which most women fetched water. There were only two wells in Intake, one at the priest's house, the other at Knight's Acre. When the river ran high, anybody could dip a bucket from any where along the bank, thus saving a bit of a trudge, but when the water lowered, women – always the water carriers – went to the Steps, cut into the clay bank and reinforced by lengths of sawn timber. Awaiting the winter rains now, the river ran slow, but steadily, level with the fourth step from the bottom.

To this place, Mistress Captoft, her thumbs already tied together, was brought. A few people crossed themselves to ward off the evil eye, most hissed and jeered. Women held up their small children, so that they might see and remember.

The bound thumbs held her hands in the attitude of prayer and though she was shaken by fear and deathly pale, she was still thankful. Not to be burnt. And still to be clothed. And in a way she was resigned; she *had* sinned, in loving Benny; had confessed and been absolved too seldom. Now, if only she could drown quickly ... Some time in Purgatory – for who would buy a Mass for her? – and then Heaven; a reunion of disembodied spirits all within the aura of the glory of God. Her parents, the brother she had loved and who had died before he was four; kind old Master Captoft. In Heaven where there was neither marriage nor giving in marriage.

As somebody tied her skirts about her ankles with a cord, she prayed again. God, let me die quickly. Lord into Thy hands I commend my spirit . . .

She fell with a splash and went down like a stone. Was under long enough for some people to have doubts. The innocent drowned, didn't they? More people crossed themselves. Then, some way down river but well within view, she rose to the surface and seemed to be riding on the water, bobbing a little, as though taking leave of Intake with a curtsey this way and that. A witch, all right.

They were prepared for that. Plough ropes with nooses all ready, young men, swift of foot and practised in catching one wanted animal out of a number, all set to run along the bank and take her, alive, to the fire, also ready in Bert Edgar's yard.

And then the impossible happened, just where the river made a slight curve, but still in the sight of all, Mistress Captoft was literally taken up, seemed for a breath-space to walk the water and vanished into the forest on the further bank.

Nobody lived, or had ever lived, so far as anyone knew, on that side of the river. Along the bank where the curve of the river deposited silt at certain seasons, there were trees, and there were trees too on some islands of higher ground so that looking across the river the far side gave the appearance of being wooded. There were, however, stretches of dangerous swamp. Nobody at Intake had first or even fourth hand experience of the place, but some old tales had survived. Once upon a time . . . Stories of men stepping on to what looked like green pasture and sinking to the knees, the thighs, the chest. The swamp began a few miles south of Baildon and extended, growing less and less wooded, to the coast. There it changed into sand dunes. Because of its reputation as a dangerous place it was avoided even by charcoal burners or refugees from justice. No wolf howled there, no fox barked, no deer flitted. Waste Wood belonged to birds, squirrels, and snakes.

It was plain that Mistress Captoft had not been saved by any human intervention.

*

'Sick it up,' old Hodgson said, thumping her back. He loosened and lifted the noose from about her body, and with his knife cut the cords. She was sick, dizzy and bewildered, drenched and terribly cold, but in her right mind. Blue-lipped and with teeth chattering she tried to thank him, but he cut her short.

'Never mind that now. We gotta get on the move.' He removed the outer one of the two rough coats he was wearing and pushed her arms into it. 'Soon warm up,' he said. 'Drink this.' He removed the plug from a small leather bottle and she gulped down a dose of what felt like liquid fire. He unhitched and wound the rope which he had fastened to a tree-trunk. He had had faith in his eye, and in his judgment, but had not trusted his strength to haul her in unaided; she was a well-fleshed woman and wet clothes weighed heavy. 'I gotta be back in my bed by sun-down and the ford's a way up. You all right, now?' Telling her to keep exactly behind him, he set off at a good pace. The path which he had trod-den down and hacked out earlier in the day lay clear ahead; it'd have been different in summer, when vegetation could spring back into place within an hour. Once he paused and said, 'Careful now. That ain't grass. Jump!' He did so him-self, surprisingly spry for an old man whose stiffness of joints had for years prevented him from doing any heavy or un-pleasant task. His daughter-in-law had once said, very sourly, 'The only thing about him that ain't stiff is his jaw. He can allust eat.' Ted Hodgson had added, 'And his tongue!' He was a carping old man.

Now he jumped over a space where the swamp was en-croaching and waited to see how she managed. 'Well done!' he said, and set off again. Here, because the swamp was creeping in, the screen of trees grew thinner, and Intake, on the other bank was visible.

'There's the village,' he said. 'The ford ain't so far now.'

It was not a ford in the proper sense of the word – a place where a river is shallow enough to be crossed by foot. Long centuries earlier some indefatigable Roman engineer had planned a straight road, and a bridge which would shorten by twenty miles the distance between Baildon and Col-chester. The fact that on the other side of the river the land was swampy had not deterred him; he planned a causeway.

With thousands of others he had been recalled when the barbarians threatened the Empire and his work had never been even half completed. His length of straight road – though its solid foundations and its paving stones remained almost intact, had been forgotten, neglected, overgrown; and of his planned bridge only some piers remained, worn smooth by the river. Old Hodgson – Young Hodgson then – and another boy had discovered the stones one day, a day between haymaking and harvest, when even hardworked little boys had a few leisure days. They'd spent a happy afternoon, jumping from one stone, only just awash, to another, and then gone home and forgotten all about it.

The other boy was dead, and Old Hodgson had only remembered when he had to.

They crossed, and were in Layer Wood.

'Now mind what I say,' Old Hodgson said. 'I take this short cut, straight back to the village and get myself to bed. *You* have a longer road. You can't go near the village. So walk straight on and you'll come to a pool; bear to your right then and you should come out not far from the back of Knight's Acre.' It was dusk already under the trees and he'd never known a woman who had any sense of direction or who wasn't scared of the dark, so despite his own urgent need for haste he spared her another minute, telling her the way again and adding, 'And there's nowt to be scared of; there ain't the wolves about there used to be.'

'I can never, never thank you sufficiently; but I shall remember you in my prayers.'

'If *they* ever guess what I been up to, it'll take more'n prayers,' he said, and trudged away.

The steer sold well. Henry went along to Master Turnbull's office and deposited half the price. Master Turnbull could see more sense in putting money aside for a living girl than for a boy who had vanished eight? yes, eight years ago; he was only sorry that the whole of the young lady's fortune had not been entrusted to him, with no consultation with the Bishop of Bywater. He could have done better for her. He would have repudiated hotly the term money-lender – the Jews had been money-lenders, usurers, until they were banished, nearly two hundred years earlier; Master Turnbull was a manager of money, his own and that of sensible people, like Master Tallboys who entrusted him with sums, great and small. He was scrupulously honest; knew that small sum added to small sum mounted up; believed that money, properly handled, could breed money and that a man should be flexible. He was fiercely anti-clerical. But when he had once mentioned the pity that it was that a Bishop should ever have been involved, Master Tallboys had given him one of those candid blue looks and said in a way that robbed his words of any offence, 'No doubt you could have done better. But you could not have obtained a place for her in Sir Barnabas Grey's household.' And that was true. A law man who was not also a churchman was still regarded as a man of inferior breed; but Time would see to that. Master Turnbull, always alert to the drift of things, was pretty certain that the day of the middle class man would come. Maybe not in his time, but in his son's.

Henry bought – since he had the waggon – some household things which Mistress Captoft had asked for – and thank God he could now pay – even for small luxuries. Even for a cask of wine. Reared for the most part in great poverty, he always felt slightly guilty when he spent anything on what was not an absolute necessity. Mistress Captoft had, in a way, imposed standards on him for which he was not yet ready. Admirable standards; it was true that Godfrey needed new clothes; that Katharine deserved the good servant's Christmas dole of stuff for a working dress. He didn't grudge, but even spending what he could afford *now* reminded him of the past when he could afford so little, and made him think of the future, always uncertain. When he felt like this he was always disgusted with himself, and gave a thought to his father, who once, for the first time in his life, with a hundred pounds in hand, had built Knight's Acre, sparing nothing, even the pargeting. Sir Godfrey had spent his last penny on the house – and then could not afford to live in it. It was Walter who had made the farm, the thing which had sustained the house for more than twenty years, and must continue to do so.

The lightened waggon rattled along; even the older horse was now headed for his stable, his manger, and the paces matched better. And Henry knew why this stretch of road depressed him. With no need to urge or guide a horse he had nothing to do but think. Ordinarily he could avoid much thought by flinging himself into work, or sleep. Too much to remember; it didn't do to remember.

The road curved slightly and he saw, coming towards him at a smart trot, very different from its usual sedate movement, Mistress Captoft's mule. No mistaking that unusual silvery grey. And astride it, Godfrey, his hair all aflutter, and some rags too. And what in God's name had happened to his face?

He'd taken a fall. Naughty, over-venturesome boy! Yet he was not riding like a boy who had been thrown. He wheeled the mule expertly so that he was level with the seat of the waggon which Henry had brought to a halt. His nose looked crooked, there was blood. And when he spoke it sounded as though he had a heavy cold in his head.

'Change with me, Father. Go and save Mamma-Captoft from those horrid, rough men.'

'What men?'

'They were rough with her. You go. I'll take the waggon.' He was already scrambling out of the mule's saddle on to the waggon seat.

Henry was capable of thinking quickly when he had to. Abductions were not uncommon. In fact when Robert was lost everybody's first thought was that he had been stolen. Violent and lawless men did take people, and hold them to ransom, sending messages – such and such a sum, in a hollow tree; under a stone. It had never yet happened at Intake; but there was a first time for everything.

'Which way did they go, son?'

If into Layer Wood a difficult search and perhaps futile.

'Into the village.'

That sounded strange. Local people didn't abduct local people in broad daylight. Still, they could have set off in the direction of the village, then veered off into the woods.

He was now on the mule; saddle too narrow, stirrups too short.

'Father, hurry!' Godfrey said. Henry set the mule to a gallop.

The boy with many knights among his ancestors, shouted, 'Take a *pitchfork*'! But by that time he had set the horses in

155

motion and his snuffly voice did not carry above the clatter of twelve hooves and the creaking of wheels.

The people of Intake, like all people faced with the unknown and the awesome, sought comfort and courage in human company. Clustering and murmuring like a swarm of bees, they moved from the river bank into the village, into Bert Edgar's yard, where the firewood was stacked and ready. Somebody brought a brand from the kitchen and set it alight. The warmth and the brightness dispelled some of the dread. A spirit of hysterical hilarity began to grow. They had all seen an amazing, a terrible thing; they were all acutely conscious of the Devil only just across the river, but here they all were, untouched so far. Survivors. Johnson, a man prosperous enough to own a horse, took his son and another man to his place, next door to Edgarsacre and came back with a cask of October ale – last year's and very potent. That struck the right note. *Make a feast of it*; fetch mugs, fetch food. Everybody bring what was available. Unrecognised a feeling of competition sprang up. The bee-swarm scattered – but nobody went alone through the deepening dusk. You come with me to my place, then I'll go with you to yours. Even men felt that way tonight.

At Hodgacre, Bet Hodge said to Jill Edgar who had accompanied her, 'I'd better just look in on the old man.'

Holding a lighted candle she opened the door of the room she so coveted. Selfish old pig, he refused to share even with his eldest grandson, a quiet boy who did not snore.

'And about time too,' the old querulous voice said. 'Here I laid, stiff as a plank and nobody to bring me so much as a drink of water.'

'Thass wrong, Granfer. I looked in time after time. You was allus asleep.'

He gave an inner chuckle. She could be lying. She could be telling the truth. If she *had* looked in that was proof that he'd made a good mommet, mounding up, under the bedclothes what, from the door could well be mistaken for a sleeping man.

'Is there anything you want now?'

'Is there anything I want,' he echoed sardonically. 'Yes.

My dinner. Four rashers, cut thin and well frizzled and two eggs, turned in the pan. You should know by now.'

She had been undecided which little cask of home-made wine to take to the feast; the pale, flowery cowslip or the rich dark blackberry which she had been saving for the old man's funeral feast. Now she knew that it was safe to take the blackberry; the old man was tough as hickory wood; he'd live for years; she'd have time to make more and see it well-ripened.

On some of the farms the pigs were feeling as neglected as Old Hodgson had pretended to be. They squealed and were fed.

The young nimble men who had run, with ropes, to dredge the witch, dead or alive out of the water, said that they'd seen nothing. One minute she'd been there, bobbing on the surface of the water, the next she'd been in the thicket. Later this story was to be embellished, and, passed down through two generations, it included a vivid picture of the Devil, cloven hooves, horns, tail and all, leering out of the thicket.

One thing was certain, even at the end of this confusing day. Mistress Captoft was being punished, wherever she was. Satan, Old Scrat, might have saved her, from the water, from the fire, but everybody knew that those who sold themselves into his service, were in the end abandoned. He was the Father of Lies, the past master of deception.

The impromptu feast was well under way when Henry arrived. The grey mule was over-fed and underexercised; urged on by a kick or a slap, it would gallop a bit, then begin to blow, a warning sign to anyone who knew anything about four-legged things. Breath must be recovered, then the easy, ambling pace resumed, more urging, a short gallop and blowing again. The younger of his two horses, despite the miles it had already done would have been a better mount, Henry reflected, blaming himself for not thinking of that before. But at last he was at Intake, the lane going on towards the village, the track diverting to the right, towards the church, the priest's house and Knight's Acre itself. And there the mule who for years had turned here, gave proof of its breed's proverbial stubbornness. Nothing would budge it.

Angrily, Henry dismounted and continued his journey – about a quarter of a mile – on foot. He intended to go from house to house asking whether anyone had seen, or knew anything of Mistress Captoft. He was spared that tedious business by the light and the noise coming from Bert Edgar's yard.

It was, he thought, like a scene from Hell. Faces reddened and distorted by the glare; drunken laughter; the smell of meat being toasted at the end of pitchforks, or sharpened stakes. Amidst so much noise one voice, however loud, would be lost. He walked to the fringe of the crowd and brought his work-hardened hands together in a clap. Those near enough to hear, jumped and fell silent, and the quietude ran, like panic through the rest. Suddenly everyone, except a wailing baby, was silent and staring towards Henry. At any time he was a good head taller than any one of them, and now that most were sitting or squatting, he loomed enormous, and with his face lit from below not unlike the Devil they were dreading. And it was only Master Tallboys! There were gasps, even sniggers of relief.

'Does anybody here know anything of Mistress Captoft?'

The Intake dumbness clamped down; what you didn't say couldn't be held against you.

'She was taken from my house,' Henry said, 'and roughly handled.'

He was not accusing them. He still couldn't believe that any Intake men would do such a thing. He'd come here for information, possibly help, if Layer Wood had to be searched. And a fine lot of help he'd find here, he thought, looking at the blank faces, the drunken faces.

'Did anybody see strangers?'

Somebody hushed the baby and for a moment the silence was not just merely an absence of sound but a positive thing. Then Jill Edgar, down-trodden for years, but now borne up because she had been first at Bert Hodgson's good black-berry, said, 'She was took for a witch and swum.'

That broke a barrier. Varying voices intermingled to tell the astounding tale; the fair trial, the test, and the Devil himself snatching the witch away into Waste Wood.

Henry listened to the babble sceptically. When he was young and impressionable Walter had derided anything that could not be seen and handled as nonsense. Even Sybilla herself could never get him to Mass. Hell, he said, had been invented to make people behave, and Heaven to cheer up their miserable lives. As for witches and warlocks and ghosts, for them Walter had only one word: Rubbish.

So now Henry thought only in practical terms. That poor woman somehow struggling out of the water and finding herself in Waste Wood, where she would find no shelter, no succour. She'd be drenched and half drowned; she'd die of exposure in this bitter wind.

He had no knowledge of the ford. He knew that there was no bridge and that the only way for someone who could not swim was to go down to Bywater, hire a boat and cross the mouth of the river, land among the sand dunes and work one's way upstream through the swamps and the trees. It could take days. There must be a quicker way. There was. Hire a boat, with men who would row in relays, and come upstream that way and land near the spot where she had disappeared. That meant getting down to Bywater this evening and setting out at first light tomorrow morning.

He stayed just long enough to ask two questions.

Where was she last seen?'

They could all answer that. Just by the first curve after the Steps.

'Who fetched her from my house?'

Dead silence.

'God damn you all,' Henry said and set off for home, now running, now walking with his long loping strides which were almost as fast. He had actually reached his own ground when he saw a faint, bobbing light, heard his son's treble voice call 'Father', and David's deeper one shout, 'Master! Master Tallboys!' Henry shouted back and the hero of the day burst into tears.

'We thought . . . something had happened . . . to you. The mule . . . came home alone.'

'Thank God, you're safe, sir,' David said. 'Mistress Captoft, too.'

'She mended my nose,' Godfrey said, gripping Henry about the thighs.

'You *have* had a day,' Henry said. 'Come on, up you get. I'll give you a ride home.'

'How *is* Mistress Captoft? Henry asked.

'All right,' David said. 'Very quiet.'

They'd all had a day. Katharine had made a mutton and apple pie, ready to serve at midday. Joseph came punctually. Jem had not stayed for dinner; he said he'd come early to help load and steer and there was something he had to see to down in the village. So the three of them had waited, expecting Mistress Captoft and Godfrey – assumed to have gone for a walk – to arrive at any minute. It was utterly unlike Mistress Captoft to absent herself from a meal without warning. Joseph had become impatient and finally, unwillingly, Katharine had cut the pie. Then it was discovered that the mule had gone and Katharine and David had assumed that Mistress Captoft had taken Godfrey, riding pillion, to Nettleton. The observance of Saints' days varied from place to place; she had probably been asked to stay to dinner there. Dusk began to threaten, worry to mount. Then, almost simultaneously, two things happened. Mistress Captoft, soaked through, and unusually silent, had come in, demanding a bath.

She was a fastidious woman; she took at least six baths a year, using a cut-down cask. While the water was being heated and carried up, Godfrey arrived with the waggon – and a flattened nose and one of his last milk teeth hanging by a thread. Mistress Captoft, cutting her bath short, had dealt with the nose; tweaking it back into shape and fixing it with a plaster of linen, heavily smeared with flour and water paste. She had also plucked out the loose tooth, saying that it was no loss; it would have fallen out soon, anyway. After that the mule, empty-saddled, had come clattering into the yard; and then Godfrey had begun to talk about his father who had gone to Intake ... about the two bad men whom he had hit with the poker, and the one who, with that same poker had broken his nose and practically knocked a tooth out.

Now, all safe again under one roof; everything would have been made plain, except for Mistress Captoft's unusual reticence and curious attitude. She gave Godfrey his due: 'He behaved like a hero. You may be proud of your son, Master Tallboys.' But she repudiated, absolutely, the idea of vengeance.

'Godfrey said there were two men,' Henry said. 'Both from the village. Did you recognise either?'

She said, 'No.' Adding hastily in her mind; God forgive that lie; told in a good cause; to tell the truth would be to start a feud. *Blessed are the peacemakers; for they shall be called the children of God.* Struggling home, soaked, muddy, her teeth chattering, Mistress Captoft had undergone a spiritual experience. God had, through the instrumentality of one grateful old man, saved her from the water and from the fire. In future she would belong to God and to Him only.

She said, with unctuous piety, new to her, and to Henry infuriating, 'We must forgive, as we hope to be forgiven.'

'A fine sentiment! My boy's face was smashed in. Am I to forgive that?'

'Yes. *Vengeance is mine*, saith the Lord.'

She was equally secretive about the identity of her rescuer. Someone who had reason to be grateful to her, she said; and to name *him* might lead to trouble, the people of Intake being so ignorant and misguided. And, while praising Godfrey's courage in going to her defence, she tended to make light of his hurt. His nose was as yet hardly more than gristle, and, attended to so promptly, would show no sign of injury. To make a fuss, to put thoughts of malice and vengeance into his mind would be infinitely more harmful.

Whoever, long ago, had devised the Tallboys badge – the hare defending its young, and the motto 'I Defend What Is Mine', had not chosen haphazardly. Henry felt that the whole affair was an affront to him. No doubt everything the silly woman said was true, in a way saintly, but he could not feel so. Somebody had come to his house and taken away a woman who, though no kin to him, was living under his roof and therefore under his protection; and when a boy, little more than a child, had gone to her aid, somebody had jabbed him brutally in the face. Henry, who would have described himself as a peaceable man, knew that he would never rest easy until the insult was avenged.

There was another aspect, too. The people of Intake being so ignorant and – Henry rejected Mistress Captoft's tolerant word, *misguided* – so bloody barbarous, they might try again. He couldn't be on guard all the time, and David was a lame man, easily thrown off balance. Therefore they must be shown, made to understand, taught a lesson.

Of his intention he said nothing to Mistress Captoft, suddenly so sickeningly pious. The thought did flash through his mind that the one person who would understand completely was Joanna – but she was far away.

In the morning he questioned Godfrey again. The white plaster stood out like a little white snout. On either side of it dark bruises showed. That anybody should have *dared*! Godfrey had nothing to add to his former account. Two men, one bigger than the other; he'd hit the smaller. 'I lamed him, Father. I hope I hurt the other one too, before he jabbed me.' He might, Godfrey said, have seen the men before, in church, but he did not know their names.

Henry waited for Jem Watson to come to work; get him talking and he might let slip something useful; but Jem did not come.

The whole village, except for Old Hodgson and the children who had been given only a sip of this, a sip of that, slept late that Thursday morning. Children got up and foraged for themselves on what was left after the orgy: Old Hodgson would have done the same, but thought it wiser to maintain his pretence for at least another day. Lying wakeful, and hungry, he wondered about Mistress Captoft; had she found her way home?

One early morning sound was not heard in Intake, and when, thick-headed, bleary-eyed men eventually lurched out into their yards, they saw why. No healthy, hungry squealing pigs. Some dead, more lying down, waiting to die.

They all knew, by the rule of thumb, taught by experience, that swine fever was catching, and, called to inspect Bert Edgar's pigs which were suffering from swine fever that wasn't quite swine fever, they had kept their distance while uttering sympathetic or exclamatory words. But that the disease could lurk in a place where no pig was had not occurred to them and on the previous day, intent upon the trial, then upon the feast they had given no thought to the matter; they'd leant against, brushed against the empty sty; some had even stood in it to get a bit of shelter from the wind. Then, after the swimming, or after the feasting, they'd seen

162

to their pigs . . . Now the incredible disaster had struck. This would be another year when bacon must be bought. Stunned, made apathetic, they stood about in groups, asking how? asking why? Because they'd made a mistake and fixed on the wrong woman – whom God, not the Devil, had reached out and saved? Curiously no suspicion now attached itself to Mistress Captoft. Superstition could swing like a weather-cock.

Into one of these miserable little groups Henry came. He was looking for a lame man. The other, the real culprit, the one who had jabbed Godfrey might not be so easy to find, but Henry was reasonably sure that a little pressure, or a little bribery would persuade the lame man to give a name to his confederate. And *he* would be smashed into pulp.

There was a lame man, leaning on Nature's own crutch, a forked bough. And there too, was a man – recognisable; Bert Edgar, who'd once worked at Knight's Acre, with his left hand roughly bandaged.

'You hit my boy,' Henry said. Not quite a statement or quite a question.

'What if I did? He lamed Ted. He'd hev lamed me. Bruk my thumb for me.'

'All right,' Henry said and began to loosen his belt.

His belt was the weapon that Bert Edgar used most often upon his wife and his unwanted children and he saw meaning in Henry's action.

'You hit me and I'll strike back. I still got one good hand.'

Henry pushed his own left hand behind him, into the back of the belt, loosened to admit it, then tightened to control it. He was being fair, chivalrous, though long ago he had turned his back on all that chivalry meant.

Ah. Then began a fight that was to be long remembered together with the witch-swimming, the baconless year.

Instinctively everybody moved back, even Ted Hodgson on his crutch, to form a ring, an amphitheatre with no seats.

There never had been; there never would be again, such a fight.

Actually Henry was doubly handicapped; he'd immobilised his left arm; Bert, while not wishing to engage his injured hand, had an elbow free; and Henry had never given or received a blow in anger since he and Richard had fought with the miniature spades which Walter had made for them, and Walter had said that the two of them were too much to control; one must go. Richard went and Henry had lived peaceably, whereas Bert Edgar had been in many fights, both as boy and man. Village squabbles easily erupted into blows, and since he was usually the victor he was always ready to carry a quarrel to the limit. He was sturdier than many of his kind because, having only one brother, he'd fed better in his childhood than members of larger families. He had indeed the build of a bull and although Master Tallboys was superior in height, possibly in reach, too, Bert did not doubt his ability to floor him.

That was what made the fight so memorable. Most people knocked flat by Bert Edgar, stayed down, either because they were knocked silly or thought it prudent not to get up. Master Tallboys went down no fewer than four times, but he kept getting up and rushing in again. He was savage enough but quite unskilled. Bert had learned the art of dodging and some of Master Tallboys' blows never found their mark at all, or simply glanced off; almost all of Bert's landed and the final outcome was all too easy to foresee, especially when one of Bert's punches split Master Tallboys' eyebrow and blood poured down, blinding one eye.

It was time for the Elders to exercise their authority, as was their right and their duty when it looked as though a man might be killed. Death in a fight was always the subject of an inquiry and nobody wanted that. The Elders had the power to stop a fight that had gone far enough by calling upon all good men and true to intervene, an order traditionally obeyed. It was occasionally obeyed in a way that led to more damage, for most bystanders took sides and in intervening dealt pretty roughly with the man thought to be in the wrong. Amongst these watchers opinion was rather divided. Bert Edgar was one of them, but in the crowd that had rapidly gathered there were those who had, in the past, suffered from Bert Edgar's fists and would not have been sorry to see him floored, just once. There were a few others who, while not completely on Master Tallboys' side gave a grudging admiration to a man who, put down four times, and clearly outmatched, wouldn't stay down. It showed pluck.

Before the Elders could act, Bert Edgar made the most dreaded move of all. He was getting tired of the fight which had lasted longer than any he could remember; knock a man flat four times when once was usually enough. In this kind of fight there were no rules – you could punch, make painful hacks at shins, even bite if chance offered. So he played one of the oldest tricks; took a step back, seeming to invite a blow and then brought his knee up sharply into Henry's crotch. It should have been over then, but it was not. Seemingly Master Tallboys did not feel, or heed the dreadful pain – about the worst anybody could inflict. Instead he seemed to rally, came forward and aimed a blow which did reach its mark. Smack on the point of the chin. Bert Edgar reeled and fell and stayed prone. Breaths that had been withheld during that last minute were let loose audibly.

Henry said, short of breath, 'Anybody who touches anything of mine will get the same.' Then, wiping the blood out of his eye, with the back of his hand, he turned and walked away. *Walked*.

It took some doing, for a blow *there* was the most agonising of all. But pride demanded that he should walk away, and not until he was out of their sight, try to discover what damage had been done – nothing so far as he could make out – and limp a little.

Mistress Captoft dealt expertly with his other injuries, but at the same time admonished him with trite pious phrases about violence simply leading to more violence and the only way being to forgive and forget.

Regarding his swollen knuckles with some pleasure, Henry said, 'Well, I can forgive him now. I think I broke his jaw.'

'Retaliation might come in a way you could not so easily avenge. If you found your horses hamstrung or a cow's udder mutilated in the night ... You could not fight the whole village.'

That was worth thinking over.

'I shall buy a truly savage hound,' he said. But not today. The thought of riding just now was something to shrink from.

Sitting opposite her at dinner, it occurred to him that Mistress Captoft looked different; washed out seemed an apt term; some of the brightness had gone from her hair, much of the colour from her face. And she was wearing, not one of her usual fanciful headdresses but a cap of white linen, very plain and unbecoming; as was the charcoal-coloured dress, devoid of all ornament. Her ordinarily hearty appetitite seemed to be impaired and she took no wine.

Jem Watson turned up in time for dinner and for half a day's wages. The orgy of the previous evening had made food in the village short; the loss of the pigs would mean tightened belts for all for some time to come; and that made a paid job, with a midday dinner a thing to be valued.

Mistress Captoft, in her forgive-and-forget mood, had said the least possible to Katharine and David, but she had spoken fairly freely to Henry who in any case knew what had happened. She had named no names, but what she had said had been in the presence of Godfrey to whom the whole affair was a drama in which he had played an admirable part. It was he who supplied the vital bit of information which Jem carried back to the village that evening.

'You coulda knocked me down with a feather, when *she* come walking into the kitchen, perky as a robin. And then I heard, from the boy. *Somebody chucked her a rope and pulled her out.*'

The Devil, they decided, would not have used such an ordinary thing as a rope. Why should he, with all the forces of evil magic at his command?

And all Intake had been here, on this side of the river, barring Old Hodgson, stiff in his bed and a woman even more crippled.

Barring Father Matthew and his ugly boy.

Joseph, the Knight's Acre shepherd, could be entirely discounted. He'd been seen going about his work just as people turned away from the river bank. Besides, he knew nothing.

But the priest had not been seen. And he *knew* what was planned. Had seemed to approve. His excuse for not being present – that the Bishop had ordered him to do nothing – had seemed all right at the time. Now it sounded very flimsy.

They were all extremely vulnerable. So much had happened in so short a time; the peasant stolidity had cracked and must be melded together again by some communal belief and purpose.

Abruptly the mind of the mindless mob thought it saw everything. Father Matthew wasn't one of *them*, he had only pretended to be so. With equal suddenness everybody decided that actually they hadn't liked him very much. He was *greedy*, always looking in at about suppertime and eating as much as a man who had been ploughing all day. The popularity which Father Matthew had gained by seeming unlike a priest, rebounded with horrible force. He wasn't like a priest because he wasn't one.

'Even to the words,' Old Ethel said. 'I've noticed.' And she should know, for the habit formed when she was Father Ambrose's housekeeper had never been broken. She never missed a Mass.

'I don't *know* the words,' she admitted. 'I ain't no scholar. What I *do* know and *can* say is that there's things he don't say like the good old man did. Nor the new one, neither – I mean the new one *before* him.'

That remark struck a note in some minds. Weren't there some shocking tales about church ritual being garbled, Pater Nosters said backwards, the Host itself being used for evil purposes?

One thing linked with another. What about that boy he kept? So ugly – except for the fur, the living spit of the thing in the picture; and talking as though his tongue was too big for his mouth. Could be his familiar. And if Father Matthew was a witch it would account for his being able to cross the river; witches could fly, couldn't they? Well, then, say he was a witch – or should it be wizard? – what had they ever done to *him* that he should kill their beasts? Plain as the nose on your face; they hadn't ploughed his glebe.

Then where did Mistress Captoft come in? They were two for a pair; in league with each other. Then why had he called her an evil woman and gone down to ask the Bishop what to do? He'd done it to draw attention from hisself and who knew that he'd ever been near the Bishop? He'd *said* so; but the Devil was the Father of Lies, so naturally them in his service would tell lies. Or it could be they'd fallen out – rogues were said to fall out – and he wanted to teach her a lesson, let her nearly drown and then save her, just to show who was master.

Another thing, too. What about his own pig?

A lot hinged on the well-being of that one animal; if that was ailing or dead it'd prove ... No it wouldn't; he'd be cunning enough to strike his own pig, just to fool them.

The talk went on and on, and round and round. It served to take their minds off the dismal prospect of a winter when bacon must be bought.

One thing emerged fairly clearly, to Old Hodgson's great delight, there was no talk of further action against Mistress Captoft. Once suspicion had fastened upon a man this almost entirely male-dominated society could regard her as women were generally regarded, helpless tools, willing or un-willing. Irresponsible creatures.

Henry, whose notice and solicitude would have meant so much – only a week earlier, said, 'But you have eaten almost nothing. And you look poorly. At least take a cup of wine.'

'Thank you, no. To speak frankly, Master Tallboys, I am weaning myself from the lusts of the flesh. On Monday I intend to go to Clevely and ask for admission there.'

'Clevely! You mean the nunnery?'

'Where else?'

'That is impossible,' he said. 'Years ago when my father was looking for a place for my sister, he went there and came away without even stating his errand. I remember it well. He said the place was a ruin, and the few nuns left either deaf or blind or senile. Time will not have improved it.' Henry knew he was right there. The time of lavish gifts to religious houses was over. Shrines at which miracles were said to be per-formed, like St. Egbert's at Baildon, and maybe St. Edmund's in the town that bore his name, were still patronised and prospering, but places like Clevely ... Who'd leave money to restore and support a place where the most that could be hoped for was a few prayers, mumbled by old women who couldn't tell Sunday from Monday?

'But that, Master Tallboys, is just what I need. In such a place what money I have will be welcome and useful and by living in discomfort – as I doubtless shall do – I shall give proof of my gratitude to God. For sparing my life.'

Something in Henry's mind asked: To what purpose? Alive just in order to be miserable? And something else asked: 'What about *you*? What is *your* life, Henry Tallboys? Work like a horse; eat; sleep; get up to work again. To what purpose?

He knew the answer to that. He had Knight's Acre; he had his son. What more could a man ask?

He said, in that deceptively stolid manner, 'I'd sleep on it, if I were you. And I'd think about Lamarsh, a different place altogether. Water-tight at least.'

Saying that he gave her one of his rare, singularly sweet smiles; a joke; come on, share it!

He didn't care where she went; or when – just this little, typical male interest in whether a roof was water-tight or not. And to think that she had dyed her hair, painted her face, latched herself in an iron corset in order to attract him! The thought shamed her to the core. God be thanked, he'd never noticed her antics!

Maude Grey cried very easily and was inclined to take advantage of this ability. Free-flowing tears could often cut short a scolding or forestall another blow. So she cried as she obeyed her mother's injunction to use her utmost power of persuasion upon Joanna. Joanna, being tactfully prepared for betrothal to Lord Shefton, had simply said, 'He is too old.' After that she had listened unmoved to Lady Grey's earnest and reasonable arguments, and to Sir Barnabas's more jocular, light-handed attempts at persuasion. So Maude had been entrusted with the task. The young who wouldn't listen to their elders, might take note of a near contemporary. Maude had been told exactly what to say and she said it.

It could be such a happy occasion, Joanna. Christmas *and* a betrothal. We shall all be so deeply disappointed.' Tears gathered and spilled.

'Why *disappointed*, Maude? Disappointment can only come from a failed expectation. The only ones I can see in this case are Lord Shefton's, and he deserves disappointment. Old enough to be my grandfather! And those teeth! They stink.'

Diligently, obediently, Maude mentioned all the advantages to be set against age and ill-smelling breath; a castle, four other abodes, one in London, access to the Court; the fact that it could only be a short servitude; an old man could not live for ever; and with his death Joanna would be free, and rich; even her own dowry untouched and much added.

Like everything else about this place, this way of life to which Henry had condemned her, false and mercenary. Hateful.

'I won't do it.'

Maude cried harder. 'The lady, my mother will be angered with me. She will say that I did not try hard enough to persuade you.'

'Why should she expect you to succeed when she had failed?'

'She thought that as we are much of an age, and friends . . .'

'Surely even *she* could not expect me to enter into such a marriage simply to save you a beating, Maude.'

'No, but I could say – and I do say it with all my heart – *I wish he had chosen me.*'

'So do I, with all *my* heart.' I should have been spared all this; and Maude would not have minded; poor down-trodden girl, knowing nothing of love; thinking only of the castle and four other abodes – and being a Countess, taking precedence over her mother!

Maude said, using the disrespectful *she*, 'She has her mind set on it, Joanna. And when her mind is set . . . She has ways of enforcing her will.'

'Not on me! She could order me to keep to this room and live on bread and water for a year. And I still wouldn't do it.' She had intended to keep her secret, something hidden and private and precious in this alien world, but now, to save further argument, to save poor Maude from rebuke, she revealed it, harsh, abrupt, conclusive. 'I couldn't. I was betrothed before ever I came here.'

In the only sure privacy that their way of life afforded them, in their bedchamber, Lady Grey said to her husband, 'I do not believe it. It is an invented story. Why, it is only a few days ago since I had a letter from her guardian, His Grace of Bywater, fully approving and congratulating me – us – on such good management; on attaining such a match. Would he have written thus, knowing her to be already betrothed? When he consigned her to our care, was not the ultimate aim to see her suitably married?'

'So I understood.'

'The whole thing,' Lady Grey said, dealing with pins and lacings as though they were the offenders, 'has been a mystery. And a burden. For one thing she now denies that the Bishop is her guardian, or that she has one at all. Grand talk about her lineage – but all Spanish. Such airs and graces, with no backing at all. And now, just when I thought the whole thing settled, and the way made clear for Maude, this happens. I shall write to His Grace of Bywater again, first thing tomorrow, and send a fast rider.'

Riding, but at the mule's pace, Mistress Captoft went along the track which led to Clevely. It went downhill and there were trees, and a curve, so that one saw the place suddenly. Henry had prepared her to some extent – a decayed, ruinous house, full of old women, but she had not envisaged such complete decay, something resembling a broken down haystack. Still her spirit did not falter. She dismounted and rang the bell, which was briskly answered by a nun who in no way fitted Henry's description: a brisk, able-bodied woman, little, if any, older than Mistress Captoft herself. They exchanged greetings and each recognised in the other a mirror image.

'I wish to speak to the Head of this House,' Mistress Captoft said.

'That, I regret to say is impossible. Our Prioress is unwell; keeping to her bed.'

A kindly way of describing that state of senility which much resembled a vegetable existence.

'I am Dame Isabel. At such time, I am in charge. If you would be seated and tell me the business that brought you here . . .'

It was both invitation and challenge. Those about to dedicate their lives – and their fortune to God, should not be easily deterred. So Mistress Captoft seated herself on a bare and not very stable bench, in a room, presumably the convent's parlour which not only smelt of damp and decay but gave visible evidence of it; a frond or two of fern in a crack in the wall, another growth, small, woolly surfaced mushrooms along the skirting where rotten wall joined rotten floor. Most deplorable, but such things could be remedied. Mistress Captoft was fully prepared to bring her money, her energy – all that she had, to the remedying. So, under the steady and unsympathetic stare of Dame Isabel's eyes – one always thought of bluish, greenish, greyish eyes as being cold, but brown ones could look like pebbles at the tide's edge – Mistress Captoft explained her situation and her intention. And having offered her all, she was repelled.

Dame Isabel said, 'Decisions taken upon impulse – as this sounds to me to be – are often regretted. I feel that you would be wise to think again. And even then, this is hardly the place. Clevely has not taken a novice for at least twenty years, so far as I can ascertain. We have no Mistress of Novices, no facilities for instruction. I am sorry.'

She said the last words with finality. She did not want the woman here. Even in her present subdued mood, the very contours of Mistress Captoft's face betrayed her as a masterful, managing creature, who, once admitted, in whatever capacity, would be a threat to the absolute authority which Dame Isabel exercised over the other inmates by right of being young and active and in full possession of all her senses and all her wits. She was also a woman of good family and had brought a little money with her. The decayed house was not quite so near the brink of starvation as it had been when Sir Godfrey visited it.

'You are rejecting me?'

'Not I. Circumstances.'

Since Henry had proved so unsympathetic to her plan, she had confided in David, telling him that she could doubtless arrange to take him since Clevely sounded the kind of place where a handy man would be welcome and useful. He'd looked glum, but made no protest. She had hastened to explain that it would make little difference to him; he would not be bound by the convent's rules, he would simply be doing much the same work in a different place.

He was cleaning out the stable when she arrived home and limped forward to take the mule. He still looked glum, but there was a question in his glance. She could not bring herself to tell him that she had been rejected; nor, in her present mood, could she tell a downright lie. So she said, 'My plans are somewhat changed.'

On the way home she had thought of Lamarsh, and might have ridden there, but it lay in the other direction and the days were short now. Tomorrow!

She had also thought that perhaps in the very rejection God had given fresh evidence of His will, and power. The poverty of the place had not dismayed her, but she had not cared for Dame Isabel. Something in her manner, her voice, her glance. And a good nun must consider herself utterly subject to her superiors.

The glum look vanished from the man's face and was replaced by an expression not easy to name.

'There're other ways of serving God, madam,' he said across the mule's neck.

'I wish I knew one,' she said rather bitterly, for on the last stage of her journey it had occurred to her that at Lamarsh – or any other religious house – there might be a Dame Isabel, or even worse. In fact the impulse was already weakening, as two such different people as Henry Tallboys and Dame Isabel had foreseen.

'I could tell you one,' David said, half shy, half eager.

'It is too cold to stand and talk here,' she said. 'When you are finished here, come into the hall.'

It was a cold day, and ordinarily, on such a day, after such a ride she would have taken a glass of mulled wine; but since her miraculous rescue she had abjured such luxuries, had even eaten sparingly, denying herself, preparing herself for further privations.

Now she was tempted, but she resisted the temptation, for although her nature was not all of one piece, soft volatile layers as it were alternating with more solid ones, on the whole she did not lack determination.

Warming herself by the fire, she was still determined to leave Intake, partly because of what had happened – though she had forgiven the people concerned; and partly because *now*, she was uncomfortable in Henry's presence. Those deliberately planned attempts at enticement she now saw for what they were, shaming and shabby. Thank God he had been so blind!

173

David came in, washed and changed into the clothes he wore when waiting at table. From the time when he had first begun the outdoor work which had restored his manhood and his self-esteem, he had been meticulous about not bringing the odours of stable, byre and sty into this part of the house. Master Tallboys was not so particular; he'd wash his hands and if his boots were very muddied or muckied, drop them at the kitchen door. For other fripperies he had no time – which was understandable.

Aware of his lameness, Mistress Captoft said, 'Sit down, David. I don't know what you have to say, but I warn you. Little acts of charity, bread and broth for beggars and washing pilgrims' feet – that was not what I had in mind.'

'Nor I, madam. What I had in mind was a great enterprise.'

'Oh,' she said. 'What?'

'Something new. So far as I know nobody ever gave a thought to poor sea-faring men. And I don't mean cripples like me. I mean . . .' he began humbly, diffidently, fumbling for words, but he warmed to his subject and began to speak with passionate emphasis.

'Say a ship out of Lowestoft or Yarmouth or any other place further north, is forced to put in at Bywater, and glad to be. Maybe a short time – just a wait on the weather, or a long – while she's being tacked together again. There's no pay till they're back in the home port. There's only pay when she puts in where she started from. Waiting men are in poor case. Take the others, out from Bywater, back in Bywater and paid off. Where do *they* go meantime? Oh, I know the inn sign, Welcome To Mariners, but the ordinary chap ain't welcome there. So it's the Lanes, low down ale houses and bad houses for him! In my time I've seen some good men ruined that way. And there's some like me, not so crippled and not so lucky. As I was, thanks to you, madam. Ones with smaller injuries, or sick; chucked out to live or die. Beggars get broth, pilgrims get their feet washed, but I never knew anything done for the poor ordinary sailor.'

'Nor did I. Though I lived for a time in Dunwich.' She brooded. Dunwich seemed a long way, and a lifetime, away.

'Sometimes,' David said, 'there's a prize money. And I always thought that if I was lucky *that* way, I'd get hold of a house somehow and throw it open to all. I mean sailors. But I never had a stroke of luck till that day I fell in with you, madam. So I never could, But *you* could. And it wouldn't be all out-go. There's them that could pay, and glad to, for a decent meal and a clean bed. And I'd work like a galley slave.'

The seed fell upon fertile ground, rooted, sprouted, grew tall and branched out, like the grain of mustard seed in the parable. Far, far more useful, she thought, than immuring herself in a convent where her gift for management would be lost, subject to somebody else's managing will, and her money absorbed into some general fund over which she would have no control at all.

'It is worth thinking about,' she said. David knew the tone of dismissal, got up and went away and Mistress Captoft went straight to the cupboard and poured herself a glass of wine. And very heartening, after four days' self-imposed abstinence.

Sipping the wine with relish, she thought of the other rules which she could now relax. She could wear her gay dresses, her trinkets, her becoming head-dresses. And *still* be doing God's work by providing a service to mankind, a thing no-one else had ever thought of. Behind it all she could see clearly the hand of God at work. That drastic purge which inspired such gratitude in Old Hodgson; the terrible experience which had brought her to her senses and made her anxious to serve God in a positive way; her rejection at Clevely, and now the moment of true illumination brought about by a serving man whom she had saved from starvation. It all wove together, making a neat and pleasing pattern.

And think of the gratitude those poor men would feel. Consider David, so grateful that he had been willing to go with her to Clevely, little as the idea had appealed to him. Her volatile, impulsive mind looked into the future and she saw herself, busy, managing, competent, imposing a firm but gentle rule on dozens of men, all like David, all deeply grateful, all calling her Madam. And, as she had once thought of Amsterdam, she now thought of Bywater and tasted in anticipation the joy of living in a town again; of being able to look out of a window and see something going on; of being able to shop every day. She thought of the house she would need, a big house, in one of the larger streets, or better still on the quay itself. She had no doubt, in her secret heart, that it was there, just waiting for her.

Henry had also taken a ride that morning, and as he expected, sitting in the saddle was extremely painful. Fortunately he had only to go to Muchanger, where a man named Walker had much the same name for breeding dogs as Tom Thoroughgood had for horses.

Ordinary dogs were, of course, obtainable anywhere, especially in the market – but there you might get a stolen dog, a stray dog, a dog spoiled by pampering, or by ill-useage. Henry wanted a properly trained guard dog, for what Mistress Captoft had said about sly retaliation by the maiming of animals, had been sound good sense. The Walker guard dogs were well-known, a careful cross, stabilised over the years, between hunting hound and mastiff, with the virtues of both breeds. It was said that Dick Walker was so knowledgeable that one glance at a litter of puppies could tell him which were worth rearing and which not, and his training was so painstaking and patient that by the time he had finished with it any dog of his could tell friend from foe, and both from neutral, simply by scent.

'You caught me at a bad moment, Master Tallboys,' Walker said, when Henry had given his name and stated his errand. 'I got puppies of course, useless at the moment, and one, nearly a year old ... Should be just right, but I ain't sure whether I oughta sell him. He's *slow*. Not on his feet, I don't mean. Slow to learn. I allus reckon about eight months. But this 'un fared a bit slow. I don't really know why I bothered with him except that he's a handsome dog and got the makings – given time.'

'May I see him?'

The dog produced was handsome; physically the perfect cross between the litheness of the hunting hound and the solidity of the mastiff; coat neither rough nor smooth, just ruffled and brindled in colour, grey, dark and almost russet hairs blending happily. Eyes of clear amber which took on a greenish hue at the sight of Henry, the stranger.

' 'S'all right. *Friend*,' Walker said. 'Well, if you like, sir, I'll show you how far he's got, then you can decide for yourself.'

He began to remove his own sheepskin jacket, thought better of it. 'No, that wouldn't be a fair test. He know my scent. If you'd put yours down, just there. Now we'll see ... You! Guard.' The dog obeyed, sniffing the coat cautiously and then standing by it.

'Now,' Walker said, 'try to take it.' Henry attempted to do so and was confronted by a mask of sheer hatred; eyes green as grass, muzzle wrinkled back showing sharp fangs.

Walker said in the rather worn voice of one who has said the same things many times, and must say it again, ' 'S'all right. Give over!' The dog again obeyed and Henry retrieved and thankfully donned his coat. The wind was even colder today.

'I reckon,' Walker said, 'I was right about him, after all. He got the makings. You want him? Mind no pampering. And best that *one* person do the feeding. Then show him what you want guarded; beat your bounds as they say and I reckon he'll do. I'll get a collar for him.' He always sent his dogs out into the world equipped with collars; for dog often fought with dog and they always went for the throat. He produced a band of leather, three inches wide and set all over with sharp steel spikes. Naturally there was a charge for collars too. And for the bit of rope to be attached to the ring of the collar in order to lead the dog home. All in all, Henry reflected he had been a bit extravagant.

Godfrey was waiting in the yard.

'For me, Father?' The perfect reward for having been brave, even when his nose was pulled back into shape and the loose tooth tweaked away.

Dismounting painfully, Henry said, 'Yes. If you feed him. But remember, he's not a pet. He's a guard dog.'

'I'll call him Guard,' Godfrey said. The attraction between the boy and the young dog was mutual, immediate, irrevocable.

Mistress Captoft did not really approve of dogs in the house. Her husband had had six, all of careless habits, but about Guard she was lenient. No concern of hers, after all, she would soon be gone. And Henry, seeing that the purpose of that painful ride was about to be defeated, was lenient, too. Poor little boy, no brothers or sisters, no friends; his mother dead, Joanna, of whom he had been fond, gone away, and Mistress Captoft about to go. Only Father would be left and Father was a busy man. So, if the boy wanted to share his supper with the dog – giving him, Henry noticed – all the choicest pieces, did it matter so much?

'I have changed my plans, Master Tallboys,' Mistress Captoft said. Once again she could not bring herself to say that she had been rejected at Clevely. Instead she spoke, enthusiastically about what she intended to do.

'So tomorrow,' she said, 'I must go down to Bywater and find a house.' Then, suddenly she clapped her plump white hand, now with all the rings back in place, to her mouth.

'Dear me,' she said, 'what with this and that, I *forgot*. While you were away, Master Tallboys, a messenger from the Bishop arrived. His Grace wishes to consult with you and hopes you will go to see him as soon as is possible and convenient. I gathered that the matter is urgent.'

Another and a longer ride tomorrow, Henry thought, pain stabbing at the thought, though he sat comfortable now, a cushion under him. Well, it must be faced. And he should be better tomorrow. The fight had taken place on Thursday; tomorrow would be Tuesday. All his other hurts were practically forgotten, even the deep split in his eyebrow healing fast. Only the invisible wound ached on. It was not better on Tuesday and he was quite glad that riding to Bywater in Mistress Captoft's company, he was obliged to match the pace of his horse to that of her mule.

In the yard of the inn, with its deceptive name, Henry said, 'I hope you find a house to suit you, Mistress Captoft.'

'I am sure I shall,' she said, and went off, as confident and light-footed as a girl keeping tryst with a sweetheart. Moving less easily, Henry went up the slight incline towards the building which was beginning to justify the name of palace.

The Bishop liked Henry; an honest man if ever there was one; a man with dignity, too.

'It was good of you to come so soon,' he said. 'You have had an accident?'

'Oh, this?' Henry said, touching the half-healed wound over his eye. 'A mere nothing, Your Grace.'

'I only hope that the matter upon which we must consult is a mere nothing too.'

'It concerns the girl? Joanna?'

'Yes. I thought it unnecessary to trouble you when Lady Grey first wrote to me. From the first a *suitable* marriage was the objective, was it not? And when I heard what Lady Grey had achieved, I thought she had done admirably – for a demoiselle of only moderate fortune and no family. A chance in a thousand. Or so I thought. I wrote to congratulate Lady Grey upon her good management; and Lord Shefton upon his good fortune. Now,' His Grace's voice became acidulous, 'I receive *this*!' He tapped his long, oval, cleric's nails on the last communication, a slightly frantic one, which Lady Grey had sent him.

'Give me the gist of it, my Lord.'

It was difficult, in Henry Tallboys' presence, to remember that he fell, as the saying was, between two stools. He was completely illiterate, like a peasant; yet he had the manner and speech of a nobleman, or a knight – and there were many of them still – who, illiterate themselves, always had a clerk at their heels.

'The gist of it is that the girl refuses, pleading a previous betrothal. If true, a valid plea. But I knew nothing of it. Did you?'

Henry thought of that makeshift, haphazard, unwitnessed promise, made over the kitchen table.

'Lord Shefton, you say? Is he known to you, my Lord?'

Claiming rather more than he should – for the truth was that Lord Shefton had no friends; he had sycophants, political and business associates, a vast circle of acquaintances, but no friend, His Grace said, 'Yes, Master Tallboys; Lord Shefton is a friend of mine. Indeed it was through him that I secured a place for the girl in Sir Barnabas Grey's household . . .'

And now, if what she says is true, made a fool of myself.

Henry sat, looking stolid while his mind spun. It was exactly what he had always wanted for Joanna; another, more comfortable way of life, and a suitable marriage. She'd been gone for two years. She must, by this time have outgrown that silly, childish infatuation for him . . . Living in a wider world, she must realise that a few hasty words across a kitchen table did not constitute a betrothal and if she had fallen back upon it as an excuse for avoiding marriage to another man, it must have been in desperation.

'Be so good, my Lord, as to tell me something of this Lord ... Shefton.'

Quite unconsciously, Henry, who had come here to be questioned, had taken control. He had, from both his parents, inherited a dominant streak. Most of Sir Godfrey's friends in the past had thought him feckless, improvident, practically simple-minded, but when he spoke they had listened: Sybilla's friends had pitied her, poor, for years without a roof of her own, and four children; not a penny to spend; but when she gave an old head-dress a new twist or altered an old gown, others had instantly, anxiously copied.

'He is immensely rich,' the Bishop said. He elaborated on that. 'Extremely powerful too. He has the King's ear – or rather the ear of those to whom the King gives heed. And as regards this marriage – that is when it was promulgated – generous beyond belief.'

'Of what age?' Henry asked, brushing wealth, power and generosity aside.

'Not young,' the Bishop said.

'That tells me nothing. How old?'

The irritation which His Grace had felt ever since he had read Lady Grey's letter – which made such mockery of the two he had written – rose to the surface.

'Really, Master Tallboys! One cannot go about among friends, looking at teeth, as with horses!'

'I know,' Henry said. 'But with friends you can gauge within a year or two, surely. Is he about your age? Older? Younger?'

His Grace could have chosen any answer since Master Tallboys and Lord Shefton were unlikely ever to meet, but there was something about the directness of the question and the straight blue stare, and about his own feeling of suppressed irritation that made him tell the truth.

'Older,' he said shortly.

'By how much?'

'Really, Master Tallboys,' His Grace said again. 'How could I know? Five years, possibly six.'

'I see.'

To Henry the Bishop had always seemed old, and now, looking across the table, seeing the jowls under the jaw, the folds below the eyes, the brown blotches on the plump hands, the paunch, he thought: Add five years to *that* and it's easy to see why the poor child was desperate; they must all be out of their minds!

In fact the Bishop had aged in a way which only he knew about, in the last couple of years; it was no longer hard to be celibate, it was difficult, impossible, to be anything else. Joanna had been the last female to rouse the least response in him; and his fulsome letter to Lord Shefton, dictated by self-interest, had been written with a feeling of envy, and some cynicism; what the fellow was getting was something pretty to look at and something to warm his old bones in bed. No more. His letter to Lady Grey had been far more sincere. To have extracted such terms from a man with a reputation for miserliness was indeed an achievement.

'We seem to have wandered from the point,' he said, taking charge of the interview again. 'I asked you if you had knowledge of a previous betrothal?'

Henry seldom acted on impulse; most of his behaviour was governed by good sense, or, as when he took Moyidan Richard, and later John and Young Shep into his home, by a recognition of responsibility. He felt responsible now. He must save Joanna, and could see only one way of doing it.

'Yes. I knew of it.'

Colour that almost matched that of the ruby on his finger began at His Grace's jowls and ran upwards.

'And you did not see fit to inform me? By such deception, Master Tallboys, you have placed Lord Shefton, Lady Grey and myself in a ludicrous situation. When I was exerting myself to find a home for the girl, an attempt to find her a suitable husband was part of the bargain; Lord Shefton's proposal was made in good faith and Lady Grey had done her utmost to arrange a marriage settlement of exceptional generosity. Now this!' In anger he rose and began to walk up and down behind the table, the silk of his gown rustling. 'Why the secrecy? Tell me that.'

Henry, trained by Sybilla – one did not sit while one's elders or superiors stood, rose too – with the now familiar twinge.

'She was so young at the time,' he said. 'Too young to know her own mind. Ignorant, too. I thought it likely that she might change.'

'Which she has not.'

'So it seems.'

His Grace saw a glimmer of a possibility of doing Lord Shefton a singular service. He dropped back into his chair and Henry re-seated himself.

'A betrothal, as you know, is a solemn ceremony. But it may be annulled – by mutual consent. The girl may be unaware of this; but if the man concerned would withdraw, it is possible that she could be persuaded to do so. As you say, she was, still is, very young. Then this most desirable marriage could be brought about.'

Desirable? A man nearing seventy at least. And how would she feel, poor child, having made that last, desperate stand, only to be deserted and betrayed.

'He will not withdraw, my Lord.'

'How can you be so certain? A little money often works wonders. And money would be available. As I say, Lord Shefton is very rich.'

'He's not a man to be bought,' Henry said.

'How do you know? Most men have their price. Who is he?'

'Myself, my Lord.' There; now I am definitely committed.

His Grace of Bywater sat silent for a moment, fighting his rage. In the Bible there was a very cogent question: *Doest thou well to be angry?* The answer was: No! *You did ill to be angry,* especially as age crept on. And quite apart from the physical risk which men past their prime ran by indulging in anger, there was the fact that rage made one splutter, choose the wrong words. Choosing his very carefully and speaking in the cold, distant way in which he would have rebuked a clerk who had made an error, he said, 'I perceive that I was mistaken in thinking you different from your brother, that rogue and thief whom I most misguidely protected. Deceit and deviousness are plainly characteristic of the Tallboys family.'

Henry stood up – that twinge again, and said, with more edge to his voice than even the experienced, sophisticated man on the other side of the table could produce, 'I cannot

182

sit here and listen to insults levelled at my family. Richard was plainly in the wrong. But your protection of him was well-rewarded, I think. You now have Moyidan, have you not? As for my deceit. What was it except that I kept silent over a betrothal I thought premature? All right, I said a *suitable* marriage. That was what I wanted for her. And had one been proposed – and she agreeable, I should have welcomed it, and withdrawn, wishing her happiness ...' He could have said much more, challenging the Bishop to go to Baildon, or anywhere else where the name of Henry Tallboys was known and ask if on a single occasion, he had ever acted deceitfully or deviously. But he knew that if he stopped to say this, he would be dismissed, ordered out of the place which had once been one of his childhood's homes.

'I have answered Your Grace's questions, and ask leave to withdraw,' Henry said, and bowed – that hurt too, and made for the door leaving His Grace more annoyed than ever. He controlled himself and sat brooding. He must, of course, write to Lady Grey and say that the girl was right and that nothing could be done. But he must also think of a way in which to get even with that insolent, arrogant, homespun-clad fellow who had flung Moyidan into his teeth. He rang his bell sharply and of the clerk who came, hasty and willing, demanded that every paper and parchment concerning Moyidan and Intake should be brought to him immediately. What had once been a single, rather faded document, a deed of gift – with conditions – granted to a few serfs – giving them leave to go and hack themselves holdings out of the forest, and to call themselves freemen, had now, over the years gathered accretions as a ship's bottom gathered barnacles. All in order. Even the one thing which His Grace had hoped not to find. For as Henry withdrew, the Bishop had thought of the venery laws – who might or might not shoot a deer in Layer Wood. It should have been possible to catch Henry Tallboys there. But it was not; for written sideways along the margin of the oldest parchment, was an addition. Henry's Uncle James had been a meticulous man, and he had made a note of the fact that he had granted his brother – Sir Godfrey – his heirs and assignees, permission to take a certain number of animals, at the right season. Even in his wrath the Bishop realised that it would be unwise to question that clause now when ostensibly Moyidan was being held in trust for the young heir, and he was merely a custodian.

Later, when his rage had subsided a little he puzzled over Henry's motive for behaving as he had done. It certainly was not money, for he had had the girl's person, and her fortune completely in his own control. To enter into a betrothal, then send the girl with the better half of her dowry away, never mentioning the betothal, practically *inviting* other marriage offers ... turn it which way you would, it made no sense at all. In the end His Grace found himself forced to accept the man's own explanation; he was betrothed to the girl, but felt it to be premature, had sent her away so that she might learn more of the world, meet other people, and would have been prepared to withdraw, to release her should occasion arise. In fact, Henry Tallboys of Knight's Acre was what the Bishop had, until today, judged him to be; a man of exceptional integrity. The honest man whom he had accused of deceit and deviousness! Regretting the words now, but almost immediately justifying himself; chagrin speaking, the flash of anger provoked by the thought of those congratulatory letters, His Grace of Bywater, who was far from stupid, reflected that honest people were so rare that there were no well-tried rules for dealing with them.

Perversely, now that he had regained calm, it pleased him to think of the dignity with which the honest man had taken leave. Neither hurt nor humbled.

Henry was neither hurt nor humbled. Plain, downright, damned angry. He'd stipulated a *suitable* marriage and the fools had tried to rig up a match between a girl who wouldn't be fourteen until June of next year and some old man doddering on the verge of the grave. Disgusting! Disgusting too that suggestion that another man could have been bought off; that every man had his price. It simply was not true. He thought of Walter. Of his own father whose story had to be patched together since he was a man so unhandy with words; but Henry knew that his father, offered riches and honours as a reward for betraying his own kind, had chosen slavery instead. For the first time in his life, Henry felt a

184

fleeting wish that he could have known his father better, admired him more, been less critical. Too late now.

Mistress Captoft did not observe that Master Tallboys was even more silent than usual on the ride home. She was so happy, ebullient, and talkative. She did not even bother to ask him what his errand had been or what had been urgent about it.

'I found *exactly* what I wanted. It was there, waiting for me, as I knew it would be. A big house, and old, at the upper end of the harbour.'

Pulling himself out of his brooding, he said, 'The Knights' House? A vaulted hall, like a church?'

'The very one. How did you know?'

'I went there, once or twice with my father. Long ago when I was young and the war was at its height. Invasion from France was expected and knights were stationed there. My father was in command.'

He hadn't given the place a thought for many years, but he remembered it vividly now. The atmosphere, men young and not so young, all, Sir Godfrey included, merry. Eat, drink and be merry for tomorrow you die. Shining suits of armour, swords, lances ready against the wall. Vast amounts of food and wine on the table and no sparing of candles. Perhaps even then his father, taking him there had hoped to woo him into knighthood, away from the farm. And if he had been thus cajoled, joined that boisterous, glittering company, where would he be now?

Dead. And Knight's Acre gone to ruin; fallow for a year with grass and pretty little flowers, sappy, expendable; and then, longer neglected, developing the tougher growths, going back to the wild.

'Yes,' Mistress Captoft said. 'It still has that name. The Knights' House. So similar to Knight's Acre that I was immediately aware of the significance and of the several vacant places on offer, decided to see it first. Of course I was *guided*.' She smiled happily and then ran on. 'Of course it is in a state of sad disrepair, but the fabric is sound enough. Nothing wrong which a little money and labour cannot restore.'

It was in fact a stone building, built – though nobody now

remembered this – to house a new Order of nuns who had come to England just after the Conquest. The Order had been short-lived and the design of the building had made it unsuitable as a family dwelling; the huge hall, intended for refectory and living place, the one sizeable parlour, briefly occupied by the Abbess, the many small rooms which that particular Order preferred to the communal dorter. During most of its long lifetime it had been used for non-domestic purposes, fish-curing, wool-storage, flax-retting, the making and mending of sails.

'It could have been built for my purpose,' Mistress Captoft said, 'and I have hired it on very favourable terms. The owner is an old man and said he favoured short tenancies. I could see why, with each change of tenant he can raise the rent. A short lease would not have suited me at all; I should just have got things ship-shape. So I offered him five years' rent in advance – with an option of buying at the end of that period.'

She did not feel it necessary to add that she had callously reminded the old man that at his age money in the hand was better than expectations in the future, and that the final disposition of the property was, to put it mildly, unlikely to concern him very much. She had done so however, and that reminder of mortality, added to the unfamiliar business of dealing with a woman, a woman who used words like *tenure*, had unmanned him.

'Finding the house took no time at all; but I thought it wise to go along to a lawyer. Then I had to find a carpenter, and a plasterer. That is why I am a trifle late. I should like to open the doors on Christmas Eve. It would be apt, would it not?' More than apt, she thought happily; the anniversary of the day when at Bethlehem there was no room at the inn.

'Most apt,' Henry said, politely breaking away from his own preoccupation. 'And I hope that everything concerning the house will go as easily as the finding of it.'

Not a word about missing her. He was one of the ungrateful.

'I shall leave you in good hands, Master Tallboys. I shall take David with me, and leave Katharine with you. She was an able cook when I found her and now she is trained to my ways. She will keep you comfortable.'

The decision to leave Katharine at Knight's Acre had been taken, as usual on impulse, but for two excellent reasons. It would have worried Mistress Captoft to ride away and leave a man and a boy with no woman to care for them; the other reason was more worldly. Men straight from the sea or from destitution were hungry for other things besides food, and Katharine though no longer in the full flush of youth had a certain comeliness which might lead to trouble. Most sailors could turn their hands to practically anything, as David had proved, and some cooking was done aboard ship. Mistress Captoft did not doubt that she would find two men, like David, slightly disabled, capable of manning the huge kitchen which had two hearths and one oven. They, she had decided, would be permanent, so that they could learn her ways. Fully able-bodied men could stay only for a limited time, dependent upon circumstances; that was a thing which she must discuss with David – as also she must discuss the name the house would bear. Knights' House was completely wrong.

The idea that she herself, one female amongst many men, might constitute a disruptive element in the happy family that she had planned never once occurred to her; she would walk among them, benefactress, nurse, hostess, Madam. Invisibly armoured.

The news that she was to be left behind dealt Katharine Dowley a shattering blow; for nothing but gratitude to Mistress Captoft, and dread of being thrown out into the world again, had kept her in this – to her – sinister house.

At first, being basically a woman of good sense, she had tried to explain herself to herself by saying that it was the *quiet*. She had gone from the Lanes – six to a room – to the inn, again six or seven to a room, an attic with a rough canvas screen between men and maids. As cook, eventually she had been given a little room of her own, but not isolated; seven steps up the other servants, six down the guests. Never before had she known silence, or that it could in itself be menacing.

She was often alone in the house and at such times the feeling became so acute that she'd drop what she was doing and run out into the yard, with some made-up excuse to talk to David, and if possible get him to come back inside with her; she wanted him to taste something, or help her to lift something. She hated being in the hall alone; she dreaded the stairs. She went to enormous pains to time her comings and goings so as to be within the range of another human being. Her bedtime was never of her own choosing.

Mistress Captoft, always considerate, would sometimes say 'It's a beautiful day, Katharine. You should take the air. Go for a walk in the woods; the bluebells are in flower.' After just one such walk Katharine never ventured into the woods again – if anything they were worse than the house. Quiet and dim, and full of nameless threat. After that she never went further than the garden, where some job could always be found, or made, and even there she was aware of the wood, as though some hidden watcher had an eye on her. Not a friendly eye.

So when talk began about the move to Bywater, Katharine was filled with joy: and correspondingly downcast when she learned that the move was not to include her. She wept and implored. She had never mentioned her fears to anyone, they would have sounded so ridiculous, put into words, so Mistress Captoft interpreted the tears, the near-hysteria, as devotion to herself.

'I cannot possibly take you with me. What would Master Tallboys do?'

'He could get another woman.'

'Doubtless he could. But not one trained by me, capable of running this house so smoothly that I shall hardly be missed.'

Missed! Katharine thought of the days, no David clattering about in the dairy, or whistling in the yard, sitting by the dying fire in the evening. Joseph, the shepherd, came to eat his dinner and then went away; Jem left at sunset; earlier on market days. Imagine a market day with Master Tallboys and the boy just a little late, dusk falling and she alone here with whatever it was that watched and waited, still watching, still waiting, ready to close in. She'd be alone with the dog and although a big fierce dog should be a comfort to a woman alone, a Guard had proved otherwise to her. She did not doubt that he would tackle a robber, or a wolf, but with fear-sharpened sensibility, Katharine had seen that he, dumb, four-legged beast that he was, *knew*. In the hall, on the stairs, and at one place in the yard, down went his tail, up went his hackles.

'I implore you, Mistress. Take me with you.'

The chastisement of servants was common practice but Mistress Captoft, even in her husband's house, had never agreed with it. A man or a woman who must be struck in order to be made to work, or to behave properly, was not worth employing. So now the hand she laid upon Katharine's shoulder was kindly though, because impatient, gripping.

'Stop it,' she said. 'Bywater is not the end of the earth! When I have things in order there – and the days lengthen – I will come to see you. To see how well you are managing. And perhaps Master Tallboys, when he has business in Bywater, will ride you down, so that you can see me. We are not parting for ever.'

This well-meant but mistaken remark merely produced more sobs, more hiccuping pleas.

'If you can't do with me in your new place, Mistress, just let me come along with you and stay, till I find another job.'

Exasperated, Mistress Captoft gave Katharine a little shake.

'Be sensible, woman! Who would employ you? Without a good word. The landlady at the inn would not give it. And how could I? If you leave, without reason, an easy place; a comfortable home and an undemanding master. Mop your eyes and nose and let's get to work. There is the mincemeat to make. What with this and that, I am so busy as to be almost distraught.'

No sympathy, no understanding.

Glorying in her busyness which so far from driving her distraught, was a stimulant, Mistress Captoft jogged down to Bywater, harassed the workmen, complained and wrung her hands over the delays. Sometimes she lodged at the inn – for days were short now. There was a time when one step forward looked like two steps backward; boards which looked sound proving rotten as pears, old leprous looking plaster which broke away as soon as new was applied. The well in the courtyard behind the house took two men a day and a half to clear of the rubbish which various transient tenants had flung into it, and another two days for the sullied water to be wound out. She had furniture to buy. All but the sick, she decided, must lie on straw-stuffed mattresses on the floor; the sick must lie higher to save stooping when they were being attended. For them beds were needed. She must have a long solid table and some benches for the big room; she must have mugs and platters and cooking pots, and blankets, and stores of such things which – experienced housewife as she was – she knew might be obtainable now, just before Christmas and then, later in dead winter, either not for sale at all or costly beyond belief.

She had money. Throughout her widowhood her income had exceeded what she spent. She could have gone to Amsterdam and set up house at a moment's notice. This was a more expensive enterprise – but rents were due to her at Christmas.

Presently it was evident to her sensible eye that, despite harassment and lavish expenditure, the old house would not be fit for occupation before Christmas. The next date worth noticing was Twelfth Night. The eve of the Epiphany. Again an apt date, for it marked the end of another journey – that of the Three Wise men from the east, with their gifts of gold, frankincense and myrrh.

'Your room and mine, David, should be ready before then,' Mistress Captoft said. 'And by that time we should have found a name.'

They had decided against *Hostel* – a bit on the religious side; *refuge* smacked of charity; *Infirmary* sounded as though only the sick were welcome; and *Home* indicated a permanence impossible to provide.

'I have thought about it, Madam. *Sailors' Rest.* If you like it I could do a bit of a board to hang over the door, for the sake of them, like me, who can't read. Not that it'll be needed. The word'll spread like wildfire.'

'If we are to open by Twelfth Night, David, you and I must move in well before. There is still work to be done and men must be harried – or bribed, to lift a finger over Christmas.'

Twelve Days of riotous idleness celebrated a winter festival which was far older than Christmas and which was still observed by those who lived in great houses, and by those who lived close to the land. The winter ploughing completed, the pig killed, there was little to do in that dead season. In towns and among people who worked for wages, the custom was dying out, but a pretence was kept up and any man who did so much as drive in a nail between midday on Christmas Eve and Twelfth Night was conferring a favour which must be returned in the form of extra wages, or a gift.

Mistress Captoft began to pack again, watched by Katharine's gloomy, increasingly wild eye. David painted his gay and eloquent sign-board.

Stordford was one of the great houses where Christmas was kept in traditional fashion. The holly, the ivy and the mistletoe brought in and hung on the walls. The Yule Log, a great tree-trunk, dragged to the hearth, there to be kindled from a piece carefully saved from last year's; it would smoulder throughout the night, be prodded and encouraged by the application of thinner, more easily combustible wood into a blaze. It would last through the Twelve Days and would leave a charred fragment from which next year's Yule Log would be kindled. At Stordford everything was ready, even to the boar's head, stripped down, cooked, reconstructed, with burnt sugar whiskers, blanched almonds for teeth and preserved cherries for eyes. But although Lady Grey's preparations were as thorough as usual, her mood was far from festive; she had Lord Shefton to face, with only the feeble excuse that she had known nothing, that she and her husband had been grossly deceived.

Immediately upon the receipt of the Bishop's letter, confirming the truth of Joanna's story, she had proposed sending the wretched girl away, but Sir Barnabas said that would not be honourable; they had engaged themselves to keep her until she was fifteen, or married, and although the girl had been secretive and the Bishop negligent, they must stick to the word of their bond. On any matter concerning codes of behaviour she deferred to him. She then visualised the horrible embarrassment of breaking the news to Lord Shefton when he arrived, with the marriage contract and the ring. He must be forewarned. 'I shall write at once,' she said;

adding hopefully, 'It may be that in the circumstances, his Lordship may wish to cancel his visit altogether.'

'My dear, that would be unwise. There is no need to ruin Christmas.' He named two of his other guests – both valued business associates – who were very anxious to meet Lord Shefton.

'But imagine how he will feel! The very sight of the wretched girl makes me sick.'

'He should have a stronger stomach, at his age,' Sir Barnabas said, easy-going, as always. She knew for a certainty that she would have the distasteful task of breaking the news, and facing the first brunt of his Lordship's displeasure. Once that was spent, Barnabas would appear, probably with a joke: Well, who can now say that no female can keep a secret? That kind of thing.

At Intake the hostility towards Father Matthew continued. He could understand the withdrawal of hospitality: the loss of their pigs, the necessity to buy fresh stock, had hit them hard. But a seat by the fire cost nothing, nor did civility. He still made visits, but he was never invited into any house and nobody showed a disposition to chat with him. Possibly they blamed him for encouraging the idea that Mistress Captoft was a witch – and he still believed that he had been right. Nobody had told him that she had been saved by a rope, so he regarded her survival as supernatural. Innocent women drowned, witches swam. Certainly they blamed him for not being present; perhaps they thought that merely by being there he could have frustrated the Devil.

Maybe they were resentful because his pig was alive and well.

Some of them had already replaced their stock, at fearful cost, winter prices, pre-Christmas prices. (Some nights and days of iron frost had killed the disease, though nobody knew that.) Father Matthew knew that there were pigs in the styes again – he could hear them, but even when he tried to take a friendly interest in new pigs, he was rebuffed. Never once asked to come and look them over.

The witch-swimming had had two indirect results. Young Hodgson was still lame and Bert Edgar's jaw had – and always would have – a lump about the size of a pigeon's egg. Did they blame him for these things?

Attendance at Mass, once so much improved, dwindled, was reduced on one Sunday morning to Master Tallboys, his son, his shepherd and the old woman called Ethel.

And then, suddenly everything changed. Led by Ethel, getting lame, poor old woman, almost the whole of the village came trooping in.

It was understandable, the priest thought as he went through the ritual, that a woman, weakened by age – and possibly some privation, for in hard times the old and the young were the first to suffer – should need a stick to lean upon. But need she strike the floor with it from time to time?

Ethel had said, 'You all listen. Every time he say a word different, I'll bang with my stick and you count.'

Quiet and stealthy as bloodhounds they were now on *his* trail. On the way home there was a bit of an argument about numbers. Six times? No, five. You went to sleep and missed one. How could I go to sleep standing up. I ain't a horse! Old Hodgson, that recognised good hand with a tally stick, said seven. And with that, in itself a magic number, most people were inclined to agree. Seven times Father Matthew had said words wrongly. All their suspicions were confirmed.

They had no intention of swimming him. No story, however-far-back-reaching, told of a man being swum as a test. It only applied to women. The test they intended to apply was very old.

And no need in this case to send two men. One little girl would do.

The little girl – the first of Bert Edgar's unwanted daughters, knocked on the door of the priest's house – once so stoutly guarded by Mistress Captoft – and said to the ugly boy who opened it, 'Father's wanted. Down in the village.'

She had been told what to say and she had learned to be obedient.

It was another bitterly cold evening. Streaks of red sunset, no warmth in it, merely the promise of frost again – were just visible beyond the stark black trees.

193

'Who is it?' Father Matthew asked, already reaching for his cloak. It was good and warm, lined with coney fur.

'I don't know. I was sent to say, Father's wanted.'

'Somebody took ill?' he asked, thinking about the stole, emblem of unworldly authority, and of the Host to be brought from the church.

'I don't know,' the little girl said again. 'I was sent to say Father's wanted. And I said it, didn't I?'

He thought it as well to be prepared.

Old Father Ambrose had carried all that was necessary for the administration of the last rites in an ancient, broken down basket; Father Benedict, on those errands from which even Mattie's vigilance and doses had not protected him, had gone out armed with a stout leather satchel. Father Matthew had a container even more suitable, a bag, beautifully embroidered. For before he was appointed to the living at Intake he had held subservient offices and some kindly women had felt sorry for him, so rustic, ill-provided, and temporary. One of them had given him his cloak, another had embroidered the bag.

Out in the cold, holding his bag in his left hand, Father Matthew lifted the right-hand side of his coak and enclosed the little girl in it.

'Walk close to me, child,' he said. She was clumsily wrapped against the biting wind, but he could feel the sharp bones of her shoulder.

'Where are you taking me?' he asked.

'To home,' she said, her voice very small. It was not a question to which I don't know would suffice as an answer, and yet in replying properly she felt she was disobeying her orders. Father Matthew was rather fond of children. So he asked her name, trying to overcome her shyness. Her name was Emma and she felt obliged to say it; asked how old she was she could rightly say I don't know.

Innocent decoy, she led the way into Bert Edgar's yard, and recognising it he thought. No wonder she is so thin! In a time of shortage, as this was, Bert Edgar was not the man to deny himself in order to see that his children were fed. It took little time to cross the yard, but Father Matthew had time to think that when he last saw Jill Edgar she was pregnant and might now have miscarried and be at death's door. All those poor little children, he thought.

His guide opened the door and said, with curious formality, 'He's here.' He stepped into the kitchen and found himself confronted, as Mistress Captoft had been, by the village Elders.

There were more candles than usual in a farmhouse kitchen. And a fire heaped high and bright enough to make the candles unnecessary. Seven men, stern-faced, at the table.

He knew, from the friendly days, about the Elders. How they had decided to buy a new bull; how they had decided to swim Mistress Captoft. He had never seen them in session before, had not even known who, exactly, composed this body of authority. Now he recognised them all; ordinary peasant farmers, so like his own father, brothers, cousins that he had instantly felt akin to them, and they, he thought, with him. Now something had happened to them—not unlike what happened to *him* when he officiated at the altar. It was something there was no word for. It was the thing, not of this world which had been conferred upon him at his ordination, the thing which Mistress Captoft had with one word, ill-chosen? Well-chosen? Yes, well, since the intention was to insult, insulted.

Old Hodgson was active again, and was the Eldest Elder. Sawyer, now so daft as not to know Christmas from Easter as the saying went, had been asked to stand down. No difficulty there; he had not even realised that he was being thrust aside.

The word for which Father Matthew fumbled, narrowing his eyes against the light so sudden and so brilliant, was *power*. These seven simple men were invested with it; not as he had been, when ordained, but power none the less. Seven men, of one mind, that mind governed by the most resolute character.

In this case Old Hodgson. In *his* opinion the priest had been largely to blame for the ordeal inflicted upon Mistress Captoft, and so deserved all that was about to happen to him. And more.

The charge – again delivered in that curiously legal and

formal way, startled and dismayed Father Matthew as much as a similar one had dismayed and startled Mistress Captoft. The Elders had held preliminary meetings and decided to use the word wizard. There had been some argument about what form of accusation should be brought against him regarding Mistress Captoft; should he be charged with working with her and saving her from her rightful fate, or with using an innocent woman as a cover for his own activities and thus almost bringing about her death? Old Hodgson was for leaving her out of it altogether. 'Surely there's enough agin him without dragging *that* in,' he said. But his was a lone voice. Old Gurth said, 'But she was saved, by a rope. Who chucked it if he didn't? And why should he chuck it if he weren't hand-in-glove with her?' It looked to Old Hodgson as though the trial of the priest – for which he was as eager as anyone – might lead to more trouble for Mistress Captoft. 'We got no proof that there was a rope. Only something the youngster said, or made up.' 'Then how did she get out?' 'Willow root,' Old Hodgson said. 'I seen 'em, so hev you, this side of the water. Long and thin and grey. Woman that'd been dowsed like she'd been wouldn't be in much state to judge. Got herself tangled in a willow root and took it for a rope.' Old Watson said, 'Well, if so. How did she get back to this side? Our Jem saw her, the very next day.' 'Same way the priest got over there in the first place. Flew through the air.' Old Hodgson saw that he must come to her rescue again. 'I dunno,' he said. 'If you remember I was laid aside just then. Had a bit of time to think. And I fare to remember, when I was tiddler, my father, or maybe it was my granfer, saying something about a place, upstream a bit, where there was stones in the water, stepping-stones, like. I recall my mother telling me not to go near 'em. And I never did.' If he must tell a lie it might as well be a good one.

There remained a difference of opinion. Out with the beans!

Each Elder came to the meetings armed with a few beans, some black, some white. With these, if an agreement could not be reached, votes were taken. The Eldest Elder carried, symbol of his office, a worn leather bag, into which each closed fist dropped a bean in such a way that secrecy was maintained. White meant yes, black meant no, and the matter upon the vote was taken had to be framed in such a way that yes or no could be the answer. Old Hodgson unwillingly produced the bag; it looked as though Mistress Captoft's innocence must be questioned, after all; unless he could twist the words about a bit.

'Now,' he said, 'we ain't met together to try Mistress Captoft a second time. It's him. So I'll put it to you this way – Did he fool her as well as us?' It was the best he could do.

They all wanted the case against the priest to be made as black as possible, so when the bag had gone round and come back to Old Hodgson and he tipped the beans on to the table, all seven were white.

He thought smugly; I not only make a good mommet. I got a way with words, too.

So now Father Matthew stood charged with being a wizard; with having overlooked one bull and forty-one pigs; with garbling church ritual; with harbouring a familiar; with trying to shield himself by accusing an innocent woman.

Like Mistress Captoft, he was given the chance to defend himself and he took it. He was particularly vehement about the boy, Tim.

'I had temporary charge of a parish. A backward place.' That should flatter these hard-eyed men, implying as it did that Intake was not backward. 'The poor boy was living like a stray dog. Hunted about by other boys. Jeered at, stoned. One day, he came to me for shelter and I discovered that he was not the idiot they had taken him for. I could understand what he said and he could understand me. I took him in and he has been my servant ever since.'

Talking of Tim brought back to his mind the time when the village was friendly, and Jem Watson, the first to see that evil picture, had remarked upon the resemblance between the strange animal and the boy.

'I never accused an innocent woman,' he said with some vehemence. 'You – or your neighbours did that. Poisonous brews, you said. And I agreed that she was an evil woman, that the picture was an evil picture.'

So far he had been dealing with them on their own level. But when he came to refute the charge that he garbled church ritual, he remembered that he was a priest, a member, however humble of the vast, powerful Church. A King, Henry II and St. Thomas of Canterbury had fought out a bitter battle about clerics being subject to secular law. St. Thomas, simply by being martyred, and becoming a saint, had won. So now Father Matthew could say, with confidence, 'If you have any complaint against me, you should take it to my Bishop.'

The wrong thing to say at Intake, that curious community, born of freed serfs, told by Henry Tallboys' great-great-grandfather to go and hack little fields – if they could out of the forest.

'We don't need outside interference, ' Old Hodgson said. 'We hev our way of doing things. And we decided to put you to the test.' And it was in a way – a fairer test than that to which Mistress Captoft had been subjected. She could sink, innocent and drowned, or swim and be burned. No middle way. Whereas trial by ordeal offered a chance. Merely by submitting to it he proved his faith in his own innocence; and if that failed and his guilt proved, he would be regarded as sufficiently punished; the real test was the willingness to take the test; the real punishment, crippled feet or hands, for the rest of his life.

'Red hot,' Old Hodgson said. 'To be carried nine paces.' He indicated the iron bar heating in the fire.

Father Matthew broke into an icy sweat, feeling already the searing pain across his left palm – it must be the left, less useful hand. His bowels stirred and a slight fear added itself to the greater; was he going to disgrace himself before them all?

Speaking, so dry-mouthed that he sounded rather like poor Tim, he said, 'I refuse.'

'Then you're guilty and know it,' Old Hodgson said.

Old Gurth said, 'Look outa the winder.'

Father Matthew looked. Someone had lighted a huge fire.

'Refuse and you burn altogether. Self-confessed wizard.'

A terrible tremor began in the marrow of his bones and worked outwards; his knees gave way. God. Mary, Mother of God. Christ. His trembling hand went to the crucifix upon his breast. A gift from his mother; made specially for him; made by a carpenter and crudely carved. Perhaps by its very crudity more expressive than most of sheer physical agony.

'I swear,' he just managed to say, 'on the Holy Cross of Christ, I am innocent.'

And what was that worth from one who even at the altar said the wrong words?

'Prove it,' they said.

Suddenly a most extraordinary thing happened. As his hand clenched upon the crucifix — one village carpenter's representation of another village carpenter's dreadful death, calm took the place of terror. He knew he was innocent; God knew he was innocent.

In a different voice, firm and clear, Father Matthew said, 'I will.' He knew he could do it – with the help of God.

Somebody said, 'Is it ready?' and somebody else said, 'Yes. White hot.'

Old Hodgson took Father Matthew to the door and flung it open.

'From here to that wand. Nine paces; I measured 'em myself.'

The wand of peeled willow gleamed white in the firelit yard; and all the assembled faces were red on one side, black on the other.

There was a sound, like wind rustling through corn.

One of the Elders, holding the cooler end of the iron in a cloth-protected hand thrust the glowing, white-hot end towards Father Matthew who took it in his *right* hand. The surest proof of faith in God that he could produce; faith must be all or nothing.

His hands had been hard as horn before he ever left his father's poor holding, and nothing in the following years had done anything to soften them. Even at school, where those with a gift for penmanship, or for advanced learning had been indoors, he'd been out, using a spade, a scythe, a hayfork. Even at Intake – well, poor Tim couldn't do everything; Father Matthew had handled the broom, the bucket, kept the church speckless. He'd used a spade, too. The only reason why he had not ploughed his glebe himself was that he had no plough, no draught animal – and no money to hire them.

He took the glowing, white-hot end of the bar without hesitation. Set out on the nine paces.

They had been measured by Old Hodgson, who was old,

and who, despite his daughter-in-law's asseverations that he was an old fraud, just wanting to sit about and watch other people work, *did* suffer from rheumatism. Nine of his paces could be covered by a man in the prime of life, as Father Matthew was, in about five. But the priest did not hurry. Faith must be all or nothing.

He reached the wand, and there laid down the still glowing bar. Then he held up his hand, unscathed. When they had all had time to look and understand, he acted as though he were in church, not in a farmyard crammed with his parishioners come to watch him being burned, or hurt.

He held up his crucifix and spoke the first words of the salutation they all knew: 'Ave Maria.'

Mistress Captoft, frivolous, worldly woman, had found it easy to forgive. Father Matthew could no more forgive the people of Intake than he had been able to forgive Mistress Captoft for her insult. All the arguments he had used then went through his mind again, and were argued down. This time with the added assurance that he was right, they were wrong, and must be shown to be wrong. They would be shown, for they were now clay in his hands.

Now his glebe was ploughed, and cross ploughed as was the custom with land long neglected. No nonsense now about ploughs needing repair, oxen needing a rest, or being lame. Converted at last, awed, penitent, admiring, they came willingly and when the ploughing was done, offered seeds. A handful of this, of that. Ill-spared, he knew, for he had been reared on a holding where even the best harvest must be cut three ways; how much to sell for cash money in order to buy such essentials as salt; how much to eat – to keep alive through the winter; how much to plant. He knew all about that.

And always, under his right hand, so miraculously saved from the white-hot iron, he could feel that little sharp shoulder blade.

Something must be done for the children.

There were some, he knew, who still fed well. There were families, where, before the pigs died, hams and bacon had been preserved and pork laid in casks of brine. But every housewife was not foresighted, or had, until disaster struck, needed to be. With other pigs coming along in the sty such hoarding was not necessary. They were the ones who now suffered most; and as Father Matthew knew, the time-honoured custom of sharing a fresh carcass now proved to be an added hardship for some. There was a lot of meat on a pig, killed at the right time, so one man would bargain with another – You have so much of my pork now and pay me back when you kill your pig. It was practical and sensible, but now there were many such debts which would never be paid, or at least not for a long time. The new pigs had of necessity been bought for breeding, not for eating.

It was the children with whom Father Matthew was concerned. The adult people could go hungry for all he cared. And he was so wretchedly poor himself. The ancestress of Master Tallboys who had built the church had endowed it as she thought, generously. But the value of money had declined steadily since her day and his stipend hardly served to keep him and the boy on the most meagre fare. When he had eaten so heartily in the farmhouse kitchens it had been less from greed than from genuine hunger. So how could he feed others?

Well, he had one apparently prosperous parishioner and he must appeal to him. It went against the grain; Master Tallboys had always seemed to him – as to so many others – a cold, remote man. Certainly he attended Sunday Mass, and brought his son, but the priest sensed something perfunctory about this performance of duty. And he was not a giver. Never once, in two years, had he pressed a coin into Father Matthew's hand with the almost ritual remark: For the use of the poor, Father. And lately, of course, Knight's Acre had simply meant Mistress Captoft. Still, he must go there and ask. First thing tomorrow morning.

He was surprised to see preparations for a move going on. A waggon, bigger and sturdier than Master Tallboys' stood in the yard; the carter, the lame man, Jem Watson and Master Tallboys himself were loading it. The boy stood watching, holding a great dog by the collar. As Dick Sawyer had said, Guard was not yet fully trained and despite assurances that the carter had a legitimate errand, was a friend, seemed to distrust him. Carter and waggon had arrived overnight, ready for an early start.

Mistress Captoft was carrying out various small parcels and wedging them into crevices between larger articles; she was also supervising and admonishing: Mind this, mind that, it would balance better if placed on this side. Her greeting was preoccupied but quite without animosity. He had been included in the general forgiveness.

Henry said, 'Good morning, Father.' Civilly, but with a question in it.

'I should like a word with you, Master Tallboys.'

'I think the heavy things are out now,' Henry said with a glance at the waggon. 'Come in and sit down.'

Henry was glad of an excuse to sit for a while. His injury was far less painful than it had been; he could ride now with only mild discomfort, but lifting still sent sharp pangs.

'I have come to ask your help. For the poor.'

Something like humour, but not quite, crossed Henry's face.

'What poor?'

Father Matthew hastened to explain; and Henry listened, with some scepticism. He had never regarded the villagers as poor. Not as he had been, and still was, in a way. For generations they had been singularly favoured, their rents fixed, for perpetuity, at some ridiculous figure by some old document. Henry's father, Sir Godfrey, the best knight in England, had always depended upon what he could win, and had been married for eight years before he had a house of his own. However, when he died, Richard, second son, trained lawyer, ordained priest, had found a flaw in that old parchment, and most of the tenant farmers had been told to buy their holdings or get out. They'd all found the money from somewhere; Henry, wanting to keep the flock together, had been obliged to borrow in order to give Richard, and John, their share of it in money. Paying interest on the loan, paying back the loan had kept him very poor. Also the holdings in Intake could all be run by families, he had to hire labour.

And even now, when the place looked so prosperous, what with putting money aside for Robert and for Joanna, he was as short of cash money as ever.

'You have so much, Master Tallboys; your swine did not sicken. And it is the Christmas season. A children's festival. I would like to give the little children of Intake a meal, now and again. So ask your charity.'

'It would have to be in kind, not in money, Father.' He was not the man to go into detail, to say that most of his money was really held in trust. He thought of the sheep-fold where his depleted flock, and Robert's – separately marked, had been joined by Joanna's, unmarked. And Joseph had recently mentioned an old tup or two, rams growing old, fit only for butchering. Joseph loved his flock, lived with them, talked to them, would sit up all night during the lambing season, or when a sheep ailed; but he was completely unsentimental about them. He or she had had a good life and must go. 'We all come to it, Master,' Joseph said.

'I can let you have a sheep. And a sack of flour.'

Better than nothing, Father Matthew thought. Not what he had hoped for, but better than nothing.

He had been so intent on his errand that the only thing he had noticed about the Knight's Acre hall was that it looked a bit bare, and the horrible picture was still there. Over the hearth. Hearth. Abruptly he was reminded of the tax called Peter's Pence because presumably it ended up in Rome, in the revenues of St. Peter's direct inheritor, of office, of authority, of everything – the Pope.

A penny a year on every hearth.

Father Matthew suddenly realised that he had not been strict enough. Peter's Pence had never increased during his time – nor, judging by the records, during Father Benedict's or Father Ambrose's. And yet the number of hearths must surely have increased over the years; some young couples built a dwelling apart, some were content by adding an extra room to the family house.

Anxious to ingratiate himself in a parish he had sensed to be hostile – and now knew to be so, he had never questioned the number of hearths. Nor had the tax collector questioned his returns. But in future he would be less lenient. He might even . . .

It was a shocking thought, but he toyed with it. Why not? Extract the last possible penny from the men he could not forgive, and spend the difference between last years' returns and this upon the children.

Henry thought about the sack of flour. If he acted quickly

enough the carter, a sturdy fellow, with a little help from David, could heave it into the waiting waggon, and drop it off at the priest's house. He was about to rise and go to arrange this when Mistress Captoft rustled in, cloaked, hooded, gloved.

'I apologise for interrupting you,' she said, 'but the man is ready to go. I could not leave without a word. Master Tallboys, I thank you for your kindness when I was in such distress; and for your hospitality. I hope that whenever you are in Bywater you will look in upon me.'

'I will indeed – though I seldom go that way. I wish you all happiness in your new life . . .' Then even at this moment of leave-taking, practicality took over and he mentioned the sack of flour.

'Certainly,' she said. 'No trouble at all. But a whole sack! That will leave you short.'

'No matter,' Henry said, 'I have wheat I can take to the miller.'

Even Father Matthew, ignorant as he was of such things, saw that this was no parting of people who had ever conspired together, or been intimate. There again he had been completely deceived by those false village people.

As he watched the sack being tucked under the sailcloth covering which protected Mistress Captoft's possessions, another thought occurred to him. Every village priest could claim as his right the cloth – blanket or quilt, in which a dead person, awaiting interment, had been wrapped. That was another rule which he had never enforced. But he would in future.

'Tell my shepherd,' Henry said, 'when you want the sheep. He'll know which one to kill.'

Katharine watched the waggon leave and then ran upstairs. She, too, was ready, immediate essentials in a bundle. She was taking only what could be easily carried on a long walk. Leave the two light-weight summer dresses, leave the old soiled working one. Leave the worn down-at-heel shoes and also the new ones, not yet broken in, wear the middle pair. Some faint echo of the fury which had made her fling the spit, stirred in her as she stole from the house, as though she were a thief, making off with what was not her own. No justice in this world! All those years, working conscientiously and indeed very skilfully at The Welcome to Mariners, one moment of madness to which she had been driven, and out on her ear. Then this place, so seemingly ideal except for that something, no name for it, no explanation, which brought the goose-pimples out even on the warmest days. She'd prayed God, give me strength to face it whatever it is. God, let Mistress Captoft change her mind about taking me. No answer. So now she must steal away and go back to the house by the tanyard, where she'd be welcome, just so long as her meagre savings lasted. After that ... No time to think, now. It was a bright day for the time of year and she felt that she could just brace herself to the necessity of skirting through the fringe of the wood, thus avoiding observation. Being careful of direction, she should come out in the lane, somewhere near the water-splash. After that she should be able to keep up, preserving a cautious distance, with the heavily laden waggon. Mistress Captoft and David were unlikely to look back; the carter certainly wouldn't. In their wake she could creep into Bywater, to Tanner's Lane – a place where at least nobody was alone, with the silence and the watching bearing down.

Once again, in this seemingly fated kitchen, no fire on the hearth, no pot boiling, no woman in charge. Henry said, 'I must have misunderstood. I thought Mistress Captoft was leaving Katharine. She must have changed her mind.'

Bread and cheese again. Only as a stopgap, of course; the larder was well stocked, and Henry, who had never attempted it, believed that cooking was largely a matter of common sense. And time. Which he could spare just now.

Lady Grey had thought of the perfect way of saving Lord Shefton the embarrassment of meeting that wretched girl again; of punishing the girl for her deceit, and of solving the problem presented by Lady Agnes during the Twelve Days when service was slovenly or resentful.

'You will absent yourself from the hall and the company entirely and spend the Christmas season in attendance upon the Lady Agnes. By night as well as by day. You will sleep on the truckle bed in her room.'

Maude or Beatrice, sentenced to such a dreadful fate would have wept, implored, grovelled. Joanna made a faultless curtsey and said, 'As your ladyship commands.'

There were dungeons below the castle keep, and condemned to one of them, bread and water once a day, she would have gone happily. The fact that Henry had confirmed the betrothal had produced such a state of euphoria – the more so because it had been preceded by a period of uncertainty. She knew more of the world now; knew that a betrothal to be binding must be witnessed and that even then there were ways of rendering it void. So in the days between her desperate statement to Maude and the arrival of the Bishop's letter, she had lived on a knife-edge of trepidation. For after all, in two years Henry had shown no sign of acknowledging her existence. She knew that he could not write – but Mistress Captoft could; and he must have realised that within six months of her arrival at Stordford, she would have learned to read. That was one of the things she had been sent into exile to learn, and nobody knew better than Henry how quickly she could learn anything she gave her mind to. No message, either verbal or written, had ever come and presently she had ceased to expect one. But nothing, no power on earth – even Henry's repudiation of her – would make her marrry that old man with his rotten teeth and bald head and spindly shanks. So she had taken the risk, and back the answer had come. The right answer. All the other desperate things she had planned – including going to London and forcing her way into the presence of the King, who, though ageing himself and said to be completely under the thumb of his latest mistress, was still the fount of all justice – these could be put away. Henry had stood by her.

She went cheerfully to wait upon Lady Agnes upon whom the final humiliation of old age and its infirmities had come. Completely bed-ridden now, with all that implied ... Even servants sometimes wrinkled their noses. And the dutiful visits had become shorter and shorter. The old woman's spirit had flagged; why bother to stay alive. Why not make the will – the thing they were all waiting for – turn your face to the wall and give up?

'I have come to spend Christmas with you, Lady Agnes,'

Joanna said, radiating not resentment or reluctance, but happiness of such strength that it communicated itself even to an old bed-ridden woman whose joints had failed her and whose only hope of happiness lay in Heaven. And in her more desolate moments Lady Agnes knew that between now and then there lay the moment of death which – though she sometimes accepted it, angrily; have done with it all – she dreaded; and after that Purgatory. Not that she'd been a great sinner, and when she could bring herself to make her will, she intended to leave something to the poor, and another sum for Masses for her soul, which should shorten her time in Purgatory. When she thought about it – as lately she had been inclined to do, she thought it curious that though the joys of Heaven and the pains of Hell had merited exact descriptions, Purgatory had never been clearly defined; it was left as vague, as unimaginable as the Limbo to which unbaptised infants were consigned.

Upon such morbid meditations the presence of the girl– whom she had always liked, rather better than her grand-nieces – broke like a ray of sunshine at the end of a dismal day. Like a breath of fresh air, which became actuality, for Joanna, realising that she must live, eat, sleep in this room, made up the fire, wrapped an extra blanket over the old body, and flung open the window. The pure clean air – mild for the time of year, and not a good omen, streamed in and the room freshened. Then, because she was so happy herself – happy even to have escaped the noise and bustle of the hall – Joanna set herself to make Lady Agnes comfortable if not happy.

'If you could hold on to me ... Put your arms round my neck ... I could get you on to this stool and fluff up your bed.'

Somewhat cautiously Lady Agnes embarked upon this operation. Over the last two years she had observed, idly, how differently girls developed. Maude had put on flesh, become curved but remained short of stature. Beatrice would probably go the same way; this girl, mature-looking, when she arrived, two years ago, had grown upwards, a full two inches, and thinned out in the process, taking on a look of frailty which was, Lady Agnes learned, completely deceptive. Strong as steel.

'Just let yourself go. I've lifted heavier weights than you.'

'Where?'

'At the farm.'

'I understood that you came from Spain.'

'My mother did.' With those words began the story, the series of stories, which afforded the invalid more entertainment than she had had for a long time. The manner of life depicted was outside her experience, almost beyond the reach of her imagination, but the girl had the knack of description, and a gift of mimicry. The place, the people all came to life. Except Henry, though it was of him that Joanna spoke most often. He remained an enigma.

'Why did he not give you a ring when you became betrothed. It would have saved a deal of bother.'

'It would have been an expense. And he thought me too young. I don't suppose the idea that somebody else might not think me too young ever once occurred to him. Henry is very . . . singleminded.' It was not an adequate word but she could think of no other.

Sir Godfrey's name had inevitably been mentioned, and Lady Agnes could remember him; very handsome, extremely brave, but so single-minded as to be almost simple. So devoted to his wife – when at last he had decided upon marriage – that he'd missed some good opportunities of pleasing ladies who could by influence have advanced his career; so no sinecures had come his way, and he'd died poor; his son ploughed his own acres!

It was all fascinating and Lady Agnes was insatiable. Tell me more about . . . What happened after that?

They were well-fed, well-supplied with firewood. That will was still to be made! Much of the service was provided by young squires because Christmas turned everything topsy-turvy. Maude and Beatrice made their morning visits as usual. Nothing to say for themselves, anxious only to get away. Lady Agnes' keen eye did, however, presently perceive a slight change, an improvement in Maude. She looked less sallow. Possibly applied colour, or a reflection of the hue of her latest new dress which was rose pink.

One day, two, three days after Christmas when Joanna had finished the dramatic story of how Griselda had found that hoard of jewels, the old woman said, 'You must see mine, my dear. Not that I can show you a ruby an inch wide.' She had a feeling that upon this subject the girl had tended to exaggerate, but what matter? There was drama in the tale of gems lying hidden, being used as playthings, and then being discovered and tumbled on a kitchen table.

She handed Joanna a key. 'It opens the small compartment in my clothes chest,' she said. 'Inside there is a box; bring it to me.'

Lady Agnes's jewels were well enough, but set in the English style, flat into the gold, so that some light and sparkle was lost. Now it was her turn to reminisce; wedding gifts, birthday gifts; the pendant her husband had given her when her first and only child had been born; a boy, dead of the whoop before he was two. There was something sad about this recountal of glad days, grievous days, the visible evidence of things outlasting their owners. It was difficult to look so far ahead, and see herself, old and ailing. Henry too ... No, such an unthinkable thought must be put away.

Lady Agnes, out of the less important items at the bottom of the box, selected a ring. It had no sentimental associations for her for she had won it from another lady at a tournament – each had wagered an ornament upon the outcome and her knight had won. It was a ring, a plain gold band with a cluster of small garnets set together, rather like a squashed raspberry. If she remembered rightly, she'd worn it only once; at the banquet which followed the tournament, just to show that she had won it, being a better judge of a man and a horse.

'I want you to have this,' she said, holding the ring towards Joanna who made no move to take it, but backed away and said, 'No. It is kind of you. But I could never wear it.'

'Why not?'

'Am I not in disgrace enough already? If Lady Grey thought that I had taken advantage; turned a penance to pleasure, the very worst might happen. She could send me back and then the bargain ... the agreement between Henry and me would fall to the ground. I must stay here, another year and a half. Until I am fifteen. Henry honoured his part, I must honour mine.'

Still fingering the ring, Lady Agnes said, 'It would be a guard against unwanted suitors.'

Joanna said, with a touch of savagery in her voice, 'There will be no need. I know now. Lady Grey flung at me the charge of being deceitful, of having encouraged Lord Shefton. That is untrue. *She* placed me by him at table; *she* told me that it was discourteous to refuse a choice tit-bit, offered by one's neighbour; or to refuse to stand up and dance when invited. It was at her bidding that I behaved in a manner she now chooses to denounce. I am wiser now, and need no ring as guard. But it was a kind thought.'

'Put them back, then,' Lady Agnes said. She retained the squashed raspberry ring, pushing it, with some difficulty, on to her little finger – the only one it now fitted. Strange to think that on an evening, long ago, she had shown it off, not only as a win from a wager, but as a ring far too big, her fingers being more slender than those of its former owner. A double triumph.

Lord Shefton was a self-indulgent old hedonist but he had been properly reared. Never, never lick a wound in public. As Lady Grey had expected, the task of breaking the unpleasant news had been left to her and she, fearing some display of displeasure, was relieved by his apparently calm acceptance of it.

'You are in no way to blame, Lady Grey,' he said gallantly. 'The fault, if any, lies with His Grace of Bywater who was, to say the least, negligent.'

Under the surface venom seethed. By withholding a vital piece of information, the negligent fellow had made Lord Shefton look a fool, and nobody did that with impunity. Let this Christmas season get over and the official wheels turning again and the Bishop of Bywater's affairs would be looked at by an eye eager to find a fault. It would be found. For just as all men had a price, all men had a vulnerable point.

Lady Grey was much impressed by his lordship's manner, and also by the fact that the rotten teeth had been removed. His breath was no longer offensive, and when he smiled, some new teeth, somewhat irregular, but clean and white and sound, could be seen.

It had been a painful, tedious expensive and rather hit-or-miss operation, but Lord Shefton had faced it bravely. There was a toothpuller in the Strand who specialised in the extraction, and replacement of teeth – mainly for vain, ageing women. Well fortified by wine and some pain-killing potion, Lord Shefton had submitted to the crude, but swift surgery, while a number of boys, each willing to sacrifice a tooth, or even two, for sixpence each, sat waiting. Pluck out the old rotten one, dab the socket well with salt; take the young tooth and press it in firmly. If it took root, well and good; if not it was simply unfortunate. It was not an operation that could be repeated. Lord Shefton with six seemingly well rooted had had above average good luck.

Nothing, of course, could restore his youth, but as she observed the new teeth and was grateful for his courtesy in not blaming her, there hung at the back of Lady Grey's mind the details of that marriage settlement.

She still wished her daughters to make good and happy marriages. And with Joanna safely out of the way, she had dared to hope that perhaps Sir Gervase Orford, another guest for Christmas, might look at Maude with a favourable eye. He was personable, well-connected, and from the point of view of money just right; not rich enough to despise Maude's dowry, not poor enough to covet it.

She was forestalled. Lord Shefton's pride recovered, like an angry snake, from the blow which had been painful but not mortal. He could still make it seem as though the quarry he hunted and which had escaped him, was not indeed what he wanted, and the easiest way to do that was to pay attention to Maude. Meek and submissive, she was not to his taste, not even pretty, but she was *young*. And of late there had been a dearth of young virgins – either girls were growing more wilful, or parents more indulgent. He had, before settling on Joanna Serriff, had a set-back or two. Now, with the marriage settlement properly drawn up in his baggage, and the ring in his pouch, he had, he realised, not too much time to spare. Time enough however to make a defeat look like a victory. Let everybody, except Sir Barnabas and his lady, think that *he* had changed his mind; it only meant the scribbling out of the name *Joanna Serriff*, and the substitution of *Maude Grey*.

True to her principles Lady Grey said, 'Maude should be

consulted.' And Maude, crushed down, rebuked, scolded, smacked, even beaten on occasion, gave the correct answer – 'As you wish, Mother.'

'No, Maude, this is the decision of a lifetime. You must take it.'

Free! Away from here. Countess of Shefton; taking–if they ever met after the wedding, precedence over her mother.

'Then I agree,' Maude said. 'When it was Joanna, I wished myself in her shoes.'

'Forget that,' Lady Grey said, commanding her daughter for almost the last time. 'You are *sure*?'

'Yes. I am sure.'

The ring, Lord Shefton admitted to himself, was not quite right. Out of his hoard he had chosen a ring for another finger, the finger of a girl whose eyes varied; emerald, sapphire, crystal. So he had brought an aquamarine. Had he foreseen what would happen he would have chosen something of warmer shade; a topaz, or one of the rare flawed yellow stones rightly called Cat's Eye. He had, of course, jewels of greater worth, the Shefton diamonds were quite famous, but a betrothal ring should not be ostentatious.

Maude displayed her aquamarine and told her news with a blush and show of animation which transformed her into something approaching prettiness. Lady Agnes wished her happiness with a heartiness which concealed some doubts. However, she reflected, there would be compensations; escape from her mother's domination, a grand title – and it could not be for long.

Joanna embraced the girl whom she had always thought of as poor Maude and of whom she was mildly fond, and said, 'If you are happy, Maude, I am pleased for you.'

Maude said, 'I could jump over the moon for joy.'

Beatrice, simpering, said, 'It will be my turn next. These things always go in threes.'

'And when is the wedding to be?' Lady Agnes asked.

'They are discussing it now. Sometime before Lent.'

It was possible to celebrate a wedding in Lent, but it was not regarded as an auspicious choice.

Impatient, now, Lord Shefton said, 'Would Candlemas Day be too soon?'

Lady Grey could understand impatience. He was old. And now that the decision had been taken – by Maude herself; *no* pressure brought to bear – had she not practically invited the girl to refuse? – it would be a thousand pities if death intervened between Maude and the title, that marriage settlement. Certain observations of rites were supposed to precede a wedding, but when one had a household chaplain ... There would be no difficulty there! Aloud she began to muse about the weather. These few exceptionally mild days – including Christmas Day itself, spoke of a hard winter still to come. Roads impassable ... snow probably, and then as it melted the slush and mire. And if Lord Shefton had welcomed the idea of a short betrothal, how much more would he – and everybody – welcome Twelfth Night? Without actually seeming to do so – and there lay the secret of her power – she had it all arranged. A *little* less food for a few days, and she had enough provisions for a splendid wedding feast. And Maude had another gown, as yet unworn. Guests were already here – neighbours within easy distance could be invited. Family ties were frail. Stordford had never been a family place; Lady Grey's relatives were too modest and Sir Barnabas's too grand.

Twelfth Night it would be.

Above stairs, Lady Agnes had fallen into a strange, unusually quiet mood. It had come upon her with the reflection that Maude's marriage, happy or otherwise, could not last long. She and Lord Shefton were near contemporaries, and that thought struck home. For the last few days, her bed made so comfortable, her mind distracted by Joanna's tales, she had felt better, lively. Now melancholy set in. It was strengthened by the thought that she must give Maude a wedding present. And how to decide about that? It must be something, out of that locked box, good enough to pass muster, and yet not good enough to be wasted, because ignored amongst those that Maude, Countess of Shefton would for a short time own and wear. A short time ...

'I want Father Gilbert – the chaplain,' she said suddenly, just as Joanna was beginning to light the candles. Aware that the chaplain had come to the sick-room on Christmas morning, Joanna said, 'Are you feeling worse?'

'I'm as well as I shall ever be! *And* in my right mind.' There was a touch of tetchiness. 'This is business. Tell him to bring pen and parchment and two copying clerks. Then stay out of the room, but within call.'

On her withered yet knuckly fingers Lady Agnes checked over the details of the will, about which she had been brooding all day. First, a generous bequest, fifty pounds, to the chaplain himself – that would ensure that the document was not mislaid or overlooked. One had to be wily about such things. Fifty pounds for a hundred Masses to be said for her soul; fifty for the poor – to be administered at Father Gilbert's discretion. Maude would want for nothing and in any case would have received a wedding present; possibly the pearls. To Beatrice a hundred pounds to be paid when she married, or reached the age of eighteen. Over Barnabas and Gertrude she hesitated. Certainly they had housed and fed her, but they could not be said to have been very *attentive* since she had been stuck away here; hurried little visits. Fifty pounds a-piece. Oh, and Roger, of course must not be forgotten, though she remembered him only somewhat dimly, he'd been from home for so long. Still men needed property and property needed a man to see to it, as she had learned, employing middlemen. So, to Roger – my nephew, my manor of Foxborough . . . And *that* also would ensure that this will was executed correctly. But she owned another, bigger manor, nearer London and now almost entirely devoted to supplying the rapidly growing city with fresh, immediately consumable food. She had not seen it since her fall had disabled her, but to judge from the returns it was prosperous, though the house – actually the house to which she had gone as a bride, which she and her husband had occupied whenever business or pleasure had drawn them towards London, was now, according to her agent, all chopped about and let out to working people who toiled on the land, or trudged into the city to earn a wage. 'My manor of Finchley,' Lady Agnes said, 'and everything else of which I die possessed . . .'

Joanna had spent the time sitting at the head of the stairs, hugging her secret happiness and oblivious to the sound of voices and laughter coming up from the hall below. She felt the wind change. Real winter on the way, and if the old beliefs were anything to go by, it would be a severe one. She remembered one of Tom Robinson's rhymes.

> If the ice in November'll bear a duck,
> There's nothing to come but mud and muck.
> Warm weather at the year's back end
> Snow drifts later on do send.

The chaplain and the clerks eventually emerged, all looking pleased. He had his legacy, and for witnessing the signature the clerks would each receive two shillings. Joanna went back into the room and made up the fire.

'Now tell me a story,' Lady Agnes demanded. 'A merry one if possible.'

Well, if not actually merry, there was a comic side to the story of Young Richard stealing from market stalls and being thoroughly beaten by everybody who could get in a blow.

'But he was Henry's nephew, you see and was a Tallboys; so Henry thought he was responsible, and offered to pay. *Everybody* on the market claimed to have been robbed, if not that day, last week, a month ago. And that was most unfair; Richard certainly hadn't stolen pots or pans. Henry hadn't enough money so he sold Richard's pony and cleared the family name. That *was* fair, but it started some talk about Henry being unkind and the poor boy stealing because he was hungry. That was a black lie. Much good it did him though!' Her eyes flashed green malice and she laughed, showing those sharp teeth. 'He was sent to school at Eton, where he says he is half-starved and frequently flogged. He may be lying again, but I hope with all my heart it is true!'

Now that the will was made the old woman felt better; it had been the prospect of parting with her belongings which had depressed her. Once more she was easily entertained.

'You bear him a grudge. Did he steal from you?'

'That would have puzzled him! No, he tried to be friends. Once he tried to give me a string of blue beads. I told him to go and hang himself with it!'

'You *are* pretty, my dear, but when you are spiteful your face changes. You look like a wolf.'

Joanna laughed again.

'Once I tried to *be* one.' She began on the story of her futile attempts to make magic brews so that she could turn herself into a wolf – like the old woman at Nettleton in Tom's story – and go to Moyidan in the night and scare Young Richard into behaving better to poor little Robert.

'I could *see* how unhappy Robert was, though Moyidan is five miles from Knight's Acre. Henry didn't believe me. But I had seen right.'

That kind of seeing, she decided, was something she had outgrown. Homesick as she had been and still was for Knight's Acre, much as she had thought about it, and during the last few days talked about it, calling it so vividly to mind and describing it, it had been just the ordinary eye of memory that she had used.

Supper came and Lady Agnes was sufficiently restored to complain both of the quantity and the quality.

'Very meagre,' she said, surveying the food – enough by Knight's Acre standards to keep two people for four days. 'I can see what is happening. Everything will be saved towards the wedding feast. We are all to go hungry until Maude is married. And this venison is green! It needed two days in the ground to sweeten it. Eaten like this it is very bad for the bowels.' Nevertheless she ate her share and a good portion of Joanna's slipped unostentatiously on to her plate. Lady Agnes noticed, but did not protest. The girl would have her reward. But not yet! The melancholy mood had lifted and the old woman thought that if she could survive starvation until after the wedding, and if Joanna could continue to be in disgrace, she was good for a long time yet.

Next morning they learned that the time of threatened scarcity would be short. Maude was to be married on Twelfth Night.

'Indecent haste,' Lady Agnes said when the girls had gone giggling away. 'I suppose my lady was afraid the bridegroom might take a fit from excitement! It would be scandalous were it not well-known that Maude has never done a thing, or thought a thought, without her mother's permission. She is a virgin – and likely to remain so.' She sniggered.

For some reason which she did not understand, Joanna

disliked that kind of talk. It was part of the falsity which pervaded this kind of world. Outwardly so prim and proper, and in company behaving as though they were all the Virgin Mary, no less, in the privacy of the solar they let themselves go, with sly hints, a special tone of voice, even a peculiar kind of smile.

Puzzling to a country-bred girl whose knowledge of sex was as simple and straightforward as the act itself, as performed by animals. Bull mounted cow, boar mounted sow; the female swelled with her burden and delivered it. With people something more was involved, fondness, loyalty – all that Joanna felt for Henry, and now hoped that Henry felt for her; but none of it funny. So why should the prospect of poor Maude's endless virginity make her great-aunt cackle in that special way? Never mind. Amusement however ill-justified made for good humour; and this morning good humour was needed, for the insufficiently earthed venison had had the predicted effect.

'I'd like my box again. I have decided to give Maude my pearls. With the wedding so hasty, she will have few gifts. Few guests who are not already here. I am a member of the family and must make the best show I can.'

Joanna opened the chest within the chest, brought the box and laid it on the bed. Fumbling amongst her treasure, Lady Agnes muttered on, 'Too good really; it is a sacrifice. If they are quick enough and haste seems to be the order of the day, Maude will wear the Shefton diamonds. But no better pearls. And of course these will be hers, when the wife of his eldest son wears the diamonds and . . .'

Abruptly she became aware that she had lost her audience. The girl stood there, looking exactly – curious the tricks one's memory played – exactly like a knight who, in the mêlée with which a formal tournament often ended, had been transfixed by a lance; held upright for a moment in the saddle by the weapon that had killed him. Just for a moment, there, and yet not there. Before he toppled.

She said, 'What is the matter?' and knew the answer to the question even as she asked it. It was pain; that terrible griping in the bowels which resulted from the eating of green venison, inadequately earthed. The girl had eaten less of it, so her attack had come later.

When she said, in a dazed way, 'I must go,' Lady Agnes knew why and where.

But it had happened again. That inside eye which Joanna had thought outgrown. Seeing again.

There, far more real than the room, the bed, the old woman handling her treasures, was the Knight's Acre kitchen, all cluttered, muddled and Henry, thinner, older, and in some way hurt, trying not to limp. No time to lose.

Joanna ran swiftly down the stairs and across the hall. The men guests had had a table set up near the fire and were playing some game with dice. The women, she guessed, were in the solar, busy with dresses and head-dresses. She slipped through the hall like a shadow, unseen and into the vast courtyard with its many stables. The wind struck its first blow, but she did not notice. She needed a horse, and above all, she needed to be unobserved. And she needed to be quick; no time for argument, explanation, even to stable-boys, so she avoided any building from which came sounds of activity and ran on until she found a stable holding horses only. The one nearest the entry was a big black animal and his harness, freshly oiled and polished, hung on the wall behind him.

The gentle ambling palfreys which she and the Grey girls had ridden were always brought, ready to be mounted, to the door; it was two years since she had slipped in a bit or buckled a girth, but she was too anxious to consider that she might have difficulty, that this was a different animal from Henry's old farm horse, or Mistress Captoft's mule. Her confidence served her, communicating itself to the animal who was of tricky temper and capable of taking advantage of the slightest hesitancy or nervousness. As it was he submitted docilely.

She had come to Stordford escorted by a man who knew the way and she had been too wretched, already suffering the first pangs of homesickness, to take any interest in her surroundings. All she knew was that the road she must take lay roughly towards the east. Straight into the wind. How rash, how foolish, how like a hen running round without its head, she had been to rush out dressed as she was for indoors; her velvet dress, provided just before she fell into disgrace; little kid slippers on her feet and on her head nothing but a head-dress which the wind snatched away, and sent soaring – like the butterfly it was intended to resemble – into the hedge. But she excused herself; if she had tarried to dress for the ride, she could have been caught, prevented. And at least she had, by accident, hit upon just the horse for this venture. She steeled herself against the cold. Henry needed her and she was going to him as fast as she could, on a horse that could gallop, the kind of animal she had never ridden before. And he had never carried so light a rider ...

She was out in the world, without a farthing, not certain of her way, depending upon the light for her direction on one of the shortest days of the year, but fear – the sense of ill to come, defeat inevitable – had no part in her nature. Sir Godfrey – her father, though nobody knew that – had never gone into a joust, or a serious battle expecting more than a trivial hurt; and Tana, her mother, had faced incalculable risks in her plan to get them both across the mountains, out of Moorish Escalona and into Christian Spain. The child of their union had been born as nearly without fear as a human being could be; and also without fear's concomitant, self-concern; that she was cut to the bone by the wind mattered nothing.

At Intake Father Matthew was a bit fearful – of the weather ... of the numbers who might come to his feast; of the possibilty that no child would come. Still he had done his best and chosen the day when Master Tallboys' gift of an old sheep and a bag of flour could be used to the best advantage. He had announced that on the Tenth Day of Christmas there would be a dinner for every child of Intake, under eleven years old. Nothing careless about the date chosen or the age limit. A peasant himself, Father Matthew knew how the rules ran. So far as they could in their crippled state, the people of Intake would keep Christmas. Two, in some places; three, days of full plates. Then would come the lean time, with what food there was being hoarded for Twelfth Night, and given mainly to the men who must be strong on Plough Monday when work would be resumed. But even then, Father Matthew knew from his own experience, there would be something for the children; the greasy salty liquor in which pork had been boiled, a bone to gnaw, the tough outer hide of ham or bacon to chew on. Knowing it all he planned his time and his age limit with care. Any child over eleven was a potential worker, worth feeding.

Tim, whom everybody except Father Matthew had despised and rejected, again proved his worth; sound common sense; he could not, he said, in his thick-tongued way, make enough bread on the oven floor for so many, but he could make pad loaves, one above the other, towers of bread, each layer separated from the next by a liberal sprinkling of flour. 'And, sir, it'll save cutting; they'll just pull apart.'

The sheep, Tim said, was too old to be roasted. It must be boiled, very gently.

Only the church itself was large enough to be used for this feast, and in the morning Father Matthew made ready, placing upon the alter a bowl of flowers, sprung from some roots which Mistress Captoft had planted and left behind when she moved. They had never flowered before, but this year unaccountably they did; braving the wind, elegant, delicate. A drift of white alongside the onion bed. A strange flower and unknown to him but he hit by accident on the name by which it was eventually to be called. Arranging them in a silver bowl – one of the gifts which Sir Godfrey had made to the church in memory of his wife – Father Matthew remarked that the drooping white petals looked like snowdrops. And as he spoke he cast a weatherwise eye at the sky. Real snow threatened.

Just across the track, in the sheepfold, Joseph was making preparations for the bad weather he knew was coming. Ordinarily only ewes about to drop lambs were sheltered from the weather, but this year the old shepherd built an enclosure capable of holding the whole flock, and his constant demands for more straw bales kept Henry and the waggon busy.

Once, as he unloaded, Henry caught a whiff of baking bread and savoury stew coming from the priest's house and realised that he was quite hungry himself. His attempt at cooking had not been successful. He had not realised that pork taken straight from the brine cask needed a good soaking before it boiled, and he was ignorant of timing; the pork had been difficult to carve, and was hard to chew, the bag of dried peas boiled with it, like little stones. He'd tried cooking a fowl on the spit, but he was ignorant of the need for basting, and of the fact that even a wind-up spit needed some attention. He left it, turning as it should, and then went out to feed his animals; the un-wound spit became stationary, half the fowl was charred almost to a cinder, the other side almost raw.

The best of the spoiled stuff must go to Godfrey who was growing; next to Jem, an inveterate grumbler, next to Joseph who never grumbled – that seemed unjust, but it was the way things went; Henry ate the worst, stuff which even his hearty appetite could not make palatable. Jem had not suggested, as he had done on a former occasion, that he should go home for his dinner, for food was not plentiful there, now; he had stayed at home on Christmas Day and the day following; he intended to stay home on Twelfth Night. That was all.

Now, as Henry smelt the proof that somebody in the priest's house could cook, Joseph spoke of food, too.

'I'll not come to my dinner, Master. If I work straight through, they'll lay snug tonight. Another thing, too. If the weather take the turn my nose tell me, maybe I shan't be able to come down for a day or two, so I'd be obliged if you'd bring me a store of bread and cheese, a bit of frying bacon if you can spare it. Then I'll manage. Oh, and a little flour, in case things get really bad.'

He had managed on his own in the past and could do so again. His diet was not quiet so dreary as it might sound. The hard Suffolk cheese toasted well, and a spade made a good frying pan. Given flour he could make dough cakes to cook on the stones that made his hearth in the centre of his now snug and waterproof hut. Over the willow branches which shaped and sustained it, he had, working at odd times, plastered clay, inside and out: then he had turfed it on the outside – choosing a time when pasture was plentiful, so that the removal of some turf from the edge of the fold had not robbed them, his charges. In the turves there had been living roots, grass, weeds, wildflowers; they had reached out towards each other, woven themselves together in a tough outer hide, wind and weatherproof. Joseph as well as his flock would lie snug whatever happened.

Henry said, 'Have you enough for today, Joseph?'

'Yes, I was thinking forrard.'

'So must I,' Henry said. For even bread was running out now. Flour too. Tomorrow he must take action about such things.

The children came trooping in, rather shyly, for this was something new and their Intake blood made them distrustful of innovation. The little girl, Emma Edgar, whose thin shoulder had put this whole project into motion, came in, carrying a child, rather over a year old, on her out-thrust hip, the traditional carrying way for females who must carry a child unable, or reluctant to walk, and yet have one hand free for some other task. To her free hand another child clung.

After the briefest Benediction, asking God's blessing on the food, that Father Matthew could remember from his seminary days, the meal began. Tim went around – important for once – distributing the circles of bread, crusty on the outside, spongy in the centre, so that they made natural receptacles into which Father Matthew, following, could drop – from a ladle which Mistress Captoft had not thought it worthwhile to remove – cubes of meat, some lean, some fat. He had spent an hour carving and chopping and removing bones. It must all be as fair as he could make it. The meat was dished up in a luscious gravy into which onions, long and gently cooked had disintegrated; there were shreds of finely chopped mint, too, the whole thickened, almost glutinous with flour.

Moving about amongst his young guests, Father Matthew reflected that his fears that after the humble feast he and Tim would have clearing up to do, were completely unfounded. A crumb of bread dropped was instantly retrieved; if a drip of gravy fell a finger dabbled in it, was licked, applied again, licked again until no smear remained. He thought: Well in one thing I was right; they are hungry.

Feed my sheep. Christ had said that. And in his seminary somebody had explained the symbolism of it. Father Matthew had never understood what symbolism meant; but he understood hunger and determined that during this bad time, and in any other bad time, children must be fed. He'd defraud the Peter's Pence collector, sell his warm cloak and his beautifully embroidered satchel. He'd beg, cajole, threaten.

The candles on the altar took on a brighter glow as the day darkened, prematurely. Snow, looming in the offing for two days, was now about to fall.

He dismissed them with the briefest possible blessing and told them to hurry home. He expected no thanks – his own manners were poor – and was not surprised when they ran off. All except the little girl, Emma Edgar. The baby on her hip had gone to sleep, still sucking a gravy-soaked crust. The other child, crammed and half somnolent, dragged on her hand. Another man would have seen in her, perhaps, the symbolism of womanhood, burdened almost from the first by the claims of the helpless young. But Father Matthew's mind did not work that way. He said, 'Run along, Emma. You will be left behind.'

She said, 'Father. Did you see? She was there, too.'

'Who?'

'Our Lady. Just there.' Having no hand free the child jerked her head towards the slab of black marble, so distinct from the grey stone of the church floor. 'All blue, with lilies.'

He saw that snowflakes were already falling, big ones drifting down with the apparent idleness that concealed real purpose, so he hurried her along, saying, 'Yes, yes, my dear child. Now hurry along and catch up with the others. Ask one of the boys to give your little brother a pig-a-back ride.'

Then he turned back and looked at the black marble slab which, he had been given to understand, covered the last resting place of the Lady Sybilla, Master Tallboys' mother, dead and buried in old Father Ambrose's time; her death if recorded at all, was recorded on a page in the Parish Book, so over-scribbled as to be illegible. For a grown woman, even a very small woman, the black slab was, Father Matthew thought, quite inadequate. More like a child's grave covering. No mark identified it. Sir Godfrey, ravaged by grief – and remorse – had complained about his sweet Sybilla lying under cold stone: Tana had taken this literally and believed that his grief, all that now stood between him and her, might be eased if Sybilla lay under marble. So Henry had been commissioned to buy marble and the only piece in Baildon was this, left over from a job the stone-mason had just completed. The lack of inscription was due to the fact, that guided by old Father Ambrose, Sir Godfrey's memorial to Sybilla had taken a more practical shape – the restoration of the church, the proper furnishing of the altar.

Father Matthew did not know that Sybilla had always brought what flowers she had to the church – a custom kept up by Griselda, faithful imitator; but he did know that lilies were the flowers most closely associated with Our Lady, even called by her name, Madonna lilies. And blue was her colour. He did not doubt that Emma Edgar had seen a vision. And what about those white flowers, springing up over-night at the edge of the onion bed? A sign of approval of what he was doing and intended to go on doing.

The thought flittered through his mind that the vision might be used to advantage; people would come to see the place, and hope to see what Emma Edgar had seen; they would leave gifts on the black slab. Many places of pilgrimage had grown from such humble beginnings.

But the first person who must be informed was his Bishop and Father Matthew shrank from another interview with that unfriendly man: he would not believe; he would mock; he would say: Last time it was a witch in your parish, now it is a child who sees visions! There was a further consideration. Suppose the Bishop believed and the word spread and people came with their presents, in no time at all, Father Matthew would find himself pushed aside. He could not actually be displaced; only an act of gross immorality could rob him of his living, but a man – or more than one man – with smoother manners and more learning would be appointed as custodians of the shrine. What little power he now had would be lessened and his plans would come to nothing.

He had his share of peasant shrewdness as well as the credulity, stubbornness, conservatism of his breed; better not start anything of which the outcome was uncertain, better not say anything not absolutely necessary.

The black horse, his first exuberance expended, settled down to a steady trot, which ate up the miles. But now the short day was ending and Joanna realised that she had not – as she had hoped – covered the distance in one swift ride. She was still in unknown country and at every crossroads was obliged to rein in and ask direction, worthless, because so far she had not encountered anyone who had ever heard of Baildon. On such a bitter day only people who were compelled to venture out were abroad; a woman feeding some cooped hens, a man milking a goat, a boy scattering scanty wisps of hay to some sheep in a bare pasture. She did not ask at houses, because that meant dismounting and that she had done only once, for a most necessary purpose, and she was so stiff with cold that getting out of the saddle, and then back again was painful, even perilous. So much so that at a place where a stream crossed the road, much like the water-splash in the lane to Intake, she let the horse drink, but did not get down to drink herself.

At each divergence of the road she was obliged to rely upon her own judgment, holding to east as well as she could.

She remembered that on that miserable journey to Stordford she and the bishop's man had stayed for a night at a religious house which had a hostel for travellers; but either she had not reached it yet, or, taking the wrong road, had missed it.

She knew from her experience of Stordford that large establishments kept open house for *bona fide* tavellers, but although she saw several big houses, windows already lighted from within, she dared not ask hospitality; people in such places formed a close-knit network and she still feared pursuit, though she thought that thanks to the black horse, she had, so far, outdistanced it. She knew that she was a conspicuous figure, dressed for indoors on such a day, a girl riding what was plainly a man's horse.

And, in the fading light, the horse was becoming troublesome. Under-exercised since his arrival at Stordford he had accepted her, as someone knowledgeable, smelling right and prepared to let him gallop. Now something inside his shapely head informed him that he was not being taken either towards his own stable, or the one which was his temporary home. He expressed his disapproval of this procedure by tossing his head and occasionally jibbing, trying to turn.

Another crossroads. There'd been no sun all day, yet cloud-blotted as the sky was, there had been just that difference in the quality of the light to distinguish east from west, north from south. That shadowy guidance was now lost. A choice of ways and nobody to ask. Wrong! Out of the greyness more solid shapes took form; a well-head, a man with a bucket.

She asked the question she had already asked so many times: Which road for Baildon? And this time instead of the – Dunno; never heard of it – she received, in turn, a question.

'Would it be Bury St. Edmund's way?'

'Yes,' she said eagerly. 'They lie in the same direction.'

'Then I can tell you. I been there. Bury, not Basildon. Carried my boy there; years ago when he was a bit of a cripple . . .'

Joanna had no time or inclination to listen to the marvellous story of how a crippled boy, carried to St. Edmund's shrine, had been miraculously cured and was able to walk home.

'Which way?'

The man moved his free arm and then said, 'No. You and me's facing different ways. Let's see.' He turned himself about. 'To your right,' he said. 'Then sharp left. It's a lonely road.'

It was also, mercifully, sheltered; great thickets of trees on either side acted as screens from the wind. Though she was now so cold as to be almost numb; the only part of her body that had any feeling left was where, between saddle and stirrup, her legs were warmed by the horse. She thought what a fool she'd been to rush out so ill-equipped, yet had she lingered to clothe herself properly, she might have been intercepted, prevented from setting out at all.

Could horses see in the dark? One might think so from the way in which Henry's old horse jogged home in the winter afternoons, but then he might know his way. How long could a horse go without food She was reasonably certain that she had snatched this one from his stable before the dilatory, Christmas-season service had reached him. Was his slowing down of pace due to his becoming weak from hunger, or to his carefully picking his way. She bent stiffly and made encouraging noises, promising him everything, everything, if only he'd keep going and get her home.

Presently she began to worry about that turn to the left. Would she miss it?

At Stordford she had not been missed immediately. Lady Agnes knew what green venison could do. Then as time went on she suspected that Joanna had been dragged in to help with the wedding preparations. They'd need fresh garlands and even a girl in disgrace could be allowed to prick her fingers on holly. The fire burned low, and presently her bladder needed relief. She began to shout, and was either unheard or ignored. Weeping with rage and self-pity, she reached for her stick. It was no longer of use to her, but she cherished a half hope that one day she might hobble again, and it always stood propped within easy reach. She seized it and beat upon the floor, upon the frame of her bed.

It was some time before the noise she made was noticed, and then only by a servant, half tipsy, as was the usual state at this season.

'Where is the demoiselle Joanna?' Lady Agnes demanded. The woman stared stupidly. How could she be expected to know? She rendered the essential service and went away.

In due course one of the pages brought up the dinner – prepared for two, the old woman noticed. She put the question to him, and he said, 'With the others, I suppose.'

'Ask your mistress to come to see me. At once!'

In the hall, dinner was already served at the high table, and at his place, below the squires, above the servants, his own awaited him. Despite the *at once*, he saw nothing very urgent about the message and decided to eat before delivering it. Then for a time he could not find Lady Grey who, in her own words, was obliged to be everywhere at once, just now. A wedding at such short notice took a great deal of organising. When the message reached her she went at once, and found the old woman alone, shedding tears of self-pity, rage and frustration. The fire was almost dead, now, and although the tray had been, placed in its usual place, on a table near the bed, much of its contents was out of reach of Lady Agnes' restricted motion.

Curiously, the urgent question was not immediately asked. Lady Agnes had never liked her niece-by-marriage, and now, in her disturbed state, embarked upon a virulent, if slightly incoherent denunciation. It was deliberate neglect; to place the girl here so that servants thought they need do nothing. And then to withdraw her, leaving a poor bed-ridden woman to die of cold and hunger. Just because she had had a visit from the Chaplain, they thought, no doubt that she had made her will, and the sooner she died the better. Well, they were wrong; she had made no will, and when she did, this piece of ill-treatment would be remembered.

Aunt Agnes must be soothed. With her own hands Lady Grey mended the fire, promised food, freshly cooked to be brought up at once; denied all blame for what had happened, accusing Joanna as fiercely as she had herself been accused. Another trick, typical of that false little jade, to pretend to accept banishment from the hall so cheerfully pretend to be so dutiful, and then to do *this*. She was skulking somewhere. She would be found, severely reprimanded.

Only half-pacified, still unwilling to believe that Joanna, whom she liked, of whom she had become as fond as the limited emotion of old age would allow, had deserted her, Lady Agnes calmed herself enough to say, 'She may have taken a fit and fallen somewhere. She looked – just before she left me – very strange.'

'In all her time here, she has never had a fit to my knowledge. She is capable of pretending *that*, too! ' Horrible, hateful girl. And too leniently dealt with, Lady Grey now realised. She should have been cuffed and shaken, stood with her hands on her head, facing the wall until she dropped, as Maude and Beatrice had been. But I was in a difficult position, Lady Grey thought, excusing her weak handling – she was neither my child, nor my legal ward. She chose, at this moment to ignore the fact that from the very first there'd been something which had warned her that Joanna was not Maude, or Beatrice ...

Even now she was not, however, sufficiently aware of the difference to consider the possibility that the hateful girl had, in mid-winter, left Stordford alone. She was hiding, sulking somewhere, doing her clever best – and even Lady Grey could not deny that in certain ways the wretch was clever – to make a confusion.

Outside the window the fading light changed; not a

brightening exactly, a lightening. The first snowfall of the year. How wise to have settled upon Twelfth Night!

Downstairs again, giving orders, arranging everything, Lady Grey said, 'Beatrice, go up to Aunt Agnes. She needs help; all her jewels are scattered on the counterpane; help her to sort them and put them away.'

Then followed the resolute, but discreetly conducted hunt for Joanna. Discreet because Lady Grey did not wish the name to be mentioned in Lord Shefton's hearing; once it had been erased from that marriage settlement, and Maude's substituted, it would have been in the worst of taste to remind him. So she shut him away, with Maude, her father and a waiting woman named Mabel to play with the Tarot cards while the rest of the household played another game. Not hunt the slipper ... not simple hide-and-seek, but, under Lady Grey's expert handling, just a game. *Find Joanna.*

Joanna was not found. What was presently discovered was that Sir Gervase Orford's best, big black horse was missing.

Sir Gervase cuffed his squire about the head, but otherwise took his loss lightly, saying, 'Whoever snatched Blackbird will have his hands full and by tomorrow will be only too glad to turn him loose. The best example of biting the feeding hand I ever met with.'

Only Lady Grey made any connection between the disappearance of the girl and the horse. And, seeing further than Sir Barnabas, she broke down, once the privacy of the connubial chamber was achieved.

Since her marriage she had never been the victim of self-pity; she regarded herself as a most fortunate woman, but now she was sorry for herself.

'Just when we were all so happy, this must happen. And you know what will be said – unless she is found and brought back immediately. That we so resented her behaviour – as regards Lord Shefton – that we bore on her too hard. Or even ... even that for the sake of that half-dowry lodged with you, we did away with her. Such stories are not unknown. Years,' she said, weeping, 'years upon years, I have done my best. And now this! More than any mortal should be asked to bear, having done her best.'

Sir Barnabas said, 'My love; you are over-wrought. Too much excitement in a short time. Too much to do. Such fancies, indeed.' He patted her and made soothing noises, behaving towards her much as he would have done to a startled horse. It did not occur to him to feel any compunction about having left everything to her, even the breaking of unwelcome news to Lord Shefton. Gertrude had always handled such things, leaving him to be merry and carefree. When she continued to fret, weeping in the graceless way of one to whom tears did not come easily, he began to think about age; that process so rightly known as the change, when amiable women turned shrew, and shrewish ones torpid, when slender figures thickened and sturdy ones shrivelled. Being fond of her, he thought: Poor dear. And made up his mind to be patient with her. 'Come, come,' he said, 'calm yourself. At first light tomorrow, mounted men shall go in search of the little hussy. She cannot have got far. In this weather.'

The snow which had begun in the afternoon, had thickened as night fell and the wind veered to the north and by morning Stordford and all the surrounding country lay deep under snow. Two feet deep, more where it had drifted. Any kind of search or pursuit was impossible now.

At Intake though the clouds still threatened, the east wind still triumphed; as the knowledgeable said, it was too cold for snow. But it would fall, as soon as the wind changed. Henry knew that he must make the best of this time. Take a sack of wheat to the Nettleton mill and while it was being ground, drive on into Baildon, where surely the bakers would be back at work.

Knight's Acre had known its ups and downs but Henry could not remember a shortage of bread. Let this Christmas season get over and the first thing he would do would be to hunt for a good sensible woman.

Heaving the sack of wheat into the waggon caused a pang which exacerbated his general feeling that something was wrong with the world. With him? So when Godfrey asked, 'Can Guard come?' the answer was sharp.

'No, he cannot. He stays here and does his duty. If you can't bear an hour's separation, you stay, too.'

The dog was already ruined; actually sleeping on the boy's bed.

'Guard, you guard,' Godfrey said, climbing into the waggon. He wanted to go with his father, out of temper as he seemed this morning. And he cherished a secret hope that during their absence something might happen to prove that Guard was not ruined. A wolf perhaps ... Unlikely; he'd never seen one himself.

Like most other people who did business with Henry, the Nettleton miller respected him without liking him much. A just man, a civil man, but cold and aloof.

'I'll call back,' Henry said. 'I have to go to Baildon to buy bread.'

'Buy bread!' What an astonishing thing, for a man who grew his own wheat.

'The woman who had charge of my house left – and took the maidservant with her,' Henry said, giving an explanation, not a bit of gossip, or a complaint.

The miller cast a glance at the lowering sky and said, 'There's no need for that, Master Tallboys. My missus is baking this very minute. She'd be glad to let you have a loaf or two.'

'I wonder if she'd tell me how to make it.'

Again astonished, the miller said. 'I'm sure she would. Glad to. Though I say it, she's a dab hand at a loaf.'

'Then I'll go in, if I may.'

The miller looked at Godfrey and said, rather diffidently, 'Would the young master like to come with me and see the mill at work?'

'Oh, yes please,' Godfrey said, answering for himself.

Moving a bit stiffly, Henry went towards the kitchen door, cursing Bert Edgar. Whatever the injury was, it would seem to heal itself, he'd forget about it until he lifted something heavy. Then it seemed to re-open and pain him again for a day or two. There was no outward sign of injury, and several applications of Walter's horse liniment had no effect at all. When the pain was there it was there until it chose to go. Most jobs, thank God, did not provoke it, he could lift a forkful of hay, a shovelful of manure without strain.

The miller's wife welcomed him warmly. She knew him – as she knew all the mill's customers by sight and by name and cherished a kind of romantic feeling for him. She thought him extremely handsome and his expression, which her husband thought surly, she thought was merely grave and rather sad. Not unlike – God forgive her if it was blasphemous – the picture of Christ on the wall of Nettleton church. (Griselda, years earlier, had felt precisely the same about Henry's father, and the feeling had saved his life by prompting her to do what she could for him when he was thrown out into an innyard barn to die.)

This morning she thought he looked not less handsome, but less well than usual. Certainly thinner. More lined. The man she saw most of – her husband – weighed on his own scales, just over fourteen stones and had a broad rosy face. You couldn't actually say that Master Tallboys looked pale, his face was too weathered for that, but she thought, in a slightly muddled way, that if he could look pale he would look pale. Maybe the cold.

'Sit here, by the fire, Master Tallboys,' she said and thought of mulled ale and ginger cakes, luxuries that a prosperous, childless couple could well afford.

Henry explained what he wanted of her – and his voice which she had never heard, close-to, before, was just what she expected – beautiful.

'My bread's in the oven now,' she said, almost as though in getting it in so soon she had been at fault, 'but of course, I could tell you.'

'I should be deeply obliged.'

'We'll have something to warm us as we talk,' she said. Not that she needed warming, but he certainly did.

As he accepted her hospitality and listened to her talk, Henry looked about him and saw how comfortable everything was. It was a kitchen; cooking hearth and wall oven side by side along one wall, shelves of mugs and other crocks and kitchen tools along another. But because it was living room too, the settles on either side of the hearth were cushioned and the table – now that the bread-making was over, wore a gay scarlet cloth.

He realised that in his own home two ways of life had always run alongside, the life of the kitchen, the life in the hall. Usefulness on one side of the wall, comfort on the other. Never really united, as they were here. Vaguely he meditated the possibility of bringing his own cushioned settle into his kitchen, but the thought of lifting made his pain worse. The sense of failure – never too far away – clamped down. He'd made a mess of everything he undertook. And, remembering the reproachful glance that his son had shot at him, as he climbed into the waggon, after hugging the dog, he was in a fair way towards making a mess of parenthood, too.

'They should be about done, now,' the miller's wife said. 'I'll show you how to test a loaf.' She did so and was satisfied. Then with an air of modest achievement, she withdrew all the loaves and ranged them, even and golden and sweet-smelling on the table. 'There's another thing to remember, Master Tallboys. They must be quite cold before they're stored away.'

She'd told him all he needed to know, but all the time she had been conscious of the incongruity of it; this handsome, dignified man, with his beautiful voice, turning baker!

'Can't you get somebody to do for you?'

'Oh, I shall in time. Once Christmas is over.' He did not again explain about Katharine's unexpected departure; but he did give his rare and singularly sweet smile, as he added, 'Until I find somebody, the boy and I must eat.'

Godfrey and the miller came in; both aglow. It had pleased the man to show, the boy to see, how the mill worked, how the flour was sieved.

'I helped, Father. Didn't I?' He turned his sweet, confident smile upon his new friend.

'You did that. Good as a 'prentice.'

Then the boy's eye fell upon the bread. 'Please, can I have a piece?' Except for those infrequent occasions when Griselda's rage with life in general had touched him for a moment, and lately father's criticism of the handling of Guard, Godfrey had never known anything but indulgence, so he made his request with assurance.

'You've earned it, by all accounts,' the woman said, cutting him a great crust of bread unlike any that had come his way before; for who should have the best, most finely sieved flour, if not the miller's wife?

He ate it with zest, and was then aware that something had happened. What? A moment before, the miller and his wife had both looked at him smiling. Now their faces had changed, though they were both looking at him still. Was it wrong to have *asked*? Apart from Mistress Captoft's little offerings he had never eaten a bit of food outside his own home. So how could he know? He must ask Father.

'That boy was *hungry*,' the miller's wife said, with surprise in her voice.

'Never knew a boy that wasn't,' said her husband.

Don't talk about, don't think about, boys. Married ten years and nothing to show for it; though they were both healthy and hearty and fitted together as hand to glove.

She'd done what was to be done. Prayed, of course. Gone to Bury St. Edmund's and taken a long look at the famous white bull, one glance at which was supposed to bring fertility. Consulted a wise woman, drunk her potions and crawled three times under a low crooked branch; borrowed a petticoat from a woman who had borne eight and reared four. Finally she had made a pilgrimage to the Shrine of Our Lady of Walsingham – a long journey for people of her kind, and the last lap of it walked barefoot.

All useless. They'd put the thought away; never spoke of it; pretended not to care. But it was such a pity, with the mill, and some savings to leave.

What Godfrey had sensed was a momentary dropping of this pretence. Watching the boy gnaw hungrily into bread of her making affected the woman exactly as showing how the mill worked had affected the man.

She said suddenly, 'I'm going to Canterbury!'

It was a name known, like Bethlehem where Our Lord was born, or Calvary, where He died. Or like London. Far off the mind's map.

'Thass the wrong time of year,' the miller said. He'd hoped, been disappointed, hoped again, been disappointed again so often, that now he would *not* lend himself to it any more. 'Spring is for pilgrimages.'

'All the better,' the intrepid woman said. 'The fewer asking favours the more notice Blessed St. Thomas can give.' She looked out of the window and saw that it had begun to snow, and she thought, undeterred – The harder the conditions, the more I show my faith. I'll walk knee-deep if that is what is asked of me.

For Joanna the snow had begun earlier, at a point where the wind from the east had finally failed in its battle against the wind from the north. As always the snowfall, bringing its own potential disasters and difficulties, released a slight, spurious warmth; she was soon wetted through to the skin, but not so rigidly cold, and the big black horse gave no trouble now.

Here was Baildon, the church by whose buttresses she and Henry had stood, enjoying their pies; the market place, all veiled by the snow; the way out of the town, known as the Saltgate; then the road, partially sheltered by the trees of Layer Wood. Turn into the lane, down into the water-splash ... The horse showed an inclination to stop there and drink, but she forced him on. Not far now and he could have everything, buckets of water, a mangerful of oats.

Turn on to the track; the church, the priest's house and then, now plainly seen, now obscured by the whirling snow, was Knight's Acre. Exactly as she had in her nostalgic hours remembered it.

The place where I was born!

And of all the women who had approached in various circumstances and with wildly different feelings, Joanna, though she had no way of knowing it, was the only one who could feel just that link with the stark, slightly forbidding house. Sybilla, for whom it had been built, had thought it over-large; Tana had thought it small; Griselda at first approach had known a faint feeling of homecoming, having very vague, childish memories of such a house. Mistress Captoft had approached it in a business-like manner, a place in which to live, a place to manage, and eventually to leave; Katharine Dowley knew it to be a horrid, haunted place. Of all the people in the world – now that Robert was dead – only Joanna and Godfrey could claim Knight's Acre as their birthplace.

Tears which Lady Grey's cutting remarks and other evidences of disfavour had failed to provoke, now ran scaldingly down Joanna's cold face; but they were tears of joy. She was home! In a minute she would see Henry. And nothing, nothing would ever get her away again.

She had still one obstacle to overcome. Guard was on guard. As his breeder had admitted, he was not yet fully trained, and he had been subjected to the petting which was held to be ruinous, but he knew that the house and yard had been left in his charge and that it was his duty to challenge, if necessary, defend. He stood, alert, in the yard, and from time to time went on patrol, doing so in a curious manner. He never went through the usual opening of the yard, between the end of the out-jutting house and a kind of mound. For him it was the worst of the three bad places, and he could only face it with Godfrey's hand on his collar. So when he left the yard he went around the other out-jutting end of the house, through the garden, to the front, along the track on the far side of the house until he came, from a different direction, to the bad place again; then he turned and retraced his steps.

The other bad places were in the hall, and on the stairs, but he was never alone there, though once or twice, he'd been worse than alone. He'd been with a woman, herself so frightened, that he could smell the fear on her. She wasn't here now.

He stood in the yard, having just finished one of his patrols, when he heard sounds; not the ones he was awaiting. Different. Strange. He moved as near the yard opening as he could go without stepping into the bad place and waited. A horse and a rider, both unknown. Had he not, as his breeder had said, been a bit slow to learn, or had he fully completed his training, the dog would have known that people bent on mischief did not approach in this fashion, open and confident, coming by right, coming home. So from the yard side of the entry he stood and challenged, but the intruder came on; Guard braced himself to defend.

Sir Gervase's best horse, though considerably reduced in spirit by twenty-six hours on the road without food or water, had enough strength left to resist the urging forward towards an unfriendly dog. He jibbed and tried to turn, repeating almost exactly the action of another horse, in the same place, action which had led to a fatal accident. Joanna's mother had been taken unawares. Her daughter was not. Nor was she in a mood to tolerate a second's delay, for she had seen, between the swirls of snow, that the chimney was emitting no smoke, which meant no fire, which meant no meal. Something badly wrong, and she had been right to come.

Guard, muzzle wrinkled back to show sharp fangs, eyes gleaming green, found himself face to face with himself as Joanna, brought almost broadside on, by the horse's attempt to turn, leaned low, her face a mask of hatred, too, green-eyed, sharp-fanged ... Wolfish, as Lady Agnes had re-marked.

She said, 'Get out of my way,' and thought what to do if the brute disobeyed. He wore a spiked collar; one twist and he'd choke! Menace from the intruder and the proximity of the hated place were together too much for the half-trained dog; he backed away. Joanna pulled the horse round and they entered the yard. Anxious as she was to get into the house and find out what was wrong, she was obliged to dis-mount slowly and clumsily, almost immobilised by stiffness and cold. She entered the kitchen with the stumbling, uncer-tain gait of a very old woman.

She spared only a glance – and that a glance of recog-nition. The kitchen was exactly as she had seen it. She stumbled across the hall and heaved herself upstairs, fearful of finding Henry in bed. His room was empty and his work-ing clothes lay tumbled on the floor. For a moment relief was as sharp as pain; then apprehension struck again. This was not a market day in Baildon. So where had Henry gone in his tidy, market-going, church-going clothes?

Not – oh, God! – not to his grave. Her mind rebutted the hideous thought. No! I should have known! I should have seen that, too. She had seen him injured in some mysterious way and the next thought that came into her head was that Henry had gone to consult the physician in Baildon. And the next immediate thought was about her own state. Unless she changed immediately from these wet clothes, she would need a physician herself! Wet clothes, as she knew, and be-lieved, for it was a belief shared by all classes, could lead to anything, from stiff joints to the lung-rot.

She found, not what she wanted, but what was needed, in the room that had been Katharine's. Two summer frocks, clean, and the old working one. Hastily, she stripped and snatching a blanket from the bed, towelled herself dry and almost warm. Then she put on all that Katharine had left.

Shoes. No good, far too big. But she remembeerd the rule, instituted long ago by Sybilla, and adhered to by Griselda; dirty footwear left by the kitchen door and indoor shoes donned. Moving more briskly now, the friction of the blanket had restored her circulation, she padded, barefoot into the kitchen and found that the rule still held. A pair of small slippers, Godfrey's? Yes, of course, fitted her well. Re-clad, re-shod, she thought first of the fire, which – as was the way with fires – was less dead than it looked. A core remained, and fed, poked into activity, it began to blaze, with every flicker showing more of the desolation which had overtaken this once-so-orderly place. There was the big black pot, swung aside on its hook and in it under a shroud of congealing fat a lump of meat and some peas like pebbles. In the larder the carcass of a fowl which only people in sheer desperation would have tried to eat. No bread. No flour. And what could one do without flour to make even a pancake, or a hasty pudding?

One could pull the black pot over the fire and hope that further cooking would soften the hard meat and the peas. And one could begin to restore the kitchen to some kind of order.

Henry halted by the sheep-fold and left two of the four loaves which the miller's wife had given him, refusing his offer to pay, some flour from the new sackful, and the cheese and frying bacon which Joseph had requested and which he had not bothered to stop and deliver on his way to Nettleton.

The bacon looked so meagre that he felt he must apologise for it.

'Just to tide you over,' he said. 'I've got another side in the smokehole. I'll bring it up tomorrow.'

'If this lay – and it will – don't you fret about me, Master. Worst come to the worst, I'll kill the other old tup.' He looked at the snow, now falling heavily, and at the sky. 'This'll be bad, but we've lived through worse.'

Back in the waggon, Henry thought about the sack of flour which the miller had heaved in so easily. The thought of hauling it down, carrying it to the larder and after that climbing up to take the fresh side of bacon from the smoke-hole, sent a pang through him.

That is sheer fancy, he told himself sternly. You are making altogether too much of a trivial hurt. How do other people with a real disability manage? Think how active David was, with his lame leg!

The curtain of snow was irregular, sometimes indeed the flakes appeared to drift upwards. In one such interval he saw his home plainly, smoke issuing from the chimney. All it conveyed to him was the idea that the fire, left very low had flared up during his absence. There was nothing to warn him of anything unusual as he drove into the yard. A more experienced dog than Guard might have indicated the presence of a stranger in some fashion, but Guard was overwhelmed with delight at the sight of Godfrey and had no other thought.

Thinking of the sack, and at the same time despising himself for his weakness of will, Henry took the waggon as near the kitchen door as possible, which was not very close, for at some time in the past Walter had occupied some of his scanty leisure in laying a kind of platform of flint stone, so that Sybilla could feed her hens and even reach the well without stepping into the mud.

'May I put the horse and waggon away?' Godfrey asked.

'You may.'

'Then you can have just a little ride, Guard. Up, boy, up!'

'Bring the bread when you come,' Henry said, and dragged the sack on to his shoulders. The pain knifed him.

There was now enough snow on the cobbles to muffle his footsteps, and Joanna was scrubbing the kitchen table. a number of things, each small, had combined to reassure her. The ease with which the fire was revived was proof that it had been lit that morning. Then she had thought: That poor horse! After all I promised him! There was an empty place in the stable; one horse, the old one she remembered, and which seemed to remember her, stood there, half asleep, but there was evidence in the manger, and in the freshly-dropped dung, that there had been two there earlier on in the day. The waggon was gone. Put this alongside the fact that there was no flour in the house, and no bread, and it was more than likely that Henry had gone to the miller's, wearing, as he always did when he stepped off his own land, his decent clothes. Godfrey's absence was not significant; Henry had this fixed idea that the way of life which he had deliberately chosen for himself was not suited to other people, and might well have sent his son elsewhere, as he had sent Robert, and herself.

When the door opened they took one another by surprise. His surprise greater than hers because she had been prepared for the haggard, pain-stricken look just as she had been prepared for the state of the kitchen. He had had no warning at all.

His face was scored by the marks of pain, and others, more grim, his determination to ignore it; a stern set mask of endurance which changed as he dropped the sack just inside the door, not reflecting the relief he felt at shedding the load, not to welcome, but to blank dismay. Total, absolute.

She'd come – or so she had imagined, to help, to rescue him from whatever troublesome situation he was in. She had intended to say: It is all right, Henry. I am here, I'll see to it all. The words were still-born.

Henry said, 'Joanna!' No gladness; no welcome.

They had sent her home. By that impulsive, thoughtless acknowledgment of a completely nonsensical betrothal he'd ruined her prospects, he thought, and here she was in a filthy old frock scrubbing a table; the very fate he had tried to save her from.

Joanna was thinking too. Better not mention that inner eye about which he had always been so sceptical. Better not mention the betrothal, nobody, not even Henry, could have greeted the woman to whom he considered himself betrothed in quite that way.

'They sent you home?' he said.

Quick, quick, a plausible tale.

'Nobody sent me. I came of my own accord. I incurred Lady Grey's displeasure and was given a punishment that was intolerable. I will tell you all, later. That is flour? Good! We can have dumplings.'

Godfrey came bursting in, 'Father, there's a strange horse ... *Janna!*' He flung himself at her, just as Guard had flung himself at him. Between Godfrey and Joanna a curious relationship had existed; for a long time Griselda, his Mumma had stood between them, and as he grew the boy had seen the girl doing all the things he longed to do, working in the yard and the fields, going with Father to market. Then, for a short time, with Mumma dead, he had been allowed to work – as well as he could – and to play with her. She knew a lot of games. He sensed, with a child's sure instinct, that she had no great feeling for him, and that he had no hold on her. She'd play if she wanted to, otherwise not. He was not important to her, as he had been to Mumma, and soon after, to Mamma-Captoft.

Nevertheless, he had missed her and was glad to see her; eager to see the connection between her and that horrible horse.

'He tried to bite me when I took our horse in, Janna did you really ride home on him?'

'How else?'

They talked about Guard, too.

'How did you get past my dog?' In some indefinable way Godfrey felt that Guard had not quite lived up to his name and had proved Father right about spoiling by petting.

'Oh, he had sense enough to know that I belonged here. How long have you had him?'

That led smoothly on to the story of the rough men, his own heroic behaviour on that memorable day; how Mamma-Captoft had gone away and taken Katharine with her.

The child's eager chatter, his complete ignorance of all undercurrents, eased the awkward situation. There was no need for Henry or Joanna to say much over the poor meal; even supplemented by the dumplings and recooked, the ill-prepared pork and peas were something to satisfy hunger and no more.

Covertly, now and again they glanced at one another and quickly glanced away.

Two years! He'd aged by far more. Even now, with lines of pain and the lines of determined effort easing away a little, and the look of absolute dismay gone. Just above his ears the fawn-coloured hair had a few silvery streaks in it, and cheek-bones, jawbones and the bridge of his nose were sharper. None of this made him less desirable.

241

In her he saw almost no change at all. A mite taller perhaps, maybe two inches. He'd always thought that she was pretty and too fragile-looking for the life she had been obliged to lead, out of doors while Griselda lived and then here in this kitchen – the life he had always thought so unsuitable and done his best to alter. So far as he could see Stordford had left no stamp on her at all.

Outside the snow, now determined, fell heavily. Every flake was welcome to Joanna, if to nobody else. It would hinder the pursuit and give her time to convince Henry of two things. That she was indispensable here; and would never, never go back.

'Milking time,' Henry said. He stood up, walked into the dairy, came back with a bucket, walking in the ordinary way, no limp, no concealed limp.

But, not to be ignored was the sack of flour dropped just inside the door, not taken into the larder and emptied into the bin. That routine act she performed herself, quite easily because although she had that delicate look she was actually as strong as steel.

What about bacon? Had Mistress Captoft, so busy and pernickety only two years ago, actually gone off leaving Knight's Acre with no bacon; no ham in the smoke-hole?

She had not. Joanna climbed up and fumbling about in the dark cavity, found a half side of bacon and a ham. The ham could stay there for a time she thought, but she unhooked and hauled out the side of bacon, rubbed it clean and with a knife sharpened on the hearthstone cut rashers so thin that at the touch of a hot pan they would contract and crisp.

When Henry came in he brought a spade with him.

'If this goes on through the night it'll mean digging our way out in the morning.' He noticed that the sack had gone and the bacon brought down. He protested that he had intended to see to both these things, presently; yet he was glad to be spared the effort and was ashamed of himself again. He remembered how, working with him and Jem Watson in the fields she had always strained herself to the utmost, making up for lack of size and strength by sheer determination. He decided that over his mysterious injury he had been weak-willed. And that called up a very ancient memory indeed:

Sir Godfrey coming home here to Knight's Acre – his first return – wounded in the knee. He'd been glum, full of self-pity, irritable. And he had limped. Limped right up to the time when he was invited to go to a tournament in Spain, and then the limp had vanished overnight and his usual sunny, optimistic temper had been restored.

Contrast that behaviour with that of his mother, Sybilla, who had taken a fall which had lamed her for life, never coddled herself, never complained. He really must, he decided, make an effort to follow his mother's example, rather than that of his father, and to begin *now* by being more resolutely cheerful.

It was not difficult, for Joanna had set herself out to be entertaining. She had always had, even as a child, an eye and an ear for anything ridiculous, and a gift for mimicry; she'd lightened his mood many a time.

Godfrey offered her an opening. He'd exhausted his account of what had taken place here during her absence, and now, happily stuffed with fresh fried bacon and more of the excellent bread, asked, 'What have you been doing, Janna?'

'Learning tricks. I'll show you one.' She stood up, selected a wooden bowl, placed it on her head, walked the length of the kitchen, made a curtsey, turned, came back and sat down again on the bench.

'That looks easy,' Godfrey said.

'You try!'

He poised the bowl on top of his head, took two careful steps, and dropped it.

In Lady Grey's voice, Joanna said, 'How can you ever acquire graceful deportment? Come here.' She gave him two purely playful cuffs about the head. 'Now try again, and remember, no supper until you have managed it.' He recognised the smacks for what they were; and in all his life he had received only two or three smacks from Griselda – quickly compensated for by some small treat. He'd never encountered what he still thought of as roughness until the rough man had jabbed the poker at him. But he had the ordinary child's appetite for drama – and no Tom Robinson to satisfy it with stories.

'Did she hit you, Janna?'

'No. I could do most of those tricks – even when it came to

carrying the bowl with water in it, and not a drop to be spilled. Poor Maude was clumsy from nervousness. Now and then I pretended to shield her. Lady Grey couldn't well hit one and not the other for the same fault. There were other punishments.'

'What?'

'Missed meals; poor meals; no riding; no tennis. That sort of thing.'

Henry had taken no part in this conversation, but he had been listening. And thinking of all the beautiful, butterfly ladies at Beauclaire. Had they all been similarly trained by a process not unlike the harsh breaking-in of young colts? It was something which he, eager to get Joanna into a different, easier way of life had certainly not visualised.

Speaking after a long silence, he asked, 'Joanna, what did you do to incur a punishment that was intolerable?'

She was prepared for that question, knowing that sooner or later it must arise. And she was cautious. Lady Grey might not wish to reclaim her, but the big black horse had an owner; somebody from Stordford would track her down and arriving at Knight's Acre, have a story to tell. Her story must not conflict. And since Henry, in the moment of meeting, had seemed to wish to ignore their betrothal – more sophisticated, now, she knew that unwitnessed it was meaningless, she had ready a story in which Lord Shefton and anything to do with betrothals played no part at all.

'I offended her ladyship. How? Why? Who knows? I did it constantly. But this time the punishment was extreme.'

Ruthlessly she sacrificed Lady Agnes. No mention of the relatively happy hours of reminiscences exchanged; no mention of the proffered gift of the garnet ring.

'Imagine,' she said, 'being set to wait upon a cross, demanding old woman, completely confined to her bed. In one small, malodorous room. I slept on a servant's truckle bed. What food was carried up to us, she had the best of. With Christmas being celebrated in the hall. No servants to do anything.'

That was another trick she had learned at Stordford – how by leaving something out here, and emphasising something there one could tell a story actual enough to be uncontradictable, and yet not much like the truth. The ladies did it all the time. It was not difficult for her to make life at Stordford, where she had been genuinely miserable, sound a great deal more horrible than it had been. Henry, listening, thought that this was not all what he had intended. He also decided – as Joanna hoped he would – not to send her back there.

'Did you learn nothing of use?'

'Oh yes. To read and write and keep accounts without the aid of tally sticks. I failed with the lute. Her ladyship said I was all thumbs. As to embroidery, she was not prepared to waste good silk on me. I patched linen and darned. Hours and hours.' She sounded very plaintive and withheld the information that the length of time spent was due to her dilatoriness and that usually Maude, so devoted, furtively finished the task set.

She did not mention Lord Shefton; that was too close to the betrothal which Henry, from a distance, had acknowledged and thus saved her, and yet at the moment of their meeting, seemed to put away. She needed time.

Henry did not mention Lord Shefton either. It was just possible, he thought, that Joanna had been less than fully informed; Lady Grey sounded quite capable of making such an arrangement, merely asking the girl, belatedly, whether she was betrothed. Getting a displeasing answer and venting her spite.

It was a subject better avoided.

And it was avoided while the snow fell, for about twelve days. Such a snowfall as even Joseph the shepherd or Old Hodgson could not remember. It was the most hampering kind of all, dry and fluffy, no midday sun came to melt it a little, no midnight frost hardened it so that it could be walked upon. In the low house at Intake it was up to the eaves and at Knight's Acre level with the high set windows.

Morning after morning Henry, aided by Godfrey who used one of the small spades which Walter had made twenty years earlier, dug a path to the well, the byre, the pigsty and the stable. Father Matthew and his ugly boy kept a path clear between the house door and the church, and at the rear, to their pigsty. In the village men dug paths to their beasts, to their neighbours and to the river. It was possible to scoop up snow and melt it but the water thus produced had a curious flat taste and was considered to be unhealthy.

It was a time out of time and at Knight's Acre there was no hardship. They had food enough; apart from tending the animals there was no work to do. Joanna spoke of games played at Stordford and Henry said, 'My mother had such toys. They may still be in her chest.'

And Henry vaguely remembered similar games, played at Beauclaire, never at Knight's Acre; everybody too busy. Pretty things; painted cards, cubes of ivory with black spots; a chequered board upon which small carved figures moved this way and that. His mother, might have keep them at the bottom of her clothes chest.

Father Matthew and Tim had little in reserve. At best their housekeeping had been haphazard. Before disaster fell upon Intake, and before the priest had been forced to regard all the grown people there as enemies the village had supplied his small needs. Apart from what he'd been offered in friendly fashion, he had always paid for what he had, a little coarse flour, a bit of belly pork.

Now, cut off, he had the remainder of the sack of flour, given by Master Tallboys, and the bones of the old sheep. Tim, whom the whole world had despised and rejected, did wonders with those bones, cracking them to get to the marrow, boiling and boiling them into a kind of glue, onion flavoured while the onions lasted.

Down at Bywater, Mistress Captoft's ideal arrangement for opening The Sailors' Rest on Twelfth Night had miscarried: not because her workmen were dilatory or she and David lacking in foresight. The weather was to blame; the east wind bringing battered ships in and preventing any seaworthy vessel from leaving. And word of her enterprise had spread about. As soon as her furniture was seen to arrive, and smoke issue from the chimney, she was besieged.

Inevitably there were applicants who had never been to sea in their lives. Mistress Captoft, cautious of beggars, knowing many to be fraudulent, yet saw them as pitiable with that keen wind fluttering their rags.

She was grateful to David when he said, 'Madam, best leave this to me. Once open it to all comers and half the beggars in England'll be on the doorstep. People like that,' in a word he dismissed all who were not seamen, 'can go anywhere. The religious houses give them alms. I was thinking of sea-faring men who've got to be here, waiting for a ship or chucked out, sick or injured. Best leave this to me. I can tell a sailor a mile off.'

Very willingly she left the business of selection to David. She had enough to do.

For one thing she was obliged to make a penny do the work of two; a new experience for her. Paying the five years' rent in advance, buying the absolute necessities for the house and paying for the repairs had practically exhausted her savings. It was in no way an alarming situation, for her rents were due at Christmas and her reliable agent in Dunwich would send the money to her promptly. There would also be, as David had said, men straight from the sea and able and willing to pay a little. No such had yet appeared; her household so far consisted of men much in the state in which she had found David, or men off battered ships, driven into Bywater by the east wind. They would not be paid until they were back in the port from which they had embarked and although some ships' masters did their best for their men, some vessels were unsafe and many stores were ruined.

Mistress Captoft found herself shopping for food at the worst time of the year and for the most expensive commodity of all – *fresh* food.

David did not know what caused scurvy, the sailors' scourge though it was known on land too in winter, especially among the poor; he did know what cured it. Any fresh food, anything that had not been salted. In his time he'd seen chance-come-stuff, fresh fish, fresh meat, a basket of cabbages, a few onions – and down in Spain, oranges or lemons, work miracles on men apparently dying, their sight failing, their teeth dropping out of spongy gums, their legs too weak to support them.

To the rear of the old house there was what had once been a garden. The various transient tenants had not tended it and weeds had overrun whatever had once been planted there. Nettles and a small plant which, broken, had an onion smell, but no fat, swollen root. Next year this garden would

247

be cultivated, there would be rows of cabbages, onions, carrots. Plots of herbs. Next year the apple crop would not fall into the grass and nettles; whole, unblemished fruit would be gathered tenderly and stored; bruised or wasp-bitten ones sliced into rings – all the injured part cut away – and strung on strings, dried in a cooling oven and then hung up.

But this was this year and Mistress Captoft must do the best she could for what was in reality a large family which grew as the weather worsened and the east wind flung battered ships into Bywater, and then the north wind held up any ship not southward bound.

Leaving, as David had suggested, the sorting of seamen from others, she had said, 'Try, David, to find at least two men who can cook. Men who will stay.'

He had found two, both like himself, beached through an infirmity more obvious than real. One had an empty eye-socket – unsightly, but did that matter in a cook? The other had only half a hand, but like many maimed men, given a chance, he could do as much with one hand and a half as any other man could do with two. Both evinced the gratitude upon which Mistress Captoft had counted, both were prepared to make the most out of little.

In fact, the men in general were splendid; well worth helping, Mistress Captoft decided as she literally tightened her girdle, losing flesh as she shared not the privation, exactly, but the limited food.

The snow did not pile up in Bywater as it did further inland. It fell, lay for a while, and then with each coming in of the tide, cold as the water was, seemed to melt away. What was happening only a mile or two from the coast was made clear by a brisk, active young man who had a home to go to. He stayed overnight, paid his fee, expressed his thanks and set out for Stratton Strawless, where his home was. At dusk he was back talking of snow ankle deep, knee deep, thigh deep, and worse with every step. Soft fluffy stuff, ready to gulp down even the most determined man.

Then Mistress Captoft understood why her rents had not arrived from Dunwich.

Even in this terrible weather now and then a bold, or

desperate fisherman, would venture out in search of herring. The hauls were small, so near to the shore, but brought in, silvery blue and often still half alive, were the subject of sharp competitive demand. When the price rose to the incredible height of a penny for six, Mistress Captoft decided that she could no longer afford herrings. David then remembered a time when a whole crew of scurvy-stricken men had been saved by some edible sea-weed. He could not remember its name but he would know it again, he said. So he and some able-bodied men searched the beach but failed to find the kind they were looking for. David realised later this was not the same kind of coast as the rocky shore where the life-saving weed abounded. This flat sandy shore did, however, at low tide, yield food of another kind, and even in blizzards men would go out to dig cockles. Others walked miles in search of nettles, for though the garden had seemed to have an inexhaustible supply, with so many men, some in desperate need of green stuff, and all craving it, even nettles were scarce.

The men, as Mistress Captoft never tired of saying, were wonderful during this time when storm-battered ships kept putting into harbour and none went out. They would rather eat half, they said, than that some poor fellow should be turned away; as for lying two, or even three to a narrow bed, 'Don't you fret, Madam. We lay closer than this aboard.' Mistress Captoft shared in their resolute good humour, was in a way enjoying the shifts and contrivances. She had abandoned her little parlour which now had three makeshift beds wedged in amongst the ordinary furniture. And a man sleeping on the settle. Just occasionally, however, she would wake in the night and think, uneasily about the debts she was incurring – no household could survive without flour. She would wonder too, how long this extraordinary weather could continue; and how long her credit would last. She was not yet well-known here – or known only as what Bywater people called half-cracked, a woman who had bitten off a lot more than she could chew. She had heard of a man who had killed a pig and when she went immediately and offered to buy half of it, to be paid for later, her best ring as a pledge of good faith, he'd looked at her very oddly indeed. More, perhaps, than other people, those who lived in a seaport were suspicious; for there was a pattern of thought, the sea offered a quick escape to cheats and debtors. All outsiders were suspect, and anybody you hadn't known from childhood upwards was an outsider.

Such night thoughts she put resolutely away and thumped her straw-stuffed pillow – her down-filled ones had gone to contribute to the comfort of sick men. God had brought her here, every step guided; He would provide.

The men made things; apparently aboard every ship there were slack times when a man must occupy himself as best he could, with whatever skill he had, on what material was available. Sitting in The Sailors' Rest, by the good fire of driftwood, they still made things. Trinkets. Useful things. Spoons with handles, beautifully carved, combs of bone indistinguishable from those of horn or ivory, crucifixes as realistic as Father Matthew's, necklaces of shells, little salt boxes with hinges of cloth or leather, salt must not come into contact with metal, instant corrosion was the result of that. Many of these things, lovingly worked over were presented with a kind of gratitude that approached love, to Madam. She wallowed in the gratitude she had always craved. Now she could wallow in it; they were all grateful; they all called her Madam; they were her children, they must be fed. But Bywater was now like a town under siege. Everybody within the narrow area that was not snow-covered had either marketed what they had to spare, or was hoarding up, for fear that this terrible winter would never end. The market on the quay was deserted.

The cooks at The Sailors' Rest had stopped making bread and reverted to what they called hard-tack. 'Take longer to chew, Madam, and stay by you better,' the one-eyed man said. 'But of course, I'll make you a proper loaf.'

'Oh no, William,' Mistress Captoft said bravely. 'Bread must be for the sick, only. But it was a kind thought . . .'

She was worried about her ailing guests, some of whom had made such good progress on a diet of fresh herrings, the occasional cabbage, and the nettles, and now appeared to be slipping back. They needed more than bread; things like sops-in-wine and good chicken broth.

There were two places in Bywater from which help might be obtained – the Bishop's Palace and the inn. Gossip had already informed Mistress Captoft that the Bishop was not an open-handed man; he had withdrawn his support from the two charitable institutions which good old Bishop William had founded. Also, Mistress Captoft had a personal grudge against him – he'd never once paid a visit to Benedict, even when a hunting expedition took him past the church at Intake. The idea of appealing to him for help was repugnant to her. So it must be the inn, where at least she was known.

She was in her bedroom, dressing for out-of-doors when her gaze fell upon the collection of little trinkets which the men had made and presented to her. An idea sparked. She remembered that her husband had often said that she had a good head for business. It was worth trying, anyway. She filled her basket with a representative selection of the articles, and set off, not to beg humbly for credit, but to make a business proposition.

The landlady of The Welcome To Mariners had a similar good head. In normal times men straight from the sea, with money to spend, were the best of the inn's customers; but there were others; dealers, carters, pedlars. Pedlars! What pedlar would not be glad to acquire a few such unusual, easily portable things?

'How much are you asking, Mistress Captoft?'

'Not money,' Mistress Captoft said in the easy take-it-or-leave-it manner of a first-class bargainer. 'Once the roads clear I shall have all the money I need. It is just that due to the weather, and the number of men temporarily stranded, and also the fact that I underestimated what I needed, my supplies are running low. I am compelled to barter. For this lot I am asking only a cask of good red wine, a fowl – a boiler would do – this week, and next . . .' Greed shone in the landlady's eyes. Wine was not expensive in itself, it was the duty on it which made it costly and she had a very workable arrangement with the collector of dues; her wine cost her next to nothing. As for fowls, except when cooped for fattening, they cost nothing either; many horses and donkeys in the yard had nosebags and many grains were dropped.

A flurry of doves passed the window and Mistress Captoft went on, her sentence apparently uninterrupted, 'and four doves each week for the next month.'

'You drive a hard bargain, Mistress Captoft.'

'If I am asking too much,' Mistress Captoft said, and made as though to collect what she had displayed.

'But I sympathise with your situation. I agree.'

They looked into one another's eyes and understood, just as Dame Isabel and Mistress Captoft had looked and recognised.

'Will there be more?' the landlady asked, thinking of how, after this lapse, custom would increase.

'Oh yes, I can guarantee a continuous supply. I have, alas, a number of men who will never go to sea again. And they like to be occupied. The poor fellow who made this,' she touched a necklace of cockle-shells, 'has only one foot. Far worse than losing a whole leg, for which a wooden stump can be substituted ... I will send two men along for the wine; but I would like to take the fowl with me.'

The landlady rose and shouted an order; then she came back and suggested that she and Mistress Captoft should take a drink together – the usual way of sealing a bargain. Mistress Captoft refused, pleading lack of time. Some sense of honour was left to her and forbade her to drink to a bargain which she was prepared to break at the first possible moment, for even as she sat there, making it, another thought had occurred. If these things were saleable in one place, why not in another, only a short distance along the quay? When the time came – as it must, surely it must, when money would buy things, the articles would be sold where they were made. Walking home, light-footed, light-hearted, she planned a kind of shelf, sloping, in the window of her little parlour; it would be covered in velvet – she was prepared to sacrifice a poppy-coloured gown which had not the happiest of associations for her. Against such a glowing background the things would look well.

Knight's Acre, cut off from the world, was enjoying a period of happiness and ease from work. Both cows were in calf, so there was no dairy work to bother with. They had casked meat and smoked meat, they had flour. Joanna knew how to make salted meat edible, and she could bake. Henry worried a little about Joseph and made one attempt to reach him, but the snow was still soft then and he was, like the man making for Stratton Strawless, obliged to turn back. Then the snow froze and upon the surface of it a man could walk. He set off with fresh bread, a whole cheese and more bacon, to find that all his anxiety had been wasted. Joseph had killed the other old tup and so far eaten only the best of it – the kidneys, the liver and a cut or two from the loin. The mangled carcass hung outside his hut, on the side farthest from the sheep-fold, from which a palpable warmth arose; so many woolly bodies in such proximity.

'All in good heart, Master,' Joseph said proudly. 'And I give this,' he looked around at the snow, 'about another four days.'

'How can you know?'

'There's a new moon, about due. Fickle as women the moon is. Yes, another four-five days'll see this out. And I shan't eat half that. Take what you like, Master.'

'All right. If you're sure, Joseph, I'll take a leg.'

As the shepherd hacked away, promising that the frost would have softened the tough meat, Henry looked across at the priest's house and was aware of – not a responsibility exactly, but a neighbourly obligation.

'What about Father Matthew and his boy?'

'Alive so far as I know,' Joseph said, with far less interest than he would have shown in a couple of sheep.

'I'll take them a bit, too. If you can spare it.'

Joseph used his knife again, hacking away this time at what was known as the scrag. Not that he had anything against either the priest or the boy. He was just being sensible.

By this time hunger had shown its ugly face in the priest's house. The flour and the stripped carcass that remained from the children's feast had been eked out to the utmost. Lately they had lived on a gruel made from the pig food, a coarse meal known, rightly, as sharps, sharp in the mouth, sharp in the belly. The husks which the swine did eat, Father Matthew thought, remembering the parable of the Prodigal Son. They still had onions, but they, though flavourful and healthy, added to the wreck the gruel made of one's inside. As a result both he and the boy were weak as kittens and for the last few days it had taken their combined efforts to keep a path to the church open. That morning, after a night of frost it had been more difficult than ever. Feebly, on the verge of collapse, the priest had performed his office, going through the motions, saying the words, but all the time appealing to God in an unusual, personal way, just as he had appealed when faced with the ordeal of the hot iron; but with less strength, less confidence.

And now here was Master Tallboys, with a hunk of fresh meat in his hand. A gift from God. Very welcome, too, was the news that Joseph who considered himself to be weather-wise, predicted a thaw within four or five days.

To Joanna the news was less pleasing. The thaw would put an end to this enjoyable timeless time, the feeling of being a close family unit, apart from the world. Henry was already talking of finding a woman who could cook, starting the search as soon as he could get to Baildon. When he mentioned this, or indeed anything concerned with the future, Joanna remained silent. Time enough to protest when the moment came. She knew she would never go back to Stordford; she was almost certain that after the way she had behaved, Lady Grey would not wish to have her back, unless there was some nonsense about that dowry. But somebody from Stordford was bound to come sooner or later, if only to recover the big black horse, and then there would be talk and the word *betrothal* was sure to crop up, and that would put an end to the happy state in which she and Henry had lived for almost a month. She had been determined not to mention the word until he did, and he seemed equally determined not to refer to it. It was a terrible thought but she faced it unflinchingly – Henry did not love her as she loved him. She'd known that in the instant of their meeting. That look of dismay, the question: Did they send you home? She knew perfectly well that had Henry suddenly appeared – say at Stordford, even if he had done a murder and been fleeing from justice with a price on his head, she would have welcomed him very differently. And since that moment, when the joyous welcome had been withheld and only Godfrey had been entirely natural, she had watched Henry carefully. She was more sophisticated now and knew that special look which did not necessarily imply friendship, or any serious intention; just the hungry, *wanting* look. (That had also been a matter of preening and giggling amongst Lady Grey's ladies.)

Tana, her mother, had believed that love on one side *must* compel love upon the other, and had bedevilled Henry's father; so sure of herself, so sure that nothing stood between them except his wife that she'd poisoned Sybilla and thus cleared her own way to nothing, except a man half-crazed by grief, glad to go off to the wars and die. Joanna knew nothing of that old sad story, but she knew her own mind. She was prepared – now – to keep their relationship on a friendly basis. She'd made a mistake once; two years ago in the wood; and perhaps another, later, in making a makeshift betrothal a condition of her going to Stordford. Makeshift as it was, it had saved her from becoming the Countess of Shefton. That was enough for the moment. Let the future take care of itself.

They played various games. Henry said, quite eagerly, 'I believe my mother had such toys,' and went up to look in the bottom of the chest in which Sybilla had kept her clothes – all long ago used by Griselda.

A box containing a board and all the little mommets for a game called chess; a pack of cards, soiled by much handling and with broken corners; six dice. None used since Knight's Acre was occupied.

After supper they had merry games, and with better feeding, and the pain not provoked, the lines in Henry's face faded out. Now and then he laughed, as in the old days, coming gloomily from a bad market day, he had laughed when she had set herself, deliberately to cheer him. Brotherly, not loverly.

The snow had also isolated Stordford and Lord Shefton was restive; longing to get back to his house in the Strand and the lively company of London. He was bored and always easily aware that here at least were two people – Sir Barnabas and his wife – who knew that he had been fobbed off with second best. Being so pleased with the match they were unlikely to say indiscreet things, but he was always conscious of their knowledge.

Maude was young – attempts to deflower her had given him a certain amount of pleasure, not least because it proved his virility – almost. Not that she would ever know the difference! Out of bed she was a bore; too anxious to please;

255

her every remark predictable, her every action intended to please, and therefore unpleasing. Even now she occasionally shot anxious glances at that old termagant, her mother, anxious for approval, fearing its opposite. It was impossible not to think as snowbound day followed snowbound day, how different that other girl was, with her spark of wit, her ready tongue and her curious air of caring for nobody. To have captured *her* would have been – despite his wealth and position – flattering to his vanity. One had only to look at poor Maude to know that any husband would have done. In fact, Lord Shefton realised, he had committed the juvenile error of marrying on the rebound. In addition, one of his precious new teeth, shallowly rooted or worked too hard, fell out. At the dinner table! Rationally His Grace of Bywater could not be blamed for *that*; but for every other aspect of this dismal affair he was to blame; and would be punished. Once the snow melted and Lord Shefton was back in London.

The thaw came suddenly and floods followed. The drains under the sheep-fold at Knight's Acre could not deal with the water, so Joseph dug ditches, all slanted towards the river, and pushed the straw walls of the pen inwards to give his dear ones something to stand upon while the water drained away. At Intake some houses, nearest the river were flooded, and some animals died. The only human casualty was old Ethel who, dipping water at the Steps, now invisible under the brown gush, missed her footing and fell.

Knight's Acre, standing a little higher, for Sybilla, seeing Sir Godfrey off to choose a site and order a house had made only one request, 'Let it not be damp, my love,' did not suffer. It stood high and dry and bathed in a sunset glow, for the exceptional winter was being followed by an exceptionally early and mild spring, when Lady Grey's emissary approached it and thought: What a mean house.

Chosen for his light weight – a consideration with roads so deep in mire – and because he was young, eager, hoping to be knighted at Easter, Peter Wingfield had been sent to track Joanna down. It had not, except for the mud, been difficult. Lady Grey, dispatching him, had not sounded hopeful; the silly girl had set out on a difficult horse, in terrible weather.

'It is unlikely that she survived, Peter, but it is necessary for me to *know*. And naturally Sir Gervase is anxious about his horse.'

During his time at Stordford Lady Grey had done little to endear herself to the young squire and now he thought, with disgust: What a typical speech! It was a wonder she hadn't mentioned the horse first.

Joanna's trail was not difficult to follow; many people remembered catching a glimpse of her, so unsuitably clad, so strangely mounted. 'Went by in a flash. Riding like the Devil was on her heels.' To some she had spoken, asking direction to a place they'd never heard of. Baildon. At each point where his questions received satisfactory answers, the young man thought: Alive so far! and ploughed on through the mud with rising hope. Because of the heavy going and the need to ask for information, his progress was slow and he was obliged to spend two nights on the way; one at the kind of big house which Joanna had avoided, one at a miserable inn. Where, he wondered, had *she* spent the night? The nights? In no likely place. Nobody at any great house, or any inn, or the religious house, knew anything of a bare-headed girl on a big black horse. It looked as though she had feared pursuit. And it would have been difficult to decide even which road she had taken on leaving Stordford, but for Lady Agnes' certainty that she would have made for home. Joanna's tales had been so vivid and the old woman's interest had been so keen that she could practically describe the road from Baildon to Intake.

After a lifetime of fairly decisive action, the poor old woman was now suffering the pains of a mind divided within itself. The way she had been abandoned on that dreadful day was disgraceful: it made her angry to think about it, and when she was angry she had every intention of changing her will. Then she would remember those few happy days the services rendered so cheerfully, so different from that of hirelings, and her mood would change. The girl must have had some *reason* for acting as she had done, and Lady Agnes was eager to know what it was. When Lady Grey said, 'It is not that I want her back. I never wish to set eyes on her again. It is simply that inquiries must be made, for appearances' sake,' Lady Agnes said, 'I should be very glad to see her again, if only to know why she deserted me as she did. After being so kind and looking after me better than I have been looked after since I was forced to take to my bed.'

It was a back-handed slap and Lady Grey was bound to admit that the girls – as she called them – were far less dutiful than they might have been. There was no need for Maude . . . and of course the Countess of Shefton could not be commanded, but Beatrice's future was still not assured. To the watchful mother it often looked as though Sir Gervase were less interested in Beatrice than in ingratiating himself with Lord Shefton. Naturally he gave Beatrice – the daughter of the house – the ordinary, courteous attentions to which the silly girl responded a trifle too eagerly. You could, Lady Grey reflected, train a girl into almost everything except dignity: and that for some obscure reason – she never blamed her own handling – both her daughters lacked. Maude was behaving like a stray dog to whom some kind person had given a bone and a casual pat on the head. Mortifying indeed.

Doggedly making his inquiries, Peter Wingfield came to the point where a man remembered directing a girl on a big black horse towards Bury St. Edmund's. Apparently at this point she had no longer been riding as though pursued by the Devil.

'They both looked a bit weary like,' the man said. 'But she perked up when I pointed the road to Bury. She smiled. She said. "Thank you. That'll do," and set off like a shot. Pretty girl.'

Baildon. She wouldn't need to ask direction here, and he, thanks to Lady Agnes' good memory, need only shout, 'Which way to Intake?'

And now here he was, thinking what a mean house, for he had been born in a castle, served as a page in another, become a squire at Stordford. He, like so many of his kind, was a younger son, must make his own way in the world, make an advantageous marriage, hope that some legacies might come his way. He was at home in his world, and in his world a plain house like Knight's Acre, stark against the background of leafless woods, was something new. Even the approach raised a question. It had a main door, not unimposing, and a way leading to it, between evenly planted rose trees.

But that path looked unused, and there was no light in any window, though the afternoon was darkening now. He decided to take the more worn trail around the side of the house. At the entry of the yard he was challenged by a large dog, and from nowhere a boy – about the size Peter had been when he had left home to become a page – ran out and took the dog by the collar pulling him aside and at the same time offering his own challenge. 'Who are you? What do you want?' Then a man appeared.

'You are from Stordford? Come in. You are expected. Godfrey, run in and tell Janna that we have a guest. We'll be there as soon as we have looked to the horse. My name is Henry Tallboys. I bid you welcome to my house.'

'I am Peter Wingfield, sir.'

'You have had a dirty ride. I'll throw down some extra straw. Given enough dry litter, horses clean their own legs. The rest we can deal with tomorrow.'

'The demoiselle Serriff . . .?'

'She arrived safely, and is well,' Henry said, leading the way into the stable. 'And so, you see, is the horse. I shan't be sorry to be rid of him.' While the young squire unsaddled and unbridled his horse Henry forked down the extra straw, brought a bucket of water, put oats and hay in the manger. 'Now for you,' he said. 'Come this way.'

'. . . covered in mud,' Godfrey was saying. 'And I'm sure Guard would not have let him in if I hadn't been there.'

So the bad moment had come. She faced it calmly. She would never leave Knight's Acre again.

Calm, Peter Wingfield reflected presently, was the keynote of this most peculiar household which could have been part of a tale. Eating at a bare, scrubbed table, in a kitchen, eating food cooked by the demoiselle Serriff, with whom he had never before been within speaking distance. Lady Grey believed in order. Each to his place. Sitting at the table with the family and favoured guests Joanna had seemed as remote as the moon, but it was in order, in fact it was traditional that young men, mere squires, or just attained to knighthood should worship from a distance. It was good for them; it gave them something to aim at. It did not prevent them – human nature being what it was – from consorting with and making occasional use of milkmaids, goosegirls and such, but it did, in most cases, forefend incautious marriages.

In every way, Peter Wingfield had been a strict conformist, observing all the rules; he had therefore cherished an unrequited, unspoken devotion to the demoiselle Serriff. Now he was at the same table with her, eating food she had cooked. She wore a hideous black dress; (Joanna had washed it on the day after her homecoming) and when he had entered the kitchen it had been protected by an apron. Any other well-born lady he could think of would have been embarrassed. She had been calm, smiled at him, said, 'Good evening. 'You're ... Peter.'

'Peter Wingfield, at your service, demoiselle,' he said, and made his most formal bow.

'I have water already heated. And I hope you are not superstitious about eating hare.'

Then Henry had lighted a candle and led Peter up to the barest sleeping chamber he had ever seen and gone away, to return with hose and jerkin of homespun.

'A bit big for you, I fear,' he said. 'But they'll serve while your own dry out.'

There was that curious calm about him, too.

On the bare scrubbed table there was not a thing that would have been out of place in a clod cottage – except the wine, which was a surprise. But Joanna – her apron removed – presided with gracious dignity. Even the little boy, at an age where boys had usually to be cuffed into good manners, had that same peculiar quality, handing the salt in its plain wooden bowl, without being asked.

Talk seemed easy. Of all those she had left behind at Stordford, Joanna inquired only of two.

'Lady Agnes? I was sorry to leave her so hastily. But I had reached the end of my endurance.'

'Understandable,' Peter said, relaxed by the calm, and the wine, and something within him, moving from an empty, distant, purely formal devotion to something far more real. 'All of us in the lower part of the hall, when we heard, thought her ladyship had been over severe.'

So far, so good! Joanna had expected a more formidable messenger. More informed. More vocal about betrothals.

'Severe,' Godfrey said, exploring a word not entirely unfamiliar, for now and then Mistress Captoft had used it. If he didn't try harder, pay more attention, she would be forced to be severe to him. 'Cruel? Did Lady Grey ever box *your* ears?'

'No. By the time I went to Stordford, I was a bit too big for that. And at Jerningham, where I served as a page, the lady, our mistress held that to give us a cuff on the ear would soil her hands. She would say: This boy spilt the gravy, or let the dish wobble . . . Then we were beaten, by the steward. Or his deputy. It did us no harm.'

'And the wedding?' Joanna said, stepping out on to ground that could not be avoided for ever; 'how did it go?'

'Well,' Peter Wingfield said, remembering the extra, rather wild festivities which had marked the double occasion, a wedding *and* Twelfth Night. Remembering, too, the malicious talk that had run around. For what those at the lower end of the hall did not know, they were ready to invent; and as the story went, that decrepit old man had set his lecherous eye on Joanna Serriff, and been fobbed off with Maude Grey. Common talk, but it should explain why, just at Christmas Joanna had been banished. Feeling for once free of all rules, Peter Wingfield said, 'It was unfortunate that one of his lordship's new teeth should fall out, only three days after.'

Godfrey said, 'Mine fall out, too. But better ones, bigger ones grow. Look!'

He smiled, showing the new tooth which was taking the place of the one Mamma-Captoft had said had been ready to fall anyway.

It was then that Peter Wingfield realised that in addition to the calm, the unruffled manner, the three people with him at the table shared another thing – a marked physical resemblance. Difficult to define, but unmistakeable . . . They were of three generations. Like most people who came into contact with Henry Tallboys, Peter Wingfield overestimated his age; wind and weather, and worry, and responsibility – and tragedy, had given Henry the appearance of being well on into his fourth decade. Their colouring varied too. Henry had inherited his father's fawn coloured hair, and there was grey just above his ears; Sir Godfrey's fawn colour, mingled with Tana's crow black had produced the dark copper, the dead-leaf colour of Joanna's hair; and Godfrey was almost golden, Henry's fawn colour muted by Griselda's – which until the child's birth, had been the bright pale colour of fresh straw. Their eyes varied, too, Peter Wingfield saw, looking from one to the other in the light of four candles which Joanna had set on the table, an extravagance to honour the guest. All blue, but different blues. Master Tall-boy's almost sapphire, or cornflower; the demoiselle's – well who could describe, even to himself, eyes which were so changeable – grey-blue, blue-grey, greenish; and the boy had a limpid almost a periwinkle-blue look. It was not so much colouring as shape, Peter Wingfield decided, the way the hair grew, in the same way from foreheads identical, except that the man's was grooved; and that smile.

The conversation at the table was light; nothing of any importance being touched upon. Afterwards Godfrey said eagerly, 'There are four of us now. Joanna, we could play that game you said needed four, couldn't we?'

They played a lively game of Naib, using beans as counters, and Godfrey won outright. He was the only one whose mind was wholly concentrated on the game. Then Henry said he must take a last look round and lit his lantern. 'I'd better take Guard out, too,' Godfrey said, adding with that enchanting smile, 'I enjoyed that. Thank you, Peter.'

As soon as they were alone Joanna, her manner changed, said, 'Were you sent to take me back?'

'No ... At least ... No. My orders were to find out, if possible, what had become of you.'

'I am glad of that. Because nothing, nobody would get me away. And I should not wish to make you fail in a set task.'

It was the custom to test young men aspiring to knight-hood not only in feats of arms, but in other ways; per-sistence; diplomacy; self-control; behaviour when drunk.

'Her ladyship was naturally anxious about you, demoise-lle. There was a difference of opinion. If you had gone afoot, the snow would have ... hampered you, and forced you to seek shelter. Then there was the horse. Sir Gervase held that you could *not* have taken him; and held with equal assurance that *had* you done so you would have been thrown.'

Youth spoke to youth across the card-scattered table and they both laughed.

'No,' Peter said. 'I was told to seek, if possible to find, but of retrieving there was no mention. Although the word goes round that Lady Agnes feels her loss.'

'And with good cause.' She must, she knew, be ruthless where Lady Agnes was concerned, make her appear to be the scapegoat. If she had a chance, once this innocent, young, terribly young man was about to mount, she'd send a little message to the poor old woman. Until then let Henry accept, undisturbed, the tale she had told him. Let the word betrothal, with all that it would bring to the surface, remain unspoken.

'If,' the young man said with great diffidence, 'the thought of returning to Stordford is repugnant to you, my mother, I know, would welcome you. My father is dead, but my mother is able to maintain a substantial household. And she is ... kindly.'

'Like you,' Joanna said and smiled. And Peter Wingfield understood what it was about – the family smile which made it distinctive. It *flashed*, swift, sudden and brief across faces not ordinarily set in cheerful lines. Serious faces, even the boy's.

'A kind offer,' Joanna said. 'But one I cannot accept. My place is here. And here I intend to stay. It is my home.'

And the young, terribly young young man had a thought, sudden and brief as the Tallboys' smile; I wish it were mine, too! A mean house he had thought it at first sight, and about that he had not changed his mind; it *was* mean, ill-furnished but there was something, the quiet, the calm and the dignity. He had the fanciful, but none the less positive feeling that if the King of England suddenly arrived here, Master Tallboys would greet him courteously, see to his horse, bring him in and offer what he had. It was a fanciful thought, for the King was growing old now and made only short Progresses and even in his best days could never have dreamed of visiting a mere farmhouse, miles from anywhere. But Peter Wingfield entertained the thought, comparing favourably, in his mind, Knight's Acre with all the other places he knew; the crush and bustle, the jostling for place, the eagerness to be noted, the craving for promotion, the constant chase, even amongst those already rich, for money; money and more money. For a moment he viewed his own future – knighthood at Easter, attachment to the household of some great lord, an advantageous marriage, and perhaps with good luck, a manor of his own, or the castellanship of a castle – with distaste.

He was shrewd enough, however, to recognise that this sudden desire for the simple life, the abandonment of ambition was only a passing thing and directly connected with the girl seated opposite to him at the table. In the course of an evening his distant conventional devotion, no more than an attitude, had changed into something warm and genuine. He thought: I am in love! And he knew that young men in love often did rash things. But even as he warned himself to be careful, he began to wonder whether it would not be possible to have the best of both worlds. Joanna *and* his career, if she had only a small dowry.

Henry came back, extinguished the lantern and said to Godfrey, 'Off to bed with you, son. Joanna, you too, please. I wish to have a private word . . .'

She was not much perturbed. Peter was too young, too low in the hierarchy of Stordford to know much. He was unlikely to bring up the mention of betrothal and thus force Henry into the open before he was ready. That was the thing she dreaded.

'Remember, Peter, to turn your clothes again before you go to bed. They'll be ready to brush in the morning.' The mud-spattered garments had been hung well to the side of the hearth, within range of the warmth, out of reach of any direct spark.

Into the coarse mugs Henry poured some more of the wine which he had, in a moment of exuberance, bought to share with Mistress Captoft.

'Whether you can help me or not, I don't know,' he said with the directness that was characteristic of him, 'but there are things I need to know before I decide upon *her* future. As a child, she was singularly frank and open. Now she is reticent. I do not even know why Lady Grey imposed a punishment which even you considered over-severe. Do you know?'

'By hearsay only,' Peter said cautiously. '*Not* kitchen gossip, Master Tallboys.' And how odd, that here, in a kitchen, such emphasis upon rank should seem necessary. 'Squires' talk,' he said, 'but we are trained to keep eyes and ears open, to make rational judgments by deduction, even by elimination. It was considered that Lord Shefton was enamoured of the demoiselle and wished to marry her; came armed, for Christmas, with a marriage contract and a betrothal ring. Which she refused, and was therefore banished.'

'Tell me something of him – what you *know*, that is.'

'He is immensely old. Past seventy. Extremely rich, but said to be close-fisted.' Nowhere else would Peter Wingfield have spoken so frankly of a man of the kind to whom young knights looked for preferment. Nowhere else would he have added, 'There was an alternative story, sir. That Lady Grey coveted such a match for her daughter ... There may be truth in that, since it came about, betrothal and wedding so hard on each other's heels.'

'I was badly advised,' Henry said. He got up, laid a log of the kind unlikely to spark on the fire and turned Peter's clothes about. Some of the mud, dried to dust, fell on the floor. 'I wanted the best for her. I said a *suitable* marriage. This I did not regard as suitable. But I have her future to think of. And now, what with one thing and another, I cannot feel, in good conscience, that I can send her back to Stordford.'

'I agree, sir. But there are other places.'

'None known to me. That was the trouble,' Henry said. 'I always wanted the best for her. I chose my way of life and it suits me. I wanted something easier for her. And when I discovered that she had means of her own, I wanted them used to her advantage. But the only suitable place I knew was my Aunt Astallon's; Beauclaire – totally destroyed in the civil war. So I sought advice, which was bad. This situation is the result.'

Peter Wingfield was young enough, and at the moment infatuated enough to regret, very mildly, that two things in that speech pleased his ear. But he knew his world. Young knights, with no prospects took service with a great lord, were housed, fed, equipped: there were prizes to be won at tournaments, loot and ransom money to be gained in any real fighting; but such sources of income were uncertain. A wife with means of her own was very desirable; equally desirable was that she should be of good family; and although Beauclaire was a ruin now it had been famous in its day, for splendour and hospitality. Even its end had been dramatic. Lord Astallon, the most neutral of men, had suddenly and inexplicably opted for the side of Lancaster, a lost cause. People still talked of the long siege which had been necessary to reduce it.

He began to speak of his mother, in her comfortable dower house near Winchester; not a large establishment, but lively and gay, ruled by a gentle and accomplished woman. He had reason to speak well of his mother who, out of her necessarily limited means, sent him money from time to time. Such gifts would cease with her death when everything would revert to his eldest brother, but by that time ...

'I am sure my mother would welcome the demoiselle. I am equally sure that she would be happy there.'

'It is a kind offer,' Henry said; but he looked dubious. It would be, like Stordford, another shot in the dark. His ignorance of the world which he himself had avoided, and yet wished Joanna to inhabit, clamped down like a fog. Such different standards! Even this pleasant, likable boy had seemed to see nothing fundamentally wrong in the mismating which Lady Grey had proposed between a very old man and Joanna, and had achieved between the very old man and her own daughter.

At the same time he could not help thinking that he himself had made a marriage of convenience, if ever man did. Not that he and Griselda had been so ill matched until Godfrey was born. There'd been no ecstasy, that rare thing, but they'd got along together well enough, until she had centred everything on the child, and begun to go a little queer.

'A kind offer,' he said again. But how could he *know* that this unknown Lady Wingfield might not turn out to be another Lady Grey? Stordford Castle, to his ignorant ears, had *sounded* perfect.

He thought too of how happy Joanna had been since her

return. How well she and he and Godfrey had fitted together. No echo, no sign of the thing that had so disturbed him. At least, he thought, I was right *there*; Stordford cured her of that fancy!

'It needs thinking about,' he said. 'And perhaps the person most concerned should have some say in the matter.'

'It was the only time in his life when he had deliberately tried to shuffle off responsibility.

The young man smiled; fairly sure of his ground now. In his world girls did what they were told. Joanna *could* have broken that rule by refusing to marry Lord Shefton – but the other story was far more likely. Lady Grey had wanted him for Maude.

'Surely, sir, as her nearest male relative ...' He had worked it out; the family resemblance, the differing names; uncle, or cousin. He was totally unprepared for the effect of those few innocent words. The man stared blankly, rather wildly and then said, 'Good my God!'

The realisation of how very blind he had been seemed to affect his physical sight and he put a hand across his eyes. Seeing it all now.

Peter Wingfield, so worldly wise, thought of illegitimacy. He had plainly touched a very sensitive spot and hastened to make amends.

'I am indeed very sorry, sir, if I have said anything untoward. But ... But the family resemblance is unmistakable. But if I have mentioned anything I should not ... I assure you, sir, you may rely upon my discretion.'

Henry was furious with himself for letting loose that exclamation. A second's thought and he could have said something casual about resemblance between cousins. Too late for that now!

He said, gruffly, 'No discretion is called for.' More than in his present shattered state of mind he could not find words for. And yet he must, because he knew what the boy was thinking?

He thought: All along, I have been blind as a bat and as stupid as an owl, and I've let my mind sink to peasant level. Dumb.

He divided the wine between the two mugs, making a bid for time. Reaching for the right thing to say.

'No,' he said, in a more ordinary voice, 'it is nothing needing discretion. No bar sinister or anything of that sort. It was simply that by reminding me that I am now her nearest male relative, you brought to mind an obligation which I had forgotten.'

Even in his own ears it sounded a feeble explanation and he was aware that the boy was regarding him with curiosity, almost concealed by good manners, but not quite.

Anger with himself, with the world, with this innocent cub, seized him again. He reached for a candle and held it out.

'You'd better get to bed. You've had a long day,' he said.

The remaining candle, its overlong wick in a puddle of tallow flared and faded, flared again. The fire died down. And still Henry sat with his head in his hands, mulling over the past, thinking of the future. Need she ever know? Would she mind? Did it matter? No. If, as he hoped, she had forgotten that scene in the wood, and the makeshift betrothal made across this very table. Forgotten – except in time of need, as when faced with a distasteful marriage. And about *that* she had been reticent. Why not about all else? And all because he had been blind and stupid. Walter said knaves and fools were punished – fools first.

Once back in London, Lord Shefton did not waste a moment. Even before Maude made her first public appearance as his Countess, he had made his opening move against the Bishop of Bywater.

His teeth had failed him, and he allowed rage and vanity to hurry him into an unsatisfactory marriage, but his memory was good for matters of this kind, his mind still subtle. He could remember a summer, two years ago, when His Grace of Bywater had been in London, trying to arrange the futures of two young people. The girl had not been brought to London, the boy had; a big boy, handsome in a loutish way and surly; apparently quite ungrateful to His Grace for bringing him to London and making efforts to get him into Eton College. Introduced as Richard Tallboys, the boy always added, 'of Moyidan.' This apparently trivial business had impressed itself upon Lord Shefton's mind, partly because he yearned to correct so unmannerly a boy;

partly because he had suggested that Sir Barnabas, who owed him money should take the girl who, later, on his first visit to Stordford, had attracted him so much.

A very short visit to the appropriate office, gave Lord Shefton all he needed to know about Moyidan in the County of Suffolk. Later in the day he had a conversation, not with any great official or favoured courtier, but with one of the virtually faceless, nameless men, one of several known to have the King's ear. The word Moyidan was not spoken. Even the crucial remark was made in a most casual manner. 'I have sometimes wondered,' Lord Shefton said, 'if the law regarding young heirs is not often broken, to the detriment of our Lord the King.' That was all; but enough.

Edward of York, Edward IV, was the richest man in England, just as he was reputed to be the tallest, and in youth the most handsome. After the victory which set him firmly on the throne, Edward had confiscated all Lancastrian property. But he was a man who loved splendour; his wars were costly; he had faithful adherents to reward and mistresses to please; he also liked to be independent of Parliament which meant managing without the grants which it could give. When the faceless, nameless adviser murmured something about an un-tapped source of wealth, he had the King's ear indeed. In theory all heirs under age were the King's wards. He might never see them, or know their names, but a wardship, like many other things, was a property, to be bestowed as a favour, or sold. There was a lively trade in such things.

Wheels were set in motion. A Commission appointed.

Maude must be made to seem the chosen one. In cloth of gold, and with all the Shefton diamonds on display, she made three dazzling appearances, all on occasions when little more than appearance mattered. Her mother's training had fitted her, to some extent, for this puppet role; anybody who, after many failures – sharply punished – could carry a brim-ming bowl of water on her head, could wear a coronet. And before anyone could get beyond this glittering facade and discover that Maude had nothing to say for herself, no spirit, nothing to compensate for her lack of beauty – or even pretti-ness, she was whisked away to Shefton Castle in the wilds of Shropshire, where she enjoyed the first real freedom of her life and in a humble, quiet way, enjoyed herself very much indeed.

In London the rumour ran that she was pregnant, and men some fifteen years younger than Lord Shefton, looked at him with awe and envy. Life in the old dog yet.

Official wheels could grind slowly, but where the King's express order and a possible source of revenue were concerned they could be speedy. Moyidan and its history was soon under review. It was in the hands of the Church now; but prior to that it had been managed by another cleric – Sir Richard Tallboys, properly ordained, and an M.A. of Cambride University, presently engaged in one of those pleasant, undemanding jobs at the Chancellory. It might be as well to consult him.

Sir Richard showed no shadow of loyalty to his old friend, the Bishop of Bywater, who had saved him from scandal and procured him his present post. All Richard's actions, since his boyhood, had been dictated by selfishness, and ambition. Ambition never satisfied; even his present post, pleasant enough, almost a sinecure, was in fact a cul-de-sac. But it did enable him to keep an ear to the ground, and he had qualified as a lawyer as well as a priest. He could tell, by the framing, the tilt of a question what answer was desired. He also had charm.

Quite disarmingly he admitted that while in charge of Moyidan, he had mismanaged it to some extent. 'But, my lords, with good intention, I may have been mistaken in thinking that in spending money immediately available upon improving the property, I was actually investing for the boy's future.'

'His Grace of Bywater knew what you were doing?'

'Oh yes. And he approved. He visited me often, and when the place was comfortable, stayed.'

All the Commissioners had a vision of a young man being given enough rope, while he spent money, not his own, and the Bishop watched, gloating over what he would, at the right moment, take over for himself.

'The boy was your Ward?'

'Not officially. His grandmother, my aunt ...' He made quite a piteous story of how poor old Lady Emma had appealed to him to take charge and hold the estate together until young Richard attained his majority. It was one of those shuffling arrangements which, over the years, had leached away revenue that should have gone into the King's coffers. Not quite typical because in this case the unofficial guardianship had changed hands.

'The boy, the direct heir, is now at Eton.'

'That I did not know. I left him at Moyidan with as good a tutor as I could find. I assumed that in taking over the castle and the manor, His Grace of Bywater took charge of him too. If I may *stress*, my lords, I was never his guardian. I am not even head of the family. I have an elder brother.'

Some Commissioners were old and liked to sit in comfort, drawing up charts, comparing figures, while younger, more vigorous men did the riding and the digging for facts. All were busy; for the investigation proved that more young heirs had slipped through the King's net than anyone would have believed possible. There were some heiresses, too, and would have been more had not self-appointed guardians tended to marry off wealthy girls at an early age, on the principle of the highest bidder being the buyer.

The Bishop of Bywater did not defend his action as regards Moyidan and its heir: to have done so would have been to admit that defence was needed; he simply described the shocking state of affairs which had existed before he took control and explained that only by prompt, firm, remedial action had he avoided a scandal which would have damaged the Church. He mentioned a lawyer, of anti-clerical views, who had been poised to attack Sir Richard Tallboys for gross mismanagement. On the whole he was rather fairer to Richard than Richard had been to him; that was largely because he was more aware of the need for solidarity within the Church. He did not mention the ugly word *embezzlement*; he spoke of inexperience, of muddle due to lack of experience. He said that so far from profiting from Moyidan, he had incurred expenses. He rang a bell and asked that every paper relating to the Moyidan inheritance should be brought and displayed; and since he had a passion for detail, it was a formidable pile. The Commissioner, a man better with figures than with written words, flinched a little.

'Your Grace regarded the boy, Richard Tallboys, as a ward?'

'A ward? No; of course not. Why should I? I – well, one might almost say that I inherited him, together with other encumbrances. But I did the best I could for him. I secured him a place at Eton College. In fact,' His Grace said, made irritable and therefore incautious, 'I did my best for them both.'

'Both? Two? Co-heirs?' Such cases had been discovered. A few early, and rather sudden deaths had been revealed, too. In the place where such statistics were reckoned the sinister words, 'died of the small-pox', were gradually revealing the fact that unofficial wards were particularly prone to such ailments. Well above average, possibly as much as thirty per cent higher than the death rate even amongst cottagers' children; fifty per cent higher than the deaths, in similar age groups in a class which could afford red flannel as wrappings, bed hangings, and curtains, sops-in-wine, and the attention of a physician.

'No,' His Grace said, the ground firm underfoot again. 'The girl was in no way concerned with Moyidan. She was ...'

He told what he knew of Joanna's story; of the tumbling out of the jewels; of Henry Tallboys, 'a most ignorant fellow,' asking advice as to how such wealth could best be employed to the girl's advantage. And how Joanna's dowry had been deployed. Roughly two-thirds of the money in Sir Barnabas Grey's keeping. A third, by the girl's own wish, invested at Knights Acre, all running about on four legs.

The Commissioner believed that he had inadvertently stumbled across an heiress of whom there was no record; a find indeed! Leaving the pile of papers unstudied, he asked direction to Knight's Acre and set out at once. He took a list of the livestock entrusted to Master Tallboys.

It was now April, and the mild weather had encouraged grass to grow, all the animals were at pasture; lambs were skipping in the fold, the herd of cattle in the meadow included five young calves. Knowledgeable about such matters the Commissioner noted the healthy look of all these beasts – they had been well-cared for during the lean months.

Master Tallboys had no records to show, but everything was clear in his head; he could distinguish the animals entrusted to him on Joanna's behalf from his own, and a man apt at counting soon saw that both flock and herd had increased considerably.

'I have always regarded the girl's beasts as separate from my own,' he said. 'The fleece money from her flock I have put aside intact. I've sold animals from time to time; from what they fetch I take what I think compensates for their food and my labour, I put that aside too. Master Turnbull, the lawyer at Baildon, keeps the accounts and invests the money for her.' Henry gave the Commissioner his straight blue stare. 'My better horse is hers, too. As soon as I am able I shall add its worth to the money accumulating.'

'That, sir, is correct,' Master Turnbull said. 'Master Tallboys is the most meticulous man I know. He is honest to his own detriment.' The lawyer's trade brought him into contact with many men with varying standards of honesty. His own was high, for he wished to leave to his beloved son not only a comfortable fortune but an unsullied name. But even he felt that Henry, still putting away certain, much smaller sums, to be kept for a boy of whom nothing had been seen or heard for almost eight years, was carrying honesty to the point of folly. 'You wish to see what has been done with the money?'

For anyone to whom written records mattered, fire particularly in the night, was a threat. However careful one might be oneself, damping down, or raking out fires, a neighbour might be negligent. Master Turnbull had faced this hazard by having chests made, so much bound about by iron that they would not ignite easily. They were small enough to be lifted, if not with ease, with sufficient determination, by one man, and four slept under his roof every night; himself – still able-bodied, two clerks and a man-servant.

From one of these chests, which he did not lift, but stooped over, he produced every parchment and paper relevant to the business in hand. He was as dedicated a record-keeper as the Bishop. Here, in black and white – the black his own ink, home-made by rotting walnut husks steeped in vinegar, was evidence not only of Master Tallboys' exceptional honesty but of Master Turnbull's financial acumen. Money received; invested; withdrawn; re-invested; mortgages; foreclosures; loans, interest on loans. It was, in fact, a record of ruthlessness as well as of honesty, but the Commissioner was not concerned with that. He merely thought that if Sir Barnabas Grey had been only half as clever in handling the major part of the girl's fortune, this obscure Joanna Serriff would be a considerable heiress. And *he* had discovered her!

Presently another Commissioner, willing to ride, and less averse to wading through closely written pages, had discovered a fact which might exonerate the Bishop of Bywater's over-hasty action in regard to Moyidan. Apparently he had not simply taken the place as a summer residence, or a hunting lodge. The Abbey at Baildon was involved. And this was tricky ground. Between the secular Church, as represented by Archbishops and Bishops, and the heads of the great monastic establishments, like the Abbey of Baildon, there had always been a gulf, now widening, just as cracks in a wall, almost ready to tumble would widen. The monastic establishments – many of them founded by orders vowed to holy poverty, had become enormously rich, and over the years, increasingly independent. The great breach was yet to come, but the climate for it was already building up.

The Abbot of Baildon did not feel that solidarity – or the need for it which the Bishop of Bywater had felt. He belonged to a wider community – the Benedictines. Part of an old Order, so old that Charlemagne himself had been their patron, and there were Benedictine houses as far away as Poland.

The Abbot of Baildon was sufficiently self-assured that he dared to keep even the King's Commissioner waiting for a while. And then, when the confrontation came, he, very gently, but inexorably threw His Grace of Bywater to the wolves.

'Yes,' he said, 'some suggestion was made, and I welcomed it. Purely on account of Moyidan's situation; Moyidan being nearer the sea. And it is fact that for some people – particularly those born within reach of the sea, the air from it has a recuperative effect. I considered that. Also the fact that it was rusticated and that any member of this community who had transgressed might there, in isolation, meditate and repent. But I soon saw that it was not a workable idea. To put it very bluntly; when His Grace was in residence ill-doers ate too well; and when he was not convalescents were too meagrely fed. The place was not organised well, and I decided to ignore it.'

As one little prop to the Bishop's well-planned scheme, the Abbot of Baildon had failed absolutely.

Down in Bywater, the better weather had eased things for Mistress Captoft. Her money arrived. Shipping began to move; able-bodied men went away – some of them thanking her with genuine tears. 'Never, never shall I forget you, Madam.' 'Madam, I'll remember you and your kindness, in my prayers, till the day I die.'

She paid her debts, but was otherwise careful with money. This harsh winter had taught her a lesson. She supervised the reclamation of the garden. It was hardly likely that two winters in succession could be so savage, but she would be prepared. She'd have her own fowls next year.

Articles made by those who had gone, and by those who could never go, looked well, as she had thought, displayed against the red velvet with which David had covered the sloping board; and, now that Bywater was busy again and the market in full swing, trade was brisk. Her little parlour was once again her own, but it was also a shop and she derived some amusement from the thought that by all known standards, she had fallen. Trade, as pursued by her husband was one thing; petty shop-keeping another. But she did not care. She was enjoying everything; even a face to face row with the landlady of The Welcome To Mariners who one afternoon, in the dead hour, dinner done with, supper hours away, walked down to The Sailors' Rest and accused Mistress Captoft of renegading on a bargain.

'You promised me a continuous supply,' she said. 'And now I have four pedlars clamouring and nothing to sell them.'

'The supply is there,' Mistress Captoft said, indicating the display in the window. 'Buy what you wish.'

'Buy?'

'Buy,' Mistress Captoft said. 'I certainly did not promise a continuous supply in return for such things as I was, in a desperate moment, forced to accept. The wine was the worst I ever tasted; the two fowls hardly needed their necks wrung – they were dying of old age. The doves mere skeletons with feathers.'

Allowing for a marginal exaggeration, these were true statements. Mistress Captoft had said to David that she could understand why the system of barter was dying out, it allowed of too much lop-sidedness. The truth did not make the accusation more palatable and the landlady lost her temper. She used terms which were questioned not only Mistress Captoft's integrity, but her legitimacy and her standard of morals. Mistress Captoft, who with one word had so shocked her Father Matthew, contrived to maintain a look of incomprehension, and almost had the last word.

She said, 'I am sorry. I understand only English.'

The landlady drew breath and said, 'Bawd!' Then realising that it was inapt in the circumstances, simply repeated the uncivil word as she retreated. She said it loud enough and often enough for David, hurrying to see who was shouting, and why, heard it twice, and limped in, expecting – hoping? – to find Madam in need of comfort.

'It was the landlady from the inn,' Mistress Captoft said. 'She objects to our board. Our shelf, David. She wanted a monopoly; but this way we cut out the middle man – or woman in this case.'

He thanked God that he had been mistaken; or that she had not understood. Which? He did not know; never would know. The weeks of hardship had made him feel very guilty and once or twice he had tried to apologise: Madam, this is not what I mean. *You* eating hard-tack!' But she had always smiled and said she had never been happier. And she *did* look happy.

Then she did something which annoyed him. One of the scurvy-sufferers, instead of making a saleable trinket, had carved out of a log of driftwood another sign for The Sailors' Rest. A huge thing, big enough almost to be a ship's figure-head. And it was coloured, as ships' figureheads were, with crude colours, so well-mixed with oil and cow-heel glue as to be resistant to salt water, rain and wind. David's own painted sign, hanging, creaking in the wind, showed a sailor, recognisable by his head wear and clothes, lying at ease on a mattress. A sailor at rest. The figurehead thing was different, just a head, with a recognisable sailor's woollen cap which could be pulled down over the ears, homespun, buffish in colour – as most were; the drab colour set off the face, reddish brown, and the eyes, blue, as sailors' eyes mostly were. The mouth of this crude and yet powerful image wore a carved smile, the red of the lips darker than the face.

'I like it,' Mistress Captoft said, after she had thanked the man who had made it and seen him off to whatever fate awaited him; scurvy again with no cure handy; or shipwreck, or accident. Actually, anxious as she was to restore and heal, every parting with a man restored and healed, hurt her. While they were under her roof, for a long time or short, they were her children and she felt towards them the helpless protectiveness, the defeated possessiveness of mothers the world over.

'It must be nailed up,' she said, 'above the shop window. It will attract attention.'

It would also make David's swinging sign, already bleached, look like a shadow.

'It will give the wrong idea, madam. In no time at all this will be called *The Jolly Sailor.*'

'And would that matter, David? Were we not, even during the worst times, jolly together? Sharing what little we had? Making merry over the hard-tack, and three of a bed? I think the sign apt. And being so conspicuous, a further annoyance to that woman.'

The next inmate to arrive however, was not attracted by the implied jollity.He came because he was in very poor shape and, as David had foreseen, news of The Sailors' Rest had spread.

He was a big man, both tall and broad; he was in good health – for his ship had been only just out from Hull, when he'd ducked his head, below deck – a thing he'd done many times before; but this time was different; he couldn't straighten his neck again. Worse than that every movement, even the effort to walk, caused agony. No ship bound for Lisbon could afford a useless hand, so he'd been put ashore at Bywater; not utterly destitute, for the captain was a humane man. Somebody had said, 'Make for The Sailors'

Rest, mate. Madam there'll cure you if anybody can.' So here he was, having been obliged to ask direction because it was impossible for him to lift his head to an angle from which either sign would have been visible.

For once Mistress Captoft was at a loss, never having met with his condition before. Flesh wounds, even broken bones she was prepared to deal with; but there was no wound; and had his neck been broken, the man would have been dead. As usual when she was in a difficulty, she called for David, and he, having so recently suffered defeat over the matter of the sign, was delighted to be able to say that he had seen a man or two in this state before; and he knew the cure.

It sounded very drastic.

'Hanging by the neck!' she exclaimed. 'But David, surely that would kill him.'

'Not properly done, madam. Hung people die one of two ways. They hang till they choke and that's a long business or the jolt'll break their necks. We shan't let him hang long, and we won't jolt him. I'll make a kind of collar.'

Cautious, in case of accident, Mistress Captoft asked the man if he were willing to submit to being half-hanged; and he said anything, even a real hanging would be better than this.

The operation took place in the kitchen, supervised by David, watched by Mistress Captoft and two or three reasonably able-bodied fellows who had orders to act immediately if anything seemed to go wrong.

The leather collar, well padded with straw was fixed to the man's neck, and to a rope, slack, at the moment, tied to a beam from which next year hams and strings of onions and bunches of dried herbs would hang.

The man – he gave his name as Dan Rush, stood on the kitchen table, David beside him. David moved the rope a little way along the beam and said, 'Step on to the stool.' Dan did so and the rope lost its slack. 'Now on to the cask,' David said. And then, 'Cask away!' Mistress Captoft held her breath as the big man hung suspended. She heard, or imagined she heard a slight click, no more than the turning of a key in a lock.

'Hold him,' David said, and the two men ran forward to take Dan's weight while David unfastened the collar.

Dan stood on the kitchen floor, straight and tall, dumb-struck. He turned his head from right to left, bent it towards one shoulder then the other.

'By God!' he said, in an awed voice. 'A bloody miracle. I'm cured! I'm cured!'

He rushed over to Mistress Captoft, flung his great arms round her, kissed her on both cheeks; thumped David and the other men on the shoulders. He was beside himself with joy. He danced.

He was a newcomer, David reminded himself; not yet aware of the rules of the house – many of them drawn up by David himself. One concerned the language unsuitable for use in Madam's presence, a rule that rendered many men practically dumb for the first forty-eight hours at least, since profanity was their natural tongue.

Another rule concerned drinking. David knew how easily men of quite mild disposition, quiet fellows, could become aggressive and noisy after that drop too much; and not only that, men of ordinarily clean habit became filthy, vomiting the least of their offences.

Ale was served at The Sailors' Rest – even during that bad time when food ran short. Mistress Captoft had laid in stores and every morning each man broke his fast with a mug of very weak ale and a hunk of bread. Ale of a slightly stronger kind was served at supper.

Anybody who wanted more than this was free to go out and buy it. Mistress Captoft said she did not wish men to feel constricted as in the ordinary charitable institution. And on the whole the matter was – at this stage – largely academic, since most of those seeking shelter were destitute. Of the paying clients there had as yet been few. But David was prepared for the future. Like many people he associated drunkenness and immorality generally with the keeping of late hours, so supper was early, soon after the Vespers bell, and at the first sound of the Compline bell the door of The Sailors' Rest was barred for the night. This gave David a chance to judge the state of any latecomer.

On the first night after his miraculous cure, Dan was slightly late and slightly tipsy. He had spent a lot of time hunting about Bywater for a present for Madam, something pretty and not too expensive, for what money he had must last until he found a ship again. Also he had plans for the next evening when he would, as he expressed it, feel more like himself. The days of agony when even to eat or drink was an effort, and the drastic, sudden cure had somewhat unmanned him. Tomorrow!

He found his trinket at last, a piece of amber, small, but genuine – he knew by the light weight and the warm feel of it that it was not a bit of the coloured glass so often sold as amber – slung on a thin silver chain. He then went to an alehouse and drank just enough to make him, in his exuberant state of mind, a little more exuberant. Not, David realised, being a just man, quite drunk enough to warrant the slammed door and the inexorable sentence: Get into the gutter and sleep it off, which in the last four months three bad characters had earned; but tipsy enough, and late enough to be admonished; tipsy enough to resent admonishment. He said, 'Get outa my way, you little runt. It ain't your house anyway. It's hers. And I've got a present for her. Where is she?'

'I am here,' Mistress Captoft said from the top of the stairs. There was, as she had planned, only one *she* in the house.

'Brought you something,' the big man said, exhibiting the frail trinket on his huge horny palm.

She took it with exactly the unselfconscious, innocent assurance that she had accepted the homemade gifts of other grateful men – things which had formed a nucleus, given a start to, quite a flourishing little business.

'How very pretty,' she said. 'But there was no need. To see you better is reward enough. Now; you are late, supper is over. But there is bread and cheese in the kitchen.'

'And if you must be sick, do it out of the window,' David said.

The big man went off in search of the food and David followed Mistress Captoft into the little parlour, now, save for the counter, her own place again.

'Madam, you heard what he said?'

'In part. His voice was somewhat slurred.'

'He called me a runt!'

'David you are not so small as to resent that, surely. To a man of that size, I suppose we all look small.' She moved to the court cupboard and poured wine into two silver cups. She could afford decent wine now, if she spared on dresses. 'Sit down, David; drink and forget *runt*. I have been called worse things in my time. There is an old song that children sing: *Sticks and stones may break my bones; but names can never hurt me.* Shrug it off, David; he will soon be gone. And as soon as he goes I shall put this,' she indicated the bit of amber and slender silver chain, 'into the window, for sale with the other things.'

All right; all right; but she had not said what she should have said. *Out he must go,* to quote from another children's game.

She did not say that; she said instead, 'David, we must remember that the poor man was only this very day released from a crippling disability.'

Yes – and to whom were thanks due for that? David Fuller. Pushed aside, called *runt* and reminded – as though he needed reminding – that he was not the master of this house.

Nursing his wine and his grievances, too painful to be put into words, David sat and brooded, his mind like balanced scales tipping this way, that way. Mistress Captoft had saved him from starvation, given him a chance to rehabilitate himself, ventured out on this whole enterprise, at his suggestion, and when the thing looked like being a failure, he had apologised. And with things at their worst, she had said that she was happy. Had indeed looked happy. As he had been. Until now, when gratitude, devotion, a desire to serve, protect, had suddenly changed; just as a bowl of sweet milk could be changed by the addition of wine into syllabub, by a little rennet, into cheese. It was not his house, but he took a large part in the running of it, upheld, both by warnings and by his own example, that respectful awe with which the men regarded her. It was to him that she turned for help and advice in any material difficulty; and for comfort and cheer in those rare moments when her spirits were low. When men were bedridden, it was he who had undertaken the tasks which he considered unsuitable for a lady to do; when men were delirious he'd taken care always to be there. Now she had stood by and heard him insulted, and gone out her way to be pleasant to the tipsy fellow, accepted his gift, bothered lest he should go supperless to bed. Just because he was a huge, handsome brute.

Mistress Captoft observed that the glass of good wine was doing little to lift David's gloom. Being a woman she did not understand the offence in the word *runt*; she had stated a fact when she said that to a man of that size everybody else must look small. The remark about who owned the house was also a fact. To mention it was not perhaps in the best of taste, but then the man was not completely sober, and had not been under her roof long enough to have learned that mannerliness was the rule here.

Then her gaze fell upon the bowl of cowslips which stood on the table between the two chairs.

'Oh, David,' she said quickly, 'it has been such a busy day, I neglected to thank you for the flowers. They gave me great pleasure. I love the scent.' She leaned forward and put her face to the posy.

'There was just the one bunch. It looked a bit lonely alongside the cabbages.'

The gloom did not lighten. She thought about how he had exerted himself over the hanging cure; scrambling up on to the table, reaching up to move the rope so that it was exactly above each decreasing level, table, stool, cask. His badly mended leg, she knew, served him well enough, with the properly built up shoe, but it was susceptible to changes in the weather, and to fatigue.

'Is your leg paining you, David?'

'No more than usual, thank you, madam.'

A perfectly ordinary, civil reply, but cold, but offhand, as his remark about the cowslips had been. Best to take no notice.

'I'd advise an early night for you. For myself, too.'

In the morning Dan woke; stretched, turned, reached both arms above his head. No pain! Cured! He could remember the cure with perfect clarity; also the hunt for the right gift; after that his memory was hazy though he had not, by his own standard been drunk. The way the man who had organised the miracle looked at him, however, indicated that something was wrong; and now he came to look at it, the man who had helped with the miracle, and the man who had tried to bar his way later on, were one and the same.

He made his graceless attempt at apology.

'No offence meant, mate.'

'You're no mate of mine.'

'You helped to cure me.'

Something of last night's business, or something looming in the future, threw a shadow.

'Worst day's work I ever did,' David said.

One of Mistress Captoft's projects – based now on experience – was the reclamation of the stables where the knights' horses had stood, in that brief, lordly interlude between times when humbler animals had been there. She thought it unlikely that next winter – or any in the foreseeable future – would be quite like the one they had just survived, but just in case, she wanted the stables put into such a state of repair that men could sleep there and not three to each narrow cell, and some in her private parlour as well as in the big communal room. The work on the stables was being done, not by hired labour – altogether too expensive – but by those of her guests fit for work. And of those, Dan Rush, yesterday a cripple, was by far the strongest and most able. He could carry a plank with which two ordinary men must struggle, sweating, as though it weighed no more than a stool: he could hold a supporting post steady and upright, dead true, while the hole into which it was planted was filled in and resolutely stamped down. Merely exerting his size and strength was, after the helplessness, a pleasure. And there was the evening still to come.

The evening held promise for David as well as for Dan. The big man was not present at the supper table, and tonight if he came back one second late, drunk or sober, the door would remain barred. And the mild wind which had brought the cowslips into bloom had shifted; sudden and keen, it now blew from the east. A night on the beach would not be pleasant – but no worse than the dog watch aboard ship. It might however teach the big brute a salutary lesson; David might not own the house; he did govern the door. And what could have been a weak place in the defensive action – Madam interfering and being sentimental, was, most fortuitously, forestalled. Madam had one of her headaches. *Her* headache, but part of the tiresome process all women suffered if they lived long enough. It took various forms, hysteria, inexplicable pains; some completely honest women took to stealing; some, married, became pregnant and bore children known as tails' ends.

Madam merely had headaches, for which, naturally, she had a palliative.

While the headache raged she lay in the darkened room, took some drops of the stuff which dulled but did not remove the pain, and waited, subsisting on water since the very thought of food nauseated her. She had had three attacks since coming to Bywater and David knew that there was nothing he could do except tiptoe in, see that there was water in the jug and ask, solicitously, 'How is it now, Madam?' If she had taken the drops recently she would give a mere drowsy murmur; fully awake she would say with resolute cheerfulness, 'Getting better, thank you.' Which was true, for her headache never lasted more than twenty-four hours.

'Mind how you move about, mates,' David reminded the men as bedtime came round. 'Madam can't bear noise when her head is bad.' Down in the big communal room noise didn't matter, for Madam's bedroom was immediately over her little parlour and the old house had thick walls and floors. Following the example of those who had been here on an earlier, similar occasion, the men shed their footwear and crept upstairs, stealthy as thieves. David made his final visit to Mistress Captoft's room. She was asleep, not merely drowsy. She would be perfectly well in the morning, he thought, as he stole away to his own bed.

Mistress Captoft woke in the dark, and, like Dan some hours earlier, was delighted to find herself free of pain.

When there were sick men likely to need her in the night she kept a candle burning, but there was no such man now, so she reached for the tinder box and not too steadily, made a light. She was slightly confused, as always after the head-ache and the doses of lovage-and-opium. She was unsure whether it was night or day until she listened. No sound from the quay. Night then! A conclusion confirmed when she moved, a little shakily, to the window and opened the shutter and looked out into the night; a clear night, with a lop-sided moon and many stars. Yes, it was night. And she was, as always after a spell of headache, ravenously hungry; not the natural hunger quite explained by the fact that she, a woman of good appetite, had fasted through a day and part of a night. The hunger — she had observed this before — was in some curious way connected with the headache, as though it had stolen something from her, something which must be replaced before recovery was complete. And it must be either cheese, or ham. Nothing else would do. She pulled on her loose robe and pushed her feet into her slippers, just as she had done many times before, called up suddenly to tend the sick, and then, taking her candle, went down to administer to herself as she had so often administered to others. But not for her, sops-in-wine, or chicken broth, or egg custard. Such items of good invalid diet still roused faint echoes of nausea. She wanted cheese, or ham.

She padded her way, silently, down the stairs, into the kitchen. A walk she made twice a day in the ordinary way, tripping lightly, but tonight, in the silence, and the loneliness, a dragging effort which to her momentarily disturbed mind, held the creeping threat of old age. When I am old, crippled, dead, what will become of them all? What will become of The Sailors' Rest? And my property? I must make a will — but to whom shall I leave it all? David? But he is only younger by a few years. That would be no solution ... She carried this wretched problem into the larder and immediately shrugged it aside, for there, on the shelf was a ham.

She had no knife, but she needed none. At the narrow end of the well-cooked ham the meat had come away from the bone, and just lay there, ready to be plucked away, not in slices, in hunks. Mistress Captoft pulled, crammed the meat into her mouth, ate as though she had starved for a month and immediately felt better. Strong, restored, good for another twenty years! It was a recognised fact that any woman who got over this particular hurdle lived on and on. And why should she worry about the future? God had brought her here; He would take care of everything.

Carrying the candle in one hand a piece of ham in the other, she retraced her steps and was at the foot of the stairs when the door knocker banged. Without hesitation she set the candle on a little shelf and slid back the heavy bar, greased by David to make it run smoothly.

Destiny blundered over the threshold.

Dan's much anticipated evening had been a disaster. He'd begun moderately and sensibly, with a couple of mugs of good ale at a house in one of the lanes, a recognised drinking place which sold liquor only. There a mere hint of his other need brought simple instructions and he found himself in the house by the tanyard; the house belonging to Katherine Dowley's cousin. Here he was supplied with a drink for which he had not asked, and was not required to pay. 'It's on the house, mate,' John Dowley said. ''t'll set you up like nothing you've ever had before.' He enlarged, in a gross fashion, upon the manner of setting up.

For John Dowley it had been a hard winter. His eldest daughter – the mainstay of the establishment – had got herself a husband; his second had run away. His third was quite old enough in the eyes of everybody but her mother. That down-trodden woman had suddenly rebelled in a shocking way. 'Over my dead body, till she's twelve,' she said, and was prepared to back her defiant words with force, armed by anything that was to hand. Then that fool Katherine had arrived. She brought a little money with her, but then the snow began, traffic with the inland ceased, shipping, except for a few battered ships seeking shelter, was at a stand-still; and food prices doubled. When the land roads and sea roads were open again, he had only Katherine to work with and in the end he had talked her round; for, with nobody to say a good word for her, she had failed to find a job. She had finally seen the necessity, but she was doing the business no good. One dissatisfied customer had expressed his complaint in plain language. 'Any time I want to bed with a sack of chaff, I can do it in my own barn. Free.'

Resourceful, John Dowley had found a way to get round this situation.

Dan Rush was sipping it now. It looked like water, had no particular taste or smell, just a faint oiliness on the tongue. Dan had moved about quite a bit; he knew ale, weak, medium, strong; he had from time to time drunk wine, red and white and yellowish and on even rarer occasions, some stuff called brandywine.

He sipped this unknown stuff, waiting for it to take effect – not that he needed it. John Dowley knew the effect. It made men unaware of whether the bulk in the bed behaved like a woman, or a sack of chaff.

Dan was aware that this was not what he had promised himself. And after that there was a gap, even in what he remembered. He came to full consciousness, lying in the gutter. Being sick. After that he felt better, though angry because the body bought and paid for had been such a bad bargain, so unresponsive. It was night, but a moonlit night, and in the quietude he could hear the sea, the waves coming in, breaking, and then the outward, dragging sound. He set off towards it.

At one corner there was a stone drinking trough, meant for cattle or pack animals. He stopped by it and drank, splashed water on his face. He was sober enough to realise that he had been drunk. He he been robbed, too? Yes. Not a farthing left. It was common practice. Brothels and thievery went together. Few men complained. Ordinary decent citizens didn't wish it to be known that they had frequented such places, and men just passing through had no time to bring a charge. Sailors least of all.

But just wait till morning, Dan thought, and that man by the tanyard would have something to think about.

The water had the curious effect of making him drunk again and lustful again. But it was dead night now; everything must wait.

And here, opening the door to him was a woman. Lightly clad, smiling, saying. 'You are *very* late.'

He fell upon her like a tiger.

Apart from that horrible affair at Intake which Mistress Captoft had pushed to the back of her mind, and had almost forgotten, there was nothing in her life to prepare her for such an assault. She'd had loving parents, a kind if ineffectual old husband, a gentle lover. She should have been helpless, managing at most a scream, but as her loose robe fell open and her night-shift tore, the real Mattie Captoft took command. She even remembered which side the big man's head had lolled. She went limp, deceptively, put up a

287

soft hand in what might have been a caress and then *pushed* with all her might. If his neck clicked again she did not hear it because he yelled as pain shafted through him. His hands lost their grip and stood there, huge and helpless as he had been when he arrived. She skirted past him and opened the door again and pushed him out and down. No effort at all. A child could have done it.

She closed and bolted the door quietly, hoping to keep all secret, hoping that David and all the other men were too sound asleep, would perhaps only half wake, attribute the cry to a couple of mating cats who did sometimes make such human noises that two or three time Mistress Captoft had been almost sure that the function of The Sailors' Rest had been mistaken and that an unwanted infant had been left on her doorstep.

In this hope that the noise might be ignored, she picked up her candle and turned towards the stairs, and there was David. Very lame without a shoe. Wearing nothing under the snatched up quilt.

She was very conscious of the torn shift, and of the marks on her neck and bosom – not kisses, bites. She tried to pull the edges of her robe together and was surprised and dismayed to find that *now* she was more tremulous than she had been when she first rose from her bed. Her mind was shaking too, wavering between a desire to laugh, and a wish to cry.

David seemed to take the stairs in three hops, put his arm around her, and said. 'Did he hurt you?'

'I hurt *him*!' she said, and laughed, but too unsteadily to deceive. He guided her into the little parlour and sat her in a chair; then he went back for the candle, carefully knotting the quilt around him. Back in the parlour he poured wine and held it for her to sip. She would have been incapable of holding it herself. He did not ask *what* had happened, he seemed to know without being told. He said, 'Why did you open the door? So late.'

'I didn't know. I didn't know *he* was still out. People do come at night. Sometimes.'

'And I've told you and told you; not to go to the door alone, after dark. Why didn't you call me?'

'I was there. I'd been to get something to eat. There was

the knock. I answered it. I didn't think, David. I didn't know how late it was. I was still confused. You know how I am when my headache lifts.'

'You should have called me for that, too. Something like this was bound to happen, sooner or later. You so pretty and kind, and a rogue in every dozen. And what a rogue'll see – in us – is a woman with no man to protect her, and a man with no authority.'

Some rancour, older than that inspired by yesterday's little affair, sounded bitterly in his voice. It was just the damned money, he thought, just the damned money, which she had, and he had not. All the wrong way round. Not, he realised sensibly, that money was responsible, except indirectly, for this state of affairs. He was to blame. He'd suggested this refuge for sailors; partly because he felt strongly about the seamen's plight, but, in even greater part, because he didn't want her to go burying herself in a convent. The last place suitable for her. But he had not visualised her here, the one woman amongst so many men. The dangerous situation he had done his best to make harmless by his own behaviour, by his insistence upon the behaviour of others, by making everybody think that Madam was practically as holy as the Virgin Mary. And he had been very vigilant. But the landlady of The Welcome To Mariners had a carrying voice and though, thank God, Madam had misunderstood, David had understood only too well.

He'd given her an opening; it was for her – because she had the damned money – to make the next move.

Mistress Captoft, able now to manage her winecup with one hand while clutching the edges of her robe together with the other, took one of her impulsive decisions. Why not? He is completely devoted to me; honest, industrious, clean. And apart from that lame leg, not a deformity, the result of an accident, a fine figure of a man.

She did not think, and if the thought had ever occurred to her she would have repudiated it with scorn, that the near-rape had fired old hungers which she had thought never to feel again.

She said, 'That could be easily remedied, David, If you would ask me to marry you.'

*

That decision at least she was never to regret. Happy ever after. For once it was true. David absolutely the head of this house, a stern, but genial autocrat; and Mistress Fuller no longer craving for vicarious motherhood. Just in time; on such a narrow edge of time that she found it, for a while, difficult to decide whether it was pregnancy or the end of all that, presently knew and presently bore a good strong boy. They named him Benedict, for as Mistress Fuller explained, two Davids in one family would be a bit confusing. 'And the name will commemorate a relative of mine of whom I was once very fond.'

At Intake, life drifted on, busy and for a time uneventfully. Peter Wingfield's visit had left no trace; the word betrothal was never mentioned. Occasionally Joanna thought that perhaps Henry was waiting for her birthday in June. She would be fourteen then. Now and then she had the darker thought – that it would never be mentioned. Henry looked at her often, sometimes broodingly, often fondly, but never in *that* particular way. However, as day followed happy day, she became resigned and told herself that it did not matter; that she would be content if things could just continue as they were; to be with him, here at Knight's Acre, would be enough. She rejoiced in being free again; in every change which the lengthening days brought to the fields and to the woods. She resisted all his suggestions for hiring what he called kitchen help. 'Why? Don't I manage to your liking?'

'You manage splendidly. But I don't like to see you doing such rough work.'

'When I complain it will be time enough to change. After all, your mother managed single-handed for years.'

'And I didn't like that either. It aged her. And how do you know about my mother and the hard times? You were not even born.'

'Tom Robinson told me. All about the plague, how the one good old servant died and your mother had the nursing to do, as well as the work.'

Henry looked at her curiously, wondering whether Tom resident here in the house when Sir Godfrey came back after that long absence, bringing Tana with him, had ever noticed anything which he himself – younger than Tom – had missed, blind as he was by such conflicting emotions, infatuated at first sight with the beautiful lady from Spain, and disgruntlement at losing his place as head and mainstay of the family.

Not that he needed proof in words or reminiscences, of the thing which the young squire from Stordford had seen and spoken of, in all innocence. It was there, and he could see it now as he looked at Joanna and Godfrey – and at himself, in Sybilla's small looking glass. Allowing in differences in sex and in age . . . the family likeness was strong.

And it had been just as strongly marked, Henry now realised, belatedly, between Joanna and Robert. Now and then people had said that they might be twins – the girl bigger and more lusty as girls often were. They *were* born on the same day, but to different mothers; Joanna a full term baby, Robert premature, hardly expected to live; Tana had suckled them both, and for some people that had explained the exceptionally close bond between them. Wet nurses were supposed to leave a mark on their nurslings. That was why they were carefully chosen.

What Peter Wingfield had in innocence and ignorance said, explained everything – even that scene in the wood, Joanna flinging herself into his arms and declaring a love which, in *her* innocence and ignorance, she had misinterpreted. It explained, too, the shame he had felt because for a moment his body had responded. He had thought it was shameful because she was so young. Now he knew differently.

Apart from this burden of knowledge and how it would affect the future, Henry enjoyed that spring, too. Joanna's housekeeping was on the happy-go-lucky side; there was always something to eat, but no trouble made of it. Even the inevitable mending she tackled with goodwill.

'Somebody once complained that my stitches were like hedge stakes,' she said, snipping off the thread after making a patch. 'And so they are. But they hold.'

The casual, happy, drifting time was disturbed by something that neither Joanna nor Henry had forseen. It was the first Wednesday in June and with Godfrey, they had gone to market; the last market day before the sheep-shearing and the haymaking ended such outings.

On the way home – at the end of a financially satisfactory day, Joanna had referred to that other day, when that horrible boy Richard Tallboys of Moyidan, had had such a well-deserved thrashing. And at the end of the journey, turning into the track alongside the house, she said, 'Well. Speak of the Devil!' For there Moyidan Richard was, being held at bay by the dog which had found that with *this* intruder, there was no need to venture on to the hated strip of ground. A snarl and a show of teeth were effective.

Leaning across Godfrey, Joanna grabbed Henry's arm.

'Don't keep him, Henry. He'll spoil everything. Send him back where he came from. Remember how he behaved last time.'

'We must just hear what he has to say for himself,' Henry said. 'He may have nowhere else to go.' He did not feel particularly welcoming. Even at a time when he felt sorry for the boy he had been unable to like him much; there was something surly, uncouth about him. Inclined to whine, too. And of course he had stolen in Baildon and told lies about his treatment at Henry's hands. And there was truth in Joanna's words about spoiling everything. Henry thought in a flash about what would be spoiled – the easy, friendly, happy atmosphere that had prevailed here for hard on six months. Joanna loathed the boy and would not hesitate to show it. There would be rancour again. However, Dick was family and there was no choice. And maybe school had improved him.

They were now level with the entry, where Dick stood, leaning against a rather poor horse which showed signs of having been hard ridden. Forcing some heartiness into his voice, Henry said, 'Hullo, Dick. This is a surprise. Hop down, Godfrey, and tell your dog it's all right.'

Consciously showing off, Godfrey did so. His own recollections of this cousin were very vague for Dick's stay had been in Griselda's time and she had disapproved of him almost as much as Joanna did – but for different reasons, and had kept her son apart from that pauper as she had insisted upon calling the heir to Moyidan. Godfrey had heard about him – even this very afternoon and was somewhat surprised to see that a bad *boy* could be so big, so almost a *man*. And rather handsome, too.

Poor old Lady Emma had thought her grandson the most beautiful, wonderful thing on earth. He was the child of first cousins – a thing forbidden except with a dispensation – but she got her way around that, because her son, Richard, had fallen in love with Sybilla's dim-witted daughter and wouldn't eat until he was told that he could marry her. Since the boy himself was little better than half-witted, Lady Emma had lived in dread of what such a marriage might produce. She knew nothing of the drover's encounter with one of the Little People on a warm, wild-strawberry-scented afternoon. That Little Richard, as she called him, was strong and sound and in full possession of his wits had been such a surprise, such a relief that she had doted upon him slavishly.

She would still have thought him handsome if she could have seen him. In height and precocity of maturing, he was typically a Tallboys, and there were black-haired, dark-eyed men in her family. And she would have attributed his surly look to the treatment he had suffered since her death. Possibly she would have been right. The boy himself thought that nothing had gone right with him since his grandmother died.

And nothing was right with him now. Joanna was as unfriendly as ever, and when he offered to carry something that she was unloading from the waggon, she spoke to him for the first time, four words. 'Look to your horse!'

Uncle Henry was more civil, but he asked too many questions

'Now tell us, why were you sent home?'

'I don't know. Honestly, Uncle Henry, I don't know.'

'Had you given trouble?'

'No more than usual. No more than any other boy. Just a prank. We were starved, you see.'

'You don't look starved,' Henry said.

'It was not the food at school that kept me going. There was an old woman who came in from Windsor with loaves and pies. And she was a cheat; sometimes there was no meat in her pies. She tried that trick last week, and one of the boys said that if she had sold meat pies, with no meat, on the open market, she'd have been in the stocks but because she was in the school yard, we had no redress. So we punched a hole in her basket and put her head through it.'

Godfrey thought the picture thus evoked amusing and laughed. A mistake, for Joanna gave him a cold look and said, 'I see nothing funny in that!'

'What was unfair was that I was the only one to be punished. Three of us did it. Only I was dismissed.'

To a degree he had again been a victim of circumstance. The Provost of Eton had a wide circle of acquaintances and had heard two rumours. One concerned the possible closure of the college because, somewhat belatedly, Edward of York saw it as a Lancastrian foundation, a possible centre of Lancastrian sympathy. The other concerned the enquiry into the wardship business. The presence in the College of one of what were beginning to be called illegal wards might be detrimental.

Of minor, but still relevant consideration, was that Richard Tallboys, though greatly improved, showed no promise as a scholar and was regarded as a trouble-maker. The latest prank formed the perfect excuse.

The Provost, a man of scruples, first made certain that the boy had somewhere to go; for he was one of those who had spent vacations at school. Assured that Richard had an uncle, he provided a mount, money for boy and horse for the journey and dismissed him.

At roughly the same time, earnest discussions about the fate of young heirs and heiresses were under way. One of the nameless, faceless men, suggested to the King that the usual method of disposal of wardships, as rewards for service, as a sign of favour, or in return for a 'gift' was not the most profitable way of taking advantage of what this net of inquiry had dragged up. Guardianship was earnestly sought after because for some years – dependent upon the age of the ward – the guardian had the use of the estates, and short of actual peculation, was free to benefit himself. Why should not these benefits accrue to the King? If the lands, the businesses, the stored wealth received the same treatment as most of the confiscated Lancastrian land had done, there would be an immediate, and welcome increase in the King's revenue.

Edward saw the point in this argument; but he saw something further, a chance to endear himself and the Yorkist cause to a certain section – small but potentially important – of the growing generation. This was important, for though the struggle between York and Lancaster had apparently ended at the Battle of Tewkesbury, it had not yet ended in the minds of men. Just across the Channel, in Normandy there was a young man with the very unroyal name of Henry Tydder, or Tudor, who called himself Earl of Pembroke and claimed the throne of England through his descent from John of Gaunt. This descent was somewhat devious, but enough to make a rallying point for discontented Lancastrians.

A man skilled in the craft made a map of England, colouring the lands already belonging to the King and looked after by his agents, in pale blue; and the lands of the recently discovered wards in pale yellow. Where a yellow patch was within easy distance of a blue one there was no problem, the already-tested-and-proved-to-be-honest agent could simply assume more responsibility, duly rewarded. Where the yellow patch was isolated, a new agent must be sought.

Moyidan was such a patch. In that remote corner of Suffolk, while the war was on, people had been neutral, or, facing a French invasion to support the Lancastrian cause, Yorkist. An agent must be found for Moyidan, honest and competent and capable of putting into action the King's policy of so treating all his young wards that they would grow up, grateful to him and devoted to the Yorkist cause.

The King was so enamoured of his policy that his new wards' idiosyncrasies were taken into account. Some were studious and must be provided with books and tutors, a spell at one of the universities if they so wished. Boys of differing nature could train as knights. All were to be well fed and well clad, be treated as the heirs that they were, so that years after he was dead and his son ruled England, they would remember their kindly guardian. Some of them would remember him as their saviour; Richard of Moyidan was far from being the only young heir in England whose patrimony had been mismanaged.

There were young heiresses, too. Their personal wishes were less regarded, for apart from a few exceptional cases, their hold on what they had inherited was only a temporary thing. When they married everything they possessed would pass into the control of their husbands. Foresighted as he was, the King did not regard females as politically important. In such matters a woman was what her husband was. He chose to forget that the toughest and most indomitable Lancastrian of them all, his most resolute enemy, had been a woman, Henry VI's wife. He also overlooked the fact that women were the mothers of men and that the first seven years of a boy's life, spent in his mother's company, could be formative. So he disposed of the heiresses rather casually. Some marriages, based on the usual bargain basis, roughly the equivalent of a cattle sale; how much for this girl *and* her property? A far more profitable way, in the long run, was to put the girl into a convent, handing over some part of her dowry; cash on the nail. Most religious houses were already feeling the effects of inflation and realised that a pound today was worth two at some unspecified date. Some were so rich in land that they did not desire more acres and would take only money – usually only a fourth of what was due to the girl; others were so poor that anything was welcome. Dame Isabel, who had so summarily rejected Mistress Captoft, saw no threat to her own position in the admission of a young girl who would bring with her not a large fortune but a steady income.

It was in connection with this steady income that Henry Tallboys' name was mentioned in the wider world. One third of Joanna Serriff's dower was being discussed and the question came up – Would it be better to sell the stock, or leave it where it was, to be dealt with as it had been in the past? The Commissioner who had visited Knight's Acre said, 'Leave it. Master Tallboys is a splendid manager; and a strictly honest man.' He told – rather amusingly, the story of how, in the course of a few hours, he had met *two* men of complete probity.

It was a virtue rare enough to be remarkable; and one which few men could afford in their official capacity, however honest they might be in their private lives. All the Commissioners understood that this whole project had been mounted in order to enrich, this way or that, the King. The rest of this particular girl's dowry was lodged with Sir Barnabas Grey of Stordford Castle. It would be taken away from him and the girl, or the convent would never see more than a token sum. By manipulations at which these men were adept most of that money would find its way into the King's purse.

Simply one, not very important case. As one Commissioner with a fanciful turn of language put it: Heirs with land were like sheep that could be sheared once a year; heiresses were like sheep killed off; the most profit must be made on the carcass. All in a day's work ...

Somebody, however, remembered that mention of an honest man, and when it became a question of finding a steward for Moyidan, Henry's name came up again.

Before any move was made, the man's antecedents, and particularly his political affiliations must be scrutinised.

Henry could not have had a better record. Son of Sir Godfrey Tallboys who had died alongside his liege lord, that passionate Yorkist, Lord Thorsdale, in the memorable year when the tide had turned. In fact, upon the face of it, it rather looked as though this man, son of a knight – and a famous knight in his day – now a working farmer, might be regarded as one who had *suffered* for the Yorkist cause, one of those who had borne his decline of fortune bravely and not come begging, as so many had done. He deserved an appointment; he should have it. Two hundred pounds a year? Surely ample, a dazzling sum to such a man. It was by such judicious cutting of corners that the King's men served the King.

Henry was not dazzled. He was, to start with, annoyed by being visited, again, and just at the busiest time. Up in the fold the shearers were busy and he was needed there because shearers were so hasty, not bothering to keep the marked fleeces apart which was important because his flock had three owners, Joanna, Robert, and himself.

At the same time the hay-making was in progress; this year a splendid crop; there had been rain at the right time, sun at the right time. Henry was needed in the hayfield, too. Jem always slacked off unless supervised, and Dick – who now preferred to be called Richard, was a lazy young devil. He did not seem to understand that he must earn his keep.

And now on one of the busiest days of the year, when Henry had decided that running to and fro between fold and field was in itself a waste of time and had allowed Joanna to take charge; to see that the sheep regarded as Robert's and those regarded as his were marked – hers, far more numerous, were left unmarked, and Henry was swinging his scythe, there was this man – not the one who had come to count animals earlier in the year. Another one.

They sat in the hall, relatively cool even on this warm day and drank buttermilk, all that Henry had to offer at the moment. And when the man had said what he had come to say, Henry was not dazzled.

He said, moodily, 'My aunt, the Lady Emma, put much the same proposition to me and I refused. I felt I had enough to do, here.'

Lady Emma had offered no salary; she had simply promised to will to Henry, as reward for his stewardship, what was indisputably her own – a bit of land, of small value, even as a sheep-run because it was remote, with no means of access except through Moyidan.

'Two hundred pounds a year, Master Tallboys, is a considerable sum. And added to it there would be a percentage on the increase. That is the rule. Any steward-in-charge of an estate belonging to one of the King's wards, is entitled to five per cent on the overall productivity.'

And still the man was not dazzled or cajoled. He said, 'It needs thinking over. One thing I should make clear from the start. If I did take on the job, I should not live at Moyidan.'

Why not, the Commissioner wondered, looking round the stark, comfortless hall; the walls bare except in two places; one narrow hanging and one wide one. The narrow one had been old Bishop William's house-offering to Sybilla all those years ago, the large one Mistress Captoft had left, because at The Sailors' Rest the only place where it could have found a place was in the big communal room, and she thought – correctly – that it would put ideas into the heads of lonely men.

There was the one settle with cushions, sadly frayed; an imposing court cupboard, completely bare. A stark room. And the Commissioner had a shrewd idea of what the beds were like in this house. He had lodged, the night before, at Moyidan from which the Church in the person of the Bishop of Bywater had withdrawn without protest, but taking with him, as indeed Sir Richard Tallboys had done, some few things which he could rightly claim as his own and which would not be missed. Even so, compared with this, Moyidan was still palatial. However, if this curious fellow preferred to live here . . .

'That, of course, would be for you to decide, Master Tallboys. The distance is small. You could ride over once or twice a week.'

'If I undertook it, I should go every day.'

'That would be very good. And of course the upkeep of the horse, or horses, would be an allowable charge against the estate. When may I hope for your decision?'

'Give me two days. This is my busiest time, shearing and haymaking. Two days from now . . . You are at Moyidan? I will come there, in the evening.'

'I could wait upon you, Master Tallboys.'

That sudden, flashing blue smile appeared and Henry said, 'No. I must come to you. I must see what, if I decide to take over, I am taking over. So I will wait upon you. The day after tomorrow. In the cool of the evening.'

The Commissioner rode back to Moyidan carrying with him the thought that this Henry Tallboys was not only honest, but cautious and hard-headed; a suitable man for the post.

Next day was Joanna's birthday. Nothing was said of the betrothal, but Henry had remembered the day and had a present for her. One which represented both thoughtfulness and ingenuity. A new gown of blue linen, of the very finest weave -- almost like silk, and with bands of real silk around the skirt, the bodice and the sleeves.

'It is the prettiest I ever had, Henry.'

'Try it on.'

She went into the hall and there shed the dress she was wearing – one that Katherine had left behind – and donned the new one. It fitted perfectly. Sounding, and looking, rather well-pleased with himself, Henry explained how such a fit had been achieved.

'I bought the stuff in the market; then I accosted a woman who looked likely to know and asked if she knew a good sewing woman. She did. After that I kept watch for a girl of your size and shape.' That girl had not been easy to find; those tall enough were either too thick or too thin, but he'd found one at last. 'Glad enough to earn fourpence,' he said. 'Twopence for being measured, twopence for being fitted. I'm glad you like it.'

She was deeply touched by the gift, and the trouble he had taken, but when she tried to express her thanks, looking at him with glowing eyes, his face seemed to cloud over and he said, 'Work won't wait; even for birthdays.'

She changed back into her working dress and went to the fold, where the shearing should finish today. Henry began scything, thinking as he worked. Turning over and over in his mind the proposition made to him by the Commissioner. It was impossible for him to ignore the fact that the farm's easiest times had coincided with his father's two brief periods of steady, paid employment. In fact he had resented Sir Godfrey's earning more, just by riding about and supervising Lord Thorsdale's property at Bywater, than he could wrest out of the land, however hard he worked. Equally plain was the thought that the land remained after the well-paid, easy jobs had vanished.

Knight's Acre was bigger now, and stock needed constant attention.

Two hundred pounds a year was not to be sniffed at.

One of his reasons for refusing to look after Moyidan when Lady Emma appealed to him, was that he had not enough learning: that no longer held good, for Richard was, or should be, capable of looking after that kind of thing. He'd work, once he saw that it was to his own advantage.

If I don't take the job, who will?

Last time he had been able to suggest his own brother, Richard. And what a calamity that had been.

Five miles, twice a day, even on a good horse – a permissible expense, would consume valuable time.

On and on, round and round, as the scythe sang through the sweet smelling hay.

Godfrey ran up.

'Can I leave off for a little? I want to look for wild strawberries, for Janna's birthday supper. I'm well ahead of Dick anyway.'

'Off you go. The best place is on the bank or the water-splash.'

In his mulling over the future he had deliberately avoided the inclusion of Joanna in his plans, either way. Any kind of looking ahead so far as she was concerned brought the inevitable, dreaded confrontation to mind.

He honed his scythe, and imagined *that* bad moment over and looked ahead again, fitting Joanna in.

In charge of Moyidan, and with a salary, he could change his way of life; entertain; give her chance to meet people, find some man to her liking – and to his!

But I can do that without splitting myself in two, half at Moyidan, half here; the divided loyalty which he feared. In two years' time – and that would be time enough, she was only fourteen – with reasonable luck, this would be a prosperous place, too. Luck, he knew, no farmer could count upon, always at the mercy of the weather. Good this year. Heavy hay, enough to keep a lot of sheep, a lot of store cattle through the winter. Other crops thick and promising, too; the oats thick and silvery, ready for cutting next week; the barley and wheat standing tall and just about to change from green to pale buff, to golden. He *knew* that two weeks' steady rain could ruin everything; no, not everything; rain could ruin a harvest, but it made the grass grow, and animals could find their own food, perhaps as far as Michaelmas. It was not unknown, in a wet season, for a second hay-crop to be gathered in.

He reached his decision. Stay here. Be his own man.

Up in the fold, Joanna was supervising, and when able to, doing a bit of cheating. Like Griselda, like Master Turnbull, she regretted Henry's stubborn determination to go on saving for Robert. She knew that Robert was dead. She'd gone to Moyidan to save him from the misery he was enduring; they'd lost their way in the wood and he had died. He'd never been strong and a night in the blizzard had killed him. She had told no-one.

Now she was doing a little bit to put matters right by shuffling a few fleeces, with Robert's mark, and a few unmarked ones – her own – into Henry's pile. Nobody noticed.

The shearers were rather more hasty than usual, and less sure of hand and eye; for by custom shearers were provided with ale as well as food, and towards the end of a job were inclined to indulge. No good leaving ale behind. Joseph was busily applying new markings to the closely shorn sheep. Nobody noticed for a while that Joanna had ceased to supervise; stood rigid, a marked fleece in her hands, staring straight ahead of her.

It had happened again. This time an almost exact repetition of what she had seen before – a mounted man bringing bad news.

Blinking her way back into the ordinary world, she saw the shearers pushing their shears into canvas or leather sheaths and Joseph putting the ochre mark on a sheep, the last to be shorn. And beyond, just turning from the lane into the track, a man on a horse.

She said aloud, 'Too late!' She could not possibly reach the house first, and even if she did warn Henry he would take no notice. He would ignore her, just as he had done before. With a shrug she resumed the sorting of fleeces which had piled up around her. What was going on in the house?

Henry, working bare to the waist as men did in hot weather, saw the horseman approach, and turn towards the door in the house-front. By his clothes and the quality of the horse, someone of importance.

Hell and damnation! More waste of time. He laid his scythe down and jumped across the bank which formed the edge of this field' rounded a rose-tree and stood between the visitor and the door.

'I wish to speak to your master.' A natural enough mistake, faced by a field worker, bare-chested, sweaty and with hayseeds in his hair. The mistake did not ruffle Henry: the man's manner did. Damn it all, he thought, even to a servant he should have said Good morning. Some of Sybilla's teaching had taken root.

With an edge to his voice, Henry said, 'Good morning. My name is Henry Tallboys.' He opened the door and holding it, allowed his visitor to enter; indicated a seat on the shabby-cushioned settle.

The Commissioner found himself at a disadvantage. He

was not a man to whom an apology came easily. He took refuge in an extra pomposity.

The search for, the disposition of all these submerged heirs and heiresses, had fallen into departments. Heirs to estates large, moderate, small; boys who bore titles those who did not. And heiresses, sub-divided according to fortune and rank.

This Commissioner dealt with girls consigned to convents.

Henry listened, incredulous, to the arrangements that had been made, in a distant place, for Joanna. Clevely! And he to keep her stock and pay what he had formerly done to Master Turnbull to the nunnery.

Boiling rage must be mastered. He mastered his and said simply, 'I shall never agree to such an iniquitous arrangement.'

The Commissioner, hostile, and in a strong position, said, 'Master Tallboys, you cannot contest a decision made by the King's Commissioners. It is in perfect order. Perhaps you would like to look ...' He produced from his pouch some papers.

God damn me, Henry thought; I can't read!

'I have no need to look. I know the facts. The girl was left without parent or guardian. So now she falls into the King's hands. And he deputes people like you! Did *you* ever take a look at Clevely?'

'I have not yet had the opportunity. I think one of my fellow colleagues inspected it and other places deemed suitable.'

Suitable! Years ago his father had considered it unsuitable for dim-witted Margaret; more recently Mistress Captoft had considered it unsuitable for herself. Henry had never seen it. But quite apart from Clevely's suitability, what about Joanna? Less suited to life in a nunnery than even Mistress Captoft had been. Young, lovable, loving: so active so eager for life and for freedom.

'I will not allow it.'

'It is not for you to allow or to prevent.'

'Oh! They want the dowry, don't they? Sooner than have this happen I'll slit the throat of every beast she owns and leave the carcasses to rot!'

Plainly a violent, unreasonable and ignorant fellow.

'To do that would be to incur severe penalties, Master Tallboys. This demoiselle is now officially a ward of the King and her property is tantamount to Crown property. To damage or destroy it would be perilously near an act of treason.'

That shot went home. The big man emitted a sound curiously like a groan, and on his unpadded bench, slumped a little.

In summer, especially in a hot summer, most of those able to do so left London where the plague-threat increased and retired to their country properties. The King himself went on Progress, sometimes visiting his own outlying manors, more often staying with favoured subjects who paid dearly for the honour; enormous feasts and costly entertainments being essential. The Bishop of Bywater did not expect to meet Lord Shefton in London during a hot June. Ordinarily he would not have been there himself, he would have been at Moyidan, cool and shady. From this pleasant place he had not been expelled. No such forthright term as confiscation or sequestration had been used; no admonition administered. He was a cleric, and so were most of the Commissioners. Dog did not eat dog; and amongst men of education a mere hint was enough. The Bishop had simply withdrawn.

He knew that unless he absented himself from London entirely he must, inevitably, encounter Lord Shefton sooner or later. He hoped later, when that bit of what looked like negligence on his part – but was actually quite understandable ignorance – might be forgotten. Yet here, on a June evening, in the grounds of a mutual friend, a pleasant garden running down from the Strand to the river, they met.

His Grace of Bywater had always liked to speak of the Earl of Shefton as his friend, but between them the links had been tenuous, and that letter of congratulation had been sycophantic in intent, the watering of a tender, but frail plant. In effect, it must have seemed a blunder, too. Or a bit of the perfidy so common in sophisticated circles.

Had Lord Shefton ignored him completely, or merely recognised his existence with a distant nod, the Bishop would not have been surprised, would indeed have been slightly relieved. But Lord Shefton came and greeted him with the utmost affability; far more friendly than he had ever been.

The Bishop had no inkling – and neither had anyone else – that this re-organisation, this search for illegal wards, this re-adjustment of property rights, had been instigated by one man, with one trivial, spiteful aim.

Lord Shefton was far too cunning a man to have shown any interest in the operation which his casual words had launched. He saw the machine lurch into action and knew that sooner or later the last tiny grain would be ground. The mill of officialdom, like the mills of God, ground slowly, but they ground exceedingly small. In this case they had ground more swiftly than usual; otherwise His Grace of Bywater would not be here; he'd be at Moyidan. Moyidan was a word which had never once crossed Lord Shefton's lips.

The lime trees were in flower, and the roses breathed out their evening fragrance, it was one of those rare evenings when supper could be served out of doors. An evening for confidences. Their host had provided excellent food and wine and presently the mood was mellow enough to embolden His Grace to speak of and to explain the awkward little incident, and his own mis-timed letter. He mentioned the name Henry Tallboys, the man who had so grossly deceived him.

It was the first time that Lord Shefton had heard of Henry. His pride and vanity, as well as his well-bred desire to put Lady Grey at ease, had forbade his asking: Who is the man? His identity did not matter; a betrothal was a betrothal and must be accepted; the whole affair made to seem of no importance whatsoever. His Lordship's rage had centred upon the Bishop of Bywater whose negligence had brought the embarrassment about.

'I assure you, Your Grace has no need to apologise. A mere tentative approach on my part. Taken perhaps a trifle too seriously by Lady Grey.'

To this amiable, understanding friend – yes, friend, now! – the Bishop could say things which convention prevented his saying to a fellow cleric. He told the whole story of Moyidan, how he had saved it from wreck, cherished it, enjoyed it, and then been edged out. By this time dusk had fallen and servants were bringing candles which burned steady in the still, sultry air. They did not however give enough light for the Bishop to see that Lord Shefton's intent expression was tinged with gloating.

His Lordship had made light of his loss, so in the end His Grace felt obliged to make light of his, saying, with just the right touch of irony, 'Imagine my delight when I learned from a friend, one of the original Commissioners, that this same Henry Tallboys had been chosen as custodian of Moyidan and guardian by delegation to its heir. With a salary of two hundred pounds a year – and of course, whatever he can squeeze.'

The realisation that all the steps taken to punish the apparent culprit had simply resulted in the enrichment of the real one was too much. The red rage ran up, reddening the scrawny throat, swelling the shrivelled face; it could only go so far: stopped short by the bony skull it checked and exploded.

Heat-stroke, they said. Old men – and although nobody knew Lord Shefton's exact age, he was certainly old – were unduly susceptible to extremes of heat and cold. Somebody sped off to the west to inform Maude; somebody rode in another direction to inform his heir. Maude had been trained not to reveal her real feelings, but to cry for almost nothing, so nobody, even those nearest to her, knew how joyful she was behind the tears. Free, not just for a short time, but for life; free, rich and independent, about to embark upon the youth which had been stolen from her.

When the latest Commissioner left Henry did not sit down with his head in his hands as he had when facing up to Peter Wingfield's revelation. That had been a shock, a thing to be accepted or rejected, a thing about which he could do nothing. This was also a shock but it concerned, as the other did not, the outer world, and demanded not deferred, but immediate action. Meantime the hay must be cut. Swinging his scythe, in the easy, seemingly effortless rhythm which Walter had brought to all such work, Henry asked himself: What sort of a world is it where a girl like Joanna could be married off to an old, old man with no teeth? Or shoved away into Clevely, which years ago Sir Godfrey had declared unfit to house pigs? The answer rang loud and clear; *it was a damned rotten world.* One that could only be fought by somebody armed with its own damned rotten weapons – the chief of which was money, which he had never had, but could have now. And not only money, but some kind of prestige.

Slashing away at the last hay, as though felling enemies, Henry indulged in self-pity, an ignoble, despicable emotion as he well knew. Both the people who had influenced his youth, his mother and Walter, the ex-archer, had decried it, in differing words, but with the same meaning. Sybilla had said apropos of some crisis he had now forgotten: 'If I allowed myself to be sorry for myself it would be merely to admit myself mistaken. What I chose, I must bear.'

Walter had said, 'Once you put on that *Pity me* look, somebody'll kick you in the teeth. Try again, say to yourself and the rest, *Catch me*,' Both right, both wrong, because their lives were so limited; and both were speaking of material things. Sybilla would not pity herself, because the hardships which came her way were the result of her choosing to marry a poor knight. Walter really meant that it was no good blaming the wind or the weather or bad luck, you must be resolute and try again.

But now Henry was sorry for himself because he had had no choice in bringing about the frightful situation in which he found himself, and no amount of being resolute and trying again would help him out of it. He'd done nothing except blunder on, doing his best from day to day. And here he was, faced with a most hideous decision; at least, not a decision, since there was only one way out. And what a way!

Joanna came and stood on the bank. As he worked towards it she said, 'Dinner is ready when you are, Henry.'

'I'm ready.' He looked at her and then away, quickly. He'd heard men in the market laughing about the way their womenfolk had carried on about sending an animal, practically a pet – to market. He knew how those women felt.

Joanna had no need to ask had the man brought bad news; she knew he had; and Henry's face showed it. He could not look pale because he was so sun-tanned, but the lack of colour under the tan gave him a dirty, sallow hue: and all the lines of worry and pain were back in his face, deeper than ever. She was surprised and relieved when he said, eating hastily and without enjoyment, 'I have to go to Moyidan this afternoon.'

Richard – he now objected to Dick as much as he had once objected to Little Richard – gave his uncle an alert look. Through all the vicissitudes of the years since his grand-mother's death, he had clung, as to a tenet of faith, to the belief that Moyidan was his, and to the hope that despite everything, he would one day come into his own.

'Is it about me?'

'In the main,' Henry said curtly. He got up, tipped the pot of hot water which always stood by the verge of a well-managed hearth into a jug and went up to wash and change into his church-going, market-going clothes. The sight of them always reminded him of the young squire on whom they had hung so loosely that evening. And some of the self-pity drained away as he realised that he was partially to blame. For putting things off; for being blind.

One of Sybilla's stories which he had always thought so inferior to Walter's, skimmed back into his mind . . .

Once upon a time, long ago and in a place far away, there was a Prince who, before he could inherit his dead father's throne, must fight a lion, single-handed. He'd shirked the contest and gone out into the world to seek his fortune. And at every turn, whenever an opportunity offered, there was the same obstacle; first he must face a lion, single-handed. In the end he had thought to himself that he might as well go home and face his own lion which in the end proved to be a tame, toothless old beast who'd licked his hand!'

It was a story with a moral, as most of Sybilla's were, which was why Henry had so much preferred Walter's which never began with: Once upon a time, but with: One time when I was in France, or the Low Countries . . . Stories which made far more appeal to a boy who had never seen a lion. Or a prince. Now, donning his decent homespun, Henry saw the point of what he had dismissed as a fairy tale. Sooner or later the lion must be faced and he should have done it, back in the winter, when an innocent young man had pointed out where and what the lion was. If he'd faced up to it then, perhaps consulted Master Turnbull, this particular situation could possibly have been avoided.

*

308

The Commissioner who dealt with heirs was taking his ease in the great hall of Moyidan Castle which with its high roof, thick walls and small windows, was by far the coolest place on a hot afternoon. He sat in a cushioned chair, with his feet on a stool, and beside him on the table stood a great bowl of strawberries and a small one of powdered sugar. Sugar, at £15 a pound was a luxury, but a Government official was entitled to *some* comfort. On account of the heat he wore a loose robe and slippers.

'Why, Master Tallboys,' he said as Henry was shown in, 'I did not expect you. Until tomorrow, in the cool of the evening. You did say that, did you not?'

'Yes. But something else cropped up and I thought it better to get this over and done with. I am prepared to take the post – but not for two hundred pounds a year. Three. Is that agreeable to you?'

The Commissioner was empowered to offer more than that, particularly when an estate was difficult, encumbered by old women with inalienable rights, some of a highly complicated nature.

He said, quietly, but with incision, 'It is not what is agreeable to me; it is what is acceptable to the Commission. Three hundred pounds would raise no quibble.'

'That is settled, then. I have another condition. I want everything checked, every quarter, by a man I know to be honest. Master Turnbull, the lawyer in Baildon.'

'A wise precaution,' the Commissioner said. And most unusual! So far – and however regarded, by value and size, or alphabetically, Moyidan was low on his list – he had not met with this suggestion before, an independent accountant.

'And now,' Henry said, 'I would like to look around and take a reckoning. Two copies.'

Safely back in London this Commissioner was to say wryly: Dealing with an honest man bears hard on the feet!

In the down-bearing heat of the scorching afternoon, Henry, the Commissioner and two copying clerks, tramped miles, peering into stinking styes, byres, stables. Sheep on the open runs were less odorous, and they took longer to count and in places where the grass had been eaten away their sharp little hooves kicked up dust. A very trying afternoon.

There was, Henry noticed, a singular dearth of young

stock; but that was because, since his Aunt Emma's death, this place had not been in the hands of a practical person. First his brother Richard intent upon grandeur; then the Bishop of Bywater, using it more or less as a pantry; eating no doubt, sucking pigs, calf meat, lamb; things no *real* farmer would ever look upon as food. Only the rich, the careless, the idiots, gobbled down what represented the future.

'Given ordinary seasons and ordinary luck, I can improve on this,' Henry said grimly. 'And not for the sake of my share. In fact, in view of the scarcity of young stuff my share had better be limited for the first year.'

They were approaching the Castle again and on the permanent bridge that had replaced the drawbridge, Henry paused for a moment, remembering the day, in another life, when he had ridden here with Tana, obeying a very human wish to impress. That was the kind of memory which he had ruthlessly suppressed all these years.

Only half-humorously, the Commissioner said, 'Do you propose to count the duck on the moat?'

As though against his will, Henry half smiled.

'No. They can wait. I was wondering if you could tell me something. Nothing to do with Moyidan.'

'Whatever I can. But sitting down. And over a glass of cool wine.'

Sitting down, and with a glass of wine so cool that it misted in his hot hand, Henry told, with his usual brevity, of the other Commissioner's visit and what it concerned, ending with the question; 'Is it true that the girl can be forced into Clevely? Against her wish? Against mine?'

'I am not involved in the disposition of heiresses, Master Tallboys. But I know the general principles. Any female with property, and lacking a natural guardian – that is a father or husband – becomes a ward of the King. Things have been lax of late and the King has been robbed of his rights; but things are tightening up. That is why I am here now. And why my colleague called upon you. Yes, it is true, the King has absolute power in such matters. He could give the girl – and her dower – to any man he selected as a husband for her; either as a present or in return for a ... a consideration. He can choose her dwelling place, the style in which she lives. Not, of course, personally; through deputies.'

'Nobody else has any say in the matter? No other relative?'

'I think not, No. Brothers, cousins, uncles would merely confuse the issue.'

'Betrothed?'

'That *is* somewhat different. In the eyes of the Church, and indeed in the eyes of the law, a betrothal – properly witnessed of course – amounts to a marriage. No man in his right sense would make a bid ... hum, hum ... offer his hand in such a case. And I very much doubt whether any convent would accept such a young person, except on a very temporary basis, as a parlour lodger as the word goes. And reputable houses are becoming wary of such; with their pet dogs and their lovers, they have done much to bring calumny upon the genuinely religious.'

'Thank you, sir,' Henry said. It was just as he had thought, as he had worked it out in his own ignorant mind. Only the one way.

He was a practical, not an imaginative man, but as the formalities were concluded – the signing of the agreement between Our Sovereign Lord the King and Henry Tallboys of Knight's Acre in the County of Suffolk – his mind did run forward and shrank from what it saw.

'Now I have a favour to ask. Could you lend me a little wine?'

'Fortunately, yes. Uncertain of how or where we shall lodge, we carry our own supplies. And here a small cask had been overlooked.' Inadvertently, of course, the Commissioner thought to himself; not much that was portable had been left when the Bishop withdrew. 'Would you prefer red or white?'

'Whichever is most heartening,' Henry said.

What he had not foreseen was that Joanna was celebrating her birthday in a humble way. She had decided Henry's glum look at dinner was concerned with business at Moyiday; bad news perhaps. And bad news for Dick – she always used that name since he had expressed a preference for Richard – would be good news for her. It might worry Henry for a

311

while, he was such a family man, but he'd get over it and a cheerful meal might help.

The rose-trees, for so long neglected, no longer bore the kind of flower of which Lady Randall who had sent them to Sybilla, would have approved; but the inferior flowers were plentiful and Joanna had set a great bunch, some upright, some trailing, in the centre of the table in the hall. There was every excuse, this evening, for not eating in the kitchen – she had baked new bread there this afternoon. The hall was cooler.

Sybilla's herb garden – which included the vegetable patch, was as neglected as the rose-trees, but amongst the weeds there were a few hardy self-sown plants which, eked out by young dandelion leaves which were plentiful, made a cool-looking salad. There was ham, properly soaked, properly cooked; new bread; a great bowl of wild strawberries, fresh cream.

She wore her new blue gown.(This had evoked a remark more wistful than reproachful, from Dick. 'If you'd taken those blue beads I offered you, they would have gone well together.' She had answered him with her usual acerbity. 'How could I? The receiver is as bad as the thief!' For once a rebuff from her failed to depress him, because he was sure that any business at Moyidan must be concerned with his restoration to it. The fact that Uncle Henry looked sour and spoke shortly, did not affect him. In fact it boded favourably. He sensed that Henry had no real fondness for him and would not rejoice if his fortunes took a turn for the better.)

Godfrey decided to change into his better clothes, and Dick did the same. All was ready.

However the business at Moyidan had gone, Henry looked no better. The dingy look behind the sunburn, the lines of strain were still there.

Joanna ventured to remark upon it. 'You look tired, Henry.'

'Who wouldn't?' I've tramped all over Moyidan this afternoon. And some things I saw did not please me.'

'Never mind. Look, I set supper here. It is cooler. And Henry, I even have ale. Joseph held some back. He said the shearers had quite enough last night and it would do them no good to arrive at their next job, drunk.'

'They hadn't lacked,' Henry said. 'They sounded merry enough when I passed them in the lane.'

The food, good as it was, tasted of nothing, but he choked it down, conscious of Joanna's eye upon him. Let her enjoy this pitiable little feast!

Presently Richard, unable to bear uncertainty any longer, said, 'Am I to have Moyidan back?'

'Yes.'

'I knew it! I always knew it!'

'Not quite as you think,' Henry said, giving way to the sourness within him; taking out his spite against the whole bloody world on the boy who was in no way to blame for *this*. 'Not quite as you think, my boy. There's a lot of hard work to be done there, and you'll do most of it. You'll go first thing tomorrow morning and start cutting hay.'

'Cutting hay?

'Yes. It should have been started a week ago.'

'Moyidan is *my* manor,' Dick said, for perhaps the thousandth time. 'Who can *make* me cut hay?'

'I can.'

'Because you are . . . my uncle?'

'No. Because the King has appointed me to take charge of you, and your manor, until you are twenty-one.'

There were many stories about uncles who had usurped their nephews' rights. Richard Tallboys had, in fact, contributed one, having learned in a painful way that it was unwise to go about Eton grumbling that the Bishop of Bywater had taken Moyidan away from him. Eton was a clerical establishment and such talk was not to be encouraged. He was beaten for three serious faults: untruthfulness; lack of respect; ingratitude. Not being stupid, he changed his story and said that his Uncle Richard had robbed him.

Now he suspected that Henry, in some mysterious way, had usurped the Bishop, as the Bishop had usurped Uncle Richard.

Richard's rule had been careless, but not harsh; there'd always been enough to eat, new clothes when they were needed. There'd been Master Jankyn, the tutor, too, but he'd soon learned not to be strict with the boy who was on such

313

good terms with the servants that a blow struck at him rebounded in the form of bad service. And for a time there'd
been Robert to act as whipping boy. Life had not been too
bad then. After the Bishop had taken over, the heir had been
ill-fed, and in the end practically without shoes; but at least
nobody even then had suggested that he should work! At
last he had appealed to Uncle Henry, who had taken him in,
provided him with clothes, fed him after a fashion – but
made him work. Then came Eton, sounding promising, but
quite horrible. Then Uncle Henry again. And now Uncle
Henry for the next almost eight years. It was intolerable.

Inside this Richard Tallboys there still lived, and would
always live, the pampered little boy whose grandmother had
doted upon him; who had so often assured him he would be
rich, that Moyidan was his.

Sullen, defiant, he said, 'Another dirty trick! As though
the King would lend himself . . .'

'See for yourself,' Henry said, jerking a thumb towards the
cupboard on whose open shelf lay the two parchments, the
agreement, the list of Moyidan's resources at the moment –
and standing alongside, the stout leather bottle of heartening
red wine. The sight of it reminded Henry of what he had still
to face, and once again he groaned, inwardly.

Now the moment had come. The table, cleared of everything but the roses, two candles just lighted, the wine bottle
and two cups. The boys dismissed, summarily, to their beds;
Godfrey still young enough to be almost drunk on such a
meal and a mug of ale, Richard reduced by one glance at
that so-official, so final a document.

Outside one lonely belated cuckoo gave her last cry, and
the wild doves took up the mournful sound.

'Joanna, I have to tell you something.'

She thought she knew what it was. Everything, since her
return had been nudging towards this moment; the day
when she was fourteen, and no longer too young. When that
hasty, unwitnessed betrothal must be either acknowledged
or repudiated. In her mind she was prepared. Six months,
and the word never mentioned, glances fond, brooding,
amused, but never right. Never *wanting*.

She sat, straight and still, her hands undamaged by six months rough work folded in her lap.

'Spare yourself, Henry. I know. That was a makeshift betrothal. I forced you . . . But, my dear, I did not keep my side of the bargain. I should have spent another year at Stordford. You are absolved.'

'It isn't that. Far less simple. Joanna . . . I think no two people were ever placed as we are. That makeshift betrothal must be made anew, and witnessed. Unless you are to be sent to Clevely.'

'Clevely. The nunnery. Who could *send* me there?'

'The King . . . But that is not the nub of the matter. Honey, by claiming to be betrothed to you, I saved you from marriage to an old, toothless man. It was all I could think of at the time. And *now* all I can think of, to save you from Clevely, is to claim it again, but on sounder ground, with the priest as witness. But my dear, my sweet . . . It would be only a stop-gap, a time-saver . . . Marriage between us is impossible. We are blood kin. Your father was mine.'

There, it was said. He drew a gasping breath of relief which coincided with one of hers, let out as though she had been punched. Her lips whitened, her eyes turned black as the pupils widened. Time for the wine.

'Drink this,' he said. 'Good for shock.' His hand, holding the cup to her was not quite steady; hers, pushing it gently away, was firm as rock, but so cold that it sent a shiver through him.

'Later,' she said. 'Have you . . . known all along?'

He shook his head. 'Not the faintest suspicion. It was that young man, Peter Wingfield . . .'

'How could he know? Who told *him*?'

'The family resemblance, he said. Then I saw how blind I had been.'

'In what way?' Her colour had come back and she sounded interested, as though discussing something which concerned neither of them intimately.

'In not putting two and two together. You and Robert were born on the same day; he was premature, you were full time. That was frequently mentioned – to account for the difference in size. Your mother and mine, and the father of

315

us both, kept the secret well. But, Joanna, once he let something slip. In all, from the land of the Moors to England, the journey had taken *four* months. So they set out in September!'

'I see. Well, apart from the betrothal – and we can get around that – it isn't such a calamity, is it? I mean ... I don't mind having you as a half-brother. In fact, I'm rather proud.'

'I have always been very proud, and very fond, of you.'

He was proud of her now. None of the fuss which he had dreaded.

'As for the betrothal,' he said, reverting to practicality, 'it must be made, first thing tomorrow morning. And last until ... until this threat of Clevely has died down. The King may change his policy. Or die. A new king often alters laws.'

'Quite apart from everything else, my dear, you can't spare me to Clevely now. With Moyidan on your hands, you need me to take charge here.'

'That is true. Knight's Acre must not be neglected.'

Nothing would be neglected. Nor need be, for suddenly life and vigour and tireless energy came flowing back. There was nothing he would not tackle, nothing he could not achieve.

Joanna looked to the future, too. One aspect of it bleak, empty of hope, dead. But then that hope had been dying, little by little, ever since her return from Stordford. For the rest ... She'd have Knight's Acre which she loved; that horrible boy would be gone, the happy family life resumed. Family!

Something remained to be done. She braced herself to tell a gallant lie.

'Henry. That day by the pool. I said a lot of things that I didn't mean. At least, not how they sounded. I was too young to tell one sort of love from another.' Then she added in her own special, light way, '*And* I was half-drowned!' She smiled, and Henry smiled back.

'So I noticed at the time!'

They laughed, as they had done, years ago, jogging home from market. Two against the world.

316